PRIVILEGED LIVES

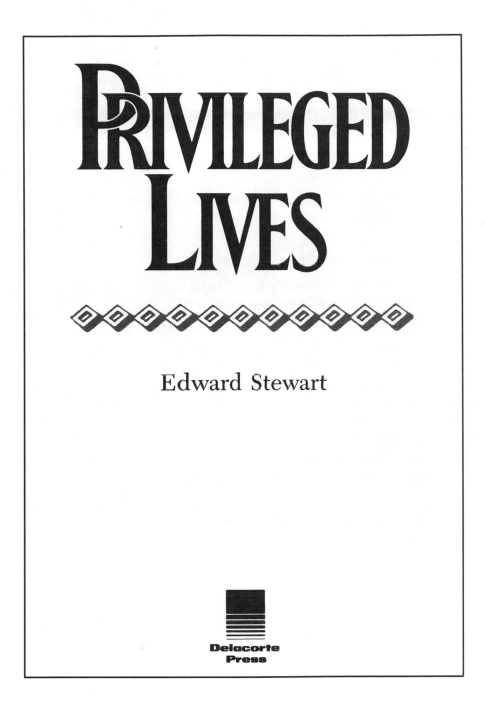

PRIVILEGED LIVES

Edward Stewart

Delacorte
Press

Published by
Delacorte Press
The Bantam Doubleday Dell Publishing Group, Inc.
1 Dag Hammarskjold Plaza
New York, New York 10017

Each character in this novel is entirely fictional. No reference to any living person is intended or should be inferred.

Library of Congress Cataloging in Publication Data
Stewart, Edward, 1938–
    Privileged lives/by Edward Stewart.
        p.   cm.
    ISBN 0-385-29652-5
    I. Title.
    PS3569.T46P7   1988
813′.5—dc19   87-30319
                                                                        CIP

Manufactured in the United States of America

May 1988

10 9 8 7 6 5 4 3 2 1

BG

For Diane Reverand

1

THE DARKNESS WAS CHARGED WITH AN UNFAMILIAR SILENCE. IN some way that Babe couldn't quite define, it felt different from the dark she had fallen asleep in.

She couldn't hear Scottie breathing beside her. She couldn't smell him, couldn't sense his weight and warmth. She turned her head.

Tried to turn her head.

The movement took unexpected effort, as though she had to push through masses of jelly.

Puzzlement went through her. It wasn't her pillow—not her goose down pillow from Altman's, freshly scented with jasmine potpourri. This pillow smelled of nothing, it had an almost aseptic absence of smell, like air-conditioned air.

And now a second puzzlement.

She couldn't see Scottie in his place beside her. There was no outline, no familiar silhouette. She reached a hand.

Tried to reach.

The hand had to crawl, finger by finger. It seemed to her that the sheet felt rougher than the combed cotton she had gone to sleep on. A dull pain went up her arm, lodging in her elbow and shoulder. She reached through the pain.

Her hand met emptiness.

She stilled a twinge of panic, told herself to think this through. Scottie had to be in the bathroom—or in his dressing room—or maybe downstairs, locking up.

Of course. Banks and Mrs. Banks would have gone to bed long ago. Scottie would be locking up.

As she lay waiting for him, she remembered the party of only a few hours ago. The champagne, the laughter, the three hundred guests. The dinner, the dancing, the drinking—far too much drinking. Calling it a day at two A.M., tumbling into a limo with Scottie. The two of them staggering arm in arm to the front door—dropping the keys—laughing—

And then . . . ?

There was a blank where the next image should have been.

Babe was aware of strange skittering sounds, voices muffled through walls. Her eyes were beginning to adjust. She lifted her head —again, a simple movement that was usually automatic took astonishing concentration.

The darkness had the wrong shape. A curtain was pulsing dimly in a space where her bedroom had no window. A floor-level nightlight that she had never seen before squeezed a tiny beam through the darkness.

She blinked, trying to make out the clock on the bedside table. The shining roman numerals were nowhere to be found. Mrs. Banks must have tidied and left the clock behind the telephone.

Babe reached toward the space where the bedside table should have been. It felt as though elastic straps were holding her arm down to the mattress.

Her fingers dislodged something solid. Glass shattered on the floor.

There was an approaching patter of heels. A door swung inward, spilling a wedge of dim light into the room. Through the opening something blurred but solid passed. It had a woman's face.

The woman glided through the dimness with the calm authority of a housekeeper. She leaned over the bed.

Babe had never seen the woman before.

I'm still dreaming, she told herself. *This is one of those dreams-within-a-dream. . . . If I concentrate I'll wake up. . . .*

The woman was playing the beam of a penlight across Babe's face.

Wake up Babe, count ten and wake up. . . .

Babe clenched her eyes shut and opened them again.

The woman was still there. She was wearing a nurse's cap. Everything about her seemed plump: the shape of her face, her arms and bust, and especially her eyes. Large and warm, ringed with dark lashes, they were studying Babe with a curious remoteness—as if Babe were a picture in a magazine.

"Who the hell are you, and what are you doing in my bedroom?" Babe said.

Tried to say. To her surprise, she had to push the words out of her throat.

The muscles of the woman's face jerked into a knot. Her hands scrabbled beside the bed, and the room was flooded in light.

The first thing Babe saw clearly was a call-button cord swaying eight inches from her face. It was hanging from the rung of a metal retainer that enclosed her like a rabbit cage.

Gradually, the space beyond the cage came into focus: not the soft peach tones of her hand-blocked silk walls, but a low-gloss, institutional white.

A man hurried into the room.

"She talked!" the nurse said breathlessly.

The man came around to the bed. A name tag angled carelessly across his breast pocket said DR. H. RIVAS. "Can you hear me?" he asked.

Babe said, "I hear you."

He pulled back. "Do you know who you are?"

"I'm Babe Vanderwalk Devens and I'd like to know who you two jokers are."

Confusion flickered in his eyes. "I'm Doctor Harry Rivas. And this is nurse Emmajean Deely."

"Whose nurse is she?"

"She's your nurse."

"And you're my doctor?"

"I'm the night intern. Dr. Corey is your neurologist. He'll be here as soon as we notify him."

"Notify him of what? What do I need a neurologist for?"

Dr. Rivas glanced at nurse Deely. "You had an accident."

"What kind of accident?"

"Don't worry about that now. You're going to be fine."

"This is a dream."

The doctor glanced at the nurse.

"You're not real!" Babe screamed.

The nurse's hand took firm hold of Babe's shoulder. Babe stared in surprise at the clear polished nails and the wedding band: it was a real hand, strong and warm, really pressing into her flesh.

Deftly and quickly, the young doctor slipped a needle into Babe's upper arm.

The pricking was real too.

* * *

Babe was sitting up in the hospital bed, trembling but awake, when a swarthy male nurse brought in her lunch tray.

"Nice to see you up, Mrs. Devens." The man moved the wheelchair away from the bed—Babe's one effort to get to the john on her own had been a disaster—and then he slid the tray onto the hospital table. "Enjoy."

She studied the meal—a bowl of anonymous yellow soup and a mysterious compote that resembled fruit.

She became aware of a woman studying her from across the room. The woman was trim and wavy blond and childishly sexy in her not very well closed white hospital smock. There was a soft slow something in the woman's glance that made Babe stare back.

Babe raised her hand and the woman raised hers at the same instant. With a start Babe recognized herself in the dresser mirror. Her face was pale and hollowed and there were dark lines under her eyes. A disturbing sense of unreality rushed in on her.

"My hair's different," she said.

"People have been moving you around," the nurse said. "Hair gets mussed up."

"It's shorter," Babe said. "Did they operate on my head?"

"Don't be silly."

"How long have I been here?"

The nurse came across the room and spoke gently. "Here. Let me." She took the spoon and dipped it into the soup bowl.

Babe watched the plump hands, wide and strong.

"Needing a nurse to spoonfeed me my soup—I'm not that helpless."

"Think you can feed yourself?"

"I'm damned well going to give it a try."

Babe took the spoon and on the second try scooped up a bit of soup and wobbled it to her mouth.

"That's good, Mrs. Devens."

"Look, you've taken me to the potty and wiped the drool off my pillow—that qualifies us as intimates. I wish you'd call me Babe."

"Okay, Babe. And you call me E.J."

"What's E.J. stand for?"

"Emmajean. Is Babe your real name?"

"Beatrice."

"Why do they call you Babe?"

"My mademoiselle called me Bébé. When I went to kindergarten the other girls thought it was a hoot—a great big five-year-old with a name like that. It got shortened to Babe and it stuck through school and college—after that it just came along with me—like an albatross."

Something had happened to E.J.'s eyes: suddenly they were crinkled and quizzical. "You said 'albatross.' You don't have any trouble remembering words, do you."

"Am I supposed to? E.J., what kind of accident did I have?"

E.J. hesitated. "I don't know exactly."

"That's bull. You do know exactly."

"Only the doctor or immediate family can tell you. Regulations."

Later. E.J.'s voice. "Visitors, Babe."

Babe surfaced, opening her eyes. She saw a woman in a navy blue dress with a single strand of pearls. The woman was holding an issue of *Town and Country.*

"Mama?" A question, not a statement.

Webbing out from her mother's eyes were small creases that Babe had not seen the night before. The hair was different too—chic and gray, caught loosely at the back of her neck by a tiny gold coil.

"Beatrice, darling."

Her mother said it as one word. *Beatricedarling.* Lucia Vanderwalk had never accepted her daughter's nickname and had loathed it when it caught on in the press.

A kiss.

Lucia's hands made a protective circle around Babe's face, small white hands with wonderfully long fingers, manicured to perfection. A little whiff of her perfume came drifting down—Tea Rose, her favorite, her only. "See who I've brought you."

Lucia stepped back to make room for a man in a three-piece gray pinstripe suit. He was a big bear of an old fellow with cheerful blue eyes and curly hair, and he was holding a bouquet of pink gardenias, grinning.

"Papa." Babe opened her arms.

With the slightly formal carriage of an investment banker, Hadley Vanderwalk III bent down and planted a gallant little kiss on Babe's forehead. "How's my Babe?" His lips smiled below the small moustache that had been brown last night but was gray today. "Gosh, you look dandy, kid."

He handed her the flowers. She didn't know what to do with them. E.J. took them and scurried off to find a vase.

Babe's parents placed chairs near the bed. Lucia spent a moment arranging herself and Babe wondered why she looked so much older than the night before.

"You've been asleep," Lucia said. "You had an accident." The voice had changed. She still had her New York Brahman accent, but there was a darker timbre than Babe remembered. "Don't worry. The doctors and nurses have taken excellent care of you."

Babe said, "What kind of accident?"

Lucia dug into an enormous petit point shoulder bag and came up with tea bags, a silver teapot, lemon slices, a plastic bag of crystallized sugar that was colored like sand on a magic beach, a pint of Dellwood vitamin-D-enriched milk. "Nurse, may we have some cups and boiling water?"

Tea was laid out on the hospital table. Lucia served.

"You can drink liquids, can't you, Beatrice?"

"Of course I can drink liquids."

"Do you still like lemon?"

"Lemon's fine."

They sat sipping. Teaspoons clinked. Babe had a sense that the scene was being acted rather than simply being allowed to happen. She suspected that the only improvisations were hers.

"You haven't told me what kind of accident," she said.

"Things change, dear heart," Lucia said.

Thoughts somersaulted through Babe's mind. She knew her mother well enough to know she was hiding something. "Where's Scottie? Where's Cordelia?"

"Cordelia is thriving. She's just fine."

Lucia crossed to the dresser and took a moment staring at Cordelia's photograph on the bureau. Babe realized that her mother was limping slightly.

"Mama, did you hurt your foot?"

"My hip. It's been this way for quite some time."

"But last night you were dancing."

Lucia sat on the edge of the bed and took her daughter's hand. "Tell me, dear heart, what was last night's date?"

"September fourth."

Her mother looked at her in silence and a mildness came into her eyes. "And what happened last night?"

"We celebrated the anniversary of my company. We had a huge party at the Casino in the Park."

"And how did East Eighty-ninth Street look when you last saw it?"

"When I visited Lisa Berensen in maternity—it was a lot of quaint old rowhouses."

Lucia walked to the window and pulled open the curtain. "Nurse, would you put my daughter in the chair? I want her to see those quaint old rowhouses for herself."

E.J. helped Babe into the wheelchair and wheeled her to the window. Babe sat staring.

Late afternoon shadows were beginning to flood the street. Here and there spots of sunlight filtered through the moving leaves of a tree. The pale new leaves had a glowing translucence, like bone china.

Suddenly the street seemed infinite under the fading sun. Everything stopped and time seemed to hold its breath. Babe sensed an extraordinary catastrophe about to occur.

"It's . . . spring," she said.

There was a flicker of agreement in Lucia's eyes. "Yes, dear heart —it's spring, and a lovely time to wake up."

Understanding came like a chop to the throat. Babe couldn't speak. Contradictions reconciled like pieces of jigsaw puzzle slipping together: the changes in her parents, the length of her hair, her surprising muscular weakness.

"I've been here seven months."

"And then some." The firm features of Lucia's face were frozen in careful neutrality. "Take another look out the window. Don't you notice anything else?"

The sky was high blue with white cumulus clouds. Beneath it the sidewalks were thronged with men and women and the streets were blocked with cars and taxis. But the cars in the street had a strange look and so did the people's clothes. There was a different skyline, rippling with changes like a flower that had bloomed overnight.

Of all the buildings on the street Babe could recognize only one old mass of masonry on the corner.

Her hands gripped the armrests of the wheelchair and she was invaded by a sense of her whole being slipping away from her.

"Do you think all that was done in seven months?" Lucia handed her daughter the copy of *Town and Country.* "You've been in coma for seven months . . . and seven years."

Babe read the date on the cover of the magazine. Her breath stopped and pain caught her ribs.

"The doctors said you wouldn't believe it right away." Lucia's eyes and voice were shot through with gentleness. "But you've come through dreadful circumstances before—your first marriage, the automobile accident. You'll come through this."

"It's not true! It can't be!" Babe's fist struck the arms of the wheelchair. "How did seven years go by in one night? It can't have happened! Where's Scottie? Why isn't he here?"

Babe felt the soothing insinuation of her mother's hand on her shoulder, as soft as milk. Lucia said, "Go ahead and cry, dear heart."

"Cry? I want to scream, I want to break something!"

"You'd be better off crying."

"Please—someone just help me understand what's happened." Babe began sobbing.

Her mother hugged her. "You've understood enough for one day."

As Lucia and Hadley Vanderwalk were leaving the hospital, an administrator by the name of Thelma T. Blauberg stopped them, introduced herself, and asked if they'd had a nice visit with their daughter.

Lucia stared for a moment at the woman's inquiring blue eyes—a little too inquiring—and curly gray hair. "An excellent visit, thank you."

"I'm so glad. Naturally, the hospital will say nothing about Mrs. Devens's recovery to anyone. But there *is* a C-3 on her file. Police notification required if victim dies or recovers consciousness. Normally we try to comply within eight hours."

2

"I LIKE IT VERY MUCH," THE MAN SAID.

Melissa Hatfield caught something in the voice. There was a "but" there. Her eyes fixed on the short man with a full head of gray hair. He was wearing designer slacks, a striped polo shirt.

The room was a thirty-by-fifty-foot cave of white light, shimmering like an image on a TV screen with the brightness set too high. Sun bounced off naked walls and inlaid floor.

"You can remodel," Melissa Hatfield suggested.

Nothing about selling apartments in the more than ten years Melissa Hatfield had been selling them had ever been easy. Real estate in Manhattan was a buyer's market and this man knew it.

"What does the maintenance run?" he asked.

"Seventeen fifty."

He coughed—a hacking sound that came from his chest. "Cold in here," he said.

Noon sun beat against the French doors, but an icy current was flowing through the air.

The man's wife called him to the terrace. "We can put a garden there."

She was pointing. Short and dark-haired, she was wearing battered blue clogs, a pullover, and a red sweater tied around her neck by its sleeves. The I'm-rich-and-I-don't-need-to-impress-you look.

Melissa Hatfield wondered if this was their idea of how to spend Memorial Day weekend: *Let's go tour some upmarket co-ops and pretend we're interested in buying.* "We can arrange terms," she said. "Ten percent down will hold it."

The man was staring into her eyes so determinedly she felt an impulse to laugh. He was trying to do it all at once: come on to her, turn down the apartment, maintain his image as a high roller.

"You're very kind," he said.

His wife crossed toward the hall, looking over the cherrywood cabinets in the kitchen, swinging them open, flicking them shut with careless slams. "Could we see the rest of the apartment?" she said.

Oh well, Melissa Hatfield thought. *It's only a beautiful Sunday on Memorial Day weekend and they got me here for nothing.*

She led them down the hallway. The bedroom door was shut.

Melissa Hatfield stopped. The door shouldn't have been shut. She opened it. The room was in darkness, needles of sunlight jabbing in through the Levolor blinds. The blinds shouldn't have been down.

She stood motionless, senses suddenly alert.

There was a faint pumping sound, like an animal catching its breath. The air smelled of something foreign, something vaguely sweet and unpleasant. Cold sweat came out on her body.

She crossed to the window. Shadows hovered like nets. The air conditioner was on full blast. She changed the setting and turned the plastic rod controlling the blinds.

In the brilliance of daylight Melissa Hatfield saw him.

He was lying on the floor, naked, hooded in black leather. A Vietnam peace symbol had been gashed into his chest. One of his legs had been taken off and the fresh stump of thigh looked like a cross section of beef carcass in a butcher shop showcase.

Melissa Hatfield's throat froze up solid and then a cry tore itself out of her, rocketing through the silence.

Seven miles away, a man lay on the beach.

He was one of four thousand souls who had journeyed from city homes down to the Brooklyn shore that day, schlepping brave little pieces of portable comfort with them. He had stretched out on an orange beach blanket, and his head was resting on a rolled blue bath towel. His eyes were shut. A yellow umbrella shaded him. A Sony transistor radio was piping whispers of Little Richard into his ear. Little Richard was his twelve-year-old daughter's choice, not his. He would have chosen Sinatra or Tony Bennett. But it was meant to be his daughter's day, not his, one of those rare days that father and daughter actually got to share, so he'd let her choose the music.

His wallet was stuffed inside his shoe, rolled into the blue towel under his head. There was a shield in his wallet. A gold shield, New York City detective.

An off-duty cop was required to carry his gun with him at all times, but Vince Cardozo was in violation of regulations. He'd decided he wasn't going to wear three pounds of nickel stuffed into his bathing trunks like an extra dick or wrap the gun in a towel and leave it on the beach when he got around to trying the water. He'd left his .38 Smith & Wesson at home.

He'd closed his eyes, telling himself it was just for two minutes. Three minutes tops. Almost immediately he'd sunk down into peacefulness, letting go of the world. Where he was, he wasn't hearing Little Richard. Wasn't hearing the waves. Wasn't smelling ocean salt or beached kelp or wind-borne suntan oil or sand that had been broiled to a sparkle.

At that moment Lieutenant Vince Cardozo was happy. He didn't know anything. Not who he was, not where he was. Didn't know that the sun was glowing, didn't know that the wind had a shine on it like twelve trumpets. Didn't know that his daughter, Terri, who had been sitting beside him twiddling the dial of the radio, had got bored and wandered off along the beach.

Lieutenant Cardozo's breathing became softer and softer. There was almost no movement in his chest. The coiled strength relaxed. The breeze stirred his hair, medium brown, beginning to gray at the temples.

White clouds sailed across the blue sky. Long swells tilted the sea up and down, sending out pinpoints of light. Out by the horizon the wind-driven whitecaps were edged in glinting gold. With a squawking cry gulls swooped in a great flock down toward the great bursts of leaves of the beachfront trees.

Something buzzed. It was a patterned buzz, a nagging seed of nightmare, two shorts and a long, pitched like a dentist's drill.

Vince Cardozo's hand awakened, located the page boy on the blanket beside him, swatted it dead.

He opened his eyes, pushed himself up on one elbow, forcing back his shoulders, opening wide. A stocky man, he prided himself on being well-built for someone of forty-odd summers. If his forehead was a bit high and smooth, he had thoughtfully balanced it with a devil-may-care moustache, giving himself, he hoped, a face sleek enough to detract from the blocky torso.

He squinted and saw Terri coming over the sand. She had dark hair and brown eyes like his and a turned-up nose, not like his. He waved at her. With the hand not holding a Diet Pepsi, she waved back.

God, he thought, *she's so damned beautiful in that yellow swim-suit.* Only twelve, tall for her age, of course; she carried herself with a grace that was impossible not to watch.

She settled down onto the blanket, looking at him with a serene humorous interest.

"Where have you been?" he asked.

"Not so far away as you." She had faintly freckled skin and there was a challenging tilt to her chin. In back of her the sky looked like no sky he had ever seen.

The pager buzzed again.

Behind her eyes was a sudden flare-up of disappointment.

"Dad," she said. "Answer it." Like her mother. Same tone, same look of good-humored annoyance.

She poked through her little plastic change purse and a minute later he felt the soft pressure of her fingers pushing a quarter into his hand. She looked up at him for a moment out of those bottomless brown eyes.

"I'll be right back," he said.

She kissed him.

At the refreshment stand he dropped the quarter in the phone and dialed Manhattan. He recognized the voice that answered. "Flo, it's Vince."

"Hiya, Vince, we got something for you."

Cardozo had no trouble finding the address. Beaux Arts Tower stood on a street of boutiques and French bakeries and antique dealers and $200-an-hour psychoanalysts, a narrow skyscraper thrusting sharply above the neighboring landmarked six-story brownstones.

The building had a glassy, upscale look. He remembered the ads: BEAUX ARTS TOWER. THE LUXURY OF THE 21ST CENTURY NOW. Built in the air space over a midtown museum, it was prime Manhattan real estate, occupied by many of the city's movers and shakers.

A large pale blue Plymouth was double-parked in front of the building. Light vibrated on the car. As Cardozo approached, the passenger door swung open and Mel O'Brien, chief of detectives, stepped out.

In his gray gabardine suit, conservative necktie, and dark brown cordovan shoes, the chief looked like a fund-raiser for a prep school.

"Very handsome," Cardozo said.

"What's that?" The chief's face was set in hard, impatient lines.

"You, Chief. Handsome."

Chief O'Brien was a man of fine bearing, age fifty-seven, tall, blue-eyed, with silver hair and a pink face. An angry pink face. "What kept you?"

"Traffic."

"I'll be right back," O'Brien told his chauffeur, a detective sitting at the wheel. If you were the chief of detectives, even your driver had a gold shield.

Cardozo and Mel O'Brien approached the building.

The chief moved with a swing to his shoulders. "Hope I didn't pull you away from anything important."

Cardozo answered, "You did."

The chief was solemnly reading his face. "What are you working on?"

"The usual. A couple dozen homicides."

"Farm them out. There's something upstairs I need you to take over right away. Murdered man in a mask."

"Mask?" That interested Cardozo. You got jaded in this job. A murdered man was ordinary, a mask wasn't.

"Bondage mask, executioner's mask, some black leather shit. Someone killed him and left him naked in one of the for-sale apartments. Took one of his legs."

"Ouch."

"You get your own task force. Borrow anyone from any precinct you want. Put together your dream team. Whatever they've got ongoing, they're liberated. And they're on overtime, starting now."

Cardozo went into the lobby, a cool art deco arcade of white Carrara marble and patinated bronze. There were man-high corn plants, lushly potted, and deep leather sofas, unoccupied. A sign said ALL VISITORS MUST BE ANNOUNCED. A nervous-looking man in a green uniform sat by the switchboard. He looked over and said, " 'Scuse me, who are you visiting?"

He had an accent that was half Puerto Rico, half New York street, and as he came forward Cardozo saw that the right side of his face was streaked with scars that had probably been fresh yesterday.

"I'm visiting the corpse."

The doorman stopped, startled, and an Irish sergeant came around from behind the switchboard. "That's okay, Hector. Lieutenant, this is Hector—Hector, this is Lieutenant Cardozo. You'll be seeing a lot of him."

"How do you do, sir." The doorman, embarrassed, lifted his cap and revealed a wig that a dime store window dummy would have been ashamed to wear.

"Floor six, Lieutenant." The sergeant held the elevator door.

In the vestibule on six, a sergeant from the 22d precinct stood guard outside the apartment. He was young, pale, and acting harried. He glanced at Cardozo's shield and handed him plastic gloves.

Cardozo twisted his fingers into the gloves. They popped on with revolting kissing smacks. As he entered the apartment, another sergeant wrote Cardozo's name, shield number, and time of arrival into the crime scene log.

The naked body, bathed in sunlight, was stretched flat on its back on the floor of the master bedroom.

The calm blue eyes, staring through a black leather mask that hugged the entire skull, were fixed on the ceiling, their gaze flat and mysterious. The mouth was locked behind a steel zipper.

Cardozo crouched for a closer look.

The mask, with its uncanny power, disturbed and fascinated him. If ever an object had suggested absolute evil to his mind, it was that crudely stitched piece of dyed hide, combining the anonymity of the executioner with the obscenity of a pig's snout.

The body was in good shape—well-exercised, lean; it was Caucasian, the body of a man in his twenties.

With the stopping of the heart, gravity had pulled the blood to the lower half of the body, causing dark blue discolorations of the parts lying downside.

The chest was crisscrossed with scratch marks. They made a circle with a Y in it, the old sixties peace sign. None appeared to have penetrated the muscle layer.

The victim's right leg had been removed. From the look of the shear marks on the startlingly white femoral bone, a buzz saw had done the job.

On the foot of the remaining leg a tag had been tied to the big toe. The tag was a standard department form, number 95. The first officer on the scene had filled in the time of discovery and relevant details.

Dan Hippolito, the medical examiner—a slim man in his middle fifties with receding, graying hair—opened the zipper of the mask to examine the dead man's lips and gums.

"When do you think he died?" Cardozo asked.

"Not more than twenty-four hours ago . . . not less than twelve."

"How was he killed?"

The M.E. looked closely at the throat. "Pending autopsy, I'd say fracture of the cervical vertebrae."

In New York City, Cardozo reflected, strangling was not one of your more usual methods of dispatching your fellow man. "I have a feeling this one died high. I want to know the drugs."

"We'll give his blood a good spin. Should have all prescriptions for you tomorrow."

A photographer was snapping pictures of the dead man. A detective was taking measurements with a pocket tape, calling out figures for his partner to mark on the crime scene sketch. A technician was outlining the corpse in chalk.

A team from the Forensic Unit was taking scrapings from the floor. Cardozo recognized Lou Stein from the lab, hunkered down searching for blood particles or traces of semen.

"What have you got, Lou?"

Lou glanced up. He was two weeks back from his Florida vacation, and his face was still mahogany beneath a fringe of straw-colored hair. "Ask me tomorrow."

Down the hallway fingerprint men armed with flitguns and makeup brushes pumped dark powder on windowsills and door-knobs, dusting for latent prints. A sergeant stood writing in a notebook.

"You were the first on the scene, Sergeant?" Cardozo asked.

The sergeant nodded. He looked all of twenty years old: freckles, blond hair, a cowlick.

"Who called you here?"

The sergeant tilted his head toward an overweight man in slacks and a peach Lacoste shirt standing near the doorway. "The super."

"The super found the body?"

"No. She did." Now the sergeant was nodding toward a good-looking, light-brown-haired woman who was taking a light from the super's Zippo. "The sales agent. She was showing the apartment to those two." He indicated a woman with a red sweater tied around her shoulders and a man in a striped polo shirt.

"Anyone else seen the body that I don't know about?"

"No one's left the apartment since I got here."

Cardozo crossed to the civilians and introduced himself. The super gave his name as Bill Connell, and Cardozo asked if he had mentioned to anyone what he'd seen in the apartment.

The super shook his head. "Not a soul. I made the phone call and came right back."

"I'm going to ask you people not to talk about anything you've seen here. Not that a man is dead, or naked, or wearing a mask, or missing a leg. We want to keep those details secret because aside from the people in this apartment, only the killer knows about them. The success of the investigation is going to depend on your cooperation."

The civilians were nodding, promising. They always nodded, they always promised, and in Cardozo's experience they kept the promise for no more than twenty-four hours.

He asked the would-be buyers short questions and listened to long, meandering answers: they were in the market to buy a Manhattan apartment, had chosen this day to drive in from New Rochelle. They were obviously scared and he had the impression they didn't know anything more than they were saying. He got their names and address and had them fingerprinted and let them go.

Cardozo asked Connell if there were any electric saws in the building.

"Sixteen and seventeen are being remodeled into a duplex. There may be a saw up there."

Cardozo sent a sergeant to search 16 and 17. "Who has the key to this apartment?"

"Till it's sold you open it with the passkey," Connell said.

"Who has the passkey?"

"It's kept in the personnel office," Connell said.

"All personnel have access?"

Connell nodded.

"Any of the residents have passkeys?"

"No, sir."

"Anyone besides personnel have access to the personnel office and the passkey?"

"I do, Lieutenant."

Cardozo looked at the sales agent. She impressed him with her lack of embarrassment or uncertainty.

"My name's Melissa Hatfield. It's my job to show the apartments. Sometimes there are prospective buyers on very short notice and I have to let myself in."

He noted things about her skin texture, voice tone, details of clothing. She wore a white dress with large woven holes in it and it looked on her the way dresses were supposed to look on fashionable women and rarely did.

"Did you let yourself in today?"

"Yes."

"I'll have to ask you some questions. Would you mind waiting in the lobby?" Cardozo turned to the super. "I'll need a list of building personnel and the worksheets for the last two days."

"I have those down in the office," the super said.

Cardozo and Connell were passing through the Beaux Arts garage. A shadowless fluorescent glow flickered across Porsches, Ferraris, BMWs, Mercedeses, and Rollses.

"Is that garage door kept locked?" Cardozo asked.

Connell nodded. "Garage users have electronic remotes to open it."

"Do the staff have remotes?"

"We have to. For deliveries."

Cardozo asked how the garage was guarded.

"Monitored from the lobby." Connell pointed to a closed-circuit TV camera poised on the cinderblock wall.

They passed the laundry room. Two washers, two dryers.

"Residents use those?" Cardozo asked.

"The maids use them."

There were two elevator entrances in the basement corridor—one marked Passenger, one marked Freight. A third door was marked Authorized Personnel Only. Cardozo opened it.

"Garbage compactor." Connell grinned. "State of the art."

"What happens after the garbage is compacted?"

"It goes into those state-of-the-art bags."

Cardozo took a moment fingering one of the black plastic bags. The plastic was sturdy stuff, a good eighth of an inch thick.

"And where do the bags go?"

"The trucking company picks them up."

Connell led Cardozo to the personnel office. Besides a desk, the windowless room held an easy chair, two metal chairs, a card table, and two filing cabinets.

"Personnel list," Connell muttered. "Worksheet . . ." He opened a cabinet drawer and looked behind a pile of racing forms.

"And the residents," Cardozo said.

"Bingo." Connell pulled out three lists.

Cardozo looked them over. "You're a resident."

Connell nodded. "The apartment comes with the job."

"You weren't working yesterday?"

"I get holidays and weekends off," Connell said.

"Where were you?"

"I spent the day at home. My wife Ebbie—she's an invalid. We don't get out too much."

Cardozo folded the lists and slipped them into his jacket pocket. He noticed a battered-looking thirteen-inch Sony TV on the desk. "Who watches that?"

Connell seemed embarrassed. "I do."

"Don't you have your own upstairs?"

"Ebbie doesn't like sports. So if there's an important game, I usually catch it here."

The room had gray concrete walls and cement floor and naked pipes overhead. It didn't look like the coziest spot for watching the Mets.

"Can I use your phone?" Cardozo asked.

"Help yourself. Do you need me?"

"Not for the moment."

"I'll be in the utility room. Out in the hall and hook a right."

Alone, Cardozo took out his notebook and spent three minutes drawing up a list of his own. He wrote down eight names, crossed out three, after a little thought crossed out a fourth.

He lifted the phone and dialed headquarters. "Flo, it's Vince." He read her the names of the four detectives. "Pull them off whatever they're doing, get them up here."

"You know what they're doing, Vince, they're having a day off."

"So was I."

"You're not going to be a loved man."

3

IN THE BEDROOM, CARDOZO STOOD ALONE IN THE SUNLIGHT GLAR-
ing through the window. He was working now, stirred by the sense of
a secret waiting to be revealed, a sense that was tantalizing and
almost sexual in its excitement.

He looked about the blank surfaces of the unfurnished room, seek-
ing some object, some detail that bore the imprint of what had
happened here.

The bedroom door had two hinges. He could remember a time
when doors had had three hinges, but nowadays builders got by with
two. He swung the door. In the crack just below the bottom hinge
something small and dark and glistening had wedged against the
jamb. He crouched. Using the tip of his gloved finger he gently
poked the dark thing.

An inch of black plastic fell to the floor.

He picked up the fragment, turned it over in his hand. He tested
the thickness between his thumb and forefinger. He wasn't surprised
at what he felt. A piece of garbage bag, similar to the ones he'd seen
in the compactor room.

He dropped the fragment into a clear plastic evidence bag.

Down the hallway, where the baseboard wasn't quite joined to the
wall, he found another piece of black plastic.

"Cleaning house?"

Cardozo glanced up. "You look lousy," he said.

In fact Detective Sam Richards didn't look lousy at all. Nattily
dressed in a navy blue blazer with brass buttons, charcoal gray summer-weight slacks, he looked like a linebacker who had traded in his
shoulder pads for a TV news anchor's chair.

But the expression on his long, unsmiling black face was grumpy, and his big roguish moustache was pulled down into a frown. There was a small pink Band-Aid on his chin.

"How'd you get the battle wound?"

"Cut myself shaving."

"Hung over?"

"Maybe. I spent last night celebrating."

"Celebrating what?"

"Having today off."

"That was premature."

"Tell me about it, Vince. Tell me why I'm alive, tell me why I'm here."

"How about if I just tell you about this killing." Cardozo described what he had seen, reviewed what he had found, and walked Richards through the apartment.

"I want you to canvass," Cardozo said. "Cover the building, cover the neighborhood, see if any of the local Peeping Toms or storekeepers noticed anything. You'll split the job with Greg Monteleone."

"Tell Monteleone I've started."

Cardozo felt he had been poking through kitchen cabinets for an hour. His watch told him it had been twenty-five minutes.

As he swung open the door beneath the sink, the inside of his nose prickled violently. Print powder came eddying up in a cloud. He sneezed once, and again, and then again.

"Gesundheit." A fortyish man in a badly cut suit the color of dry clay was watching from the corridor, amused. Detective Greg Monteleone's brown eyes were gleaming in a cheerfully soulful face that gave him the appearance of a prankish poet. "Three sneezes means good luck."

"Thanks, Greg." Cardozo opened cabinets above the sink.

"What are you looking for?"

"If I knew, maybe I wouldn't be looking for it."

"Hasn't Forensic already been through those?"

"I like to see for myself."

"Trouble with you is, Vince, you're a perfectionist, a type A personality." In his off-hours Monteleone was a voracious reader of self-help books. "You have to learn to delegate."

"I'm delegating. That's why you're here."

"You looked in here?" Monteleone had a hand on the refrigerator. In all the years Cardozo had known Greg Monteleone, he had had his hand on either a refrigerator door or a girl's leg. Monteleone pulled out the plastic vegetable and meat bins, setting them down on the linoleum and peering into the empty spaces behind them.

"Don't eat the evidence," Cardozo said.

"There isn't any evidence. Not even a goddamned beer."

Cardozo searched through the dishwasher, the drawers, the little closet for brooms and mops. His eye kept coming back to the dishwasher. It was a front-loading brown-and-cream model.

He pulled down the dishwasher door. He gave the lower basket a forward tug, and it glided easily out over the open door. He pulled on the upper basket, the shallow rack for cups and glasses. It slid almost all the way out, empty.

He gave another tug and this time felt firm resistance. He reached a hand in, probed. He pulled out a handful of neatly coiled black insulated electric cord. Now he tugged the upper basket and it slid all the way out, empty. He pulled the lower basket out, lifted it off its tracks and set it on the floor.

The water sprinkler, shaped like a small perforated propeller, sat in a recess on the floor of the washer. He realized now that only two of the paddles belonged to the dishwasher. What he had taken to be the third paddle was a mini rotary saw, wedged into the hollow beneath the sprinkler.

He lifted the saw out. "What do you think of this, Greg?"

Greg Monteleone was standing behind him, looking over his shoulder. "Black and Decker. The best." He took the saw in his gloved hands, angling the blade to the window light. "This baby cuts bone, all right."

Cardozo scratched his ear. "The killer didn't hide the body, but he hid the saw. What kind of thinking is that?"

"It's crazy thinking," a female voice said. "You have a crazy killing, so what else do you expect?"

A woman stood in the doorway. Cardozo turned and gave Detective Ellie Siegel a smile. "Glad you could make it, Ellie."

She gave him a look from her dark eyes that was not a smile by a long shot. He recognized another cop in mourning for her lost holiday.

"Detective Ellie Siegel," Cardozo said, "you remember Detective Greg Monteleone."

"Not funny," Ellie said. "Please, not today."

Greg and Ellie were good detectives; they just weren't the greatest friends. Greg got along with Ellie better than she got along with him—but Greg made it a point to get along with just about anyone who didn't insult him. Ellie made no secret of the fact that she considered Greg, in his opinions and tastes, a thug.

Greg got back at Siegel by openly admiring her looks, which wasn't hard. She had Mediterranean coloring and fine Semitic bones, and her dark eyes were just close enough together to give her gaze a strange, arresting quality. She was a woman that men watched, even when she wasn't wearing the violet body-hugging dress she had on today.

Cardozo took Siegel down to the bedroom and showed her where the dead man had been found.

"Well, Lieutenant," she said, "just what do you expect me to do about it?"

"Find the leg. It was put in a heavy-duty black plastic garbage bag. It could have been dumped down the chute in this building. It could have been tossed into a public garbage can or trash basket. It could already be landfill."

"It wouldn't be landfill, not yet. Sanitation doesn't move that fast on a holiday weekend. And it could have been dumped in someone else's garbage. I passed about twenty French restaurants between here and Seventh Avenue, and they weren't all shut. Restaurants use private garbage services."

"You can have all the uniformed bodies you need. Search the garbage cans in a ten-block radius and then search the landfills."

She pursed her lips thoughtfully. "What makes you think this leg is in one piece?"

"It may not be."

"We could be looking for hamburger?"

"We could be looking for hamburger."

"Vince, ruining my weekend is one thing, but ruining this dress I'm not going to forgive. You could have at least warned me. I'd've worn jeans."

"You don't have to dress like you're going to a tea party all the time."

"It's Memorial Day for God's sake."

"Who dresses for Memorial Day?"

"Jewish princesses."

"You didn't see any strangers going in or out of the building?" Cardozo was in the lobby, questioning the doorman. "No delivery men, no repairmen?"

"Holiday weekend, you kidding?" Hector Dominguez shook his head. Sunlight spilling through the lobby door sank into his toupee, refracting brightly when it hit the fringe of graying human hair over his ears. "Yesterday maybe three, four people went in and out of this building."

"Who?"

"Residents."

"Which residents?"

"The ones who aren't away. Most got houses in the Hamptons, houses in Europe. A few don't."

"How do you think that guy got into six?"

"He didn't get in on my shift."

"Think he came in through the cellar?"

"He'd have to get through the door; that takes a remote."

"You can buy those remotes."

"But you gotta set the code."

"There aren't that many codes, are there?"

"Anyone coming in through the cellar, it would have showed on the monitor."

Hector tapped a finger on the bank of four TV screens. Two showed the garage, and two showed the interiors of the elevators. The views of the garage were panning shots from cameras moving back and forth in automated hundred-eighty-degree arcs. The elevators were stationary shots from cameras mounted in the ceilings of the cabs.

"You were at this door from eight A.M. to four P.M. yesterday?" Cardozo kept going over it, testing to see if it kept coming out the same way. "You never left your post?"

Hector shrugged. "Maybe I went downstairs to take a leak."

"Maybe you took a leak or you took a leak?"

"I took a leak."

"What time?"

"It's not like it's a big deal you'd remember the exact time."

"You left this door unguarded?"

"I left it locked."

"Who has a key?"

"All the residents."

"So a resident could have come in, or anyone could have left, and you might not know?"

"That could happen. It's not like I was expecting a murder."

But his eyes were saying something else. They said he'd been expecting something, maybe still was expecting it.

"How'd you get those scratches on your face, Hector?"

Hector's hand went up to his cheek and a glass ruby flashed from his finger. "Man, my damned cat scratched me."

"When?"

"Yesterday, day before. I forget."

"You'd better work on that memory, Hector."

A big red-headed man sauntered into the lobby. He had florid coloring and glinting green eyes that didn't take the least offense when Hector challenged, "Hey, you gotta be announced. Where you goin'?"

"That's okay, Hector," Cardozo said. "Detective Malloy's with me."

Hector touched a fumbling hand to the brim of his cap and Detective Carl Malloy, smiling, touched a finger to a nonexistent hatbrim.

Cardozo drew Malloy aside and filled him in on the crime. "I want you to check out all the cars and trucks parked in a five-block radius."

Malloy was a constitutionally cheerful man, but at the mention of a five-block radius he drew a deep sigh. Five blocks meant better than three thousand vehicles. The sigh puckered Malloy's fire-engine red vest at its straining brass buttons. A little under six feet and a little over two hundred pounds, Malloy had trouble with his weight. He binged daily on bagels and cream cheese, claiming his doctor had told him dairy products would quiet his ulcer.

"You can have all the bodies you need," Cardozo said. "Start running the licenses through National Crime Bureau and see if anyone's got a record."

"You got it," Malloy said.

Cardozo nodded and turned and crossed the lobby. Melissa Hatfield was waiting on one of the leather sofas. She saw him and quickly jabbed out her cigarette.

"Would you mind showing me the other unsold apartments?" he asked.

"Why not? That's what I'm here for."

They took the elevator up to 12. There was a small carved drop-leaf table in the foyer, and a bowl of dried flowers had been put on it. A soothing aromatic spiciness filled the space.

She fitted the passkey into the lock and opened the door.

"Same floor plan," Cardozo observed.

"The buyer makes his own modifications," she said.

Cardozo crossed through the entrance hall into the livingroom. The air was warm and still. From the window he could see a bright gray sliver of the East River a mile away, glinting between Sutton Place high rises.

He explored the kitchen, the bedrooms, the bath. Something bothered him. "This is exactly the same as six?"

A hint of mischief crept into the line of her mouth. "Not quite. This one costs thirty thousand more."

They looked at 16 and 17 and 19. Cardozo had that same feeling— a difference. In 23 he asked, "The ceilings aren't a little lower here?"

"No, they're all ten foot eight. That's one of our selling points."

The livingroom of 29 had a pale blue oriental carpet and deep beige sofas. She explained that this one was the show suite.

"What's the price?"

"We're asking a million."

He whistled.

"It's not so high considering the view."

"You didn't build the view."

She smiled. "The buyer doesn't know that."

French windows led onto a terrace and Cardozo stepped out. Well-watered boxwoods masked a hip-high wrought-iron railing. Chains of creeping cars and trucks shimmered and rippled in the heat rising from the streets far below. From here you could see the Queens and Brooklyn shores and a surprising amount of green in a city that he had always thought of as asphalt, concrete, and glass.

"Something to drink?" Melissa Hatfield offered. "The company stocks everything."

"Scotch and water and a little ice will be fine."

When he returned to the livingroom, she was arranging bottles and glasses and napkins on the top of a carved rosewood chest that had been gutted and turned into a bar.

"Care for a nibbly?" she offered. "We have fish balls, chicken livers with bacon, cheese puffs. It only takes a minute to warm them in the microwave."

"No, thanks. I'm trying not to eat between meals." He sipped. She'd left the water out of his Scotch.

She caught his hesitation. "Sorry. I forgot you're not a potential buyer."

He let his gaze walk across the walls. There were three paintings and they reminded his untutored eye of French impressionists.

"Are the oils genuine?" he asked.

"The Vlamincks are real. The lawyer at the Metropolitan says the Renoir's a forgery. He wants to buy it himself."

"Are they safe here?"

"They're insured. If anyone steals them, Beaux Arts Properties will be richer than ever."

Cardozo pulled Bill Connell's list from his pocket. "Tell me about your tenants."

"We don't have too many tenants. Technically we're a co-op, and the law limits our income rental. There's Armani, the clothing shop on the first floor. They have five employees. They were closed for the holiday. Rizzoli, the book shop on the second floor. Four employees. Closed for the holiday. On the third floor there's Saveurs de Paris, a French pastry shop. *The New York Times* food critic likes them and they get three dollars an éclair. The concierge has an apartment on the same floor."

"What's a concierge?"

"Bill Connell, the super. He and his wife have a dinky two-roomer."

"I didn't know there was anything dinky in this building."

Her eyes lifted a moment toward his. "A little more than you might think."

Cardozo's eye went down the list. "Fourth floor. Doctors Morton Fine, D.D.S., P.C., Hildegarde Berencz, D.D.S., P.C., Seymour Black, D.D.S., P.C. Who are they?"

"Dentists."

"Closed for the holiday?"

"They close for every holiday you've ever heard of, including Ramadan."

"Fifth floor. Dr. Arnold Gross, M.D., P.C., Dr. Robin Lazaro, M.D., P.C., Paola Brandt, P.S.W., P.C., Renata Mills, P.S.W., P.C."

"Therapists. P.S.W. means psychiatric social worker. They don't have an M.D., they can't dispense drugs."

"Floor seven. Princess Lily Lobkowitz."

"Her ex-husband's Polish. It's one of those unverifiable titles. She can get a little crazy when she drinks, but I don't see her killing naked young men in black hoods."

"Duke and Duchess de Chesney. You've got a lot of titles in this building."

"I think the title's real. They're English and they're hardly ever here. Which makes them ideal in a cooperative situation. They let management vote their proxies."

"Debbi Hightower, nine?"

"She's a girl who thinks she's going to make it in show business."

"You don't?"

"Fortune telling's not my field. I only sell real estate."

"Father Will Madsen—tenth floor."

"He's the rector of that Episcopal church on the corner. Very quiet man, never disturbs a soul."

"Eleventh floor. Fred Lawrence."

"Accountant. He falsifies returns for some of the biggest guns in show biz and government."

"Why do you say falsifies?"

Her face colored. "Sorry. I'm really on today, aren't I. I don't know anything about Fred Lawrence. He strikes me as sneaky and he's an accountant, that's all. His wife wears loud, cheap clothes. Thinks she's sexy and she's not. Their child's a spoiled brat."

The twelfth floor was marked *unsold*. "I see there's no thirteen."

"We don't want bad luck in this building, Lieutenant."

"Fourteen—Billi von Kleist."

"He's president of Babethings—the clothing company Babe Vanderwalk founded. He's jet-setty. Maybe some of his friends are a little druggy."

"What kind of drugs?"

"Oh, most people are doing coke nowadays, aren't they?"

Cardozo looked at her. "I'm not."

"Neither am I. But you know what I mean."

A silence passed.

"Fifteen—Notre Dame. I take it that's not the football team," Cardozo said.

"The rock singer. You haven't heard of him?"

Cardozo scowled. "My daughter's heard of him."

"He's on tour. He's never here."

Sixteen and seventeen were marked *unsold*. "What about eighteen, Estelle Manfrey?"

"Very rich, very old, very frail—never here either. She lives in Palm Beach."

Nineteen was another *unsold*. "Twenty—Tillie Turnbull?"

"You and I know her as Jessica Lambert."

Cardozo's pencil stopped tapping. "The movie star?"

Melissa nodded. "She's a very nervous woman—always skittering around in dark glasses and babushkas. She puts her kerchief on before she puts on her makeup, so usually there's a ring of Max Factor around the kerchief. I don't really think men in black masks are her type."

"Twenty-one—Gordon Dobbs?"

"He writes books about society with a capital S. Who's sleeping with who, who got blackballed from what. He's very fastidious, very organized, has a reputation for malice that he doesn't quite live up to." She glanced up. "Are you asking if I think these people could be killers?"

"Just asking what you know about them. Twenty-two. Phil Bailey."

"President of NBS-TV and a lot else too. I drew up all the papers but I called him Philip. Phil equals Philip, right? Wrong. I had to redraw everything. His legal name's Phil. He had it changed. I checked the court records. It's that understated power trip that the really big people are on. They don't care if you know their name or their face or their income. In fact they'd rather you didn't. They don't want to be on the cover of *Time* and they don't go around blocking traffic with limousines. They're not out to impress anyone."

"But he managed to impress you."

She made a circling motion with her glass. "He and his wife are decent people. He's a powerful man. He's a polite man. A very attractive man. Men like that don't need to do the sort of thing we saw in six."

"Maybe his wife does."

"Why? She has Phil."

Her thought processes intrigued him. "You see it as a sex crime."

"Don't you?"

"Maybe." His eyes went back to the list. Twenty-three was marked *unsold.* "Twenty-four—Hank Doyle. The pro football player?"

"The same."

Cardozo was surprised. "He doesn't seem the type."

"Which way do you mean, Lieutenant? He's not the type who'd want Beaux Arts, or Beaux Arts wouldn't want his type?"

"Both."

"We gave him thirty percent off. We needed a black in the building."

"Why?"

"We had to be integrated to get federal funds."

"Are you sure you don't mean a city tax abatement?"

"No, Lieutenant. Beaux Arts Properties is smarter than that. In addition to the city tax abatement, we got federal funds for integrated, middle-income housing."

"This is middle-income?"

"According to some people."

Cardozo shook his head. "Twenty-five. Joan Adler."

"She writes about politics. She's a crusader in print, but in person she's a mouse. Always cringing in the corner of the elevator. She has a tremor in her arm. I think she may have m.s."

"I see twenty-six and twenty-seven have been made into a duplex for Johnny Stefano. Is that the composer?"

Melissa nodded. "He had a string of hit shows up through the mid-seventies. He was late with his last two maintenance payments. He may be having some kind of money trouble. I get the impression he's sexually kinky. He wears leather in the elevator. Of course a lot of people do nowadays. It may not mean much."

"Twenty-eight—William Benson."

Melissa Hatfield lit up. "He's an adorable old man. Completely unassuming. You'd never know he's built half the buildings that make New York New York. Including this building and the museum below it. Of course he's old now and has to walk with a cane, but he puts in a twelve-hour day."

Cardozo found it intriguing: Melissa Hatfield had a sharp word for practically everybody in the building—yet the president of the TV network and the old architect seemed to have won her heart. He wondered how.

He checked off floor 29, the apartment they were sitting in. Which brought them to floors 30 and 31.

"Esmée Burns," Cardozo said. "I see that's another duplex."

"Burns makes cosmetics," Melissa Hatfield said. "Very successfully."

Cardozo had a memory of dozens of small pink bottles on the bathroom shelf. "My wife used to use her stuff."

"Why'd she stop?"

"She died."

"Oh. I'm sorry."

"That's okay. I got used to it a long time ago."

"You're still wearing your wedding ring."

"In my work you wear a wedding ring whether you're married or not. It keeps things simple."

"Not a bad idea. Maybe I should try it."

Cardozo frowned at the list of occupants. "There's a lot of empty space in the building."

"We're one seventh vacant, Lieutenant. With the new tax laws, Manhattan real estate's soft."

Cardozo folded the list and slipped it back into his jacket pocket. "What did you do Saturday?" he asked.

"Me? Nothing special. Why? Am I a suspect?"

"You have access to the key."

She rose from the sofa. She had a good figure. He could see she worked at keeping in shape. "I lead a quiet life, Lieutenant. Saturday is one of my truly dull days. I slept late. I fed Zero."

"Who's Zero?"

"Zero's my cat. How's that for an alibi? He's a domestic short hair, marmalade, neutered, three legs—he had cancer last year. He's twelve years old."

"I was asking about you, not Zero. Your cat's in the clear."

"Sorry. I'm a cat person. Do you have a cat, Lieutenant?"

"Street Abyssinian."

"I never heard of that breed."

"It's more an accident than a breed. My daughter adopted him from the animal shelter."

"I hope he's had his shots."

"He's has, thanks for asking. Tell me, did you happen to go out at all yesterday?"

"I'm sorry, I can't help loving cats. I guess I go on about them. Yes, I went for a walk in Central Park."

"What did you do for lunch?"

"I skipped lunch. Had an early dinner."

"Where?"

"Where I have all my dinners—in my kitchen. Then I saw a movie."

"What movie?"

"Dark Victory—Bette Davis."

"Where's that playing?"

"I rented it from the video shop. When I got home there was a message on my answering machine. My boss wanted me to show six to some buyers today."

"You were in and out all afternoon?"

"New York's a great city for wandering when the weather's nice."

"Where did you wander?"

She walked to the window. She tossed a nod. "Way over there by the river. I love the boats, and the boys diving into the East River, and I love the seagulls, even though they're scavengers, and those islands, even though they have prisons on them."

"Are you on call every weekend for your boss?"

"I get a commission above my salary, Lieutenant. I don't feel my employer imposes on me, if that's what you're asking."

She came back to the sofa with a swaying walk, hands held behind her, out of sight.

"It wasn't exactly what I was asking. By the way, what did I say just now that upset you?"

Her gaze came round to his. "It wasn't anything you said. I know this sounds naive, but I've never seen a dead body before."

"That's not naive, that's lucky."

"I think it's beginning to hit me. Do you ever get used to it?"

"No, I'm not used to it." He finished his drink.

She took the glasses back to the kitchen.

"Which leg?" he asked.

She turned and gave him a blank look.

"Which leg did Zero lose?"

"The rear right."

"Same as the man downstairs."

"I was trying not to think that."

"It's okay to think things."

She rinsed the glasses and put them into the dishwasher. "We gave him chemotherapy, we gave him radiation. Nothing could save the leg." She closed the dishwasher. "Silly to think of a cat when a man's dead."

"Zero's okay now?"

"He's fine. Hops around, doesn't even know the leg's gone."

"That's great. A survivor. We should all be survivors."

They stood saying good-bye in the lobby, and Cardozo asked for her phone numbers at work and at home.

Melissa Hatfield took out her business card, added her home address and phone, handed it to him.

He watched her leave the building. The young woman who had come close to tears over her three-legged cat strode like a lioness past the afternoon doorman, recognizing him with the barest of nods, hair streaming behind her in a long chestnut mane. Her hand went up, swift and sure of its power. Magically, a taxi materialized at the curb to whisk her away.

In his work Cardozo had seen hundreds of New York women neurotically attached to their pets—fat women, middle-aged women, rich women who turned to their Pekinese or Persian for the warmth and meaning that no lover or job would ever give their lives.

But Melissa Hatfield didn't fit the profile. She was intelligent, attractive; she didn't need to spend an entire Saturday alone. What's more, Cardozo didn't believe she had. She didn't give off the scent of the manless New York woman; nor did she give off that sadder scent of the friendless New Yorker. He didn't think she was gay and he didn't believe her story about wandering around all day and renting an old Bette Davis movie for her evening entertainment.

He'd been a cop long enough to know that ninety-five percent of humanity lied. Even nuns gave the truth a little twist now and then. Lying didn't make a person a killer.

Still, he felt Melissa Hatfield had tried to con him and he was curious why she'd tried. He jotted a memo in his pocket notebook: HATFIELD—ALONE SATURDAY?

4

THEY DIDN'T SEE BABE WATCHING.

She stood outside the open door, in darkness, staring in.

They moved in slow motion through a soft sea of candlelight, holding champagne glasses. They wore tuxedos and gowns and rubber headpieces like children's halloween masks. Babe recognized Winnie the Pooh, Mickey Mouse, Richard Nixon, the Mad Hatter.

A butler in a John Wayne mask glided through the crowd, refilling glasses from a green jeroboam with a Moët label.

Babe could see the masks bobbing up and down, chitchatting animatedly with one another.

"Bonjour," Porky Pig said. *"Ça va?"*

That didn't seem right. Porky Pig couldn't have said *bonjour.*

For an instant Babe was lost, hovering between two worlds. Then her eyes blinked open. The dream figures faded and the hospital room came slowly into focus.

"Bonjour, ma petite." That voice again, familiar now.

Babe's gaze went to the doorway. She saw a rangy, wide-shouldered, fit-looking man in his late fifties. He came forward into the light, wearing a beautifully cut blazer and slacks and a silk tie with the insignia of the New York Racquet and Tennis Club. He bent down at her bedside to kiss her. He had gray hair and strong, handsome features, and he smelled of vetiver cologne. At that instant she recognized her old friend Baron Billi von Kleist.

"It's been quite a while." He spoke with the comfortable Oxford accent of a European aristocrat. "You look splendid. As usual."

He took a chair and sat gazing at her. He had a deep tan, and she sensed something very like compassion in his eyes.

"Stop being charming," she said, smiling as she always did when he played with her. "*You* look splendid. *I* look like an exhumed corpse."

He lit a cigarette and leaned back in his chair. He crossed one knee over the other. The press in his gray trousers was razor sharp.

"*Chacun à son goût,*" he said. "Actually, I'm here on a mission, not a visit. I've brought you an old friend—she's been seeing you faithfully twice a week while you were in the land of Winken and Blinken and Nod but now that you're awake, she's turned a little shy about picking up with you again. She asked me to bring her. Or rather, your mother told me you were back and when I said I was coming to see you, she delegated me to bring Cordelia."

"Cordelia!" Babe cried.

"Hello, Mother."

It was a woman's voice, not a girl's, and when Babe looked toward the doorway of the hospital room it was a woman, not a girl, who stood there.

Babe squinted. "Cordelia?"

Instead of an answer, her daughter shot Babe a questioning look, swaying with a moment's unsteadiness as though she had the legs of a newborn deer. Then she gathered up her poise and glided into the room.

Babe had to catch her breath. When she'd last seen Cordelia the child had been a gangly, unhappy twelve-year-old, but the young woman who walked into the hospital room was a stunning young blonde: startlingly made up and colorfully dressed in jeans and a yellow silk blouse, with jangling chains and baubles and a wide gold cuff bracelet on her left wrist.

The young beauty bent over the bed and kissed Babe. It was not a daughter's kiss, warm and giving, but reserved, precise—a kiss between countesses.

"Welcome back," Cordelia said. Her eyes were the deep, almost cobalt blue that Babe remembered.

"It's good to be back," Babe said. "Let me look at you."

Cordelia's hand slipped free of her mother's. She backed away from the bed and turned 360 degrees, like a mannequin in a fashion salon showing off a new dress.

"Don't say it. I've grown. I'm two inches too tall to be a dancer and it just killed me when I had to drop out of ballet school."

"But you're a perfect height."

"I owe that to your genes, mother. And to Billi's nagging me about posture. Just like a parent."

"Wasn't I supposed to act like a parent?" Billi said. "After all, Cordelia's my ward—and a very well behaved ward too."

"Yes." Babe remembered sitting in the lawyer's office, signing a paper making Billi Cordelia's guardian in the event of any mishap to herself. She and Scottie had almost killed themselves driving on the wrong side of the road in Gstaad and it seemed a good idea—one of those just-in-case legalities that she had never thought would actually come to pass. "Were you a good guardian?" she asked.

"You'll have to ask my ward," Billi said.

"Billi was magnificent," Cordelia said. "He kept Grandmère from nagging too hard and he took me out at least twice a month for wonderful evenings—and he hired me."

"Hired you? What did you hire her to do, Billi?"

"Cordelia will tell you all about that. She's an excellent employee." Billi rose. "I'm going to leave you two alone. I'll be back, Babe. We'll have a chat of our own."

He kissed her good-bye, and she had a sense he wanted to say something more. But he turned and left.

Mother and daughter sat gazing at one another. Cordelia's eyes were smiling, but uneasiness peeped through them.

"You're beautiful," Babe said.

"You mean I'm glossy. I have to be. I'm a professional model."

This is my child, Babe thought. *This stranger.* "Tell me everything."

"That would take days."

"Good. They say I've got weeks to kill in this place."

Cordelia shifted in her chair. Babe noticed the faint pulse under a milk white patch on the inside of Cordelia's arm, barely hollowed by shadow.

"You're staring," Cordelia said.

"I don't mean to. It's just that you were so little and lost and now you're so grown-up and you don't look lost at all."

"Do you mind if I smoke?" Cordelia said.

For an instant Babe was startled: a child of twelve smoking? Babe had to remind herself that this particular child was nineteen. She watched her daughter light a Tareyton filter king. Cordelia did it very well, like an actress in an old Warner Bros. movie—the rich bad girl—tilting her head back, propelling twin dragontails of white smoke through her arched nostrils.

Cordelia studied her mother. "You're looking well, Mother."

Babe felt jewelless, dressless, seven years behind the times. "Bring me up to date. You were twelve when we last talked. You wore braids and you were always bumping into things."

A frown flickered on Cordelia's face. "And I was going to Spence, and you were making me wear those horrid braces."

"They weren't all that horrid, and look what lovely teeth you have as a result."

"I hated them. But they came off when I was thirteen, so at least I didn't look like a freak when I went to Madeira."

"How did you like Madeira?"

"A little stuffy. I roomed with a girl from Richmond. We almost got thrown out for smoking pot." Cordelia's eyes narrowed thoughtfully, and then she dropped her gaze. "I was on probation for a term."

Babe felt an instant's anxiousness in the pit of her stomach. She hid it with an interested smile. "That probably helped your schoolwork."

"Yes, I did well in music."

"You get that from your father."

"And I did well in French and history and art too."

"You get the art from me."

"I graduated with honors."

"I wish I could have been at your graduation."

"Be glad you weren't. It rained. And guess what. The headmistress turned out to be a murderess. She's serving a twenty-five-year sentence for shooting three bullets into her Jewish lover."

Babe studied Cordelia, wondering if she was playing some kind of joke.

Cordelia smiled. The smile got as far as her eyes and then her jaw and chin tightened. Suddenly she placed her head across Babe's lap. Babe began stroking the pale golden spill of hair.

After a moment Cordelia sat up again, choking back a sniffle. "I had my coming-out that spring at the cottage in Newport. Grandpère was my escort. He looked smashing in his old World War One ribbons."

Babe wondered—why Grandpère, why not Scottie? "Grandpère's decorations are World War Two, darling."

"You know what I mean. And then Vassar accepted me. But after six months I knew it wasn't for me. So I came back to New York, and met an agent at a party, and voilà, I'm a model. I haven't made up my mind whether or not to work full time. Modeling's so dull—half of it's just standing around perfecting your bored look."

She demonstrated her bored look, and Babe had to laugh.

"Do you want to see my portfolio?" Cordelia opened a large

leather carrying case. It was crammed with glossies. She slipped them out of their plastic sheaths and handed them over one by one.

Babe studied photos of her daughter on horseback, on camelback, on elephantback, her daughter running on beaches, in Irish meadows, across Newport lawns, her daughter lounging formally, informally, in furs, in a Scaasi, in Calvin Klein jeans, her daughter smiling at dogs, at jewelry, at foreign cars, at silverware, at young men. And then there were magazines with Cordelia on the cover: *Vogue, Harper's Bazaar, Mademoiselle.*

"You're very successful," Babe said. "But you gave up college?"

"I earn thirty-five hundred an hour. College just didn't do it for me."

Babe wondered what money was worth nowadays. She wondered what an education was worth.

"I'm the logo of Babethings," Cordelia said.

Babethings—the company Babe had founded to market her designs. She wondered who was heading it now, how it was doing.

"I'm under contract. I do print ads and TV. Anytime they need a face or a voice-over, it's me. So in a way, I'm famous. I've been interviewed in *People* magazine and *Interview* and I've been on talk shows and I'm invited all sorts of terrific places."

Babe's thoughts were racing, trying to keep up with everything her daughter was telling her. "And do you have boyfriends?"

Cordelia's eyes flicked away. "At the moment there's Rickie—you'll meet him. I'm fond of Rickie, he's a smashing tennis player and he dances terrifically. He wants to marry me but I honestly don't know. His father is Sir Rickie Hawkes, Barclays Bank."

"Oh, yes," Babe said, recognizing the bank, not Sir Rickie. Doubtless the British had created quite a few new sirs since she'd gone under.

Cordelia spoke of her other interests—discos and parties and cars and Thoroughbreds and interesting people doing interesting things that got mentioned in the papers.

"And do you ever see your father?" Babe said.

"Ernst is wonderful. Every time he plays in New York I go backstage. We're very close. *Vanity Fair* did a father-daughter article on us. He played a smashing Rachmaninoff Third with the Cleveland at Carnegie last month. I saved you the reviews."

"Do you two ever have time to talk? Does he take an interest in you?"

"We talk all the time. Ernst phones no matter where he is—Budapest, Berlin, Capetown—just last week it was Tokyo. Of course he gets the time zones mixed up, so we're usually talking at four in the morning—but I do adore him."

It sounded to Babe like the same old Ernst, going as strong at seventy as at fifty-five, whisking in on a jet plane, sweeping Cordelia off to the Palm Court for champagne and cakes, pressing two tickets into her hand, tossing her to the press in the greenroom after the concert.

"And do you ever see Scottie?" Babe asked.

Cordelia froze over. It seemed precocious to Babe, a girl that young able to freeze over that hard, that fast.

"Why would I see Scottie?"

A silence fell on the room.

"Because he's your stepfather."

"But he's not—not since he divorced you."

Babe felt a jolt of pain jump through her nerves. She pushed herself up in the bed: she was shaking. She had to make herself believe that this was real: the words she had just heard, the girl watching her, the shock reeling through her.

Cordelia's eyes were fixed on her mother now, wide and observing. "Grandmère said she was going to tell you everything. I can see I've put my foot in it."

Only the thought that she must be strong in front of her daughter kept Babe from breaking into little fragments. "Of course Grandmère told me. Are you and Scottie still friends?"

Amazement and pain mingled in Cordelia's expression. "How could we be, Mother? After what he did to you?"

Babe's instincts were telling her to keep going, fake it. "Don't blame him, darling," she said quietly, telling herself she'd suspected, that she'd been prepared for bad news. "You can't expect a man to stay married seven years to a woman who might never wake up."

Cordelia's hands tightened into fists. "Why are you so kind to him? You must love him incredibly. Still."

5

"DID YOU NOTICE ANY STRANGERS IN THE BUILDING OVER THE weekend?" Detective Sam Richards asked.

"Strangers?" the woman said. "There are always strangers in the building. Those shops bring in nothing but, and that psychiatric clinic on the fifth floor produces some very strange encounters."

Sam Richards had been on the job long enough to know the world and its bullshit. Yet the word *princess* still commanded his respect. It conjured up pictures from a book of King Arthur and his knights that he had pored over as a boy. True, Lily Lobkowitz was no lady fair. She might once have been. There were vestiges—a bright blue sparkle to the eyes that nervously watched him, an attempted confidence to the tilt of her very rounded chin. But her face was lined and tired, and powder had spilled onto her dark blouse. He had a feeling she'd put on her makeup after he had rung the doorbell.

She sat very still on the chintz sofa, not regally straight but cautiously so, as though if she leaned in any direction at all she'd keep going, right onto the floor. She smelled of vodka.

"Did you see strangers over the weekend?" he asked.

"No, not over the weekend—not that I can recollect." Her teeth touched her lower lip. "Of course, I've been indoors all the time, trying to shake this summer cold."

The princess's livingroom was spacious, comfortably furnished; the plush love seat and chairs matched the sofa. A portrait of a woman with a jeweled crown hung over the fireplace. Beyond the grand piano striped awnings shaded the terrace from the bright afternoon sun.

"Did you go out at all on Saturday, ma'am?"

He had a hunch she didn't like taking deliveries from the liquor store; she didn't want the building staff to count. So she went out herself. She probably had two or three stores in the neighborhood and was careful to rotate her visits. It seemed sad, a princess spending a holiday weekend alone with her Stolichnaya.

"Did you see anything or anyone unusual?"

That same faraway look, annoyance seeping in now. "You could hardly call it unusual—Hector does it all the time."

"Does what, ma'am?"

"He leaves the door unguarded."

Sam Richards took out his notebook and turned past the page where he'd jotted the milk and eggs his wife wanted him to pick up from Shop-Rite. *Write it down,* his instructor at Police Academy had said. *No matter how dumb, no matter how insignificant it may seem at the time, it could turn out to be evidence.* "What time on Saturday?"

The princess was silent a moment. "The second time I went out for my cold pills. I'd say it was two o'clock or so."

Detective Sam Richards stepped out of the elevator.

The thunk-thunk-thunk of a fender bass came at him through the door. He pushed the buzzer politely, and when the music showed no signs of abating he pushed it impolitely, leaning his full 220 pounds onto his thumb.

A woman's voice screamed, "Who is it?" and he shouted, "Police!"

The music cut off. There was a scurrying silence.

The foyer boasted no lacquered table or little Oriental rug, none of the wealthy little amenities Richards had noticed on the other floors of the building. The door opened three inches. A young woman stared out. Her watery green eyes said she was nearsighted.

Sam Richards held his shield up above the safety chain. "Detective Richards, twenty-second precinct."

"Far fuckin' *out.*"

"Are you Deborah Hightower, the owner of this apartment?"

"Debbi." She had the husky voice of a three-pack-a-day smoker. "No *e* on the Debbi."

"Could I come in for a moment?"

"If it's about my maintenance payment, talk to my lawyer."

"It's not about the maintenance."

She undid the chain and stepped back from the door, letting him pass. She wore black nylon jogging shorts and a *Coke is it!* T-shirt, and her feet were bare.

The hallway opened into a livingroom furnished with two black beanbag chairs and two Techtronic stereo speakers. The amplifier and turntable sat on the shelf of a varnish-it-yourself bookcase that she hadn't varnished. No window curtains softened the view of the high rise across the street. Black scuffmarks on the parquet floor told of heavy furniture that had been dragged in and dragged out again. The air smelled of freshly sprayed lemon deodorizer. The lemon didn't quite mask the scent of marijuana.

Ms. Hightower offered coffee. "Instant. Sorry about that."

"Fine by me."

Sam Richards dropped onto a beanbag and stared at marks on the walls where six pictures had hung. The floor needed dusting.

She came back from the kitchen with two white plastic mugs and handed him one. He noticed that the long green fingernail on her third finger was a falsie, beginning to hang loose. She seated herself in the beanbag facing his and blew on her coffee.

"Do you know a man was murdered in the building?" he said. "We found him two hours ago in six. No ID."

"That's wild."

"Were you home this weekend?"

"Home?" She looked confused. "You mean here? This isn't home, honey, this is a crash pad. I have a share in a summer place out in the Hamptons." She sipped quietly. "But sad to say, I've been here for the last three days. I'm in a show down at the World Trade Center."

"Oh, yeah? What show's that?"

"*Toyota Presents.*" She was searching him for a reaction.

"Oh, yeah. *Toyota Presents.*"

"A lot of stars got their starts in industrials. Shirley MacLaine danced for General Motors."

"Right. I heard that somewhere." Sam Richards opened his notebook. "Debbi, could you tell me when you were in the building yesterday, when you came in, when you went out, what hours you were in the lobby, the elevator, anywhere else on the premises?"

She said she'd worked late, come home around noon Saturday, slept till an hour before the show, left the building around seven, returned early this morning.

"Did you see or hear anything unusual in the building?" It occurred to him that if Debbi Hightower had been as stoned yesterday as she seemed today, she wouldn't have noticed an elephant falling out of the sky.

She hoisted one leg up and placed a foot on the edge of the beanbag. Her toenails were pink, which didn't go with the green fingernails. "Seemed a lot less busy than usual."

"Any odd noises or people?"

She thought a moment. "Well, it's all relative, isn't it? I mean, what do you consider odd?"

"Strangers in the building?" William Benson, who owned the apartment on the twenty-eighth floor, shook his head. He was a small, lean man about eighty years of age. With elegant carelessness, his right hand twirled a pair of horn-rimmed bifocals. Gold cufflinks winked at the wrists of his burgundy smoking jacket. "No, none that I noticed."

"Any strange noises?" Detective Monteleone asked.

"I'm afraid I couldn't tell you that. Memorial Day's a wonderful weekend for working. I turned off my hearing aid."

For the first time, Detective Monteleone noticed the small beige plastic button in Benson's left ear.

Behind the eighty-year-old architect the livingroom glowed like an art gallery, with track lighting that picked out abstract expressionist and pop art paintings on the walls.

"There was one thing," Benson said, "but you could hardly call it unusual, it happens so often. I went out for the paper, and I had to use my key to let myself back into the building. Our Saturday doorman, Hector, wasn't at the door. I have a hunch he sits down in the personnel room watching ballgames on TV."

"Tell me that's not a Gestapo tactic. Tell me it's not." Fred Lawrence, the owner of the apartment on floor 11, was explaining to Detective Sam Richards how he happened to be in New York on a holiday weekend when his wife and son were out romping at their summer rental in Ocean Beach. "To phone on a Friday—not even the courtesy of a letter—and call a field audit Tuesday—knowing Monday's Memorial Day. It destroys my weekend, it terrifies my client, it wastes everybody's time. I've never let a client overstate deductions. I don't work that way."

Sam Richards nodded, shaping his lips into a conciliatory smile. "We've all had our troubles with the IRS."

"It's harassment, plain and simple." Fred Lawrence, his stomach pushing a breathless bulge into his pink Polo sports shirt, his face beet red and gaunt, was clearly a man under strain. His fringe of black hair glistened with sweat. Behind gold-rimmed spectacles, his eyes darted, never once meeting Sam Richards's. He paced the room, fingers skittering across the edges of hi-tech leather and chrome chairs and glass-topped tables.

"And then this outrage in six—how the hell did a thing like that happen? We're supposed to have security in this building."

"With your help, Mr. Lawrence, we hope to find out how it happened."

Fred Lawrence threw a startled glance at the detective. "You seem to think I have some information—well, I don't."

"What time did you return to the building?"

"Around noon yesterday."

"You parked in the garage?"

"Yes, I rent a space there."

"Did you notice anything or anyone strange in the building over the weekend?"

"As I tried to explain, Officer, I'm under a great deal of pressure, I'm extremely preoccupied, and I apologize, but the answer is no, I noticed nothing until all you police came pouring in."

Cardozo pulled his Honda Civic into the unlit alley beside the ninety-five-year-old precinct building. There was a parking space beneath the fire escape. He made sure to lock up. Unmarked police cars had been getting ripped off lately in the precinct parking lot.

He nearly tripped in the dark over a stack of A-frame barriers. They had been piled in reserve two years ago for crowd control. Crowds had come and gone, the barriers had stayed.

Above the green globes glowing on either side of the station house door the precinct flag fluttered limply from its pole, a rumpled seal of the City of New York and the number 22. The two two was one of the six precincts that used to make up the Seventh Division. Changing city administrations had moved the numbers around, but the sooty bricks and rusting iron and peeling paint were still there on Sixty-third Street, distinctly out of place in the heart of Manhattan's Silk Stocking District.

The inside of the 22d Precinct station house was as shabby as the outside, perhaps a little more so since it never got rained on except for parts of the fifth floor, where the roof leaked. For three decades City Hall had been promising to rebuild.

The Muzak was playing "One for My Baby." Cardozo disliked Muzak, and he especially disliked that tune. He didn't see why a police force that was cutting patrols to meet its budget needed canned music.

He waved to the lieutenant working the complaint desk, then followed two sergeants up the old iron-banistered staircase. The radios buckled to their hips gave off synchronized bursts of static. They were pulling a handcuffed hooker through a door. She was kicking, screeching, beginning to lose her blond wig.

Things were quiet tonight.

Cardozo paused at the second floor corridor and watched the sergeants push the woman into the precinct holding cage. She began shaking the bars, screaming that they'd stolen her motherfucking wig and her lawyer was going to kick their honky asses.

The marble steps leading to the next floor were gritty with ancient filth. On a bench in the hall a detective was taking a statement from an elderly male complainant who had just been robbed at knifepoint on Lexington Avenue.

"The city's not safe anymore," the man was moaning. Cardozo felt sorry for a guy that old and just beginning to learn.

He entered the Detective Unit squad room. The large office was crammed with metal desks and files and old wood tables. The windows were covered with grills, and the grills and glass had been painted over in an industrial green that almost matched the walls.

It was late and the room was deserted except for the detective on night duty. "What's happening?" Cardozo asked.

"There's an R.I.P. up on Madison," Tom Sweeney said. "Two Hispanics seen breaking into a chocolate shop."

Cardozo gave Sweeney a look. Most cops did their eight hours and got their asses home. Not Sweeney, at least not lately. He seemed to be in the squad room round the clock. Cardozo had heard rumors that his wife was in the process of leaving him for another woman. He felt sorry for the guy.

Sweeney said a ten thirty—reported stickup—had come in fifteen minutes ago: a Caucasian with a .38 had walked into the Bojangles on Sixtieth and taken four hundred dollars, wallets, rings, and wrist watches. No casualties.

The room smelled of coffee. Cardozo made his way to the source of the smell. "What kind of idiot would do that? Anyone sitting in Bojangles, the watch has got to be a Timex, the ring's tin. Criminals used to have brains in this city."

An evil-looking Sola for charging radio batteries sat on a padlocked cabinet. The cabinet was where detectives weary of carrying three pounds of metal could stow their weapons. Two Mr. Coffees sat quietly steaming beside the Sola. The squad split the cost of cheap drip-grind and kept the coffee makers working around the clock. Cardozo poured a Styrofoam cup of brew that looked as though it had been jelling in the bottom of the pot for two days. He ripped open an envelope of Sweet 'n Low and let the powder silt down into his coffee.

"What's that pross in for downstairs?" he said. "They made loitering a crime again?"

"Offering to sell coke to Lieutenant Vaughan."

Cardozo made a face. Another hooker trying to sell talcum powder to a plainclothesman. He couldn't believe Vaughan would bother with the arrest, the paperwork, the aggravation. "What's Vaughan want with bullshit like that?"

"You know what the CP says: we gotta increase productivity." Sweeney nodded toward the bulletin board where the two-week-old word-processed directive from the police commissioner's office had been push-pinned. "Budget time in Nueva York. *El capitano* wants to goose those percentages."

Cardozo's eyes went across the deserted room. The detention cage, butted into a corner, was empty for the moment, with a two-year-old copy of *Penthouse* magazine spread facedown on the bench.

He crossed to his office, a cubicle with precinct green walls.

His desk was the same gray metal as the desks outside. The phone was an early touch-tone model that Bell had discontinued in 1963; it had had a crack under the cradle since '73 and the tape on the crack got changed whenever it dried up. The typewriter was a model-T Underwood that you couldn't have donated to a reform school.

He frowned. A dismal-looking pile of departmental forms had accumulated around the typewriter since Saturday. Today was supposed to be his RDO, his regular day off; he was supposed to be in Rockaway with his little girl.

He sat in the swivel chair and saw that the top piece of paper was a hand-scrawled note: CALL CHIEF O'BRIEN AT HOME A.S.A.P., followed by the captain's home phone and the initials of the sergeant who had taken the call.

Cardozo dialed the Woodlawn number.

As the phone rang he glanced through the rest of the paper. Mostly it was a bunch of fives, DD5 supplementary complaint reports, the

triplicates that detectives filled out summarizing progress on ongoing cases. As unsolved crimes got stale, regulations required a minimum of two reports annually. The fives mounted up—the older the
report, the thicker the fistful of blue forms stapled to it.

A voice cut into the ringing. Gruff. "O'Brien."

"Chief? Vince. Just got your message."

"Vince, the goddamnedest thing. Remember that Babe
Vanderwalk business seven years ago—the husband tried to—"

"I was on your task force. I remember."

"Damned if Babe Vanderwalk didn't come out of her coma. The
hospital phoned. And then a lawyer phoned. Represents the family,
they don't want any fuss, they don't want any publicity."

"*Mazel tov* to the Vanderwalks. Can she talk?"

"She can talk. She's normal. Lost a little weight, joints a little stiff,
but she's all there."

"Does she remember anything?"

"Go see her and find out. I'm delegating you."

Cardozo exhaled loudly. "Chief, you just handed me a one-legged
John Doe."

"You know the background, Vince. Go to Doctors Hospital, get a
statement, and close the case. Five minutes."

"I can't control what she's going to say. Her statement may open
the case."

"Get a statement that closes the case. Go up there tomorrow. They
wake those patients up at six, seven o'clock. You don't have to wait
for visiting hours."

"Chief, I honestly—"

"Thanks, Vince, I knew I could count on you."

The receiver went dead in Cardozo's hand. He looked at it a
moment and then slammed it back onto the cradle.

Though it was seven years in the past, the Vanderwalk case still
stoked old resentments in him. He'd worked his butt off collecting
solid evidence, he'd avoided the minefields of the Miranda and Espo-
sito decisions, the jury had convicted, and then on appeal the D.A.
had accepted a plea bargain that let the killer off.

Except if Babe Vanderwalk was awake, the killer wasn't a killer
anymore.

Anyway, that's tomorrow, Cardozo reminded himself. *Today's today.*

He pushed Babe Vanderwalk Devens out of his head and began
skimming fives. They were drearily familiar: ripped-up hookers,

businessmen with no ID dead in trash barrels, family fights where somebody had taken out a knife or gun, stewardesses jumping out of their Third Avenue shared apartments—or had they been pushed? They were like old friends to him. He'd been staring at some of them for over ten years.

And they all concluded with the same words: NO NEW INVESTIGATIVE LEADS SINCE LAST REPORT.

The cases kept pouring in, dead bodies that had all been human beings, every one of them entitled to live till accident or natural death claimed them and, failing that, entitled to justice. It was his job to see they at least got justice. No homicide case was ever closed till it was cleared, but fewer than a third were cleared nowadays. That meant a backlog of over five hundred in the two two alone. A lot of killers were walking around on their own cognizance out there.

His eye went guiltily to the filing cabinet. The bottom drawer was wedged shut against an overflow of departmental orders that he had yet to get around to reading. The precinct was drowning in paper. Paper had become the measure of all things. It got you promoted, got you demoted, decided your salary, your rank, your standing in the department's eyes. Paper was where it was at.

"Hey, Vince." Tommy Daniels from the Photographic Unit came bounding through the door and clamped a hand on Cardozo's shoulder. "Got the pictures you wanted of the ten eighteen." He thrust out an envelope.

Cardozo slipped the glossies out of the manila envelope. It surprised him how young the dead man was: perhaps twenty-two years old, very blond, with medium-length, shiny hair. The eyes were long-lashed, the chin strong, almost challenging, with a cleft to it, the lips full but not quite pouting. A handsome boy. He seemed to be contentedly dreaming.

"Beautiful, hey?" Daniels said.

Cardozo looked at his photographic expert's thick black hair, his chartreuse shirt that lit up three walls of the cubicle, his face shining with an eagerness to please that would have been cute in a cocker spaniel.

"You go for guys, Daniels?"

"The shots, Lieutenant. I'm talking about the shots."

"Yeah, they're Academy Award."

Daniels folded his arms proudly across his chest. "The usual procedure with morgue lights is to use a fast shutter time, but that gives you the morgue look. I experimented, used a slow shutter, three tenths of a second, then gave the film seven minutes in a hydroxide solution. That gives the skin a glow."

"You call this skin glowing?"

"It's not your standard morgue shot is what I mean."

"Daniels, are you on speed or are you doing a four-to-one today or what?"

"O.T. Time and a half and a half on a holiday."

Leave it to a go-getter like Daniels to figure the overtime angles. "Today's not a holiday," Cardozo said. "Tomorrow is."

"The weekend's a holiday."

Cardozo shook his head, looking at a full body shot.

"The perp has got to be one weird piece of work," Tommy Daniels said. "Real EDP." EDP was the police psychiatrists' abbreviation for Emotionally Disturbed Person. "He'll walk, right?"

"Daniels, are you a coroner, are you a shrink? I got enough resentment today without your expert opinion."

"Today? You got resentment today? Tell me a day you don't have resentment."

"Very comic. Today was supposed to be my day off. I can forgive a lot, but not dragging me into this shit on my day off, and I promise you, the animal that did this is not going to walk."

"Okay, okay, I just meant the courts—you know."

"Screw the courts. We're all emotionally damaged persons—you, me—that doesn't give us special privileges to saw people up." Cardozo tapped a photograph. "Let's crop this one a little higher so he looks like he could be wearing an open-necked shirt. Put the face on a flyer: anyone having any information please contact et cetera et cetera. Run off a few thousand. We'll paste them up around town."

Daniels took back the photo. "Ten four."

Cardozo glanced at him. Cops on TV used police radio abbreviations, why shouldn't real cops. Life imitating art. Daniels in his liqueur-green shirt imitating *Hill Street Blues* reruns.

An association clicked in Cardozo's head. "Say . . . what happened to that photography van we used on the Mendoza stakeout?"

Special Services had gutted an old Consolidated Edison repair truck. From the outside it looked like the standard Con Ed nuisance, a small white-and-blue van that took a week and a half futzing around a manhole. Inside it had cameras and radios and phone-monitoring equipment.

"The one seven borrowed it."

"Borrow it back. I want a team at Beaux Arts Tower—your boys—

round-the-clock photographic surveillance. Pictures of anybody entering or leaving the premises, any vehicles pulling up to the door or taking that alley down to the garage. A logbook with dates and hours, licenses, taxi medallion numbers."

"Sounds like we got a budget on this one."

"Yeah, we got a budget."

Cardozo sat down, alone in his cubicle. He sipped a little of his coffee. He cleared a space on his desktop. He moved Tommy Daniels's glossies around like pieces of a jigsaw puzzle. He couldn't make sense of the missing leg.

Cardozo had seen corpses where the head was gone, where the tits were gone, where the dick or balls were gone. Those were the classic chop-offs.

But the leg. Why the leg?

He took a sip of coffee. He was thinking that he was getting up in his forties. Most of the cops he worked with were younger, still good at running and good at climbing fences, good at looking at stuff like these pictures and not barfing. The pressure was getting to him, One P.P. screaming for results, *The New York Times* on his ass the one time in a blue moon one of his men shot in self-defense. Fear was getting to him, too, fear of looking like a dope or a coward, fear of opening his mouth and getting in shit with the brass.

He pushed up from the desk and walked to the window.

He gazed into the black night of the shaftway. His fingers drummed on the top of the file cabinet. Had there been something about the leg the killer wanted to hide: a birthmark, a tattoo, a deformity?

Cardozo selected a photograph of the dead man's face and took it out to the desk lieutenant. "Send this over to Missing Persons—John Doe. Have them show it around, check if he turned up missing."

It was a long shot: the victim might not have been reported missing, he might not have been missing long enough to be reported, he might be missing from Wichita. But you had to cover the bases.

Cardozo went back to his office, lifted the phone, and dialed a number. He waited, jaw clenched, through eight rings. Finally a voice said, "Stein, Forensic."

"Lou, it's Vince. Got anything yet on the Beaux Arts killing?"

"Didn't Tony tell you?"

"Would I be calling if Tony was here?"

"He's gotta be there, he left an hour ago."

Cardozo came back into the squad room. "Was Tony Bandolero here asking for me?"

Sweeney angled his chin toward a half-open door across the room. "In there."

There was an unused space off the squad room. One of the detectives had found a Sony Trinitron in the garbage on the street and brought it in, and detectives on a break sat around watching TV. People in two two threw out good garbage.

Cardozo crossed the room. He could hear gunshots and screeching tires. Cop show. He wondered how detectives, grown men, could watch that stuff.

He peered into the flickering darkness. "Tony, you there?"

One of three forms heaved itself up from a chair. "Shiut. Police-woman was about to nail the arsonist."

Tony Bandolero came into the light, a heavyset man in his late twenties with limp black hair and a low, wrinkled forehead.

"How can you watch that stuff?" Cardozo asked.

"You want me to be improving myself, Vince, reading some great books? *Divina Commedia,* that's how I should be spending my coffee break? *Fangul.*"

Cardozo closed the cubicle door. "What have you got?"

"Eight partial prints."

Cardozo took the sheet and frowned. "You can get a positive ID from this?"

"If you can come up with a suspect, why not?"

"Crap. We're going to get a match, and it'll be one of the building workers, someone who had nothing to do with it."

"You don't know that, Vince."

"I know it. What else?"

"We removed human blood from the rotary saw."

"Is it his?"

"It may not be enough to type, Vince. We're going to try. But all we can definitely say at this point in time is the victim is type O and the blood on the saw is human."

"That's all?"

"Not quite. The leather mask is standard s.m. gear—what they call a bondage mask down at the Pink Pussy Cat."

"Any prints on it?"

"Leather is very tough to print."

"So where are we?"

"You're going to like this, Vince."

Tony Bandolero handed him a magazine. Cardozo leafed through.
"What the hell's this, gay porn?"

"It's a leather goods catalogue, Vince, from a Greenwich Village
sex shop called the Pleasure Trove. It is *the* place for leather and
bondage goods."

"This is part of the NYPD reference library?"

"Will you hear me out, Vince? The mask is handmade, and it's in
the catalogue, item number 706."

6

THE M.E.'S OFFICE WAS LOCATED AT THIRTIETH STREET AND FIRST
Avenue in one of a complex of cinderblock buildings near Bellevue.
A dark-haired girl was in charge of the lower-level reception desk,
talking to a cop who wanted a receipt for a drop-off.

Cardozo gave her his name and asked to see the medical examiner.

The girl smiled at him prettily and consulted a clipboard hanging
at the side of her desk. "He's expecting you. Do you know the way?"

Cardozo nodded. He couldn't help thinking she was awfully young
to be working in a morgue.

He took the stairway to the subbasement with its depressingly
familiar banks of overhead fluorescent lights and walls of latched
stainless-steel body lockers. Drains dotted the cement floor at six-foot
intervals.

This level was full of scurrying figures in white lab coats. Many of
them, Cardozo knew, were medical students on the prowl for preg-
nant Jane Does. The city let them take the dead fetuses.

As he pushed through a door with heavy green rubber lips his nose
was assaulted by a sudden stench of formaldehyde and human decay.

He saw at a glance that four of the tables in the cutting room were
occupied. Three of the bodies, two white males and a black female,
had had their rib cages split open, exposing the lungs and viscera.
The fourth was covered. Beside each table stood a scale for weighing
organs.

"Hey, Vince." Dan Hippolito crossed the room. He was wearing a
surgical smock and a rubber apron. He had pushed a curved Plexiglas face shield up over his receding hairline. "We just finished drain-
ing him and he's ready. Right over here."

Hippolito led Cardozo to the necropsy table where John Doe lay beneath a white sheet, his one leg jutting out with the foot at a slant. Hippolito gave the sheet a nudge and let it spill to the floor.

"The incisions on the chest are superficial, don't mean anything. The skin coloring and neck contusions indicate asphyxia. Like I said before, looks like he was strangled. We'll know for sure when we get to the lungs. The leg was cut off an hour, two hours after his heart stopped beating. The shear marks on the femoral bone were made by a rotary blade."

"Dan, I don't get it. Why take a dead leg?"

"That's your field. I'll tell you what happened, you figure out why. The left testicle, on the other hand, was cut off before death."

Cardozo couldn't believe he had missed it. "He lost a ball?"

Hippolito lifted the scrotum sac. Now Cardozo could see it. One testicle.

"How long before death?"

"Figure at least a year—it's completely healed."

"Did a doctor do it?"

"Either a doctor did it or a doctor stitched it."

"Why would you take a ball off?"

"A lot of reasons. Like cancer maybe."

"A guy this young?"

"The environment's not healthy, Vince. You see pathologies developing early in a great many mammals. The reproductive organs are especially vulnerable."

Hippolito pulled on a pair of heavy latex gloves. He removed the suction catheters from the dead man's wrists. He angled the overhead light and began speaking into a microphone suspended over the table.

"The body is that of a young male Caucasian, twenty to twenty-two years of age, height approximately six feet, body weight prior to drainage one hundred forty-nine pounds, light weight due to absence of right leg, which has been severed at the midpoint of the femur. Left testicle missing. Superficial cutaneous cuts."

He opened the dead man's mouth and peered in.

"One filling, upper left second molar."

Hippolito moved to the foot of the table, took hold of the ankle, and rotated it slowly.

"How is your little girl?" he said. "Still a real charmer?"

It made Cardozo uneasy to discuss his daughter in a room full of dead bodies. It seemed like inviting bad luck. "Fine, thanks. Terri's just fine."

Hippolito walked to the other end of the table and lifted the head, testing the resistance of the neck muscles. He reached up to the microphone. "Rigor mortis is pronounced, indicating death occurred at least thirty-two hours before examination." He lifted each eyelid in turn and gazed down into the unseeing eyeballs. "She must be beginning school now, your little girl?"

"Sixth grade."

"A prodigy." Hippolito studied the throat closely, then spoke into the mike.

"Contusions on front of neck, probably thumb imprints. A rash is visible around the neck." He angled the light further down the body. "And around the waist and the ankle."

"What kind of rash?" Cardozo interrupted.

Hippolito raised a hand to turn the mike aside. "Maybe an allergy, but the localization is unusual for that. Most likely some kind of abrasion."

"Think he was tied?"

"I'll have to peel the skin and see it under a microscope. Looks like a reaction to some kind of particles or granules. I don't think rope would do it, but we'll see."

Hippolito unhurriedly studied the dead arms and wrists.

"What's that?" Cardozo said suddenly.

The left hand was balled into a fist.

Hippolito frowned, pulled at each finger in turn. "I'll be damned, Vince. He's holding on to something."

The M.E. took a pair of surgical pliers, adjusted the grip around the dead man's index finger, and gave a quick twist. The finger flapped loose with the crack of a breadstick. With three more cracks Dan was able to bend the hand open.

Cardozo could see something small and white, the size of a fat caterpillar, wedged into the pulpy gray valley of the heel of the palm.

Hippolito probed the object free with a pair of tweezers.

"A cigarette butt." Hippolito frowned. "Filter tip. Check the brand." He handed it to Cardozo.

There was a ring of red around the filter.

"Lipstick," Cardozo observed.

The M.E. pointed to a plastic evidence bag. Cardozo dropped the butt into it.

Hippolito was examining the hand, shaking his head.

"The cigarette was extinguished on his palm. I'll tell you something, Vince. This happened while he was still alive. And here's what's weird."

Hippolito pointed his scalpel to a quarter-inch circle of ash and caked blood.

"He closed his hand around the burning cigarette. Normally that wouldn't happen, the reflex would be to eject it or somehow evade it."

"Could the killer have forced his hand closed?"

"See how the tendons are tensed? That shows he clenched his own hand. It's not a normal reflex to pain."

Hippolito gazed at the body.

"What strikes me is, there's a remarkable absence of defensive wounds. Not that the peace sign on the chest is life-threatening, but still you'd think that the victim would have tried to defend himself in some way."

Cardozo remembered the scratches on the doorman's face. "No skin under the fingernails?"

"A little, but it looks like his own."

"What's his own skin doing under his fingernails?"

"He itched, he scratched himself." Hippolito reangled the light. "Now we dig in. Better stand back."

He lowered his face shield. Using a high-speed circular saw, he began an incision into the chest. Blood and tissue spattered up.

Cardozo backed off. "Dan, I'm going to say good-night."

Driving home down Second Avenue, Cardozo didn't see any patrol cars. He busted three red lights.

When he let himself into the apartment, Mrs. Epstein, the neighbor, was in the livingroom watching TV. She bustled up from her chair. "Terri's alseep. Your lamb chop's in the oven, I left it on low. By now it's dry. We thought you'd be home earlier."

"I thought so too. How much do I owe you?"

"You gave me twenty last time. I owe you."

"Then we're even. Thanks."

Mrs. Epstein was a heavyset woman with gray hair, and she kept brushing a strand away from her eyes. "She's a beautiful child. You should spend more time with her."

"I'd like to."

He walked Mrs. Epstein to the outer hall.

"I hope it wasn't too lousy, whatever you had to do today."

"Not too lousy." He watched her let herself into her apartment. He waited for the click of her door, then came back into the livingroom. He tossed his manila envelope onto the table and snapped off the TV.

His gaze traveled across the convertible sofa with its hand-knitted blue woollen afghan, the lamps with plastic protecting the shades, the white spinet piano with Terri's finger exercises open on the rack, the goldfish tank, the framed oil painting of a valley near Lourdes where he'd been on his honeymoon. It wasn't the greatest room on earth, it would never win prizes for interior decoration, but every object spoke to him. He was comfortable here, the world couldn't batter down the door.

He felt too wired to go to sleep. He picked up Mrs. Epstein's paper and put his stocking feet up on the sofa. He turned to the sports page.

"Hi, Pop." Terri stood in her nightgown rubbing her eyes. "What's that?" She pointed at the envelope on the table.

"Pictures."

"Can I see?"

He hesitated, feeling the same instinct he had in the morgue, the instinct to keep his daughter and his corpses in two separate compartments of his life. "You don't want to see."

"He's dead, isn't he." Terri had opened the manila envelope and was sitting in lotus position on the rug staring at the glossy of John Doe's face.

"Honey, I told you not to open that."

"What you said was, 'You don't want to see.' "

"I meant don't open it."

"You should say what you mean."

"You're going to make a very obnoxious lawyer some day, you know that?"

She looked up at him, eyes serious. "Who was he?"

"We're trying to find out."

She rotated the glossy ninety degrees. "He was gay, right?"

Cardozo was interested. "Why do you say that?"

"Oh, because he's good-looking."

"Come on. There are plenty of good-looking straight men and plenty of ugly gays too."

"Yeah, you're good-looking and you're straight, but this kind of fuck-you good looks—"

"Hey, mind your language."

"Sorry. But he wears his looks like a prom queen. I-know-you-want-me-and-you-can't-have-me. You can tell he spent two hours a day taking care of that skin and hair."

Did they teach her this stuff in school, he wondered? Somehow he didn't think the sisters and the lay teachers at Saint Agnes would be capable of it. "You can tell that, can you?"

"Sure. Did he dye his hair?"

"I don't know."

"Was he a model?"

"A model?" Cardozo reflected on the possibility. "I don't know that either. I'll have to look into it."

Cardozo arrived at Doctors Hospital a little after seven in the morning. His shield got him past the guard and he found Babe Devens's room.

"Mrs. Devens?"

The woman sitting in the cranked-up hospital bed gazed at him with extraordinarily large blue eyes. "Yes?"

He'd never met her, but she was no stranger to him. He'd studied her life, her friends, her habits. He'd stared at that sleeping face and wondered what she'd look like awake. What her voice would sound like. Now he knew. With her pale blond hair and her clear pale skin, she hadn't aged a day in seven years. It was as though she'd been in deep storage.

"May I come in for a moment?" He didn't wait for permission. "Lieutenant Vince Cardozo, twenty-second precinct, homicide. I worked on your case."

He showed her the gold shield. There was a pause. He could feel her hanging back with that word *homicide,* staring thoughtfully at his face.

He pulled a chair over to the bed. The air in the room was fragrant with the scent of bougainvillea. A vase of bloodred blossoms sat on the dresser.

"I know this isn't the best time for you," he said, "but we'd like to close the case as quickly as possible. We thought, with your recovery, you might have something to add to our understanding."

She wasn't saying anything and neither were her eyes.

"I realize this isn't pleasant for you, and I apologize, but I have to ask what knowledge, what recollections you have. Specifically, do you recall the attempt on your life?"

"Mr. Cardozo, would you kindly tell me what in the world you're talking about?"

He looked at her. Her face was intelligent, alert.

His heart stumbled. He realized she didn't know. Suddenly he knew he'd been set up.

He rose and went to the window. Head raised, shoulders back, he stood looking out at the jagged line of buildings high in the morning light.

He rethought his strategy. As a cop he had certain skills: how to bullshit, how to observe, how to turn on a sort of street charm. It wasn't the kind of charm Babe Devens was used to, but he could manage the occasional three-syllable word and at least not have to duck if four syllables came zinging back at him.

He circled around to the chest of drawers and picked up the silver framed photograph. "Is this your little girl? Cornelia?"

She was watching him. "Cordelia."

"Cordelia. Right. You meet so many people you get names mixed up."

"You've met Cordelia?"

"Talked to her. Beautiful little child. A lot of poise. I have a girl around the same age—twelve."

"Cordelia's not twelve anymore."

"No, I guess not." He angled the silver frame. "Beautiful garden. Where was this picture taken?"

"My husband and I have—we had a home in East Hampton."

"You don't have it anymore?"

Her eyes met his. "I've been told I don't have a husband anymore."

"Mrs. Devens—I have a feeling you're beginning to figure out why I'm here."

"You think he tried to kill me."

"We think you might remember."

"I don't remember anyone's trying to murder me."

"Memory's tricky. Especially when you've been unconscious for a time."

She studied him, stretching out the slightly uncomfortable silence. A questioning look was in her eyes.

"Was it you who investigated?"

"I didn't head up the investigation. I wasn't even lieutenant then. But I did some legwork. Asked some questions. Got some answers. Don't know if the answers mean a hell of a lot. For what it's worth, I know what you were wearing that night."

"A blue gown."

"What you ate."

"Squab stuffed with wild rice. Raspberry mousse with white chocolate sauce."

"What you drank. What recreational drugs you did."

She lowered her head, like a little girl.

"Who you danced with. Who your husband flirted with."

She looked at him quickly.

He smiled. She didn't quite smile back.

"I liked the clothes you designed," he said. "I'm no expert, but I thought you made women look good. Feel good. And they didn't have to pay an arm and a leg. I know some women cops who used to swear by your stuff. It was great they could afford it. Women cops don't get paid a whole lot. Neither do the men. You going to go back to it? Designing?"

"As soon as I possibly can."

"Great. You've got a lot of fans out there."

"Mr. Cardozo, was my husband brought to trial for my attempted murder?"

"Correct."

"Was he found guilty or not guilty?"

"Guilty of reckless endangerment."

"Did you agree with that?"

"I thought it was attempted homicide and I thought the evidence bore that out. But I'm a cop—not a D.A. I collect the facts. I don't prosecute the case."

"Then you think my husband tried to kill me?"

"I think he injected you with the insulin that put you in coma. I call that trying pretty hard."

He looked at Babe Devens and he sensed she wasn't there anymore. She had gone somewhere else, into a room in her memory, and she had left a Babe Devens doll in the hospital bed. A doll trying hard not to let droplets spill down its cheeks.

"You see, I don't know any of this." Her voice was low and unsteady. "No one's told me about insulin or injections or attempted killing or reckless anything."

"There was a witness."

She sat not moving, leaning back against the headboard. Her eyes were fixed on her folded hands and then they lifted to meet his.

"May I ask who?"

"Your housekeeper found a tan bag in your husband's dressing room. The syringe and the insulin were inside."

She squared her shoulders and stared straight ahead. "I remember the ride home. I remember unlocking the front door and dropping the key. We were laughing and stumbling. I don't know what happened next. I suppose I undressed."

"You undressed and went to bed."

"And then you say my husband . . ." A furrow deepened between her eyes. "I don't believe my husband—my ex-husband—tried to kill me."

"Scott Devens confessed. The charge was bargained way down, but he admitted it."

She was staring at the wall. Cardozo knew she wasn't seeing the wall. He knew she was looking past it at something else.

"But you're not sure," she said. "That's why you're here."

"Until you remember something that contradicts his confession, I'm sure. My feeling is you'll remember something that supports it. And when you do remember, phone me." He gave her a card with his work number.

"Is it really going to help if I remember?"

"Frankly, it could be a pain in the ass. But I like the bad guys to get what they deserve."

"And the good guys?"

"They should end up happily ever after."

Their eyes connected.

"Are you a good guy, Mr. Cardozo?"

"Pretty good, all things considered."

"Maybe you haven't considered all things about my husband."

"Maybe."

"What if I remember that it was the butler?"

"That would interest me."

She was looking at him, smiling now. "You're funny. I'm glad I met you."

"I'm glad I met you." He stopped at the door. "Oh—Mrs. Devens."

"Yes?"

"Welcome back."

7

CARDOZO WAS AT THE PRECINCT A LITTLE BEFORE 8:00 A.M., IN good spirits from his talk with the heiress.

Three detectives were standing around the Mr. Coffees, yakking about Saturday's game, stretching the moment before they faced the day.

Cardozo walked over to the lieutenant's desk and glanced down at the sixty sheet—the complaints from the preceding tour.

He went into his cubicle. The two black plastic fragments he had found in apartment six had been placed on his desk in separate evidence bags, each bearing its own tag from the property clerk's office.

He opened the case folder, moved the property vouchers aside, and skimmed through the pages of the report. They all bore the heading CASE UF61 #8139 OF THE 22D PRECINCT, DETECTIVE VINCENT R. CARDOZO, SHIELD #1864, ASSIGNED. The 8139 represented the total number of cases reported as of this date to the precinct: homicides, stray dogs, stolen cars, anything and everything, solved and unsolved.

Then the facts: JOHN DOE, MALE, WHITE, HOMICIDE BY STRANGULATION, MAY 24. A photograph of the dead man's face was stapled to the page. There followed the time and place of the homicide; description of the scene of the crime; blanks for the victim's name and relevant details of life, association, and employment; blanks awaiting names and addresses of persons interviewed; names and shield numbers of members of the force at the scene of the homicide; notifications made, still blank.

Sam Richards, wearing a dapper green blazer, knocked on the open door. "All set, Vince."

Cardozo gathered his task force in the dingy but large room that served the detective squad as a spare office.

Greg Monteleone used a box top as a tray to carry five coffees, and Ellie Siegel, almost elegant in a pale blue dress, came in with a large box of assorted doughnuts.

Cardozo stood at the blackboard. He took a piece of chalk and wrote the words JOHN DOE HOMICIDE. Then came John Doe's identifying numbers: UF 61# 8139; UF 60# 6480. UF stood for uniformed force, which meant police, plainclothes or otherwise; the 60 and 61 were the departmental forms on which all reports relating to the crime would be filed.

Beneath he wrote the Forensic number, 3746-10, and the five property voucher numbers. Next he wrote the day of the murder, the coroner's estimated time of death, and the place of occurrence. He sketched a diagram of apartment six, putting a stick-figure man in the bedroom where the body had been found.

On the left of the board he listed the two small pieces of plastic, the electric saw, the cigarette butt, and the black leather mask that so far constituted the sole physical evidence in the case. He followed these by their tag numbers. On the right he wrote the word *witnesses* and put a question mark below it.

He stood back and turned to face his squad.

"What have we got? No ID on the victim. Our crime scene crew came up with eight partial prints. We're in the process of matching these against the prints of every MOF and every civilian at the crime scene. If we fail to match them, they may or may not prove to be the prints of our killer. Negative for any fingerprints on the mask. The saw we don't yet know about. The blood on it is human, too small an amount to be typed yet. Beyond that we have two shreds of black plastic, so far not a particle of fiber or hair. In short we have nothing. Okay—clockwise around the room."

Sam Richards set down his coffee. "Princess Lobkowitz, you should excuse the expression, drinks a little, so it's not surprising she didn't hear anything. However, she has a peeve with Hector the doorman. On the day of the killing, around two P.M., she had to let herself into the building with her own key. Hector should have been on duty, but he wasn't."

"Benson mentioned the same thing," Monteleone said.

Cardozo went to the blackboard and made a notation: HECTOR, NOT AT DOOR 2 PM?

"I also spoke with Ms. Debbi Hightower," Richards continued, "no *e* on the Debbi. She heard nothing, saw nothing, says she was at work at the Toyota show at the World Trade Center for the last three nights, and this kept her out till noon Saturday and nine A.M. Sunday."

"Only one kind of Friday night show goes till noon Saturday," Monteleone smirked.

Cardozo ignored him. "What about the accountant?"

"Fred Lawrence is a very angry man," Richards said. "IRS decided to surprise-audit a client, he had to cut short his holiday weekend and come back to New York to prepare. He arrived in the building noon Saturday, says he saw nothing, heard nothing. However, I think he did hear something or see something."

"What makes you think that?"

"A remark about the garage. He said he was very annoyed about conditions down there, he was going to complain to the co-op board at the next meeting."

"What conditions?"

"All he would say was, 'Nothing criminal, but goddamned annoying considering the money we pay—we could at least get a little respect.' We've all heard the attitude."

Cardozo smiled. It was the standard civilian complaint against cops.

"After which," Richards continued, "I spoke with one of the doormen, Jerzy Bronski, at his SRO in Chelsea. He says both Saturday and yesterday he worked the midnight shift, then drove his cab from 8 A.M. to 8 P.M. —he moonlights—then he slept."

"Yezhi," Monteleone said.

Richards looked up. "Beg your pardon?"

"Yezhi, not Jerzy. The Poles pronounce J-E-R-Z-Y Yezhi."

"Sounds like Yiddish for Jesus," Richards said.

"Yezl," Siegel said. "The Yiddish word for Jesus is *Yezl.*"

"Don't look at me," Monteleone said. "I'm not discussing Yiddish, that's not my department."

"My grandmother used to say *Yezl,*" Malloy said. "Every December she'd open her Christmas cards, and if there was a Jesus bambino she'd say, 'Another *Yezl.*' "

"You're Jewish?" Monteleone asked. "I didn't know that."

"Only my grandmother," Malloy said.

"Enough Jews for Jesus," Cardozo said. "Can we please get on with this?"

"I haven't been able to get to Claude Loring, the handyman," Richards said. "I went to the address the super gave me, 32 Broome Street. I spoke to Loring's roommate, who now claims to be his ex-roommate, a gentleman by the name of Perfecto Rodriguez."

"That's a name?" Greg Monteleone asked. "They call their kids Perfecto?"

"Who are you calling 'they'?" Ellie Siegel inquired.

"You know who I mean."

Siegel was glaring. "Say it, Greg."

"Latinos."

"Greg," Siegel remarked, "anyone ever told you you're a racist?"

"I can't believe a parent would call a kid Perfecto, I think it's a horrible name for anyone. That makes me a racist?"

"Ladies and gentlemen," Cardozo cut in, "stow it."

Richards went on. "Perfecto says Loring hasn't been living at that address since the first of the month. Loring left no forwarding address, Loring owes for Con Ed and telephone, Loring also left a lot of classical records and dirty laundry, will we please tell Perfecto if we locate Loring."

"Perfecto doesn't know where Loring works?" Monteleone asked. "That seems funny—we know where Loring works."

"Why are you on Perfecto's case?" Siegel asked.

"Believe me, I don't give a damn about the guy, but he seems a little dense."

Cardozo consulted his notes. "The Beaux Arts worksheets show Loring was on the job every day last week, eight A.M. to four P.M."

"I checked back with the super," Richards said. "The only address he has for Loring is Perfecto's pad on Broome Street."

"Where do they mail the paychecks?" Cardozo asked.

"They don't. The super hands them out at the building twice a month. Loring's not due at work today, but he's due tomorrow, so I figure I can catch him then."

"Unless he's left town," Monteleone put in.

"There's one other thing," Richards said.

"Go on," Cardozo said.

"I had the feeling the building personnel were holding back. I don't mean their stories didn't check out, but there was something they weren't saying. Revuelta's wife was right there beside him; every now and then she'd shoot him a warning in Spanish."

"What was the warning?"

"I didn't catch the exact words, but she was giving him that 'Keep your mouth shut' look. It's universal body language. Joshua Stinson's wife gave me the same feeling."

Cardozo looked over at Monteleone. "Greg?"

Monteleone nodded. "I got the same feeling exactly when I questioned Andy Gomez and Fred Johnson. Mrs. Gomez and Mrs. Johnson don't want their men losing their jobs at Beaux Arts Tower. You could read it on their faces. Same thing when I spoke with Herb Dunlop and Luis Morro. Dunlop has a really nice little place in Kew Gardens, a back yard, roses. All four of them can account for their movements. If you believe the witnesses, there's no way we can place them at the scene."

"What witnesses?" Cardozo said.

"Family."

Cardozo made mental note. "What about building residents?"

"Benson didn't hear anything," Monteleone said, "but he's an architect and he says he turns his hearing aid off when he wants to concentrate. Father Madsen didn't hear anything either."

Very dimly, Cardozo was beginning to see connections. Conditions in the garage, whatever the hell that meant. A doorman not at his post when he should have been. Building employees' wives nervous about cops. "Sam, go back, talk to Lawrence. Find out about these conditions in the garage. Which brings us to the leg." Cardozo turned to face Ellie Siegel. "Ellie?"

"Negative on all trash cans accessible from the street, public and private, within a five-block radius. I couldn't check Beaux Arts's garbage: it went out Sunday morning."

Cardozo frowned. "Sunday on a long holiday weekend?"

"It struck me as unusual, too, Vince, but when you look at the overtime that garbage companies get for hauling on Memorial Day weekend—twice their regular fee—it makes sense. Especially since the agent of the building owns the garbage company."

"I thought garbage was mob-controlled," Sam Richards said.

Siegel glanced at him. "You think real estate in this town isn't?"

Cardozo nudged her back to the subject. "What about commercial garbage?"

"The neighborhood has a high concentration of luxury restaurants —mostly French, some Italian. Within the five-block radius, only eight put their garbage directly out on the street. The others use locked bins. Of the eight, six hadn't yet had their garbage picked up.

All the bags contained bone, and all the bone has gone to the lab for analysis. Incidentally, this was a really disgusting job."

"Sorry. What about the other two restaurants?"

"Unfortunately, neither uses the same pickup company as Beaux Arts. We're dealing with three companies and three landfills. There were no municipal pickups over the weekend, but do you want to consider the possibility that the killer took the leg himself to a municipal landfill? That would bring us up to six landfills."

"Let's start with the three."

"We've started."

"Carl, how are we coming on the licenses?" Cardozo asked. "What've you turned up?"

"What we've turned up so far," Carl Malloy said, "is no hot cars, no cars registered to criminals."

"What you've turned up so far in other words," Monteleone said, "is you've turned up nothing."

Malloy looked at him. "Thanks, Greg. Thanks for telling me."

"Some reason for thinking the person who did this drove?" Siegel said.

"Come on, he drives," Monteleone said. "Everybody drives."

Monteleone was being deliberately provocative. He had a way with "everybody" statements that drove Siegel wild.

"My brother doesn't drive," Siegel said.

"And not every driver has a record," Richards said. "Look at me— I'm clean."

"He drives," Monteleone said, eyes on Siegel.

"The killer may be a woman," Siegel said.

"How about that," Monteleone said. "Where were you the night of the killing, Ellie? Double-parking?"

Ellie Siegel took a long sip of coffee. "It would be a real long shot if the killer's out on parole for sawing somebody else up."

"Long shots happen," Cardozo said.

"If *that* long shot happened," Monteleone said, "there's going to be one very ticked-off parole officer."

Cardozo's eyes played across the faces of his detectives. Malloy and Monteleone were reminders of the days when the force had been male only, overwhelmingly white, and for the most part Irish and Italian. Siegel and Richards were reminders of the demographic changes that had shaken the force in recent years. Though City Hall had brought unbelievable pressure to recruit women and minorities into the upper ranks, there was nothing political about their winning the gold shield of the detective and the right to work in civilian clothes. Each of the four detectives had had a distinguished record in uniform, and each—for all their differences of character and outlook —had the strong legs, hard knuckles, and patience that it took to make a good detective.

Cardozo assigned tasks.

Richards would keep knocking on doors and asking questions. He would show flyers of the victim's face to all the staff and residents of Beaux Arts Tower; he would post a flyer in the lobby. Malloy would check out the vehicles of the Beaux Arts staff and residents.

Monteleone would put in a call to the local mental institutions to see if any sex offenders had been released or had escaped within the last month.

In addition to overseeing garbage, Siegel would put her art background to work. "Take a photo of the dead man to the Photographic Unit, have them airbrush it, put him in high-fashion casual clothes."

Cardozo explained that the squad would stay on overtime, moving forward as quickly as possible.

"And I want a five on everyone you talk to."

A collective groan went up.

Cardozo was back in his office when Lou Stein phoned from Forensic. "We've been through the garbage you sent us, Vince. None of the bone is human."

"Crap. Have you matched the eight partials?"

"Three of them. One is the victim's thumb and two belong to —the name seems to be Hatfield. None of the prints from the building staff match, but we still need prints from Loring, Gomez, Revueltas, and Stinson."

"What about the saw?"

"Wiped clean. Not a print on it. But we did find a male body hair embedded in the oil on the rotor. Caucasian. Not pubic. Probably forearm. Wild. Not from the victim. Who handled the saw?"

Cardozo thought back. "I did. Monteleone did. We were wearing gloves."

"I'll still need a hair from each of you. Soon as you can, Vince."

8

STARTLED, BABE LIFTED HER HEAD FROM THE PILLOW. LIGHT rippled across the walls as curtains shifted in the breeze from the air conditioner.

"Did we wake our little girl?" Lucia Vanderwalk was standing there in a pinstripe white cotton suit and polka-dot navy blouse.

"That's all right, Mama."

The gold bracelet on Lucia Vanderwalk's wrist jangled softly as Hadley Vanderwalk helped her into a chair.

"Babe, you're looking dandy," Hadley said. "Just dandy."

Hadley was wearing a dark three-piece suit, and as he took the chair beside Lucia's she reached over to level the tilt of his bow tie.

Babe pressed the button that buzzed her bed up into a sitting position.

"Are you feeling strong enough to go over your appointments?" Lucia asked.

"I didn't realize I had appointments," Babe said.

"Hadley." Lucia held out a hand.

Hadley Vanderwalk handed his wife her oversized handbag. She reached into it and set a desk-sized ledger on her knees. The cover was gleaming morocco, with the name *Beatrice* in gold-leaf letters on the front. "A wonderful bookbinder on West Twenty-seventh did this on two hours' notice, over the holiday—can you imagine? Such craftsmanship."

She flipped almost halfway through the book, to the pages marked MAY. Babe saw that it was an appointment calendar, and many of the blanks were already filled in, in Lucia's looping Miss Porter's penmanship.

"You'll be seeing Dr. Eric Corey, your neurologist, twice a week, Mondays and Thursdays at eleven. You'll see your bone specialist daily at nine in the morning, except weekends of course."

Babe was silent, knowing better than to voice outright opposition to her mother's organizing.

"You'll see your physiotherapists daily at three, weekends included. Dr. Corey says its important to keep moving, not to lose a single day. And you'll see your psychotherapist two times a week."

"Psychotherapist?" Babe said.

Hadley lifted his gaze and stared silently at Lucia.

"Ruth Freeman," Lucia said. "She's terribly popular. Your father and I met her at a dinner at Cybilla deClairville's—can you believe the luck?—and of course we spent the *entire* evening talking about you."

The word *psychotherapist* brought back an image to Babe's mind, a flickering glimpse of a white room and strange masked figures moving in evening clothes. "I was dreaming when you came in," she said suddenly.

"How nice."

"Richard Nixon and Winnie the Pooh and Porky Pig were giving some sort of horrible party. I've had that dream before."

Lucia drew a long breath, studying her daughter carefully. "It's not unusual to have the same dream over again. I often dream of Southampton as it was during the summer of 1948. Your father gave me the most splendid birthday present—a fancy dress ball. We had Eddy Duchin and his orchestra."

"Wonderful man, Duchin," Hadley said. "Played golf every bit as well as he did the piano."

"Remember how he played 'Just One of Those Things,' Hadley? Your favorite song."

"It's *your* favorite, Mama—not Papa's."

"Your father adores 'Just One of Those Things'—don't you, Hadley?"

Hadley smiled pleasantly. "Passionately."

"You know you only adore it to please her, Papa."

"You're in a mood, dear heart," Lucia said. "Was your dream so terribly upsetting?"

"I can't remember it now."

"Why don't you discuss it with Dr. Freeman?" Lucia said. "She knows everything about the mind. She wrote *the* book on recovering from schizophrenia. She'll see you here at the hospital, of course. No one expects you to be up and running about town just yet."

"I'm not schizophrenic. There's nothing wrong with my mind. It's my brain that was in coma."

"Of course. You're absolutely right." Lucia looked into Babe's eyes and smiled her most conciliatory smile, inviting Babe's.

Babe did not smile back. "I want Scottie to visit."

Lucia's face became expressionless. Babe could feel her mother mustering the case for refusal.

"That's rather awkward," Lucia said.

"I believe I have a say in my own life."

"Beatrice, could you at least please trust your father and me? We've stood by you seven years when half the specialists in the country told us it was hopeless. Strange as it may seem to you, we're standing by you now."

"Mama, do you think I don't know what Scottie was accused of?"

Lucia floated Babe a worried look. "Who told you?"

"A detective was here."

Lucia was silent a moment. "There was more to it than mere accusation. Scottie was guilty."

"Of trying to murder me? That's absolutely asinine."

"He admitted it."

Silence wrapped itself around the room.

"He hasn't admitted it to me," Babe said.

Lucia sighed tolerantly. "The first order of the day is for you to get well."

"How do you expect me to get well if you treat me like a baby? Mama, I want my life back. And I want to start by having visits from the people who matter to me."

Lucia gloved her voice in gentleness. "But you *have* started. What do you call your father and me, and Cordelia and Billi? Don't *we* matter? Aren't we enough for a beginning?"

"I want to see my husband. I want to see friends."

Lucia leaned forward to pat Babe's arm. Her hand was cool and soft, with the touch Babe remembered from childhood, the touch that said *Trust Mama, it will all be all right.* "I know, dear heart."

"I want to see Ash Canfield."

Lucia took a moment to arrange herself in her chair, a moment of breathing deep, of recomposing the careful neutrality of her expression. "Ash is dying to visit. Of course you'll see her."

"I've known Ash since childhood and she's my best friend and I've a right to see her *now*."

"Yes, yes, dear heart." Lucia kissed her fingers and pressed them over Babe's lips. "Papa and I will take care of all that."

"Why can't Babe be permitted at least to see Ash?" Hadley asked.

"Beatrice's condition is far too delicate to allow that," Lucia said sharply.

They had returned to the Bentley. The chauffeur was driving them home.

"I couldn't disagree more," Hadley said. "Babe is damned sturdy. She could use a little laughter, though. Bet your life Ash would pep her up."

"Ash Canfield is the world's sloppiest gossip. She'll wear Beatrice out. Frankly, I'm opposed to her even knowing our daughter has recovered."

"You expect to keep the news secret?"

"For a week or two. Till we decide."

Hadley looked at his wife, interested now in what she was thinking. "Till we decide what?"

Lucia turned and stared at Hadley as if it took all her strength and all her will not to upbraid him for imbecility. "Till we decide our child's future. And I hope we shall be able to do that calmly."

"That's ridiculous. Babe's future isn't ours to decide."

Something hard was creeping into Lucia's eyes. "It is till the court decrees otherwise."

Hadley frowned. "A five-minute visit from Ash Canfield, a woman she's known since kindergarten—how on earth is that going to blight Babe's future?"

"Ash has always had an enormous talent for stirring up mischief and she has always encouraged the same talent in Beatrice."

The driver began to turn. Lucia leaned forward and rapped irritably on the half-lowered glass partition.

"Kingsley, must I keep telling you not to take Roosevelt Drive till they've finished that construction?"

Hadley Vanderwalk waited till the television went on upstairs in Lucia's morning room. Lucia denied following the afternoon soaps, and she never watched them on the TV in the drawing room. But he knew she was secretly hooked on them. She kept a VCR programmed to record them when she was out, and he knew for a fact she exchanged tapes with fellow addicts in her bridge-and-charity-ball set.

As soon as Hadley heard the familiar voices on the TV, their emotion muted through the ceiling, he lifted the telephone in the library and quickly punched out a number.

"Ash?" He spoke in a lowered voice. "Good to hear your voice, my dear. It's Hadley Vanderwalk. . . .Yes, of course we're coming to the party, wouldn't miss it. Now prepare yourself. I've a message for you from a friend in the hospital."

"Sweetie," a voice cried. "It's really true—you're back!"

Babe looked toward the door. A figure had stopped motionless on the threshold, a big-eyed, pale-haired woman in pink.

"I haven't changed *that* much. Come on, it's me—Ash!"

Recognition came flooding in. "Ash—my God!"

Arms spread, Ash Canfield took four running steps into the room. And stopped again.

The two women gazed at one another, silent and hardly breathing and not quite believing what they saw.

"Don't I at least deserve a hug?" Babe said.

"You deserve ten million hugs."

Ash leaned over the bed and hugged Babe and Babe hugged back, gratitude welling up and filling every inch of her.

"Sweetie, I've missed you. You don't know how much." Ash blinked hard. Tears were giving her contact lenses trouble and a smile made tiny brackets around her mouth. "You're looking terrific. Not a pound overweight. And not a week older, damn you. Coma must have agreed with you."

"Coma is rotten. I can hardly sit up or feed myself. My stomach has shrunk. I'm on a diet of liquid and something they call semisolids. Two male nurses have to walk me an hour a day. My memory has gaps, I'm tired half the time, I've been out of touch so long I can't carry on a conversation, don't know half the names people are dropping. And to top it off, I have to get around in that monstrosity." Babe threw a nod toward the wheelchair.

"Eventually you graduate to crutches, I suppose?"

"So the doctor promises. And then a cane."

"That will be very distinguished."

"To hell with distinguished. I want to play squash again, and dance, and ride horseback."

"You will, sweetie, you will." Ash took unsteady possession of a chair, crossing her legs.

Babe studied her childhood friend. Ash Canfield looked very different from the image in her memory: older, more made up, more flamboyant in her choice of colors and jewels.

And there was something else, harder to pin down—a nervous energy that had taken over the room instantly.

"Care to fill me in on the mystery?" Ash asked.

"Mystery?"

"Your father made me promise not to tell a soul you've recovered. I gather it's a big, big secret. I love secrets and I especially love being in on them. So spill. Who are we hiding you from?"

There was a silence.

"I don't know," Babe said quietly.

Gradually Ash's smile froze and something in her eyes shifted. She was looking at Babe as if they were both far from home and lonely and if they cared to admit it both a little afraid.

"You'll never guess who I've become." Ash's voice and everything about her had undergone a slight adjustment.

"You've married again?" Babe said.

"No, I'm still married to Dunk, but he made the Queen's Honors List three years ago. He's Sir Duncan and I'm Lady Canfield, if you please. We're mentioned in all the columns and we get asked everywhere."

"But you *always* got asked everywhere."

"And now we're able to turn down twice as many invitations." Ash turned in her chair. "Haven't you got palatial digs here!"

"I'd rather be home."

"Of course you would, but still . . ." Ash rose from her chair and inspected the hospital room, prowling like a cat stalking out territory. She peeked into the bathroom and came back carrying two water tumblers.

"In the meantime, in between time, look what I smuggled past the warden." She reached into a Bergdorf's bag and pulled out a bottle of Moët, cool and glistening. "How's about it?"

"Thanks, but I'll pass," Babe said.

"But sweetie, it's liquid."

"It will only put me to sleep."

"Ah, well." Ash twisted the wire loose, jimmied the cork with her thumbs until it popped, and quickly aimed the overflowing foam into the nearest tumbler. She took a little pillbox from her purse. The lid was mirrored, and the pills inside were pink ovals.

"What are those?" Babe asked.

"Mood elevators. I'm depressed. I have to lose twelve pounds, and Duncan's leaving me."

Babe and Ash had known one another since kindergarten. They'd roomed together at Miss Porter's in Farmington and had almost been expelled for putting a bedpan of Campbell's cream of tomato soup in the bed of a detested house mistress. They'd come out together at the New York Infirmary Ball and then roomed together at Vassar. For years they'd worn their hair the same way, worn the same dress size, shared clothes and secrets and booze and drugs, dated and loved and hated the same boys. They had both wanted to marry the same man —but Duncan Canfield had finally proposed to Ash, and Babe had instantly married the internationally famed pianist Ernst Koenig, thirty-eight years her senior. She'd done it to make Ash jealous. The marriage had lasted seven disastrous years and Ash, embroiled in her own disaster of a marriage, had never expressed the slightest jealousy. Babe had long ago forgiven her.

"Duncan's always leaving you," Babe said, "and he's always coming back."

"It feels permanent this time. And it's happening at the worst possible moment. We're giving a party for Gordon Dobbs."

"Who's he?"

"Of course you don't know—poor sweetie. Dobbsie is the top society writer in town. Charming and sweet and funny and I adore him. It's the two hundred other people I'm not up to. Ah, well, those are the risks of planning a party." Ash poured herself another glass of champagne. "But let's talk about you. Did you have any out-of-body experiences? Did you see God, or angels, or pillars of light?"

"I don't remember."

"What a waste." Ash gulped pills from her palm and downed her champagne and poured another splash into her tumbler. She became even more talkative on her third glass.

She had acres of scandal about the latest world leaders and living legends and newly famous: she told Babe who was rich this month, who was beautiful, who was robbing whom, who was screwing whom. The names had changed, but otherwise it was very much the same dirt Ash had always dished.

Suddenly she broke off. "Good jumping Jehoshaphat!" she cried. "Will you look at the time? I'm going to be late for the caterers. Do you mind?" She lifted the receiver from the bedside phone and jiggled the cradle. "Your phone's on the fritz."

"I have a suspicion Mama arranged it so it only takes incoming calls. *Her* incoming calls. I can't call out."

"You're not turning paranoid, are you?"

"She doesn't want me phoning Scottie. He hasn't been to see me, you know."

"Hasn't he." Ash looked at her oddly, and Babe could feel something close itself off in her friend.

"My parents won't talk about him. Cordelia says he's divorced me."

"Cordelia told you that?"

There was a beat's silence.

"A police detective told me Scottie tried to kill me."

Ash squared her shoulders and looked at Babe. "Then you know."

"Ash, I don't know anything. When I went to bed I had a husband and a daughter and a career. I wake up and seven years are missing. I'm groping around a room blindfolded and someone's moved all the furniture."

"Poor sweetie. It must be god-awful." Ash took Babe's hand.

"Has he remarried?"

"Do the doctors really want you discussing this?" Ash said.

"What do doctors have to do with it? It's my *life.*"

A sad smile appeared on Ash's face. "He hasn't remarried."

Babe studied Ash, with her skittering glazed eyes and nervous hands.

"But he has someone," Babe said.

"Doria Forbes-Steinman."

"That redhead with all that pop art?"

"Her hair's ash blond now and she sold off a lot of the pop art. She's gone into magic realism."

Babe fought to keep pain from edging into her voice. "Do they live together?"

"They have a huge co-op—a lot of English country antiques mixed in with deco and modern. You can see the Empire State Building from the bathtub."

"You've taken a bath there?"

"Of course not. It was written up in *Architectural Digest.*"

"Does he love her?"

"Who knows if he loves anyone."

Babe was silent a moment, remembering. "I know he loved me."

9

TRAFFIC WAS SNAGGED BEHIND A CON ED REPAIR TRUCK WHEN Cardozo finished his lunch and came out of the deli. He crossed the street against the light, threading his way through honking cabs and delivery vans. On the opposite sidewalk he turned.

His eye lingered a moment on the delicatessen. It occupied the ground floor of a pre–World War I red brick six-story walkup tenement. The building was the lone survivor in a block that manifested all three stages of New York real estate frenzy: demolition, parking lot, and construction.

Cardozo took a moment to study the building under construction. Already looming up twenty-seven stories on Lexington Avenue, it was of a type unseen twenty years ago, a scaffoldless high rise where each floor served as a foundation for the next and the owner could build as far into the sky as his lawyer could persuade the city authorities to write the variance.

He stared at the block, adding it up like an equation. There was a balance to it. At the corners, one building coming down, one going up; in the middle, one parking lot, one tenement.

And then his eye saw something else. Up on Lexington, on the second-floor level of the uncompleted high rise, the owner had erected a large sign above the heads of the churning crowd. The lettering, in generously legible wedding-invitation script, spelled LE XANADU, LUXURY CO-OP, SPRING OCCUPANCY, OFFERING BY PROSPECTUS ONLY, ADDRESS INQUIRIES TO BALTHAZAR PROPERTIES, 555-8875.

Cardozo frowned. He slipped his notebook out of his breast

pocket. He flipped through yesterday's notes and he found a business card with the same number, 555-8875.

An NYPD seal with the warning NO ENTRY CRIME SCENE had been pasted over the crack between the front door and the jamb. He sliced through it with his VISA charge card and then he took two keys from the evidence bag—a Medeco and a four-sided Fichet with teeth that looked as though they could cut flesh.

He unlocked the door and entered apartment 6.

Someone had left the air conditioner running. The air was comfortably cool. A gentle afternoon light slatted through the silver-gray Levolor blinds and glowed on the dark polyurethaned floors.

A coat of fingerprint powder lay on the tops of the doorknobs. It lay in the same fine black snow in the kitchen by the refrigerator and sink and cabinets.

Cardozo wriggled his fingers into a pair of skin-thin plastic gloves. They were a medical item. The department bought them by the gross.

He went into the bedroom.

The one-legged chalk man on the floor looked crazily wrong, a figure of bends and angles in a space where nothing else was bent or angled. The straight line where the leg had been cut off seemed inconsistent, as though the artist had abruptly lost interest in his job.

He walked around it to the window and riffled his finger along the edge of the blinds. They made a soft clacking sound like marsh reeds in a breeze. He turned the Lucite pole, changing the slant of the blinds, letting the outside come gradually in.

Five stories below he could see the museum garden, the twenty-foot reflecting pool, the bronzes of huge-boned naked women. There were tables with blue-and-white umbrellas. Museum members, clean and relaxed in their summer clothes, were strolling or sitting alone or in twos and threes with books, cups of coffee, decanters of wine.

What kind of a city was it nowadays, he asked himself. How did the pieces fit together? It was getting a lot crazier, a lot tougher than when he had been a rookie patrolman and the biggest danger he'd faced was stepping into a mom and pop fight on Saturday night in the South Bronx.

South Bronx—his first beat—five miles and twenty-two years away.

In those days in all of New York City there were maybe 300 murders a year. In about 60 percent of the cases perpetrators were found within 24 hours. The conviction rate was close to 80 percent and it took at most three months to bring a case to trial. Heroin had been the hobby of 20,000 losers north of 96th Street and Coke meant the stuff that wasn't Pepsi. The NYPD had yet to come up with the 911 emergency number or mix with computers, Knapp commissions, or civilian review boards. It had taken an average of 22 minutes for a squad car to respond to a call.

Now the murder rate was shading 2,000 a year, you were lucky to identify the corpse, let along the killer; you found perpetrators in 40 percent of the cases, the chances of getting a conviction were one in twenty, and the chances of getting that conviction reversed or sent back on appeal were 50–50. Everything was computerized—fingerprints, rap sheets, 911 calls—and the computers were down 40 percent of the time. It took a squad car an average of 70 minutes to respond to a 911 emergency. New York had become the junkie capital of the world, with one resident in ten an addict. And coke with a small *c* was so popular that even rookie cops were stealing the seizures from busts and substituting Johnson's baby powder, a fact discovered when an overworked prosecutor looking for a second wind had snorted one tenth of a gram of evidence.

New York had turned into the city of more—more confusion, more corpses, more wealth, more poverty, more drugs than ever before or anywhere else, and still climbing.

Why do I love this town, Cardozo wondered.

Maybe because someone has to.

His eye traveled to the ivied marble wall and wrought-iron fences that the museum had erected to separate its garden from the rest of the city.

And then his gaze came back inside.

He had no clear idea what he was looking for. He browsed, open to any suggestion the rooms might throw to him. He went through empty closets. He pulled open the mirrored door of the bathroom medicine cabinet. Black powder floated down and dappled the white of the sink.

He peered into the tub and then his eye went up to the shower curtain rod. Something caught his attention. He took off his shoes, stepped up onto the edge of the tub and squinted at the bright stainless steel.

Tiny scratches ran lengthwise across the distorted reflection of his nose.

He checked the rod three feet further on and found the same scratches.

A shoplifter on heroin was screaming abuse from the lockup cage. Cardozo's ears winced as he climbed the stairs. He stopped at Detective Monteleone's desk.

"Greg, the super says there were shower curtains in all the unsold apartments—clear plastic with a white border. The shower curtain in six is gone. What do you think?"

Monteleone looked up from his pre–World War II Underwood. He had rolled a virgin five into the carriage. "I think exactly what you think I think. The killer wrapped the leg in it."

"There was no spill. How did he tie it?"

Monteleone shrugged. "Rope."

"There weren't any fibers in the bedroom."

"Wire."

"There weren't any scratches on the polyurethane. And if he used the curtain, why'd we find the garbage bag fragments?"

"He spread the curtain to do the messy work, then used the bags to clean up, then got rid of the leg and the curtain." Monteleone held out a bitten buttered bagel.

"Thanks, I ate." The furrows on Cardozo's brow deepened. "I found scratches on the shower curtain rod. There used to be rings. They're gone too. Metal, not plastic. Who uses metal rings nowadays?"

"My grandmother-in-law. No one else."

"You ever tried to unhook those things? Why would he bother?"

"I don't think he would, Vince. Anyone using a shower curtain to dispose of a human leg would pull the curtain off the rings. But if the rings are gone, it's something else. Maybe the building agents were showing one of the other apartments, a shower curtain got torn, so they replaced it from six."

"The shower in the other bathroom would already have curtain rings. They'd just take the curtain."

Monteleone scratched his moustache. "What does the super say?"

"He says the last time he checked there was a curtain in six, but he doesn't remember when the last time he checked was."

"I don't think it connects to the killing."

"Somebody still took it."

"Petty larceny."

10

BARON BILLI VON KLEIST HAD TAKEN UP HIS FAVORITE POSITION: observer. Leaning against the mantelpiece, he shrugged one broad shoulder, adjusting the hang of his dinner jacket. His gaze continued to sweep the party.

Ash Canfield's livingroom was thronged with the people who controlled the look, as opposed to the power, of New York. Waiters circulated unobtrusively with trays of champagne. The mayor was seated at the Boesendorfer, rippling out Cole Porter for one of Alan Jay Lerner's widows.

"Hey, circulate. You're one of my stars." Ash Canfield was wearing her blond-rinsed hair upswept and wide on her head; long black lashes half-veiled her gaze. "Just introduce yourself to anyone you don't know."

"My dear Ash," Baron Billi smiled, "not only do I know ninety-nine percent of the people here, I know half the clothing—intimately." He had counted over a dozen of his designs being worn tonight. The gowns sent a massively mixed message—*See my body, want my body* —and *Drop dead, you could never afford me.* Tough swank—the look that Billi had pioneered after assuming control of Babethings—had not only reversed the company's sweetness-and-light image, it had tripled earnings.

"Do you know Irina, princess of Serbia?" Ash said.

"Oh, *please,* is that a threat?"

Billi saw Lewis Monserat, dealer, talking with Dina Alstetter, the sister of the hostess. They were standing in one of the open terrace doorways, their diet-slim bodies glowing in the light of a Lalique lamp.

Billi made his way across the room.

"Well, handsome Billi," Dina said. She touched a hand to her crisply waved auburn hair.

"Lovely, lovely Dina. So tan and lean. The evening shows promise —at last." Billi took Dina Alstetter's hand and ceremoniously lifted the long, manicured fingers to his lips. "And when may we look forward to your debriefing on Barbados?"

"Barbados was glorious. Karim's yacht is unbelievable. You've *got* to patch up with him. Three stewards, and my own maid."

"New York must be quite a comedown."

"In more ways than one." Dina was wearing gray silk and she kept touching the rose quartz and gold dividers of her pearl necklace. "I see my baby sister has assembled her usual collection of trend-setters and fashion terrorists—all busily dripping pearls, ashes, and borrowed *bons mots.*"

"Watch out for your own glass house." Lewis Monserat flicked flame from a gold lighter and held it to Dina's cigarette. He'd combed his gleaming black hair straight back, rather than over his forehead, and somehow the effect was to make his eye sockets look far more hollow than usual.

"Tell me," Billi said, "is that woman in the very bad fake Fortuny Princess Irina of Serbia? Don't turn too obviously—just behind you to the left."

Dina turned and her blue-gray eyes made no pretense of not staring.

Lewis Monserat looked and said the woman was one of the new curators of the fashion collection of the Metropolitan Museum, just hired away from Dallas— "Doesn't that make you want to salaam?" —and then he began pointing out the other stars in Ash's new crop of instant celebrities.

"You can always count on Ash's network," Dina sighed. "Whether you need a broker or an abortionist, a friendly judge or a caterer, Ash always knows someone who knows someone. Only do you notice there's someone very important missing?"

Billi looked around the room. "Who?"

"The host." Dina ran her hand through her hair with a look of iced merriment. "Will you two excuse me? I'm ravenous."

Dina pried her way through conversational groupings. Guests were throwing their heads back with the open-mouthed hilarity of television youth. From outside came the sound of dance music.

Taking one of Ash's Lowestoft plates in hand, Dina surveyed the buffet table.

There were candle-warmed tureens of eggs scrambled to a froth and slivered with white truffle; chargers heaped with chilled Mediterranean *langoustes; mousse de crevettes;* assorted *crudités* with a Pernod dip; ice swans of gray Iranian caviar that could only have been procured from the commissary at the U.N.; cold *filet de veau* in port jelly sliced paper-thin, with miraculously smooth béarnaise to dollop over it; boiled quails' eggs sumptuously marinated in Polish buffalo grass vodka; wine aspics; and at the dessert end of the table towers of freshly imported exotic fruit, creamy ices, and tangy sherbets in frosted crystal cups.

Rising from bunches of grapes, gazing down on the cold stuffed lobster like an embalmed maître d', was a 17th-century French marble bust of Socrates.

Ash Canfield reached into the picture, switching a cluster of white grapes with a cluster of red. She stood back, judging the effect.

"Hi, Sis," Dina said. "Quite the royal spread."

Ash smiled a little uneasily. "Help yourself."

"The mousse looks yummy. When's the host arriving?"

Ash blinked and stood frozen in a sudden cave of silence.

Dina gave her sister's hand a mischievous little pat. "Chin up. The show must go on."

"Excuse me," Ash said. "The bandleader's played that tune three times." She quickly joined the tide flowing through the open French windows out onto the terrace.

A dance floor of polished oak had been laid down. Men in black tie and women in new summer gowns whirled to the music of a nine-piece orchestra. Beyond them the city pushed up a steel and glass skyline that burned with the hard glow of diamonds on a bed of black velvet.

Ash found Gordon Dobbs by the bandstand, whispering with a sax player, jotting something in his notebook.

"Ash my dear, only you could have gotten this crowd together." As Gordon Dobbs slid his notebook back into his dinner jacket, diamond shirt studs sparkled in his boiled shirt. "I know for a fact that Jackie deFonseca sent last-minute regrets to the vicomtesse de Chambord so she could come here. Tomorrow morning all New York will be talking of nothing but."

Gordon Dobbs wrote a column for *New York* magazine. Ash viewed him as a sort of protector in a fierce and flammable world. He did not pretend to be other than what he was, and he had a reliable talent for cutting enemies down to gossip-size nuggets.

"Why the notebook?" Ash asked. "Surely you're not working."

"Bet your sweet ass I am. Working the joint, seeing who's with whom and who's not, who's saying what and who isn't."

"But you can't write the party up—you're the guest of honor!"

"My dear girl, a professional gossip has an obligation to his readers. He is on twenty-four-hour call."

Ash took his arm. "You're not going to say anything about Dunk—*please*, Dobbsie."

"I'll have to at least *mention* he was indisposed. Otherwise it'll look as though Suzi and Liz scooped me." Gordon Dobbs's dark eyes twinkled beneath curly hair beginning to gray. "And we don't want people saying you made me guest of honor just to shut me up, do we?"

"Can't you write about something else? Dunk isn't the only important person who's not here." Ash hesitated. "If I give you a very, very hot story, will you leave Dunk out of your column?"

"Depends how hot."

"Babe Devens has come out of her coma."

Gordon Dobbs's eyebrows shot up. "Are you pulling my leg?"

"It's the absolute eye-witness truth."

"So spill, spill."

Ash drew Gordon Dobbs to a corner of the terrace and filled him in on the details. "But don't you dare quote me."

"Let me have it exclusive. For a week." Gordon Dobbs recapped his pen. "And show me where people are getting that terrific-looking pink grapefruit sorbet from."

At the buffet table, Hadley Vanderwalk was helping Lucia empty the contents of two sorbet cups into one.

"Tante Lucia," Ash smiled. "Uncle Hadley. I'm so glad you could make it."

"Splendid party," Hadley said. "One of your delightfully rash impulses."

"Tante Lucia, you remember Gordon Dobbs."

Lucia had dressed in black, with a brocade jacket. She had put a pink ribbon in her hair. It was as though she still saw herself as a bright, irrepressible little girl. She had charmed her father when she was six, why not the world now? "Yes," Lucia said, "of course I remember Mr. Dobbs."

Gordon Dobbs lifted an asparagus-and-Saint-André canapé to his lips and nodded mysteriously.

"Isn't the news glorious?" Ash said.

Lucia Vanderwalk knit her flawlessly pruned eyebrows together. "News?"

"I visited," Ash said. "Didn't Uncle Hadley . . ."

"Mr. Dobbs," Lucia said, "would you excuse us?" Her narrow gaze went from Ash to Hadley and back to Ash. "Where can we talk privately?"

In the library, morocco-bound sets of Eugene Sue and Macaulay sat on shelves with beveled brass edging.

"You gave your word." Lucia's lips were set in a thin line of fury.

"My word?" Hadley seemed honestly baffled.

"That you wouldn't tell anyone about Beatrice. And of all people, you had to go and tell *her.*"

Ash's lips trembled. One hand played with the clasp of a cabochon emerald earring. "I'm sorry, Tante Lucia. I only wanted to cheer Babe up."

Lucia stood there, rigid and unyielding, staring at Ash in absolute motionlessness. "You've never been trustworthy. Not as a child, not now. If there is any publicity, if anyone or anything disturbs my daughter's recovery, I shall hold you personally responsible."

Ash looked at Lucia, her thick-lashed blue eyes fixed and blank and uncomprehending. And then something dropped like a curtain. "Would you excuse me? My guests."

Turning, Ash bumped into a chair. As she crossed the hall to the livingroom, she looked a little out of control, not quite managing things with her usual grace.

"A little hard on the poor gal, don't you think?" Hadley said. "You can't really expect to keep Babe's recovery under wraps."

"We've got to keep it under wraps, as you choose to put it, till we're sure Beatrice can cope."

"Of course she'll cope. She's as strong as a Thoroughbred and she'll be getting the best physical therapy money can buy."

"And can Cordelia cope? This is going to throw the poor child completely back into her mother's shadow."

"Do you really see your daughter and granddaughter as rival flowers struggling for the same patch of sunlight?"

"How can you ask that? In seven years have you understood one single word the psychiatrist has said to us?"

Hadley Vanderwalk took an imperturbable swallow from his glass of champagne. "You're too many jumps ahead for me, Lucia old girl."

There was a change in Lucia. She suddenly smiled.

"Cordelia," Lucia said. *"There* you are. We've been searching all over."

Hadley turned. It was difficult to say how long Cordelia had been standing in the doorway. She had her hair swept up this evening. She was wearing a bodiced blouse of Edwardian lace fastened at the collar by a cameo brooch set with a small emerald, and she looked chic and striking and strangely unconcerned.

"And you're wearing your great-grandmother's brooch," Lucia said. "I love seeing it on you."

"Anyone care to dance?" Cordelia asked.

"It would be a great relief," Hadley said.

On the dance floor, Hadley inhaled his granddaughter's perfume —Joy, the most expensive in the world. The jewels that flashed from the girl's wrists were diamonds.

"Were you and Grandmère arguing about me?" Cordelia asked.

"Grandmère thinks you're going to have some kind of crisis now that your mother's back."

"And what do you think, Grandpère?"

"I think you're old enough to behave like the young lady you give every sign of being."

"Thank you, Grandpère."

The band was playing a very slow "I'll Be Seeing You," and Cordelia danced like a little girl, her cheek angled down toward her shoulder, looking up at her grandfather.

A hand tapped Hadley on the shoulder. Hadley turned his head. The hand belonged to Count Leopold de Savoie-Sancerre, a bald, paunchy gentleman in his middle seventies with a chestful of World War II Danish military decorations.

"Doublecut, if you please," Count Leopold said. His partner was Lucia Vanderwalk, and she was frowning at her husband.

As Hadley handed Cordelia over to the count, he whispered to his granddaughter, "Pray for me." He took his wife's hand. "I seem to be running into you all over the place, my dear."

The band broke into a manically up-tempo "Darktown Strutters' Ball." Count Leopold methodically boogied Cordelia toward the edge of the dance floor. "The countess has some very fine snort. What do you say?"

Cordelia smiled. "You're on."

Countess Victoria de Savoie-Sancerre, forty years her husband's junior, was bent over a Chippendale side table in the spare guest room. Long dark hair half hid her face, and her wide-apart green eyes didn't bother looking up as Count Leopold and Cordelia came in.

"Company," Count Leopold sang out.

"Close the door." With a gold safety razor Countess Victoria was carefully pulverizing the cocaine spill on a Cartier purse mirror. An enormous ruby-and-diamond ring blinked on the joint of her finger. "Anyone know why Dunk isn't at the party?"

"Dunk and Ash are breaking up again," Cordelia said.

"Is it true Dina Alstetter had an affair with Dunk and he ditched her for Ash?"

"Years ago," Cordelia said.

"No wonder Dina's acting so smug." Countess Victoria arranged the coke into lines. "Youth before beauty."

Cordelia took a hundred-dollar bill from her purse and rolled it into a tight little cylinder. She bent over the mirror.

"Be careful," Countess Victoria warned. "I got this stuff through a Nicaraguan freedom fighter. It's eighty percent pure."

11

AT 7:59 A.M., CARDOZO ENTERED THE PRECINCT HOUSE. PANDEMO-
nium was back to normal after the long holiday weekend. The lobby
swarmed with cops, their waists thick with the dangling parapherna-
lia of the Job: beltloads of .38-caliber rounds, service revolvers,
leather-wound billy clubs, staticking radios, and handcuffs that rang
discordantly with each step. Greetings and backslaps were being
exchanged like calls on the floor of a stock exchange. Cardozo traded
a few, joining the flow up the stairs.

In his cubicle the three button on the phone was lit. It was Dan
Hippolito, reporting on John Doe's blood. "He had enough alcohol in
him to pickle an elephant. Enough coke to orbit a hippo. Plus considerable quantities of heroin and meth."

"Was he a junkie?"

"Nah, with junkies the circulation is so bad you see necrotic tissue
in the toes, but Johnny's got no punctures and five good toes."

"What does the combination of drugs tell you?"

"Nothing special. You can buy it prepackaged on the streets.
There's usually some other shit in it, but that metabolizes without a
trace."

Cardozo thanked Dan, then phoned the lab. "Hey, Lou, did you
check John Doe's hair? Any chance he dyed it?"

"It's the first thing we check with blonds. The color's real. He did
use a very expensive conditioner—high in vitamin E. But it's over-
the-counter stuff."

Cardozo drew a line through the memo in his notebook. At 8:05 he
crossed the hall for his task force meeting.

"How are we doing on garbage?" he asked.

Siegel shook her head. "No leg yet."

"And the photo?"

"Turned out pretty well." She had taken a photo of the dead man to the Photographic Unit, had them airbrush it and put him in high-fashion clothes from last month's *GQ*. She passed it to Cardozo.

He eyed it critically. The photographic boys had dressed John Doe conservatively: button-down shirt, regimental tie, tweed jacket. "Take this to the modeling agencies. See if they ever worked with him." He turned to Detective Malloy. "Carl, how about licenses?"

"Still coming up dry," Malloy said. "Except for Bronski. He's got violations on his cab—and complaints to the commission."

Cardozo smiled: the city's taxi commission was a pork barrel of bribery and embezzlement, and the commissioners—who did little besides enforcing a cabbie dress code—were presently targets of criminal indictment. "What kind of complaints?"

"Picks up passengers from any lane, busts lights, grabs other cabbies' fares. A go-getter like that, you'd think he'd hustle rides during the off-peak hours. But noon-to-two, he must have been napping. At eleven forty-five he had a fare from Broadway and Park Place to Fifty-fourth Street and Sixth Avenue. The next fare was one P.M., from Ninetieth and Broadway to Fifty-ninth and Sixth. Then one forty-five, from Fifty-fourth Street and Sixth to Twelfth Street and Third Avenue."

"Aren't those rides spaced a little far apart?" Cardozo said.

"Very much so, compared to other drivers' sheets. Another thing. Bronski leaves his first fare a block from the Tower. He leaves his second six blocks from the Tower. He picks up his third a block away. I suppose it's possible, but it seems strange."

"How was his meter for the day?" Cardozo asked.

"Low. The other drivers' sheets averaged twenty dollars more for the same shift."

"Better give it another look," Cardozo said. "Greg, what about mental institutions?"

Monteleone had checked for sex offenders released or escaped within the last month. No escapes had been reported, fifteen offenders had been released.

"Follow up on them. Find out where they were Saturday. What residents did you get hold of?"

"Jessica Lambert, Esmée Burns, and Estelle Manfrey are out of town semipermanently. Lambert's in Hollywood, shooting a miniseries about Ellie Siegel."

Detective Siegel looked up.

"Bad joke. It's about a woman sleuth. Burns always spends April and May in Paris, she has a perfume factory there. Manfrey is in a wheelchair in Palm Beach, zonked on painkillers."

"Who did you talk to personally?"

He'd spoken to Joan Adler, the mousy writer of political broadsides, who had returned from weekend house parties in the Hamptons. She had not recognized the victim's face on the flyer. He'd also shown the flyer to the Beaux Arts staff, with the same result. He had persuaded Bill Connell, the super, to let him post a flyer in the lobby.

"Today," Cardozo said, "take the flyer to the stores and the clinics. And get the names of the employees and patients."

"They're not going to want to give me those."

Cardozo ignored the objection. "Run the names through the Bureau of Records. Have the Passport Office send us photos."

"You're assuming every name on the list will have a passport."

"The ones that don't, ask the Bureau of Motor Vehicles for license photographs."

"Vince, that could be two hundred photos."

"So? We're going to have a lot of faces to match." Cardozo turned to Sam Richards. "Sam, how'd the follow-up on Debbi Hightower go?"

"I checked with the World Trade Center. She was sort of telling the truth. There was an industrial show in the ballroom of the Helmsley Hotel and it was called *Toyota Presents.*" Sam Richards passed a program to Cardozo. "But Hightower's not listed on the program. I checked the hotel's employee list. No Hightower there either. I asked the waiters and bartenders if they'd seen a lady of Miss Hightower's description. They had. She came in through an agency— Amanda's Girls—temporary staff for the show."

"What kind of temporary staff?"

"Hostess. She served coffee and smiled."

"Who was the audience?"

"Out-of-towners. Toyota dealers, would-be Toyota dealers, Ford dealers Toyota is trying to steal."

"What time did this show go on?" Cardozo asked.

"Eight o'clock."

"I don't buy Debbi Hightower served coffee and smiled at a bunch of out-of-town car dealers from eight o'clock Friday night till noon Saturday. Amanda's Girls—is that a legit business?"

"They're in the Yellow Pages—office temps. They have a New York business license."

"I'd like her to account for that time, Sam."

"She's a hooker," Monteleone said. "Don't tell me she bought that apartment on an office temp's pay."

"She's late with the maintenance," Sam Richards said.

"Lean on her," Cardozo said. "Find out who she was with. Maybe she brought the guy to her place. Maybe he saw something she didn't. Maybe he did something she didn't see. Dig. How'd you do with Fred Lawrence and that problem in the garage?"

"I finally got it out of him. He rents a space in the garage, it's supposed to be his and his alone. He got back from Fire Island on Saturday at noon, and a taxi had parked in his place."

"A taxi?" Cardozo frowned. "Why didn't he want to tell you?"

"Because he's ashamed. He says he's type A, driven, heart-attack material, can't take frustration. He went crazy and phoned the cab company. Said he was Jewish Defense League and he was going to blow them up."

"What was the name of this cab company?"

"Ting-a-ling Taxi, something cutesy like that. He'd just as soon not remember."

Cardozo was thoughtful. "Bronski's company is Ding-Dong Transport. That's awfully close to Ting-a-ling Taxi. Bronski could have had his cab parked in the Beaux Arts garage from noon to two. That would explain the low meter and why all the rides are near Sixth Avenue and Fifty-fourth. Carl, check that out."

Malloy nodded.

"Any luck finding the handyman?" Cardozo asked.

"I've got a phone call in to the super," Richards said. "He'll let me know when Loring shows."

"Maybe the handyman went to Rio," Monteleone said. "Do we have extradition with Rio?"

"If we need it," Cardozo said, "we'll get it. Sam, how'd you do with the other residents?"

Richards had been able to question Billi von Kleist, the fashion designer; Phil Bailey, the TV network president, and his wife Jennifer; Johnny Stefano, the Broadway composer. None of them could shed any light on events in the building Saturday, and none of them recognized the face on the flyer.

Cardozo sighed. "That still leaves three residents unaccounted for."

Sam Richards smiled. "Doyle's in the Betty Ford clinic, coming off cocaine. It's his third try. The smart money says he's not going to make it. Notre Dame is at the Aga Khan's resort in Sardinia, shacked up with Senator Behrend of Nebraska's wife. The duke and duchess are in Issy-les-Moulineaux with Countess Rothschild, who is terminally ill with bone marrow cancer."

"How'd you get all that?" Cardozo asked.

"I found a very good source. Maybe you'd like to meet him."

"Frankly, they're the reason we have cockroaches in the building." Gordon Dobbs was discussing Saveurs de Paris, the bakery on the fourth floor of Beaux Arts Tower. "Their croissants aren't even fresh. Don't worry, I never buy from them." He chuckled. "They didn't make any of these."

Cardozo's glance went down to the colorful assortment of tiny glazed cakes laid out on the silver platter. He bit into another one, the third he'd taken, despite his worries about softening up his gut. They were superb pastries, the sort of pastries that must exist in children's dreams. Through a mouthful of hazelnut, he asked about the super.

"Bill Connell's divine—you need a drip fixed, he has the handyman here in three seconds. His wife's an invalid, you know, and that's why he plays around."

There it was again: the superficially pleasant remark, the sting in its tail. Cardozo asked what Dobbs knew about the dental clinic on four.

"Let's call a spade a spade. They're a welfare mill. Some very peculiar people walk in and out of that office. It's common knowledge that the good doctors are, shall we say, liberal with their prescriptions for painkillers."

Cardozo sensed Dobbs had no evidence, no information, not even a reasonable suspicion: he was doing this because he wanted two cops in his livingroom, because he wanted to turn that evening at dinner to the jeweled blonde beside him and say, "Guess who came to tea at my place today . . . the fuzz."

Cardozo asked about the psychotherapists on five.

The boom of Gordon Dobbs's laughter filled the room. He rocked back and forth in his chair. "Poor souls—they're having a very hard time of it. Competition's tough. New York is licensing far too many psychiatric social workers. I mean, make up your mind! Are they doctors or mother's helpers? I spoke to one of them in the elevator, mentioned Jung and drew a complete blank. Obviously they do a lot of work for the state. Someone's paying for that space, and believe me, it's not those shabby clients of theirs."

"You wouldn't happen to be acquainted with any of them?"

"The patients? God, no." Dobbs's smile was ingratiating and seemed to say, *We understand one another, it's just you and I against the riffraff in the world.*

Cardozo mentioned Lily Lobkowitz.

"Princess Lil? Her ex-husband's Polish, she's a Copa girl from Enjay."

"Enjay?"

"Joisey. Her sister is Senator Galucci's wife. The princess has a slight drinking problem. One glass of sherry and she's off to the races. My heart goes out to the poor thing. She's never invited anywhere anymore. Her brother-in-law gave her the apartment—the poop is, she had to go to a priest and swear by the Virgin Mary to stop shoplifting from Bendel's."

Dobbs did not look at all the way Cardozo would have imagined a professional society gossip. With his dark eyes and lithe build, his curly hair beginning to gray, he looked the sort of a man who made his living as a mercenary on battlefields, not in drawing rooms. What he sounded like was something else.

"The Duke and Duchess de Chesney?" Cardozo asked.

"They're British, of course; the best sort of British. Never pull rank. Marvelous conversationalists—always in demand. They're in Paris because Countess Rothschild is dying and wanted to have someone entertaining around while she's fading. Now, to me that says a great deal."

"Debbi Hightower?" Cardozo said.

"She claims to be an actress-hyphen-model, but I doubt she could act her way out of a birthday cake at a stag party. Poor child; some people should *not* do cocaine. Off the record, I've heard that she's a call girl."

"Do you know any of her johns?"

"Well, I've seen some very sheepish-looking gents stopping on her floor."

"Recognize any of them?"

A suggestion of color crept up Gordon Dobbs's cheeks. He lifted a porcelain teacup and sipped. "I wouldn't feel right naming— No, you have to ask her. I'm sorry I brought it up; it's not my business."

Cardozo moved right along. "Will Madsen?"

"The rector of the church on the corner? He's done wonders bringing in people for lunchtime services, and their concerts are a joy. He's an absolute gentleman, never talks religion. I respect that in a man of the cloth, don't you?"

This man's asking me what I respect? Cardozo thought. "Fred Lawrence?"

"Does income tax returns for some very glam people. I must say he's worked magic for me—IRS hasn't audited me in seven years, and that's a world's record."

Dobbs's livingroom had a cool, cavelike comfort. One wall was shelved, with discreet track lights pinpointing terra-cotta idols and figurines, beaten gold masks, carved bronze and ivory, painted fragments of pottery. Dobbs was obviously a collector. The fireplace was carved marble, and curtains of silk and peach velvet made the windows here seem taller than in six.

"Baron Billi von Kleist?" Cardozo asked.

He wondered if there wasn't an instant's hesitation before the reply came.

"Billi's a marketing genius, and quite close to the White House. The first lady—I kid you not—the president's wife was at his apartment for dinner two months ago. And of course the designs he markets are truly imaginative—though I must say this latest line of his takes a little getting used to."

"Notre Dame?"

"I don't have to tell *you*, Lieutenant, that any young man in a torn Saint Laurent with punk green hair singing songs like 'We Are Going to Kill You' is utterly harmless. That whole punk drag thing is strictly for Middle America. He's Scientology, never goes near drugs or alcohol. He's always on tour—you never see him in the building. At the moment he's having an affair with the wife of Senator Behrend of Nebraska. They're at the Aga Khan's resort in Sardinia."

There were taps. Detective Sam Richards's feet clicked on marble as he moved from the foyer with its black-and-white checkerboard floor back into the light pooling by the terrace. He stood holding a teacup, staring out at the view.

"Phil Bailey?" Cardozo asked.

"Phil's president of NBS-TV—utterly unpretentious—more a businessman than an artistic type, but just as much at ease talking to David Bowie as to King Juan Carlos. His wife's a charmer. She could have been a concert harpist, but she gave it up to marry him. She's

Israeli, but very polished. I love Israelis like that. And I hear the son's a gifted architect."

Cardozo caught just an edge, like a blade winking under a sleeve: Dobbs didn't like Jews, made exceptions, had no idea that Cardozo was a Portuguese Jewish name: probably feeling damned liberal about it, Dobbs was giving him the condescension he reserved for Catholics.

"Hank Doyle?"

Dobbs lifted his hands. A gold wedding band flashed. No other finger jewelry. "What a horrific tragedy. Hank's wife and I used to have long talks in the elevator. She told him he had to choose, it was snort or Charlayne, and he chose snort. Now he's at the Betty Ford Clinic—but seriously, do you know anyone who's recovered from coke? It's just too cheap and too available. And now all this crack nonsense. Dreadful."

A bell rang. Cardozo's eyes went toward the foyer.

The front door opened and a thickset six-foot-tall blond man in overalls walked in, pocketing a key. He had a slight limp, the sort that shrapnel-wounded veterans had brought back from Vietnam. His nose had a bump as though it had once been broken.

Dobbs turned. "In the master bathroom, Claude, the porcelain faucet."

The man vanished down the hallway.

"Who was that?" Cardozo asked.

"Claude? He's the handyman. I have a leak."

Cardozo's and Richards's glances met.

Sam Richards rapped on the open bathroom door. The handyman glanced up from his work, his forehead wrinkling when he saw the open wallet and shield.

"Detective Sam Richards, twenty-second precinct. Where were you Saturday, Claude?"

Loring crouched there, frowning, then pulled himself very slowly to his feet. He laid a wrench across the sink.

There was a silence while the two men stared into each other's eyes, appraising each other.

Richards was looking at a broad-faced man in his early thirties, thick-bodied, with blond hair, sideburns, a moustache—a man who moved with all the ease of a stone wall learning how to walk.

Loring ran a soiled finger beneath his blond moustache. "Saturday I was crashing at a friend's."

"All day?"

Loring's chest pushed against his T-shirt, showing ridges of gymnasium muscle. He nodded.

"Where were you Sunday? And yesterday?"

"Same place."

"Can anyone vouch for that?"

Loring opened his mouth . . . and then clamped it shut. His eyes were red-rimmed, as though they hadn't seen sleep in a long time.

"Claude, you'd better tell us—for your own sake."

"What's my sake got to do with it?"

"There was a killing here Saturday."

"I didn't have anything to do with that."

"You have a key to the apartment where the body was found."

"Me and a few other people."

"We're talking to them."

Loring shook a Camel from the crunched pack in his hip pocket. "Who was this friend whose place you were at, Claude?"

"You going to pester her? Look, I just had a fight with my roommate, the turd threw me out. It's hard enough finding a place to sleep in this crappy town without you guys barreling in and scaring the shit out of her. What's she going to think, you bust down her door asking if I killed some poor bastard?"

Richards folded his arms across his vest, and the sleeve of his brown suit rode up, exposing a new Seiko on his wrist. "We're just asking her were you there, Claude."

Loring picked up his wrench and stood slapping it into his palm. "Does she need to know about the killing?"

"Damn," Richards said, slamming down the brakes, "look at that." A dark green van, sporting a huge logo of a blue jay, had parked by a fire hydrant. Richards regarded fire hydrants as a police parking preserve.

"Tennessee license," Cardozo said. "Wouldn't you know."

Richards found a hydrant on the corner of Sixth and Thirty-third and parked with three expert twists of the wheel. They threaded their way through sidewalk jungles of potted palms and corn plants; the jungle was for sale at ridiculous prices—two hundred dollars a tree and up—and the green foliage was thick enough to give sanctuary to an entire Vietcong brigade. The pavement was steaming in the freak summer warmth. This was the wholesale flower district, and the real estate industry, ready to boom the walkups in the area, had christened these blocks FloHo.

Loring's friend and alibi lived in a Civil War loft building with World War I paint peeling off the limestone-arched doorway. Cardozo found the button with part of a business card wedged into the name slot: FAYE DI STASIO ASSOCIATES. He pushed, and after a second push a buzzer screeched back and the glass door released with a click.

They began the climb up the rickety steps. The air in the stairwell pressed like a blanket soaked in hot water. A dark-haired young woman waited on the fourth-floor landing. It seemed to Cardozo there was something hurt and bitter in the way she was standing there, defending her door.

"Faye di Stasio?" he asked.

She smoked her cigarette and she just stared and let ashes drift down toward the floor. "Who's looking for her?"

"Police." Cardozo showed his shield, introduced Richards.

"The place is a mess." She let them pass.

A television was going. The room was steeped in the aroma of negligence, and the air smelled like an old sofa.

"You had a guest over the weekend?" Cardozo put the question in a carefully natural voice, as though it would be the most normal thing in the world for this woman to tell Vince Cardozo all about the men who shared her sleeping space.

Her gaze came up level to his. "Who's in trouble—him or me?"

"Not you. Maybe not him either."

"I'm having some coffee—could I offer you some?"

Cardozo glanced at Richards. Richards nodded.

"Won't you have a seat?" Her words were strangely ladylike coming from a woman with dirty bare feet.

Cardozo couldn't believe the poverty of the space: stained, crumbling walls, laths poking through plaster like exposed bone; window curtains decaying in the city's acid air; chairs with fractured legs bound in mover's tape.

The two policemen picked chairs that looked safe.

Cardozo let his eyes prowl the apartment. A sewing machine had been set up in the kitchen; cloth toys spilled out of three-foot cartons stacked beside the bathroom; cat food in a bowl by the door was growing a two-day-old skin. An air-conditioning unit pumped noisily in a rear window. Beyond the burglar gates tips of scraggly sumac rose in the soot-blackened courtyard.

She brought three mugs of coffee.

"A man called Claude Loring stayed with me."

"What times was he here this weekend?" Cardozo asked.

She lit a fresh cigarette and held it to one side, her elbow on the table and her wrist angled back. "Late Friday night till this morning."

"What do you mean, late Friday night?"

"Well, maybe it was Saturday morning. The sun wasn't up."

"He was here straight through?"

"Right up there." She pointed to a loft bed that had been amateurishly built over the kitchen.

"You were home all weekend?"

A silence went on too long. She nodded again.

"Never went out?"

"I was working. Maybe I went for coffee, cigarettes."

"So how do you know he was here all the time?"

"The longest I was out was ten, fifteen minutes. He's like a bear—sleeps two, three days in a row."

"You've known him how long?"

"Oh, we go back a few years."

"What kind of work do you do?"

"I run my own business—creative toys for pets."

He picked up a stuffed mouse sitting on a table: the eyes opened like a doll's and a squeal came out of it.

"You made this?" he asked.

She nodded.

"Pretty," he said. He didn't quite mean it.

Her face lit up like a hundred-watt bulb. "I'm really a cloth-sculptor. The business is temporary, till I get my exhibit."

The phone rang and an answering machine cut in. "Hello. You have reached the office of Faye di Stasio Associates." The voice was hers. "Please leave your name and phone number and a member of our staff will contact you."

There was a beep and then a man's voice, gruff. "Hey, Faye—it's me. Pick up."

She threw back her coffee and crossed the room and snatched up the receiver. "I'm sorry," she said after listening a moment, "we had some trouble. It won't happen again."

"What sort of trouble?" Cardozo asked as she came back to her chair.

"The van broke down. Nothing could go out Saturday. Today everything's ready and our dealers are claiming they lost the holiday trade, they want to cut back on their orders. What a business."

"Claude must be a help to you."

"Yeah. Claude's great."

12

"I SHOULD BE ANGRY AT YOU," DR. ERIC COREY SAID.

"Why?" Babe was sitting in a smock on a table covered with paper roller in the doctor's examination room.

"For one thing, you woke up while I was in Bermuda. Made me cut short my vacation. For another, you're in such damned good shape you're almost a false alarm. There's not much I can do for you. Nature seems to be handling the hard stuff."

Tallish, with a deep tan that set off his aquamarine eyes, Dr. Corey had a bedside manner that matched his voice: gentle, perhaps too gentle to be completely trusted. As he examined her he was slow and careful not to hurt her.

"You're my pet project. I've sunk seven years into you." He rotated her ankle. "Feel okay? Better than yesterday?"

"Much better."

"That?"

"Ouch."

"Just a pin. We want to be sure your nerves are waking up. Wiggle your big toe."

She made an effort. The big toe responded with a twitch.

"Good girl. Cross your legs." He bonged her knee with a rubber hammer.

Her leg bounded up.

"You've got fine reflexes, ma'am, and they're getting finer, and one of these days they'll be just about normal—for a woman your age."

"Doctor, how old am I?"

"That depends when you were born."

"But am I older than when I went into coma? Or did my body and mind just stay in a deep freeze?"

"Interesting question. Might take a philosopher to answer it—or a lawyer. Hey, see the shape your ligaments are in? Not bad—not bad at all. We walked you a mile every day so they wouldn't shrink."

"Thank you."

"Thank your gene pool. You're a robust woman. All we need to do now is build up your strength, exercise your muscles, feed you. How's your appetite?"

"I'm dying for some decent food."

"Good sign. We'll move you to solids gradually. Your stomach's shrunk. We have to stretch it slowly. No lobster Newburg in the first month."

Her eye went to the wheelchair. "When will I be able to walk?"

"We'll have you on crutches in a few weeks, and in a couple of months you should be able to make it on a cane."

"Months!"

"Maybe sooner."

"When can I leave the hospital?"

"We'll see." He made a notation on a clipboard. "How are you feeling—mentally, emotionally?"

"Angry to have lost seven years. Curious to know what caused my coma."

His eyes flicked up at her. "Hard to say seven years after the fact. Could have been a bump on the head, or drugs—"

"Insulin?"

He laid down the clipboard. "What gave you that idea?"

"A police detective."

He looked at her. "Police aren't M.D.'s, you know. The only people their pathologists examine are dead."

"That's not an answer."

"It's all you're going to get from me because it's all I know. Now hop into that chair and let's skedaddle you out of here."

13

A LITTLE AFTER 2:00 P.M., A TRUCK WITH THE LOGO ANDY'S DUMP-ing, Astoria, pulled onto the Fountain Avenue landfill in Queens. Its load had been held at a depot in Manhattan over the long weekend. The truck searched, proceeded farther down the area, found a dumping place under the slow drizzle, and reared up: there was a sudden intensification of the stink in the air as the debris slid down glistening into a pile on the earth.

Ten years ago there had been nothing here but Jamaica Bay, a finger of the Atlantic. Now there was a land built of garbage, raising its rotting mountains to the sun's heat, pressing its soft shore into the ocean. All day long an unending cortege of dump trucks, escorted by clouds of hovering gulls, had been depositing their contributions.

Since Sunday an army of men and women in police rain gear had laboriously explored this new land. For over thirty-six hours they had sunk five-foot steel probes into the muck, turned pieces of slime, climbed over ridges and valleys, peered into the rusted refrigerators and stoves that dotted the gray moonscape like wrecked space probes from another planet.

With a deafening mechanical scream the truck changed gears, swung in a wide U, and lumbered back out of the dump area.

Seagulls came screaming down.

Patrolman Luis Estevez, on loan to the 22d precinct from Special Services, was checking piles on the north strip of landfill. He walked a distance, moving his eyes in short arcs along the garbage until some object or shape caught his attention, moved closer to poke, then moved on.

In the mound just left by Andy's Dumping something half glimpsed caused him to turn around and take a second look.

About five feet up the new embankment there was a black glistening lump poking through the compacted putrefaction, and he wondered.

Boots sloshing, he made his way toward it.

The mountain changed shape beneath him, sucking him down.

He was six feet away before he could see the black plastic clearly, close enough to suffocate in the stench, and he had to get even closer to see the crisscrossing steel reinforcements, the paper-sheathed wire twist that held the neck of the bag shut.

He thought a minute, then bent down, placed both rubber-gloved hands around the neck and gave a strong, slow tug. Gradually the mountain yielded up the bag. The patrolman carried it down to the older landfill, where the footing was solid. He took a knife from his hip and with hurried grimness cut into the plastic.

A mass of red pulsing with maggots slopped into the open.

Meat—nothing but meat. This in itself was unusual.

His eye caught something white. With rapid efficiency he probed his blade along the ridge of white.

His face stiffened.

He knew what he had found, and it made him cold inside.

He ran back to his blue-and-white and radioed his supervisor. Police radio traffic was insecure and newspaper scavengers routinely listened in, so he kept the message brief and general. "Hey Lou," he told his lieutenant. "It's Estevez. I found something that's going to interest you."

It was early afternoon. The rain had almost stopped and Sheridan Square was swirling with Jersey drivers and pedestrians and pigeons all hell-bent on ignoring the traffic lights.

Cardozo approached the threshold of a darkened doorway and stepped into the coolness of the Pleasure Trove adult boutique.

The air smelled of banana incense. There was no sound except the whir of an air conditioner, the whisper of a radio turned to an easy-listening station. He looked around the shop.

A mousy-looking man was browsing nervously through a rack of high-gloss pornographic magazines. Two teenaged girls suddenly broke into giggles at a display case of tickler-dildos.

A salesman sat behind the counter, staring at the *Times* crossword puzzle, chewing somberly on a pencil eraser.

"Excuse me." Cardozo stood at the counter and reached into the brown paper bag that held the plastic evidence bag. He opened the plastic bag and lifted out the leather mask.

"Ugly mother," the clerk remarked. "You want to return it?" He was a slender man in his middle forties with graying brown hair and a neatly trimmed beard and moustache.

"No, but I'd like to get some information."

"We don't wholesale."

"No sweat. This is item 706 in your catalogue, right?"

"Not anymore it isn't. Last time we advertised any of these was in the March catalogue."

"But you sold this mask?"

"Is there some kind of problem with it?"

"I'd like to know who bought it." Cardozo quietly laid his wallet open on the counter.

The salesman's glance went down to the shield and came back up, altered now into another sort of glance. He picked up the mask, turning it in his hands, studying it doubtfully.

"This isn't a Pleasure Trove product. It's a rip-off. These masks are made by Nuku Kushima."

"You say that name like I should know it."

"She exhibits in SoHo galleries, which makes her masks art. Ours are home entertainment. Hers go for thirteen thousand dollars. Ours go for three hundred fifty. We sued, but she has a grant from the New York State Council of the Arts and the court decided the case fell under the Warhol principle—remember, Warhol signed two cans of Campbell's soup and sold them as art?"

Cardozo didn't remember: civil suits weren't his beat. "Could you show me the difference between your masks and hers?"

"Ours are machine-stitched on commercial leather stitching machines and hers are hand-stitched by couture seamstresses—so they don't hold up." The salesman turned the mask inside out and pulled at a seam. "Her stitching is at quarter-inch intervals. Ours is sixteenth-inch. She uses nylon thread, we use gut. Gut can take eight times the tension. See how this has already started pulling apart? This baby has sure seen some action, hasn't she."

"Are these masks popular?"

"The price doesn't make them too popular—but tourists from New Jersey are buying them since that murder." Predictably, the body in six had leaked to the press; and just as predictably, the press had gotten most of the details wrong. "We sold a few today."

"How many?"

The salesman went to a filing cabinet and pulled out a drawer. He thumbed through invoices. "Three."

"Can I see those?"

Cardozo reviewed the sales slips: there were two on charge cards. One sale was for cash. Joan Smith, 3 Park Avenue, 350 plus twenty-eight eighty-eight sales tax.

He thought about that. "Joan Smith paid cash?"

The salesman made a trying-to-remember face. "First sale today. She was here at five to ten, real impatient because I didn't open the door till ten. Some people are that way. It says ten to ten on the door, they gotta get in at five of."

"You always take the customer's name on a cash sale?"

"Sure, we send them our catalogue."

Cardozo laid himself ten-to-one odds there was no Joan Smith at 3 Park Avenue; twenty-to-one if a 3 Park Avenue even existed, it was an office building. "Do you remember what she looked like?"

"Average height, nice figure. She was dressed real SoHo punk. You know, designer garbage bag. Blond hair, natural I think; she was wearing a big studded leather belt, celebrity shades."

"What do you mean, studded belt? Like s.m.?"

"Like high-trash fashion. A lot of big fake gemstones."

It seemed strange to Cardozo: first sale the first day after a holiday weekend, anxious customer, close to four hundred dollars cash in hand. As though a leather bondage mask was one of those items you absolutely couldn't start the day without, like cream in your coffee or gas in your tank or your first cocaine fix.

"Got a phonebook?"

"Sure." The salesman hefted a dog-eared copy of the Manhattan White Pages over the counter.

The book listed plenty of J. Smiths and a few Joan Smiths, none at 3 Park Avenue. There was an N. Kushima on Prince Street in SoHo, and Cardozo wrote down the number. "I'd like to buy one of your masks," he said.

"We're sold out." The salesman's expression held a hint of guarded helpfulness. "But since you're NYPD, I could let you have the store sample—I'll mark it down to a hundred."

"Do you take VISA?"

"Sure do."

Cardozo held out his hand. "My name's Cardozo. Vince Cardozo."

"I'm Burt."

* * *

Cardozo called N. Kushima from a booth, said he was police and needed to talk with her.

"I'll be home another half hour," she said.

The woman who opened the door to him was a small Japanese with a face like a walnut; she was wearing jeans and sandals and a paint-splattered hospital smock, and her hair was tied up in a checked handkerchief.

"Come in, please." The only thing Oriental about her was the face. Her accent was pure New York, an incongruous mix of Jewish and street Hispanic. She smiled crookedly.

He stepped into a loft flooded with yellow light. The sun had come out, and the space was lush with potted plants on windowsills, on tables and stands; an eight-foot avocado tree was growing out of a ceramic urn on the floor.

The paintings on the walls were six-foot canvases with barbed wire nailed to them, Adidas jogging shoes and babies' mittens and burlap sacks impaled on the barbs, red paint and lucite-encased viscera spewing from the sacks. The intestines looked real, as though they'd come from a butcher shop or autopsy room.

She stood there looking at him looking at the paintings.

"Yours?" he asked.

"Of course."

"Is that the way you feel, or just the way you want other people to feel?"

"Ours is a savage age. I'm sure a policeman sees sights far more dreadful than any of these. I'm having a cup of miso, would you care for some?"

"No, thanks."

"Please." Her gesture encompassed chairs and scattered floor pillows. She sat in a peacock chair, drew her legs up, and looked at him. "How may I help you?"

He took the two leather masks from their bags and laid them on the floor in front of her. "Do you recognize these?"

A frown of caution darkened her forehead and she sipped carefully from her cup. With her foot she pushed the Pleasure Trove mask contemptuously aside. "That one is a vulgarization." Her foot hovered above the other. "This one is mine."

"How can you tell?"

"How does a mother know her children? I made it. It is me."

"How many did you make?"

"Only five. Five is my limit—above that I am a whore."

"Who bought the mask from you?"

She was sitting there, sipping her miso.

"I know nothing of who buys my works."

"I want the buyer."

"My gallery handles all sales—Lewis Monserat on Prince Street.

Cardozo carried the masks through narrow SoHo streets filled with rushing, lurching traffic.

The Lewis Monserat Gallery on Prince Street was quietly impressive, with a high skylighted ceiling, a calm atmosphere, and no visitors.

The receptionist sat at a large desk, a prim woman wearing a blouse with a Peter Pan collar. She smiled at Cardozo's approach, but when he showed his shield and asked to speak with Mr. Monserat the smile was gone.

"I'll see if he's in."

She went into another room, closing the door behind her.

Cardozo used the time to look at the exhibit, paintings of faceless figures who seemed to get smaller and lonelier as the canvases got larger.

The woman reappeared and ushered him into the rear office.

A man with a head of black hair that looked as though he'd marinated it in olive oil rose from behind a desk and held out a hand. "Lewis Monserat. How can I help you, sir?"

He was wearing a very well-cut, expensive Italian suit. His large, expressive eyes gave Cardozo permission to drop into the studded leather chair.

Cardozo took the Kushima mask from the brown paper bag and placed it on the desk.

"You sold this. Who bought it?"

Monserat reached out and lifted the mask. He turned it over, then inside out. When he finally spoke, his voice had quiet resonance. "This has a slight resemblance to the work of my client Nuku Kushima, but—"

Cardozo cut him short. "Miss Kushima has identified the mask. Who bought it?"

Whatever had been cordial in Monserat's manner abruptly vanished. The silence in the room was suddenly flat and harsh.

"It's against gallery policy to release our client list."

"I'd appreciate your reversing that policy."

"Wait one moment, please." Monserat rose and went out into the gallery. Cardozo could hear him making a phone call.

On the desk, a nineteenth-century carriage clock struck four delicate chimes.

Monserat returned. "You cannot compel me to release that information without a court order."

"Who says?"

Monserat's gaze met his levelly, coldly. "My attorney—Mr. Theodore Morgenstern—I'm sure you've heard of him?"

"Would you get him on the phone, or do I need a court order for that too?"

Smiling acidly, Monserat picked up the telephone. He dialed, handed Cardozo the receiver, and sat back.

"Ted Morgenstern," an officious voice said.

"It's Vince Cardozo."

He and Morgenstern had collided in courtrooms, in judges' chambers, before grand juries: often enough to hate one another's guts. A public yet shadowy figure for over three decades, Morgenstern had made his reputation and fortune acting as broker in business deals, criminal justice deals, political hostage deals, international arms and spy deals, real estate deals—and those were just the deals that were public knowledge.

"We're investigating a capital crime," Cardozo said. "It wouldn't take me two hours to get an order compelling disclosure of that list."

"Then I suggest those would be two hours most well spent, Lieutenant. It's about time you so-called law enforcers learned to operate within the law."

It took less than twenty minutes for Cardozo to learn that he wasn't going to get a court order compelling diddly-squat—not in two hours, not in twenty. His judge, Tom Levin, was not in the court, not in chambers, not reachable. Levin's secretary, sounding harried over the phone line, said she'd do her best to page him. Her voice was not hopeful.

As Cardozo touched the receiver down into the cradle, Carl Malloy burst into the office. He was moving like a bouncing ball, his hair lifting from his forehead and flopping down again.

"Vince, we've been going crazy, where you been, we've been beeping you all afternoon."

"The hell you have, I just put fresh Duracells in that beeper this morning." Cardozo's glance went to the unopened package of Duracell batteries lying on top of the fives. "I'm losing my marbles."

Malloy's eyes met Cardozo's, keen and wild. "Vince, we found the leg."

There was an instant of absolute silence and Cardozo's stomach had the crazily exhilarated sensation of free fall.

"Where?"

"It was out in a landfill in Queens, the truck picked it up Sunday from Beaux Arts Tower. We traced the truck, we traced the garbage, we traced everything, it all dovetails."

"What shape's the leg in?"

"Call Dan Hippolito, he's looking at it right now."

Just as Cardozo reached for the phone a button began blinking and a voice from the squad room shouted, "Vince, phone call for you, on three!"

"Who is it?"

"Some guy."

"Jesus, can't anyone around here take messages?"

There was a crackle and Dan Hippolito's voice came on the line. "Vince, I've looked at this new bone material. It's human, a right male thigh. How are you, by the way?"

"I'm fine. What have we got?"

"We can type the blood from the marrow, it's O, same as John Doe. There's some skin tissue, pretty ragged, an educated guess is that it's Caucasian or very light black or Hispanic."

"In other words the whole human race."

"It's not Oriental. There's a mark at the fracture, characteristic of a rotary blade, and there's an approximate match with John Doe, but it's approximate, because bone tissue was compressed in the compactor."

"Is there anything you can see that the killer wanted to hide: a birthmark, a tattoo, a deformity?"

"Vince, there's no way you're going to get a birthmark or tattoo off of this. It's hash. This new tissue isn't going to tell us why the killer wanted the leg off. So far as deformity is concerned, the femur is reasonably intact, God only knows how, and there are no breaks, no bends, no bone pathology. There's a fungus in the fat cells of the marrow, but hell, this meat's been rotting for three days and it's been buried under every parasite in the city of New York. So take it from there, Vince, that's the best I can do."

Cardozo felt a wave of disappointment rising in his gut. "Thanks, Dan."

"Give my love to your daughter."

"I'll do that."

14

CARDOZO PHONED MELISSA HATFIELD AND ASKED HER TO HAVE a drink with him after work.

"I can meet you at six fifteen at Morgan's," she said. "Fifty-third and Sixth. Know the place?"

Cardozo knew it. Ten years ago Morgan's had been Reilly's, the watering hole for his precinct. Reilly's was the corner lot that had not sold out to Rockefeller Center. For four decades, dwarfed by gleaming million-dollar art deco skyscrapers, the two-bit, two-story grungy bar with blinking Schlitz signs and Miss Rhinegold posters in the window had been a zit on the face of Prometheus. Cardozo had loved Reilly's: not just because the owner had stood up to John D. Rockefeller, Jr., but because the drinks weren't watered, because you could get corned beef and cabbage from eight in the morning till four the next morning, and most of all because of the customers: maintenance men, Rockettes on break from the Music Hall, secretaries and off-duty police and firemen, people who did a dollar's work for a dollar's pay and didn't expect to get famous or bribed or laid for it.

Those days had ended when Reilly died and Reilly's became Morgan's. The zit became a beauty mark. White wood siding went up over the crumbling brick, green New England shutters got nailed to the siding, red ruffled checkered cafe curtains appeared on bronze rails. Cardozo had gone back once and once had been enough.

Tonight he arrived five minutes early. He wanted to see Hatfield come in, wanted to watch her for that one moment before she knew he was looking.

Morgan's was doing the kind of business Reilly had only dreamed of: SRO. Cardozo had to push through the shoulder-to-shoulder Happy Hour crowd.

The bartenders worked in front of five-foot pyramids of the booze of eighty nations. They had pirate moustaches and Jack LaLanne bodies, and their red-checked open-necked shirts matched the cafe curtains. They came on to the female customers, bending close to catch the order, and gold chains twinkled in hairy cleavages. With the male customers they were macho and curt.

"What's yours?" a six-foot linebacker radiating cologne snarled.

"Scotch and water," Cardozo said.

He left a dollar tip—he knew what this city did to a guy's budget and he believed even shitheads deserved a decent wage. There was no thank you.

Attitude, Cardozo thought—New York's gift to the world. Everyone was handing it to everyone. Park Avenue socialites stepping into limos, Puerto Rican checkout girls in the supermarket—their eye met yours with that same unlovely, unmistakable message: drop dead. It was turning into a worm-eat-worm town.

Cardozo took his drink and looked for a place to sit. There were electric hurricane lamps on every checkered tablecloth. Faces bent into the circles of light—faces struggling to look sophisticated, faces struggling to look beautiful and successful, faces running on cocaine and faces beginning to blear out on Stolichnaya. Faces trying to connect with faces.

He found an empty table; it looked like the last one in the place. On the wall where Reilly had hung the first dollar bill the bar had ever earned and the bounced checks of famous clients there was a nautical compass and a brass barometer. A clock ding-donged the time in ship's bells. Cardozo wanted to cry.

A short, slight girl with long dark hair and an order pad tried to interest him in the day's special fish. He told her he was waiting for a friend, and even though he wasn't ready he sensed the girl worked on a percentage and he ordered another drink.

Melissa Hatfield stepped through the twin brass doors. She was carrying a very full ebony crocodile attaché case and she was wearing a gray dress belted tight enough to give it a little flare at the hips. She went straight for the bar. Men moved aside and hopeful eyes traveled with her and she knew it. She passed directly under the glare of a hurricane lamp and there was a moment when the gray of her dress became red roses, orange roses, green leaves, thorns. She looked good under the light and she knew that too. She smiled at the barman.

The body-built pirate ignored the bald gent who had been waiting five minutes for a Rob Roy. He poured Melissa Hatfield a white wine on ice, topping it with a showy, dead accurate shot from the soda gun. He handed her the drink, smiling.

Melissa Hatfield paid and turned. Her glance swept the pandemonium. Cardozo rose and signaled with a raised hand. She saw him, smiled, came across the room. Men stepped aside for her.

She dropped the briefcase beside the table. "Three closings in TriBeCa," she said. "More paperwork than the nuclear test-ban treaty."

Cardozo couldn't tell whether she expected sympathy or congratulations. Maybe both. He rose.

"You don't have to be gallant, Lieutenant."

"Vince," he said. "Call me Vince."

She sat down.

He watched her sip her drink with a sort of elegant disdain and he let his intuition roam. Melissa Hatfield had an aunt in the Social Register and she'd parlayed the connection into a career of putting people down in small ways, selling luxury real estate to hungry overnight millionaires.

"Pretty dress," he said. "Silk?" He knew it wasn't.

She knew he knew. "Taiwanese synthetic. It's trick printed. You're supposed to see roses in certain lights."

"It works. I saw them."

"Bloomingdale's expected them to be a big seller last year. They weren't. I got this for eighteen dollars off a gypsy rack on Thirty-second Street."

It was interesting what people volunteered about themselves. She was telling him she wasn't dumb about money the way her clients were. She was telling him not to lump her with them. He sensed that was important to her.

"Where do we go from here?" she said. "Dinner and a Broadway show? Your expense account or mine?"

"Not tonight. Tonight's business."

Her eyebrows arched. "Don't tell me you're going to make my day and buy one of the apartments in Beaux Arts Tower. I could swing a discount for you. You'd add a little safety to the building."

He noted the controlled tapping of her finger on the ashtray. She had mastered her eyes so they didn't skitter when he fixed his gaze on her.

"Only rajahs and Philippine dictators are buying into this co-op market." He moved the hurricane lamp to the wall. He laid a nine-by-eleven manila envelope on the table. It was marked NYPD OFFICIAL BUSINESS PENALTY FOR PRIVATE USE $50.

Her glance went down to it.

"I took another look at six this afternoon," he said. "How often are the unsold apartments cleaned?"

"I don't know, but I can check."

"Did six look cleaner to you than the others—except for the obvious difference?"

"Except for the obvious difference, no. It looked about the same."

"Is the air conditioning left on in the unsold apartments?"

"Never. That wastes electricity. I come in a half hour before the showing and turn it on."

"Did you turn on the air conditioning in six?"

"No. I didn't have time to get to the building early."

"But it was on."

"Somebody must have—left it on."

They both understood she was talking about the killer.

"How many times did you show six this last month?"

"Only yesterday." She added, "Manhattan real estate's soft these days."

"Melissa, the card you gave me says you work for Beaux Arts Properties. Who's Balthazar Properties? They're putting up a co-op on Lex and Fifty-third and they have the same phone number."

"That's us too."

"Why do you have two different names?"

"We have eleven different names and we have eleven different companies. It's not illegal. We limit the liability. If one building springs a leak or goes bankrupt it doesn't endanger the other properties."

"One company for each property?"

"I'm not Nat Chamberlain's accountant. I know of eleven companies. I know of eleven properties in this city that are secured as of closing business today. I doubt that's the whole picture."

"You like working for Nat Chamberlain?"

"I wouldn't work for an employer I didn't like—any more than you would."

"What makes you so sure I wouldn't?"

"You're not the type."

"You seem to think you know how to size people up."

"I'm not in your league, but I'm good."

"What can you tell from a face?"

"Whether the sale will go through."

"Take a look at the pictures in that envelope."

He saw her hand wanting to hesitate, and he saw her not allowing it to. She opened the envelope and drew out the two glossies. Her eyes went from one to the other and narrowed.

"I take it this is the dead man?"

"You should have my job."

She shifted the photos around on the table. The face in the photographs had a classic male beauty, and death gave it a patrician glaze, like a Roman head in a museum case.

"He's handsome," she said finally. "Too bad."

"If he'd been ugly, it wouldn't have been too bad?"

Her gaze came up to his. "If he'd been ugly he wouldn't be dead."

"You know something I don't."

"This isn't how ugly people die. This is how ugly people kill."

Cardozo sat back and sipped his Scotch.

She asked, "Was he as young as he looks?"

It interested Cardozo: people kept seeing everything but death: he was young, he was good-looking, that was what they saw. "The coroner thinks he was twenty-two, twenty-three."

Her eyes didn't tip anything, but the silence did. A silence that long meant she was having to think. She picked up a glossy again. "Christ. Why are they all dying so young?"

"Who do you mean, *they*?"

"People like him, young, dying . . ." She was in her mind and didn't speak for a minute.

Someone young died, he realized. Someone close to her. "Tell me something, Melissa. You looked at those pictures and whatever you saw, you couldn't make it go away. What was it?"

She let out a breath. "It's hard to put into words. Sometimes you see somebody but you never realize you're seeing them because they're always in the same context."

"Like who?"

"Like the man at the newsstand; the doorman you pass on the way to the subway; the woman who runs a bookstore and you wave as you go by. And then one day you see that person lifted out of their context—and you don't know who they are or why you should even think you remember them. You stare at them and they stare at you and it's almost hostile, like hey what are you doing off your shelf? My work isn't like yours, it doesn't call for a trained memory. I see a face, I do business with the face, if the deal falls through I forget the face. But with this one there's something . . . I feel I could have seen him. But it didn't have anything to do with work."

"When?"

"I don't know. There's no feeling of time connected to it."

"Where?"

"In an elevator."

"What elevator?"

"I don't remember. All I get is elevator."

"Beaux Arts Tower?"

"No. Definitely not. Anything to do with our buildings I remember. But if I saw this man, I was off guard, not paying attention. It's as though we looked at each other, smiled, and agreed not to say hello. You know the way it can be with strangers in the city. What I mean is, this was friendly but the distance was very, very controlled. I wish I could be more specific, but all I get is that kind of a question mark feeling."

"Melissa, I want you to do something for me. Keep those photographs. Keep looking at them. Keep putting that face into every elevator you walk into. In one of those elevators you're going to remember. And as soon as you do . . ." He reached into his wallet, thick with a wad of VISA carbons, and fished out one of his cards. "Those are my numbers. Work phone on top, home phone on the bottom. Call me. Day or night." He smiled. "But not too late at night."

An eye of light gleamed in the dark. Cardozo adjusted the lens of the projector. The image cleared, showing late afternoon New York sky, pale and cloudless. Hard bright sun splashed down onto the Fifty-third Street pavement, across the deco facade of the Museum of Contemporary Arts and the marble-faced lobby of the high rise next to it.

Cardozo was going over yesterday's hidden-camera photos of Beaux Arts Tower.

On the wall of his cubicle, men and women hurried toward destinations he could not see. Examining their images, Cardozo was fascinated: reading the truth and the falsehood in the human face—that was the most challenging puzzle of all.

He pushed a control button and the carousel turned, dropping a new slide into the projector.

It was a photo of a fortyish man with thin sandy hair and a light-weight tan suit. The man was entering Beaux Arts Tower, but he was looking behind him.

The man's skin was tinged with shadows: the bones in his face showed bluishly and gray speckled his hair. In his hand he held a briefcase. It looked expensive, genuine pigskin.

The man gave Cardozo a long steady gaze.

It was unmistakable: the gaze was coming straight at him.

Cardozo switched off the projector.

The feet of his chair let out a spine-jangling shriek as he slid back on the linoleum floor.

He stood in darkness. He swung open the door, walked into the light of the squad room, poured himself a cup of Mr. Coffee coffee. There was no Sweet 'n Low.

He went back into his cubicle. He closed the door. He switched on the desk light and looked down at the log that Tommy Daniels's photographic team had kept.

Each person going in or out of the building was recorded in the notebook and given a number. Some of the entries had names, where names were known. The license plate of every car pulling up at the door was recorded, as was the license of every vehicle entering or leaving the garage. Each entry was accompanied by a time, and each number cross-indexed to a photograph of a person or automobile.

Cardozo reviewed the list.

The number of the man in tan was 79. No name. Cardozo wondered. Tommy Daniels had sworn that no one would make the truck, but Cardozo knew how men sitting on a plant could get bored, how they could get careless.

Cardozo snapped off his lamp, turned the projector on, looked at 79 again.

Something in 79's eyes met Cardozo's almost like an act of defiance.

Shit, Cardozo thought. *He made the truck.*

It was much later.

Girders whipped past as Cardozo drove over the Brooklyn Bridge: the tires of his Honda went from asphalt to exposed steel infrastructure and the humming in his ears jumped up an octave.

He took the first exit, swinging down into Brooklyn Heights. A rough warm wind was bending the leaf-heavy trees as he parked.

The rain had made up its mind to stop. There was moonlight in the sky. The street was dark, but it was a warm darkness, not the dread-inspiring night of Manhattan. Streetlamps cast islands of illumination. Noble nineteenth-century town houses, merchants' homes, framed the tree-lined street. The scene had the order and unreality of a stage set.

A church bell chimed the late hour. In the distance, a group of well-dressed young Jehovah's Witnesses was returning to their dormitory.

Cardozo lifted the lock of the hip-high wrought-iron gate at number 42, noting that it was purely decorative, nothing protective about it. It swung back smoothly. Trees overhung the flagstone walk.

Judge Tom Levin, in pajamas and a bathrobe, opened the door.

"Hope I didn't keep you waiting," Cardozo said.

"Hell no. Come on in."

Slippers slapping on carpet, Levin led Cardozo into the sitting room. Cardozo sat in a corduroy-covered chair.

Levin's fifty years had given a firm set to ascetic features that in youth had probably seemed soft. "Scotch?" he offered.

"Why not."

The judge rose, got glasses from the sideboard, tonged ice into them, added Johnnie Walker. Cardozo watched him.

The glow of a streetlight fell in leafy patterns through the tall window.

The judge brought Cardozo's glass back to him. The judge sat and smiled and raised his glass in an unspoken toast.

"What brings you here, Vince? You sounded angry on the phone."

"I'm on the Beaux Arts Tower killing."

Levin arched an eyebrow. "Lucky you."

Cardozo explained that he needed a court order to get Monserat's list of purchasers of the Kushima bondage masks.

"Who's Monserat's attorney?" Levin asked.

"Ted Morgenstern."

Levin rose and stood by a window staring down into the small garden behind the house, where ferns grew under the oak trees.

"That prick," he muttered.

Judge Levin was a Harvard grad, an ex-liberal. He kept a licensed thirty-eight revolver, and he kept writs, subpoenas, and court orders in blank at home, so he could execute them at any hour of day or night.

He crossed swiftly to his writing desk. The forms were there, in the second drawer, awaiting only the specifics, which he now bashed in on an old Olivetti portable.

Judge Levin handed Cardozo the order. "This should add a little misery to his life."

15

"I TOLD BRONSKI WE HAVE A WITNESS PLACING HIS CAB IN THE garage of Beaux Arts Tower—so who was his fare and why did he falsify his sheet and put Fifty-fourth and Sixth?" Detective Carl Malloy was wearing a Kelly green vest today. "Bronski swears the sheet is correct: he says he had to take a pee, so he went to the building to use the men's room. He didn't want to mention it to us because it's against building regulations to, you know, use the place as a facility. He would never have parked his cab in the garage except it was a holiday and he expected most of the residents to be away for the weekend."

Malloy hesitated.

"I still get the feeling he's holding back. I went back over his taxi sheets. On the day of the killing and for three days before, he had the same fare—a pick-up at Broadway just before noon and a drop-off at Fifty-fourth and Sixth at twelve-thirty. Even allowing for midday traffic, that's a hell of a long time."

Something clicked in Cardozo's mind. "Where on Broadway?"

"Sometimes the sheet says two twenty-five, sometimes two fifty."

"The Federal Building's down there," Ellie Siegel said.

"So's the World Trade Center," Cardozo said. "And Sam, you said those are the same days Debbi Hightower was in the Toyota show?"

"But the show was from eight at night till ten thirty." Siegel frowned. "What are you saying, she slept over?"

Richards looked at the others. "Didn't Gordon Dobbs say she's a hooker?"

"What's the mystery?" Greg Monteleone gave a little grin. "Debbi's been getting free cab service after she turns her hotel tricks, and Bronski's been ripping off Ding-Dong to get a little daytime nooky."

"Maybe he's her pimp," Carl Malloy said.

"Do pimps have intercourse with their hookers?" Ellie Siegel asked.

"If they're good girls, once a month," Sam Richards said.

"A white pimp?" Monteleone said. "Give me a break."

Irritation began to gather in Ellie Siegel's eyes. "Greg, white pimps exist."

"In this town?"

For an instant Ellie Siegel just stared at the ceiling.

"On the other hand," Monteleone conceded, "I don't think it proves Bronski and Debbi are chopping up naked guys."

"You don't know that, Monte," Malloy said. "You don't know these two."

"I know they're dingbats."

"Dingbats don't murder?" Siegel challenged. "Greg, how the hell did you ever make detective?"

"They promoted me before affirmative hiring let you in."

"Carl," Cardozo cut in, "will you keep after Bronski, see about those fares?" Heaving his body up out of his chair, he signaled Monteleone and Richards to come with him.

In the corridor a detective was interviewing a hysterical female complainant who had received a ransom note for a missing dog. In the squad room Detective O'Shea was doing day duty, and Detective Moriarty stood at a cabinet looking for a case folder.

"Hey Vince," O'Shea called, "Lou Stein sent over a lab report. It's on your desk."

There was a lot else on Cardozo's desk: a two-inch stack of new departmental orders and a blue paperbound book that looked like an addendum to the state telephone listings, in fact a revision of the penal law pursuant to last trimester's state supreme court decisions.

Greg Monteleone picked up the penal code and shoved his mouth into a lopsided grin. "What did their honors decide about that guy getting a blow job in the van at the Holland Tunnel?" He flipped through pages. "What's sodomy, seven seven oh nine?"

"Consensual heterosexual sodomy's legal," Sam Richards said.

"Not in public."

"A van on a public thoroughfare is private property with a reasonable expectation of safety from search and seizure—State of New York versus Offernaty, 1985."

"Not if the door's open," Cardozo said. "State of New York versus Moony, 1986."

"Who gets a blow job with the door open?" Richards asked.

"This guy does." Monteleone's large Mediterranean nose came out of the booklet. "Marvin van Peters, do you believe that for a name?"

"It's a gag for *Screw* magazine," Sam Richards said.

"Give me that book," Cardozo growled.

Monteleone was hooting and jumping. "Innocent, he's innocent! Hey, fellas, hit the tunnel!"

Cardozo grabbed the penal-code update. "If you gentleman would be kind enough to give me a little undivided attention?"

He patted the slide projector.

"Know how to work this thing? Today, instead of watching *Police-woman* reruns, you, Greg, and you, Sam, are going to look at these." He held up a box of slides. "Each time you come to a face you recognize, you enter the name here in the logbook, okay?"

He showed them the logbook from the surveillance truck at Beaux Arts Tower. Turning to yesterday's loose-leaf pages, he explained the logging system.

"And when you've finished, you're going to take the license numbers and names from the log and run them through the National Crime Bureau."

He tossed the penal-code update back to Monteleone.

"Enjoy."

Cardozo took the lab report with him and hurried down the marble staircase. Nodding to the duty officer at the portals, he left the station house, turning into the alley at the side of the precinct. He walked around his Honda and crawled in behind the wheel. He slammed the door and took a moment to read the lab report.

Lou Stein had found no match between Loring's, Stinson's, Gomez's, or Revuelta's prints and any found at the murder scene.

The Lewis Monserat Gallery was deserted except for the well-groomed receptionist, who looked up at Cardozo from the Gabriel García Márquez paperback she was reading at her desk. Today he noticed that she was in her late forties.

"Mr. Monserat will not be in this morning," she said.

"All I need is the list of buyers of the Kushima mask."

"Only Mr. Monserat can give you that."

"Miss," Cardozo said, "this is a court order." He handed her the document.

"I'm not a lawyer, I don't understand this."

"You read English."

"There's nothing I can do without Mr. Monserat's permission."

"You can hand that list over right now, or you can phone your lawyer and tell him to meet you in twenty minutes at the Tombs."

She flinched and went to a mahogany filing cabinet. After a moment's lip-biting she pulled out a sheet and handed it to him.

The list of buyers of Nuku Kushima's artwork *Bondage IX* showed three institutions: the Franklyn Collection in Washington, D.C.; the Walter Kizer Museum in Los Angeles; and the Museum of Contemporary Arts in New York; and one private collector, Doria Forbes-Steinman, with a Manhattan address.

"Miss Kushima told me there were five masks," Cardozo said.

"There were four made and four sold."

"I'd like to look in that file."

"You have no right to—"

Cardozo moved around her and searched the *K*'s. He flipped through invoices for woodcuts, oils, conceptual pieces, and lithos. He slowed down at Leather Sculptures.

The gallery had placed Kushima *Body Halters* with three institutions; *Blade-Tipped Black Leather Boots* with two institutions and two private collections; *Executioner's Gloves* with one institution and four private collections. *Razor-Studded Vest* had been a slow-moving item, one private collection; *AC-Powered Nipple Clamps With Leather Thong* had gone to two museums and two private collections.

Bondage IX (mask) had four purchasers. The sheet was freshly typed.

"How many masks did you make?" Cardozo asked.

Nuku Kushima's slender little body blocked the doorway of her loft. "Four."

"Yesterday you told me five."

"I could not have said five because I made only four. Four is my artistic limit."

He stared at her inscrutable lying little face and wished to hell he'd carried a hidden tape recorder when he'd questioned her. Not that the tape would have had any legal value, but at least he'd have had something to confront her with. As matters stood, he had nothing, and she knew it.

"Would you be willing to repeat that in court, under oath?"

There was nothing in her eyes: no truth, no falsehood. Only a Zen emptiness. "Naturally."

Cardozo made a detour to the Mr. Coffees and poured himself a cup that his stomach didn't need but that his nerves craved.

Ellie Siegel sat at a battered desk trying to negotiate over the phone with a computer in Washington, D.C. She raised her eyes to Cardozo's and they were curiously and wonderfully green.

"Hey, Vince," the desk lieutenant called. "Two slashings last night. One in the one eight, the other in the two one."

Cardozo treated himself to two envelopes of Sweet 'n Low. "What's it got to do with us?"

"Looks like a serial killer. O'Malley thinks the perp might have chopped a hooker in the two two."

"Not in the last six months—but tell O'Malley he's welcome to look through our files."

Cardozo shut the door of his cubicle and began dialing the phone numbers on the Monserat sales sheet.

The curator of the Franklyn Collection in D.C. told him the Kushima mask was on exhibit in the basement, in the New Trends show. An assistant curator at the Walter Kizer Museum in L.A. said the mask was presently on view with recent acquisitions.

The New York Museum of Contemporary Arts had a recorded message announcing the screening times of D. W. Griffith's *Orphans of the Storm,* part of a retrospective honoring Lillian Gish.

Cardozo took his coffee into the squad room and sat on the edge of Siegel's desk. The computer at the other end of the phone line had put her on hold, and she gave him a weary smile.

"Ellie, you used to teach art."

"That's why I'm a cop."

"How can a bondage mask be art?"

"Because critics and dealers say it is."

"Then why isn't a toothbrush art?"

Her eyes sparkled with mischief and intelligence. "Vince, you're a beautiful Philistine. A toothbrush *is* art, has been since the MOMA exhibit in seventy-six."

"An artist can do anything and call it art?"

"Some artists would call the murder in Beaux Arts Tower conceptual art."

Cardozo was thoughtful. "You think an artist did it?"

"He or she would have to be a very dedicated artist, a rebel against the commercial establishment."

"Why do you say that?"

"No signature. No commission for the dealer. Dealers get up to sixty percent."

Cardozo took a long swallow of coffee. "Doria Forbes-Steinman seems to have gone into art collecting in a big way."

"Sure, she's what art critics call a major force."

"I haven't kept up with her since the Scottie Devens trial. Have you?"

Detective Siegel flicked hair out of her face, casually. "A little. I'm the same as any other supermarket shopper stuck in the checkout line. I grab a *National Enquirer* from the rack."

"I don't read the *Enquirer,* so fill me in."

Siegel lowered her long, dark, curling lashes. "She and her husband aired their differences in civil court, so Doria's past is now part of the public record. Turns out she's a charming colleen, Vince, a breath of Killarney from deepest Transylvania. Her full name is Doria Bravnik Forbes-Steinman. Bravnik is Yugoslavian, like her. Forbes is the name of the British foreign service schnook she claims was her first husband."

"He wasn't her husband?"

"A gal like Doria stirs up vicious rumors. The issue's moot, because once her British passport got her to New York, she *divorced* Forbes and married Steinman."

"What does the *Enquirer* say about Steinman?"

Ellie looked embarrassed, as though it was an admission of depravity that she knew so much rumor. There was something about Siegel that seemed unsoiled: her face was sophisticated, cynical even, without being malicious. It was that quality that had drawn Cardozo to her.

"If some of those Wall Streeters are overnight millionaires," she said, "Steinman's a five-minute billionaire. But it isn't enough nowadays just to have money. You have to do something to get written up in *Manhattan, inc.,* so Doria and Steinman collected modern art. They played artists like stocks and they bet lucky. By the time of the Devens trial they'd built up what the press calls an important collection. Doria left Steinman six years ago and took half the collection. She hasn't divorced Steinman, because divorce would disinherit her two Forbes children, who Steinman agreed to support when love was in bloom. The kids are stowed in a Scottish boarding school at his expense. Steinman sued Doria for her half of the collection and the lawsuit had the art world lined up in warring camps."

Across the squad room a telephone jangled. Detective DeVegh, receiver balanced between shoulder and ear, called out, "We got a squeal. Who's up this morning? You catching, Ellie?"

"Ellie's on a case," Cardozo said, curtly, and DeVegh gave him an excuse-me-for-breathing look, and Cardozo asked Siegel, "Tell me about the Steinman lawsuit."

"Vince, you really have time for this b.s.?"

"I want to know everything about these people, including what underarm deodorant they use."

"Lewis Monserat, the art dealer, testified for Steinman. Doria threw the slop bucket at Monserat, accused him of being a little bit more than an art dealer."

"How much more?"

"Doria said Monserat was a certified necrophile, a pederast, a porno film maker, a child prostitution ringleader, a Nazi collaborator who turned his own mother in to the Gestapo. Monserat's lawyer pointed out that Spain was one of the few European countries not occupied by Nazis, and she waffled and said maybe Monserat just murdered his mother."

"She said this in court?"

"Affirmative. Doria had her day, irrelevant and inadmissible though her testimony may have been. The one legally damaging shot she did get off was to claim Monserat used her to bid up his own clients' paintings at auctions."

"Did Monserat sue?"

"He threw the slop bucket back. Said Doria's maiden name was Schinsky, she was a Belgrade hooker, she was already married to a certain Mr. Bravnik when she married Forbes bigamously and got her exit visa out of the Eastern bloc. If Monserat was telling the truth, the marriage to Steinman was bigamous too."

"Did Doria sue?"

"No one sued, they all gave interviews and went on talk shows. Doria got more exposure than Monserat, because by then her name had surfaced as the other woman in the Scottie Devens trial. The smart money was betting Doria was the reason Scottie tried to put his wife under."

"I was betting that too," Cardozos said quietly.

Siegel flicked a dark-eyed glance at him. "So? It looked like a pretty sure thing to me too. You're looking unhappy."

"Just thinking. Is Doria still living with Scottie?"

"Last I read in the supermarket, they were an ongoing item." Siegel's smile was a miracle—world-aware and world-mocking but self-aware and self-mocking too. "It's the real world out there, Vince —it's a different mind-set: glamour and art and high fashion and beautiful people doing their beautiful thing—not us poor schleppers in the twenty-second precinct."

"Who got the Steinmans's art collection?"

"Doria got to keep her half. Including that mask."

A butler led Cardozo into the livingroom of the Fifth Avenue duplex. The room was large and plush and sunny, with yellow chrysanthemums on the Steinway. The breeze of an air conditioner stirred the folds of dove gray window curtains. Track lights lit three oil paintings of the same cathedral, each panel done in dots of a different primary color, like a monster comic strip.

A woman came into the room.

Cardozo looked at Mrs. Forbes-Steinman, and he saw a statue, its broadly beautiful face smiling at him. She extended her hand: her slightly plump arm was covered with bracelets of light blue sapphires.

"I have great respect for the police." Her voice was low and cultivated and bore a residual middle-European trace.

He would have loved to have answered, *And I have great respect for women who give good head.*

"How may I help you?" she said.

"You own a Nuku Kushima mask?"

"Bondage Nine."

"Do you have it here?"

"Naturally. Would you like to see it?"

"Very much."

He followed her into a hallway. Through an arch he could see the butler and a girl in a maid's uniform silently setting a dinner table for twelve.

The mask had been fitted over a wig stand and was sitting on a teakwood pedestal. He noticed a faint pattern of minuscule lacerations around the eyes.

"How did it get scratched?" he asked.

She sighed. "Would you believe the Nicaraguan girl used lemon Pledge and a Brillo pad on it?"

She was standing close beside him and he turned his head and studied her. Everything about her struck him as exact, smooth, artificial, extremely tense. Even her skin, which was a pampered pale olive shade.

"Could I ask you a question?" he said.

She regarded him pleasantly.

"You're an educated woman," he said. "You have taste. Why do you own this? It's ugly, and what it stands for is ugly."

She laughed, showing white even teeth in the subtly reddened line of her mouth. "I suppose by the same token you could say Picasso's *Guernica* is ugly."

"This isn't Picasso's *Guernica*. This is the facial equivalent of a thumbscrew."

"Beautiful art is often ugly. I know that sounds like a cheap paradox, but it's my belief that the point of art isn't to please, it's to . . . arrest." Her perfume filled the stillness. "I admire a work of art the way I admire a person. It has to take me without my permission, command my attention. The Kushima commands my attention."

"You bought this through Lewis Monserat?"

Her large, thoughtful eyes came to rest on him. "My husband and I bought it through Lewis Monserat. The court awarded it to me as part of our settlement."

He took note of the word *settlement* and realized that Doria Forbes-Steinman had her own way of tilting the truth. "Have you bought other pieces from Mr. Monserat?"

"I've bought from a great many leading dealers—Leo Castelli, Andre Emmerich, Ileana Sonnabend, Andrew Crispo when he was still in business. In fact, I came within a hairbreadth of owning the Brancusi head that Andy Crispo sold the Guggenheim; the deal was set, but Andy was in trouble with the IRS, and the Guggenheim offered a half-million more. I said, 'Andy, I can't hold you to our bargain, I release you, you need the money.' There's a lot of heartbreak in this business."

"But did you buy other pieces from Mr. Monserat?"

"I'm so tired of being linked to that monster." Doria Forbes-Steinman sighed. "Yes, I bought other pieces from Lewis Monserat—unfortunately."

"Why unfortunately?"

"He has fine pieces. But he's not the sort of man I like to deal with."

"Why not?"

"In Europe, where I come from, he has a reputation. He's a criminal. More than that. He's evil."

"Is that your way of saying you dislike him?"

"I dislike his deeds. Being a pageboy at Goebbels's wedding—don't you think that disgusting?"

"It's not a crime."

"Renting bodies from funeral homes—that may not be a crime either," she said, "but it's vile. Child pornography may not be a crime in our enlightened era, but that's disgusting too. Or don't you have children?"

"I have a child."

She looked at him, half smiling. "Then we're in agreement."

The sky was high and cloudless and the sun was hot on Cardozo's back. Limousines blocked Fifty-third Street and he had to make his way with a stream of well-dressed men and women into the Museum of Contemporary Arts.

A reception was being held in a room of Toulouse-Lautrec posters.

He skirted the hubbub and went searching for the fourth mask. In a gallery away from the voices and music he found a collection of heads. There were faces of stone and wood and plastic, all caught in glass boxes like vivisections in sterile chambers.

Walking among them, reading from the printed catalogue, he came upon the leather thing he was looking for: *Bondage IX*, leather and steel sculpture, Nuku Kushima, American, 1941–.

He stared at the face that was not a face: eyeless sockets the size and shape of stitched buttonholes, the lump of nose flattened into a piglike snout, the queasily smooth earlessness beneath the temples, the gash of sealed zipper marking the line where lips should have been.

The mask seemed to communicate a message he could only half understand. He sensed something deeper than terror: the utter willing acceptance of catastrophe.

There was a sudden hollowness in him.

In a moment suspended outside time he heard the zippered scream of a dead man six stories above this very space.

Women's laughter broke in. The cheerful buzz of conversation flowed around him, corks were popping in another room, waiters were scurrying.

"All that redness around John Doe's waist and upper thigh and ankle—there had to be some kind of allergen attacking the epiderm. But why those areas and no others? Because that's where the elastic bands in socks and underpants chafe. Okay, but what kind of allergen?"

Dan Hippolito slipped a slide under the microscope, bent down, adjusted the focus.

"We peel the skin from the waist, the ankle, the upper thigh, study it under the microscope. Behold, granules the size of boulders."

Hippolito motioned Cardozo.

Cardozo bent over the scope. He saw boulders.

"So we pulverize the skin, spin the particles, and eureka, the foreign substance has a different specific gravity from human skin and we isolate the culprit—detergent."

Cardozo pulled his eye up from the microscope. "Detergent?"

Hippolito nodded. "Generic industrial grade nameless detergent —killer soap—cheapola of the cheapola—not sold in supermarkets, not even ghetto supermarkets, and the FDA has considered outlawing it. It's illegal in Canada, illegal in twelve states of the union. In New York it's iffy but there are jobbers—under investigation by the attorney general—who sell the powder in forty-pound cartons. Now this stuff is so corrosive that dry—*dry*—it eats through cardboard."

"So who uses it?"

"Broadly speaking, two sorts of institutions. Prisons and bottom-of-the-line Laundromats."

By the time Cardozo got back to HQ, Lieutenant Damato was beginning his blotter entries for the four-to-one tour. Of the task force, only Siegel and Malloy were still in the station house. Cardozo called them into his office and told them the medical examiner's new evidence.

"The victim took his clothes to a cheap Laundromat and used their soap," Ellie Siegel said.

"Or left the clothes for them to wash," Malloy said.

Cardozo pushed back in his chair. "So we're looking for a Laundromat that may or may not be self-service, but also has a dump-your-laundry-and-we'll-handle-it service. How many Laundromats like that are there in this city?"

Malloy screwed up his face, an expert. "Three, four hundred easy."

"Get flyers out to all Laundromats in all boroughs."

"What about Laundromats in Jersey?" Ellie Siegel said. "Hoboken's nearer than Staten Island."

"Include Hudson County."

"Prison," Carl Malloy said. "John Doe could have been just re-leased or he could have escaped."

"So? Check the prisons."

Alone, Cardozo set up the projector and began going through slides.

Behind him, a voice spoke.

"Vincent Cardozo?"

Cardozo turned in his chair. A pudgy young man in an Italian-cut summer-weight gray shantung suit stood backlit against the open door.

"Ray Kane," the young man said, "attorney-at-law." He held out a chubby pink hand. He had no visible neck; smooth baby-fat jowls overspilled his shirt collar. The shirt designer's name was appliquéd to the breast pocket, and Kane smelled as if he had baptized himself in cologne.

"How can I help you, Mr. Kane?"

"Today you walked into the legitimate place of business of Lewis Monserat and terrorized his assistant. You threatened to send her to the Tombs and you menaced her with an improperly executed order for seizure."

"I thought Ted Morgenstern represented Monserat."

Ray Kane drew himself up. "I am an *associate* of Mr. Morgen-stern's firm."

Cardozo got the picture. Ever the true power broker, Ted Mor-genstern had sent one of his small fry to handle the niggling paper work.

Cardozo slowly rose to his feet. From a standing position he could see pink scalp through Kane's thinning razor-cut hair. "Mr. Kane, I'm working."

"So am I." Kane held out an official document bearing the seal of the court.

"What's that?"

"An order demanding return of the list of purchasers of the Kushima mask."

"On what grounds?"

"Improperly seized, without warrant, no evidence of a crime." Kane smacked his lips as if he were sucking macaroons off dentures.

"A murdered man, you don't call that a crime?"

"I warn you, Lieutenant, if you try to link Mr. Monserat's name to any ongoing criminal investigation, we shall not hesitate to bring slander charges."

Cardozo picked up the receiver of his phone. "Damato, send me one of the A.D.A.'s."

Kane stared at Cardozo from contact lenses that were probably meant to change his brown eyes to blue but instead made them look like a very special effect in a sci-fi film.

In a moment there was a knock at the door. "Lieutenant Cardozo? Lucinda MacGill, assistant district attorney." The young woman held out a hand. Her pale brown hair was cut in bangs, tumbling in back to her shoulders.

"That was fast," Cardozo said.

"I was downstairs taking a deposition."

It was the job of assistant D.A.'s to take statements from suspects, and Lucinda MacGill had a stenographer with her, a man in his early thirties, tall and thin with scraggly black hair and a beard to match. He looked like he'd rather be writing sonnets but needed the bread to pay his Con Ed.

"How can I help you?" Lucinda MacGill asked.

"Miss MacGill," Cardozo said, "meet Counselor Kane."

Her lips thinned as she said hello.

"Counselor Kane is serving me a writ, and I want to be sure it's properly executed before I comply."

Assistant D.A.'s were like detectives: they caught cases on a first-come, first-served basis; or, more accurately, the cases caught them. There was no picking or choosing. How you handled what you were served determined how your career went. Lucinda MacGill looked like she could handle.

"May I see the writ?" Her eyes scanned quickly and she gave the document back to Kane. "It's properly executed."

Cardozo crumpled the Monserat list into a ball and lobbed it to the floor. "All yours, Counselor."

Cardozo sat at his desk asking himself why his jaw was clenched so tight that electric currents were stinging through his fillings, how his heart could be in two places at once, thudding in his left temple and crashing in his gut.

Because he was furious.

Over a gofer.

A gofer for a shyster who had headed the opposition on a case that had been cleared seven years ago. A case that had officially evaporated when Babe Devens woke up.

He told himself to be reasonable, think about something else, something that didn't make him angry, like the air conditioner in his cubicle that wasn't even pretending to work. Or Lewis Monserat, peddling marked-up s.m. gear and hiding behind the skirts of the law.

Had anyone who wasn't guilty of at least grand larceny ever hired Ted Morgenstern or any of his associates?

Cardozo's mind went over that a moment, flicked back to Doria Forbes-Steinman's accusations. They were wild, certainly exaggerated, but . . .

He lifted the telephone. The receiver blasted him with the strains of a vocal quartet warbling "The Age of Aquarius."

"I don't believe it. I'm getting Muzak on the goddamned phone."

He strode through the squad room into the hallway.

The redheaded proprietor of an East Side crack boutique sat on a bench, manacled to a plainclothesman. She was gazing into a simulated-gold pocket mirror, studded with phony emeralds. Her free hand, holding a puff studded with more phony emeralds, was busily powdering her face.

The same smarmy musical arrangement was drifting up the stairwell.

Cardozo leaned over the banister and shouted down, "Get that fuckin' Muzak off my phone!"

The crack boutique owner's eyes came up at Cardozo with a grin. "Way to go, man, way to go."

It did no good. it didn't even make him feel better. Now when he lifted his receiver the tune was "Yesterday."

He gave up and walked downstairs.

The computer room was the only effectively air-conditioned room in the station house. The computer rated air-conditioning because, unlike a cop, it refused to work in discomfort.

"Help you, Lieutenant?" Charley Brackner asked. A brown-eyed young man, prematurely bald, Charley was the precinct's resident computer whiz, the only person who could turn the machine on or off without blowing the air conditioning. His cheerfully condescending manner reflected the confidence of a man who had long ago realized the unique and intimidating power of the skills he possessed.

"Call up the rap sheet on Lewis Monserat."

Cardozo spelled the name, and Charley's fingers, moving in a blur over the IBM letter keyboard, fed the information into the computer. The screen flashed the word SEARCHING and a moment later the words NO FILE AVAILABLE.

"What does that mean?" Cardozo said. "There's no file or there's a file but we mortal schmucks aren't allowed to read it?"

Charley turned around in the swivel chair, patiently professorial. "It means Maisie has nothing on him."

"Maisie?"

"The computer. Either Monserat has a damned good lawyer, or he hasn't been caught, or he isn't a criminal."

"Not even a parking ticket?"

"Believe it or not, Lieutenant, eighty percent of the residents of central and south Manhattan lead law-abiding lives."

Cardozo's face and hands were dappled in reflections from the slides. When he recognized a figure he added to an earlier notation in the log. Fresh faces got new notations.

He flicked to a new slide and suddenly he sat forward.

It was as though the light had changed, as though the surrounding area had dimmed out and only the narrow waist held in a black band splashed with primary colors was in focus.

He toyed with the lens. The figure on the wall receded into a blur, came forward into sharpness.

His eyes took in the three-inch black leather belt, the outlandishly huge and brilliant red and green and blue costume jewels encrusting it.

The woman had a strikingly deep suntan and blond hair that splayed out into the breeze in a long wave behind her.

Cardozo felt a tightening around the chest.

He switched off the projector. For a minute the wall seemed to glow where the image had been.

He lifted the phone and dialed the number of the Pleasure Trove sex shop.

Burt, the salesman from Pleasure Trove, leaned back against the cubicle wall, a column of smoke rising from his cigarette up into the still air. The carousel made click after click as the slides flicked by.

The legs of Burt's chair came down on the linoleum with a thunk. "Hold that picture." His eyes were narrowed, suddenly attentive, his mouth closed so that his lips made a fine line. "That's her."

The young blond woman in the slide was striding toward the Beaux Arts lobby. She had brown eyes, strong nose and jaw. A puff of wind had driven her apricot ruffled blouse hard against her breasts, showing a firm, braless outline.

In her right hand she was holding a shoebox-sized package.

Cardozo rose. "Thanks, Burt. I appreciate it."

After Burt left, Cardozo sat thinking.

There was an easy way of putting it together. Didn't mean it was the right way, just an easy way.

Kushima had made a fifth mask, Monserat had sold it, and it had turned up as part of the personal adornment in a mutilation murder. The owner of the mask had reached the gallery, who had reached the artist, and they all were denying the mask had ever existed.

Now tie that in with the Pleasure Trove mask, bought for cash by a woman using a false name and address.

Did women ever buy leather bondage gear? Sure, statistically there had to be more than a few kinky women in the greater metropolitan area. Okay, could she have been buying it on her own for reasons that had nothing to do with the killing? Could she have been embarrassed, so she used a fake name and address?

Right away there was a contradiction: she went into Beaux Arts Tower with the mask, she came out without it.

Cardozo kept playing with combinations, and there was one he kept coming back to: the owner of the fifth mask had bought the Pleasure Trove mask as insurance, which meant he believed it was indistinguishable from the Kushimas. He'd used the unknown woman as a gofer because he could not afford visibility. In case the trail ever led to him, he'd be able to whip the mask out and say, "See, fellas? Here's mine. Must be someone else you're after."

Which meant that somewhere there was a record of that mask's movements, a trail of paper scraps that led to the killer.

Cardozo pored over the log. The girl was number 28. Name unknown. No match with patients of either clinic. Only one other picture was cross-referenced: number 43. In this one she was coming out of the building, back into the sunlight, without the package.

Those were the only two pictures of her. Both Tuesday, May 27. First day of business after the murder. Cardozo noted the times in the log. In at 11:07, out at 11:18.

He studied both slides. This time he was looking at the doorman. In the first the doorman seemed to be watching the young woman, suspiciously, difficult to say whether he recognized her or not. In the second his expression was much friendlier and he seemed to be speaking to her.

Cardozo studied the photos of the house staff, selected a slide, dropped it into the carousel. The wall lit up with a close-up of Andy Gomez.

It was almost eleven; from behind the steeple of Saint Andrew's the moon was rising into the night sky. Andy Gomez stood inside the door of Beaux Arts Tower, talking animatedly on the house phone.

"Hi there, Andy." Cardozo flashed his shield.

Andy's eyes withdrew suspiciously under their brows and he hung up the phone.

Cardozo showed him a photograph. The lab had brushed out the background so as not to compromise the surveillance van. "Ever seen this woman, Andy?"

Andy frowned. "I see a lot of women."

"Come on, Andy. You seem like a pretty alert guy to me. A woman like this came to the building, you'd remember which apartment she went to."

"Maybe I said hello to her, she's a pretty woman, but remember who she was visiting, hell no. I see too many faces."

Cardozo scanned the fives on the Beaux Arts John Doe that had come in since yesterday, put them into their own stack, reflected that time was passing and memories of potential witnesses were growing staler.

Tommy Daniels knocked on the open door. Today he was wearing a heliotrope pink shirt that brought an infra-red glow to the cubicle.

"Your photographers are doing nice work," Cardozo said. He handed Tommy the picture of the blond-haired mystery woman.

"Beautiful lady. Who is she?"

"We want to find out. Have your men in the van keep an eye out for her. If she goes into the building again, follow her and see which floor she goes to."

16

"I JUST LOOKED AT THAT BUFFET AND PUT ON TEN POUNDS. BUT I danced every ounce of it off." Lucia Vanderwalk sat smiling at her daughter. "I haven't heard such a dance band since Eddy Duchin played at my birthday. No rock whatsoever. And Cordelia has never looked prettier. Of course, she was wearing one of your gowns."

"One of *my* gowns?" Babe said.

"One of your company's gowns. Billi has kept all your designs up to date. Mercedes Somoza was wearing one too."

"I don't know who Mercedes Somoza is."

Lucia's fingers tiptoed across her single strand of pearls. "Mercedes is the wife of the new Costa Rican ambassador to the U.N. She's quite the fashion arbiter. Billi's awfully good at getting the right people to wear Babethings designs. That's half the secret of your company's success."

Babe returned Lucia's gaze with calm blue eyes. "As I recollect, the company was fairly successful when I was president."

"No one's denying that, but it's stayed a success, and that's an accomplishment nowadays. Billi's done a great deal in your absence, I hope you're aware of it. And I don't mean just the company. He's taken loving care of Cordelia—and you know and I know he's not at all a family man. But for Cordelia he's always made an exception."

"Cordelia did look well," Babe said.

"And she looked heavenly dancing with your papa and Count Leopold. You remember the count?"

Babe smiled. "A lot of military decorations and thinning hair?"

"He's bald now. But Countess Victoria has more hair than ever. It's interesting how your friends have changed. I wish you could have seen them."

Babe drew herself up to her full sitting height. "Did anyone ask about me?"

Lucia hesitated. "We haven't told people. Not just yet.

"Why not?"

There was a silence while Lucia and Babe stared into each other's eyes.

"Until your doctor feels you're fit, your father and I don't think publicity's a good idea."

"Publicity's not going to harm me."

Lucia's lips shaped a sad little smile. "Times have changed. The press are demons nowadays. They're capable of dressing up a reporter as a nurse and sending her in to change your bedpan."

"There's no danger of that. I'm not using a bedpan."

"I'm glad you still have a sense of humor," Lucia said. "You and your ready wit would have been quite the stars at Ash's soiree. Ah well, you'll have other chances. All in due course."

Another silence went by.

"How did Dunk look?" Babe asked suddenly.

"I didn't see Dunk."

"Ash said she and Dunk are splitting up again."

"Did she? Well, I suppose Ash would know."

"Is Ash in some kind of therapy?"

"That's a strange question."

"She was taking pills and I wondered if a psychiatrist prescribed them."

"Some very fine people are being helped by psychiatrists. There's nothing shameful about it. The church is no use, so where else can a person turn if they get depressed or land in a divorce or—someone dies."

"You talk as though you've been to one yourself."

"I wouldn't hesitate if I needed treatment. But of course I'm the preneurotic generation."

"Was Doria Forbes-Steinman at the party?"

In absolute motionlessness Lucia sat looking at Babe. When she spoke again her words were measured and precise. "Ash wouldn't have that woman in her house, and if she did, I would not be her guest, nor would Billi, nor would—many other people. Why do you ask about Mrs. Forbes-Steinman?"

"Ash said Scottie's living with her."

"How kind of Ash to bring you up to date."

"There was nothing unkind about it. In fact I had to pry the information out of her. She wasn't at all eager to tell me about Scottie."

A silence flowed by. Lucia shrugged. "Scottie served his sentence. Now he plays the *piano* somewhere or other."

"Where?"

"Why do you insist on discussing him? It's only going to depress you."

Babe met her mother's cool gaze, knowing that Lucia would never be ill-bred enough to tell a lie, but knowing too that she was a woman capable of withholding large scraps of truth.

Lucia sighed. "Scottie's playing at one of the East Side hotels. I honestly can't remember which one. It's not the Carlyle."

"I want to talk to him."

"I fail to see what purpose would be served by that."

"I want to know the truth."

"You know it."

"I know a few half-truths that you and the police saw fit to spoon-feed me and a truth or two that Ash let slip."

There was a beat of hesitation. Lucia looked down at her hands as they traced the gold lettering on Babe's datebook. "I honestly feel you know enough for the time being."

"All right, I'll get out of here and find Scottie myself."

Lucia slammed down the datebook and walked to the window. She stood for a moment with her back to the room. She was trembling on the brink of something but then she pulled back.

"Dear heart, you're making such splendid progress. Why risk an emotional shock that will only set you back?"

"Don't you think I've *had* emotional shocks?"

"Yes, dear heart, indeed I do. That's why I'm concerned." Lucia came back to the bedside and repossessed her chair. "You've had enough suffering. Now you have to concentrate on recovery."

"I'm going to concentrate on finding out what's happened to my life."

"In the old days, when you were born, the only way a woman could get a proper rest was to go into the hospital and have a baby. You're having a rest without any of that. Why don't you just relax, away from all stress and strain, and Dr. Corey will tell you when you're fit?"

"He'd better certify me fit today, because I'm leaving tomorrow."

"That is not an option." Lucia's voice was flat and somehow dangerous. "Your father and I cannot permit you to leave this hospital."

"I don't see that it matters what you do or don't permit."

"Then you apparently don't realize that the court has made you your father's and my ward."

"I was in coma when the court decided that."

"You're not well yet."

"Maybe I'm physically weak, but I'm conscious and mentally sound."

"Why don't we leave that diagnosis to your doctor?"

"I know my state of mind better than any doctor."

"I wouldn't insist."

"I do insist."

Her mother gave her a sudden sideways stare, hard and disapproving. "Then the court will have to rule."

Babe had to fight a moment's refusal to believe what she'd heard, and then she marveled at her mother's ability to serve up a threat so offhandedly, without even changing her tone of voice.

Lucia paused. If the threat was a bluff, she had now committed herself to it. "I'm sorry, Beatrice. I didn't write the law. It requires three doctors to examine you and to agree in their findings."

"Then have them examine me today."

"It's up to Dr. Corey when they examine you. And Dr. Corey feels you need a stay here."

Babe studied her mother with her elegantly coiffed gray hair, her strong facial bones, and dark eyes. A sick premonition hummed inside her.

"Beatrice, dear heart, why must we argue? All any of us wants is for you to be well and happy and strong."

"Has Dr. Corey told you how long he prescribes protecting me?"

"He's mentioned three months. I should suppose that's give or take a month."

Babe's voice rose. "You don't mean give or take a year?"

Her mother gave her a tsk-tsk'ing look. "Don't be a goose. Look at you. You're flushed. You've got yourself all tired." Lucia carefully adjusted the fold of Babe's top sheet. "Now why don't you be a good girl and lie back and try to nap."

When Cardozo got back to the station house at ten that evening, there was a message waiting on his desk: PLEASE CONTACT AS SOON AS POSSIBLE, BABE V. DEVENS.

He saw by the sergeant's scrawl that the phone call had come at 1:30 that afternoon.

He phoned the hospital and asked for her room.

"I'm sorry," the operator said, "no calls are allowed after ten P.M."

It was 7:30 in the morning, and Babe Devens was in her hospital room, watching the morning news on TV, when Cardozo came in.

"Lieutenant Cardozo." She looked pleased to see him.

The room was bright with morning sun. He felt an odd and sudden shyness.

"Sorry I took so long," he said. "I didn't get your message till last night."

"You're very good to come."

He closed the door. They looked at one another in silence. He was very aware of her intelligent face, her green eyes, her honey blond hair.

"You remembered something?" he said.

"No. Please don't be angry at me. I need your help."

That interested him. Babe Vanderwalk Devens needed the help of a $47,000-a-year homicide detective.

"My family want me to stay in the hospital. I want to go home."

"You don't need me." He smiled. "You're over twenty-one. There's the door."

"It's not that easy. The court put me in their custody. They have my power of attorney. Legally I'm a child."

"Haven't you contacted your lawyer?"

The silk of Babe Devens's robe made a slight rustle in the quiet room. "First of all, I can't. That phone only takes incoming calls. I had to ask E.J. to call you from the nurse's station. Second of all, he's my family's lawyer. He's working for them, not me. My parents want me in protective custody and they won't let me see anybody but their handpicked visitors. Look." She handed him a leather-bound datebook. "Mother has my life mapped out for the next month."

Cardozo leafed through the pages, admiring the neatly looping handwriting. "Maybe your folks are right. Maybe you should stay in the hospital till you're strong."

Determination flared in Babe Devens's eyes. "There's nothing I'm doing here that I can't do at home. The house has an elevator, I can take E.J. with me, the therapists can work with me there. I'll be fine."

It occurred to him that this woman knew herself and knew her limits and that if she said she would be fine then she would be.

"What do you want me to do?" he said.

"Put me in touch with a lawyer who's not Wall Street and not old money and not scared of Hadley or Lucia Vanderwalk."

Cardozo found Lucinda MacGill on the second floor taking a deposition from a woman screaming in Yiddish and Russian. A sergeant, obviously a volunteer pulled out of the muster room, was attempting to translate.

A young man handcuffed to a chair was screaming Spanish and a lieutenant was translating. Through all the screaming and translating Cardozo gathered that the young man had pushed the woman's husband under a Queens-bound F train while attempting to grab the gold Star of David from his neck.

Lucinda MacGill saw Cardozo and came over to the coffee urn. "The kid's high on crack," she said. "The husband died forty minutes ago in emergency at Saint Clare's. The woman wishes she'd never left Russia."

"You working tomorrow?" Cardozo said.

"Tomorrow's Sunday. I'm sleeping."

"If you felt like going up to Doctors Hospital tomorrow and talking to Babe Vanderwalk Devens you could earn a little extra."

"Babe Devens? You're kidding. I thought she was in coma."

"She was but now she isn't. The court made her her parents' ward. They won't let her out of the hospital. She wants to go."

"Thanks, Lieutenant. That might just pay off my car loan."

Lucinda MacGill lit one of her two daily cigarettes and smiled at Babe Devens as though they had been friends for years. "Tell me about your family. What are they after? Do they want to control your money?"

Babe Devens sat with her arms folded on the hospital table, staring at Lucinda. "They don't need to control anyone's money. They have plenty of their own."

"Some people are greedy."

"Not my parents. They're do-gooders. They think they're protecting me."

"From what?"

"All kinds of sordid realities."

Lucinda MacGill rose from the chair and began pacing. "You have a right to a sanity hearing—we get three examining doctors to declare you competent, your family has the right to three examining doctors to declare you incompetent, a judge hears the experts and decides. If the judge decides against you we move for a jury trial. You'll definitely win with a jury."

Babe's deep-set eyes darkened and there were furrows in her forehead. "What would all that take—months?"

"Months, maybe years; and a few hundred thousand dollars."

"I don't want to go through all that."

"Good. Neither do I. I work for the city and I'm moonlighting." Lucinda moved to the window. A swollen summer sun ached in the sky, edging skyscrapers in blinding silver. "There hasn't been a word about you in the papers," she said.

Babe Devens's brow wrinkled. "Should there be?"

"Well, the papers printed all the testimony when your husband tried to kill you."

"My husband didn't—" Babe Devens broke off. "What's your point?"

"Your parents are trying very hard to keep your recovery quiet. Let's make them show cause. Give them x number of days to convince a court you shouldn't be declared competent. That leaves them two options: go to court—which would entail headlines—or stay out of court—and lose custody and power of attorney. You decide. You know your family."

"They can't abide publicity."

"Good. We'll go that route."

17

AT THE TASK FORCE MEETING MALLOY REPORTED THAT SO FAR NO prisons in the tristate area had recognized the photo of John Doe. "Maybe we should go national."

Cardozo tossed a chewing gum wrapper at an ashtray. There was a growing buzz of frustration in him. "So go."

Greg Monteleone sat shuffling three squares of phone message paper. "For what it's worth, two Laundromats say they recognize the flyer. Unfortunately, they're eight miles away from one another, so unless John Doe schlepped his dirty linen by helicopter, one of them's got to be mistaken."

Cardozo told Monteleone and Malloy to each take a Laundromat and check them out.

Cardozo lowered the shade in his cubicle and set up the projector. He looked at slides, Sunday's slides, Monday's, the whole week's. He tried to see each one as though for the first time.

Again and again he referred back to his one maybe, the mystery woman in slides 28 and 43: his gaze took in the flowing blond hair, the confident face and stride, the blouse, the skirt, the belt . . . the pink-striped package that went into the building and never came out again.

He told himself that there had to be a match, that Tommy's team had missed it, that she was somewhere else too, in another photo neatly logged and tagged.

But she wasn't and she wasn't and she wasn't.

At one thirty Monteleone was back from Queens to report that the mom and pop who ran the Laundromat had made a mistake.

Two hours later Malloy was back from Staten Island. The ferry ride had been great; the woman who ran the Laundromat was an old sweetie, but she had a habit of calling the FBI and reporting that their Ten Most Wanted had left laundry in her shop. The FBI had stopped taking her calls, so she'd turned to local law enforcement.

Monday, June 2. Cardozo was clicking through slides. He compared the faces on his wall to the faces on his desk, photographs Ellie Siegel had gotten from the insurance companies that reimbursed the Beaux Arts clinics.

There should be a computer to do this, he thought.

In three hours he found only seven matches that weren't already in the log. He felt he was groping through a maze that led only to potholes.

He was yawning and blinking when Siegel walked in from the squad room wearing a big smile. She stared at Cardozo with his head resting on his forearm.

"I got something." Her face lit up the room. "The owner not only claims to have seen the victim regularly, she has his laundry."

Cardozo's smile opened like a Japanese fan, the muscles stretching one at a time, and he realized he hadn't smiled in nine days. "Where?"

The area on lower Eighth Avenue was in the throes of gentrification: gays and yuppies edging in, Puerto Ricans getting edged out. On a block of Medicaid dentists and trendy upscale bistros, the Paradise Laundromat shared the ground floor of a brick tenement with the Jean Cocteau Hair Salon and Greeting Card Boutique.

Cardozo and Siegel entered the narrow storefront. To reach the clanking washers and dryers they had to walk a gauntlet of neighborhood Latin kids pitting their machismo against Japanese video game machines.

Soap dust floating in the air prickled the inside of Cardozo's nose and made him want to sneeze.

A girl waited by one of the dryers, studying her reflection in the window of spinning underwear. She was applying makeup, careful not to get powder on the headband of her Walkman earphones.

At the rear of the store an old Chinese woman in a black five-and-ten oriental robe was sitting erect and rigid on a small wooden box.

Cardozo showed her his shield.

Her tiny black eyes studied it suspiciously.

He showed her the flyer.

She nodded, her skin as dry as old parchment, her features drawn and shrunken. *"Sí,"* she said. *"Joven."* Young.

"His name, his address?"

No reaction. Cardozo tried his Spanish, a modification of the Portuguese he'd learned at home as a child. *"¿Su nombre, su dirección?"*

The old woman shook her head in denial. *"No nombre, no dirección."*

The right corner of her mouth was drawn down: she had some kind of paralysis of a facial nerve, and that, added to her accent, made her hash of Cantonese, Spanish, and English very hard to understand.

Cardozo was able to piece together that the young man had come in regularly, every Thursday, and he must have lived nearby, because he carried such big bags of laundry.

"You have one of these *sacos grandes*?" Cardozo asked. "Give it to me. *Dámelo por favor.*"

The slant of her eyes lent them a wary expression. "Ticket?"

"No ticket."

One finger unbent. "One dollar *más.*"

She went and got a stool and pulled a green nylon bag down from a crowded shelf.

Half a laundry ticket was safety-pinned to it. The date stamped on it was May 23. The Friday before the murder. She undid the pin, her hands liver-spotted and twisted with arthritis, and dropped it into a box of similar pins.

She held out the half ticket and with a cracked Bic pen made a pantomime of signing. Cardozo signed. She made him write down his shield number.

"Eight dollars fifty cents." Her English was a hell of a lot better when it came to money.

As Cardozo pulled into the cluster of glassy buildings, the air had a tang of oncoming rain. He took the laundry up to the fourth floor.

The man from Evidence was already there, a scholarly-looking civilian in his late twenties, tall and skinny with curly red hair. He began making an inventory of the laundry. It was a curious mix— woollen argyle socks with Brooks Brothers labels, Fruit of the Loom underpants and T-shirts, Healthknit jockstraps, five-and-dime tube socks without labels.

"A lot of socks," the evidence man commented. "He must have worn two, three pairs a day."

"Maybe he jogged." Cardozo noticed that the clothes were all India-inked with the same initials—J.D.

Funny if the guy's name really *was* John Doe.

Cardozo had known evidence men who would tag a pair of socks as a single item, especially if a detective was waiting, but this man went strictly by the book, tagging each sock with its own numbered tag, tearing each tag on its two perforated lines, filling out each stub in identical, careful block printing.

Lou Stein sauntered into the room. His face still bore traces of its holiday tan, but the holiday smile was gone. Care had eaten its way back.

"We're not going to need all that," he said. He lifted a pair of underpants, a T-shirt, and a sock out of the tagged pile and signed for them.

On the seventh floor, in the soft blue glow of lab lights, Lou Stein removed the evidence tags and dropped the clothing into a bath of distilled water. Sliding the lid into place, he pressed a button. The water began agitating violently.

After three minutes Lou drained the water from the tub and fed it into another tank. He played with a bank of switches. Something began making a Cuisinart sound.

Lou beckoned. "We can watch over here."

Cardozo fixed his eyes on a computer terminal. Mathematical and chemical symbols exploded into green points of brilliance on the black screen.

Thirty seconds later a printed analysis spewed out of the mouth of a computer-linked desktop printer.

Lou ripped off a sheet of printout and resettled his spectacles thoughtfully. "The underclothes and socks show a heavy saturation of the same detergent that caused the rash on John Doe."

Cardozo stopped on the fourth floor. The evidence man was examining a shirt. His teeth were pressed down into his lip.

"What do you make of this, Lieutenant?"

Cardozo took the shirt. It was white cotton, a nice weave, oxford or chambray.

"A dress shirt with a one-inch collar," Cardozo observed.

"Most of the other stuff is initialed J.D. This one's initialed D.B."

Cardozo studied the inside of the collar with the India-inked letters. "And no label."

"What is it, a Chairman Mao?"

Cardozo didn't know. "How many of these has he got?"

"Just that one."

Tommy Daniels arranged the sleeves outward on the table like the arms of a crucified man. "I'll shoot you a beauty. Good enough for *GQ*."

"Forget beautiful," Cardozo said. "I need six prints."

Cardozo called the team into his office. He passed out the photos and then rested both hands on the edge of the desk.

There was a wide waiting silence. Three tired men and one tired woman stared at the pictures.

"Whatever any of you are doing now," Cardozo said, "drop it. Find out what the hell kind of shirt that is, who makes it, where it's sold."

It was dark when Monteleone returned. There was no mistaking the black beyond the window for the last traces of day.

"It's a clerical shirt," he said. "Priests attach their collar to that hole in the back with a collar button."

A skin of silence dropped on the cubicle, freezing out the voices and clatter from the squad room.

"The guy's too young," Cardozo said. "He couldn't have been a priest." He realized that what he meant was, a priest couldn't have died that kind of death—God wouldn't have let him.

"Everybody seems young when you get older," Monteleone said. "Hell, cops look young to me. To tell the truth, Vince, even *you* look young to me."

Cardozo sat there for a moment letting things sort themselves out in his mind. He tapped a blunted pencil against the blotter.

"Let's assume he's a priest. Priests live where they work, right? And how far would you carry laundry—five, six blocks tops, right? Let's post the flyer in all churches within six blocks of that Laundromat."

"Clerical shirts are just formal shirts without the collar or the fancy front." Greg Monteleone was sharing his research with Tuesday's task force meeting. "They come in three colors—black and white for your hoi polloi priests, and magenta for bishops. White clerical shirts always have a rabat worn over them. That's a vest. Some Jesuits and low-church Anglicans try for the dog-collar look, and they wear the black shirt with the collar and without the vest."

"We're looking at a white shirt," Cardozo said. "Is it Catholic or is it Anglican?"

"They're both the same," Monteleone said. "The only difference is who's inside. They're all sewn by Ricans and Chicanos and gook illegals in the same Yiddish sweatshops."

Ellie Siegel, looking exasperated, scratched a match loudly and lit a cigarette.

"If you're buying a standard clerical shirt," Monteleone said, "you do it by mail or you go to a Roman Catholic shop and get it off the rack. If you want to go special, outfits like Brooks Brothers make white clerical shirts to order for rich Anglicans and Romans."

"Didn't know there were rich priests," Siegel said.

"They're called bishops," Monteleone said.

"Was D.B.'s shirt custom-made?" Cardozo asked.

Monteleone nodded. "The guy at Brooks Brothers said D.B.'s was a very nice custom job. The cloth quality was extremely high, and the tapered waist isn't standard."

"The minister had his waist tapered?" Richards said.

"Maybe he was proud of his waist," Malloy said.

Siegel seemed puzzled. "Throwing a tailor-made shirt into the washer with the underwear—wouldn't you think he'd send a shirt that expensive to a dry cleaner?"

"I don't know when you last looked at a priest or minister," Monteleone said, "but the shirt very rarely shows. The black vest hides it."

"Did Brooks Brothers happen to have made this shirt?" Cardozo asked.

Monteleone shook his head. "No. But a shirt like this you can have custom-made at any shop that tailors to order."

Cardozo sighed. "Okay, guys. Hit the Yellow Pages." He adjourned the meeting and went to his cubicle.

He reviewed the new slides from the observation van. He had asked the photo team to tag any new appearances of the girl in 43 — and he noticed that there were no tags.

He switched on the projector and began going through the slides. Yesterday had been sunny. Beaux Arts Tower gave off a sense of dignity and ease, a cool monolith, its large windows tinted against the sun.

He slowed at a photo of a dark-haired man in a seersucker suit, carrying a briefcase, looking back over his shoulder directly at the camera.

Another man who had made the truck.

Cardozo stared at the photo a moment. No, it wasn't another man. It was the same man in a different suit.

He went back through the log and found the earlier notation: #79, Monday, May 26.

He dropped 79 into the carousel and clicked the picture on.

The same man was carrying the same briefcase, looking very spiffy and businesslike. His patent leather shoes looked like dancing pumps, thin-soled enough for him to have felt every pebble on the pavement.

Seventy-nine's eyes met Cardozo's.

Today Cardozo tried to look at the slide in a new way. Possibly there was something about the man in the picture that was cocksure and careless. Maybe he was looking around not because he sensed danger but because he sensed attention. Maybe he wanted to see who else thought he was looking good.

Cardozo clicked back to the other photo of the same man. This time his attention went to another detail: Hector doing duty at the door, grinning.

Cardozo clicked forward.

Hector and the caller vanished into the lobby.

Next: Princess Lily Lobkowitz entering, looking angry at finding no doorman.

Next slide: 79 leaving the building.

Three slides later, Hector was back at his post, and Baron Billi von Kleist was entering the building. Hector was smiling at him.

Next: a patient for one of the psychotherapists entering the building. Hector wasn't smiling.

Cardozo clicked forward to a photo showing a shadowy figure getting out of a cab. A woman. She was wearing dark glasses, a kerchief, tight jeans.

Next slide. Hector was signaling the woman. Next: Hector and the woman retreating into the depths of the lobby, leaving the doorway unattended.

Cardozo stopped. The taxi and the woman's dark glasses triggered an association to a killing he'd solved two years back. The Mildred Hopkinson case.

Hopkinson had been legally blind and she'd lived with her working sister in Kew Gardens. Three years ago her father had been pushed from a twelfth-story window in Manhattan and someone had left one of Mildred's gloves on the floor. It seemed a crude and cruel sort of frame; Mildred's vision kept her housebound, and with her father's death her small annuity passed to an uncle.

Cardozo had ordered a stakeout on Mildred's home and discovered she had a secret boyfriend, a cabby who picked her up every day at the side door, took her for a drive to a motel, and brought her back to that same door at three sharp.

Mildred finally admitted her boyfriend had driven her to her dad's, the old man had picked a fight, and—not seeing the open window—she'd pushed him. Two years for involuntary manslaughter.

Cardozo clicked back through the sequence of slides. He knew exactly what he was looking for. Bingo. He stopped at the shot where the woman was getting out of the cab.

No mistaking it. She hadn't paid for the ride. Another glad-to-please cabby.

Thanks for the tip, Mildred.

Cardozo went back to the first day's photos, looking for any female wearing glamour shades and babushka.

June 2—four P.M. —a woman coming out of the Tower wearing dark glasses, no kerchief.

Debbi Hightower? He put the picture aside, pulled a Hightower from the stack, dropped it into the projector.

He clicked between the Hightower and the maybe Hightower and the girl in the cab. He reached out with his imagination, raking things in.

They're dealing dope. Seventy-nine is delivering, Hector is holding, Debbi is buying—definitely using . . .

He clicked back to the cabby, a gray-capped man out of focus in the foreground. He played with the lens. He couldn't get the image to sharpen.

It was frustrating. The man was right there in the photograph and Cardozo couldn't see him. It was like a Miranda rule standing between him and a smoking gun.

He phoned Tommy Daniels.

Tommy arrived wearing canary yellow trousers and his conservative helio pink shirt. He was remarkably energetic and Cardozo envied him that.

"Do a little magic with that slide, will you, Tommy?"

Tommy Daniels popped a pink gumdrop into his mouth. It was disgusting some of the things members of the force did to avoid smoking. He played with the lens, focusing and unfocusing the image in the shaft of light.

"Stop, hold it right there, Tommy."

The face was still blurred, but the logo on the cab door was clear enough to make out: DING-DONG TRANSPORT.

Cardozo handed Tommy the slide of the woman in dark glasses. "How clear can you make that?"

Tommy tinkered with the projector. He shook his head. "I'll have to do this one in the lab."

"I'd be obliged, Tommy."

Cardozo swiveled in his chair and yelled for Malloy. "Get Bronski's cab sheet for yesterday." Cardozo read the hour from the log. "I want the drop-off at 12:20 P.M."

18

"WE'VE BEEN SERVED WITH A SHOW CAUSE ORDER OF THE MOST unbelievable malice," Lucia Vanderwalk said. "It comes from some woman lawyer purporting to act on your behalf."

"I'm sorry, Mama," Babe said, "but I obviously needed legal representation."

"Why? You have your father and me acting on your behalf."

For a moment Babe said nothing from where she sat in her wheelchair. "I'm grateful for the help you and Papa gave me while I was sick. But you've stopped being a help. I want to get out of here and you want me to stay and that's why I hired Miss MacGill."

"Then you admit you went behind our backs."

"I admit I hired a lawyer. There's no secret about it."

"This Judge Levin who signed the order is an outrageous incompetent. He ruled against Cybilla deClairville in her suit against her dressmaker."

"Judges make strange rulings. Who knows how the judge may rule when you and I go to court. Or how a jury may decide, if it comes to that."

A very bad silence rolled in.

Lucia said, "You seem to relish the idea of making this squabble public."

"I don't relish it, but I'm willing to take the chance. What I'm not willing to do is sit here and let another minute of my life tick away."

"Dr. Corey happens to be an excellent physician and it's his opinion you're not well enough to be let out of the hospital."

"And it's my opinion I am."

"You're not a specialist."

"I am when it comes to myself."

Lucia turned to her husband. "Hadley, will you reason with your daughter?"

There was a special smile at the corner of Hadley's lips. Babe understood it exactly. Her father's eyes met hers, creating a conspiracy of warmth.

"Lucia, she's an adult. As I understand the legalities of this, she ceased to be our ward once she regained consciousness."

"Is that true, Bill?" Lucia said.

Lucia and Hadley had brought Bill Frothingham, the family lawyer, with them, and Lucia gave him her lovely smile. She had a great many smiles at her disposal, not all of them lovely, but this was obviously the one she thought appropriate.

"Not precisely." A gray-templed man with penetrating eyes and a sharp-featured arresting face, Bill Frothingham had a gift for getting on well with people, or at least keeping them at bay with the sort of smile he was smiling now. "The test is competence, not consciousness. Once Babe can demonstrate competence she becomes her own ward."

"Obviously she's competent," Hadley said. "She went and hired a lawyer."

"You can hardly call it competent," Lucia shot back. "She's defying the best neurologist in the country."

"Look here." Bill Frothingham shoved his mouth into a peacemaking grin. "We all want the same thing, which is for Babe to be well. If she'll agree to spend a reasonable amount of time under medical care—

"I'm taking my nurse with me," Babe said. "I'll be under medical care in my own home."

"Don't expect a doctor like Eric Corey to make house calls," Lucia warned.

"He likes me," Babe said, "I'll invite him to dinner."

"Don't you get sarcastic with me, young lady."

"I'm telling you exactly what I plan to do."

Lucia's green eyes challenged her daughter. "And if you should need an X ray or an EKG or an EEG or a CAT scan?"

"I can always be readmitted."

"Lucia," Hadley said pleasantly, "I think we should admit when we're beaten."

19

AT THE WEDNESDAY MORNING TASK FORCE MEETING CARL MAL-
loy produced Bronski's cab sheets for June 2. The sheets said he'd
been at West End Avenue and 93rd Street at 12:20 when the photo
van placed his look-alike at Beaux Arts Tower.

"I don't believe the sheets," Cardozo said.

He passed around Tommy Daniels's blowup of the girl in the
babushka.

"A two-week vacation in Oahu if anyone can identify her."

"Debbi Hightower," Sam Richards said.

"You're crazy," Malloy said.

"How can you tell from this?" Siegel said. "It's a blob."

"Debbi's a blob," Greg Monteleone said.

"But she's not this blob," Malloy said.

"You're a real help," Cardozo said. "All of you. Get out of here."

He went back to the slide projector and began the laborious task of
going through all the photos since day one, isolating all nonresident
females wearing babushkas and designer shades.

By late afternoon he'd turned up eight possibilities and was wondering about a ninth when there was a knock on the doorframe.

He turned.

A boy stood at the door, very lost, very out of place. His look was
open and vulnerable. His hair was reddish and hung in bangs on his
forehead. He wore faded jeans, Adidas jogging shoes, and a T-shirt
with a few well-laundered holes. It was the yuppie version of the
street look.

Cardozo could see his caller was not a junkie, not a pimp, not a
pross, not a booster.

"Lieutenant Cardozo?"

"Help you?"

"My name's Dave Bellamy." The boy's voice was taut, unsteady. "The man downstairs told me to talk to you."

The boy's feet kept checking an impulse to step backward. Cardozo could see he was scared shitless.

"It's about a guy I know. Jodie Downs."

In Cardozo's mind the initials J.D. set off a little inner jingle. He began listening with his skin. He lifted a pile of rubble from a chair. "Have a seat."

The boy sat obediently.

"If you'd like some coffee—" Cardozo offered.

"No, thanks, I've had a lot more than my quota today." The way the boy said it was embarrassed, apologetic, like a drunk saying *I've had too many, I've had to have too many to psych myself up for this.*

"I saw the poster at church last night." The boy's glance fought desperately for some sort of courage, skittering off surfaces, ricocheting away from Cardozo's. "The poster said anyone recognizing this man. I recognized him. Jodie Downs. He was watering my plants for me while I was away."

Cardozo got out a pad, began taking notes. "Can I have your name and address, Dave?"

Dave Bellamy spelled his name and gave an address at One Chelsea Place— "That's the Episcopal seminary on Ninth Avenue. I'm a second-year student. I got back late from Chicago last night, I've been home visiting my folks for a week, and I went to a late mass at the Roman Catholic church on Twenty-fourth. They have a beautiful late mass. I saw the poster."

His hand going to his hair, pulling at a strand of reddish blond.

"The plants in my room were dead. Some clothes of Jodie's were on the bed, and some of mine were missing."

"When did you last see Jodie?"

Dave Bellamy had to think a moment. "The night I flew home. Friday May sixteenth. He came to my room to get the keys."

"You got a minute, Dave? I'd like you to come with me downtown and look at something."

The attendant walked to number 1473. He turned a key and applied just enough pull to bring the slab sliding out. Ball bearings screeched.

Bellamy glanced at Cardozo.

Cardozo gave him a nod.

Bellamy walked across to the slab. His step was cautious, as though the floor might burst beneath his feet.

The attendant lifted the sheet. The light drew the drained, waxen face of the dead man out of the shadows.

Bellamy stared, not moving, not breathing.

The corpse looked curiously unborn, eyes closed in placental dreaming.

Cardozo waited in a tingling state of awareness. There was no sound but the plashing of water from an unseen hose. The smell was a blend of formaldehyde and meat that had sat too long in a marinade of sickening sweetness.

Dave Bellamy just stood there with a stunned look. Then he lifted his hands slowly and nodded his head.

As they drove uptown Bellamy sat strapped into his safety belt, but his mind was somewhere else, secret and apart.

A late afternoon shade had fallen over the city. The sky was a darkening bruise behind the turrets of lower Manhattan, just beginning to glitter with electric lights.

"It's your first corpse, isn't it," Cardozo said. He felt sorry for the boy. "It's like virginity. You never get it back."

They parked on West Twentieth.

Cardozo followed Dave Bellamy into the seminary. Through a window he could see the interior of an office, the shape of a priest bent over a desk. There was an intermittent amateurish clatter of typewriter, the ringing of a phone, and then a voice of which he could make out nothing except the gentleness. The priest waved Dave Bellamy through and smiled as though he recognized Cardozo.

They passed into a peaceful cloister with stepping-stone paths and evening-dappled oaks. There were iron fences, dark, ivy-twined brick buildings and a chapel with a high Gothic tower. Green-washed light filtered through trees that had grown undisturbed for a hundred years.

They went up a stairwell with hollowed stone steps. The well smelled of centuries of cleanliness. They stopped at the fourth landing.

Dave Bellamy nervously got out his keys and opened the door. He turned on the light. It revealed neat, scholarly clutter: a desk, stacks of black-bound books that reminded Cardozo of the Penal Code, drafting lamps, a crucifix—Jesus in ivory, not suffering—over the bed. Khaki trousers and a sports shirt had been tossed down on the bedspread as though someone had just made a dash for the shower. There was a suitcase beside the bed.

"Those are his?" Cardozo asked.

Dave Bellamy nodded.

"And the suitcase?"

"That's his too."

"Do you lease this room?"

"I'm leasing it for the summer session," Dave Bellamy said.

"May I open the suitcase?"

"Sure."

Cardozo opened the bag. The top layer was underpants and tube socks and T-shirts with J.D.'s initials. The next layer was leather. A vest, a belt, a cap, gloves, all bearing the India-ink initials J.D. Then black rubber and steel. The kind of things sex shops sold and called novelties. A plastic Baggie with grass, Bambu rolling papers, some tabs of blotter paper, a contact lens holder with coke inside, a two-ounce brown bottle three-quarters full of liquid popper.

"How'd you meet this guy?" Cardozo asked.

"We're from the same hometown. Mattoon, Illinois. He was studying fashion at Pratt, I was . . . here."

"Did you know he was into this stuff—drugs, leather?"

"I knew he was gay," Bellamy said. "I didn't know the details."

"Did you know he had one of your shirts?"

"No."

"Did he take any of your other clothes?"

"Some clericals are missing."

"I take it Jodie liked to dress up."

"For laughs I'd let him put on my clericals. Just here in the room."

"Can you give me his family's phone?"

Back at the precinct, Cardozo ordered that flyers of the dead man be distributed to all the leather bars in Manhattan.

He stared at his telephone.

He knew he was making the first mistake—thinking, planning what to say. There was no way of planning it.

He picked up the telephone. He dialed and listened to the line buzz.

A voice in the the county sheriff's office in Mattoon, Illinois, answered. A moment later the deputy sheriff picked up and listened to what Cardozo had to say. A sigh traveled across the phone line. "I'll go over and tell Lockwood and Meridee Downs myself. They're friends."

"Would you give them my number?" Cardozo said. "They may have questions."

"They'll have questions all right."

A call from Mattoon came seventeen minutes later. "Lieutenant Vincent Cardozo?"

"Speaking."

"This is Lockwood Downs. Jodie's dad." The voice was strangled. "My wife and I just heard that our son . . ." The words died.

"I'm very sorry," Cardozo said. He felt scooped out inside, and freezing, and he knew with his whole body what the murdered boy's father was feeling.

"My wife and I will be in New York tomorrow," Lockwood Downs said.

"You don't have to," Cardozo said, trying to make it easier for them.

"Lieutenant, we have to."

Cardozo peered over the railing toward the Eastern information counter. He saw the man and woman standing at the baggage carousel. They were dressed in unobtrusive mourning, and somehow that seemed sad and sweetly square and very old-fashioned. She was small and pretty and straight, her body held erect in a soft white dress. The man was thin, nearly six feet tall. His clothes spoke of another time, the early Kennedy years: pepper-and-salt suit and a gray tie and a lightweight charcoal raincoat over his arm.

Cardozo came down the stairs. He held out his hand and introduced himself.

"Meridee and I want to thank you for phoning," Downs said. His voice was tight and controlled and the sun had layered brown into his deep-lined face.

"Do you have luggage?" Cardozo asked.

Mrs. Downs shook her head. She had soft reddish hair and moist green eyes and there was a light dusting of freckles across the bridge of her nose. "Just these," she said.

They were each carrying a flat little fit-under-the-seat bag.

"We'd better go see Jodie," Downs said.

"That's not necessary," Cardozo said. "Jodie's friend Dave Bellamy identified him."

"You don't understand," Mrs. Downs said. Her small forehead was smooth, her mouth and chin firmly set. "We came east to say good-bye to our boy."

The attendant raised the sheet. The parents gazed down at the shut eyes.

Cardozo could feel the wave of shock hit them. Every atom of color was driven from their faces.

They always caught you unprepared, those moments when you knew that life was not forever, that death was just around the bend. The Bible told you and life told you, but still you never felt it in your gut except when it was someone special that death claimed. Cardozo had had one of those moments. Lockwood and Meridee Downs were having one now.

A thousand years crept by.

Mrs. Downs bent to kiss the dead lips.

Downs's face lifted up and he looked at his wife so tenderly, so softly, that the look was a caress in itself. Cardozo could remember that look, the look of caring, of belonging to someone.

She threw her arms around her husband and just cried.

Cardozo drove the Downses to the Helmsley Midtown, where the airline had reserved them a two-hundred-dollar-a-day room for the night. Downs took off his jacket and ordered drinks from room service and asked Cardozo to join them.

They sat down in big comfortable upholstered chairs and chatted —that aimless surrealistic chatter that people always make in the face of death. For the Downses, it was the beginning of a release. For Cardozo, it was his job.

Cardozo had the impression the Downses had been a hopeful upward-bound kind of family. He handled real estate and contracting, she had a nurse's certificate. They lived in the west end of town, the good end. They spoke with open pride about their white-shingled house on Lincoln Street. It had two baths and a full cellar, and it was theirs, mortgage paid in full.

Downs said, "I don't believe in debt. I guess that's un-American of me."

"Jodie grew up in that house," Mrs. Downs said quietly. She shook her head. "It seems unbelievable. There was a time only a little while ago when Jodie was still here, in this world, and now he's not."

"His whole life, wiped out," Downs said. "You look back, you see a street paved with might-have-been's and if-only's. The phone rings, and you expect it'll be him saying, *Hey, Dad, send a hundred bucks.*"

"He was always short of money," Mrs. Downs said.

Cardozo began to learn a little about their son. He didn't push into it—just let it come.

"He played French horn in the marching band," Mrs. Downs said. "He was too slender to make the high school football team."

"But he worked out with weights," Downs said, "until he made the basketball team."

"He was popular with girls too," Mrs. Downs said, wistfully. "The gay thing—that came later."

Cardozo ran his mind over Jodie's life. "How did Jodie lose his testicle?"

Downs was silent. Cardozo sensed in him a puritanism that had lost confidence in itself. It was his wife who finally broke the silence.

"Jodie came to New York three years ago to be an actor. He met a man in a bar. He took the man home. The man drugged him and slashed him."

"Did the police ever find this man?" Cardozo asked.

Mrs. Downs pushed the hem of her dress down past her knee. She shook her head.

"After that Jodie enrolled in fashion school," Downs said.

Cardozo understood the dark in which the Downses were adrift. He rotated his glass, making the ice in his Scotch shudder, knowing he was about to hurt them more.

"Something else happened to Jodie," he said. "You didn't see it. But you should know." He could hear someone's wristwatch ticking. "His right leg was amputated."

Mrs. Downs's lower lip trembled. She blinked hard. Downs stared at Cardozo in silence.

"It was done after death," Cardozo said, as though this was some sort of pitiful comfort.

Downs sat stone still, a sad broken mountain of a man, not a tremor in his face, not a movement except the narrow glazing over of his eyes.

"Was there anything on that leg—any distinguishing mark, a tattoo?"

"Nothing I know of," Downs said.

Mrs. Downs lifted her drink from the end table. She sipped slowly until it was drained halfway down to the ice cubes. "They tied Jodie up and terrorized him and he was completely at their mercy and they didn't care. And then they got their thrills. No one should have to die that way—for nothing, for no reason except some drugged-out lunatic wants to know what it's like to be God."

She moved to the window. She stood with her back to the men.

"Who killed our son?" she asked in a voice so calm and matter-of-fact that Cardozo was chilled.

"I intend to find that out," he said.

She turned. She looked at him. "Do you promise?"

"Now Meridee," Downs cut in, "all the lieutenant can do is his best—"

She pushed off her husband's hand. "Lieutenant, do you have a child?"

"I do," he said. "A girl."

"An only child?"

"That's right."

She took Cardozo's hands in hers. "Then you'll find Jodie's killer? You'll see—he gets what he deserves?"

Cardozo knew exactly what she was going through. His eyes promised. "I'll find him. He'll get what he deserves."

Cardozo returned to the precinct and felt an unaccountable craving for sweets. He ordered in blueberry pie and milk.

He sat reviewing the task force's fives and then he phoned the one nine and asked for Detective Barry MacPherson. The mumble that came over the line was either a bad connection or a mouthful of cheese blintz.

"Barry, you had an attempted homicide over there, first week in June, three years back."

"We had nine attempts and six successes, I remember the week well. So does my wife. June third's our wedding anniversary. That was the year we didn't get to go to Colorado. This year we didn't get to go to the Bahamas."

"Keep plugging. Maybe next year you won't get to go to Paris." A delivery boy brought the pie, sticky and sugary, a purple disaster. Cardozo made a face. "The victim's name was Jodie Downs, twenty years old, ex-aspiring actor, fashion design student, gay. He picked up a slasher in a bar, lost one of his balls."

"Ouch."

"You weren't by any chance on the case, were you, Barry?"

"It's hard enough remembering the ones who die. The survivors I have a very short retention for."

"He's dead now."

"Can't say I recall him."

"Jodie Downs."

"A lot of stiffs under the bridge in three years."

"Could you messenger me whatever paper you've got?"

"You got it."

Ellie Siegel came into the cubicle. She stood there a moment just staring at Cardozo. "Ever heard of the Rawhide bar?"

"Tell me what I'm missing out on."

"Eighth Avenue and West Twentieth." She sailed an interoffice memo down onto the desk. "The bartender recognized the flyer. His name is Hal. He's tending bar till eight. So you got time to enjoy your pie."

Cardozo shoved the paper plate at her. "You enjoy it."

She looked at the purple stain sinking through the crust into the cardboard. "Vince, you know your problem? No self-respect, putting junk like that into your gut. Some night I'm going to cook you a decent meal. You're too young to be going to pot."

"I'm not going to pot."

"Mr. America you're not."

"Who's talking, Miss Universe? I get my share of propositions."

"You'd get better propositions if you ate right. Knock off ten pounds and maybe you'd even get a shiksa to marry you."

"You're a pushy Jewish broad, you know that?"

"I'm as Irish as you."

"I'm not one percent Irish."

"So we match."

"You think you're going to get me with insults, you really think insults are going to give me a hard-on?"

"Who needs you, Vince? You're a macho bitch."

Cardozo pushed through the door. He took a deep breath, tasting the air, disliking the smell of spilled beer that seemed to have gone a stage beyond rot.

The bartender hefted himself up into a standing position. A black-moustached giant, steel studs sprayed across his leather like diamonds, he came down the bar, passing a damp cloth along the wood. The rag stopped two swipes away from Cardozo. "What'll it be?"

"Diet Pepsi."

The bartender gave Cardozo the can of soda.

The shadows in the bar were deep—almost night. Tatters of street light played through the synthetic buckskin that had been rigged across the windows.

"You're Hal?" Cardozo asked.

"That's right."

"You know this guy?" Cardozo laid a flyer on the bar.

The bartender put on granny glasses and they gave him a look totally at odds with the piratical black beard. A tiny loop of steel glimmered in his right ear. He studied the flyer a moment, then folded his glasses back into his vest pocket. "Yeah. I know him."

"Tell me about him." Cardozo showed the bartender his shield.

"Jodie and I dated."

"And?"

"Are you a narc?"

"Homicide."

Shock hit the bartender's face. He leaned down against the bar. "He's dead? How?"

"We want to find out."

The bartender began to wipe a glass. From the pool table, clear and clean as the tap of a woodpecker, came the contact of a cue on an ivory ball, then the rumble of dead weight dropping down a felt-lined pocket.

"He never mentioned any threats?" Cardozo asked.

"He didn't get threats. He got propositions."

"Who'd want to kill him?"

"I don't know. Me, sometimes."

"Where were you the twenty-fourth?"

"Week ago Saturday? Same place I am now. Right here."

"Where was he?"

"The Inferno."

"What's the Inferno?"

"Sex club on Ninth. He practically lived there. It's where we met."

Wind-whipped rain spattered down, making soapsuds in the gutter outside the precinct house as Cardozo hurried from the alley into the lobby. His cubicle was hot and still. He stood with his finger on the light switch, trying to guess from the mound on his desk how much departmental garbage had come in. He pressed the button. The light flung his shadow across the wall and filing cabinet.

The Jodie Downs file was on his desk, along with a note from Detective Barry MacPherson of the nineteenth please to take care of the hospital report.

There were four pages of NYPD letterhead covered with amateurish, misaligned, misspelled typing—clearly a departmental job—and there was a sheaf of public health reports, slightly better typed, with photographs attached.

The police report was grim, sad reading.

Jodie Downs had reviewed mug shots and sat at twenty-one lineups and had not been able to recognize his attacker. The assailant had never been found. The Identi-Kit picture, based on Jodie's description, showed a stocky, well-built man in his late twenties, with strong jaw, dark curly hair, a high smooth forehead, a moustache covering a sensual full upper lip. Possibly Hispanic or Italian. There was nothing real about the perpetrator: he was a dream, a stud who swaggered through a million male fashion drawings and probably ten million gay jack-off magazines.

Police and Lenox Hill Hospital psychiatrists profiled Downs as a bewildered and guilt-ridden young man, unable to reconcile the contradictions in his own personality, compulsively drawn to the temporary self-obliteration of drugs and sexual acting out.

Cardozo looked at the photographs and felt sick. They'd been taken, he supposed, for insurance purposes—in case Jodie Downs had sued for loss of his testicle.

Cardozo went to the door and hollered for Monteleone.

A moment later the light from the squad room outlined Greg's solid frame.

"Greg, you used to work Vice Squad. What do you know about a place called the Inferno?"

"You got six hours, Vince. It doesn't open till midnight. Doesn't get swinging till two."

"What goes on there?"

"What doesn't go on. It's a sex club. Sex and drugs."

"Gay?"

"Vince—it's got everything. Maybe no animals, maybe no liquor license, but believe me there are categories of behavior there that even the Supreme Court couldn't put a name to."

"What kind of dress?"

"Dress? You kidding? Leather bra or booties is optional—but your basic party wear at Inferno is skin."

"You don't have to look any special way to get in?"

"You could look like Godzilla and get in. In fact that's the kind of membership they want."

"Were you a member?"

"Sure. The whole vice squad of New York's a member."

"Are you still a member?"

"I haven't received an expulsion notice."

"Good. You're taking two guests tonight."

"Vince. I'm a married man."

"You don't have to break your marriage vows."

"That place is what Cardinal O'Connor calls an occasion of sin."

Cardozo shot Monteleone a look. "His Eminence is a member too?"

Monteleone leveled a smoke-colored gaze at him. "I want overtime and a half. Hardship pay."

"Screw you. And find Ellie. Tell her she's invited. One A.M. sharp."

20

"WE'RE PUBLIC NOW." THERE WAS PRIDE IN BILLI'S VOICE. "OUR stock is traded on the New York Exchange. And doing very handsomely."

"How much of ourselves do we own?" Babe asked.

"We control, naturally. We've kept the lion's share. Twelve percent."

"That's a lion's share?"

"Nowadays. And I'll tell you something else. We hold a hell of a lot of IBM, and the crash didn't touch it."

"But we're designers," Babe said. "Not a brokerage house."

"Indeed we are designers. Designers plus." He plunged into a whirlwind description of the plusses: the new products and services, the plans to expand and diversify, something about Canadian lumber.

Babe rested her forehead against the palm of her hand. Her eyes were so heavy that they were weighing down her entire head. "Billi, I'm sorry, it's too much coming at me at once."

Billi was silent a moment. Long black lashes half-veiled his gaze.

She saw she'd wounded him. "Don't misunderstand. I love what you've done—no, that sounds phony and frivolous. I can't even follow what you've done, but I trust you. I always have."

She'd almost married Billi. He'd proposed marriage after her divorce from Ernst Koenig, before her romance with Scottie. She'd never said yes, never said no—except by marrying Scottie, which was as decisive a no as a woman could give—yet he'd remained her friend and business associate.

"I just feel helpless, Billi. So completely cut off and out of things."

"But you're not." He rose and turned off the air conditioner and opened the window, letting in a rush of city air that seemed noisy and vital compared to the lifeless cool purity of the stillness in that room.

She could smell the world out there, the streets alive and bustling and active, the people living and real and seven years older than she remembered. She yearned to catch up, to be part of it again.

"You're going to get yourself out of here," he said. "And you're not going to yield an inch to those parents of yours. It's not that they're against you. They're just frightened for you."

"Why?"

"Because a lot's changed in seven years. A lot of people are thrown by the new society, the new behavior, the new money."

"There's never anything new about money."

"Nowadays there's a great deal." A shadow crossed Billi's face, and there was a curl of disdain to his tone. "The new *nouveaux* aren't the type you remember. They entertain on Park Avenue and they invite gossip columnists and press agents. They deal on Wall Street and bank in Geneva, shoot in South Africa, shop in Hong Kong, eat in Paris. And flaunt it everywhere. Ostentation is the rage—and it's the biggest reversal to rock society since drugs. Some people can't cope —they're clinging to the old ways for dear life. Lucia and Hadley pretend we're still living in the time of *The Forsyte Saga* and *Gaslight*. And they're not the only people fooling themselves."

Billi stood a long moment beside the window, his eyes squinting against the rays of the sun. His arms were locked around his chest. There was something held back in his voice and it didn't go with his words.

"Take our friend Ash Canfield," he said. "She looks quite the lady with her Chanel suits and her little hats and she has that eager, childlike quality. She thinks life should be a coming-out party—but she's flustered and bored when the band's not playing, so she turns to drink and drugs. She's living a nightmare—destroying her body, her mind."

Babe was silent, thinking of the Ash she had known years ago and the Ash she had seen last week.

Billi turned. He looked at her. "But you're not frightened, Babe, and you're not helpless. You never have been. You're going to be fine. Cordelia's got the same stuff as you. She's going to be fine too."

"Cordelia's changed."

"She's grown up."

"I know. I'll have to get to know her all over again."

"You're going to enjoy that."

"I hope so."

"*Dis donc,* do I detect just a little note of self-pity?"

Babe's hands played with a loose strand of her hair, and then she attempted a little smile and couldn't manage it and she settled for a little shrug. "You detect a symphony of self-pity. Billi—what happened to my life?"

There was a play of small muscles of Billi's forehead; in his eyes was a mingled expression of deep grief and indignation. Babe had always felt that his sarcasm was a cover, that he was a gentler, kinder man than he gave himself credit for or wanted others to see.

"It didn't just happen to you, Babe. It happened to all of us. What it is, or was, is a matter of opinion. You're going to have to find out for yourself. And it's going to hurt. No one can make it any easier for you."

"Least of all Billi von Kleist, who's going to be the perfect tight-lipped gent and not tell me a word."

"Scottie was my friend too."

"Was?"

Billi crossed back to the bed and took her hand. A wave of his vetiver cologne went past her, and she drew the first easy breath she'd taken in three days. No matter how many worlds came crashing down like dropped trays, she could always count on Billi von Kleist and his cool common sense.

"Let it go, Babe. Start letting go of it right here and now. It's over, gone. Get on with the present. Get back to work."

His eyes were probing into hers: they were a fiery blue that seemed to scan her and read her like sonar.

"No matter what else happens," he said, "no matter what else you discover has happened, hold on to work. Work is the last, the most important, the only frontier. Everything else comes and goes —but work stays. The one friend, the one parent, the one child, the one lover. It's the only thread we've got to guide us through this labyrinth we call a life."

21

THEY WERE STANDING IN THE MEAT-PACKING AREA OF MANHAT-
tan, a neighborhood of industrial buildings and warehouses just south
of 14th street. The air had the smell of badly refrigerated death.

Derelict-looking buildings lined the block. A phonebooth was the
major source of light.

It was a sweltering night, sidewalks still steaming from the rain.
The worst of the storm had blown over, but a trickle still fell, glittering through the headlights of passing cars, triple-parked meat
vans and idling limousines.

A steady stream of figures scurried under umbrellas from taxis and
limos to a darkened building at the end of the block.

"What'll the jet set think of next," Siegel said.

The entrance to the Inferno was through a wooden shed that had
been built out over the sidewalk. Monteleone led Cardozo and Siegel
past a mean-looking bouncer and down a flight of cement steps that
curved not into the cellar of the building but in the opposite direction, into a catacomb under the avenue itself. The steps were narrow, but not as narrow as what came next, a dank space lit by flash-
lights barbed-wired to the cement walls. Members were backed up
in a line, waiting to show their ID's to the director of admissions. He
sat behind a four-foot raw wood carton that bore the stencils COFFEE,
CAFE, PRODUITO DO BRASIL, and he wore a leather patch over one
eye.

He lit one neatly rolled joint from another. He glanced at the line
of customers. This was his moment, his island of power. Nothing was
going to hurry him.

The people behind Cardozo were talking about how much Fifth

Avenue office space was going for per square foot. They looked like
stockbrokers, lawyers, small-time civil service grafters who had
snorted a line, kicked the traces, and bolted off the ten-to-six Mon-
day-to-Friday path.

Monteleone showed his membership card. "Two guests."

The admission man's olive, broadly ugly face took on a look of
calculation. "Twenty bucks."

Monteleone pulled twenty from his wallet and signed the register.
Cardozo noticed that he signed the mayor's name.

They moved on into a dim area where members were taking off
their clothes and handing them over to the clothescheck.

"Check your clothes." Monteleone was already out of his trousers,
wearing ridiculous plaid boxer shorts. "Keep some money in your
socks. Drinks are three bucks each."

A brave smile deepened the lines of Siegel's face. She pulled off her
blouse.

Cardozo stripped down to his Jockeys.

They moved into the next room. It was cavernous. The low ceiling
rested on wooden beams that came from the dirt floor at crazy
angles. The acid rock thundering from a dozen speakers gave the
cavernous space the feel of a coalmine that might collapse at any
moment. Definitely a space for people who liked to live near the
edge.

The bar was a bunch of crates arranged in a circle. Naked figures
were sitting and standing and posing.

Beyond the bar was an area packed with waterbeds and hemmed
in by sections of steel fence, suitable for padlocking your playmates
to; there was a six-foot wading pool of the sort you see on suburban
back lawns; there were deck chairs scattered around, card tables
where members could take conversation and drug breaks.

"So you think this is where Jodie Downs met Mr. Right," Monteleone said.

They stood there, three uncomfortable cops in their underwear,
without guns, without shields, keeping their eyes open.

Gradually details began standing out.

A man with an IV in one arm and a glucose bag hanging from a
head-high walker was talking with a woman sitting on the bar. She
lazily stroked his shoulders with a whip.

"Pig city," Siegel muttered. "Absolutely new dimensions in
chazerei."

Across the room, a woman was walking over a naked man with

football cleats. A few solo acts prowled the dark corners, sniffing for action.

Cardozo felt like a fifth wheel on a spaceship. "Anyone want a drink?"

Nobody objected.

On his way to the bar he passed a man in a sling getting fist-fucked by a fat, bare-breasted woman in an executioner's hood. At a nearby card table women naked under their black raincoats were discussing how their husbands got off on this fister, how much better she was than the fister at Plato's.

Cardozo stood at the bar.

It took a few moments before the bartender asked what Cardozo wanted.

"Three Scotches."

"Dream on, little boy." The bartender ripped the flip tops off three Schlitzes and didn't bother wiping the spatter off his nose or off the bar.

Cardozo put down twelve dollar bills.

The bartender crumpled them up in his fist like a wipe-up towel. "You're new?"

Suddenly Cardozo was looking at the bartender, seeing him. He was a heavyset man in his late twenties or early thirties, with dark curly hair, a jaw that needed shaving, a moustache covering a full upper lip. Jodie's Identi-Kit.

"Yeah," Cardozo said. "I'm new."

"Stan," the bartender said.

Cardozo accepted a tough handshake. "Vince." His real name was easier than trying to keep false names straight.

"You're with them?" The bartender threw a nod toward Monteleone and Siegel.

"Yeah."

"Enjoy yourselves."

Cardozo took the drinks back to his coworkers. Now that his eyes and nerves were adjusted he noticed a half-dozen other men who looked like Jodie's Identi-Kit. Clones.

"It's not a funny thing, make believe, is it," he said.

"It's a Petrie dish," Siegel said.

"I'm going to mingle," Monteleone said, and he was gone.

"No one's enjoying themselves," Cardozo said. "I thought orgies were supposed to be fun."

Siegel looked at him. "Vince, you're so touchingly square."

"Yeah." He had a feeling of being outside everything, of not belonging to the same race as these people. "Why did Jodie Downs do it? Why do any of them do it?"

"The sex? It's an excuse to do drugs."

"Why do they do drugs?"

"So they can enjoy the sex."

"Ellie, the exasperating thing about you is you sincerely believe you got it all figured out."

"I haven't got anything figured out. But I don't freak as easy as you and I got my eyes open. You said we're looking for a killer?"

"Inferno is the last place we know Jodie was seen alive. We want to know who he talked to, who he left with. Our witness is there. It could be our killer is there."

Friday, June 6. Thirteen days since the murder. It was already a long hot morning in the task force room. Cardozo turned slowly in his chair and rose to his feet.

"I'm moving the photography van from Beaux Arts Tower to the Inferno. We're going to photograph every person going in or out of that club. We're going to compare those photos with the Beaux Arts photos. We're looking for faces we can connect to the murder scene. We're also going to stake out the Inferno."

"You might as well dust for fingerprints in a toilet bowl," Monteleone said.

Cardozo shot him a look. "That toilet bowl holds evidence. We'll dust."

Cardozo outlined the rotating schedule he had worked out: the members of the task force would appear singly and in groups at the Inferno, night after night, till they became familiar faces.

"Tonight Siegel will apply for membership, they'll remember her from last night, and she'll take Malloy as a guest."

"Thanks," Siegel said.

"Tomorrow night Malloy takes Richards."

"Aren't they going to connect us?" Malloy asked. "A bunch of squares hanging around not doing coke, not partying?"

"So? We're voyeurs, that's how we get our kicks."

Cardozo passed out Xeroxes of Jodie's Identi-Kit attacker.

"This is the type of man he was attracted to. So we look for Inferno patrons of this type. We win their confidence. We ask if any of them knew Jodie, noticed who he was with that last night."

The detectives filed wearily out of the room, holding copies of the fantasy face.

Lucinda MacGill, assistant district attorney, was waiting for Cardozo in his cubicle.

"It's improper and it's dangerous." Her tone was objective, noncommittal.

"So's life," Cardozo said.

"We're not talking life. We're talking criminal code. You don't have probable cause to put an observation truck outside that club or to send plainclothesmen in."

"I didn't ask for your permission. I asked how can I do it without blowing the case."

"Any first-year public defender will make a civil liberties issue that the NYPD hasn't got the right to photograph consenting adults going to and from their private revels."

Cardozo's eyes snapped to the ceiling and scanned wearily back and forth.

"And, Lieutenant, if you're going up against that sleazebag Ted Morgenstern on this, you can expect to get the Bill of Rights thrown at you."

"Why do you say I'm going up against Morgenstern?"

"The State Liquor Authority records are public and they're computerized. According to the records, Morgenstern's firm represented the Inferno in their application for a liquor license."

"The patrons of the Inferno are snorting coke."

"Name ten members of the United States Senate who aren't."

"Right out in the open?"

"The Inferno is not out in the open. It's a chartered fraternal organization under the laws of New York State, and like your home or mine it's private."

"Private for ten bucks."

"A trespass case could be made if any MOF goes in there with a false ID."

"All the members are using false ID's."

"They're not all trying to make a bust."

"It's an orgy pit."

"So are a lot of Park Avenue bedrooms."

"I've spent my life working in the sewer. Till the Inferno I thought I'd seen all sizes and shapes of shit. I'd like to know how much Morgenstern paid who to get that liquor license."

She studied him, looking to see if she'd made any dent at all in his cop's head. Not a hopeful look. "I'm talking to a brick wall."

"The brick wall has ears."

She lifted her half-tinted fashion glasses, revealing the flash of two intelligent watchful eyes. "Your photography van is illegal. If you find evidence, destroy the photograph and find the evidence another way. Anything you or your plainclothesmen discover inside the club is entrapment. It can't be used. Any recordings you make are for your reference only and they've got to be destroyed. Ditto for any notes or memos. The key word, Lieutenant, is destroy. I'm telling you now, because after you send that van in, I'd be an accessory to obstruction. As for any memos, recordings, or photographs already in your possession, you're on your own there. You have to read any suspect or potential witness his rights. And remember, the potential witness enjoys the same expectation of noninvasion as the suspect."

"You're asking the impossible."

"I'm not asking, Lieutenant. You can't take a step without probable cause, and Miranda is a minefield. I've seen valid cases destroyed because cops used their common sense instead of listening to their lawyers. Play it my way, or your killer walks, and you're the man who walked him."

Cardozo watched her leave the cubicle: a nice, easy walk. *She's going to go places,* he thought. *Definitely.*

On a long, lined yellow legal pad in a tight tiny scrawl Cardozo recorded every question he could think of. He was curious about the wide-open sex scene at the Inferno—especially in the light of AIDS. Who owned the club, why hadn't it been shut down?

He took Melissa Hatfield's business card from his wallet and punched her work number into his phone. He asked if she'd care to join him that evening for another drink.

"What's the occasion?"

"You thought you maybe knew the victim or had seen him."

A silence.

"I'd like to show you some new photographs. They might jog your memory."

When Melissa finally spoke her voice was unexpectedly bright. "Could I possibly persuade you to come up to dinner at my place tonight?"

Melissa Hatfield's address was a high rise on East Sixty-sixth, with a uniformed doorman and a sign saying all visitors must be announced.

Cardozo waited while the doorman announced him, eyeing him as though he were a mugger.

He rode to the twenty-ninth floor, rang her buzzer once, and waited.

When she opened the door, there was something different about her hair; it seemed to float around her face. "Come in," she smiled.

Her apartment bore the small graces of civilization: it was clean, cozy, softly lighted, with a pale Oriental rug and a spinet piano and bookcases and framed posters that looked like French and German art shows.

Not a million dollars, but in a way better: intelligence, taste, knowledge of what made her comfortable and what didn't.

A great lump of tabby cat was moving on the sofa.

"That's Zero," she said.

Even with one leg missing, the animal was huge and very much a presence. "Hi, Zero." Cardozo patted it on the scruff of the neck.

"Please," Melissa said. "Sit."

He sat down in a leather chair that was a little cracked and cat-clawed. A knitted gray shawl had been thrown over the area where the damage was concentrated. Given the perfection of the rest of the room the chair was almost out of place, like an old relative at a birthday party of children. It had the look of a favorite chair.

"Drink?" she offered.

"Scotch and water."

"I remember." She vanished a moment and came back with two glasses and handed him one.

She sat.

He sipped. The drink was incredibly strong. "Still trying to sell me an apartment?"

"I figured you could use it."

"An apartment?"

"A drink."

"It shows?"

"You look lousy. Great but lousy. The way a cop's supposed to look."

He sensed that she might be coming on to him in her sweet lady-like style and he didn't want to encourage it. "Can we get the cop stuff out of the way?" he said.

"Fine by me."

He showed her a photograph of Jodie Downs in his all-American jeans and high school sweatshirt.

She looked at it very sadly, a long time. She took a cigarette out of the crystal box on the polished maple tabletop and lit it.

"Bad habit," he said.

She exhaled twin jets of smoke. "Tell me," she said. "About him."

"His name was Jodie Downs. He was a student at Pratt. Ring any bells?"

Her eyes turned murky gray and she kept smoking. "None."

"He also had a fondness for very kinky, very sleazy sex clubs. Maybe that rings a bell?"

"Look, I work in a crooked business with opportunistic people, but I don't go to sex clubs. It's not my scene."

"Okay, so we know that wherever you remember his face from, it wasn't a sex club. And we know his name. Let's put it together."

"I was wrong," she said. "The man I thought he looked like is alive —he sells me my *New York Times* every morning at the newsstand on Sixty-sixth Street."

The last time Cardozo had questioned Melissa Hatfield she'd told him she led a lonely life and the claim hadn't fitted with his impression of her. Again he felt a dissonance between what she was saying and what his instincts were telling him. He believed her that she didn't go to sex clubs, but he didn't believe she'd never seen Downs's face. She was holding something back.

Cardozo was aware of the purring of the cat at his feet.

Melissa handed back the photograph.

"What do you feel when you see a dead man like that?" she asked.

"I feel I have a job." He sloshed his drink, helping the ice melt.

"I felt anger, hate, and doom," she volunteered.

"Why doom?"

"If it can happen to him it can happen to anyone."

"It's not going to happen to you."

"Oh, no? There's a lot of death around."

"That's a cheerful thought."

"I'm a cheerful girl."

"Okay, cop stuff concluded." He knew he wasn't going to trap her. The only other way to go was to talk trivialities, get her to lower her guard and maybe let something slip.

He said it was a hot day, and she said it was turning into a hot night.

Through the window behind her the summer light was fading and the sky above the horizon of penthouses was going from violet to blue. She said even with air conditioning there was sometimes no way to get cool except to go out to a movie, and they began chatting about their favorite films, and it was as though they were taking a stroll nowhere special, just heading the same way together.

After the third round of drinks she asked if he was hungry.

"Thought you'd never ask. I'll eat a zoo."

"Not on the menu. Will cold pesto salad do?"

The salad was delicious. It brought back the intense and uncomplicated pleasure of eating. Cardozo lifted his glass of chilled white wine. "To the cook."

She raised her glass.

"Melissa," he said, "is it easy for you to check a deed?"

"What kind of deed?"

"Who owns the building at Thirty-four and a half Ninth Avenue?"

"What's at Thirty-four and a half Ninth Avenue?"

"A sex club called the Inferno. If I check, it looks like the police setting up a bust. If you check—"

"It looks like Nat Chamberlain setting up a new luxury co-op. Sure, I can find out."

The strident jangle inched into Detective Greg Monteleone's awareness. He rolled onto his side to squint at the digital readout on the Japanese clock-radio.

It was two minutes after one A.M.

His wife was stirring beside him in the bed. As he searched for the switch on the lamp her sleeping hand went out, trying to stop him.

His finger connected with a plastic button and there was an exploding cone of light, horrible light.

Gina lay shading her eyes in shock, blinking at him. "Don't answer," she moaned.

His eyes apologized. He snatched up the phone in his fist and brought it to his ear. "Monteleone."

A voice said, "It's Will Madsen."

Monteleone had to think before the name clicked into place. The Episcopal priest whom he'd questioned in Beaux Arts Tower. "Yes, Father."

"There's been something on my conscience. I did see something the day of the murder—something I didn't mention." Madsen sounded nervous. He also sounded drunk. "I hate to make trouble for other people."

"I certainly can identify with that."

"Could we meet somewhere? Now?"

Monteleone wasn't going to bicker about the hour. Information on murders was a seller's market. "Where would you like to meet, Father?"

22

TASK FORCE MEETING, SATURDAY, JUNE 7, FOURTEEN DAYS AFTER the murder.

Siegel was winding up her Inferno report, telling how she'd connected with one of the hard-core regulars. "He's bisexual, and he knows everything that goes on in that place. He wants to see me again."

"Good," Cardozo said. "Did you make a date?"

She regarded Cardozo steadily for an instant. "We left it open. He's not going to forget me."

It was Malloy's turn. He seemed shaky and nervous as he drew a deep ragged breath.

"The bartender—Stan—gave me free beers. Real chatty type. Offered me coke, I said my doctor told me to lay off. He gave me his home phone."

"Did you give him yours?" Cardozo said.

"Told him I was married, said he couldn't call me at work or home. That turned him on."

Monteleone smirked. "Carl, you're so hard to get."

"Date him," Cardozo said. "Get close to him."

Malloy's Irish eyes were thoughtful. "Okay."

Monteleone's turn. "Had a talk with Father Will Madsen. He seems to be a periodic lush. Turns out he's been withholding a piece of information, but this morning around one A.M. he got drunk and spilled. The day of the murder, a little before noon, he saw Debbi in the lobby flirting with Hector Dominguez."

"The guy with the dead muskrat on his head?" Sam Richards said.

"What a lousy rug," Malloy said.

Monteleone continued. "When Madsen was passing through the lobby again, Debbi was back, totally crazed. She was trying to claw Hector to pieces. Madsen feels very guilty telling this. It's taken him two weeks and a few fifths of Stoli to come forward."

Cardozo pondered, trying to stick events together.

"Remember those scratches on his face?" Siegel said.

Cardozo nodded. "Hector said the cat did those. Greg, when did this happen?"

"A little after 2 P.M."

Silence came down, broken an instant later by the sound of Richards making a hacking attempt to recover from coffee swallowed the wrong way.

"What did Madsen mean, Debbi was flirting with Hector?" Cardozo asked.

"He said it looked like Debbi was coming on to the guy."

"He didn't say coming on," Siegel said. "A priest wouldn't use that expression."

"He said flirting. That means coming on, right?"

Siegel made an impatient face. "Flirting is courtship, Greg. Coming on is hard cruising. One is flattering and one is demeaning."

"Got it," Monteleone said. *"Gracias mucho."*

"Like she was offering herself?" Cardozo said. "Like she was willing to make it with Hector?"

"Father Madsen seemed to think so."

Cardozo was thinking of the possibilities, everything going through his mind at once. He had three facts: at noon a not very bright upscale hooker had been trying to wheedle good graces from a Neanderthal doorman, and two hours later she was physically attacking him. And sometime during those two hours a man had been murdered on the sixth floor.

"What turned Debbi around in two hours?" Cardozo said.

"I saw someone change like that once," Siegel said. "It was a psychotic break brought on by cocaine."

Sam Richards's lower lip moved. He ran his tongue along it. "There's another witness—he'd be able to shed some light."

Cardozo looked at him. "Who's that, Sam?"

"Jerzy Bronski's taxi was parked in the garage. He says he was taking a pee, but it stands to reason he was boffing Debbi, right?"

Cardozo picked up the telephone. He dialed. The line buzzed eight times.

"Ms. Hightower's residence," a woman's harried voice said.

"Miss Hightower, please."

"This is her service. She won't be back till Sunday evening."

"What time Sunday evening?"

"Who's calling?"

"Her father."

"Hello, Dr. Hightower. I didn't recognize your voice. Debbi will be back after eight o'clock."

A wave of annoyance swept Cardozo. He set his coffee down. He looked at the Beaux Arts Tower service personnel work schedule. Hector Dominguez would not be working until Monday, 4 P.M. to midnight.

He phoned Hector's home number and after two rings thought better of it and hung up. Save that one for face-to-face. He pulled the fives on Jerzy Bronski.

The sky had turned dusky gray. Heat waves rising from the street were tinged with the neon of shop signs.

The garage occupied a corner lot. There was a cardboard sign in the glass pane of the dispatcher's door: DO NOT ENTER.

Cardozo entered. He flashed his open wallet and asked for Jerzy Bronski.

The dispatcher, tufts of black hair poking out from his sweat-soaked T-shirt, glanced over from his desk. "Not back yet."

Cardozo sat uninvited in the free chair.

Stuttering fluorescent light flicked the peeling wall.

At quarter after eight a tall, slender man came in with his taxi sheets.

"Visitor," the dispatcher said.

Jerzy frowned at Cardozo, a sharp line jagging down between his eyebrows.

Cardozo rose and introduced himself. "Good meeting you, Jerzy. How about some coffee?"

"How about a drink?" Jerzy said.

Three minutes later they were settling down at a table on the glass-enclosed terrace of the Sazerac House across the way.

Jerzy tapped a Lucky loose from a crumpled pack and laid the pack on the table beside the metal ashtray. He lit the cigarette, striking a match from a book one-handed. He leaned back against his chair. "It makes me look bad, cops coming into my garage asking about me like I was a criminal."

"Jerzy, believe me, for a guy who moonlights his ass off the way you do, you're looking great."

Jerzy shaped an O with his mouth and blew out a perfect smoke ring.

"We know you've been making it with Debbi Hightower," Cardozo said. "And we know you were with her the day of the killing."

The legs of Jerzy's chair came back to the floor and denial began gathering itself in his face.

"We have a witness who can place your cab in the garage." Cardozo went out on a limb. "And who saw you take the elevator up to Debbi's. Hightower isn't the point, you weren't breaking any laws that we're interested in enforcing. What we want from you is information."

Jerzy's finger drew a track in the condensation that had formed on his glass of Scotch and water.

"Why did Debbi attack the doorman?"

Jerzy was silent.

"We know you falsified your cab sheets. We know you were driving Debbi home every day after she hooked in the hotel. We know, but Ding-Dong Transport doesn't need to know."

Jerzy's expression was undecided: he wanted to save his ass but he didn't want to wind up parking it in a fry pan. "She freaked out," he said.

"Why?"

Jerzy mopped his face with a dime store handkerchief that needed to see some action in a washing machine. "A delivery was late."

"Jerzy, I'm not a narc, so let's get this out of the way. It was coke, right?"

Jerzy put his drink down. He spoke quietly. "She's one of those chicks that live on the stuff. We were having a great time, and then she flipped." He imitated the intonation of Debbi flipping. "Gotta see my dealer, gotta see my dealer."

"Who's her dealer?"

Jerzy sucked in breath, hollowing his cheeks. "Do you have to drag me into this? You've been watching the building, you know who runs the coke in that place. He promised her the stuff: she went down and he didn't have it. She flipped out."

The third time Cardozo buzzed, the decibel level of punk rock dropped to something approaching bearability. The door opened a crack. A young woman's face stared at him above the safety chain.

Her blond hair fell to her shoulders, curly in a way that suggested she had just bathed.

She looked curiously at his shield and then curiously at him.

"They said the police were coming up."

"I am the police."

"You're not the black dude that was here before."

"No, I'm not."

"He was nice."

"So am I."

She worked her eyelashes. "What's this about?"

"Just a few questions."

"The place is kind of a mess—the maid's been sick."

"That's okay, we can talk here in the hallway."

"What the hell, you're not my mother, you're not going to criticize. Are you?"

"Promise."

She stepped back from the door, her loosely tied bathrobe a swirl of Day-Glo ruffles.

The furniture in the livingroom was minimal: beanbag chairs, bookcases, lonely objects in a dim cavern. Magazines and show business newspapers littered the floor.

She sank onto a beanbag chair and he sat on the other.

Her eyes fixed on him in uneasy expectancy.

"You had a fight with the doorman a week ago Saturday," he said.

"That's not true."

"Come on, Debbi. We know why you're wearing a false nail and we know how Hector got his face scratched. We have a witness."

"Who?"

"I'm not going to tell you that."

"I have rights."

"You don't have those rights till I arrest you, Debbi. I'm asking you some questions hoping maybe I won't have to do that. Just tell me what you and Hector were fighting about."

Her eyes became pools of evasion. "Hector's an s.o.b., that's what we were fighting about."

"Debbi, we know about Hector's sideline."

She got up from the beanbag. "No way I'm going to get into this conversation."

"We know he's dealing coke to you."

The face was defiant now, eyes blazing. They were blue-gray eyes, a wild blazing blue-gray. "I'm calling my lawyer."

A beige decorator phone lay on the floor at the end of a tangled plastic line. She didn't make a move toward it.

"Debbi, we're not interested in the coke. We're interested in what happened in this building a week ago Saturday when a man in six was murdered."

"I don't know anything about that."

"Does the name Jodie Downs mean anything to you?"

"No."

"Inferno?"

"What inferno?"

She said it without a capital I. That satisfied him.

"Why did you attack Hector?"

She didn't answer.

"Debbi, I don't care about that coke, but some friends of mine would care a whole lot."

Behind the bright glitter of her mascaraed eyes, he caught a sudden note of pleading.

"In my business, I have to stay alert. So sometimes I do a little coke." She grinned nervously. "Sorry 'bout that."

His mouth smiled back at her. "A lot of people do coke. Hell, cops have been caught doing it."

"Tell me. It's strictly personal use. I don't deal."

"We understand that, Debbi. We're not accusing you of dealing."

"I was expecting a gram of coke. I prepaid. With Hector you prepay. He said he'd have it at one thirty. All right, I was a little late picking it up—but that's no reason for him to sell it to someone else."

"Who'd he sell it to?"

"He said it was a real good customer who needed it real bad, needed it more than I did."

"Do you have any idea who?"

"Look, I make it my business not to know other people's business, you know what I mean?"

"Someone else in the building?"

"I absolutely don't know that."

Broome Street was dark as Cardozo stepped out of the car. A summer wind gusted along the pavement, swirling sheets of newspaper. Tiredness was all through him as he let himself into the apartment.

"You look beat." Terri walked toward him, and the soft cone of the hallway light sculpted her out of the darkness. She had a springy step and her body radiated a comfort with itself.

His arms went around her, folding her to him.

"You had a call. A woman." She handed him the piece of paper with the number.

He sensed her attention and looked at her sideways. Her oddly adult, humorous eyes met his and the flicker of a smile passed between them.

He went into the hallway and dialed. His reflection in the mirror told him he needed a shave and he'd been sweating into his shirt a few hours too long.

On the second ring Melissa Hatfield answered.

"Am I calling at a bad time?" he said.

"No, I'm watching TV." Behind her cheerful voice something solemn was waiting to come out. "I checked into that address. Thirty-four and a half Ninth Avenue is leased to a company called Pegasus International, and Pegasus is renting the adjoining cellar space to the Inferno Fraternal Society."

Holding the phone receiver in one hand, Cardozo stretched to pick up a pencil. He found a blank space on a junk mailing from the Museum of Modern Art. "Who's Pegasus?"

"I think they're a paper company. They're leasing on a month-to-month basis, which is unusual for a building, to say the least."

"Who are they leasing from?"

There was an odd pausing before she spoke again. "They're leasing from us. Balthazar. We picked up the building about four months ago. They were already in occupancy. We've picked up a few odd lots in the meat-packing district. My boss, Nat Chamberlain's, trying to put the lots together. So he leases month to month. When he gets enough property he'll rip down and put up a condo."

"Doesn't Chamberlain care who he rents to?"

"The theory is in case there's a stink he can claim he didn't know who Pegasus was renting to. It's like Mayor Koch or President Reagan not knowing their handpicked deputies are breaking all the laws. I could check the Pegasus incorporation papers, but it'll be the usual New York labyrinth."

"Don't bother with that. You've told me enough. Thanks."

"Vince, I enjoyed last night."

"So did I."

* * *

At one o'clock the following morning, Detectives Carl Malloy and Sam Richards entered the underground premises of the Inferno Recreational Club, signing in as Mr. Warren and his guest, Mr. White.

23

ON SUNDAY, THE EIGHTH OF JUNE, A LITTLE AFTER 8:00 P.M., BABE Devens's nurse wheeled her out of the side entrance of Doctors Hospital to a gray stretch limousine double-parked on 89th Street. The chauffeur came around to help the nurse lift Babe into the back seat. Lucia Vanderwalk watched, and something locked in the stern planes of her face.

The back of the car smelled of fresh roses. Babe and her father sat facing traffic, and Lucia and the nurse took seats facing Babe.

They took the FDR Drive south. Seven years had made their difference, but Babe was relieved to see that the city was still there. The same East River was awash with reddish light. The same jagged skyscrapers loomed dark purple against the fiery sky, pillars holding up the sunset.

The limousine swung off the drive, smoothly catching green lights all the way to Fifty-seventh Street, where children were playing in the little riverside park. Babe smiled at the peaceful scene with its golden long-ago glow.

One block north a dense group of people stood clustered on the sidewalk, shouting and pushing and spilling over into the street. Advance copies of *New York* magazine, available that day, had carried a column by Gordon Dobbs reporting Babe Devens's recovery. A white-panel truck was double-parked just ahead of Babe's town house. The blue lettering on its side said WCBS-TV NEWS.

"Revolting," Lucia muttered. "Hadley, you were going to see that this didn't happen."

"It's a free country, my dear."

Honking a path clear with his horn, the driver brought the limousine to the curb. The crowd surged toward the car.

The chauffeur came sprinting around to open the door. Lucia stepped out, slicing space with her handbag, holding reporters at bay.

The chauffeur quickly set up the wheelchair and then E.J. helped him load Babe into the chair. E.J. steered the chair across the pavement and Hadley, walking with a slight limp, went ahead and pushed the buzzer of number 18.

The crowd pressed in. A bearded man in fatigue trousers came dashing forward, balancing a minicam on his shoulder. Babe looked up into wild, snapping light. Mikes thrust themselves into her face.

"Looking great, Babe!"

"Did Scottie do it, Babe?"

The door of number 18 was opened by a stranger who regarded Babe with a look of extraordinary gravity.

The wrought-iron grill clanged shut and then the front door closed. Street noises were blotted out, and Babe found herself once more in the house she had left only a week ago, a week that other people called seven years.

"Beatrice," Lucia said, "this is Wheelock, your new butler."

The man's face was gray, composed like a stone, and he seemed tall and cadaverous in his servant's cutaway.

"How do you do," Babe said.

"How do you do, ma'am. Welcome home, ma'am."

"Where's Methuselah?" Babe hadn't thought of Methuselah, the highland terrier, till this moment. Suddenly she missed his running leap, his paws mauling her dress, his damp breath and warm animal smell in her face.

"Methuselah had to be put to sleep," Lucia said.

There was a stab in Babe's heart. She wheeled herself into the hallway. Her eyes took in the familiar framed pictures on the wall, the Sheraton table, the umbrella stand. They all told the bygone story of yesterday.

"I want to see the house," Babe said.

"Of course," Lucia said. "E.J. will help you."

"Thanks, I can manage this chair myself."

Babe rode up alone in the elevator, the same mahogany-paneled elevator she remembered, yet in some elusive way different. It took her a moment to see that the floor buttons had been replaced, black numbers on white and not the white on black she recalled.

She stopped on each floor and wheeled her chair along the corridors.

Every room, every passageway, was quiet and mysterious and changed: spotless new coverings on the chairs in Cordelia's room, not quite the same blue as before; a firescreen in the guest room, copper where it had been brass—one by one the little shocks built up, signs that the house had been shut for years and hurriedly reopened.

A lump of mourning lodged in her throat as she wheeled to the open doorway of the master bedroom.

She hesitated at the threshold of the well-furnished, handsome room, pulling in sensation through every pore. A scent of dried-rose potpourri drifted to her. Her eyes traveled across the canopied double bed, the bentwood chairs and loveseat with their shapes that were like chamber music made visible, the shelf of Limoges figurines.

She saw herself in the mirror wall, an unfamiliar woman in an unfamiliar wheelchair, saw her own dismay at these reminders of the life she had built young and lost young.

She wheeled forward to the chest of drawers. Her mind was in motion, counting and registering and remembering. Her eyes looked down at the silver-backed hairbrush and mirror and comb, then played across the space where Scottie's things should have been.

She felt the beginning of a spear going through her breastbone.

She wheeled to his closet and opened it, needing to persuade herself it was true. A pleasant masculine smell of well-cared-for closet floated out, gradually translating itself into darkness, emptiness.

To her right, a last pale remnant of evening fell through the window. *Just one night,* she thought, *and everything's gone.*

In the aching stillness she felt the vibration of something more, some other absence.

She wheeled to the door that opened on the other half of the enormous closet, her side. She pulled it open and sat there, tasting coolness and enclosure and a shadow that devoured all solidity. She reached her hand out in front of her and swept the rack of gowns— that rack that should have been gowns.

Her fingers touched night.

"We gave them away," a voice said.

Babe turned and saw her mother watching her from the hallway. A taste of betrayal flooded her. "You gave my clothes away?"

Lucia's eyes met Babe's carefully. Babe detected hesitation on her mother's face, quickly giving way to decision.

"Only the gowns. It was seven years ago, dear heart—not yesterday. What were we to do? We weren't sure you'd recover—and fashions change—and so many people need clothing."

"I designed most of those gowns."

"And you'll design others."

Lucia took charge of the wheelchair, steering Babe back down the hallway into the elevator. She looked at her daughter as though she were very anxious to play this scene well. "Times change, dear heart."

"Why have you hired Wheelock? What happened to Banks?"

"We couldn't keep Banks on salary for seven years."

"And Mrs. Banks?"

"You'll like Mrs. Wheelock every bit as well."

The elevator hummed down the shaft toward the second floor.

"There've been offers for this house," Lucia said, the brightness of her voice signaling that the subject was herewith changed. "Real estate values have shot up in this city—tenfold and more."

"I'm not interested in selling," Babe said.

"But you can't live here."

"Why not?"

"You've got to face facts. Scottie isn't coming back."

"There are other people in my life."

The elevator stopped on the second floor. Babe took the wheels of the chair and gave it a hard push forward, out of Lucia's grasp.

Her eyes inventoried the drawing room, sweeping familiar antiques and leather-bound books. The boiserie was hung, as always, with the Pissarro, the Sisley, the Flemish flower paintings.

But the ivory-pale wall panels were a slightly fresher ivory than she remembered, the carpets were a little brighter, and there were cut begonias in a vase on the Boesendorfer she had bought for Scottie, who had never allowed anything, not even a photograph, to be put on that piano.

On the mantelpiece above the unlit fire, the ornate ormolu clock that had never ticked before was marking time with audible ticktocks.

The room was tidier than Babe had ever seen it. She was reminded of those rooms in her friends' houses that were always camera-ready, in the hope that *Architectural Digest* or *The New York Times Sunday Magazine* would drop by.

As she wheeled across the Aubusson, Bill Frothingham rose from the chair by the fireplace. "The house is looking grand, Babe. As are you."

"It's nice of you to welcome me, Bill. Did Mama ask you here for any particular reason?"

"I asked Bill," Hadley Vanderwalk said, and Babe turned and saw that her father was standing by the sideboard making himself a whiskey sour.

"Oh, it's business then?" Babe said.

"Just a little something that ought to be taken care of," Hadley said.

Babe wheeled herself to the sideboard. "I'd like a drink before I hear about this little piece of business that can't wait till Monday." She tonged ice into a highball glass.

"Are you allowed to?" Lucia said, coming into the room.

"Ginger ale, Mama."

"Let me help."

"Too late."

The ginger ale fizzed up over the edge of the glass. Babe sopped up the overflow with two swipes of a cocktail napkin. She saw that the napkin had a monogram embossed on it, Babe Vanderwalk's curling *B* and *V* surrounding Scottie Devens's large *D*.

An immaculately uniformed gray-haired maid came in to pass a tray of hot hors d'oeuvres.

"Beatrice," Lucia said, "this is Mrs. Wheelock."

The maid gave a thin smile, her eyes opaque and unreadable.

Babe took a chicken liver wrapped in bacon and speared with a toothpick. "Thank you, Mrs. Wheelock. How do you do."

Bill Frothingham opened his briefcase and took out two documents. "How's your right hand, Babe? You remember how to sign things?"

Bill handed Babe the documents and she saw that they were two copies of a divorce petition, signed by Scott Devens as petitioner and by Hadley Vanderwalk exercising power of attorney for Beatrice Vanderwalk Devens.

"The divorce was granted on the assumption that you wouldn't regain consciousness," Bill Frothingham explained. "But since you have—"

"And thank God you have," Lucia said, folding herself into a tapestry chair of leafy green.

"Since you have, thank God," Bill Frothingham said, "your signature would be a good idea."

For a moment Babe's mind darted ahead, skimming possibilities. "But since I *am* conscious, and haven't signed, are Scottie and I divorced?"

Bill Frothingham's heavy eyebrows creased. "Certainly you are. The state granted the decree."

"But is it valid if I don't sign?"

"You have to be reasonable, dear heart," Lucia said.

"Being reasonable seems to be a way of letting other people make decisions I should be making myself."

Bill Frothingham was somber. He placed his hands together, interlacing his fingers stiffly. "It was Scottie who petitioned for divorce. Your signature is a formality. All it means is that you acknowledge you were informed."

"I don't think that's all it means." Babe stared coolly at the lawyer. "Scottie petitioned for this divorce thinking I would never regain consciousness. Doesn't the whole thing have to be reviewed? Surely the law gives Scottie a chance to reconsider?"

"Scottie doesn't deserve a chance to reconsider," Lucia said. "And he certainly isn't getting one."

"What about me? What if I *want* to be married to my husband?"

Looks were exchanged.

"You're being perverse, Beatrice. You know perfectly well what Scottie tried to do to you."

"No I do not. All I know is what you *claim* he tried to do, and he'd be in jail if the court had agreed with you."

"I see we're in for a painful conversation." Lucia sat on the edge of the chair, bristling with resolve. "Your husband," she said, "your dear charming Scottie, confessed to the court that on the night of the celebration, after you passed out—"

"I did not pass out," Babe said.

Lucia went at her own unhurried pace, like a clock during a tempest. "I beg your pardon, dear heart, but four men had to help you to the car. There were witnesses aplenty. Scottie brought you home and while you were unconscious, he injected you with insulin. Enough cc's, the experts said, to kill a normal person. Well, either the experts aren't particularly expert or you're not especially normal."

"Thank God," said Hadley.

"Since you didn't die," Lucia continued, "Scottie couldn't very well be tried for your murder. So your papa and I did the next best thing. We had him indicted for attempted murder."

Babe sat stiffly forward in her wheelchair. *"You* had him indicted?"

"We gave the state every possible encouragement," Hadley said.

Babe considered the implications of this. "You mean you hired lawyers and detectives to help the prosecution?"

"To help *you*," Lucia said. "You're our only child. What if we had lost you?"

"But I'm not a child and the only people who've lost anything through all your helpfulness are Scottie and me."

"Child, child," Lucia said in a voice Babe remembered from long ago, the voice that was at once soothing and subtly undermining.

"Scottie was charged and convicted," Hadley said.

"Then why isn't he in prison?" Babe shot back.

"He appealed on a technicality," Bill Frothingham said. "The court allowed him to plead guilty to a reduced charge of reckless endangerment."

"It would have been negligent homicide had you died," Lucia said.

Babe's voice rose a little. "What was the technicality?"

"Evidence was improperly introduced in the first trial," Bill Frothingham said. "It was disallowed in the second."

"They couldn't very well convict without the evidence." Lucia's tone made it clear she considered this unjust.

"What evidence?" Babe demanded, angry at her mounting sense that she was not being told the whole truth.

More looks were exchanged. The room seemed awash in shadows and denial.

"The syringe," Hadley said.

"Scottie did it for money," Lucia said. "He wanted your fortune and he wanted to live with that horrid Doria Forbes-Steinman woman."

"I can see by Babe's face she doesn't believe a word of this," Hadley said. "It's all coming at you too quickly, isn't it, kid."

Lucia sat there cool, unmoved. "If she doesn't believe us perhaps she'll believe *The New York Times.*"

Lucia went into the other room and returned with an armload of newspapers. She placed them in Babe's lap.

Slowly, Babe read an article in one of the seven-year-old late city editions. It soberly set out the details of Scott Devens's arraignment for attempted murder.

"How handsome he is," Babe said, "even in this terrible photograph."

"I never liked Scottie," Lucia said. "I never pretended to. Your papa never liked Scottie. The only people who liked him were your café society friends, and that was only because he played Gershwin so divinely on the piano. Playing Gershwin is hardly a reason to marry a man you know nothing about."

"It wasn't just those people who liked him," Babe said. "I liked him too."

"Naturally *you* liked him," Lucia said, impatient now.

"And Papa liked him too."

"He did play a good game of golf," Hadley said.

"Your papa does not like Scottie now," Lucia said. "No one likes him except Doria Forbes-Steinman, and she's a fool."

"Maybe not such a fool," Babe said.

"Not such a fool as you, perhaps."

Babe skimmed news reports of Scottie's denials, his appeal, his second hearing before Judge Francis Davenport, and his subsequent confession to reckless endangerment.

"Frank Davenport heard the appeal?" Babe said. "How was that possible? Didn't they know he's a friend of yours?"

"He's not a friend anymore," Lucia said. "Two months, can you imagine? A man tries to murder another human being and after two months they let him out of prison. You'd have thought, after all we'd done for him, Francis Davenport could have arranged a little bit more for us. But Francis said the law's the law, foolish and unjust as it is. I say Francis Davenport is Francis Davenport, foolish and unjust as *he* is. You really can't count on friends anymore: you can't count on anything except family. Thank God we've still got family."

"It's unbelievable," Babe said. "Frank Davenport should have been barred from trying the case."

"Babe, please just read this." Bill Frothingham handed her another document.

Babe studied the yellowed Xerox. It was Scott Devens's signed confession that he did *recklessly, willfully, and knowingly endanger the life of Beatrice Vanderwalk Devens by not calling for assistance when I knew she was in proximate danger of death.*

"He didn't confess to injecting me."

"It was a plea bargain," Bill Frothingham said. "His lawyer wasn't going to let him admit to a potentially capital offense."

"But there *was* a witness, and there *was* evidence," Lucia said.

"What witness, what evidence?" Babe cried. "You told me the syringe was disallowed."

"On a sleazy technicality."

"Then who was the witness?" Babe said. "There's no mention of any witness in these newspapers."

"I didn't give you all the papers."

"I'm not a child! I want to know and I have a right to know. This is *my* life, *my* marriage!"

"Scottie's admission to the lesser charge," Bill Frothingham said gently, "was tantamount to a confession of attempted murder. The word *knowingly* is a diplomatic way of saying he knew there was insulin in your blood."

"And *willfully,*" Lucia said, "means he put it there. And if it hadn't been for that dreadful Ted Morgenstern the syringe would have been admitted into evidence. Anyone Morgenstern defends is guilty. Everybody knows that. Why else do you think Scottie went to him?"

"Who was the witness against Scottie?" Babe said.

In the silence that fell, distant sounds came to Babe distinctly and with remembered meaning: the summer breeze softly rustling the curtains, the wood beams of the house creaking with obscure strain, the hum of the elevator.

"You don't need another shock," Lucia said.

"You think one more is going to finish me off? How you've changed in seven years, Mama—and you too, Papa, sitting there afraid to say a word without her permission. You weren't afraid to tell me not to marry Scottie. You weren't afraid to hire detectives to dig up his past. You weren't afraid to tell me everything sordid and disagreeable you could unearth about my first husband. Where was all your concern then? Why are you so worried about my feelings now?"

"Because you're ranting and hysterical," Lucia said.

"Maybe I'll stop ranting when you tell me who testified against Scottie."

In the silence a new voice spoke.

"Why not tell her? It's not a secret, is it?"

A young woman with blond hair stood in the doorway.

"Cordelia," Lucia said.

Cordelia was wearing green suede boots and jeans and a lace blouse, and an amethyst necklace. Cordelia crossed to Babe's wheelchair and kissed her mother on the forehead.

"Hello, Mother, you're looking well. I was supposed to be part of the welcome home committee but the traffic in from the island was terrible." Cordelia went to the sideboard and foraged among bottles. "Who drank the *mandarine*?"

"There's *poire*," Lucia said.

"Poire's for after dinner."

"You haven't eaten?"

"Didn't have a chance. Marshall Tavistock's plane broke down. Anyone mind if I finish the Fernet-Branca?"

"I was telling your mother," Lucia said, "that you don't live here anymore."

"Haven't for years. Are you going to sell the place, Mother? You really should."

"I like the peace here," Babe said. "And the view."

Cordelia dropped into a chair covered in glazed blue chintz and swirled her glass, studying the waves in her aperitif. "The Argentinian ambassador to the U.N. would buy in a minute."

"I'm not selling."

"It's awfully big for one person," Cordelia said.

"Maybe you'll want to move back," Babe said.

"Doubt it."

There was a silence, and Babe said, "I hear you have a beautiful loft. I'd like to see it."

"When you graduate to crutches you can. The elevator's not working."

"That elevator will be repaired long before your mother's on crutches," Lucia said.

"I don't know. Mother's moving awfully fast." Cordelia smiled. "I see you've been reading old newspapers. Am I in any of them?"

"No," Babe said. "You're not in any of these."

Cordelia's glance went coolly around the room. "Who's going to tell Mother? No one? Bill, is your drink all right? Grandpère, Grandmère, your drinks?"

"We're fine," Hadley said.

"The sooner we get it into the open," Cordelia said, "the sooner we'll never have to talk about it again."

"Agreed," Hadley said.

"Cordelia—" Lucia said, a warning in her voice.

"Really, Grandmère, why should Mother have to get it from the public library? She might as well know what everyone else knows. Sooner or later someone is bound to tell her anyway."

"Let it be later," Lucia said.

"No," Babe said. "Now."

"I agree with Mother," Cordelia said. Her eyes met Babe's. "It was me, Mother. I testified against Scottie at the first trial."

For a long moment Babe couldn't react, couldn't believe it. Refusal welled up in her. "But you were only twelve."

"I suppose that's why no one believed me."

"They believed you," Lucia said.

"Well, it didn't stick, did it."

"That wasn't your fault."

"Anyway, now Mother knows and we don't need to discuss it, do we? Unless Mother wants a discussion."

"I don't understand." Babe's voice faltered. She made a hacking attempt to grasp this, to understand. "Cordelia . . . saw Scottie . . . ?"

"I saw him come out of the bedroom with the syringe. That famous syringe. I hope they've got it in a museum somewhere."

"You *saw* him?" Babe tried to gain some particle of comprehension. "But you were—so young, so little."

"Being twelve doesn't mean I was blind—or a dolt."

Babe shook her head slowly. "I don't see how . . . I just don't see . . ." She fought for some sense of direction.

"Mother, this could get very boring. Everyone in this room except you has heard this cross-examination nine hundred times before."

Babe couldn't move. She needed something to point her feelings at and it wasn't there.

"I'm sorry, Mother. Truly I am. How did we get onto this subject anyway?"

"It's all because your mother doesn't want to sign the divorce petition," Lucia said.

"Yours and Papa's divorce petition," Babe said.

"Is Grandpère divorcing you, Grandmère? How adventurous for you both."

"Please, Cordelia," Lucia said. "We're discussing something serious."

"Why doesn't everybody just lighten up," Cordelia said. "This room is a morgue."

"If Beatrice would sign the petition," Lucia said, "she'd certainly lighten up Bill's workload—only Bill's too much a gentleman to say so."

"I can't sign something I don't understand," Babe said.

"You understand perfectly well," Lucia said. "You just don't want to admit you made a mistake marrying that man."

"You're right," Babe said. "Because I don't believe I did make a mistake. And I won't believe it till I hear it from Scottie's own lips."

"Babe," Hadley said gently, "just what do you expect Scottie to tell you?"

"He can tell me he tried to kill me."

"He's not going to tell anyone that," Lucia said. "Not now when he's off scot-free."

"Then at least he can tell me face-to-face he wants a divorce. He can meet me in Bill's office—and he can bring his attorney if he's scared of incriminating himself. But unless you produce my husband, and unless he tells me this petition is his doing and his desire, I'll . . ."

The air in the room was suddenly a wall of ice.

"You'll what?" Lucia said.

"I'll contest this divorce."

24

MONDAY EVENING CARDOZO DROVE OVER TO BEAUX ARTS TOWER.
Hector Dominguez was lounging against a pillar in the lobby. His
belly was getting big for his green jacket.

Cardozo motioned him to the side of the lobby. Hector hesitated
before stepping away from the door.

"I can't get your cat out of my mind, Hector. I hate to see an animal
falsely accused."

Hector's eyes met Cardozo's carefully.

"What was the cat's name?" Cardozo asked.

"Estrellita."

Cardozo took Hector's arm, holding him back lightly. "We know
about both your jobs. You've been dealing dope in this building. We
know who your customers are and we know who your supplier is."

Hector's soft red face flared into a hard red face. "Bullshit."

"Relax, Hector. We're not interested in the dope. On Saturday the
twenty-fourth you sold Debbi Hightower's coke to someone else.
Who was the other customer?"

Hector's blink rate began edging up. "What customer? I'm a doorman."

"Someone came into this building that you haven't told us about
and you sold them a gram."

Hector looked at him. A thick knotty artery pulsed in his temple.
"You're crazy."

"I need the name, Hector."

"I ain't got no name."

"You withhold evidence, Hector, and I promise you, I will get
angry about the coke."

"That Hightower, she's a coked-up whore. She'd say anything to save her skin. I'm a family man, I'm not going to get dragged into this. You want to accuse, talk to my lawyer."

"I'm going to keep it one on one for the time being. Let's take a walk. I'm parked by the hydrant down at the end of the block."

Hector took a sidelong glance at Cardozo. "Man, you gotta be kidding."

"No kidding, Hector. I need some answers from you and I can see this isn't the right atomosphere."

"I'm working, man."

"So am I, man, and you call me Lieutenant, okay?"

Cardozo motioned his guest to a straight-backed chair, keeping the swivel chair for himself. He started off nice-guy. Standard operating procedure.

"Smoke if you want to," he offered.

Hector took a pack of Marlboros out of his shirt and lit one. Cardozo pushed the ashtray across the desk.

"Truth time, Hector. Who bought the gram?"

"You got the wrong guy."

Cardozo picked up a handful of paper from the desk. He began leafing through the latest interdepartmental memos. Ten minutes went by. He looked up.

Hector was showing no agitation except for the way he stubbed out one cigarette before lighting the next.

"Why are you shielding them, Hector? Who'd you sell Debbi Hightower's gram to?"

There was no ventilation in the cubicle. Hector's brown eyes squinted against the smoke of his cigarette.

Cardozo leaned forward and bent the neck of the desk lamp up. The reflector aimed the full glare of the hundred-watt bulb straight into Hector's face.

Hector didn't wince or blink.

"We have photos, Hector. Pictures of your distributor making the drop. Pictures of you dealing."

"This is bullshit. I want to talk to my lawyer."

"All I need is a name, Hector. And then you walk out of here."

"I don't know any fucking name." Hector's voice was sliding up into a whine. "I didn't sell any fucking gram, I don't deal coke. Hightower's lying."

Cardozo went back to his reading.

In fifteen minutes Hector said, "Can you move the light? It's in my eyes."

Cardozo slammed a fist down onto the desktop. The lamp jumped and Hector started two inches out of his chair.

"Tell me the name!" Cardozo shouted. "Come on, you stupid Spic meathead! Stop wasting my time!"

Cardozo yanked Hector's right arm up behind his back and marched him out into the squad room.

"Hey, man, you're hurting me."

Cardozo pushed Hector over to the duty desk. Sergeant Goldberg looked up. "Need some help, Vince?"

"Yeah—cuff this scum and put him in the cage."

This was pure police theater. The law said suspects could not be caged without being arrested, and most suspects knew this. But the press published so many horror stories of police brutality that suspects could never be sure the cops would go by the law. The press—by creating uncertainty—helped cops. The scenario was this: Cardozo would go back to his cubicle and Goldberg would say to Hector, "You look like a good guy to me, I'm not going to cuff you or cage you." And Hector would sit there staring at that empty cage, believing it was only Sergeant Goldberg's good heart that was keeping him out of it and knowing that a good heart, like patience, could wear out.

Cardozo shut his door and spent the next hour reviewing van photos of the ins and outs at the Inferno.

Details nudged his attention. This man's hat, that woman's bracelet. He was surprised by the number of limos with black windows, lined up outside the warehouse like a cortege heading for a burial in Queens.

He compared Inferno and Beaux Arts photos, noting in the log that the comparison had been made and that the match was negative.

A voice cut into his concentration.

"I want to talk to my client."

Cardozo swiveled around, flicking on the desk lamp.

Ray Kane was wearing a madras jacket and green trousers. He carried a tan raincoat over one arm.

"Which client is that, Counselor?"

"Hector Dominguez."

"Does Hector know he's your client?"

"I'm his attorney of record in a matter still pending before the third circuit."

"What matter is that?"

"I don't have to disclose that."

Cardozo drew himself together and stood. "Dominguez has no right to counsel till he's charged. The law gives us eight hours to detain him."

"You've used up three of them."

"And I'll use up another five."

"Lieutenant, you have no probable cause."

"I have plenty of probable cause."

"I'd like to hear what it is."

"The fact that a man of your distinction, an associate of Ted Morgenstern, is representing a lowly doorman."

They stared at one another, each holding the other in the icy challenge of his gaze.

"You move Mr. Dominguez to arraignment in half an hour or I'm bringing habeas corpus." Kane turned and with a waddling stride marched from the room.

Cardozo found Assistant District Attorney Lucinda MacGill working night shift in the second-story squad room.

"I'm holding a man called Dominguez," he said. "I don't want to charge him, but he has information in a murder. Is he entitled to counsel?"

"Since this is a capital charge, it would be advisable." She leaned forward to lift her coffee cup from the desk, and fluorescence from the overhead lights flashed in her hair. "If you deny him counsel but don't charge him, you're in a gray area."

"Gray I can live with." Cardozo placed both hands on the desk edge. "An eager beaver from Ted Morgenstern's firm is representing Dominguez in a case pending. Can we find out what the charge is?"

MacGill set down her coffee and motioned Cardozo to come with her across the corridor. She went to a computer terminal and punched in data. A moment later the screen came up a field of glowing green type.

"Is that Hector or Hernando Dominguez?" she asked.

"Hector."

She punched in more data. "Raymond L. Kane the Third is representing Hector C. Dominguez, felony conviction possession of cocaine intent to sell, three-year sentence suspended, Dominguez cooperated with the D.A."

"Cooperated how?"

"Doesn't say. He's released in Kane's recognizance."

"So what's my situation if I don't let Kane talk to him?"

"Nothing you get from Dominguez can be used to charge or detain him."

"I'm not interested in Dominguez. Can the information be used against another person?"

"That depends. Does it incriminate Dominguez?"

"Of dope dealing, yes."

"It'll be thrown out, violation of Dominguez's Fifth Amendment right not to incriminate himself."

"Hector sold a gram of coke to an unknown person in Beaux Arts Tower at two P.M. the day of the killing. I need the customer's name."

"You feel this unknown person might be what—a witness to the killing?"

"I feel anyone in that building at that time might be the killer. It has to be checked out."

"You're in a bind, Lieutenant. If Dominguez gives you the name and it is the killer, you haven't gotten that information legally and your investigation is tainted."

"Once I get that name, I can go for the suspect on other grounds."

"What grounds?"

"I'll be in a better position to know that when I have the name."

"Aren't you going at this bass-ackwards, Lieutenant?"

"Got a better way to suggest?"

"You have no choice. At this point you have to charge Dominguez with withholding."

"Why? I can hold him eight hours. The threat of that cage could change his mind. It's changed other people's."

"You realize the odds are very strongly against you."

"I've been on the force twenty-two years. I'm immune to the odds by now."

He met her eyes. They were deep green and speculative, and he knew the thing they were speculating about was Vince Cardozo.

"Maybe you don't remember who's on night court," she said. "Judge Joseph Martinez."

Martinez, one of seven Hispanic judges in New York County, claimed that city police discriminated against Hispanics. Waging a one-man campaign to redress the wrong, he routinely dismissed all but the most heinous charges against Hispanics, and when he did not dismiss, he set ludicrously low bail. Cops had nicknamed him Let-

'em-Go Joe; prosecutors had attempted through three city adminis-trations to unseat him. He had the mayor's protection because he delivered the Hispanic vote.

"Unless you charge Dominguez," MacGill said, "Martinez will grant habeas."

"If I charge Dominguez he has a right to talk to Kane and I'll never get that name."

"If you don't charge him, Kane teams up with Martinez and they get you on false arrest. We're talking about *your* skin now, Lieuten-ant."

Cardozo stared at the green print on the screen. "Okay. Withhold-ing evidence in a felony."

MacGill rose and approached the bench. Her untroubled gaze met the judge's. "Your Honor, Hector Dominguez is withholding impor-tant evidence in a murder case."

Judge Martinez had a bored, square-jawed face, silver hair, and a sleepy Pancho Villa moustache. He folded his hands on his breast and closed his eyes.

"I was not informed of my client's detention," Ray Kane said. His madras jacket flopped open, exposing a well-rounded swell of shirt-front. "I was denied visitation. Hector Dominguez was not even questioned, but was held incommunicado for four hours. The police are harassing, plainly and simply, and violating my client's constitu-tional right to protection against unreasonable search and seizure."

Judge Martinez opened his eyes. "Counselor Kane, a dull roar will suffice. Is any of this true?" he asked MacGill.

"Your Honor," Lucinda MacGill said, "the people have probable cause to believe that Hector Dominguez—"

"Your Honor," Kane interrupted, "Lieutenant Vincent Cardozo had the audacity to call my client a Spic meathead."

Judge Martinez leaned back wearily in his chair, gazing down into the courtroom, at the benches rustling with handcuffed hookers and pushers, cops, defenders, A.D.A.'s. His eyes found Cardozo and black lightning went out from them.

"I have two grounds for throwing this out. One, Lieutenant Cardozo's behavior constitutes a prima facie case of police brutality. Two, Mr. Dominguez should have been charged before and not after four hours of detention."

Not even a ripple disturbed Counselor MacGill's surface. She had perfect control of her face. "Your Honor, police interrogation would be impossible if every potential or unwilling witness had to be charged before questioning."

"Tell it to the Supreme Court, Counselor." Judge Martinez brought his gavel slamming down. "The Spic meathead walks. Next case."

25

THE SENIOR PARTNERS' CONFERENCE ROOM CONTAINED AN ENORmous oval table and pictures of New York Harbor and the Statue of Liberty on one wall and a yellowed photograph of the Stock Exchange after the anarchist explosions of 1894 on the other.

Davis Hobson and Michael Williams, seniors of the firm, were waiting, looking grayer and a good deal heavier than Babe remembered them, and in addition to Bill Frothingham there were three junior associates.

"You're looking well, Hadley," Davis Hobson said. "How are you exercising?"

"By mixing my own martinis," Hadley said, and there was laughter.

"And you, Babe," Davis said. "You're looking younger than ever. As are you, Lucia."

"There should be place cards at this table," Lucia said. "Where are we supposed to sit?"

"Our team's on the north side," Bill Frothingham said, "and Scottie's is on the south."

Scottie, Babe realized with a sudden thickening in her throat. She looked at the man she had assumed to be an associate and she felt the shock of seeing someone she ought to have recognized and had not.

He came toward her, tall, dark-haired, easy-striding, the man who had once been the most important force in her universe. His dark, wide-set eyes and high cheekbones still combined into a strikingly handsome face. Perhaps it was the fault of the ceiling light throwing shadows into his eye sockets, but Babe wasn't prepared for the gauntness, the lines.

"It's been a long time." Scottie's voice was soft, and his mouth widened the promise of a smile just a fraction.

"Babe, have you met Ted Morgenstern?" Davis asked. "Ted's representing Scottie and we thought he ought to be here too."

The man she had taken to be the third junior associate stepped forward. "A great pleasure to meet you at last," he said, taking her hand. He had a deeply tanned face, and his glowing eyes seemed to probe into her, trying to read her intention.

Babe forced a smile.

"Shall we get on with it, then?" Davis Hobson said.

Those who were standing sat, and E.J. positioned Babe's wheelchair at the table next to Lucia.

Davis Hobson suggested changes in various clauses of the divorce agreement "in view of the fact that Babe Devens is alive and well, thank God."

Ted Morgenstern agreed to the changes in a flat voice.

Babe tried to follow the discussion. She saw the room as though from far away, through opera glasses that had accidentally been reversed.

Scottie was looking across the table at her. She pushed her wheelchair back.

"Beatrice," her mother said, "you asked for this meeting, now don't drift away. This concerns you."

"I'm listening," Babe said.

She wheeled to the window. She listened quietly for several minutes as Bill Frothingham suggested further changes in wording, and then she turned her chair around.

"Scottie," she said, "take me to lunch."

Scottie knew of a decent French restaurant two blocks away. E.J. steered Babe's wheelchair through the midtown mob thronging the sidewalk. Only a few people bothered to recognize Babe and stare. At the restaurant door Babe asked E.J. to be a sweetie and vanish for an hour.

E.J. hesitated. "You'll be all right?"

"Of course I'll be all right. I'm with Scottie." Babe reached back and touched his hand.

E.J. cast a doubtful look at them both. "All right."

It was a wise choice of restaurant: there was a wide entrance hall, no stairs, a darkly gleaming bar on the left. The main room had a high

ceiling and walls painted a soft orangey pink, like the inside of a
perfectly ripened melon.

The luncheon crowd was beginning to thin out. Scottie was able to
get a nice table by the window; the maître d' removed a chair and
Scottie angled Babe and her wheelchair in its place.

"Something to drink?" the maître d' offered.

"Just wine with the meal for me," Babe said.

Scottie nodded, indicating he'd take the same.

And then there were just the two of them, silent at their table.

For Babe, it seemed only hours since she and this man had clung to
each other and felt the deepest oneness of body and soul. And now
Scottie was remote, sitting stiffly in his chair, regarding her wordlessly with his deep-set brown eyes. She couldn't even guess at his
feelings.

"I didn't expect this," he said. "Frankly, I never expected you to
want to see me again."

The waiter brought menus and they ordered *gravlax* and *cervelle*.
Scottie ordered a bottle of Gavi de Gavi white wine.

She couldn't help but be aware that he was noticing the other
tables, watching the diners who were pretending not to be sneaking
glances their way.

"Are you sorry you came to lunch?" she asked. "Sorry you're here,
alone with your ex?"

His brows gathered together. "Why should I be sorry? You're the
one who's taking a chance."

"Am I? Are you going to kill me over *gravlax*?"

"Not funny, Babe."

There was a silence. When finally the food came, Scottie raised his
glass in an unspoken toast and then asked her if she didn't think the
wine's flinty taste perfectly complemented the *gravlax*.

"Did you?" Babe asked. "Did you try to kill me?"

"Is that what we're here to discuss?"

"I don't know what we're here to discuss. I miss you, Scottie."

"I'm sorry."

"Don't you miss me? At all?"

She would have liked him to say that he missed her horribly, but all
he said was that after seven years he had gotten used to most of the
changes in his life.

She told him it hadn't been seven years for her. She'd gone to sleep
with a life and a family and a husband and she'd woken up the next
day to find it all whisked away.

"You'll adjust," he said. The look on his face was determined and cold.

The waiter brought the second course, *cervelle* bubbling in beurre noir with capers and beautiful lemons that looked as though they'd been carefully halved with pinking shears.

The waiter refilled their wineglasses, and when he was out of earshot Babe said, "You couldn't have wanted to kill me. I couldn't have misjudged you that badly."

"Do you really want to discuss this over lunch?" he said.

"When else are we ever going to have a chance?"

"You do realize the attempted murder charge was reduced," he said.

"Mama says your lawyer used a technicality to get you off."

"Your mother has never made a secret of her feelings about me. I pleaded guilty to reckless endangerment and nothing else."

"I don't understand why you pleaded guilty to anything at all."

"I couldn't face another trial. My lawyer said a deal was the best way out of it."

"I spoke to the detective who investigated. Vincent Cardozo. He's positive you tried to kill me."

"Babe, you're going to meet a great many people and every one of them will have an opinion. I could tell you yes, I tried to kill you, or no, I didn't, and knowing you you wouldn't believe me whichever I said. Either you accept the court's finding, or you decide for yourself. Nothing I can say is going to help you make up your mind. And as far as I'm concerned, the case is closed."

"It's not closed for me. I have to know."

"It's history now, Babe."

"It's *my* history. *My* life that went down the tubes. *My* marriage."

"You still have your life."

"Do you love Doria Forbes-Steinman?"

His eyes had a sad, overcast look. "Why are you asking these questions? What's done is done."

"Have you stopped loving me?"

"Babe, it's useless. I stopped loving you long ago, long before the coma."

"I don't believe that."

"You've never believed things you didn't want to hear. Two years before that night I'd stopped wanting you, stopped wanting to sleep with you or even be with you. You must have sensed that."

"Were you sleeping with other women?"

"Only Doria."

She was afraid that if she moved the hurt and frustration inside her would explode. "Why did you stop wanting me?"

"It built up over the years. One day I realized I had to have something of my own, something that wasn't your career or your celebrity or your money."

"You had me."

"Hardly. Nothing was going to get you away from that office of yours—and the interviews, and the photography sessions, the showings—the whole nonstop emergency. It was like being married to a surgeon. You were always on call for other people."

To hear him tell it, the marriage had been years of living in her shadow, of wiping his own desires out of existence. As she listened, she felt a great dull void forming between them. Her voice grew low and weary.

"Were you jealous?" she asked.

"Not even jealous. I felt worthless."

She realized that she knew nothing about him. Suddenly there was an emptiness inside her so deep that she could almost feel wind blowing through her. "I never knew that. Never had the slightest idea. Do you feel worthless now?"

"No."

"Doria's done that for you?"

"I've done it for myself."

"Why didn't you tell me you were unhappy?"

The muscles of his face tensed into a furrowed, faraway look. "I did —and you never heard."

It made her angry that the blame was being heaped on her, and she felt argument edging into her voice. "I'm not a mind reader. If you'd told me my work was hurting our marriage, I'd have changed."

"Babe, this isn't the nineteenth century. Women have careers."

"They still want marriages."

"It's a little late for our marriage."

She looked at him and wondered if she would ever, ever stop missing him.

"You don't want me, Babe. You didn't want me then and you don't want me now. You're just upset at losing something that you thought was yours. Believe me, you'll get used to it and you'll be glad not to have me moping around."

"I never accused you of moping."

"You're blind. We went into marriage wanting two different things. It was bound to come apart."

"What was it you wanted?"

"I wanted it to go on the way it was in the beginning. When we were courting—funny word, isn't it—you adored me. We made love every minute we were alone. And when we were apart we were on the phone ten or twelve times a day. Once you phoned to tell me to look out the window because there was a beautiful storm in the north. In those days I was the center of your life. Everything you did, you wanted to share with me. You can't imagine how lucky I felt, how important, how loving and how loved. And then, when we married and you had me, the rules of the game changed. We made love on weekends—period—unless we were houseguests, and then we didn't because the sound might carry through the walls."

"That was only once, at Cybilla deClairville's, and you know how old-fashioned she is."

"It was more than once."

"Scottie, if it was my fault, I'm sorry."

"You're a remarkable woman, Babe. You can go years without seeing there's a problem, and then when it's finally pointed out to you, you don't just try to solve it, you take responsibility for causing it. You're very much like your mother in that respect. Neither of you seems to recognize that there are some facts in this world that you didn't create. And a great many you can't control."

"Someone caused our problems. They didn't just happen. Maybe I was too busy and too blind. But if I seemed to take you for granted, I never took you for granted in my heart."

He sat hunched, staring into space. She felt she was pleading with him, pleading ignobly.

"I loved our time together," she said. "I loved our conversations over breakfast and the walks in the country and sailboating and traveling. I loved all those meals in our favorite little restaurants. I loved the times we were alone and I miss them."

"I loved them too." He was silent. "But I don't miss them."

Emptiness swirled around her, and she was sure she would drown in it. "I don't believe you," she said. "You're changing things, you're rewriting the past. You *were* happy with me. You *do* miss me."

"Babe, you're wrong."

"I couldn't be that wrong. I'm not an idiot."

"Yes you are. Don't you see, Babe?"

"See what?"

"For God's sake, I did what they accused me of."

First puzzlement, then shock filled her. "What are you saying?"

She looked at him, drawing back into her wheelchair as if she could shrink away from the words. There was pain in her like a fistful of pointed needles.

His face was a mask of dead calm expressionlessness. "I tried to kill you."

26

WHEELING HERSELF OUT OF THE AIR-CONDITIONED RESTAURANT, Babe met a curtain of hot, blinding light. She sat blinking and thought she was going to faint, but her grip on the arms of the wheelchair held her.

Willing herself to be calm, alert, she maneuvered her chair slowly along the sidewalk, allowing the crowd to press past her.

As Babe came out of the elevator her mother was waiting in the law firm's reception area, face set, eyes filled with total disgust. She laid down her copy of *Town and Country* and stared at her daughter, moving nothing but her unforgiving green eyes. "You have knocked me absolutely speechless." She spoke evenly and with enormous anger. "You look dreadful. What did that wretch do to you?"

Babe drew herself up stiffly in her wheelchair, feeling naked and vulnerable. She couldn't get out, so she'd have to get through. "It's a long story." *All those years,* she thought. *Gone like one tick of the clock.*

"You always find a reason to disgrace yourself, don't you."

"Mama, please. Let's not have a fight now."

"All right, we'll have it later."

Lucia led the way to Bill Frothingham's office, and Babe wheeled behind her.

Bill Frothingham offered his best smile. His hands grasped Babe's tightly and she squeezed back, grateful for his touch. She hadn't realized till that moment how much hurt and rage there was in her.

She reached out and took the pen from the silver Tiffany inkstand. "Where do I sign?"

* * *

Babe handed back the two volumes of *NY-P-3567 PEOPLE V. SCOTT DEVENS.*

"There was an appeal," she said. "Could I see that record?"

The librarian looked at her chair and then at her. He was a man of about fifty and he had a pinkish porcelain face. "You'll have to give me the number." His breath had the disinfectant smell of eucalyptus oil and she instinctively knew he had been drinking on his lunch hour.

She gave him the number, neatly typed on a sheet of Bill Frothingham's firm stationery.

He vanished into the stacks, throwing one doubtful look back at her. Finally he returned, empty-handed.

"I'm sorry. Those records are sealed."

The limousine stopped at the Greene Street address and the driver came around and helped Babe into her chair. The sky above SoHo was bright blue.

There was an art gallery in the elegantly renovated storefront on the ground floor. Babe glanced at the paintings in the window— hyperrealistic still lifes of food wrapped in plastic, spattered with supermarket price stickers. The name of the gallery owner triggered a memory—Lewis Monserat: she knew him from dinner parties and gallery openings. Then her mind corrected: that had been seven years ago; she *had* known him.

Babe's driver wheeled her into the vestibule. The elevator—a refurbished freight lift—was waiting.

"Thanks, I can manage from here," Babe told the driver. She pressed six, Cordelia's floor.

Cordelia opened the door and looked at her mother with a surprised and happy smile. "Mother—why didn't you tell me you were coming?"

"I won't stay but a minute."

"Let me show you around. Do you need help with that chair?"

"No, I'm getting pretty good at it."

Cordelia went on ahead, and Babe wheeled behind.

"This is the living space." Cordelia's braceleted arm swept out an arc, tinkling like a wind harp with gold and plastic and dime store charms. "And that's the sleeping space, and there's the eating space. It's all partitioned space, you see. Someday the plumbing will be done, and then I can get on to something fun—like putting up shelves. Would you like coffee? I was just having a cup. It's French roast, I get it from DeLuca's downstairs."

"That would be wonderful."

Babe watched her daughter at the gas range, neatly setting up the Melitta and spooning coffee into the gold mesh filter and then sprinkling cinnamon on top and finally, careful as an action painter dribbling color on a canvas, pouring in the boiling water.

Babe sat holding a hand-painted Provençal mug. Feeling embarrassed, almost shy, she stared down at the coffee and then she looked up at her daughter. "Is Lewis Monserat still alive?"

Cordelia laughed. "Of course he's alive. Why?"

"I used to know him, and I saw his name downstairs."

"He's the most successful art dealer in town."

"He always was."

Cordelia sipped. "How's your coffee?"

"Perfect." Babe hadn't tasted her coffee. She tasted it now. "Cordelia—I was wondering—I was wondering if you'd want to—if you'd consider living at home again."

Cordelia came across the room and knelt at Babe's wheelchair and hugged her mother's knees. "Oh, Mother, that's so sweet of you. I had a feeling you were going to ask—but I don't think so, thanks."

Babe sat motionless, looking at the floor that had been taken down to the bare oak and varnished, then again at Cordelia.

"I love you, Mother—and I understand—really I do. But you've got to understand *me*. When you—went away—my world fell apart. I did the only thing I could. I learned how to take care of myself. Now that you're back you want to take up from where you left off. You want me to be twelve years old again, and don't you see, I can't be. I've accomplished too much. I have my life, my career, my home—I can't give them up."

"I wouldn't try to make you dependent."

"Oh, Mother, semantics isn't going to get me back to Sutton Place. I've grown up. I've moved on. And there *was* a lot of pain, more than you realize, and I'm not going to go back to it."

Babe sat hovering between hurt and acceptance.

Cordelia unhooked a set of keys from a peg over the kitchen sink and pressed them into Babe's hand. "Look—these are yours. Keys to my place—so you won't ever feel shut out."

Babe's hand closed around the keys. "I know now how hard it must have been for you." A burning lump had stuck like half-swallowed food in Babe's throat. "I read the transcript of the first trial."

"Why in the world did you do that?"

"I'm sorry you had to go through it. It must have wounded you terribly."

"Wounds heal, Mother. But they've got to be left alone. Your wounds *and* mine."

"They told me the transcript of the second trial is sealed."

Cordelia looked at her mother.

"What happened at that trial?" Babe asked.

"You don't actually think I remember."

"You must remember *something.*"

"I was twelve years old and scared to death. I don't remember any of it, I don't *want* to remember any of it. And I really think you should put all that behind you too."

It was raining when Babe got home. As the elevator lifted her upward, there was a gentle throbbing between her eyes.

She wheeled down the hallway into her bedroom and sat staring out the window. The low slate roofs of the neighboring town houses glowed damply.

She picked up the phone and dialed Ash Canfield. A machine answered. "Ash," she said at the beep, "it's me, pick up."

Ice rattled in a glass. A voice said, "What's up, sweetie?"

"That's a terrible message, you sound dead."

"I can't help it, I feel dead. You don't sound so full of beans yourself."

"I was down at the courthouse reading the trial transcript."

"Yuck."

"They've sealed the record of Scottie's second trial."

"Just as well. You don't want to poke around in all that muck."

"I want to know what happened."

"It's no secret what happened. Scottie got off with a week at that country club where they sent Martha Mitchell's husband and now he's playing the piano at the Winslow and he's a great hit with all the ghouls in town."

"How did he get off?"

"How do I know?"

"Come on, Ash, you always used to know everything."

"I still know everything. I just don't happen to have the details at my fingertips. But I can get them."

"How soon?"

"Are you still attached to that wheelchair and nurse?"

"Just the wheelchair."

"Meet me for lunch Friday at Archibald's."

"What's Archibald's?"

"A very posh, very in, dining spot on the Upper East Side. And the food's half edible, too."

27

THURSDAY NIGHT AT THE INFERNO. POUNDING MUSIC HAMMERED through Siegel's skin. The smell of liquor and sweat seeped through her pores.

Her friend with the clone moustache was really letting her have it, his whole philosophy of living and loving. "Nothing beats good sex," he said.

"Nothing," Siegel agreed.

"I was married for eight years but it wasn't good sex. Good sex is what it's all about."

Siegel's ears were filled with the roar of the place. She excused herself, said she'd be right back. She found Richards on a bench monitoring the stream of members coming into the bar. Sound, fury, and movement poured by in a smellifluent cascade.

He slid her a glance, motioning her to look toward the bar. A blond, heavyset man with a droopy moustache was standing six feet away.

"The handyman," she said. "Claude Loring."

And then she saw something else.

A man was moving with a shambling gait away from the bar. He had two wings of black hair over his ears, and he had dark, haunted eyes. He was badly out of shape in his Jockey shorts.

Siegel sat there right on the brink of recognition and then a little memory popped out. "Lewis Monserat. The art dealer that handled the masks."

Richards peered. "Think they're together?"

"They're sure not together tonight," Siegel said.

"Loring knows me," Richards said.

"Okay, I'll take Loring. You take the king of the New York art world."

Lewis Monserat prowled, and an aura of tension came off him like mist. His hands kept kneading one another. Whatever he was on, it seemed to Detective Sam Richards that it could not be one of the joy-making chemicals.

The art dealer looked unbelievably thin, his ribs standing out and his flesh sunken in except for the potbelly.

He found a corner that fascinated him. He hunched his shoulders and stared into the darkness as if trying to count how many shadows were writhing in it.

Siegel had to work hard to keep Loring in sight: he was moving in a sort of dance, weaving in and out, disappearing into the crowd, reappearing again. He paused to observe group action, scored coke, did coke, dealt coke.

Then he leaned silhouetted in barlight against a pillar, erect, solitary, like a pillar himself. His gaze moved smoothly from face to face, body to body, shadow to shadow. It stopped.

Siegel followed the direction of his eyes.

A group of dancers had taken over an area by the bondage poles. One of them was taller than the others, a lanky boy of twenty or so with fine, curly light hair. He exuded a scrubbed blond healthiness.

His coloring reminded Siegel of Jodie Downs.

Loring watched the boy dance and then he watched the boy go to the bar for a beer. The boy took his beer to one of the empty tables along the wall.

Loring followed. He planted himself before the table. He gave the boy a long steady gaze that was open and hungering.

The boy was staring at the label on his beer can. There was something about him that seemed unsoiled: his face was not yet calculating.

Loring said something. The boy brought his gaze up. Loring grinned lazily. Color stole slowly up the boy's face.

Loring lit a joint. He moved forward and held it out. The boy accepted it and took a long drag.

Loring sat down. He looked at the boy. He asked something.

A little line of wariness ran from the boy's eye down to the corner of his mouth.

Something stretched between them like a wire, alive with current, taut, ready to snap.

The boy shook his head.

Loring nodded and got up. He walked away without looking back at the boy, boring his way through the crowd and out into the clothescheck vestibule.

The boy was sitting there, eyes lost in the semidistance, sad, peering, as if he had no place in the whole world to go.

Siegel could see Loring on the bench in the vestibule, wrestling his foot into a boot. A moment later Loring was pushing his way up the stairs.

Suddenly the boy seemed to make up his mind. He was moving quickly through the crowd now to the clothescheck. Siegel saw him claiming an armload of denim.

She realized the next few moments were going to move very quickly. She pushed her way to the clothescheck, got her clothes back, and quickly dressed.

The boy was already halfway up the stairs, wearing some of his clothes, carrying the rest.

Siegel climbed the dimly lit stairwell, a fog of body heat pressing against her as she came out into the mugginess of the street. A thick robe of mist trailed through the parked cars. Footsteps echoed on the cracked pavement.

Loring was walking a jagged lane through the limousines and trucks. He passed through a cone of light from a streetlamp. Light pinged off the studs in his jacket.

The boy appeared in the gaps between parked trucks, trying to catch up.

Loring stopped at a parked van, a run-down Ford with a blue-jay logo on the side. He unlocked the cab door and hoisted himself up and in. He did not shut the door.

The boy was running now.

Siegel crossed the avenue, keeping the two in her sightline.

The boy reached the door of the truck. He looked up.

Loring made a bored face, slouching down deeper into the driver's seat. He swung his boots up onto the dashboard.

The boy was standing there, looking at Loring, his eyes expectant and young. Loring turned and looked at him. He reached a hand down and helped the boy swing up into the truck.

Siegel came closer to the truck, close enough to see the license number on the Tennessee plate. She wrote it in her notebook. She circled around to the front of the truck, weaving like a junkie.

The jagged line of warehouse roofs bit up into the smoky sky.

She crouched against a wall as though she were a bag woman resting. An ambulance screamed through the night.

Loring took out another joint. His mouth smiled and his moustache smiled too. A cigarette lighter flicked. For an instant the cab filled with light, drawing out of the dark two faces huddled near the flame.

The faces stayed close. The joint went back and forth.

Loring put both hands on the boy's head, turning it, and kissed him.

Then he bent forward to twist a key in the ignition. The engine made a sound like eight dozen winos hawking phlegm.

The van pulled away from the curb. Siegel shot up off the sidewalk into the street. She raised a hand and jumped into the headlight beams of a cruising yellow Checker cab, ready to flag it down by body block if necessary.

The cab jerked to a halt. Siegel jumped in, flipping her wallet open to the shield. "Follow that truck."

The Iranian-looking driver nodded.

The van trundled east through the potholes of Fourteenth Street and then north through the potholes of Sixth Avenue. It parked at a hydrant on the corner of Thirty-third.

"Let me off around the corner." Siegel tipped the driver an extra five.

As she came around onto Sixth Avenue she saw movement in the van. The boy was bending his nose down to Loring's hand, taking a hit of coke.

The truck door opened and Loring and the boy stepped down.

Siegel hung back in a store entrance.

Loring led the boy across the sidewalk to the arched doorway of a six-story loft building. A moment later they were inside and the door clicked shut behind them.

"The kid came down alone two hours later," Siegel said. "I called it a night and went home. Sorry, Vince. I felt as wrecked as he looked."

"You did a good job," Cardozo said. There was a detail in her report that nagged at him. The van.

"Loring's our boy," Monteleone said.

Cardozo made a skeptical face. "If it was Loring, then how do you explain Monserat?"

"What's to explain?" Monteleone said.

"He sold the mask and lied about it."

"A lot of people lie."

"Monserat is in very bad physical shape," Richards said. "Whoever did that to Jodie Downs, they could haul weight."

"Loring is built," Malloy said.

"Also," Richards went on, "it may not mean anything—but Monserat is a very inhibited guy. He watches, he jacks off, that's it."

"Just comes and goes," Monteleone said.

The linoleum let out a screech as Siegel shoved her chair back. "Greg, anyone ever tell you you're disgusting?"

"My wife Gina, every night. And she loves it."

"Ellie," Cardozo said, "could you come with me a moment?"

Siegel went with him into his cubicle. He switched on the slide projector and went quickly through the preceding night's photos. Taxis and limousines and meat trucks flicked across the wall, and scurrying between them, like roaches fleeing the light, were men and women with maniacal dead eyes, phantoms plunging through a shadowy doorway into the age-old search for kicks and oblivion.

He stopped at the first photo of Claude Loring: it showed a beefy blond man in jeans and a two-day beard, licking a candy bar. There was a space at the curb, a view of trucks clogging the avenue. A van was parked across the avenue. On the side of it was a huge logo of a blue jay.

"That's Loring's van?"

Siegel nodded. "That's it."

Cardozo stared a moment at the blue jay, and then he called Richards.

"That van with the blue jay, Sam—where have we seen it?"

Richards's gaze came up at the image on the cubicle wall. A frown darkened his forehead. "The day we talked to Loring's alibi—the girl space cadet over in the flower district—that van was parked outside her place, at the hydrant."

"Right," Cardozo said. "Tennessee license. Didn't she get a phone call—her machine answered and she picked up?"

Richards had to think a moment. "Like she knew what the message was going to be and she didn't want us to hear."

"What was it she said about deliveries?"

"Someone was on her ass because she missed her weekend deliveries. She said her van was being repaired."

* * *

At first Cardozo was aware only of a sheet of silence. Then, faintly, through gray cinderblock walls, came the slamming and buzzing, the humming and thumping of an inhabited building.

He was standing in the garage of Beaux Arts Tower, the belly, listening to the digestion that kept the animal going.

His glance moved from shadows into the acid greenish pools of fluorescent light, sweeping Rollses, BMW's, a floor full of TV commercials sprung to three-dimensional life.

There were names stenciled in white on the wall by each parking space. In the space marked LAWRENCE, a handsome red Porsche sat.

Cardozo mentally erased the Porsche and put a yellow cab there, a cab with the words DING-DONG TRANSPORT on its side.

After a moment he walked past the garage door to the service elevator. He gazed up at the closed-circuit TV camera making scans of the garage. Mounted on the wall ten feet above the concrete floor, it panned slowly his way.

He stood in the empty loading bay till the camera lens had him head-on. He realized that if a truck were parked in that place the camera wouldn't pick up either side panel. Which was why a doorman watching the closed-circuit TV wouldn't have seen a truck with a blue jay painted on the side.

Cardozo had a sense of pressure behind his eyes and at the same time he felt light-headed, almost dizzy. He was finally beginning to see both sides of the coin.

He phoned Jerzy Bronski's garage and had them radio Jerzy. Twenty minutes later Jerzy was sitting on a bench on the esplanade in Carl Schurz Park, his face dark and still, drawn down on one side as though by the weight of the cigarette he was smoking.

"Thanks for waiting," Cardozo said.

"I almost didn't."

Cardozo sat on the bench. His eye went to a tugboat sliding past on the shining gray water of the East River. "Pretty place. You come here a lot?"

Jerzy's thin lips were set in a taut line. "I don't come anywhere a lot. I hold down two jobs and today I'm pulling two shifts at the wheel of that wreck they call a Chrysler. Already I lost twenty dollars sitting here on my tush."

"Look at it this way, Jerzy. Now you have friends at the precinct. It could come in handy."

"Maybe it'll pay my rent?"

"It might even pay your dealer."

Jerzy gave him a look. "You said I was home free on that."

"You are. But I need a little help."

"I already helped. And guess what, Debbi knows it was me that talked to you."

"She didn't learn it from me."

"Give me a break. Debbi's no Einstein, but she's no dumbo either."

Cardozo let that one sail right by. "Saturday, May twenty-fourth, the day the man was murdered in six and Debbi didn't get her coke. Why did you park in Fred Lawrence's space?"

"All right, maybe I parked in someone's place. It's a crime?"

"Why didn't you use the truck bay?"

"Must have been someone already parked in the bay."

"You remember who?"

Jerzy had to think a moment. "A van."

"Can you describe it?"

"A van's a van."

"Some are big. Some aren't. Some are red, some are green. Some are blue."

Something made Jerzy's eyelids twitch and he raised them. "It had a bird on it, a blue bird. I remember that bird."

"Was it a blue jay?"

"It was a bird that was blue, you tell me if that's a blue jay."

Cardozo showed Jerzy the print. "Is that the van?"

Tommy Daniels had done a good job enlarging the van, cropping the foreground.

Jerzy's lips shaped a thoughtful pout. "It's the same bird. Maybe it's the same van. How do you tell one beatup '78 Ford from another?"

"Did you notice anything about the license plates? Like were they out of state?"

Jerzy gave him a look. "Give me a break. Do I look like a traffic cop?"

"You said Claude Loring was crashing here the whole weekend and you missed your deliveries because your van broke down."

"That's right." Faye di Stasio was wearing an old T-shirt and a faded pair of jeans and Cardozo had a feeling she had thrown the clothes on two minutes ago when his buzz at the downstairs door had woken her.

Cardozo handed her the photograph. "Is this your van?"

She looked at the photograph, then stared with confused eyes back at him. "It could be."

"That blue jay is your company logo, isn't it?"

Her eyes were dark and nervous. She nodded.

"So what would it be doing on someone else's van? Aren't logos registered, like trademarks?"

"That's right, but—"

"So it's your van."

"I suppose."

"You recognize the street in that photo?"

"No."

"Did someone else park your van there?"

"I guess."

"Who do you loan your van to?"

"Claude."

"What does Claude borrow the van for?"

"To get around."

"Was he the one who wrecked it?"

"No one wrecked it."

"But you missed your deliveries Memorial Day weekend."

"The van broke down but it works now."

"What was wrong with it?"

"It wouldn't start. The brakes were slipping. You know, the usual van shit."

"Who repaired the van?"

"Some shop repaired it."

"What shop?"

"I don't know. Some shop Claude took it to."

"When did he do that?"

"The week before Memorial Day."

"And when did he bring the van back?"

"The week after."

"Can you show me the bill?"

"I don't know where the bill is."

"You do a lot of coke, don't you."

She blinked her eyes, held herself still. "Did I miss some kind of connecting link?"

"I said you do a lot of coke. Claude does a lot of coke too."

She leaned forward. Her smile took a long time to stretch out to him. "You're kidding," she said, and then, studying him, "Okay, you're not."

The silence was heavy. Light spilled across the floor: a cat strolled into it. She gave the animal a look as gray as driftwood. She went into a small room beyond the kitchen. She came back with a cigarette.

"You ever met Claude's dealer?" Cardozo asked.

She found an ashtray. "Claude has a private life, I don't butt in."

"He never told you about the doorman at Beaux Arts Tower—the guy that wears the rug?"

"I'm not feeling well and this conversation isn't helping."

"The doorman with the really bad rug sells Claude his coke. You never been to Beaux Arts Tower?"

"Why would I have been to Beaux Arts Tower?"

"I think you've been there." Cardozo crossed to the bathroom door and nudged it open. The odor of three-day-old cat litter drifted out. He flicked on the light and pointed to the tub. "I think you stole that shower curtain from them."

"I don't know where that shower curtain came from."

"It came from Beaux Arts Tower."

"I didn't steal it."

"Then how come it's here and not in apartment six where it belongs?"

"Claude gave it to me."

"You're saying Claude stole it."

"I didn't say that. I mean I don't know where it came from. So don't try to tie me in with someone else's petty larceny."

"Screw petty larceny. I'm talking homicide."

"I'm really not following this."

"You helped Claude. You loaned him your van and you let him crash here. And he gave you coke and that shower curtain and a little wine and booze and frozen dinners from the show suite, right?"

She just stood there looking at him. "That's not murder."

"No, it's not. But killing a guy is."

Suddenly her fingers weren't behaving. She dropped the cigarette. She bent and picked it up, leaving a fresh burn among a million old marks on the floor. She sank into a chair.

"You're an accomplice," Cardozo said.

"Knowing someone is not being an accomplice." She looked distant, isolated, sitting there, her skin pale, her face locked in gold-framed glasses with a faint raspberry tint to the lenses.

"You admit you know," he said.

"I admit I know him."

"The killer."

"Claude. I don't know anything about a killing."

"If you haven't figured out about the killing by now your brain's running slow. If he was innocent, why did he ask you to lie?"

She was having difficulty swallowing.

"Lying about where Claude was and where the truck was is aiding and abetting. That's a felony. Why do you want to help that schmuck?"

"He's a friend. I help my friends."

Cardozo had a feeling she meant there was nothing she wouldn't do not to be lonely.

"Maybe I should call a lawyer," she said.

"You can call a lawyer from jail or you can talk to me here, now, just the two of us."

"I don't know anything."

"I could bust you for coke. I'm carrying a warrant to search." He tapped the bulge of the .38 under his jacket.

"Why are you doing this to me?"

"Because of what he did to a guy."

"You don't know that."

"I'll tell you what I know. Your van was seen at Beaux Arts Tower Saturday May twenty-fourth. It was seen in the garage and it was seen on the security monitor and twenty people have identified that photo. That same day seven people saw Claude Loring in the building and one of them sold him a gram of coke and you snorted that coke. So don't tell me Claude Loring was sleeping his buzz off from Friday night till Tuesday morning. It's you against twenty-seven eyewitnesses."

"You have your witnesses, you don't need me."

"But you need me. If the D.A. brings charges on your first statement, you'll be buying coke in prison and not on the street."

She brought her head down slowly between her hands. She huddled as if she didn't want to exist.

He let her hurt for a long moment. "Tell the truth now," he said, "and we'll forget that first statement."

Her head came up and she gave him a pathetic, vacant stare. "I can only tell you what I know."

"That's good for a start."

Her fingers became still. Her face sagged, white as a flag of surrender. The silence was broken by the sound of the cat scratching violently in its litter box.

"Claude wasn't here till Saturday afternoon. He showed up around four."

Her eyes closed. She looked drained, waxen. She squeezed her lids shut to hold back tears.

Cardozo took down a brief statement longhand and had her sign it. The statement wasn't worth a fart legally, but psychologically it would be a powerful weapon in breaking down Loring.

"Do I have your permission to search the van?" he asked.

"Looks to me like he panicked," Cardozo said. "Hitting on Hector for coke so hard that Hector let him have the gram and screwed up Debbi's delivery. Hector wouldn't have done that unless Loring had been in a very bad way."

A shadow rippled across Lucinda MacGill's face. "So we're talking murder two."

"No, stick with murder one for a minute. Loring planned the killing. Afterward he tooted a few lines to pull himself together, started taking the body apart with an electric saw, freaked, went to his girlfriend's to crash."

Her look seemed to wonder at him. "Leaving the body half dismembered?"

"It was a holiday weekend, no one was going to be around, he turned the air conditioning on so the body wouldn't cook, what was the rush."

"You're conjecturing that he reasons this way."

"Coke can lead to some pretty off-the-wall thinking. And we don't know what other drugs he was doing."

"What other drugs do you think he was doing?"

"Does it matter? Drugs aren't a defense."

"Unfortunately, some judges and juries have accepted them as an absolute defense in gay murders."

Cardozo let out a long, slow exhalation. "I think he was using downside stuff. Smack, ludes, something that put him out for two days. So instead of getting the rest of the body into the garbage over the weekend, he was passed out for two days, and by then the body had been found. So he asked Di Stasio to alibi for him."

Lucinda MacGill studied the handwritten statement. A silence fell on the cubicle. There was only the sound of phones ringing outside in the squad room.

"Di Stasio's statement is enough to bring Loring in for questioning."

"I want to go into Di Stasio's van. Loring transported the victim to Beaux Arts Tower in it and it could hold evidence."

Lines of disapproval ran downward from the corners of Lucinda MacGill's mouth. "You can't get into it. Di Stasio was unrepresented by counsel when you questioned her."

"I'm not accusing her of murder."

"Anything she does to incriminate Loring incriminates her of shielding him. She's entitled to counsel and she didn't waive her Miranda rights. If Loring is in possession of the van when you search, and if he borrowed it in good faith, he has an expectation of privacy. Violating it makes the state's case tref."

There was a pause. She kept staring at him.

"You make my life tougher than it needs to be, Counselor."

"That's my job. Get a warrant, Lieutenant."

Cardozo lifted the phone receiver and pushed the digits of Judge Tom Levin's number. The call clicked through.

"Judge's chambers."

"Amy, it's Vince Cardozo. Where is he?"

"Right here."

A sudden jovial baritone came on the line. "Make it fast, Vince, I have a jury coming back in."

"I need a warrant to search a van."

"What do you expect to find?"

"If I'm lucky, evidence in a murder. Lucky or not, drugs."

"You got it. Tell Amy the details."

Cardozo told Amy the color, year, and make of the van, the number on the Tennessee plates, the name and address of the owner.

"I'll messenger the warrant to you right away."

"Amy, I want to marry you."

"That won't be necessary, sweetie."

28

THE BAR AT ARCHIBALD'S WAS FOUR-DEEP IN PEOPLE. BABE WAS
aware of heads turning as the maître d' wheeled her through the
crowd to the corner table.

Ash, in a froth of pale raspberry chiffon, was sitting with a half-
finished Manhattan. She was wearing pendant diamond earrings that
glowed like soft little lights beside her head.

"Hi, doll." She leaned to kiss Babe on the cheek. "How about some
champers?"

"What's the celebration?"

"I've reconciled with Dunk." Ash signaled the waiter. "André,
we'll have some Moët."

Babe opened her napkin—it was peach linen, matching the tablecloth and the walls—and looked around her. The atmosphere was
one of frenzied chatter, with women wearing gold at noon and
people waving and shouting from one table to another and everyone
squirming in their bentwood chairs to get a look at whoever was
coming in.

At a corner table, in an ugly web of cables laid across the floor, two
men in blue jeans and workshirts were aiming a portable searchlight
and a shoulder-carried minicam at a fat man and a garishly
overmadeup woman. The man and woman wore full evening dress; a
heavy diamond-and-gold necklace lay across the woman's half-ex-
posed bosom, and heavy emeralds dangled from her ears. A third
man in jeans was holding a microphone over the vichyssoise, catching their conversation.

"What in the world is that?" Babe asked.

"They're probably filming a segment of *Life-Styles of the Rich and Famous,*" Ash said.

"During lunch? Don't the customers object?"

"Object?" A bubble of laughter broke from Ash's throat. "Half the people here would kill to get on that show."

Babe was puzzled, and Ash seemed amused by the look on her face.

"This is what's in," Ash said, "so get used to it: Shrill Is Beautiful."

Ash explained that the maître d' seated all the right people in the front room; climbers and nonentities were put in the rear dining room, affectionately dubbed Managua by those who didn't have to sit there.

"Some have offered bribes of a thousand dollars to be seated in front. Over there by the pillar is the royal box. That's where Nancy sits when she's in town. And Jackie, and Liz."

The waiter brought champagne. A moment later he brought another Manhattan that Babe had not seen Ash order. Ash didn't seem to notice it wasn't the same drink she had just put down.

"To us."

Ash lifted her champagne glass to Babe's. They clinked.

They began laughing and talking about things, remembering things, wandering down familiar paths.

"Lasagna of shrimp, scallops, and spinach in saffron sauce?" Ash peeped at Babe over the top of her menu.

"I think cold poached salmon for me," Babe said.

Fifty-five minutes later a tall handsome woman stopped at their table. "Is everything satisfactory?" She had deep-set eyes and black curly hair that came to her shoulders.

Ash, poking dubiously at her shrimp, raised a glance at the newcomer and smiled. "Faith—look who I've brought you."

The woman stood there in her dove gray crepe de chine dress looking at Babe. Expression left her eyes and was replaced with guardedness.

"Babe," Ash said, "it's dear old Mrs. Banks."

For a moment Babe's breath stuck in her throat. She told herself it couldn't be: the woman was too poised, authority emanated from her like a perfume, Mrs. Banks would be in her sixties by now. But then she saw the faint erasures on the face, the surgical blankness around the eyes and chin and forehead. She realized this ice statue was her old friend and servant.

"Sit with us," Ash pleaded. "Do have a glass of champagne. This is auld lang syne."

Mrs. Banks gave just a nod of her head. The deep red ruby on her brooch was the size of an acorn. She pulled out a chair and sat and Ash poured an inch of champagne into a water glass and pushed it toward her.

"You're looking well, Mrs. Devens." The tone of Mrs. Banks's words fell in an emotional dead center, without a trace of remembering or affection.

"You have a lovely restaurant," Babe said.

"God's been good to me. So have the columnists. But then, that's what I pay a press agent for."

"Could we meet sometime?" Babe said. "Have tea and talk?"

Mrs. Banks fixed her with a stare. "I don't talk about the past."

"It's true," Ash said. "A publisher offered Faith a fortune to do the book on you and she turned him down."

"Enjoy your meals," Mrs. Banks said.

And without touching her champagne she had gone on to another table.

"Isn't it too divinely much?" Ash said. "Mousy old Mrs. Banks! Everyone calls her Faith now and she gets interviewed and invited everywhere."

Babe watched her former servant greeting patrons, moving through the tables in a pattern that was planned and intricate and swift. She was so caught up in the transformation of Mrs. Banks that she didn't pay attention to the relaxed, good-looking, vaguely aristocratic man who had approached the table. He tapped Ash on the shoulder.

Ash turned, saw him, and whooped. "Dobbsie, you devil, where have you been?"

She offered her face and he kissed her.

"I've been holding poor dear Jeannie Astor's hand. Her poodle died."

"Well, tell her not to overeat. She always stuffs when she's depressed. Dobbsie, this is Babe Vanderwalk. Whoops, Babe Devens. She knows all my secrets, so you can be as dreadful as you normally are."

Dobbsie's dark eyes met Babe's. "How do you do?"

Babe held out her hand. "How do you do?"

He took the hand lightly. "Gordon Dobbs. Better known as Dobbsie."

"Dobbsie and I go way back," Ash said. "It was love at first sight." She tapped an empty chair. "Sit," she commanded.

Dobbsie drew out the chair and sat, taking a moment to adjust the crease in his gray cotton slacks. He looked at Babe, his gaze interested and curious, and he smiled a half smile. She saw that his receding brown hair was going gray at the temples.

"Babe is my absolutely oldest chum in the world," Ash said.

"And the two of you were hellraisers at Miss Spence's," Dobbsie said, "smoking cigarettes in the back of study hall."

"You only know that because I told you," Ash said. "Tell him about the school uniforms we had to wear, Babe. Tell him."

"They were gray flannel skirts," Babe said. "With green woolen blazers."

"Not the skirts," Ash said, "tell Dobbsie about the socks."

"They were gray too," Babe said.

"Scottish wool from Abercrombie's," Ash said. "Our family chauffeurs took turns driving us to school together—and in the back seat of the limo we'd scrunch down—"

"And undress," Dobbsie said.

"And exchange left socks," Ash said. "And on laundry day my fräulein and Babe's mademoiselle went out of their respective *skulls* trying to solve the mystery of the socks that wouldn't pair off!"

"You two were quite the lost generation," Dobbsie said.

"Well, we were almost not confirmed," Ash said. "Really. We used my father's CBS passes to get into Elvis Presley on the Ed Sullivan show and we passed Elvis's autograph around confirmation class."

"And Reverend Endicott Lewes phoned our mothers," Babe said.

Ash imitated Lucia. " 'Where did you get *hold* of such a terrible thing?' "

"I don't see that Elvis was so terrible," Dobbsie said.

"At the time he was considered a threat to the morals of the republic." Ash giggled. "He was certainly a threat to mine."

"Come on, you were only twelve," Dobbsie said.

"I'd already had the curse."

"Excuse *me.*"

"Mr. Lewes didn't think we were ready to be confirmed into the Episcopal Church," Babe said.

"Our mothers were terrified we'd have to become Methodists," Ash said.

"You jest," Dobbsie said.

"Our fathers had a talk with the bishop," Ash said. "It cost an *entire* stained glass window in the Cathedral of Saint John the Divine to smooth the whole thing over."

"And for six months," Dobbsie said, "you both were punished by not being allowed to have dessert at Sunday supper at the Cosmopolitan Club."

"How did you know?" Ash cried.

"I have sources," Dobbsie said.

"Oh, I told you, I know I told you, you wrote it all down the way you're writing it all down now."

Babe observed Dobbsie's hand, half-hidden by the tablecloth, writing on a small notepad on his lap.

"Babe, tell Dobbsie about sneaking off to Arthur Murray's to learn the twist."

"We sneaked off to Arthur Murray's to—"

"And at my big sister Dina's coming-out, Lancelot and Doonie Farquharson were so impressed with our wild dancing that they took us to the penthouse suite and ordered up martinis from the King Cole Room. And when we got back to the party Lester Lanin was playing "Good Night, Ladies" and everyone was convinced we'd gone all the way with the Farquharson boys right there in the Saint Regis!"

"I should hope to hell you had," Dobbsie said.

Suddenly Ash seemed almost shy. "Oh, no one did that in those days. It was the fifties, after all."

"Come on, Dina's coming-out must have been in the sixties. Didn't you two flower children at least star in a few freakouts or one or two love-ins?"

"It was the *early* sixties," Babe said.

Ash, pink-faced and sparkling-eyed, was deep into her fourth glass of bubbly. "I was a virgin till I met Dunk, and Babe knew it."

"And you knew I was a virgin," Babe said.

Ash giggled again. "Till *you* met Dunk. No, we are not going into that, that is *too* sordid. And Dobbsie you will *not publish it*!" Ash reached under the table and grabbed Dobbsie's pad. She frowned at it. "Shorthand—how did you learn that?"

Dobbsie gracefully lifted his pad out of Ash's hand. "By studying."

"Why do you know shorthand?" Babe asked.

"It makes my work a little easier."

"Dobbsie writes books." Ash cupped her hands around her mouth and pretended to whisper. "He wrote the book that Mrs. Banks wouldn't. The book about your murder."

The silence was dense and extraordinary until Dobbsie burst into a comfortable basso rumble of laughter. "Ash didn't mean that the way it sounds."

"Oh yes I did. Dobbsie is the only man in town who doesn't call a spade a gardening implement. Murder it was and murder he called it. And Scottie didn't have the guts to sue."

Ash rose teeteringly from her seat.

"You two get to know one another. I have to go to the little girls'."

Dobbsie watched her weave through the tables. "What a sensational woman. I'm absolutely in love with Ash. Pity she's drinking so much."

"Ash has always liked to get tiddly at lunch."

"Tell me when she's *not* tiddly. The only gal who comes back for seconds at Communion. Poor kid, the reconciliation's just not going to work."

Babe had a premonition she was about to hear something that was going to make her feel disloyal to Ash.

"Ash ran away from Silver Hill three times." Dobbsie had lowered his voice. "She won't admit she has a problem. Dunk's really just enabling her. She's got to hit her own bottom and admit the booze has got her licked. But she's so chock-full of denial. Refuses to join the Fellowship."

Fellowship, Babe sensed, had a capital *F.*

"I'm a member." Dobbsie lifted his glass of Perrier and lime. "Not ashamed to admit it. Most sensible thing I ever did in my life. Haven't touched a drop in eleven years, grace of God."

"That's admirable," Babe said, feeling a compliment was desired. The minute she said it she had an odd sense that she had just turned a corner.

Very smoothly, Dobbsie leaned across the table until his face was only inches away from hers. "There's a terrific meeting at Saint Bart's. Yes, Saint Bart's, where you two almost flunked Confirmation. Liz and Lee and Liza and Mary are regulars. I've tried to get Ash to come with me, but she says she can't sit in a room with Bowery bums. As if it were a poor person's disease. Twixt thee and me, half the Social Register has the same problem and you'll find a hell of a lot of them in the Fellowship. The first step is, you've got to admit you're powerless over the sauce and *get spiritual.* I've been trying to twelfth-step Ash for six years."

"Ash can be contrary," Babe said.

"I hope you don't mind my being frank," he said. "About her problem."

"I think there are times when it's appropriate to be frank."

"Babe, you're terrific. Just the way Ash described you. Now Ash said you want to know about Scottie's trial."

"I want to know what happened after they closed the courtroom and sealed the record."

"I can give you a few facts and some gossip and some theories. Why don't we get together and talk about it at my place, so I don't have to lug my notes around town."

He gave her his card. She looked at the address.

"But that's the museum," she said, surprised.

"It's the museum plus Beaux Arts Tower. We're going through a little notoriety these days—had a murder over Memorial Day weekend."

Ash returned to the table. Her eyes were clear, bright, and calm, and she was walking a straight line. She settled smoothly into her chair. There was a curious smile on her face. She signaled the waiter for another bottle of Moët.

Dobbsie chatted about some Texans who were funding the Metropolitan Opera's new *Il Guarani* and who were hooked on cocaine, and then he saw a woman across the room and waved. "That's the Duchess de Chesney, used to be Anita Starr, showgirl slash schoolteacher slash porno star, now *there's* a story I want to get. Will you girls excuse me?"

"Have you got his book?" Babe asked as soon as she and Ash were alone.

"Dobbsie's book on you? It's divine, of course I have it."

"May I borrow it?"

29

THE LAMPLIGHT LAY STILL AND LIQUID ON THE BEDSHEETS. Propped on two pillows, Babe opened *Mortal Splendor: Inside the Babe Vanderwalk Devens Affair.*

She read slowly, carefully.

It is in the nature of beginnings, Dobbsie wrote in his prefatory note, *that they begin . . . somewhere. Every comedy, every tragedy, every act of life-giving or life-taking, has its beginning in some other event. The Freudian tells us it all began in the unconscious where forgotten childhood trauma festers. The Marxist tells us it all began in the class struggle that shapes the destiny of every human, be he capitalist drone or proletarian drudge. The Bible tells us, not unwisely, that it all began in the cataclysm of the Creation.*

Where then did the chain of events begin that climaxed in Babe Vanderwalk Devens's drug-induced coma?

In the needfulness of a six-year-old little princess who had every luxury but parental love? In the ambition of a Kentucky mountain boy who preferred martinis to beer, the music of George Gershwin to the twang of a guitar? In the grinding three-hundred-year poverty of Appalachia? In the Babylonian glitter of New York City that has dazzled and appalled the world ever since the Robber Barons burst upon the scene?

Maybe the Bible gives us the clue. Maybe it all began . . . in the beginning.

Babe frowned and turned the page. In the first chapter, "By Their Roots Shall Ye Know Them," Dobbsie examined bloodlines.

Through marriage licenses he had been able to trace Scott Devens's ancestry back through three impoverished Kentucky generations; he said that research further back had been made impossible by "a wall of illegitimacy."

Dobbsie then turned to Babe's family tree. He had unearthed the name Pieter Isaak Valk in the register of the Shearith Israel Synagogue of Amsterdam—a remarkable congregation where, almost seven decades earlier, the name Jan Jakob Astor had been similarly inscribed—*Jan,* of course, being the Dutch form of *John.* (The name *Valk,* Dobbsie explained, was related to the Dutch word for falcon, which also served as a slangy Lowlands pejorative for a sharp operator. *Imagine,* he said, *a young American called Peter Isaac Shark, and you have the picture.)* Pieter Isaak, the youngest son of a peddler, had been bar mitzvahed in 1830 and in 1833 had emigrated to New York on a ship of the Dutch West Indies Company. He went into the fur-trading business, hauling barrels of Dutch rum into the Indian reserves in upper New York State and Quebec; he bartered liquor for animal pelts, shrewdly extending credit to the tribes, and forged a monopoly.

In 1848 Valk, now a stock market millionaire calling himself Peter Isaac Vanderwalk, rescued the United States Treasury from bankruptcy, forming a consortium to buy up the largest bond issue ever floated by the federal government. From 1860 to 1864 he bankrolled Abraham Lincoln's Union government in its struggle against the Confederacy.

At age sixty-eight, Peter Isaac married Isabella Hadley, the twenty-three-year-old daughter of the president of the New York Stock Exchange. On the wedding day, Isabella's father, under grand jury indictment for embezzlement, was able to make good all discrepancies in the Exchange's books, effectively mooting the charge.

Because Vanderwalk so openly used his power, society considered him a robber baron and shut him out.

Dobbsie told a story dating from the 1880s, when the Astors and the Vanderbilts had sworn they would never say more than two words to any Vanderwalk.

Mrs. Astor and Mrs. Vanderbilt, competing for the position of absolute leader of New York society, had filled their mansions with quantities of European art and sculpture. But one prize eluded them: neither could persuade her husband to spend the half-million dollars which the Austrian chancellory was asking for its Rubens *Adoration.*

Isabella Vanderwalk determined to exploit the situation and make her long-delayed mark in society. At his wife's insistence,

Vanderwalk paid the Austrians a half million and hung the painting in his Fifth Avenue mansion.

Society faced a dilemma: how to view the Rubens without appearing to accept Vanderwalk's hospitality. Finally Mrs. Astor's friends decreed they were willing to visit the Vanderwalk mansion, but only between two and four in the afternoon, taking no food or refreshment. Mrs. Vanderbilt's friends decreed they were willing to visit between four and six, with the same condition.

Vanderwalk thereupon announced that he would give the Rubens to the Metropolitan Museum, with an endowment to keep admission free. However, he gave both the Vanderbilt and the Astor factions one last chance to see the painting privately: he invited them to dinner at his home the evening before the gift was to be made. (It was well known that Mrs. Vanderbilt and Mrs. Astor never entered the same private home or sat at the same table.)

After agonizing whether it was better to dine with one's enemies in the home of a robber baron or to rub shoulders with one's inferiors in the Metropolitan Museum, society opted for the more comfortable humiliation, dinner.

The etiquette of the time required that invitations had to be returned, and by accepting Vanderwalk's, New York society obligated themselves to invite him and his family into their homes.

There was, however, no obligation to *speak* to a Vanderwalk.

Mrs. Astor and Mrs. Vanderbilt both arrived at exactly 8:15. As they had sworn, they said only two words to Vanderwalk: "Good evening." They had arranged that any other messages would be communicated by their banker, Pierpont Morgan.

The ladies found the Rubens hanging in the grand salon, covered by a gold velvet curtain. Pierpont Morgan asked, "Do you not have something to show these ladies?" Vanderwalk answered in his Dutch accent, "Whatever the ladies like." The ladies said nothing. "Well, then," Vanderwalk said, "I will show them a fine dinner."

After the four-hour twelve-course seated banquet, Mrs. Astor and Mrs. Vanderbilt again stood before the curtained *Adoration,* and Pierpont Morgan again asked Vanderwalk, "Are you absolutely sure you do not have something to show these ladies?" Again Vanderwalk said in his Dutch accent, "Whatever the ladies like." The ladies still were silent. "Well, then," Vanderwalk said, "I will show them some fine dancing."

The guests repaired to the ballroom, where the New York Symphony played the latest waltzes and quadrilles. At two in the morning, when a light breakfast was served, Pierpont Morgan spoke in great anger to his host. "Sir, to put it plainly, have you not an *Adoration* by Peter Paul Rubens to show us before we go home?"

Vanderwalk looked astonished. "Indeed I had, but at midnight it became the property of the museum, and the workmen removed it."

"Why in God's name did you not uncover it?"

In his Dutch accent, Vanderwalk replied, "Out of consideration for Mrs. Vanderbilt and Mrs. Astor. They have criticized me, in society, for displaying my possessions."

"Mrs. Astor and Mrs. Vanderbilt would not have criticized you tonight."

"Bless me, but I am buffaloed. The ladies had only to say the word."

Over the next two years, Vanderwalk's five hundred guests dutifully invited him and his Mrs. to five hundred dinners; at none of the gatherings was one word beyond "Good evening" addressed to either of them.

Till his death, Vanderwalk remained an unregenerate embarrassment, speaking English with a thick accent, cheating at cards, dining with dirty hands and dripping food on himself, calling for Dutch rum with his meals, even though fashion insisted on French wine. Old Vanderwalk even went so far as to tell bawdy stories in mixed company that included the wife of President McKinley; for this he was roundly scolded in his *New York Times* obituary.

With the expansion of wealth and the slackening of moral codes that resulted toward the end of the 1890s, the entry requirements for New York society shifted. It was enough to have money and not to have been convicted of a crime. The New York that had shut Vanderwalk out welcomed his young wife, his son, and his dollars.

Vanderwalk's son, Hadley Vanderwalk, Sr., attended Princeton University, married a Rockefeller, produced three sons, built a telephone and telegraph monopoly, served in World War I and in the kitchen cabinet of three presidents, never drank or smoked, financed Lend Lease, and spent a lifetime living down his father's reputation.

But perhaps Hadley Vanderwalk, Sr.'s most fateful act, Dobbsie wrote, *was to bequeath to his youngest granddaughter—Beatrice Wilmerding Vanderwalk—half of all the aluminum in the United States—making her, at age three, one of the ten richest women in America.*

As Babe read on, she felt she was seeing herself in a fun-house mirror. The person that Dobbsie called Babe bore only a distant, distorted resemblance to the self she remembered and knew.

As a five-year-old, Dobbsie reported, Babe had been photographed by Cartier-Bresson, playing with her two hundred dolls, her thirty-two doll houses, and her two thousand doll gowns; the photographs had appeared in *Vogue*.

At eight, Babe was given her first pony; at ten, her first Arabian mare. Photographs appeared in *Town and Country*.

At twelve, Babe was given her first yacht, the sloop *Cygnet*. Each summer, for the four weeks that the family lived at Hampton Court, their fifty-two-room summer "cottage" in Newport, she had at her disposal her own captain and two-man crew. At sixteen, old enough for a New York State driver's learning permit, she was given her first Mercedes-Benz. The car had a refrigerated glove compartment.

Babe had her coming-out at Hampton Court. Hadley Vanderwalk, Jr., spent one and a half million dollars providing three orchestras, a quarter-mile-long buffet, and a dozen bars for his daughter's twelve hundred guests. Babe wore a seven-thousand-dollar gown designed for her by Yves Saint Laurent; she was featured on the cover of *Life* magazine curtsying to the duchess of Windsor, and news cameras of the three networks covered the event.

It was not surprising, Dobbsie said, that Babe—an only child—grew into a rebel. For homes she had had the old Flagler mansion off Fifth Avenue; the Newport "cottage"; the house in Palm Beach, scene of the family's Christmas celebrations; the winter chalet in the Swiss Alps and the summer "chateau" on the French Riviera. As an infant she had played in sandboxes with Rockefellers and Vanderbilts. Educated at America's finest institutions—Spence, Farmington, Vassar—she had broadened her circle to include the children of board chairmen of AT&T, ITT, IBM, United Fruit, TWA. Never separated from those patrician playmates for longer than a summer vacation, she took privilege for granted—above all the privilege of flouting the very conventions that legitimized her own wealth and status.

At nineteen she defied her parents and plunged into a scandalous marriage to internationally renowned concert pianist Ernst Koenig, a thrice-divorced man thirty-eight years her senior. Vassar expelled her.

Dobbsie felt that this first marriage was more than an adolescent acting-out: it was a cry for help, an ominous signal that Babe Vanderwalk wanted in marriage what she had missed in childhood—nurture by loving, as opposed to paid, hands. In Koenig, she had tried to turn a father figure into a husband. Her alchemy had failed, and the solution, she must have decided, was to reverse the transformation. With one failed marriage securely under her belt, she packed her eight-year-old daughter into a Swiss boarding school and set out to find a husband she could turn into a father.

Scottie Devens, Jr., a new chapter began, *is the kind of man women can't resist: good-looking, polished, not doing everything he could with his gifts—a perfect candidate for rescue.*

Dobbsie chronicled Scott Devens's troubled childhood as the son of a Kentucky dirt farmer, his rowdy high school education, his early involvement with "Cuban elements" in Miami. This part of the book was full of quotes from unidentified sources: "Scottie Devens's closest chums," "a former sweetheart who wishes to remain anonymous," "the mother of his aborted child," "a Rumanian diplomat and drug courier"; "there are even those who swear . . ."

Like two oppositely charged particles in a cyclotron, it was inevitable—according to Dobbsie—that sooner or later Babe Vanderwalk and Scott Devens would collide.

The *Paris Review* was holding a Vietnam peace rally–fund-raiser at P. J. Clarke's, a perpetually trendy bar on New York's Third Avenue. Babe, doing her bit, was passing drinks. Scottie, doing his, was playing cocktail piano.

The room was overcrowded. Reports vary as to who pushed whom —*some say that Jackie Kennedy stumbled against Mrs. Leonard Bernstein, others swear that Truman Capote gave Mrs. William Paley what he intended to be a joking shove.*

In the ensuing thirty-second domino effect, drinks were spilled, dresses were ruined, friendships were suspended, and love began: Babe Vanderwalk was shoved onto Scottie Devens's keyboard. Never missing a beat, he continued playing "I've Got a Crush on You"—on Babe's abdomen.

Pieter Isaac Valk, the little Jewish boy from Amsterdam, had not been able to earn social acceptance in a lifetime of unremitting work; Scottie Devens, the hard-drinking ivory-tickling WASP from blue grass country, had it handed to him in five seconds.

Three weeks after that meeting, Babe married Scottie, and together they embarked on the lives of jet set royalty. Within a year Babe discovered she had a gift for designing clothes, and Scottie discovered he had a yen for Doria Forbes-Steinman.

This part of the book was full of things anyone could have known: who owned what, who made how much, who worked where, who knew whom, who lived with whom. It was also full of things Gordon Dobbs had obviously invented: descriptions of people's houses that were quite simply inaccurate, the underwear people wore, the way they smiled and the way they kissed, the exact things they said to one another during chance encounters at huge parties.

Scottie's romance with Doria, Dobbsie claimed, became serious five and a half years before Babe's coma. He described excursions the lovers had made to Paris, Antigua, Acapulco, quoting various unnamed socialite gossips, bellboys, doormen, private investigators.

Dobbsie then described the "crime" and the trial, summarizing the prosecution's case in detail.

Cordelia Koenig, Babe's daughter by her first marriage, was awakened at three in the morning by strange sounds emanating from the bedroom shared by her mother and stepfather. Peeking into the hallway, she saw Scott Devens tiptoeing from the bedroom into his dressing room. He was carrying a syringe.

When Babe Devens failed to awaken the next morning, an ambulance was dispatched from Doctors Hospital.

Babe was admitted to the hospital, comatose, with an abnormally high level of insulin in her blood. Emergency room personnel administered one massive glucose injection at 9:00 A.M. and a second at 10:12 A.M. Babe failed to respond.

A little after noon that same day, Cordelia confided to the maidservant, Faith Stoddard Banks, what she had seen the night before.

Mrs. Banks searched the closet of Scott Devens's dressing room and found a tan alligator carrying case. Within this case she discovered a syringe.

Mrs. Banks phoned Babe Devens's mother, Lucia Vanderwalk, who phoned her lawyer, William Frothingham. In turn, Frothingham phoned Harrison Jonik, a former New York City detective with thirty years' experience who had gone into private practice.

Jonik conducted his own search of the closet and discovered that the tan alligator carrying case contained not only a syringe but three bottles of insulin and one of liquid Valium.

The bottles and syringe were turned over to ChemLab of Union City, New Jersey. Encrusted solution was found around the needle. The solution was shown to contain Valium, ammobarbital, insulin, and salinated water.

Dr. Wallace Walker, a prosecution witness and chairman of the Department of Endocrinology and Diabetic Research at Southern Queens Hospital, testified that Babe Devens's coma was the result of a "massive injection of insulin." He based his findings on Babe's blood sugar and insulin levels. Under normal circumstances a patient receiving two such massive glucose injections over a period of seventy-two minutes would show a rising blood sugar level. But Babe's blood sugar level had failed to rebound, a clear indication that she had been injected with a toxic quantity of insulin.

Dobbsie's account of Scottie's defense was little more than a summary of unrelated and unsavory cases that Scottie's lawyer, Ted Morgenstern, had defended. Dobbsie detailed Morgenstern's ongoing skirmish with the IRS and the New York Bar Association's repeated attempts to disbar him. There were two pages quoting Morgenstern's denial of rumors that he was a homosexual and had had four face-lifts.

Dobbsie described the six days of jury deliberation that led to the guilty verdict. He cited rumors that Charles ("Chassie") Rockefeller, a drinking and polo buddy, had not only posted Scottie's bail but had ponied up a million dollars to retain the dean of Columbia Law for advice in masterminding Scottie's appeal. He quoted Scottie's statement that he still loved Babe more than any other woman on earth, and were she to regain consciousness tomorrow, he would be back in Sutton Place, with Doria's blessing, at the side of his lawful wife.

Dobbsie next quoted from a magazine article by the well-known hostess and social commentator, Dina Alstetter:

Two days ago, when I was visiting the stately Sutton Place town house where Babe Devens sank into her final sleep, Babe's thirteen-year-old daughter, the remarkably poised Cordelia Koenig, asked me if I'd like to accompany her and her grandmother to see "Mommy's room." I followed them into a bedchamber done in marvelous Billy Baldwin earth tones, with a Renoir flower painting *(Les Trois Roses)* supplying contrasting accents of green and yellow.

There on the dresser were Babe's silver-backed brush, comb, and handmirror—heirlooms that belonged to her maternal great-grandmother, the beloved philanthropist and cofounder of Saint Vincent's Hospital, Yvelise Wilmerding of New York's original Four Hundred.

On Scottie's side of the double bed was a silver-framed photograph of a teenaged Babe Vanderwalk at a Waldorf Democratic Party fund-raiser, dancing an uninhibited Charleston with then-President of the United States Lyndon Baines Johnson. Beside the photo was a small, strikingly handsome lacquer box, designed by Erté, intended to hold shirt studs and cufflinks. I opened the box. Inside was a matchbook from the Colony, with the phone number of "Jeanne" scrawled within the cover, and an unused bottle of injectable insulin—manufacturer S. Merck, lot number R-4756-18.

Dobbsie pointed to the poetic justice in the fact that *these ill-matched twain—the "shucks-ma'am" boy from Kentucky and the bejeweled, dumpy siren from Marshal Tito's workers' paradise—are bound together, forever, by the secret which was no secret at all—except to that stone lady wearing the blindfold.*

For that bond, say many who know both these upwardly driven social overachievers, has already turned into a hard-drinking, hard-cursing, fist-fighting shackle. "I wouldn't invite them anywhere," says one prominent Manhattan hostess. "Not because of the murder —I couldn't care less—but because of the filth they scream at one another in public."

Arthur Schlesinger, Jr., won't sit down at the same table with them. Neither will Brooke Astor.

And don't mention their names to actresses Celeste Holm or Dina Merrill.

Dobbsie found some consolation in the fact that, *whether or not justice will ultimately be done in the courts of man-made law, justice has been achieved in a more poetic sense: Scottie and Doria have been sentenced to lifelong doses of one another.* "It's a far more horrible punishment than the crime," says a Coty-award winning designer, "especially for him."

On the final page of the book, in a somber concluding note, Dobbsie said he had begun his research convinced of Devens's innocence, but an exhaustive analysis of the record and thirty thousand pages of interviews had forced him to change his mind.

The real mystery, he said, was not who had injected Babe Devens, but how any sane man or woman could question the considered verdict of twelve impartial jurors. *How much longer,* he concluded, *will society ignore the drumbeat of reason and step to the danse macabre of money?*

Babe closed the book.

Dobbsie's cunning interweaving of fact and conjecture astonished her. The man was a shrewd and ruthless master of implication. If the book had been commissioned by the prosecution, it could not have been more effectively calculated to damn Scottie Devens.

Babe telephoned Ash. The machine answered and beeped.

"Ash, it's Babe. Are you sleeping?"

"Not now I'm not." Ash's voice sounded as though she had just crawled out from under a half-dozen Nembutals. "Hi, doll. What time is it?"

"It's early, I'm sorry. I've just read Dobbsie's book."

"Don't you love it? Champagne truffles all the way."

"I think it's horrible."

"Then you must still be in love with that bastard Scottie."

"Maybe, but I doubt it. I didn't know your sister wrote magazine articles."

"And books. Dina's been an oral journalist for four years. She tape-records people and her secretary types up the tapes. She interviewed Pope John Paul for *Sewanee Review;* it's been anthologized to hell and back. And she did a *great* book on Sid Vicious for S and S. She had help on that, Dobbsie edited it a little."

"She certainly did a job on Scottie. I suppose she had help on that too."

"She was just trying to be obliging."

"Who was she obliging?"

"Your family. They wanted the insulin in the lacquer stud box brought out and none of the papers were touching it."

"But Ash, there was no insulin in the lacquer stud box."

"How do you know? You weren't exactly *there.*"

"Because there wasn't any lacquer stud box. Scottie used a little ceramic bowl to hold his cufflinks and studs."

30

CARDOZO NUDGED RICHARDS AND NODDED OVER THE HEADS OF the crowd. "Here he comes. Old Faithful."

The tall, thickset blond man moved down the stairs with a drunken cockiness, an almost falling-down swagger. He had an enormous smile on.

It was close to three in the morning and Cardozo and Richards had been waiting for him almost two hours.

Loring stood a moment in the confusion of the vestibule, rocking back and forth as though physically colliding with the amplified waves of music.

"Tripping on the moon," Richards observed.

Loring stumbled out of his clothes. Pushing an armload of denim in front of him, he jostled into the clothescheck line.

The clothescheck man flipped Loring's jeans and T-shirt and jacket over a hanger and slid Loring a numbered chit. Loring stuffed the chit into his right tube sock and slid a dollar back across the counter. Cardozo made careful note which end of which rack the hanger went onto.

The clothescheck man cheated a look at Cardozo.

Unencumbered now, Loring narrowed his eyes and scoped the scene. The main room was mucky, rutted, steaming like a basin in a public pissoir. Shadowy figures grouped and regrouped with the urgency of viruses stalking vulnerable cells. Loring zigzagged into the party area, helping himself to every available wall and pillar.

"Stick with him," Cardozo told Richards. "Don't let him leave."

Richards went after Loring.

The clothescheck man watched Cardozo with a bemused look,

studying him. Cardozo let his face open into a warm, wide grin. He crossed to the counter.

"Hi." The clothescheck man's eyes were cheerful and his mouth had a tough, defiant twist. "You alone?"

"Not now," Cardozo said. "My name's Vince."

The clothescheck man leaned against the counter and looked at him. "Arnold."

Cardozo accepted a bone-crushing macho handshake.

A smile slopped down Arnold's face. "You're new?"

"Just heard about the place."

"Who told you about it?"

"You just checked his clothes."

"Claude?"

"You know him?"

"Everyone knows Claude. He's wild."

"You ever partied with him?"

"Hell no. He likes kids."

"You don't?"

"I'm into grown-ups." Arnold's eyes were probing. "You?"

Cardozo shrugged. "A little of everything."

"I got some nose whiskey, premium blow."

Cardozo grinned. "Why not?"

Arnold called, "Hey Herb, cover for me!" He opened a door, and a bright wedge of light fell across the clothes racks. He motioned Cardozo into the rear room.

A naked overhead bulb spotlighted a clutter of mops and crates and empty bottles. The brick walls were covered with decomposing movie posters. The air smelled of mildew.

Arnold placed a pocket mirror on a ledge. He took a vial out of his hip pocket and tapped a spill of white powder onto the mirror.

He offered Cardozo a tiny pink-striped cocktail straw.

"You'd better put that coke away before you make some cockroach very happy." Cardozo pulled his shield out of his sock. "I'm a cop."

The word caught Arnold like a shot. "Shit."

"Relax, I'm not busting you." Cardozo reached into his wallet between charge cards and lifted out a scissored-down photo of Jodie Downs. "Know him?"

Arnold's forehead wrinkled. He took the photo and held it nearer the light bulb. "I remember him. Snooty kid. Used to come here every night. Haven't seen him in a few weeks."

"Did you ever see him with Claude?"

"Maybe once. Yeah, once. Sure. The last time he was here they left together."

"What night?"

"The night the sound system blew. That makes it—Friday. Memorial Day weekend."

Cardozo hurried up into the light drizzle. In his pocket he had the key ring from Claude Loring's jeans. The asphalt had the gleam of sweating skin, and the lights of slow-moving limousines reflected in it like dropped torches.

The glow of a streetlight caught the tail of the Ford van parked across the avenue.

Cardozo threaded his way through traffic. Tommy Daniels was waiting for him in a niche in the wall.

There were seven keys on Loring's key ring. The first four didn't fit the van door and the fifth did.

Cardozo swung the door open. Daniels clambered up behind him into the van.

Cardozo held the flashlight and Daniels took the pictures, snapping the dashboard, the glove compartment, the seat, the floor of the cab.

"Get a good shot of these." Cardozo played the flashlight beam across two dark baseball-sized stains on the carpeting on the passenger side.

After Daniels had photographed the stains Cardozo took a penknife and began cutting the carpet away from the floor.

"Hey, Vince. Paydirt." Daniels was holding a piece of rag. "This was under the seat." He shook his head, turning the cloth in his hands. "Underpants."

Cardozo grabbed the shorts. He felt something jump in his gut. They were stained with grease and with something else that had caked and was beginning to flake, and the India ink initials on the waistband were J.D.

"The bloodstains are all type O, same as Downs," Lou Stein said two mornings later. "I recovered residual skin and urine from the fabric, chromosomes match. Downs used a lousy Laundromat. Sad for him, nice for us."

"Thanks, Lou. Sorry to be throwing all this overtime at you."

"I can use the extra income. The county reassessed my house."

Cardozo broke the phone connection and punched another number. Judge Levin answered on the third ring.

"Tom, I need two arrest warrants."

The hacksaw mimicked the screams of a skewered hamster. Claude Loring was lying on his back in the kitchen of apartment 11, cutting through a drainpipe. He was wearing a Levi's shirt with the arms scissored off, and sinew tensed darkly under the tanned skin of his forearms.

"Claude." Richards nudged a foot against Claude's workboot.

Loring's head came out from the cabinet under the sink. Wariness flickered over his features as he lifted off his Walkman earphones.

"Want to talk to you," Richards said. "Down at the precinct."

"I'm working," Loring said.

"So am I. We have a warrant, Claude." Richards turned slightly, nodding toward Ellie Siegel. "Claude, Detective Siegel; Ellie, Claude."

The flat of Loring's thumb ran back and forth over the edge of the saw. He heaved himself to his feet. He gathered up his Walkman and pushed a button, extinguishing the tiny voice of the soprano chirping from the earphones. "Let me wash."

"Better help him wash," Siegel suggested to Richards.

A woman came into the kitchen and shot the officers a look that was outraged and ice-cold. "Hey, the duke and duchess of Argyll and Diana Vreeland are coming to dinner—what about my sink?"

Cardozo borrowed a chair from the squad room and placed it against the cubicle wall, facing the desk. He fooled with the angle of the drafting lamp, swinging it up and down till it cast a glow that struck him as right.

"Close the window," he told Richards. "We don't want the air to smell too good."

"Believe me, Vince, you got no worries."

Cardozo took the evidence bag containing the black leather mask and placed it in the top desk drawer.

He surveyed the cubicle and nodded.

Richards went out and brought Loring in.

Loring looked uneasily around the cluttered little space of the cubicle.

"Have a seat, Claude." Cardozo indicated the straight-backed wood chair against the wall.

Loring sat. There was a tightening of muscle in his face.

"Have a smoke." Cardozo pushed the ashtray across the desk.

Loring fumbled a pack of Camels from his shirt pocket. He hung a cigarette inside his upper lip. Before he could light it Richards held out a flaming Bic. Loring bent into the light, inhaled, pulled back.

Cardozo started quietly. "How well did you know Jodie Downs?"

There was a blank on Loring's face. Cardozo had seen a lot of blank faces in the line of questioning, and this was a very familiar sort of blank. It was a holding where a reaction should have been.

"I didn't know him." Loring's eyes locked with Cardozo's.

"Ever hear the name?" Cardozo asked.

"No."

"You sure?" Richards asked gently.

Loring threw him a nervous little smile that wasn't a smile, but it was a chance to get his eyes away from Cardozo's. "Yeah, pretty sure."

At that moment Richards became the good guy.

There was a good cop and a bad cop in every interrogation; the suspect always did the casting. These first few moments of sitting, looking around, always showed who he felt less threatened by. In a long interrogation cops might flip roles as a strategy to confuse the suspect and wear him down, but they always started by taking the parts he assigned.

"Ever see this face?" Cardozo handed Loring a photograph.

Loring looked at it. "I don't know. Maybe."

"That's Jodie Downs," Cardozo said. "He was gay. You're gay, aren't you, Claude?"

Loring's eyes were scooting around in a nest of unsmiling smile lines. "Doesn't mean I knew him."

"What kind of sex do you like to have?"

"Same as a lot of people."

"Rough sex?" Cardozo asked.

There was a blaze of silence.

"You go to some pretty rough places," Cardozo said.

"What's rough?"

"The Inferno."

"Yeah, I've been to the Inferno."

"Jodie Downs was in the Inferno the night before he showed up dead in apartment six. So were you."

Loring swallowed.

Richards stood before Loring and smiled at him. "Coffee?"

Loring nodded.

"Milk and sugar?"

"Thanks."

Richards brought back coffees for everyone.

Cardozo stirred his coffee. "Claude, where were you Memorial Day weekend?"

"It's in the report," Richards said. "Claude was crashing at a friend's."

"Who was this friend, Claude?"

"It's in the report, Vince. Her name's Faye di Stasio."

"You were there all weekend, Claude?"

"Yeah." Loring's voice had shrunk.

"Can you prove that?"

"Read the report, Vince. She backs Claude up."

Cardozo shifted folders. "Jerzy Bronski's interrogation says something else. It says that at two P.M. on Saturday, May twenty-fourth, Claude's van was in the garage of Beaux Arts Tower."

"I don't have a van."

"You have Faye di Stasio's van." Cardozo leaned back in his chair and looked at him. "Claude, why did you lie to us and say you spent the weekend at Faye's?"

"It wasn't a lie."

"Then it was your ghost that bought a gram of coke from Hector Dominguez?"

Loring's shoulders stiffened.

"Don't fuck with me, Loring!" Cardozo shouted. "I didn't bring you here to get jerked off!"

"Vince," Richards said, "take it easy. Please."

"I *am* taking it easy!" Cardozo opened the desk drawer and slammed the evidence bag down onto the blotter. "Where'd you get this, Loring?"

Loring stared blinking at the black leather mask. His voice was tight. "I gotta crap."

"First you gotta give me some answers."

"You let me go crap or you're going to have one smelly office, Officer."

"The name's Lieutenant and you can shit in your yarmulke for all I care."

"Vince, let him crap. He's going in his pants already."

"All right, crap. Go with him, Sam."

*   *   *

Richards and Loring were back in six minutes.

Cardozo pretended not to notice Loring's uneven breathing, the first sign of panic. "You might as well tell us about Hector, Claude. He's told us all about you."

Claude's eyes went to the mask on the desk and then scooted away. "Okay, I buy coke from Hector."

"You bought coke that Saturday."

"I was strung out, I needed some."

"When were you in the building?"

"Two o'clock."

"I need the exact time, Claude. When did you drive your van into the garage and when did you drive it out?"

"I got there at quarter of two and I left at quarter after."

Cardozo sat forward and gripped Loring's face in his hands with barely contained fury. "Jerzy saw your van in the garage before noon."

Loring threw Cardozo's hand off. "Don't you fuckin' touch me, cop!"

"Then don't you keep me hanging by my dick! Tell me the truth!"

Loring began to break. "Look, I was freaked, maybe I wasn't certain of the time . . ."

Richards took over, his voice gentle. "What freaked you?"

Claude's teeth left dents in his lower lip. "I had a fight with my roommate. He threw me out, threw my records and tapes on the street."

"Why'd he do a shitty thing like that?"

"The bastard met someone else."

Cardozo cut in. "How'd you feel about that, Claude—angry? Angry enough to get coked up and kill the first kid you could drag out of the Inferno?"

"I wasn't anywhere near the Inferno that weekend, I was crashing at Faye's! I was out for half an hour scoring coke!"

"Claude," Richards said, "we know it was more than half an hour."

"Okay, maybe a couple of hours."

"That's not what your friend Faye says." Cardozo handed Loring the handwritten statement he had taken from Faye di Stasio.

For a long, long moment Loring stared at the page, not breathing, nothing moving but his bloodshot eyes.

"I have to sit here and take this shit?" he screamed. The sheet was fluttering wildly in his hand.

Cardozo lifted the phone. "Send her in."

A moment later Faye di Stasio stood in the doorway. Behind her dark glasses and the disheveled jeans and T-shirt she wore like camouflage, she seemed scared and vulnerable.

"I told them the truth, Claude." There was a desperate apologetic plea in her face. "They know."

Claude dropped his head into his hands.

"Claude," Cardozo said, "the clothescheck saw you leave the Inferno with Jodie Downs the night before the murder."

Claude hugged his arms across his chest.

Richards crouched down, facing Loring knee to knee. He put a gentle hand on Loring's shoulder. "There's nothing to be afraid of, Claude." Richards gently lifted Loring's head up from his crossed arms. "Whatever's bothering you, you can tell us. Let go of it, Claude. We're here to help you."

Something was happening to the play of moods across Loring's face. The fear and hostility had left his eyes and were replaced by a dreamy wondering. Suddenly his face fogged in and he slumped violently forward.

Cardozo shot to his feet. "What happened in the john?"

"He crapped is what happened," Richards said.

Cardozo grabbed Loring's left arm. His eye ran along the road map of veins. "You let him shoot up!"

"He didn't shoot up!"

"Then he swallowed something!"

Faye started to speak, hesitated, bit her lip. "He carries ludes," she said.

Blind rage flooded Cardozo. "Claude!" he shouted. "How many did you swallow?"

An asbestos curtain had dropped around Loring. Nothing was getting in or out.

Cardozo lashed out with his open palm, slamming the wall half an inch from Loring's face.

Loring's eyes flicked open. They slid toward Cardozo.

"Get a tape recorder," Cardozo shouted.

Richards brought a tape recorder from the squad room. Cardozo pressed the start switch.

"This is Lieutenant Vincent Cardozo interrogating suspect Claude Loring. Claude, before making any statement you have a right to consult an attorney. If you can't afford an attorney, we will provide one. Do you wish an attorney?"

Loring stared at him with the unblinking eye of a potato.

The telephone jangled. Richards was nearest. "Yeah?" He covered the receiver. "Vince, it's his lawyer."

Cardozo took the receiver. "Vince Cardozo."

"My client is to make no statements," Ted Morgenstern said.

31

"LIFT! COME ON, YOU CAN DO BETTER THAN THAT!" WITH A PROD that was not all that gentle, the therapist encouraged Babe to perform the leg movement.

Just as she managed to extend her knee, her leg went off to the side. She stared at the defiant limb, helpless and puzzled. Her vision began blearing at the edges.

"Keep going." The therapist was smiling, but he smiled only with his lips. His eyes were carefully assessing. "Come on. You nearly did it."

Blinking away tears of frustration, Babe brought the leg up again, awkwardly, hardly breathing and just a bit afraid. This time, to her amazement, she was able to complete the movement.

Just as an exhalation of relief escaped her, Mrs. Wheelock knocked on the door and said that the man from Viewerworld was here.

Babe glanced toward the therapist.

"That's enough for today," he said. He unhooked the weight from her ankle. "We don't want your ball-and-socket joints to go on strike."

"Mrs. Wheelock, show the man where it goes," Babe said. "I'll be right there."

Babe transferred herself into the chair. The therapist stood watching, not moving, not speaking, not completely masking a mild disapproval in his expression. She had told him not to help her even if she begged.

She wheeled across the room. The therapist, holding the door, suddenly blushed. He had forgotten his agreement: he had helped.

"Sorry."

She smiled. "See you next time. Thanks for not being easy on me."

In the bathroom Babe stretched to turn on the shower and adjust the water temperature. She reached her right arm and grabbed one of the eight handles temporarily bolted into the stall. She pulled herself halfway up and reached the left arm to another handle.

Once she was standing, it was a fairly uncomplicated maneuver to lower herself onto the aluminum stool that had been bolted to the floor. She used one hand to steady herself and the other to soap with. The tingling spray gradually washed the bone-soaking numbness of her joints.

She allowed herself three minutes in the shower. Then, groping along handles installed in the walls, she centered herself on a foam-cushioned stool. As she dried herself, she glimpsed herself in the mirror, forehead and mouth taut with effort.

Once dry, she wheeled herself into the dressing room. To give herself tangible goals, she had placed crutches against the wall. She stared at them now. Though it was hard to believe it at the moment, one day she would graduate to them. Next to the crutches she had placed a malacca cane and next to that a pair of Ferragamo half-inch heels.

It took her nine maddening minutes to dress.

By the time she wheeled into the guest room on the floor above, the workman had uncrated the viewer and placed it near an electrical outlet.

He looked around at her. "Do you have any film we can try?"

Babe had converted this room into her special library, and it was here that she planned to learn her way back to the present. Seven years of back issues of *U.S. News and World Report* occupied a half wall of shelves, *Vogue* and *Harper's Bazaar* and *W* another. *The New York Times* on microfilm took up two entire bookcases that had had to be placed free-standing, like library stacks.

Babe handed the man a microfilm box.

He threaded a roll of film into the machine and demonstrated on-off, focus, and forward and reverse. Babe carefully absorbed the instructions.

When the workman had gone, she closed the door. After three minutes' search she found the box of microfilm she wanted.

She switched the viewer on. The cooling fan hummed faintly and a cold milky light fell onto the angled screen. She carefully threaded her tape in and fitted the sprockets to the guidewheels.

Behind her the wall of the old house creaked.

Turning the knob carefully, she scrolled to the report in *The New York Times,* seven years ago, on the fashion page, of her party at the Casino in the Park.

Babe stretched a hand up from her wheelchair and pushed Gordon Dobbs's buzzer.

A manservant admitted her.

Gordon Dobbs was sitting in the livingroom at an old cherrywood table that served as a desk. A telephone receiver was cradled between his shoulder and his ear and he was scribbling furiously on a pad. He was wearing a jade silk robe over his slacks and shirt, and he turned to acknowledge Babe with a cheery wave.

He silently mouthed the words *just a minute* and pointed to the receiver, indicating that he was trapped with an intolerable bore.

Babe wheeled into the room. Her eyes took in the framed pictures on the wall. Gray birch logs waited for winter in a fieldstone fireplace flanked by neatly loaded bookshelves.

"Aha—exactly on time," Dobbsie said, hanging up the phone. "And in that contraption. How do you manage?"

"I hired a car and driver."

"The only way to do things nowadays. Would you like an armchair?"

"Thanks, but I'm comfortable."

"Coffee?"

"Please. With lots of sugar and cream."

Dobbsie rang a small enameled bell and told the manservant to fetch two coffees.

Babe had noticed that over a third of the books in the shelves were English and foreign-language editions of Dobbsie's books. "I see you're very successful with your readers," she said.

"Yes indeed. Folks in Kansas and Osaka can't get enough of the private lives of society's public people."

"Tell me something: do you honestly believe Scottie did it?"

Gordon Dobbs lit a thin brown cigarette with a gold lighter. "My dearest darling, I *know* he did it."

"I'm not so certain as you."

"Naturally not. You weren't at the trials."

"Tell me about those trials."

For a half hour Dobbsie described the trials. He had an excellent memory for who had been wearing what. He did not know why the second trial had been closed, and he didn't even have gossip as to why the record had been sealed.

"There are too many gaps," Babe said.

Dobbsie poured fresh coffee. "If you have any doubts, I suggest you read my book."

"I've read your book. And I don't like it."

Gordon Dobbs smiled. "I do enjoy candor. Tell me what you don't like."

"To begin with, the tone."

A thoughtful look touched the corners of Dobbsie's mouth. "I felt the tone was appropriate. I was describing money, influence, power —all the things that make people marry and murder one another."

"Your research was slanted."

He took off his glasses and spent a moment thoughtfully regarding her. "Give me an example."

"The insulin in the stud box. In all the years we were married, Scottie never had a stud box. He used a ceramic bowl."

Dobbsie frowned. "I got that detail from an article by Dina Alstetter, published in *SoHo* magazine. Second serial rights were picked up by newspapers and magazines across the country. The same as with my book. Except I had a national TV tour and Dina didn't."

"Scottie couldn't have put the box there. Mama made him move into the Princeton Club the day I went to the hospital."

"Who else could have put a box of insulin on your bedside table?"

"I don't know who, but it's absurd to think Scottie would incriminate himself so carelessly, so stupidly. That box was planted so that Dina would find it."

"I happen to know Dina pretty damned well. We've worked professionally together and we toured the Sid Vicious book. She's a totally sweet gal—and she would not print a lie."

"Maybe not knowingly."

"Babe, even if Dina was careless—which I find highly unlikely—magazines check their facts. People who tell fibs in print get slapped with big fat libel suits."

"After the second verdict I'm surprised Scottie didn't sue you."

"Not bloody likely. He's a crook—as well as a liar and a murderer manqué. The civil rules of evidence are far more relaxed than the criminal. He'd have lost. Unlike Oscar Wilde, he knows when to stop."

"Then what's to keep *me* from suing you?"

Dobbsie glanced up at her. "What in the world for?"

"Libel."

"I never libeled you."

"What do you call that tan alligator bag in the closet? Scottie never owned a bag like that. So the implication is that it was mine. And whose drugs were in it? The state never proved that Scottie used drugs. So the implication is that the liquid Valium was mine too."

"I never said that."

"But you published it. The implication's right there in print, with your name on the book. And now I'm back from the dead, civil rights restored."

A hint of hesitation flickered in Gordon Dobbs's handsome face. "What would you hope to gain in a lawsuit?"

"Answers to questions."

"Like what?"

"Like why you wrote that book the way you did. What did you stand to gain by prejudicing Scottie's appeal?"

Gordon Dobbs was looking at Babe carefully now, and she knew he was estimating her power to hurt him, weighing it against her usefulness to him, calculating what sort of fresh tack to take with her.

"You're right to be suspicious of the book," he sighed. "I signed an agreement with your parents' lawyer. Bill Frothingham set up the interviews and gave me the information."

Babe heard Dobbsie out in silence, fighting to control her growing anger.

He explained how Lucia Vanderwalk had hired an ex-police detective who had extremely good connections and wasn't bound by the law. He explained how the detective had reconstructed the crime. He explained how the reconstruction had formed the basis of the book.

"In return I let Bill Frothingham see the manuscript. He vetted it for errors. There was no obligation to change anything, just to consider your family's suggestions. They allowed a great deal to stand that wasn't at all favorable to your great-grandfather."

"Did my family pay you?"

"Yes, I received a consideration."

"Naturally they let you publish old family scandal—no one would think they were behind the book. But how could you have put your name to someone else's accusations?"

"Frankly," Dobbsie said, "I believe Scottie was guilty. The book was published after the first trial, so it certainly didn't harm him. He got his appeal. He got his reduced plea. He got everything."

"Of course it harmed him. Coming from my parents it would have been revenge and no one would have paid attention. Coming from you it was news and hundreds of thousands of people believed it. Why else do you think my parents paid you?"

Dobbsie took Babe's hands in his. "I'm a bad person, Babe, but I'm not an *unusually* bad person. I lay no claim to your respect, but I do hope for your friendship."

"Did my parents pay Dina too?"

"I have no idea," he said. "You'll have to ask her that yourself."

"Do you know what I can't understand?" Babe said. "Why did the insulin in the stud box show up after the first trial and not before?"

Dina Alstetter gave a cold little smile that wasn't a smile at all. "It would have showed up anytime anyone had had the sense to look."

"And you were the first to have the sense?"

"I was the first to have the curiosity."

"I'll tell you what I think," Babe said. "I think that bottle of insulin was planted long after my coma."

Dina Alstetter exhaled. She didn't move or even show a reaction. "Why would anyone have planted it?"

"So you could drive another nail into Scottie in print."

"That's rather naive of you, Babe." Dina Alstetter's hair was long, straight, and dark and she gave it a quick toss. "It's not my habit to allow myself to be used."

"If the insulin wasn't a plant," Babe said, "why wasn't it evidence at the trial? Why didn't the police even find it?"

"Because the police are not particularly effective at their work." Dina Alstetter rose smoothly from the chair. She wore designer blue jeans and a bodiced lace blouse, and most of her length was in her legs. She walked to the window of her Beekman Place sitting room. Sunlight poured through in a dazzling slant. "Babe, you've been away an awfully long time. A lot has changed in this city."

"I'm aware of that."

"You may not know that I've taken up investigative journalism since my divorce. I've won awards. I've even been mentioned for a Pulitzer. I'm not trying to impress you, but you should have some awareness that I enjoy the respect of the journalistic community—I may be Ash Canfield's sister, but that doesn't mean I'm some neophyte dumb enough to run a story that's a plant."

"Did my parents pay you to publish that article?"

Dina's head whipped around. "Absolutely not."

They stared at one another.

"Did the police ever look at the bottle?" Babe asked.

"As a matter of fact, they didn't. I don't suppose New York's Finest get around to reading *SoHo* magazine."

"And you didn't take it to them?"

"My lawyer advised me not to."

"Then who has it now?"

"I have it."

"I'd like to see it."

Babe wheeled herself across the sidewalk, steering clear of shade trees and uniformed maids walking poodles. The neighborhood was a luxurious preserve of solidly built pre–World War I co-ops, with the odd brownstone town house sprinkled in.

The Provence Pharmacy stood on the corner of First Avenue. As Babe approached, the automated door opened onto a splash of yellow and green *frictions de bain* on special, piled in neat pyramids.

A cool breeze of perfumed air conditioning fanned her face.

The young druggist behind the counter looked at her wheelchair with frank curiosity. "Help you?" he offered.

Babe took the bottle from her purse. "I phoned the manufacturer," she said. "They told me they sold this lot number to you."

The smile on the druggist's face dimmed. His hair was richly dark and clipped almost in a crew cut. His face betrayed a residual sprinkling of teenage acne. His eyes met Babe's for just a second longer than necessary. "It's possible," he said.

"Is there some way you can check?"

A frown slipped across his face. "I can see if it's in the computer," he said doubtfully.

"I'd be grateful," Babe smiled.

He went behind a glass partition and two minutes later he came back holding what looked like a three-inch cash register printout. "We filled this prescription almost six years ago."

Babe's heart gave a skip behind her ribs. "Could you tell me who you filled it for?"

32

"YOUR HONOR, THIS IS A WHOLLY IMPROPER ARREST," TED Morgenstern's voice boomed into the half-empty courtroom. Cords stood out at the base of his extraordinarily wrinkled neck. "Lieutenant Cardozo interrogated Mr. Loring without counsel and without advising him of his Miranda rights."

Watching Morgenstern, Cardozo felt a sort of weary, sick recognition: not only of the face that was never without a tan, the hawk eyes, the thin nose and lips, the gray-fuzzed shaven head crossed with wrinkles and scars, but of the delivery, the cranked-up outrage, the whole farce of legal nit-picking that masqueraded as a struggle against injustice.

Lucinda MacGill, tall, showing a mouthful of fine white teeth, moved with a tennis pro's grace toward the bench. Her hair bounced lightly. "Your Honor, Lieutenant Cardozo wasn't obliged to read Mr. Loring his rights until arresting him."

"From the *moment* Lieutenant Cardozo waved a warrant in my client's face, Mr. Loring was effectively under arrest!" Morgenstern made a heroic gesture that threw open the jacket of his tux, revealing mother-of-pearl shirt studs and a blue silk cummerbund. It was unlikely dress for court, but Counselor Morgenstern obviously had no time to rush home and change before tonight's dinner-and-dancing date.

Behind Judge Joseph Martinez's eyes was a sudden flare-up of interest. He lifted his chin and cocked his head slightly to one side, arching his graying moustache. "At what time did Lieutenant Cardozo wave an arrest warrant in Mr. Loring's face?"

Cardozo rose from the front row of pale varnished benches.

"Shortly after ten this morning Claude Loring was shown a warrant issued by Judge Levin."

Judge Martinez's eyes were cold and assessing. "When did you read him his rights?"

"After talking with him and determining there was cause for arrest."

"What time, Lieutenant?"

"Around noon."

"By which time," Ted Morgenstern broke in, "Mr. Loring was suffering acute methaqualone poisoning."

Lucinda MacGill stood there, tall, light-haired, alert and sharp. "The police did not drug Mr. Loring. He went to the men's room and drugged himself."

"One thing at a time, Counselor. Did Lieutenant Cardozo interrogate Claude Loring for two hours without reading him his Miranda or allowing him counsel?"

"Five hours, Your Honor," Ted Morgenstern interrupted. "I didn't see my client until three o'clock this afternoon at Saint Clare's Hospital."

Cardozo's eyes connected with Morgenstern's and hate flashed between them. The emotion was more than personal: it was a natural instinct, an antipathy between alien species.

They both knew the city: who the players were, how things got done, what worked. The difference between them was that they played on different teams for different rewards. Morgenstern had the notoriety, the plugs in gossip columns, the town house in the East Sixties, the dukes and duchesses to dinner, the limo. Cardozo had the citation for bravery, the forty-seven thousand salary, the walkup apartment, Mrs. Epstein going dutch with him on lamb chops, the Honda Civic.

"For three hours no one could see Mr. Loring because he was unconscious," Lucinda MacGill said. "That was Mr. Loring's *choice.*"

The judge's head had tipped back, his mouth slightly open. "It's the police's duty to safeguard any person in their custody. In this duty, as in his Miranda obligations, Lieutenant Cardozo conspicuously failed."

Without a beat of hesitation Ted Morgenstern stepped forward. "Your Honor, I request that this charge be dismissed."

"Murder one? Dream on, Counselor."

"In that case I request reasonable bail for Claude Loring."

Lucinda MacGill stepped toward the bench. "The people oppose bail for Claude Loring. He's a sociopath, impulsive and unreliable. To free him before trial could put innocent citizens at risk and it could result in his absconding."

"Your Honor, it could be a year or more before this case comes to trial. Are the police asking a South African–style preventive detention?"

"Your Honor, I resent the attempt to turn this arrest into an act of political repression. Mr. Loring is accused of a serious and brutal charge, the taking of an innocent human life."

"*Genug,* young lady." Judge Martinez waved an impatient hand. "Let's weigh risks. There's the risk society faces if Mr. Loring is free on bail. As he has no previous record, that risk is minimal. Then there's the risk Mr. Loring faces if he remains in police custody. So long as we have right-thinking gay-bashing hombres like Lieutenant Cardozo on our force, that risk is considerable. Bail of one hundred thousand dollars is granted."

Outside the courtroom, Cardozo's white-knuckled fist came up and slammed into the wall.

He stood there a moment, hardly breathing, hardly moving. The light slanting down from the fluorescent strip in the ceiling flickered.

A chip of plaster flaked down.

He punched the wall again.

Cardozo was reading the five on Midge Bailey, a new homicide.

No sign of forced entry, of struggle or violence. Nothing missing from the apartment. Eighty-seven dollars and a VISA card and a MasterCard in her purse.

The woman next door had been almost apologetic for having called the police. *The dog was howling. The door was open.*

Cardozo studied the crime scene photos of the fifty-five-year-old housewife. He had spent his career digging around in the mud of low tide, but when he saw a human being worked over the way someone had gone over Mrs. Bailey, he realized he knew nothing whatsoever about the things that crawled on the ocean floor.

The phone gave two sharp clangs. He reached over, dragging it closer by the cord, lifting the receiver. "Hello?"

"Lieutenant Cardozo?" A woman. Cultivated voice.

"Speaking."

"This is Babe Devens."

Cardozo settled himself back in his chair. "Well, hello."

"Am I calling at a bad time?"

"You're calling at an excellent time. What's the trouble?"

"If you have time, I'd like to talk to you."

"I have time," he said. "Talk."

"Could we meet?"

"Mrs. Devens, what are you doing in half an hour?" He knew a restaurant on Sixty-seventh Street: bad food, watered booze, good privacy. "There's a place near here called Danny's."

Cardozo walked up Lexington toward Danny's Bar and Grill, not thinking about Midge Bailey, not minding the mugginess, not minding the red light that stopped him on Sixty-sixth, enjoying the sunshine and the skimpy, bright clothes on the women.

Danny's was almost deserted this time of the day, and Cardozo was aware of a tight expectancy in his chest as he pushed through the door into the air-conditioned dimness.

The late afternoon light made the restaurant a mysterious dark blue pool. A few early drinkers had taken up places at the bar, huddled in their separate solitudes. A jukebox was crooning softly.

When his tired eyes adjusted he could see down the rows of deserted tables. There was sunlight in the window and it outlined Babe Devens sitting at a far table.

She saw him, and a nervously ingratiating smile flashed across her face.

"Good to see you up and around," Cardozo said.

"I'm around." She tapped her armrest. She was sitting in a wheelchair. "Not quite up yet."

"That'll come in no time." He pulled out a chair and sat down facing her. "You're looking terrific."

"Thanks. I have a feeling if I can stay far away from hospitals, I might learn how to live again."

The owner, a burly Irishman with enormous sideburns, came over to take their orders.

"What are you having?" she asked Cardozo.

"A draft Michelob."

She said she'd have the same. He hadn't figured her for the draft beer type, but when Danny brought the drafts he liked the way she drank hers and seemed to enjoy the taste.

"What's the trouble?" he asked.

"It's not exactly a police matter. It's just that you helped me, and I wanted to thank you in person, and . . ." She pushed her glass around on the table. "I've been trying to see the records of Scottie's second trial. They're sealed."

Cardozo frowned.

"It isn't usual, is it, to seal court records?"

"Not unless you're a Kennedy and you accidentally drowned a campaign worker who absolutely was not your mistress and the judge is a friend of the family."

"Scottie doesn't have that kind of clout."

How pretty she is, Cardozo thought, the soft blond hair slanting across her forehead and the large inquiring eyes fixing him with their cool wondering stare, and the bright mouth, silent and expectant now.

"Your daughter was a minor at the time," he said. "The judge might have been protecting her from publicity."

"That doesn't make sense. She was a minor during the first trial, and those records aren't sealed."

That stopped Cardozo for a moment. He tried to match the precociously sexy model in the Babethings ads, the teasing face, the seminude glossy body peeling out of the hip-hugging jeans, with his notion of childhood. Cordelia couldn't have been older than fourteen when those ads began. "There could have been new evidence introduced in the second trial—testimony that gave evidence of another crime, or prejudiced a case already in the courts, or libeled somebody. Hard to say. Judges have pretty broad leeway. They don't often seal records, but when they do they're not called to account for their decision."

"Is there any way I could get to those records?"

"You could sue. You could petition the court."

Frustration showed in her face. "Lieutenant Cardozo—"

"I wish you'd call me Vince."

"If you call me Babe."

"Okay, Babe."

"Vince—"

That first names broke the odd little pocket of tension that had built up. She smiled, and he had a sense she would be a very easy person to be with.

"You testified at the first trial," she said. "Did you testify at the second?"

"The honor of my presence was not requested at the second. By then the fix was in."

"The verdict was rigged?"

"What verdict? The state bought the plea bargain."

"How was that arranged?"

"Your husband's attorney made the D.A. an offer and the D.A. accepted. In my opinion the state had the evidence to lock your husband up and in the second trial they threw it away."

She was looking at him. Her eyes were not saying anything. He could sense that inside this lovely quiet woman there was a huge amount of determination.

"At the first trial Cordelia was the only eyewitness against Scottie," she said. "He was convicted on her testimony. But at the second trial that conviction was reversed. And Cordelia's testimony is sealed. Why? What did she say?"

"Why don't you ask her?"

"She doesn't remember."

"Doesn't remember or doesn't want to?"

"A little of both, I think. It was too painful for her."

Cardozo nodded. "I can see that. A lot of people abandoned your little girl. By the way, who took care of her?"

"My parents raised her. But legally she was the ward of a family friend—Billi von Kleist."

Cardozo's eyebrows went up. "Why did she have a guardian?"

"Scottie and I were almost killed in a car crash—our fault, we were driving drunk. Billi was a good friend, and we thought in case anything ever really happened to us, there should be someone to look after Cordelia. Billi adored her, and she adored him, and so I appointed Billi. I never thought it would actually come to pass. But then I went into coma, and Scottie was charged, so Billi became Cordelia's legal guardian."

"But Von Kleist let your parents take care of her?"

"He's not a family man. All he really wanted to be was a friend to her. The sort my parents could never be."

"You don't think too highly of your parents."

"I think they're confused people. They mix up the nineteenth century with the twentieth. I think they put Cordelia up to testifying against Scottie. They've always disliked him. I think Cordelia lied in the first trial and told the truth in the second."

"What truth?"

"I think she cleared Scottie."

Cardozo shook his head. "No way."

"Scottie was framed," Babe said.

"You really want to believe that."

"It's not just because I want to believe it." She opened her purse and placed a small blue bottle on the table. "Somebody put this in a box beside my bed after the first trial. Insulin. A friend of mine by the name of Dina Alstetter found it. She mentioned it in a magazine article. The article was quoted in a book that smeared Scottie. The author of that book is a man named Gordon Dobbs."

"Gordon Dobbs," Cardozo said thoughtfully. He turned the bottle in his hand, studying the faded label and the still-legible lot number. "Well well."

"He told me my parents paid him to write the book."

"Not surprising. They were out to get Devens. They paid a retired police detective too." Cardozo kept turning the bottle, studying it. "Where did you get this insulin?"

"My mother let Dina keep it and Dina gave it to me."

"Peculiar," Cardozo said. "Why didn't your mother give it to the police?"

"I don't think this bottle existed when the police were investigating. I think this bottle came later—when Scottie appealed."

Cardozo studied the lot number on the label and then he held the bottle upside down, testing the seal.

"The manufacturer gave me the name of the pharmacy that bought it," Babe said. "The pharmacist won't say who he sold it to. He says records are confidential."

"Pharmacy records aren't confidential," Cardozo said. "Not from the police."

"If someone did plant this bottle—"

"All it would prove is that someone planted this bottle after you went into coma."

"But doesn't it prove he's innocent? If Scottie were guilty, why would anyone *have* to plant proof?"

"There could be reasons. It'd be a sure way to create doubt about his guilt."

She shook her head. "There's no doubt about that. I had lunch with Scottie. I asked outright if he'd tried to kill me. He said he had."

"So he finally got honest. I guess that settles it."

"Not the way you think. I was married to Scott Devens for five years. I know when he's telling the truth and I know when he's lying. When he said he'd tried to kill me, I saw something in his eyes, I saw it written on his face. Maybe that sounds strange to you, but I'm an artist. I have a trained eye, I see things that most people miss."

"What was this something you saw in Scott Devens's face that the rest of us missed?"

"I saw a Scottie I'd never seen before—a man who can't stand up for anything—not for his own feelings or convictions and worst of all not even for himself or for the truth. He doesn't respect himself anymore. He's sold out. He's not the Scottie I married."

"So he's lying?"

She nodded.

"Isn't that a very peculiar lie to tell?"

"He knows how to make me hate him."

"And do you? Hate him?"

"I hate him for thinking so little of me he could imagine I'd believe him. And I hate him for thinking so little of himself that he'd allow his good name to be taken from him."

"Why would he do it?"

"I guess he's always wanted an easy, glamorous life. Now he has one. Maybe he was paid."

"Who paid him?"

"I don't know. Who profits besides Scottie if Scottie lies? The only person I can think of is the person who—" Her words broke off.

"The person who tried to kill you?"

She sighed. "Do you think I'm crazy?"

"I think you have some interesting ideas." Cardozo held the clear colorless liquid in the bottle up to the light. "What did you say the name of that pharmacy was?"

"You sold this," Cardozo said. "Who bought it?"

The druggist took the insulin bottle. His frowning eyes traveled from the label to Cardozo's shield. He went wordlessly behind a glass wall and Cardozo watched him push buttons on a desktop computer.

A machine made muffled tap-dancing noises. The druggist returned and, still saying nothing, handed Cardozo a three-inch printout. Cardozo's eyes skimmed the dot-matrix letters that spelled PROVENCE PHARMACY and the lot number of the insulin, followed by the name of the prescribing doctor and the prescription number.

The name Faith S. Banks leapt off the paper, jabbing him between the eyes like a fork prong.

He stood frozen, recognizing that something was very much off. His mind backed up six and a half years. Banks had been Babe Vanderwalk's maid. Her evidence had been central to the case against Scottie Devens. She'd found the brown bag in Devens's closet and given it to the Vanderwalks' private investigator. It had held the syringe, insulin, and liquid Valium.

"Have you filled any other prescriptions for this woman?" Cardozo asked.

"We've been selling her insulin for twelve years," the druggist said. "She's a diabetic."

Back at the precinct, Cardozo pulled the records on the Devens case.

The bottles of insulin found in the brown bag had had their labels, including the lot numbers, removed. The contents had had to be analyzed before they could be positively identified as insulin. There had been no fingerprints on the bottles.

There was no mention in any of the fives of Faith Banks's being diabetic.

Because nobody asked, Cardozo thought. Nobody thought of asking if anyone in the house had a legitimate supply of insulin.

But we must have asked, he thought. *You don't not ask a thing like that.*

Cardozo puzzled, drinking coffee after coffee, till he was getting a high-pitched note inside his ears like a cricket playing a violin.

We must have asked and Banks must have lied.

He felt his way further.

The insulin bottles in the brown bag had been stripped of identifying marks. But the Alstetter bottle had been traceable straight to Banks. How come?

What came to him was that the first bottles had been part of a careful frame aimed at convincing the police; the fourth insulin bottle had been a careless embellishment, executed long after the Vanderwalks' professional investigator had gone home, aimed at convincing an amateur magazine sleuth named Dina Alstetter.

Cardozo lifted the phone and dialed Judge Tom Levin's number.

Cardozo followed Judge Levin into the sitting room of his Brooklyn Heights town house. There was a fresh bottle of Johnnie Walker black label on the sideboard, glasses and ice waiting.

The judge handed him a glass.

The transcript was sitting on the table, a brown binder with the label already beginning to peel off. *People of the State of New York v. William Scott Devens.*

Cardozo took a seat in the corduroy easy chair, his eyes bent to the transcript. He sipped Scotch and made notes on a small lined pad.

After page 73, when the defense was moving to introduce a medical report into evidence, there was a blank page.

Cardozo turned to the next page. It, too, was blank. He riffled quickly through the remainder of the transcript. All blank.

"Tom," he said, "would you take a look at this?"

Tom Levin took the transcript and stood turning pages. "This is downright interesting," he muttered.

"Why would anyone steal pages from a sealed record?"

"Because sealing a record is bullshit. Every day of the week people like me get into sealed records, and whoever wanted this record sealed was making sure people like you didn't read it."

Cardozo read the newspaper articles on Babe Devens.

According to the *Post,* she had returned to her life of luxury among the rich and famous of New York. The *News* said her five-bedroom town house on Sutton Place was assessed at 4.2 million dollars. Her neighbors included two U.N. ambassadors, the world's leading operatic tenor, a movie star, and a cousin of the queen of England. *People* magazine said that before her coma she and her husband had thrown parties for some of the biggest names in society and show business. Any day now she would return to her rightful place as queen of the glitterati.

The guests in the photographs of Scottie and Babe Devens's last party looked to Cardozo like a bunch of rouged-up clowns, living in a world that rained diamonds and tinsel and cocaine.

He couldn't picture her in that society. Didn't want to.

He pushed the buzzer of number 18 Sutton Place, a gray slate town house with French château turrets. A stiff-necked butler let him in.

"Would you care to wait in the sitting room, sir?"

"That's all right, Wheelock. Here I am."

Cardozo turned. Babe Devens was wheeling herself out of the elevator, hair honey blond and eyes sky blue, and his heart gave a little jump of pleasure. Her blue silk afternoon dress shimmered faintly. Smiling, she stretched out her hand. "You're very kind to come."

He took the hand, held it, and said "Hello," and when she looked at him strangely he realized he'd forgotten to let go.

"Do you think it's too warm for iced tea on the terrace?"

"The terrace is fine by me," he said.

He followed her through a room that looked as though someone had robbed a museum to furnish it. The thought came to him that if he accidentally knocked an *objet* off a table he'd be busting two hundred thousand dollars. He felt clumsy and intimidated, and he made up for it by adopting a careful swagger.

She used her chair smoothly, her movements strong and practiced and precise. He opened the terrace door for her, and she wheeled her chair to a little wicker patio table.

A row of boxwood bushes and small dogwoods just beyond the flagstones afforded a token sort of privacy, marking the space off from the rest of the park. Beyond the hedge a tree-fringed lawn stretched almost to the river.

Cardozo sat and Babe rang a small silver bell.

He raised his eyes up to where lingering summer sunlight caught the roofs of the city. *Wouldn't this be the life,* he thought.

A uniformed maid appeared.

"Mrs. Wheelock, we'll have our iced tea here."

The maid returned, bringing a carved-glass pitcher beaded with condensation and two tall glasses packed with ice cubes and fresh mint sprigs.

Babe poured, her arms braceleted and bare but in the sunlight downed with light blond hair.

"Help yourself to sugar or NutraSweet."

The edge of Cardozo's sleeve brushed her hand and her hand stayed there on the table as though nothing at all had happened.

"You don't have to keep your jacket on," she said.

He hesitated. "I'm wearing a gun. Your neighbors might think it was funny, you sitting here with a man with a gun."

"They think it's pretty funny my sitting here at all. If they don't like your gun they can call the cops."

He laughed and felt warm and happy inside. He took his jacket off, put it over the back of his chair, and hoped to hell there was no ring around his collar.

"It's pretty here," he said.

"I love this place. It has water, sky, trees. You wouldn't think there's nature in the city, but there is." She took a swallow of tea. "You should know this—I'm not going hide it. It's so good, it's so nice just to talk to you."

He looked at her, and the hair on the back of his neck came alive as though the lightest finger he'd ever felt had passed over it. "It's nice for me too," he said.

"You're the only one who doesn't treat me as though I'm permanently damaged."

He sensed strength in her, not the willed force of sinew, but something gentler, surer, like a flower coming through rock. "You're not damaged at all."

She looked at him and he sensed gratitude. The shadows of the row-houses were crossing the lawn, stretching toward the river wall.

He took out his notebook. "Down to business, okay? A judge let me see the record of the second trial. Ted Morgenstern pleaded your husband innocent."

"I thought Scottie pleaded guilty to a lesser charge."

"He started out pleading innocent. This time the syringe wasn't allowed in evidence. Which didn't leave the state many cards to play. The state called four witnesses. The doctor. Your housekeeper, Mrs. Banks. Your daughter. And Billi von Kleist."

Her eyes came up, surprised. "Billi testified against Scottie?"

"Not exactly against him. He said you left the party drunk, you left with your husband, it was two in the morning, he offered to go home with you, your husband said no thanks. The doctor said you were injected with a near-lethal dose of insulin sometime between midnight and four o'clock that morning. Cordelia said she saw your husband coming out of the bedroom at three in the morning. Mrs. Banks said Cordelia woke her up at three fifteen. So far it's the same case the state presented in trial one—minus the syringe. Then Morgenstern takes over. He moves to put in evidence a psychiatric report on your daughter."

Babe wrinkled her brow.

"The psychiatrist's name was Dr. Flora Vogelsang. Do you know her?"

"I've never heard of her," Babe said.

Cardozo's glance flicked up at her. "Vogelsang's still practicing. Has an office over on Madison Avenue. It looks like she examined your daughter, prepared a report for the defense, and came to court to back it up with her testimony."

"What did the report say?"

"I don't know. The trial record's missing from that point on. Someone substituted two hundred blank pages. No way of knowing if the report was accepted into evidence, how Vogelsang testified; no record of the tender of a plea bargain."

Babe's eyes were intelligent and questioning. "Why would those pages have been taken?"

"Someone's covering their—their behind. But you don't have to be Albert Einstein to put it together. Your daughter was the eyewitness against your husband. Morgenstern couldn't defend his client, so he did the next best thing—he attacked the witness. Bringing in the psychiatrist means he attacked her sanity. The upshot was, the state couldn't use her. So what do you do. No eyewitness, no syringe, no case. You buy the plea bargain."

When he had laid it all out he could feel the almost physical touch of her attention.

"I can't believe Scottie would let his lawyer . . . He loved Cordelia, she was a daughter to him."

"He was saving his skin."

"Wouldn't the jurors remember what was said?"

"They didn't hear it. The judge would have cleared the courtroom. Morgenstern would have questioned Cordelia and pulverized her, the state would have seen it was hopeless and accepted the plea bargain, the jury would have been sent home."

"Cordelia's changed. I'm sure it has to do with that trial." Babe Devens sat looking at Cardozo, her face anxious now and determined. "I wish I knew what that psychiatrist's report said."

"I'd like to know too." Cardozo stood up and slipped back into his jacket. The seersucker cloth was still warm from hanging in the sun. "By the way—do you happen to know if Faith Banks had any health problems while she was working for you?"

"None that I know of," Babe Devens said. "Why?"

"That insulin you gave me was hers. She's a diabetic."

The twilight was already dusky gray. Sunset was near. The darkening leaves hung quivering on the trees and shrubs and night was coming down very gently.

"I never knew that," Babe Devens said.

"It's not the kind of thing you'd necessarily notice. She just wouldn't eat sweets or drink alcohol."

"That's true—we offered her champagne and she wouldn't touch it."

"The insulin in the brown bag could have been hers. I hate to admit it, but your ex-husband could have been framed. Which isn't necessarily good news. Did you change the locks on the house?"

Babe's glance came up at him watchfully. "If someone still wanted to kill me, they've had plenty of opportunity."

"I'm not saying it's likely. I'm saying be a little extra careful, stay alert."

She nodded. "I had the locks changed."

"Don't give away too many keys."

"I haven't. I won't."

"And if anything starts worrying you, or if there's anything you need—"

"You're being extraordinarily kind, and I appreciate it. But I don't want a guard, if that's what you're offering."

"Or any other way I can help."

She shook her head. "I've imposed on you enough."

"No you haven't."

She smiled.

"Okay," he said. "Stay in touch. Or I'll be worrying."

"Don't worry about me. Please."

He glanced over his shoulder. "Does that gate go to the street?"

"Slam it hard. It locks itself."

After a moment he turned and crossed the lawn, passing under the leafy trees, and then he was lost to sight.

Babe Devens's head hummed with wondering. She had seen Vince Cardozo fewer than a half-dozen times, but already she felt something she couldn't put into words. She thought of his dark eyes, his look of weariness, of taking life sadly. She thought of his offer of protection and for some reason it made her feel a little safer.

The iron gate clanged. A pulsation seemed to pass through the darkness. She sat there a long time, wondering things about Vince Cardozo and staring at the space where he had vanished.

33

Judge Francis Davenport held his head back, a look of brooding fierceness coming from thick gray brows and black eyes. "Counsel, I hope you have your arguments a little better prepared tomorrow than you did today. This court will stand in recess till ten o'clock."

The silver-handled gavel came slamming down. The judge squinted into the court and said, "Babe, come in, won't you?"

Babe thanked the clerk who helped her wheel her chair into the judge's chambers.

"Aren't you looking splendid," the judge said. Out of his robes he was a thickset man, heavy-jawed, with silver hair and a patrician accent. "What an absolutely great surprise."

She angled her head up, offering her cheek to his lips. "Uncle Frank, I need help."

She could see a wave of guardedness hit the judge. He was obviously afraid she'd come to ask about Scottie's trial.

"You know, Babe, I was at your baptism at Saint Bartholomew's. I've always regarded myself as your ex officio godfather."

Her family's money had put Francis Davenport on the bench and kept him there: he was in no position to decline to perform a favor. All he could do was tactfully dissuade her from asking.

"I happen to care about you very dearly," he said.

"I know that, Uncle Frank, and I'm grateful."

The judge heaved a short sigh filled with resignation. "What kind of help do you need?"

"You have police department contacts, don't you?"

"I have a few friends among the force."

"What can you find out about a lieutenant detective of homicide named Vincent Cardozo?"

The judge pushed his lips together. "Probably a little."

"He's a native New Yorker, as native as you, Babe. Grew up on Charlton Street, in Greenwich Village."

Judge Davenport was sitting by the unlit fire in Babe's drawing room, consulting a small leather-bound notebook.

"His father was a Portuguese Jewish immigrant who came to this country as a steam press operator. By the time of his death Baruch Cardozo was a senior administrator in the post office."

"Baruch," Babe said, savoring the strangeness of the name. "That's a Hebrew word. What does it mean?"

"Sorry, Hebrew isn't one of my languages. They called him Barry for short. Lieutenant Cardozo's mother was an Italo-American, native born, a lay teacher at Saint Anthony's school, where Vince had his primary education. Vince was an only child. He's nominally Roman Catholic. His father observed High Holy Days at the Village Temple till his death and was given a Jewish burial."

Warm summer twilight floated through the windows.

Judge Davenport turned a page of his notebook. "Vince was very popular with his schoolmates. Spoke back to the teachers, was not popular with the sisters. Ran with the neighborhood gangs. Had a few scrapes with the police when he was a teenager. No felonies of course. Went to Fordham University, political science, graduated cum laude. Graduate work at John Jay College of Criminal Justice— he still has twelve credits to go for his degree—entered the Police Academy, joined the force, worked his way up from patrolman to lieutenant detective in homicide. He's highly thought of; his clearance rate is one of the highest."

"What's his private life?"

The judge was staring at Babe with a curiosity bordering on disapproval. Clearly the web of connection between her and this homicide cop was eluding him.

"Vincent Cardozo's private life is quiet. Thirteen years ago he married Rose Romano."

Babe pulled herself upright, spine straight, her back not touching the wheelchair.

"Rose was a schoolteacher, like Vince's mother. He and his bride moved into a small apartment on Broome Street, not far from where Vince grew up. A year later they had a daughter, their only child,

Teresa. Teresa goes to grade school at Saint Agnes, highly intelligent."

"Are Vince and Rose Romano happy?" Babe asked. She felt remote from the man they were discussing and the life that surrounded him. Her sense of him was sketchy, unfinished; she felt a need to give him definition.

"From all reports, they were extremely happy."

The past tense caught her. "Are they separated?"

A silence flowed by and Judge Davenport gave her a glance with a trace of warning.

"Five years ago on Christmas Eve Rose Cardozo discovered that the tape deck they were giving Teresa was defective. She went to Crazy Eddie's in the Village to replace it. She never came home. Christmas Day a patrolman found her in the basement of a high rise being constructed on West Street. She'd been assaulted and stabbed seventy-three times with a sharp instrument."

The words caught Babe with physical force. "His wife was murdered?"

Judge Davenport drew in a deep breath and nodded grimly.

"Did they find the killer?"

"Never."

A knot twisted in Babe's stomach. *He's living with that,* she thought. *He's faced that and he's gone on.*

When the judge had gone, Babe took the elevator upstairs. She wheeled to her dressing room and reached resolutely for her crutches.

"Oh Billi," Babe sighed, staring out at the city sliding past the limousine windows. "Sometimes I think too much has changed. I wonder if I don't need a thousand years' more sleep."

"You're doing exactly the right thing. All you need, my little princess, is to get smack back in the saddle."

Babe prayed as the limousine drove west on Forty-seventh and south on Broadway. She prayed when the driver stopped and opened the door for her. Getting out, she found she was still horribly awkward with her crutches.

Billi cleared their way through the stream of humanity. Taxis and construction trucks blocked the Thirty-ninth Street crossing. The air was full of a thousand accents and smells. There was an energy to people's walks, an animation to their faces. It was as though the city was alive again after a long holiday. People gestured with their hands more than Babe remembered. The population of the city had become more Mediterranean and Caribbean. Faces were darker, sensuality more explicit.

Billi held open the do-not-open steel-and-glass door of a smoked-glass skyscraper on the corner of Thirty-eighth.

Babe hesitated, remembering her little boutique on the ground floor of a Park Avenue town house. *Do I really want to do this?* she thought, and the answer came, *Yes, I really want to do this.*

"Sixth elevator," Billi said.

On the way up to the twentieth floor, Babe's ears popped four times.

Billi steered her toward a door with a huge gold Babethings logo. He kissed his fingers and pressed them over her lips. "Welcome home," he whispered.

"Good morning, Mrs. Devens," the receptionist called out, as though they were old friends, and Babe smiled back, feeling all kinds of uncertainty.

Billi guided her along a corridor opening onto various complexes of smaller rooms. "We have three floors," he said, "but this is the main floor. Don't worry—even I can't find my way around."

To Babe it seemed a hi-tech warren of glossy white mazes. Low, indecipherable voices came from behind closed doors bearing unfamiliar names and titles. There was a muffled sound of activity, like distant traffic. Somewhere a million phones were ringing.

Billi explained the changes: the expansion into new space, the in-house publicity department, the computerized operations, the new products—perfume, diet programs, videocassettes, how-to-shop manuals.

Babe listened, nodding, feeling hope and doubt in her heart and praying that only the hope showed on her face.

People were scooting around in Italian-cut suits and overstated jangling baubles. They looked like teenagers. The median age of employees seemed to be eighteen.

Billi made introductions, and baby-faced strangers said, "Good to have you back, Mrs. Devens," and Babe had a pained flash that something once familiar had turned alien, like a beloved child grown into an unknown adult.

"Come see our cruise line." Billi took her through the laboratory. The clothes being assembled on a hundred-odd tailor's dummies looked like costumes for a futuristic Hollywood gangster film, abandoned at varying degrees of completion. "One thing hasn't changed." Billi smiled. "It's all still done in a last-minute dash. God knows how we're going to get a hundred fifty pieces ready by September."

Babe picked up the hem of what appeared to be a Turkish skirt. "Who does our beading now?"

"It's still done by hand."

"This has to be redone, it's uneven."

"Oh, that's nothing. A few beads are always dropping off—the work's done in India and shipped back."

"India?" Babe touched another half-finished dress. "Where do we get our linen?"

"China."

"*Mainland* China?"

He laughed. "Of course."

"And our lace?"

"Everything's from China. Linen, lace, silk. The labor's cheap, knock wood, and they keep their delivery dates."

Babe could recall the distinctive touch and smell and look of Irish linen and French lace and Italian silk, textures she had used and mixed as an artist might combine pigments.

"What does this sell for?" She touched another dress.

"Twenty-four hundred."

She stared at Billi with disbelief. "Wouldn't we sell more at eighteen?"

"Babe, our clientele has expanded beyond a hundred of your WASPy best friends. Our hungry customers wouldn't want *anything* for eighteen. They're insecure. Twenty-four guarantees that it's good. All our pricing's done by a top market analysis firm."

She could feel there was something she wasn't tuning in on. In their silent way these clothes were telling her that fashion had gone its own independent way while she'd been asleep.

"We're selling a hundred times the volume we did seven years ago." Billi held a door for her. "And that's just the clothes. Licensing brings in a good third of our gross."

"What do we license?"

"All kinds of goodies. Perfumes, chocolates, wines, gourmet frozen dinners. You'll have some at lunch. Where you'll also meet our designers."

"Funny—when I went to sleep *I* was our designer."

"And now you're our star."

Billi took her down yet another corridor, stopping to introduce her to people whose names she couldn't even start to remember. They all seemed to be bursting with projects for designing and publicizing and promoting.

"My little garret," Billi announced.

With its gleaming glass and plastic surfaces, Billi's office gave the impression of a surgery. On a chrome desk, buttons on two telephone consoles were flashing. On two walls, transparencies hung by steel clips beside illuminated viewing screens.

Babe leafed through the designs stacked on an easel by the window. The clothes were sharp-edged and aggressive, with jolting contrasts of color and extreme juxtapositions of texture. She stopped at a sable jacket worn with jeans. "Whose are these?"

"Mine."

"You drew them?"

"No, no, no. I have a *cabine* of five designers—they submit sketches and fabric ideas. They have twenty-five people working under them."

She let the sketches fall back against the easel, thinking of the days when she had run the Babethings boutique and atelier with a total of fifteen tailors and seamstresses and beaders. As she turned she noticed the large black eye of a computer terminal on the table next to the drawing board. "What's that monster?"

"State of the art three-D simulator," Billi said. "We use them to store designs, compose, revise. It's quite handy. It'll help your drawing."

The computer screen reminded Babe of the surface of a stagnant pond: murky, dark, with infinities of microscopic menace swirling just below. "It won't help *my* drawing," she stated firmly.

"Babe, *chérie*, once you get your footing I'm going to see to it that you give progress a try. Now come along. One last stop." Billi took her down a hallway and swung a door open.

She stood letting her glance scan the room. Her sense of déjà-vu carried a disturbing adrenal kick.

"It's my old office furniture!" she cried. "You kept it!" She gripped Billi's hand where it lay on her shoulder. "Billi—you angel!"

She lurched forward, caught her balance, then went slowly around the room, touching the gilt beechwood chairs, the antique French desk, the grandfather clock—all as familiar as the props of a recurrent dream. Placing her crutches against the wall, she sat at the desk and pulled open a drawer.

"I didn't dare clean out those drawers," Billi said. "Though they certainly could have used it."

"You'd better not have." Babe foraged happily through the familiar rubble of pens and doodads and scratch paper and cloth swatches. When she found a picture postcard she gave a delighted yelp.

"What's that?" Billi said.

Babe looked at the postmark. "It's from Mathilde—from Brittany. She went back for a week's vacation to that old farm of hers just before I—before my coma."

Mathilde had been the matron of Babe's atelier—a wonderfully capable seventy-year-old Frenchwoman whom she'd hired away from Saint Laurent. "I wonder how she is. Does anyone ever hear from her?"

"I heard Mathilde was dead."

Babe's heart gave a little stab. "Oh, no."

Billi shrugged fatalistically. "Well, she was old."

"How's work?" Dr. Corey's hands moved over her in slow, careful motions, touching her with rubber hammer, icy steel stethoscope, inflatable plastic tourniquet with crackling Velcro clasps.

"I'm getting in a few days a week," Babe said. "Trying my damnedest. But it's like learning a language all over again."

"You're learning a lot of things all over again. You ought to be getting pretty adept at it."

"I wonder," Babe said. "I've been having some trouble."

"Trouble with what?"

"Memories."

"Forgetting things?"

"No—just the opposite. Remembering things."

"That's a good sign," Dr. Corey said.

She smelled rubbing alcohol, then felt the cool touch of damp cotton, followed by the jab of a needle in the crook of her arm. She was aware of a slow uneasy warmth spreading outward from the skin puncture as blood was drawn up into the cylinder of the syringe.

"But these memories are like shadows," she said. "I can't get a focus on them. It's as though they were someone else's, not my own."

"You're a shrewd observer. The fact is, we all have memories that aren't our own."

Dr. Corey withdrew the syringe, offering her a smile. She wanted to believe that smile.

"Freud has a case of a nearly illiterate Austrian servant girl. She

remembered and recited entire chapters of Leviticus in perfect bib-
lical Hebrew. She'd never studied Hebrew and she could hardly
speak her native German. It turned out she'd been employed by a
Lutheran pastor. At night while she was sleeping he'd stomp up and
down his study, declaiming the passages—ergo her memory. She
heard Leviticus without realizing she'd heard it. The girl was considered a prodigy until Freud found the explanation."

Babe ran her fingers up and down her arm, touching the little
circular bandage Dr. Corey had put over the vein. "But the girl *was* a
prodigy. The memory *was* hers."

The column of the doctor's neck swelled. His tone became explan-
atory, as though he were addressing a student. "The memory of the
pastor was hers—but the memory of Leviticus wasn't hers in the
same sense. She'd suppressed the pastor but retained the sound, not
the meaning, of his nocturnal recitations. Memory is an idiot with
one hundred percent retention. Like an old relative who babbles on
too long. On the other hand, consciousness and understanding are
selective. It's the selecting process—the selecting *out* of links—that
gives us the impression of uncanny recall."

"I'm not following that."

"I'll give you an example. One patient of mine—president of a
leading brokerage house—remembers President McKinley's assassination even though he was born forty years later. What he doesn't
remember is that his grandfather witnessed the assassination and
loved to talk about it."

"How do you know he heard his grandfather if he can't remember?"

"His mother remembers her father telling the child when he was
four years old. The shooting terrified the child, but he adored his
grandfather. So in his mind he separated the two."

"But Leviticus in Hebrew really exists, and McKinley's assassination really happened. What about things that didn't happen? Is it
possible to think you remember them?"

"Absolutely. You could remember a dream. And you might even
remember it as a fact. After all, in their own terms, dreams are as real
as a tree or a Pythagorean theorem or the sound of a violin. Dreams
happen. All physical and mental data coexist in the universe."

"You sound mystical."

"There's nothing mystical about common sense." Dr. Corey was
silent, as though lost for a moment in some limitless space of conjecture. "Or maybe there is. I've never given it much thought."

Her eyes came around to him, cautiously. "Could I have dreamt while I was in coma?"

"During certain stages of coma, absolutely. The mind has to keep busy or it goes crazy."

"Why would I dream about a cocktail party with guests wearing joke-store masks?"

"Because that might just possibly be your considered judgment of cocktail parties. Pay attention to those little warnings your unconscious sends you. Often they're right on target."

Phones were ringing and echoes were spilling in from the corridor; there was an unending chatter of humans and computers and printers as Babe let herself into her office. A rush of emptiness, like an air current, swirled up to greet her.

She had stacked the sketches of the last three seasons' cruise lines in five enormous piles on her worktable and desk and chairs. They were part of a program she had worked out for herself to try to recapture her edge. As she stared at the piles she felt an emotion somewhere between hopelessness and defiance.

She gave herself a five-second you-can-do-it pep talk, hung up her jacket, leaned her crutches against the wall, and sat down.

She began with last year.

As she puzzled over the 150 sketches, her eyes tightened into thin, frustrated slits. All she saw was crude stripes and checks, strident op-paisley and industrial-strength colors, willfully eccentric tailoring that would be impossible to execute without sags and cinches. It all seemed to be part of the three-thousand-dollar look.

She felt a queasy wobbling of her own judgment, as though somewhere in her long sleep she had lost track of how reality was built, of what cause led to what effect.

She had in front of her the printout of Babethings' profit sheets: it showed that hundreds of rich young women—and probably some wanting to be young—bought these skirts and jackets and blouses.

Babe was puzzled. How did designs like these make any woman feel female or beautiful or successful or good about herself? Where was the affirmation? Could Babethings' customers, the women who had made the company a thirteen-million-dollar grosser, all be fashion masochists?

I'm cranky, she told herself. *Maybe I shouldn't be doing this today. Maybe I should relax and fool around with a piece of blank paper and a plain old* caran d'ache.

She cleared the worktable.

"Okay—genius at work."

She arranged herself at the drawing board in a spirit that was iffy but hopeful.

She started a design immediately, a pale blue spring dress, but she didn't care for it and crossed it out. She began another design and again came to a blank wall. Her hand had trouble putting down the shapes she saw in her head. She drew a simple blouse and it was impossible for her to draw the collar. She tried it without the collar and it looked as though a guillotine had chopped it off.

After an hour she had gotten no further than simple outlines, increasingly simple, it seemed, and increasingly uninspired.

Finally she had to admit that determination was getting her nowhere. With a decisive slap she closed her sketchpad on the pages of crossed-out designs.

A sense of utter futility filled her. *I'll be damned if I'm going to go on a crying jag in this office,* she told herself.

As she pushed the draftsman's lamp away from the worktable, the picture postcard that she had attached to the extendable arm fell to the drawing board.

Her eye went to the photograph of the old farmhouse in Brittany. At that moment one of those little messengers Dr. Corey had warned her about blipped something from her unconscious.

She picked up the card and frowned at the partial postmark, piecing together the name of the town.

Fingers trembling, she opened the phone book and looked up the directions for international dialing. She called information in Brittany and in her best school French asked if there was a listing for Mademoiselle Mathilde Lheureux.

A moment later the phone was making the French two-buzzes-in-a-row signal.

A voice answered. *"Allo?"*

A band of surprise tightened around Babe's throat. "Mathilde—you're alive!"

"Bien sûr I'm alive. Who is this?"

"It's Babe, Mathilde. I'm alive too."

An instant's astonishment blipped from Brittany up to a satellite over the Atlantic and down to Manhattan. "But they told me you were dead!"

"They told me *you* were dead!"

"Well, what do they know. *Chérie,* you must take the very next plane and come visit."

"I can't. I'm working. You come visit me."

"I can't. I'm rebuilding the farmhouse. The timbers are beautiful but old. Like me. Three hundred thousand francs to put in steel supports. What can I do? It's my home."

They chatted for almost three quarters of an hour, and when Babe hung up, she felt cheerfulness bubbling in her blood.

She bounced into Billi's office. "Billi, guess what—Mathilde's alive!"

Billi looked up from his desk. He seeemd quite unexcited. "How in the world did you find that out?"

"I phoned her."

"Well, well, imagine that. Is she going to come visit us?"

"I'm afraid I couldn't persuade her."

"Too bad. Would have been fun to see the old grouch again." Billi steepled his fingers together. "Say, Babe, would you care to give me the benefit of your expertise on something?"

He showed her a sketch of a pink silk cocktail dress with an extraordinarily long and very high waist, worn with a matching quilted satin bolero. Granted, fashion sketches tended to a sort of impressionistic exaggeration, but the thought came to Babe that this was an attractive sketch of an extremely impractical outfit.

"One of my designers put a 1954 Chanel on the computer and reworked it," Billi said.

"The bolero looks like something Valentino would do," Babe said.

Billi smiled. "He did. Two seasons back. We changed the color and shaped the collar a little."

Babe felt her lips draw together. "Are we using it?"

"Well, we have a few gaps in the cruise line, and it wouldn't be too hard to crash. What do you think? A fond *hommage* to past elegance?"

Babe had been trying her best to keep an open mind, to get a feel for what was happening in today's fashion. But more and more she had a frustrating sense of inability to judge the direction that design had taken, or at least that Babethings had chosen to take. The company designers were making brilliant statements, but the fact that the statement had to be worn by a living woman was simply an obstacle to be ingeniously and expensively conquered.

"It's rather . . . witty," Babe said. And if Billi included it in the line, she would have to wonder if she understood anything about today's fashions.

"Witty," Billi said. "What an apt observation. What ever did we do without you for seven long years, *ma petite*? Yes, we'll use it. A little blandness to spice the line."

34

CARDOZO WAS OVERSEEING THE CASE OF AN UPPER EAST SIDE
slasher victim that Monteleone was handling, and it took him to Dr.
Flora Vogelsang's neighborhood, a bright half mile of antique shops
and art galleries. The air was thick with the smell of money burning,
the jostle of women who spent a thousand dollars on a wristwatch,
men who paid five hundred for a wallet.

In the lobby of 1220 Madison a doorman sat with hunched shoulders on a stool by the buzzers. Cardozo approached.

"Help you?" the doorman challenged.

Cardozo opened his wallet, flashing the shield and a twenty-dollar
bill. Bribes were not tax-deductible, and they couldn't be recovered
from petty cash. They were an inescapable expense of the Job.

"Does a child psychiatrist by the name of Dr. Flora Vogelsang live
here?"

Cardozo moved through a corridor thronged with delivery boys,
derelicts, off-duty cops, neighborhood office workers. It was the standard showing for the noon lineup, an easy way to make five bucks if
you resembled the precinct's suspect of the day.

He stepped into the viewing room. This was the see-through side
of the one-way mirror. A white-faced young woman was sitting there
shredding a Kleenex.

"Thanks for coming, Miss Yannovitch." Cardozo put on his most
sympathetic voice and face. "I know this isn't easy for you."

Tammy Yannovitch was the next-door-neighbor of a woman whose
murder was being investigated. Yannovitch had reported seeing a
male Hispanic entering the elevator just before she'd heard her

neighbor's dog barking; she'd gone into the unlocked apartment and found the body. A patrolman had caught a male Hispanic trying to break into an apartment three buildings away, roughly the same description, carrying an upholsterer's knife.

Cardozo spoke into the mike. "Okay, bring 'em on."

On the other side of the mirror seven Hispanics filed into the room and stood blinking into the light.

Tammy Yannovitch opened her purse and put on her glasses, and right away Cardozo knew her ID was going to be worthless.

"You wear those glasses often, Miss Yannovitch?"

"Only when I go to the movies." She stared at each of the seven, squinting through her pink-tinted Coke-bottle lenses. "It's hard to be sure—I only saw him that split second."

"That's okay. Take your time."

She took her time, said she thought maybe it was number two, maybe it was number four. The men stepped forward and faced right and left and she still wasn't sure.

Cardozo was looking at number six. The man was wearing a Miss Liberty T-shirt, and black hair curled from his enormous head. His features were thick, as though a sculptor had laid them on with a trowel. The lobe of his right ear was missing and with his heavy, rounded shoulders he was brutish in appearance.

"I'm sorry," Miss Yannovitch said. "I can't be sure. I'd hate to get an innocent man arrested."

Cardozo laid a consoling hand on her shoulder. "That's okay, Miss Yannovitch. Thanks for your trouble." He turned to Sam Richards. "Take number six up to the squad room."

Cardozo went to the computer room and asked the sergeant to call up the sheet on Waldo Flores.

Two attempted rape. One conviction.

Multiple possession and use of stolen credit cards.

Multiple possession of stolen goods.

Multiple possession of controlled substances. One conviction.

Multiple possession of controlled substances with intent to sell.

Multiple living off immoral earnings of female.

It was an interesting sheet for a man of Waldo Flores's range. There was not a single breaking and entering. So, obviously, Waldo was an expert B and E man.

Cardozo went to the evidence room and checked out two vials of crack.

Flores was waiting upstairs in the squad room.

"Hey, Waldo." Cardozo slapped a hand on his back. "Been a while. You're looking good. Come on in here. Let's talk."

Waldo's eyes were serious, questioning. "Lieutenant, I just came by to earn five bucks. Anyone fingered me, they're crazy."

"I forget how you like your coffee. Milk and sugar? Make yourself comfortable, amigo."

Waldo sat in a chair. "This place is a Turkish bath. How do you stand it?"

"A cheerful attitude is the secret, Waldo. God gives me the courage to change the things I can and the serenity to accept the things I can't. And why don't you give me your jacket if you're too hot. Nice denim. Is it a Calvin?"

"It comes from the Army Navy."

"You've been boosting at the Army Navy again?"

"I charged it."

"Whose charge card?"

"I want to see a lawyer. Get me a nice lady lawyer with a big soft ass."

"Let's put your pretty jacket right here on the back of the chair. How's your coffee?"

"You drink this shit or you save it to brutalize minorities?"

Cardozo had to smile. There was something likable about the guy, a kind of engaging street sass.

"That's top-of-the-line precinct coffee. I'm doing my best for you. I'm even going to help you out of the jam you're in."

Waldo frowned. "Who says I'm in a jam?"

"Your rap sheet says you're an expert B and E man."

"That sheet's a horse's ass. I been booked for fencing goods I didn't know was stolen; but breaking and entering, no way."

"I know, amigo. You got a way of finding twenty-two-inch TV's on the street that's uncanny. I have a serious offer to make you. How'd you like to do a job for me?"

Waldo flashed two surly dark eyes. "You think I'm going to go for some crazy entrapment? Man, you been smoking."

"Do this for me, and we drop the crack charge."

"What crack charge?"

"You're holding, Waldo."

"Bull*shit*."

Cardozo heaved himself up from the chair and went to the door. "Sam, would you come in here a minute?"

Sam Richards sauntered into the cubicle.

"Does Mr. Flores look like he's holding two vials of crack in the right pocket of that jacket?"

"One way to find out." Richards reached into the denim jacket and pulled out two vials.

"You planted those," Waldo screamed.

"Take them and label them, would you, Sam?"

Cardozo brought two more cups of coffee, and this time he shut the door.

"Here's the deal, Waldo. There's a little old lady that has her home and office in a building on Madison and Eighty-seventh."

Cardozo explained exactly what he wanted from Flora Vogelsang's files. "Thursday would be a good night to hit her."

Waldo looked into space. He'd served time on two felonies. Nothing mattered to him now except staying out of jail.

"Any dogs? Any cats?" His voice was low and wispy, like his balls had been cut. "I don't go in where there are any pets."

"No dogs, no cats. This lady's a loner."

The kid at the pizza counter had dyed his hair magenta and he had a safety pin in his ear and he was spending too long arguing on the payphone. When he finally slammed the receiver down and came over to Waldo it was like he was doing someone a favor.

"What'll you have?"

"Pizza—ever hear of it?"

"What do you want on it?"

"Nothin'."

Twelve minutes later Waldo stood on the corner of Eighty-seventh Street. His eye scanned glitzy shop windows, lit for the night and tucked away behind antiburglar grills. There was a phonebooth halfway down the block. Balancing the pizza box on top of the phone, he dropped a quarter into the slot and dialed.

Among all the windows shimmering with light there was a four-window row of darkness on the twelfth floor of number 1220. The four windows stayed dark and the ringing went on and finally a machine answered and a woman's recorded voice said, "Hello, you have reached the office of Doctor Flora Z. Vogelsang."

He hung up. In his mind he was rehearsing the moves.

Traffic sped by. Headlights lashed the street. In the lobby of 1220 the doorman was sitting on a stool, reading *The Enquirer*. A cab stopped in front of the building and a man wearing an army jacket and designer sunglasses got out. Waldo saw his chance.

He ran, dodging horn blasts and headlights. The doorman was on the intercom, clearing the man in the army jacket. "Pizza for ten-D," Waldo called out.

He got into the elevator and pushed twelve.

At the door of 12G he untaped a narrow flexible copper rod from his chest.

Ninety seconds later the door swung inward and Waldo scooped up the pizza box and stepped into the dark apartment.

He set the pizza on the floor and crept along the corridor, nudging doors open. Behind the fourth door he found the office.

A rug stretched before the file cabinets, muffling his feet. The drawers made liquid hisses as one by one he pulled them out. He took the penlight from his hip pocket. He crouched down. The pin of light slid along the rows of manila files and stopped at the divider marked K.

A moment later Waldo had the KOENIG, CORDELIA folder in his hand. He tipped the pages out, folded them, tucked them under his shirt.

A button on the desk telephone winked lit.

Waldo raised himself from his crouch and quietly lifted the receiver. The machine had already answered and the recorded voice was saying, "Hello, you have reached . . ."

After the beep a live voice said, "Doctor, it's Hildy, I've got to talk to you, please pick up."

There was a click. "Yes Hildy? Is this an emergency?"

Waldo's heart lurched.

"He phoned." Hildy was sobbing. "Robert phoned."

"Hildy, sooner or later you're going to have to break with Robert. This might be an excellent opportunity."

Dr. Flora Vogelsang finally got Hildy off the line and hung up the phone. "Meshuggener," she muttered.

She lit a Pall Mall, smoked half of it, and realized she wasn't going to get back to sleep by natural means.

She slid her feet into her slippers.

Waldo crept to the doorway. A shaft of light spilling into the hallway caught the pizza box on the floor.

An old woman stumbled into the corridor. She didn't see the pizza. She turned on the bathroom light. There was a rush of water and

Waldo saw her through the open door gulping tablets, then downing a tumbler of water.

The bathroom light clicked off and the old woman stumbled back. Her slipper pushed the pizza but she didn't look down. She leaned on the doorframe, one hand to her abdomen, and burped. A moment later the bedroom light went out.

Waldo waited five minutes. Sweat was pouring off him. He inched down the hallway and picked up the pizza box.

The bedroom door was half open. He peeked in.

Light came through the filmy window curtain. The old lady's hair was a frazzled spill of gray on the pillow. She lay on her back, hands folded across her as if she had died in her sleep.

Waldo couldn't believe there was any sleeping pill in the world that worked that fast.

He went down the hall to the bathroom. The bottle was on the ledge above the sink. He shoved it into his pants pocket.

"Whoever gave you your information, you should shoot them." Waldo Flores's dark eyes stared at Cardozo above the rim of his cup. "Vogelsang was home."

"Did she see you?"

They were sitting in a booth at Danny's. The ripped blue Naugahyde benches had been bandaged together with electrician's tape.

"No way. She was too zonked on downs to see the walls." Waldo reached into his I LOVE NEW YORK T-shirt and pulled out three sheets of paper.

Cardozo flattened out the pages on the Formica tabletop. Creased down the middle and smeared with red grease, they bore the letterhead FLORA Z. VOGELSANG, M.D., PH.D.

"These are a fucking mess, Waldo. What did you do, slaughter a canary on them?"

The air conditioning was blasting. Waldo had to cup his hands around the match to light his Winston. "Excuse *me*. I musta forgot to wear my kid gloves."

Cardozo flipped pages.

"Hey, Lieutenant, I gotta get back to the garage."

"So? There's the door."

"I could use a hundred."

For an instant Cardozo's eyes hardened. "Here's twenty."

*　*　*

PRIVILEGED AND CONFIDENTIAL
Re: Cordelia Koenig
psychiatric evaluation
age: 13-2
occupation: student
tests administered
　Wechsler intelligence test
human figure drawings
Rorschach
thematic apperception test
EKG
blood analysis
urine analysis
vaginal smear

Cordelia Koenig was agreeable, attentive and polite, with something of a precociously socialized manner. Indeed, in the "grand" manner of a far older woman, she attempted to put the examiner at ease, complimenting the examiner on "your lovely office," recognizing a flower vase as Meissen, suggesting that the examiner "take your time" and inquiring if she was answering questions too quickly.

Based on observation alone, the examiner had the impression of an obsessive albeit well-contained preadolescent person, whose hostilities are quite unconscious, and at variance with her social intent.

Miss Koenig's work on the Wechsler reflects superior intelligence. Her full-scale score is 131, very superior, consisting of a verbal score of 130, superior, and a nonverbal score of 129, superior. The similarity between scores tends to obscure fluctuations in functioning, indicative of an emerging disturbance.

The projective tests reveal a shrewd, manipulative, resentful, and confused preadolescent whose modes of adaptation are unstable and tenuous. Her efforts at accommodation are forced and, at times, inappropriate—a fact of which she is obliquely aware. Impelled by aspirations for prestige and approval, she attempts to integrate both her accurate and her bizarrely inaccurate perceptions by linking objectively unrelated aspects of reality and at times grossly distorting these to fit her preconceived matrix of meaning.

Miss Koenig is very much concerned with the problem of self-importance, unconsciously intermixed with furtive rebellious impulses and an urge for extraordinary, godlike powers: in this regard, she equates female fertility with the power to bestow life and/or death. Consciously, in reaction-formation, she is unable to accept all but the most benign, loving, "good daughter" aspects of herself, despite an awakening realization that the aggression against which she so defends herself originates not in a hostile environment, but *in herself.*

Adroit at deceiving both others and herself, Miss Koenig relies on intellect to rationalize away the darker side of her own nature. Given her age and history, and the marked narcissistic infantilism of her parents and parent substitutes, it is not unusual that her identities and identifications are many and unstable, but overall they point to profound sexual bewilderment, morbid preoccupation with biological processes, and a denied longing for exotic, spectacularly attractive female roles.

Miss Koenig exhibits marked erotic inclination toward her father and toward any man who can be seen as a father surrogate. This, of course, clashes with her image of herself as a model of dignity, self-containment, and aristocracy. She is impelled to irresponsible, hedonistic activity, associating spontaneity (doubtless through observation of her elders) with liquor and psychoactive drugs.

Unconsciously, as revealed in her human figure drawings, Miss Koenig feels herself to be at the command of a cold, absent paternal figure and of a cruel, watchful maternal figure, both of whose nurturing is fiercely desired and seductively withheld. She saves her deepest conscious resentment for her father, but on an unconscious level she sees her mother as a dreaded rival upon whom she must humiliatingly depend for survival. Her strongest conscious need is to be noticed; her strongest unconscious need is for the infantile gratifications of affection, specifically to be fed (primary orality).

Miss Koenig is fending off feelings of despondency, helplessness, aggression, and guilt, despite her persistently positive denial. She wants to take flight from the unbearable contradictions of consciousness and to find respite in unconsciousness, without, however, any loss of prestige and importance. Sudden perceptions of consciously disdained but unconsciously coveted forms of sexual exhibitionism indicate a dangerous rift in her distinction between the imaginary and the real.

Diagnostically, Miss Koenig reveals an obsessive-compulsive character disturbance, with marked decompensation in intellectual and emotional functioning.

The physical examination reveals Miss Koenig to be in exceptionally good health except for a transient infection (gonorrhea). For this I have put her on a series of antibiotic injections, the standard remedy in young adults. The physical prognosis is excellent.

The psychiatric prognosis is less happy. While Miss Koenig shows a degree of resiliency and rational recoverability, her primary orality, obsessive distortive tendencies, and feelings of worthlessness indicate an inadequately substructured personality. Adolescence will almost certainly see the onset of major depressive episodes, with or without concomitant acting-out. Long-term psycho- and psychopharmacological therapy, as well as close monitoring, are absolutely indicated.

Flora Z. Vogelsang, M.D., Ph.D.

"Mrs. Devens please. Lieutenant Cardozo calling." He took a stinging hot swallow of coffee.

There was a click and then her voice was on the line, that wonderfully warm voice, coming alive at the sound of his.

"Nice to hear your voice, Vince."

"Just a quick question. Who was your husband's doctor seven years ago?"

He could feel her wondering why he was asking.

"We both used the same doctor—Fred Hallowell on Park."

The manager pointed Cardozo into the depth of the garage.

Cardozo's steps echoed. It was a dimly lit space, badly ventilated, smelling of gasoline. Light reflected on the floor, pulling murky rainbows out of the oil spills.

He watched the lower half of a man wriggling under a blue '86 Pontiac. He nudged the man's foot with his own.

The rest of Waldo Flores wriggled out.

"Pontiac's looking good, Waldo. Maybe I'll bring my Honda here for a tune-up."

Waldo looked as though he wanted to give Cardozo a mouthful of the greasy wrench he was holding. "We don't do Hondas."

"That's a shame. What I'm here about, Waldo, I have another job for you." Cardozo handed him the piece of paper with Dr. Frederick Hallowell's Park Avenue address and office hours. He explained that there would be a number of cards in Scott Devens's file and all he needed was the card for September of seven years ago. "Go in over the July Fourth weekend, okay?"

35

AT 12:35 CARDOZO WAS SITTING IN DANNY'S BAR AND GRILL working through a Reuben sandwich with a Diet Pepsi, lemon on the side. He'd already decided dessert was going to be strawberry cheesecake when Ellie Siegel came through the door.

She sat at the table and plunked her Crazy Eddie shopping bag on the empty chair next to her. She looked at the menu. "Think I have time for crabcakes?"

Danny, the owner and waiter, said sure, crabcakes took five minutes. Siegel ordered crabcakes and potato skins and asked Cardozo if she could have a glass of Chablis on duty.

"Think you can handle it?" he said.

"Make that a double," she told Danny. She then got comfortable in her chair and said, "Okay, Vince, why have you invited me out for a fancy lunch? What's bothering you?"

"This." He handed her Vogelsang's report.

As Siegel read, her features creased into a frown. When she had finished she leaned back in her chair. "That was then, Vince. This is now."

He felt a naked flash of anger. "It doesn't stop mattering just because a D.A. bought a plea."

"But is it any business of yours? Vince, you got a job."

"Babe Devens was my case. I blew it."

"You didn't blow anything. You're only a cop. You don't control the D.A."

"I'm a detective and I didn't even *sniff* this."

"You're homicide. This is child abuse, morals, narcotics—and it's a hell of a long time ago."

"The creep that fucked her should go free just because he's been on the loose seven years fucking other thirteen-year-olds? If that's the law, the law's nuts. I have a girl who's going to be thirteen and I'd murder the guy that touched her."

"First of all, there's no way you're going to find out who molested Cordelia Koenig six years ago, and second of all the girl in this report is not your daughter."

"The guy in this report is the guy that tried to kill Babe Devens."

"Mrs. Devens didn't die."

"He took seven years from her, he should be allowed to do that? Fuck the kid, take seven years from the mother?"

"Okay, life's not fair."

"You scream about porno hurts women and sexism on the job hurts women but when it comes to something in real life that hurts two real women all you can say is life's not fair. You take my breath away, Ms. Siegel. You really do."

Siegel raised her eyebrows at him. Her gaze was interested and curious and cool. "Vince, there's no homicide here, this doesn't connect to any ongoing investigation. She's one of two million people in this town who was battered when she was a kid and she's been using it ever since as an excuse for getting high and getting by. Why are you fixating on her?"

Cardozo handed Siegel the pages that Waldo Flores had brought him that morning: Dr. Frederick Hallowell's record on Scott Devens's September checkup seven years ago.

She took the document with an expression of mild expectation, and she read it with a look of mild surprise. What impressed Cardozo was how very mild the surprise was.

"Looks like Scott Devens gave his stepdaughter the clap when she was thirteen," she said.

"Looks it." A terrible sense of loss possessed him.

Siegel stared at him, her face registering concern. "Vince, are you all right?"

"Yeah." He didn't know what was happening within him. He didn't want to think about it. "Yeah. I'm fine. Am I acting weird or something?"

"Or something."

"I don't know why this hits me the way it does. I feel I've been sandbagged. How many corpses have I seen, how many raped kids, why does my mind say no to this?"

Her eyes hooked his. "Vince, we both know that where Cordelia is headed will be a hell of a lot worse than where she is now. The road she's taking, there's only one direction—down. I think you should talk to her mother."

He thought about telling Babe. The whole thing was taking on a numbing sadness.

Siegel touched his hand. She had a firm, clear gaze, no agitation, no uncertainty. "It's not as though you had to tell her her kid's dead—yet."

She was on crutches and she seemed happy to see him. "Iced tea on the terrace?"

"No—no iced tea. Let's talk inside."

She looked at him with an expression of curiosity, then led him into the large den beyond the dining room.

"You're doing well on those crutches," he said.

"I add a half hour a day. It takes a human being two years to learn to walk—I'm hoping to do it in two months."

He admired her: she accepted that the game was tough, but she had a quiet determination to keep playing.

"Drink?" she offered.

"You sit, I'll fix them," he said. "What'll you have?"

"Scotch and a little water. There's ice in the bucket."

It was a handsome bucket, silver, engraved with the emblem of the New York Racquet and Tennis Club and beneath that the words SCOTT DEVENS, SQUASH CHAMPIONSHIP, 1978.

He fixed two stiff Scotches and handed her one. She was sitting in an armchair, crutches resting against her and forming a little barricade.

Outside the windows, sun splashed the private park.

"How much pain can you take?" he asked.

"How much are you offering?"

"The psychiatrist's report on your daughter."

Her whole expression changed. She was looking him straight in the eye, the way people do when they're scared of showing they're scared.

He opened the manila envelope. It was a calculated risk: it meant showing her that people she'd trusted had taken her life apart.

He handed her Flora Vogelsang's pages.

Her blue gaze went slowly across the sheets, and there was an ache for her in his chest.

She didn't move except to turn the pages. She didn't say anything or even show she was reacting. But he could feel her taking it in, and he could feel her world turning dark.

When she'd finished she looked more numb than anything else. The shock didn't seem to have happened yet. She just sat swaying a little against the chair.

"Strange how it catches you unawares. A minute ago I was happily making lists of guests for my first party, and now . . ."

She sat looking across the room at him.

"There's more," he said.

She looked up, hands hanging a little way from her body, breathing shallowly, lips parted, braced for the second blow.

He gave her the other document.

After the first paragraph she stiffened. Behind her eyes came the sudden flare-up of understanding.

At that moment Cardozo felt a tightness in the back of his throat, an overpoweringly tender melancholy for her.

"We know why your parents accepted the plea bargain. They weren't going to let this come out."

Her face held like a struck mirror determined not to break apart.

"It takes money to keep a secret. A lot of people knew this one. Dr. Vogelsang. Ted Morgenstern. Your ex-husband. Your daughter. Maybe the D.A. Maybe even the judge."

She mused on that. He watched her pulling in.

"You're thinking something," he said.

"I wonder if Mrs. Banks knew. It might explain . . ."

"It might explain what?"

She told him about Mrs. Banks's restaurant, her clothes, her new face and manners and social set.

Suddenly Cardozo's mind was making connections. He asked questions: where did Babe's parents bank, did she know where Scott Devens and Mrs. Banks had accounts, where did Cordelia get her money and where did she keep it, how close were the Vanderwalks to Judge Davenport?

"I've always called him Uncle Frank. My mother was angry that he didn't give Scottie a harsher sentence, but they were certainly close till the trial.

Cardozo's face darkened. "They're your parents," he said, "but they're sons of bitches. I think we should take them."

"Take them?"

"Confront them. Get this cleared up for once and all."

* * *

The taxi stopped before a five-story German schloss in the middle
of a block of French châteaus. A Mercedes limousine was parked at
the curb, in front of iron gates bearing the sign, NO PARKING ACTIVE
DRIVEWAY 24 HOURS A DAY. Cardozo calculated it was the kind of
house that went nowadays for six million and change.

He paid the cabby and helped Babe and her crutches onto the
sidewalk.

Babe turned. "All I told Mama was that I was bringing a friend for
tea. She'll be dreadful with you. She says I only introduce her to men
I've decided to marry. I never allow her any input, she claims."

"I'll handle it."

Babe gave him a nervous smile and the smile he gave back was not
nervous at all. She pressed the brass doorbell. Murky clouds scudded
across the sky and thunder rumbled overhead.

After a moment a butler opened the door: there was the merest of
stiff-backed bows. "Good day, Mrs. Devens."

"How are you today, Auchincloss? Please tell my parents that
Lieutenant Cardozo and I are here."

"Certainly. Would you care to wait in the drawing room?"

The butler vanished, and a panting chow chow came running up,
barking, darting its black tongue over Babe and her crutches, then
sniffing at Cardozo's trousers. The dog preferred the trousers.

"If Jill annoys you just push her away," Babe said.

Cardozo let the dog play with his cuff. His gaze took in the marble
staircase, the paintings, the narrow blue Oriental carpet that seemed
designed precisely to fit the hallway and leave a six-inch border of
gleaming dark parquetry.

He followed Babe into the drawing room. The walls were vivid
orange—an unusual color for a room, bright and haunting. The sofas
and chairs were ivory-colored satin. The teacups and service were
waiting on the coffee table.

"Well, we're the first here," Babe said.

Cardozo could see she was fidgety. For distraction, he asked about
a Japanese urn under the Steinway. Babe said the urn had belonged
to the last mistress of the last king of Rumania.

Cardozo began to get a sense of the house. Everything was rich,
fantastic, beautiful. The *tchotchkes* of the world's rulers had fallen to
the Vanderwalks in astonishing quantity. Not just the urn, but Queen
Victoria's fan, in a glass case above the door; Winston Churchill's
watercolor of Somerset Maugham's villa, in a gold frame that must

have cost a patrolman's annual salary. Babe said the tea service had been designed by Paul Revere for the empress Josephine.

A woman in a navy blue dress came through the doorway, fixing Cardozo with pale blue eyes. "How do you do—I'm Beatrice's mother, Lucia."

Her face was like an artist's painting, the white of her skin contrasting delicately with her gray hair and pale crimson lips. She wore a single strand of pearls. A tiny circle of diamonds pinned to the silk dress caught the light and threw out flashes of color.

"How do you do, ma'am," Cardozo said. "Vince Cardozo."

A man in a navy blue blazer sauntered into the room. Babe introduced her father.

Hadley Vanderwalk had the look of a gray-haired American aristocrat, tall and lean and sharp-featured, his skin tanned by years spent on yacht decks and golf courses. There was something pleasant and intelligent in the set of his mouth.

Lucia Vanderwalk moved to a sofa and took a seat by the tea service. It was a signal for the men to sit. Her hands moved powerfully, gracefully, over the silver, seeming to communicate with it.

"Tell me about yourself, Leftenant." She pronounced his rank that way, British. *Lef,* not *lou.*

"I was born in New York, I grew up in New York, I became a cop in New York."

"Homicide or vice?"

"Homicide."

"You look familiar." She stared at him, something more than ordinary interest in her eyes. "Ceylon or China?"

He realized she was talking tea and he figured what could he lose. "China."

She poured from the teapot on the left. "Lemon or milk?"

"Lemon, please."

"Sugar"—she glanced at him— "or NutraSweet?"

"A little NutraSweet, thanks."

"Yes, I use it too."

She handed him a cup. It was almost weightless. The china was as delicate and fine as the skull of a newborn baby.

"Please help yourself to sándwiches. The dark bread's *petit-suisse,* the light's watercress. No one's allergic to watercress, I hope?"

Petit-suisse, Cardozo discovered, was cream cheese with a pleasantly tart accent.

Lucia Vanderwalk distributed tea and directed conversation.

Cardozo gradually got a feel for the Vanderwalks. They were wealthy liberals. They'd hung a sign on their lives—Do Not Disturb. They knew social inequity existed and they dealt with it by electing Lena Horne and Paul Newman to the country club.

Lucia struck him as a woman who knew exactly what she wanted —she didn't use words like "maybe" or "perhaps." Hadley struck him as the sort of husband who would defer to his wife's judgment in every matter but the important one—money.

"The Metropolitan Museum is doing just as much as any settlement house for the people of this city." Lucia Vanderwalk's glance, level and confident, turned diagonally across the table toward Cardozo. "Perhaps you don't agree, Leftenant?"

"You're right," he said pleasantly. "I don't agree."

Lucia Vanderwalk tilted her head questioningly. "Have you *been* to the Metropolitan?"

"I investigated a robbery there ten, twelve years ago."

"But have you ever been there *un*professionally?"

He met the dowager's adamantly tolerant gaze. "I don't have much time for things that don't connect to work. Wish I did."

"Sounds like you fellows are on the job twenty-four hours a day," Hadley Vanderwalk said.

Cardozo nodded. "Pretty much."

"But you're certainly not working now," Lucia Vanderwalk smiled.

"As a matter of fact, I am."

There was a drawn-out, smiling silence. Lucia Vanderwalk observed Cardozo with interest.

"Seven years ago," he said, "I helped investigate the attempt on Mrs. Devens's life. That's why you recognize me."

Lucia Vanderwalk's lips pulled into a thin line. She turned her eyes coldly toward her daughter. "Beatrice, this is shabby and absolutely irresponsible. You could at least show a little consideration for your poor father!"

Hadley Vanderwalk did not look the least bit troubled.

"If you and your husband had refused to plea-bargain," Cardozo said, "the D.A. would have prosecuted on the original charge. Why didn't you refuse?"

"Are we going to go into all this *again*?" Lucia Vanderwalk sighed.

"Did you have sudden doubts about the evidence? Or about Scott Devens's guilt?"

Lucia Vanderwalk's eyes defied Cardozo. "Neither my husband nor I had the slightest doubt whatsoever. Nor have we now."

"After the first trial," Cardozo said, "you invited a writer by the name of Dina Alstetter into your daughter's house. Mrs. Alstetter found a bottle of insulin in a stud box in the bedroom. You let her keep that bottle."

"Yes, she wanted to write a magazine article about it."

"Didn't it occur to you that the bottle should be taken to the police?"

"I am not going to submit to cross-examination in my own living-room."

"Your daughter's house was searched and there's no mention of that stud box or that bottle in any of the reports."

"What finds its way into police reports is hardly my responsibility."

"The insulin in that bottle was prescribed for Faith Banks."

Lucia Vanderwalk's face arranged itself into a careful blank. "Evidently my daughter's housekeeper was a diabetic. Is that a crime?"

"Isn't it a little odd that the evidence at the trial was insulin that Mrs. Banks found in Scott Devens's closet?"

"I fail to see the oddity."

"Mrs. Banks never told the police she was a diabetic. And the insulin that she claimed she found was never traced."

Lucia Vanderwalk tapped her fingers together. "Mrs. Banks's health and medications are all very mysterious I'm sure, but what has my daughter's former servant to do with me or my husband?"

"Quite a lot, ma'am. You two paid Faith Stoddard Banks two hundred fifty thousand dollars. The money was transferred to her bank account the day after Judge Davenport closed the second trial to the public. On the same day you paid a half million into Scott Devens's account. You've been paying him a quarter million and Mrs. Banks fifty thousand every year since."

Lucia Vanderwalk exhaled loudly. "Hadley," she commanded, "will you kindly say something?"

"I'm amazed at Lieutenant Cardozo's research," Hadley Vanderwalk said imperturbably.

"Tell him it's not true!" his wife cried.

"It's not true." Hadley Vanderwalk paused to light his pipe. "The money went to Ted Morgenstern."

A disbelieving expression flared on Lucia Vanderwalk's face. "Hadley, how can you be so stupid?"

"Morgenstern took his percentage—a large one," Hadley

Vanderwalk said. "He passed the rest on to Mrs. Banks and to Scottie. Morgenstern's a clever man. He organized a syndicate to back Mrs. Banks's restaurant. He organized another to back Scottie's career. Both have been profitable, I understand. Morgenstern gave us a chance to invest. We foolishly turned him down. Principle, you know."

Cardozo took out his notebook and made a show of consulting his notes. "At the second trial Ted Morgenstern introduced a psychiatric and physical examination of Cordelia made by Dr. Flora Vogelsang."

"That record is sealed!" Lucia Vanderwalk cried.

Cardozo gave her a long, slow look.

Mrs. Vanderwalk took a cigarette from a crystal box. "Dr. Vogelsang, for your information, is a vicious old Freudian and she should be burnt at the stake. She called Cordelia mad. Can you imagine, from inkblots and projective I-don't-know-what's she had the gall to accuse our granddaughter of inventing stories. I'm ashamed for Beatrice to have to hear this, but Dr. Vogelsang claimed Cordelia hated her mother and was in love with her stepfather. It was the most revolting oedipal offal, the lot of it."

"Ted Morgenstern introduced another medical report into evidence," Cardozo said. "Dr. Frederick Hallowell's. That report showed that Scott Devens was infected with the same disease as Cordelia—gonorrhea."

"Must we?" Lucia Vanderwalk snapped. Her finger tapped a furious bolero against her pearls.

"Yes, Mama," Babe Devens said. "We must."

"What were we to do?" Lucia Vanderwalk pleaded. "Let the papers get hold of it? Tell the world that Scott Devens had intercourse with his stepdaughter, a twelve-year-old? We had to protect the child."

"Babe, you have to understand," Hadley Vanderwalk said. "We thought you were lost and gone. We had to choose. Justice for our dead daughter—or a chance for our granddaughter. We chose Cordelia. Maybe it was wrong, but given the circumstances, that was the best decision we could make at the time."

"The second trial would have destroyed her," Lucia Vanderwalk said.

"Cordelia had no comprehension of what Scott had done to her," Hadley Vanderwalk said.

"She was only a child." Lucia Vanderwalk stubbed out her cigarette. The ashtray was Steuben. The table was Chippendale. The cigarette was Tareyton filter. "Scott seduced her with drugs. Terrible things—marijuana, cocaine . . ."

"Injections of morphine," Hadley Vanderwalk said. "At twelve she was an addict."

"You have no idea," Lucia Vanderwalk said, "how hard that child has had to work to put her life back together, to put all this horror behind her, how hard she's worked to get off drugs. It took courage and persistence. You're not going to undo the healing of seven years, surely you're not!"

Babe absorbed the plea quietly.

"Don't blame us for cooperating with Ted Morgenstern," Hadley Vanderwalk said.

"If we hadn't, he would have attacked Cordelia's innocence." A sigh settled on Lucia Vanderwalk's lips. "Destroyed it."

"Her innocence?" Cardozo felt the ambiguous weight of the word, felt its several facets. "Why do you say her *innocence?*"

"A child's innocence matters!" Lucia Vanderwalk's face was a mask of determination, mouth and jaw set. "A child's belief in her own innocence matters!"

And suddenly Cardozo saw. "My God. Morgenstern got Devens off by accusing *Cordelia!*"

Lucia Vanderwalk's face stiffened.

"He accused your *granddaughter* of the attempted murder! Cordelia, not Devens!" Cardozo felt a wave of certainty pass through his chest. "And you were afraid it was true. From the beginning you were afraid. That's why you hired your own investigator. To protect your grandchild. Your investigator planted evidence. And to keep the accusation alive when Devens appealed, you planted evidence yourself."

"Lucia," Hadley Vanderwalk said without the slightest sign of stress, "you don't need to deny this, you don't need to make any comment at all."

Lucia Vanderwalk was hardly breathing. "I will not permit this poison to be stirred up again."

"Cordelia confessed," Cardozo said. It was a wild shot.

"Never," Hadley Vanderwalk said.

"Oh yes she did," Cardozo said. "She confessed to that psychiatrist."

Neither Vanderwalk answered. Lucia's body appeared to be jerked by some invisible force into boardlike rigidity.

Cardozo kept putting it together. "Mrs. Banks helped you frame

Scott Devens. He agreed to stay framed, but he held out for the plea bargain. You paid him and Mrs. Banks off and you had the record sealed. And just to be double sure, Ted Morgenstern had blank pages substituted."

The air in the room congealed into a shining stillness. Lucia Vanderwalk seemed not even to be breathing.

Cardozo could imagine her instructing the cook in the morning, reading the mail before lunch, taking an afternoon walk around the garden, putting on a fresh dress, hammering out a deal with Ted Morgenstern over Ceylon tea and watercress sandwiches.

"You did this for yourself, Mama," Babe said quietly. "Not for me, not for Cordelia."

Lucia Vanderwalk had a voice like a terrorist's captive reading a prepared statement. "Your father and I did it for the family. There are some ghosts that we keep at home."

"I do remember something," Babe said, "something about Cordelia. Only it's foggy." She had a numbed, desperate look, as though a puff of breath could have erased her. "Cordelia was standing by my bed. I wasn't conscious, but I knew she was there, and I was trying to wake up, because something horrible was happening . . . and I knew I had to reach out my hand and stop her . . . but I couldn't come to the surface."

She was sitting in the big chair by her fireplace, taut, trying to appear calm, trying not to cry.

"It's strange, I was afraid for *her*—not myself."

Raindrops made a whispering sound against the windows.

"Your twelve-year-old daughter about to commit murder," Cardozo said. "I'd be afraid for her too. It's natural. You love the little monster."

Her eyes held a stillness, an expectancy, as though a second blow were about to fall and there was nothing she could do but accept it.

"Look, this is me, Vince. You don't have to impress me. Stop trying to be your mother. She's a lousy role model. Go ahead, bawl. Your husband went to bed with your daughter and it looks like your daughter tried to kill you. Come on, cry, scream, curse."

Tears were finally welling in her eyes, finally starting to roll down her cheeks. All she needed was a nudge.

"And they talk about Jewish mothers," Cardozo said. "Your mother sacrificed you for your daughter, and she's twisted that around to make *you* feel responsible for it." He knelt beside her.

"Your daughter's a guilt-ridden zombie because one subject your mother has never allowed to be aired—*never*—is what Cordelia did and why. There's no atonement, no forgiveness for her. Lucia Vanderwalk won't allow atonement or forgiveness when a family reputation's at stake. Imagine a child being alone with a secret like that. I'd say you have grounds for matricide or nervous breakdown or at least a few tears. You have Medea for a mother and an emotional paraplegic for a daughter and you haven't had one moment of honest unmanipulating love in your whole life. Go ahead. Let me hear a few sobs. Loud and clear. I'm not going to tattle on you."

Babe stared at him. Her body gulped in a breath and she dropped her head into her hands. She closed her eyes and started shaking as though a wave had hit her.

She was dismayingly beautiful in her tears. Her defenselessness called out every protective instinct in him. There was a sudden sweet tightness in the back of his throat. He became aware that what he felt for her was not a passing attraction nor even simply desire. An excitement and a tenderness that were far more than sexual moved him.

He took her hand and pulled her toward him and suddenly he took all of her and closed her tight into his arms. They embraced, their kiss growing in intensity, and he felt her breasts through the soft fabric of her blouse.

That was it. They were across the physical frontier peacefully and without effort. There was a long soft lingering moment of knowing that one day they were going to make love.

And then they pulled apart.

She looked at him. He wanted her to remember his eyes. He wanted her to see what was in them: that he was with her, that he cared.

"Vince," she said, "isn't there a drug that acts as a hypnotic—while people are under they recall buried memories?"

"Sodium pentothal."

"The police use it, don't they?"

"Sometimes."

"If I saw Cordelia injecting me seven years ago and I've forgotten —wouldn't sodium pentothal make me remember?"

"It might."

Something nervous and uncertain played across her face. "Could a police doctor do it?"

He saw determination in her and he saw, too, that she was scared out of her skin. The last thing on earth she really wanted to know was who had held that syringe.

He nodded. "I'll set it up."

36

CARDOZO PUSHED THROUGH THE REVOLVING DOORS OF THE CRIMI-
nal Court Building into air conditioning and Muzak and the dimness
of high vaulted ceilings. He was heading toward the elevator when a
voice from the newsstand called "Vince!"

A suntanned man with black curly hair put down the change for a
New York Times and strode forward, tall, smiling, moving with purposeful grace in his dark summer suit.

Cardozo shook the hand of Alfred Spaulding, D.A. The D.A.
steered him into a waiting elevator. "The Beaux Arts handyman is
willing to confess to killing Jodie Downs. Morgenstern wants to talk
plea bargain."

"Come on, Al. We have Loring without a confession."

"But with a guilty plea we don't have to go to trial. And there's no
chance of some crazy jury finding him innocent. We go straight to a
hearing before a judge and Loring gets sentenced. Nice and neat."

The elevator deposited them smoothly on the eighth floor. They
made their way down the wide, bustling corridors. The D.A.
stopped, his hand on the knob of the familiar frosted glass door.
"Let's just walk through the motions, hear Kane out."

"Al, why am I here? What do you want from me?"

The D.A. twisted the knob and motioned Cardozo to go first.
"Vince, you know Lucinda MacGill."

Lucinda MacGill was wearing a gray linen suit and her body and
carriage radiated presence and competence. Cardozo shook the
hand she offered. Her eyes were intelligent and there was a warning
in them. She flicked her head just a degree toward the inner office.
Cardozo followed her glance.

It was an old-fashioned room of casement windows and leather chairs and oil portraits of dead justices. Lockwood and Meridee Downs were sitting at the conference table. Lockwood Downs got up from his chair as Cardozo came into the room.

"I didn't know you were in town," Cardozo said.

"We got in last night." Lockwood Downs's eyes were weary. "We were hoping you'd call."

Wariness stirred in Cardozo and he didn't know if it was for himself or for the Downses. His eyes went to the window, where Ted Morgenstern stood whispering with his chubby associate, Ray Kane. They were both wearing Armani summer suits and they emanated a lazy awareness of their own power, like Roman emperors on a picnic.

The D.A. waited till everyone had sat. "Counselor Morgenstern has an offer."

"I'll plead Loring guilty of manslaughter"—Morgenstern steepled his fingers together— "if the state will allow mitigating circumstances."

"I'm sorry," Lockwood Downs said. "I'm in real estate, not criminal law. Could someone explain why my son's death would be manslaughter and not murder?"

"Murder involves malice aforethought," Morgenstern said.

"The question is whether or not Loring planned to kill your son," the D.A. explained.

Downs's face was drawn, lined with fatigue. "How can Mr. Morgenstern prove Loring didn't plan it?"

"It's up to the state to prove he did. Mr. Morgenstern has to prove very little."

"And what is a mitigating circumstance?"

"Anything that diminishes Loring's responsibility. For example, if he had a mental condition that impaired his judgment."

"Or took drugs," Morgenstern said.

"Took drugs?" Downs sounded incredulous.

Ray Kane handed Morgenstern a sheet of paper.

Morgenstern slipped a pair of bifocals over his nose. "We have a very strong precedent. On Palm Sunday, 1984, Christopher Thomas —a cokehead who had been free-basing for two years—massacred ten people in their Brooklyn home. A jury accepted the defense of diminished responsibility by reason of cocaine intoxication. They found Thomas guilty of ten counts of manslaughter. Now we'll all admit that that case was a good deal more heinous than what we're dealing with here."

Cardozo looked at Lockwood Downs, flailing in the dark side of the moment. His wife reached across the table and clenched her husband's hand.

Nothing came to Cardozo in words, only a knobbed something inside his ribs, a buried quiver of knowing he wasn't just going to sit there with the parents and see the son's murder whittled down into justified assault.

"What in hell is Counselor Morgenstern talking about," Cardozo said, "body count? Murder is murder, and it's just as illegal whether you kill one or a hundred."

Morgenstern's eyes glinted angrily in a pulp of wrinkles.

"Ted," the D.A. said, "I can see an argument for manslaughter, but you're going to have a hard time selling me on mitigation."

"Provocation," Morgenstern said.

Cardozo cut in. "Could I have a word with you, Al?"

In the other room, Cardozo shut the door. "Their son's been murdered, for God's sake, and you and Morgenstern could be pricing rugs in a Persian bazaar."

"Vince, take it easy."

"At least give them a meaningful choice. If it's manslaughter, it's manslaughter—no mitigation. Loring's already getting away with murder."

The D.A. shook his head. "Whether or not I buy Morgenstern's argument, a jury might. If Morgenstern thinks he can produce mitigation, I want to know about it here, not in the courtroom."

"You know damned well he's going to say the victim was guilty and the killer was innocent and if anyone should be on trial it's Jodie Downs, cocksucking dopester and disgrace to the human race."

"If all he has is a bluff like that we'll tell him it's no deal."

"Al, I'm not going to let you subject that man and woman to Morgenstern's tactics."

"It's not up to you, Vince. I warned them what they were in for. They wanted to hear Morgenstern out. Any decision on a plea bargain is up to them."

Back in the conference room, Morgenstern was calmly trimming and lighting a cigar. He waited till Cardozo and the D.A. took their seats. After four unhurried puffs he spoke.

"Jodie Downs had a police record. Three years ago he was picked up by a Transit Authority officer for sodomy in a subway men's room."

The shell came in on target. Meridee Downs's face froze. Lockwood Downs looked at Cardozo quickly, terrified, then dropped his head.

Cardozo hadn't known, and he realized Jodie Downs's parents hadn't known either. "Wait a minute," he said. "Was Downs arraigned?"

Morgenstern nodded, smug. "He was arraigned in night court and paid a fine."

"Let me see what's on that sheet." .

Morgenstern's assistant passed the tattered Xerox copy across the teakwood tabletop.

Cardozo's eyes scanned the lines of erratically spaced type. "Jodie Downs pleaded guilty to loitering in a public place, not sodomy."

Morgenstern's eyes crinkled into a half smile. "The arresting officer's report is more explicit."

Cardozo turned to Lucinda MacGill. "Can Morgenstern use that report?"

MacGill glanced toward the D.A. He nodded, giving permission, and she answered. "Counselor Morgenstern will claim the report shows a pattern of reckless self-endangerment. The judge will admit it as mitigating evidence. At that point the arresting officer can be called to testify."

"There's something I don't understand." Meridee Downs was gripping the table edge as though the room were somersaulting around her. "Jodie did some wrong things in his life. No one's denying that. But what does any of this have to do with his murder?"

"Counselor Morgenstern is sending you a message." Lucinda MacGill's voice was tight with controlled anger. "Unless you and Mr. Downs accept the plea bargain, he's going to defame hell out of your son."

"Harsh words, Counselor," Morgenstern said.

"Scuzzy tactic, Counselor," she replied.

"Let's bear in mind," the D.A. said, "that it's Counselor Morgenstern's job to defend his client, and this is a pretty standard defense."

"He's not defending the killer," Lockwood Downs said. "He's prosecuting our son."

"In Mr. Morgenstern's business," Cardozo said, "it comes down to the same thing."

Morgenstern continued, speaking quietly and steadily. "I have here a police report from the nineteenth precinct. This will be a very important part of Claude Loring's defense. Three years ago, on the night of June twenty-third, Jodie Downs picked up a stranger in a gay s.m. bar called the Strap on Tenth Avenue."

Meridee Downs covered her mouth.

"Jodie Downs took the stranger to his apartment on West Fifty-second Street, where according to his own admission they smoked 'five or six joints' and did 'a couple of lines' of coke. During sex—again Jodie Downs's own admission—the stranger attacked him with a razor, maiming him and cutting off one of his testicles."

Lockwood Downs listened with eyes downcast. His fingers rested on the table, tips just touching.

"Jodie Downs was admitted to Saint Clare's Hospital through the emergency room. Examining psychiatrists found Downs to be quote 'a guilt-ridden sexually obsessed young man bent on self-destruction.' " Morgenstern turned a page with a little snap. "There are photographs that go with this report, and I assure you they are the equal of any photographs the prosecution might be hoping to introduce into evidence."

Silence hit the table.

Cardozo absorbed the fact that Morgenstern had gotten hold of the report, just as he'd accepted that pages from the sealed record of one of Morgenstern's trials had turned up blank. Cardozo felt the old familiar outrage, but no surprise. He had long ago realized that Morgenstern's network was a cancer metastasizing into every institution in the city.

Smoke puffs fueled the stillness.

Cardozo realized he would never forgive Morgenstern for that cigar. For everything else, the deals, the sleaze, the distortions, maybe. For that cigar, waved in the face of these parents, no way.

"The report by the hospital psychiatrist is privileged," Cardozo said quietly. "Am I right, Al?"

"We'd have to ask the Supreme Court," the D.A. said glumly.

"Dead men," Morgenstern said, "do not enjoy doctor-patient confidentiality. In any case, we don't need the report. The doctor who wrote it, Dr. Larry Fenster of Saint Clare's, is willing and ready to take the stand in Claude Loring's defense."

The D.A. narrowed his eyes in solemn speculation. "So what kind of deal do you have in mind, Ted?"

"Negligent homicide," Morgenstern said.

"Negligent?" Lockwood Downs stared at Morgenstern disbelievingly. "You're going to claim Claude Loring killed my son by accident?"

"No," Morgenstern said. "The state is going to claim it."

Cardozo and the Downses came down the broad marble steps into Foley Square. A sharkskin-sleek gray stretch limousine was waiting by the curb and a uniformed chauffeur stepped out to hold the door.

"Is this yours?" Cardozo asked.

Lockwood Downs nodded. He seemed sandbagged. "Ours for two days. The district attorney's letting us use it."

A current of coolness reached out from the open limousine door. Cardozo was aware of the heat of the sunlight on his shoulders, aware too of Meridee Downs standing there looking like a dying leaf. "I wish I could have done more," he said.

"You did enough." Downs's voice broke. "You were there."

A truck backfired, and pigeons wheeled up into the soft blue sky of a summer's day.

"Can we give you a lift anywhere?" Meridee Downs asked.

"Sure, if you're heading uptown."

There was a bar in the back seat, and a color TV, and a tape deck, and a videocassette player. A heavy smell of perfume hovered pleasantly over the smell of leather upholstery. They sat quietly as the limo dodged expertly through Chinatown and took the FDR Drive north along the river.

Lockwood Downs drew his breath in. "I want to kill them for what they're doing."

The sun, subdued to dusky copper, slanted in through the raised windows. The U.N. and new riverside luxury co-ops whizzed past. Meridee Downs's eyes fixed on Cardozo. "Lieutenant, do you recommend the plea bargain?"

Cardozo knew what the D.A. wanted him to say and he knew what he felt like saying. "Doesn't quite balance out. Jodie lost his life. You lost a son. The killer loses a few months."

Her face was puzzled. "The district attorney told us fifteen years."

"Fifteen's the maximum. No one but Charles Manson and Sirhan Sirhan serves the maximum. Loring's going to the mat voluntarily. The minimum is the most he'll get. Eight years. Then you have to subtract time off for good behavior. Also, you have to consider early parole. So if you want to know what I think, I think the plea bargain's a mistake. I think the state can get a conviction without it."

"The district attorney said if we accept it there won't be a trial."

"There'll be a hearing. Loring will plead guilty, waive trial; the judge will sentence him."

"If we go to trial we may not win," Lockwood Downs said.

The material of Meridee Downs's dress made a rustle in the quietness. "And Morgenstern will make everyone think Jodie did it to himself, he deserved it. Lieutenant," she said, "Jodie tried to turn himself around. He tried hard. He may have done bad things, but nothing like what was done to him. He never murdered anyone."

"The plea bargain's up to you," Cardozo said. "Whichever way you decide, the D.A. will back you."

"Where we live," Lockwood Downs said thoughtfully, "they haven't even heard of alternative life-styles. 'Gay' means happy or it means AIDS. It's forty minutes from Chicago and eighty light-years from New York. We have to go on living in that town."

"But it's murder," Meridee Downs said, "not shoplifting. Loring has to pay."

"But we have to go on living," Lockwood Downs repeated.

The limousine stopped in front of the Waldorf. Swedish and Israeli flags were flying. A doorman sprinted out and held the door.

The hotel lobby glittered with lights and polished oak, brass and crystal and gold and velvet and green Italian marble.

"We've come up in the world," Lockwood Downs said bitterly.

Cardozo went with the Downses while they picked up their room-key and then he watched them cross through the ultra-well-dressed throng to the elevator.

Meridee Downs turned and gave a quick, sad little wave.

He waved back, with a sense of standing outside a disaster helplessly looking in, of watching a man and a woman mutilated by events.

He went to the checkout desk. A young woman looked up at him.

"Suite twelve twelve," he said, unobtrusively showing his shield. "Who's paying?"

The young woman cast him a look, then checked through a bin of room registration forms. She drew out a card. "Prepaid by American Express card."

"Mr. Downs's card or someone else's?"

"Pyramid Enterprises."

Back in his cubicle, Cardozo phoned American Express. He jotted Pyramid's phone and address on a scratch pad and stared at them until the association he wanted clicked in his mind.

He went through his Rolodex. His finger stopped at Melissa Hatfield's card, Beaux Arts Properties, Inc. The telephone number and address were the same as Pyramid's.

He lifted the phone and dialed.

Her honeyed, moneyed voice came on the line. "Beaux Arts."

"Melissa, it's Vince Cardozo."

"Nice to hear a sane voice. You *are* sane, aren't you?"

"Always."

"It's a madhouse here today. Never work in real estate."

"It's a promise. Could you do me a favor?"

"If it's legal."

"Absolutely. Can you tell me what Pyramid Enterprises is?"

"That's easy. Pyramid is our Delaware corporation."

He read her the American Express number. "Who uses that credit card?"

"Nat Chamberlain. It's for entertaining company clients."

At 10:45 the next morning, Meridee and Lockwood Downs stepped into District Attorney Alfred Spaulding's office. Hopelessness lay on them like a palpable shroud.

The district attorney offered coffee. He offered to send his secretary for Danish, for orange juice. They said they'd had breakfast at the Waldorf, thanks.

"There's no sense dragging this out." Lockwood Downs was holding his wife's hand. They were sitting side by side at the conference table, in a cone of summer morning light streaming through the ten-foot casement. Their faces were drained. "We'll go along with the plea bargain."

"This office will abide by your decision," the district attorney said quietly.

"If I may say so," Ray Kane said, "I think you show commendable wisdom." Kane had come alone; apparently Morgenstern had been sure of the Downses accepting the plea bargain and hadn't considered it important enough to show up for.

"We'd like to thank you for all your help," Lockwood Downs said, "and we'd like to thank Lieutenant Cardozo for his."

Lockwood Downs's eyes met Cardozo's, and at that moment the squirrel that was leaping around inside Cardozo's ribs turned into a rat.

"We know you have a lot of murders in New York." Something had happened to Meridee Downs's voice. It was like stone, as if there were no more tears in it. "We appreciate the trouble you've gone to on our behalf."

And that was it. Short, rehearsed speeches. They made their exit quickly. Cardozo was rising from his chair with them, and the next moment he was looking at an empty doorway.

He turned to the D.A. "How do you happen to know Nat Chamberlain?"

Something hovered over the D.A.'s face. "Nat who?"

"He's paying for the Downses' suite at the Waldorf. He's paying for their limousine. He's probably paying for their plane tickets. He owns Beaux Arts Tower."

A furrow appeared between the D.A.'s eyes. He turned to Ray Kane. "Ted told me your office was paying for all that."

"The office *is* paying." Ray Kane smiled, snapping the gold locks on a pancake-thin pigskin briefcase he had never bothered to open. "Nat owes Ted some favors, Ted called them in. Not to worry, gentlemen." He glanced at his watch. "I'd love to take you two to coffee, but I have a meeting with the mayor's commissioner for cultural affairs. Good seeing you both."

After Kane had left, Cardozo stood staring at the D.A.

"Why did you let Morgenstern get involved?"

"Where was I going to put them, Holiday Inn? Morgenstern has a budget for that kind of thing; this office doesn't."

"It's not right, Al. A lot of things in this case aren't right." Cardozo could feel a vein in his forehead beginning to pump up. "The plea bargain's a fucking farce. How can you buy diminished responsibility?"

"Vince, what are we going through this for? The parents are gone, you're not winning anyone's vote, certainly not mine. I accept diminished responsibility because Loring is a cokehead, he admits he was high."

"Sure, to save his neck he admits it. But tell me something. We dusted that apartment for fingerprints—and there were fingerprints of everyone on God's earth except Claude Loring. How does a man snowed out by coke remember to remove fingerprints of a crime he claims he was too snowed out to know he's responsible for?"

The D.A. pointed his finger at Cardozo. "Vince—you've done your job, let me do mine. Do us both a favor and just butt the hell out of this."

"Right," Cardozo said with disgust.

Three minutes later he walked down the steps of the Criminal

Court Building, crossed Foley Square, and rounded the corner without looking back.

"Claude Loring, Junior," Judge Francis Davenport said, "you are
accused of negligent manslaughter in the death of Jodie Downs."

Loring stood facing the bench. He was wearing a dark suit and a
conservative striped tie. The suit was new and it fit. Quite a change,
Cardozo thought, from sawed-off Levi's denim jackets. Loring was
even clean-shaved, and with the moustache gone his face had lost its
pirate glow. Gray skin was tight across jutting cheekbones; eyes were
dull sockets.

"How do you plead to the charge? Guilty or not guilty?"

Loring's voice was small and tight. "Guilty, Your Honor."

Judge Davenport leaned forward, arching his thick gray eyebrows.
He studied the defendant.

In his seat at the rear of the almost deserted courtroom, Vince
Cardozo folded his arms and watched. The image sank into his mem-
ory: Judge Davenport with his plump, pink face gazing at Claude
Loring with his wasted face.

"Mr. Loring, do you understand the legal meaning of the words
negligent and *manslaughter*?"

"Yes, Your Honor."

"You admit you took Jodie Downs to an apartment in Manhattan?
You admit you tied him up and engaged in behavior which contributed to his death?"

Cardozo looked across the aisle to where Lockwood and Meridee
Downs were sitting erect and alone. He felt the pathos of what was
happening to them. A boundary was being crossed. They'd spent
their lives not breaking laws, and till now they'd thought the rest of
the world had been doing the same. But someone had changed the
rules and forgotten to send them a telegram.

"I was very spaced out, Your Honor," Claude Loring said.

"That's well and good, Mr. Loring, but do you or do you not admit
you engaged in behavior which contributed to Mr. Downs's death?"

"He asked me to, Your Honor, and I deeply regret it."

"Did you intend to kill Mr. Downs?"

"No, Your Honor."

Meridee Downs dropped her head into her hand. Her husband put
his arm around her. The Downses' faces were telling Cardozo about
loss, about a belief in simple justice that was being murdered as
stupidly and brutally as their boy had been.

"And did you intend him bodily harm?"

"No, Your Honor. It was a scene."

"A scene?"

Ted Morgenstern rose. According to the morning's *Post,* there had been a birthday party for him the night before, eight hundred of the New York Four Hundred discoing in black tie at the Metropolitan Museum of Art, and his eyes had a puffy look. "Your Honor, a scene is a sexual encounter between consenting adults. It is a common and usually harmless transaction in the sadomasochistic community. My client was drugged and under the impression that the acts Mr. Downs requested would not lead to bodily harm."

"This is a pretrial hearing, not a trial, Counselor, so please resist the temptation to prove your client innocent of murder. Mr. Loring is pleading guilty to a lesser but still serious felony, and it is my duty to be sure he understands the meaning of the charge and of his plea."

"My client admits he performed the acts, Your Honor, without realizing or intending that they would contribute to Mr. Downs's death."

"Counselor, I'm not questioning intent to contribute to death, only intent to perform acts which reasonably constitute reckless endangerment of human life. That is after all the issue which we are here to determine. Mr. Loring, you admit that you freely consented to perform the acts?"

Morgenstern nodded yes.

Loring took the cue. "Yes, Your Honor."

"You admit to these acts and you do not dispute the state's claim that Mr. Downs's death resulted?"

Loring glanced again at Morgenstern, who nodded no.

"I don't dispute anything, Your Honor."

"Do you understand that in entering a plea of guilty you forgo jury trial and may be sentenced at the discretion of this court to the maximum term allowable by law?"

"Yes, Your Honor."

"Give this a moment's reflection, Mr. Loring. Do you wish to change your plea to not guilty and to be tried by a jury?"

Morgenstern shook his head absolutely no.

"I plead guilty, Your Honor."

Judge Davenport settled back in his chair, face set in a slumber of judicial indifference. "Let the record show that Claude Loring, Junior, pleads guilty to the negligent manslaughter of Jodie Downs. Do the people accept his plea?"

The D.A. rose. "The people accept."

"Let the record so show. Prisoner is remanded for sentencing three weeks hence in this courtroom at ten thirty in the morning." Court adjourned with a thump of Judge Davenport's gavel.

Lockwood Downs rose. His hands were visibly shaking. Up till this moment everything might have seemed a nightmare, but Cardozo could see that this was real to him now: the courtroom, the prisoner in handcuffs and a neatly fitted new suit being led out between two guards, the judge retiring to his chambers, the defending attorney in his snappy dark suit and French cuffs crossing the room to confer with the D.A. in his snappy dark suit and French cuffs, two power brokers thrashing out a merger.

Lockwood Downs helped Meridee to her feet. They stood in the aisle, pulverized, afraid to take even a step in a world where there was suddenly no support for anything or anyone.

Cardozo went to them.

"It takes three weeks to decide on a sentence?" Deep new lines had etched themselves into Lockwood Downs's face.

"Judges like to take their time," Cardozo said. "They have a theory it avoids reversible error." He didn't bother saying what he thought of the majestic crud of the law, pulsating with crimes against common sense.

"And then what happens to Loring?" Downs asked.

"State penitentiary."

As Meridee Downs looked up at Cardozo he saw her face flood with hatred.

"That's worse than a city jail?" she asked.

He nodded. "If you can believe it."

"We won't be coming back for the sentencing," Lockwood Downs said.

Cardozo could feel the man's pride, the instinct not to cause a scene, not even now when all the promises the universe had ever made him were being taken back.

"I'll be here," Cardozo said. "I'll phone you."

37

"SCARED OF NEEDLES?"

Jerry Brandon snapped the cartridge into the syringe. He regarded Babe with a hint of mischief, as though they were about to embark together on a lighthearted adventure, a trip through the funhouse of her mind.

"I can't say I love them," Babe said.

"Get ready to love. There are people in this town that kill for twenty cc's of this stuff." Brandon had gone gray and a little haggard since Cardozo had last seen him, but he still had his smart-talking police-doctor mask, cocky and charming. "Why don't you have a seat before we boost you to outer space?"

Babe sat down in the black Barcalounger. Her movements were tentative and gingerly. She was a very scared porcelain doll.

Brandon took her arm and placed the tip of the needle at the little blue vein pulsing in the crook. His thumb pressed slowly on the syringe.

Cardozo waited by the wall, out of the light. Babe shot him one scared look. "Babe," he said, "it's going to be okay."

Brandon withdrew the needle. "Count backwards from a hundred."

Babe's eyes fixed as if they had lost their sight. "One hundred . . . ninety-nine . . ."

The outer layers of her brain began shutting down. At 93 she closed her eyes.

Brandon gave the go-ahead nod, and Cardozo pressed the start button on the tape recorder.

Brandon ejected the empty cartridge from the syringe and loaded another. "Showtime." He took her arm, feeding the point of the needle into the vein. "It's yesterday, Babe," he said.

At first there was no reaction. Her breathing was slow and deep, almost hoarse. And then there was a tiny movement on her face, and Cardozo could sense something taking shape. Her lips moved. A puff of voice came out. "Yesterday."

"You're waking up. Where are you?"

For a while she lay there, hammocked on the Barcalounger, limp and passive and still. And then she opened her eyes. Her glance circled the room. It passed over Cardozo as though he were a table. "I'm in our bedroom."

"Tell me about the bedroom, Babe. What do you see?"

"It's sunny through the windows."

"What color are the window curtains?"

"Pale green. They have orange flowers."

"What do you do, Babe? You wake up and then—?"

"Slippers. On the floor by the bed."

"What kind of slippers?"

"Blue silk."

Brandon pursed his lips at Cardozo, and the nod of his head said, *My my, aren't we snazzy.* "Fine. Now let's go further back, Babe. You're in the hospital."

There was a silence as though she were processing the command and trying to locate the mental file. She frowned, and finally something clicked and she said the word *hospital.*

"You're waking up in the hospital. It's the first time you've ever woken up in that hospital. What do you see?"

"It's dark." A strange childish sort of sobbing began coming out of her. "Scottie isn't here." She shook her head from side to side, and her eyes were tearing over. "No one but me." Her wrists and fingers knotted over the armrests. Her face twisted with effort. "I can't move."

"Babe, can you see anything?"

"A window." She squinted, trying to see something. "The window's in the wrong place."

"What else?"

"No clock."

She stiffened. "A door just opened. Now there's light." She narrowed her eyes, tracking some moving object. "A woman came in. She's wearing a nurse's cap. She's leaning over me, very close." Babe's posture suddenly altered: her head came up and forward, her shoulders tensed. "Who the hell are you, and what are you doing in my bedroom?"

"You're doing fine, Babe, just fine. Everything's okay. Stay there in the hospital. Just hold it there."

Brandon came across the room to Cardozo and spoke in a lowered tone. "Where was she before the attempt was made?"

"A big blowout—it was the anniversary of her company. Press reception kind of thing. Celebrities, booze, fancy food."

"Okay, I'll walk her through the party and get her back to the town house."

Brandon returned to the Barcalounger and reloaded the syringe. "Babe—last night you were at a party. Tell me about that party."

"Party," she repeated. Her eyes were still shut and there was something held back in her voice, something half thinking and half dreaming.

"You're at a party, Babe. Now. You're at the party."

Her head drooped for a moment. "I'm not supposed to be here. They don't know."

"Who doesn't know?"

"Mickey Mouse and Winnie the Pooh and the Mad Hatter."

Brandon gave Cardozo a look. "You said celebrities?"

"Is that normal?" Cardozo said. "I thought this stuff was like truth serum."

Brandon shrugged. "One man's truth is another man's Disneyland."

Disconnected sighs were coming out of her.

"What do you see, Babe? What are you seeing?"

"Watch out for the trucks."

Brandon turned his eyes back to Cardozo, his glance asking whether or not to go on.

Cardozo frowned, puzzled: it was as though Babe had set out walking down a perfectly familiar street and suddenly for no reason had swerved into an alley. He nodded, keep going.

"Babe, what kind of trucks?" Brandon asked.

She opened her eyes, looking at the huge trucks. "Meat trucks."

At those two words, *meat trucks,* a sick nervousness began humming inside Cardozo. It was as though Babe had stepped off the map into pitch black space.

"Where are these meat trucks, Babe?"

"In the street outside the building."

Cardozo was signaling with his hands, stretch it out.

"Tell me about the building."

"The building is on the corner. The cobbled street meets the asphalt. The building is falling apart. The sign is in English and Spanish. Body parts of cows. The doorway is on the left. That's where I go in. Only they don't know."

Brandon turned to Cardozo. "I don't know about you, but I'm lost. You want to get her back to the party?"

Cardozo felt the premonition of something larger. "No—follow this."

"You go in the doorway, Babe. Then what?"

"Up the stairs in the dark. One flight. Another flight. I can hear voices."

"Whose voices?"

"Mickey Mouse. Richard Nixon."

Cardozo narrowed his eyes in speculation. The two men stared at each other.

"I open the door."

She had the face of a little girl peeking into a forbidden room. The peeking turned into a shy half-smile. The shy half-smile became a big grin.

"They don't hear me. John Wayne is passing champagne." The grin wiped off her face. She sat up in the Barcalounger, alert now. "The man is naked."

"What man, Babe?"

"The young man. He has blond hair. He's lying in the corner. They've drugged him. Winnie the Pooh and the Mad Hatter pick him up and tie him to the H."

Something began coming to Cardozo, some inexplicable sense that the nightmare at the end of Babe's alley fitted into someone else's nightmare.

"What's the H?"

"Wood. Black wood. White wall. Alice in Wonderland and Donald Duck help with the mask."

Cardozo felt evil imploding. *This isn't happening,* he thought. *I'm not hearing this. She didn't see this.*

"What kind of mask, Babe?"

"Black leather. There are two slits for the eyes and no ears and there's a zipper over the mouth. The young man can't move and he can't make any sound."

Cardozo felt blood rush along his scalp.

"Minnie Mouse has a beautiful red silk gown on. Hundreds of

sequins, hand-stitched. She takes the cigarette from her mouth and
—" Babe gasped. "And she puts it out in the young man's hand."

Cardozo's neck muscles tightened and his throat was suddenly dry.
"Ask her which hand."

"Which hand, Babe? Which hand does Minnie Mouse put the
cigarette out in?"

"His left hand."

There was dread at the pit of Cardozo's stomach. Common sense
said there was no way she could know, no way she could be saying
what she was saying.

"She closes his fingers around the cigarette. He makes a sound. A
moan."

Disbelief was thudding so hard through Cardozo's veins that the
image of Babe in the chair and Jerry Brandon bending over her
seemed to come apart before his eyes.

"Richard Nixon takes the knife from the table. It's a curved knife.
It's a melon knife, I think." Sweat needled her forehead. "Richard
Nixon walks up to the naked man and he takes the knife and he . . ."

Waves of trembling broke over her. Cardozo could feel the terror
in her, the kind that comes from knowing you have to turn your eyes
away or your mind will snap.

Brandon looked at Cardozo, asking, and Cardozo nodded. "Ask
her what Nixon does with the knife."

"What does Nixon do with the knife, Babe?"

A spasm ripped the muscles of her face. "No—I don't want to see
it!" She covered her eyes.

"You do see it, Babe. You do see it."

She brought her hands down a little, far enough to peek over
them. "He cuts the young man. The poor young man can't defend
himself and Richard Nixon . . ."

Cardozo's heart turned over in his chest. "Ask her what the cut
looks like. Ask her does it have a design."

"What does the cut look like, Babe? Does it have a design?"

She stiffened. "He cuts a circle."

"What's in the circle?" Cardozo said.

"What's in the circle, Babe?"

"There's a Y, dripping blood." She doubled over, her arms
clamped across her stomach, and made retching sounds.

Brandon touched her forehead. "Babe, go back to sleep."

A blankness flowed into Babe's eyes. She slumped back against the
Barcalounger.

"Wow," Brandon said. "What was that all about?"

Cardozo bent over her. He took her hand in his. It was cool, limp. He massaged her knuckles. It was five minutes before her eyes opened slowly. He spoke in a low voice, tinged with sympathy. "Come on. You've earned a little fresh air."

He helped her up and he helped her onto her crutches. He kept a firm guiding hand on her arm.

They walked out to where the daylight was dark gold, barred with gray. The streets were alive, bustling and active with people hurrying home from work. A Spanish vendor was selling authentic Italian ices. A small Chinese girl ran past, pigtails flying. They let the thickly peopled sidewalk carry them along.

Babe lifted her eyes to where the skyline stopped sharp against the sky. "What did I remember?" she said.

"You didn't."

With a pained blinking of her eyes she turned to him. "It wasn't Cordelia?"

"You didn't remember. Brandon tried to get you back to that night but he couldn't."

Cardozo turned off the cassette player.

Ellie Siegel was staring thoughtfully into her can of cherry Coke. "Somebody told her," she said.

"Who could have told her? Who knew about the cigarette butt in Downs's left hand? Who knew about the peace sign carved on his chest? We kept that stuff out of the papers."

"Vince, is there any possibility maybe you mentioned some stuff to her?"

"Why the hell would I mention it to her?"

"Because you're sorry for her. Maybe you wanted to make her feel important. A lot of cops tell their girlfriends things they shouldn't, little inside shit about ongoing investigations—"

"She is not a girlfriend. Jesus Christ, enough with the matchmaking."

"Would you give me back my head, please? I'm just trying to understand how there could be such a mix on that tape. She has insider details and then all that _mishegoss_ about John Wayne and Mickey Mouse. And Nixon. What's with the thirty-seventh president? Added to which, there's nothing about apartment six, nothing about Claude Loring. Devens just has isolated bits and she's filled in the rest with comic book stuff."

"It bothers me. I heard her saying those things and it locked right in to a feeling I've had all along about this Downs killing."

"The case is solved, Vince."

"Where did the mask come from? Where did that cigarette butt come from? Who was the woman that bought the mask from Pleasure Trove and took it to Beaux Arts Tower?"

"Wait a minute. Loring confessed. The evidence backs up his confession. The witnesses back up his confession. You're not going to tell me that crazy tape raises any questions about his guilt. Neither does the mask or the cigarette or the woman no one could identify. They don't make Loring innocent. No way. The woman may not even connect. The mask is a mass-produced item. The cigarette—no one's ever been convicted on a cigarette unless the charge was littering or polluting the atmosphere at the Four Seasons. The questions in this case have been answered. That's why those files in your lap are marked Case Closed."

Cardozo sat there with his Diet Pepsi on ice, sealed in a state of wondering. "Too many coincidences. Morgenstern defended the Devens murder attempt and the Downs killing. We put Babe Devens under and out comes the Downs killing."

"Vince, you're over the line. You've got a mishmash, not coincidence. Mickey Mouse is not an accessory in the Downs killing. Richard Nixon has an alibi. You're not going to get any judge to subpoena Alice in Wonderland."

Cardozo was silent, frowning.

"But assume she was there," Siegel said. "Where does it get you? Downs is being tortured and murdered, and in walks Babe Devens, up two flights of dark stairs. Forget she can't even walk *now*. Forget apartment six is on the sixth floor. Forget she had nurses watching her around the clock, forget the coma. Forget she sees the murder and doesn't see the murderer, forget what she *does* see is half of Disneyland. She's there while the handyman is taking Jodie Downs apart. Just ask yourself: what is Babe Vanderwalk doing in that place at that time? Who or whose purpose does it serve? Her own? The handyman's? The victim's? Where was she before and where did she go afterward? How come no one saw her?"

"So why did she tell that story?"

"Because you and Dr. Kildare had her flying on Medicaid angel dust."

"How did she get the details?"

"You mean how did she get the wrong details? She made them up.

How did she get the right details? Maybe she made them up too and got lucky. Or maybe there *is* something to ESP, maybe she knew because *you* knew, because you've been fixated on this case for so long that anyone who can read lips would know what you're thinking."

Cardozo put down his glass and rested his head on the back of the seat. Through lowered lids he stared at the dead TV screen.

"G'night, Vince." Siegel came across the livingroom and patted him on the cheek. "The chicken was delicious."

"The neighbor cooked it."

"It was still delicious."

He sprang to his feet and came with her into the hallway. Thoughtfully, she considered the man holding the door for her.

"Vince, I don't mean to spoil the ending for you, but Loring did it."

He nodded, eyes blank with fatigue. The latch clicked shut.

For two more hours he sat staring at photos and fives, his mind toying with connections, trying to tease the new piece into place.

"Hey, Dad—aren't you sleeping anymore?"

His daughter was standing in the doorway, in rumpled night-clothes, and he felt a rush of absurdity and guilt.

He closed the file. He walked slowly, feeling an ache in his back, and he wondered if he was turning into one of those middle-aged deskmen with back problems.

Terri followed him down the hall to the kitchen. He put a pan of milk on the burner. Hot milk, his instant sleeping pill. She got a cup out of the cabinet for him.

Cardozo stood watching his daughter. That movement of the arm she had from her mother, and the way she took charge of the stove with her head a little on one side was her mother's too.

"How you feeling, Dad?"

So was the question, and the dark-eyed look, with their implied gentle nagging.

"I'm okay."

She mixed Sweet 'n Low and cinnamon in the cup and handed him the milk. She suspected something. He knew she sensed he wasn't right.

"Get some sleep," she said.

But that night he didn't sleep.

* * *

A gob of milky light smeared on the wall. Cardozo adjusted the lens. The image leapt into focus, a tall beautiful woman with black curly hair that came to her shoulders.

Babe sat with her crutches leaning on the wall behind her, hands pushed down in the pockets of her skirt. After a long moment of deliberation she said, "There's a seven-year gap in my memory and even if I knew these people, they've changed and I might not recognize them."

"Or on the other hand you might."

Cardozo clicked to the next. A slim blond girl with deep-set eyes. Mystery woman taking mask into BAT.

Babe pulled back, shook her head no.

The next. A middle-aged man with hollow eyes and wisps of black hair over his ears.

"That's Lew Monserat, the art dealer. He's lost weight. Is he well?"

"You mean mentally? I wouldn't swear to it."

Cardozo made check marks in the log, one for recognition and another for a certain hesitation that might have masked recognition.

Claude Loring flashed onto the wall, sweaty in his sawed-off Levi's jacket, striding into the entrance of the Inferno.

It began with something vague. Babe just stared, still and silent.

The photo exuded a terrific sense of cocaine tension, cocaine power, cocaine violence, all held under tight Valium control.

Cardozo could feel she was beginning to make a connection. Her face tightened and paled. She was on the brink of something.

"His eyes look so cold. He makes me feel afraid."

"Do you know him?"

"Should I?"

"There are no shoulds about it. Maybe you've seen him somewhere, maybe you haven't."

"Seven years ago he would have been a child."

"But you feel something."

"Yes, I feel something, but . . . Vince, I'm sorry, I just can't tell. Maybe it's just that he looks so intense."

"What does that remind you of, someone looks so intense?"

"It makes me think . . . I'd like to draw him."

38

"THE DEFENDANT WILL RISE."

Claude Loring rose. Babe leaned forward. She was sitting in the front row of the courtroom, next to Cardozo. Her gaze took Loring in, from the short-cropped hair to the neat regimental tie to the tailored dark suit.

Ted Morgenstern hadn't bothered coming to the sentencing. He'd sent Ray Kane, balding and young in his Armani suit, looking restlessly at his wristwatch, as though he had a helicopter to catch three minutes ago.

Judge Francis Davenport adjusted half-moon spectacles on his nose, surveyed the almost-empty courtroom, and peered down at the defendant. "Claude Loring, you have pleaded guilty to the crime of negligent manslaughter."

Babe's eyes were pinned to the man at the defendants' table.

Claude Loring's head was bent now, his face gaunt; there was no light, no life in his eyes.

"It is the sentence of this court," the judge said, "that you serve not more than twenty-five and not less than six years imprisonment at the New York State penitentiary at Ossining, New York."

Loring's head dropped.

Cardozo calculated rapidly that Loring would be out on parole in two years. He could feel hate come out on his body like sweat.

Two guards came forward and led Claude Loring away.

Ray Kane stuffed papers into a briefcase, twirled the combination lock.

Cardozo quickly shouldered his way after the prisoner. He flashed his shield at the guards. "Hey, fellas, I want to talk to Claude a minute."

Loring turned around.

"Someone I want you to meet, Claude."

Babe came slowly across the courtroom on her crutches. She looked searchingly at Loring. Her brow wrinkled, questioning.

Claude stood squinting at her, one finger poked through his pants pocket, scratching his balls. Something was rumbling inside him, a lot of anger coming to a boil under his skull. His voice snapped out like sandpaper. "What the fuck do you want, bitch?"

Cardozo slapped the killer hard across the jaw.

A guard stepped between them. "Easy does it, Lieutenant. He's state property now."

"Can I use the phone, long distance?"

"Of course," Babe said.

They were in her livingroom. Cardozo stared a long time at the phone and he could feel her watching him, curious.

Finally he picked up the receiver and punched out a number. Three shades of white noise came over the line and then three buzzes and then the voice of Lockwood Downs from the middle of Illinois.

"Loring got six to twenty-five," Cardozo said.

There was a silence. "What does that mean?" Downs said.

"He could be paroled after he serves a third."

"A third of what?"

"A third of six."

"Two years." The voice had crumpled.

At that moment Cardozo experienced an overpowering melancholy. Lockwood and Meridee Downs would hurt. They would hurt for the rest of their lives. Every time they saw a young man in the pride of youth with all the promise of life before him, they would think, *That could have been our son.*

Cardozo felt pitifully small. "I'm sorry."

He hung up.

Babe was giving him that piercingly blue look.

"Vince—why did you make that call from here?"

She was staring at him and he wasn't sure what he was reading in that stare. Her eyes were gentle and questioning, but there was a strangeness in them too.

"I don't understand why you wanted me to hear. And I don't understand why you took me to that trial."

"So you could see the defendant."

"Why?" she said.

"Why did you think you knew him?"

"I didn't. I thought I might like to draw him."

"Still want to draw him?"

"Why are you testing me? You're acting as though I'm somehow involved."

"You *are* involved." For the next twenty minutes Cardozo told Babe about the Downs killing. He could see it was shocking her and he could see too that it wasn't connecting to anything in her head.

"This is what you said under sodium pentothal." He put the cassette player on the coffee table between them. He pushed the start button.

When the tape was over she looked up at him, frightened, eyes begging for the sort of assurance he couldn't give, a promise that the world wasn't crazy, that she wasn't.

"It's impossible," she said.

"Right," Cardozo said. "It's impossible."

Cardozo laid two lists on the table. "She ID'ed these twelve from the photo file. She was definite. These seventeen are maybe's—she didn't know their names, but she dawdled, like she knew the faces. And this is her personal address book. Don't lose it—it's a loan."

"So what do you want from me?" Charley Brackner asked.

"You have some other lists on that computer. Beaux Arts Tower and the Inferno. Can you pull the matches?"

Charley gave a happy little smart-ass grin, his way of saying the task was pathetically uncomplicated. "Sure. We create a directory called B DEVENS and when we get the names in we'll tell Maisie to COMP." His fingers began flying over the keyboard and the names began lighting up the screen.

An hour and a half later the names were on the computer and Charley typed in SEARCH: INFERNO.

The screen flashed back: SEARCHING.

Charley swiveled around in his chair and lit a Camel. "Maisie's random access," he told Cardozo. "Sometimes she's lucky and hits it on the first go, sometimes she takes a few seconds."

The screen flashed: ENTRY NOT FOUND.

"Okay, let's try Beaux Arts."

The screen flashed: ENTRY NOT FOUND.

"Not found, what does that mean?" Cardozo said.

"Not found means not there."

"I know those files are in the computer," Cardozo said.

"Did these three files have anything in common?"

"Try Jodie Downs or Downs murder."

Charley typed *DOWNS*.

The screen flashed SEARCHING and a moment later

DOWNS, JODIE, MURDER
THIS DIRECTORY CONTAINS THE FOLLOWING SUBDIRECTORIES
AND/OR FILES
BEAUX ARTS TOWER
INFERNO FRATERNAL AND SOCIAL CLUB NINTH AVENUE
LOCKWOOD DOWNS
MERIDEE DOWNS
CLAUDE LORING
LEWIS MONSERAT
FAYE DI STASIO

"Can you match Babe Devens's lists to the names in those files?"

"Sure." Charley typed in the COMP order.

The screen flashed SEARCHING.

"Son of a bitch is going to do it," Cardozo said.

"Tell you what else Maisie can do. Every time she matches a name, she can call up all files under that name and search them for new names."

"What's the point?"

"It's a sieve. Eventually the net's so fine you'll catch everything— like B. Devens mail-ordered slippers from the same dealer in Cleveland as one of Monserat's artists."

"Do it."

Two hours later Charley brought Cardozo ninety single-space accordion-folded leaves.

Cardozo looked at the quantity of print-out. His eyes had the pain and disbelief preceding sudden death. "Charley, you're a good man. Too good."

Cardozo began going over the pages.

He could feel there was some kind of connection he wasn't tuning in on. He took the pages home that night and puzzled over them.

At 3 A.M. he put his head down on the sofa cushion.

Thirty seconds later he saw Claude Loring's gaunt face, his contemptuous eyes, his lips hurling out words. Cardozo listened to those words.

What the fuck do you want, bitch?

He replayed them, catching the exact intonation. it came to him. That stress on the word *you.*

Charley Brackner was in his cubicle, fresh from a night's sleep, chewing on a prune Danish.

Cardozo dumped the ninety pages into Charley's wastebasket. "Forget this shit. Loring *knows* her. All we need to know is how Loring connects with Babe Devens."

Charley made an expert sort of face. "Everybody in the world networks to somebody somehow." He typed instructions into the computer.

SEARCH LINK LORING : B DEVENS

A moment later the screen flashed back

SEARCHING.

After sixty seconds of the flashing word, a column began running down the screen.

C LORING

BEAUX ARTS TOWER

BILLI VON KLEIST

MONSERAT GALLERY

DUNCAN CANFIELD

ASH CANFIELD

B DEVENS

"Print that," Cardozo said.

Charley gave the print command and a page clattered out of the printer.

Cardozo detached the page. "Thanks, Charley."

"Vince."

Charley's tone stopped him.

A new column was running down the computer screen.

<pre>
          C LORING
     BEAUX ARTS TOWER
     BILLI VON KLEIST
     MONSERAT GALLERY
    D FORBES-STEINMAN
        SCOTT DEVENS
          B DEVENS
</pre>

Cardozo stared at the screen. "Does Maisie read *The Enquirer*?"

"Huh?"

"Could you get that machine to amplify the link between Forbes-Steinman and Devens? Does it *know* that they're shacked up, or is there something more?"

Charley typed in

<pre>
    SEARCH LINK D FORBES-STEINMAN: SCOTT DEVENS
</pre>

The screen flashed

<pre>
              SEARCHING
</pre>

After almost a minute new material began scrolling up the screen.

<pre>
       MIRANDELLA, SUNNY, HOMICIDE
          EVIDENCE AT CRIME SCENE
             SUBJECT'S PURSE
               CONTENTS
    HELENA RUBINSTEIN BLUSH PINK LIPSTICK
         TAMPAX TAMPONS THREE
               KEYS FIVE
         FOUREX CONDOMS EIGHT
         ESTEE LAUDER COLOGNE
    EIGHTY-SEVEN DOLLARS THIRTY-TWO CENTS
             CHARGE CARDS
    MASTERCARD 5500-7843-2316 SANDRA MIRANDELLA
    VISA CARD 5647-5418-8953 JOY FEINSTEIN
       BLOOMINGDALES CHARGE 6532-098
       D FORBES-STEINMAN/SCOTT DEVENS
</pre>

"Stop there," Cardozo said.

Sunny Mirandella was the name of a TWA stewardess who had

lived in Dr. Flora Vogelsang's neighborhood. She'd been found with a slashed throat, and she was Monteleone's case. So far there'd been no collar, and after three weeks with no productive leads, Sunny had been moved to a back burner.

Cardozo called Greg Monteleone into the computer room and nodded toward the flashing cursor on the screen. "What does that mean?"

"Sunny used stolen charge cards."

"Why are there two names on the Bloomingdale's card?"

"It's a joint charge shared by Steinman and Devens. There are two cards, one name on each. Sunny was using Steinman's card."

"And the two names were still on the account? How recently were those cards issued?

Monteleone shrugged. "They're good through this year."

"Did you follow up on Steinman's card?"

"Course I followed up on it. Steinman lost it at a party."

"Pull the sheet on it."

Monteleone got the sheet. "A dinner at Tina Vanderbilt's last April twelfth. Sixty guests. Doria Forbes-Steinman went to the powder room and she left her purse on the bed. That's when she thinks the card was stolen."

"She thinks. She thinks." Cardozo thought. "Tina Vanderbilt? Charity bashes, fund-raisers, opera galas?"

"Yeah. She has a triplex on Park."

"So that would have been a formal dinner. The women wear gowns and the purses are little things, gold pony hide from Saks, you can fit the house keys and two hits of coke in. Why would Forbes-Steinman take her Bloomie's charge card to a sit-down dinner? That's a waste of purse space."

"I never claimed to understand women."

"Get me a photo of Sunny Mirandella. A nice normal presentable photo."

"We don't have any nice normal presentable photos of Sunny Mirandella. They all look like s.m. centerfold."

"Then get me her driver's license."

Doria Forbes-Steinman looked carefully at each photo: Jodie Downs, Sunny Mirandella, Claude Loring.

She was sitting on the plush gray sofa in front of the three-panel comic-strip blowup of a cathedral. Cardozo could see beyond her into the hallway, where the Nuku Kushima black leather mask was still on display on its pedestal.

"Just a minute," she said. "This man *is* familiar."

Cardozo came back across the sunny room and looked down over her shoulder. She was holding the photo of Claude Loring.

"Where was it? . . . Down in SoHo last winter. . . . He's that friend of Lew Monserat's. I saw them at the opening of the Schnabel exhibit at the Mary Boon Gallery." She looked up at Cardozo. "But my Bloomingdale's card wasn't stolen at Mary's. I bought a juicer with it the day after that opening."

"You say this man is Monserat's friend. Do you mean they were together often?"

"No, I mean they seemed to be lovers that night. Lew loves kinky trash. Always has."

Cardozo's mind went over the links. Loring and Monserat both played at the Inferno; Ted Morgenstern represented them both; and in Doria Forbes-Steinman's opinion they'd had an affair. An affair didn't seem likely: the clothescheck at the Inferno had said that Loring liked kids. But still, there was some kind of relationship between the two, some bond that made them a team. "Would you happen to have the date of that Schnabel opening?"

"It's in my calendar." Doria Forbes-Steinman got up from the sofa. "Just a moment."

She left the room and returned.

"Here we are, Lieutenant. I wrote it all down for you." She handed him the date, time and place, on a piece of stationery *from the desk of Doria Forbes-Steinman.*

"Mrs. Forbes-Steinman," he said, "there are two names on that Bloomingdale's charge account—yours and Scott Devens's."

She blinked and flinched back as if something menacing had flown near her eyes. "Is that a question?"

"May I talk with Mr. Devens?"

She folded her hands together and then unfolded them.

"Scottie's not here at the moment. The easiest way to find him would be to go to the Teak Room at the Winslow around eleven tonight. He's playing piano there."

Mrs. Vanderbilt sat in a silk brocade chair, facing an antique writing desk. She did not rise, and she did not invite Cardozo to sit.

"I hope I haven't come at a bad time for you," he said.

"Of course not." Mrs. Vanderbilt's tone made it clear it was such an obviously bad time that to mention it merely compounded the annoyance. "How may I help you, Leftenant?"

"You gave a dinner here—"

"I give many dinners here," she cut in. She looked at least ninety. Her eyes were blue and sharp and lively. Her hair was white, and it had the striking elegance of a founding father's peruke.

"You gave a dinner last April twelfth."

"That's true." She was dressed in pale pink. She gave the impression of being short, no more than five feet tall, and fashion-model thin, weighing at most ninety-five pounds. "Was a crime committed at my dinner?"

He smiled. "I doubt a crime has been committed at any of your dinners, ma'am."

She didn't smile. "That relieves me."

"Could you tell me if Doria Forbes-Steinman was here that night?"

"She has been in my home." Mrs. Vanderbilt's mouth was pale: it was two pink lines lightly sketched across her strangely glowing face. "But you'll want exact information."

Mrs. Vanderbilt turned to her secretary, a woman of fifty-some years dressed in black.

"Endicott, will you fetch the guest list for April twelfth last?"

The room was large. The ceiling was high. The walls were shimmering with French impressionists. Endicott scurried to one of the three doors.

"Endicott."

Endicott stopped.

Mrs. Vanderbilt fixed her gaze on Cardozo. "You'll want the service list as well?"

"Please," he said.

"Very well, Endicott." Mrs. Vanderbilt gave a wave.

Endicott opened a door and a miniature dachshund burst into the room. With three high-pitched barks it jumped into the lap of New York City's premiere hostess, tail wagging crazily.

"Have you ever seen such energy?" Mrs. Vanderbilt allowed the animal to lick the sapphire-cut diamond on her finger. "Isn't Robespierre just ferocious? And darling? *Sois sage, Robespierre! Sois sage pour maman!*"

Cardozo had the impression Mrs. Vanderbilt spoke to her pet in French because she didn't want the servants to understand. He couldn't think what to say to her about her dog. He was suddenly haunted by a phantom that showed up now and then, the adolescent fear of using the wrong fork at a formal dinner.

Endicott returned.

Mrs. Vanderbilt deposited the dog on the floor. *"Va t'amuser, Robespierre."*

There was something dubious and nasty in Endicott's eyes as she handed Cardozo the lists.

He took a moment running his eye down the columns of famous names. "I see Scott Devens and Doria Forbes-Steinman were both here."

Mrs. Vanderbilt's face indicated displeasure. "Mrs. Forbes-Steinman was here. Her escort was taken ill. He sent his regrets at the last moment."

Cardozo could see that Mrs. Vanderbilt was not in the habit of receiving or forgiving last-moment regrets.

"May I have copies of these?" Cardozo asked.

"Endicott, type copies for the leftenant."

"Champagne, sir?"

Cardozo showed the waiter his shield. "Water for me. Send Mr. Devens whatever he's drinking and tell him I'd like to talk when he's finished his set."

Cardozo looked around him. The decor was World War II movie palace Moorish. The tables were packed too close. Someone had paid off a fire inspector.

An amber spot picked out Scott Devens at the keyboard of a baby grand, dark and handsome in his tux, weaving a Bach fugue on "You Do Something to Me."

The Winslow Hotel's Teak Room was what publicists called an intimate space, a watering hole for people who liked to get mentioned in the gossip columns and didn't mind dropping four hundred dollars for two bottles of champagne. Gabors hung out here, and Yugoslavian princes who didn't speak Yugoslavian. Lighting was low, coming from candles on the tables and false windows with silhouetted minarets.

Devens kept smiling over his right shoulder at the front table. Cardozo dimly recognized some of Devens's party: a TV stud actor, a strikingly bizarre six-foot black fashion model, an artist who silk-screened trash cans, the publisher of a porn magazine who'd survived three bombings by Moral Majority activists. He didn't recognize the drunk woman in the gold brocade dress. She wasn't Mrs.

Forbes-Steinman and she couldn't have had anything going for her but money. Her face turned determined and anxious every time Devens looked at another table.

There was a spattering of laid-back applause as Devens closed the lid on the keyboard. He brought his Scotch to Cardozo's table.

"Very kind of you, Lieutenant—is it Lieutenant now?"

"I don't forget old acquaintances, Mr. Devens."

"Would you care to join my friends and me?"

"Let's keep it simple and you join me."

Devens sat.

"Mrs. Vanderbilt says you didn't go to her dinner on April twelfth."

Devens crossed one leg over the other. His black patent leather pumps had little bows that didn't tie anything. He didn't move a muscle in his face. "I was sick."

"Mrs. Forbes-Steinman didn't lose that charge card at Mrs. Vanderbilt's. Sunny Mirandella stole it from the apartment."

Devens drained his glass. "Who's Sunny Mirandella?"

Cardozo placed three photographs on the table: Downs, Loring, and Sunny. "Why don't you tell me."

"You've got to be joking. There's only one woman here."

"Who said Sunny's a woman?"

"I assumed . . ." Devens frowned and didn't say what he assumed.

"You can do better than that, Scottie. Her murder was in the papers and you're in her date book."

Cardozo could see Devens calculating the odds that it was a bluff, and then he could see Devens realizing that by taking the time to calculate, by not coming in fast with a denial, he'd given himself away.

"What does that convict me of?"

"You tell me."

Devens sat immobile for a moment. Suddenly he thrust out his arm and stopped a passing waiter. "Dewar's on the rocks. Double. Anything for you, Lieutenant?"

Cardozo shook his head.

"Don't you drink?"

"If I drink I smoke, and if I smoke I lose all self-respect."

"You impress me, Lieutenant. After two trials and seven years, you're still gunning for me. Why? How could you hate a man you don't even know?"

For all his fine clothing, Devens gave off the scent of an all-American whiner, a man who was hustling whatever and whoever he could. Cardozo wondered what Babe had seen in this loser and then he wondered why he was bothering to wonder.

"I don't need to know you," Cardozo said. "All I need to know is what you did to that kid."

"Sunny was not a kid and I didn't do anything to her."

"But once upon a time Cordelia Koenig was and you did."

Devens looked at him suddenly, with panic, and then he slid away into a sort of blank. "Christ. I thought we were talking about Sunny."

"We were."

"I only saw Sunny that once. I don't know anything about her except that she was sweet and maybe she was a thief and now she's dead."

"How'd you meet her?"

"I flew back on her flight from Chicago. We got to talking."

"Where were you two weekends ago when she was killed?"

"I was in the Hamptons."

"All weekend—Friday to Sunday?"

"All weekend—Friday to Tuesday."

Nice weekends in the jet set. "Can you back that up?"

"Yes I can."

"You're going to have to. Who were you with?"

Devens gave him the names, and Cardozo wrote them down in his notebook.

"Are you going to spread it around about Sunny and me?" Devens asked.

"Does it matter?"

"It could ruin me."

"Nothing's ruined you yet. Waiter, can I have the check?"

"This is on me," Devens said quickly.

"No it's not." Not taking his eyes from Devens, Cardozo laid twenty dollars in the saucer.

39

"Something or someone," Cardozo said, "links you to the Beaux Arts killing. I'm betting it's someone you know but don't know you know—some little memory that got erased when you were in coma. We've compared the names in your address book with our case files. There are a few matches, but they're people we already know— socialites on the periphery. They don't lead us anywhere new. What we need is someone who has your memories of seven years ago— intact."

"Well, that obviously isn't me," Babe said.

They were on the flagstone terrace behind the town house. Cardozo was standing there just looking at her.

"Did you ever keep a diary?"

Babe smiled. "Never."

"Can you think of any close friends, anyone who traveled in the same circles, someone who knows as much about you as you do about yourself—and who'd be willing to help?"

Babe's throat was suddenly scratchy as steel wool. "I would have said Scottie, but obviously not."

"No one else?"

"Well, Ash Canfield—I don't have a secret in the world from her. We made it a policy never to be stoned at the same party. In case one of us had to take the other home."

"Then let's ask Ash to look over these photos. How do we get hold of her?"

Babe had graduated to a cane, and she was able to climb the ramp to the *Minerva,* industrialist Holcombe Kaiser's two-hundred-foot yacht, without Cardozo's help. As they reached the deck, noise and lights hit them.

The black-tie extravaganza—one of the hardest-to-wrangle invitations of the season—was in full swing. The masts wrapped in furled sails soared three stories high.

Cardozo was aware of people looking at Babe with hungry ogling eyes, whispering speculations, and he was aware that some of the speculation was spilling over onto him.

He held out the Tiffany-engraved vellum invitation for Beatrice Devens and Escort, and a young, elegantly uniformed butler steered them toward the reception line and called out their names.

Holcombe Kaiser, their billionaire host, greeted his guests with the brisk dispatch of a ruling monarch. "Haven't seen you in a while, Babe."

A camera flashed as Kaiser's lips touched Babe's cheek.

"Too long," she said. "This is my friend Vincent Cardozo."

"How do you do, sir." It was that faintly ironic use of the word, from superior to inferior. "Thanks for bringing Babe."

Cardozo knew Kaiser only from news stories, knew he had spent a lifetime piling up dollars and publicity into the Holcombe Kaiser legend, carving himself a conspicuous place in a conspicuous society. Gray-haired, gray-bearded, radiating self-satisfaction, he looked Cardozo impersonally in the eye. "Please meet my good friend Edmilia Tirotos."

Kaiser had been a widower for over half his life, and Edmilia Tirotos, the four-foot-nine wife of the deposed Indonesian dictator, stood beside him, performing the duties of hostess. Olive-skinned, dark-eyed, her face-lifts giving her a weirdly young smile that she seemed powerless to alter, she wore a diamond tiara that must have accounted for over half the foreign debt of her former fatherland.

"Where the hell are we going to find Ash Canfield?" Cardozo whispered. "This place is worse than a lockup cage."

"Let's try the bar," Babe said.

It was not an easy task. There were open bars fore and aft, and a dozen strikingly handsome waiters circulated with trays of champagne.

At eight thirty the *Minerva* cast off, its motors churning the Hudson to vanilla mousse. The sun was setting, turning the Manhattan skyline amber.

Babe and Cardozo pried their way through the usual crowd going through the intricate steps of the celebrity gavotte, with amplified dance music played under a striped canopy by Scott Devens and his twelve-piece orchestra.

Inside the ship's saloon the crystal prisms of a ballroom chandelier scattered tinkling rainbows across oyster damask and walnut paneling, dappling the pink marble fireplace with a Rubens painting above it.

Babe found Ash Canfield on a silk sofa, a fair-haired woman in a scoop-bodiced silver gown, eyes sparkling with bold gaiety.

"So *this* is the famous Lieutenant Vincent Cardozo." Ash spoke in a whispery, out-of-breath, society-girl voice.

"I didn't know I was famous," he said, "but thank you, Mrs. —what do I call you—Lady Ash or Lady Canfield?"

"It's not a proper title, I'm only Lady Canfield, but why don't we drop the Lady and you can call me Ash. And yes, you're very famous among the inner circle of Babe's friends."

"Ash," Babe suggested, "come see the view."

"I've seen that filthy harbor. You forget, Babe, I was born in Doctors Hospital, right on the shores of Manhattan, just like you and every other little girl who ever went to Spence. Rather like Moses in the bulrushes, don't you think, Lieutenant? Or do I call you Vincent?"

"Call me Vince."

Ash linked arms with them both. "Now that we're all cozy, let's look for a bar. I'm famished for an olive."

They worked their way out of the saloon. Ash threw out greetings, chatty and frivolous, hyper-radiating giddy good humor.

Cardozo pried them a path down the corridor, through a tumult of celebrity hugs and giggles and pushing.

Babe stopped suddenly in the middle of the corridor. Her eyes had locked on a woman in a strapless gray silk gown and Cardozo wondered what her mind was telling her that he wasn't tuning in on.

There was a tangible arrogance to the straight set of the woman's mouth and thin Roman nose and cool wide-spaced green eyes. It took Cardozo an instant to recognize Doria Forbes-Steinman, and it took him an instant longer to realize that Babe was staring not at the woman but at the dress she was wearing.

"Hello, Doria," Babe said.

Doria Forbes-Steinman turned, standing there behind a wisp of smoke, finishing her cigarette. Her eyes went from Babe to Cardozo to Ash. "Why, Babe, what a surprise. No one told me you were invited."

"Obviously not," Babe said. "That's my gown you're wearing."

Doria Forbes-Steinman smiled. "Hello, Ash. Hello, Lieutenant," she said.

"If you've let the others out at the hips and shoulders as badly as this one," Babe said, "I don't know whether to sue you for theft or for butchery."

"I know exactly what to sue you for, darling—libel."

"Please do. And say hello to Scottie for me."

Giving Babe the finger, Doria Forbes-Steinman eased herself into a wave of celebrities that was sweeping down the corridor.

"If you want to sue," Cardozo said, "sue your parents, not her. It was their job to say no."

"How did she do it?" Babe said.

"Ted Morgenstern."

"It's beyond belief. *Beneath* belief."

Cardozo found an empty stateroom and herded Babe and Ash inside and closed the door behind them. It was a comfortable rosewood-paneled room, hung with soft blue paintings all bearing the powerfully legible signature of Picasso, as recognizable as the trademark on a Coke bottle. There was a single Monet, which Cardozo had the feeling was Holcombe Kaiser's way of remembering where he had hidden the safe.

"She has my husband," Babe said, "and she has my gowns."

"Let it go," Cardozo said softly. His hand reached and squeezed Babe's.

She squeezed back, gratefully, and then she opened the writing board of an antique carved French walnut secretary. She spread the three-by-five-inch photo reductions on the seamlessly inlaid surface of marble and boxwood.

Ash stood there, a wondering stare fixed on her face. "What's this, lotto? Am I supposed to pick a winner?"

"In a way," Babe said. "Would you look at these photographs and tell us if you know any of the people?"

For a second Ash seemed to have to process the request, and then she settled herself, a wobbly wisp of Chanel-scented elegance, onto the corner of the blue chintz sofa. She sneaked her glasses out of her purse. Guiltily. The lenses had thick middles to correct the far-sightedness that came with middle age, and Cardozo could see from the way she put them on that she hated wearing them.

She picked up the photos. She stared silently at each one, eyes mechanical, remote, as if she were arranging cards by suit in a hand of bridge. She separated one photo from the others. Her glance turned diagonally across the writing board toward Babe.

"This one."

"Family snapshots?" The door had opened soundlessly. A man stood in the doorway, then sauntered into the room. Snow-blond brows and lashes made his blue eyes deep and startling. He moved quickly next to Ash and put his arm around her shoulders. "May I peek?" He had the look of an overripe Nordic god, slightly inflated, the blond curls singed in gray. His plaid cummerbund did not manage to disguise the comfortably thickening waist of the tennis player at forty.

He spread the photos out side by side. "Let's see, our summer vacation in Europe—no, our summer vacation in Billi von Kleist's lobby. What dreary photos—who's collecting snapshots of big Mack trucks?"

"Dunk," Ash said, pushing his fingers away from the photos and tamping them into a neat stack, "this is Vince Cardozo, Babe's friend."

"How do." Dunk Canfield sized up Cardozo in an unimpressed glance.

Cardozo had read up on Sir Dunk: he had grown up in the world of the British formerly wealthy; family connections had gotten him admission to Harrow and a scholarship to Oxford and he looked like a lump of laid-back complacency who had never doubted his right to a life of serious unearned luxury.

Babe smoothly lifted the photos from Ash's hand and tucked them into her purse.

Sir Dunk stared at Babe with an almost childish annoyance. "Not going to let me look?"

"You wouldn't be interested," she said. "And what's all that noise upstairs?"

"The guest of honor's arriving," Dunk said. "Care to greet her?" He offered Ash his arm.

On the surface at least Dunk and Ash Canfield were a matched pair: good dressers, terrific smilers, bronzed and well-born and handsome. Babe and Cardozo followed them up to the deck.

Motor roaring, blades throwing out a blast of whiplashing wind, a silver Martin-Marietta custom helicopter was touching down on the landing pad at the stern of the *Minerva.* Crewmen had herded guests back beyond a perimeter of red velvet ropes.

The copter door swung up and out stepped Baron Billi von Kleist

—relaxed, grinning, instant master of the space around him. A blitz of flashbulbs caught him in his tails and Legion d'honneur.

With knightly consideration the handsome European aristocrat turned and held up a kid-gloved hand. It was grasped from inside the copter by the black-gloved hand of the guest of honor.

Tina Vanderbilt stood scowling in an elegant Fortuny scarlet silk evening gown that she could have worn a half-century ago.

Edmilia Tirotos and Holcombe Kaiser stepped forward. There was a *ménage à trois* of kisses. Tina Vanderbilt's dress turned out to have a large, detachable necklacelike collar of fabric roses sprinkled with silver paillettes. Edmilia deftly detached it and handed it to a waiter.

Holcombe Kaiser sprang open a Cartier's box.

Edmilia lifted out a rope of diamonds and gold and placed it around Tina's neck.

Flashbulbs went off like fireworks.

Society applauded.

With surprising nimbleness, Tina Vanderbilt curtsied to the crowd.

A whisper whipped around the deck— "three thousand carats!"

Scott Devens and the portable members of his orchestra formed a semicircle around the guest of honor. Scott gave the downbeat: saxes and violins and accordion broke into "Happy Birthday to You."

Tina Vanderbilt stood smiling politely, firmly, in the middle of a churning circle of photographers, flashbulbs, and newsmen.

Somebody said she was ninety-six and tonight was her fifth annual eightieth birthday.

There was ten minutes more dancing before the ship's horn sounded an all-hands alert, summoning the guests to dinner.

The swaying couples gradually abandoned the dance floor. The circular white tables, each set and name-carded for eight, had centerpieces of red roses floating in amber water. The air sizzled with the tart smell of champagne and hot chafing dishes.

Babe and Cardozo found their table. Ash was already there, sitting alone with a bottle of champagne and a half-full glass, looking cheerfully wobbly.

"Aren't you keeping bad company?" Babe said.

"What company?" Ash said.

"That bottle."

Ash lifted the bottle. "Are you kidding, doll? Piper's the best. Pull up a glass."

A Countess Marina of the Ukraine arrived on the arm of a Prince Ludovic of Serbia. They both had dyed blond hair and face-lifted skin that gave them the agelessly smooth look of Slavic Barbie and Ken dolls. When they introduced themselves they spoke with incongruous Hispanic accents.

Gordon Dobbs introduced Betsy Vlaminck, an imperious old fashion magazine editor in an aqua turban, and Dunk Canfield—carrying two more bottles of champagne—took the seat next to his wife.

Cardozo listened as Ms. Vlaminck lamented the whole Hamptons scene and said Oscar and Annette and Lock and Steve and Happy were moving their summer retreats to Rhinebeck, and wouldn't it be just what the Hamptons deserved if real estate values plummeted.

"Poor Lee Radziwill," Sir Dunk said. "Why she wouldn't be able to rent out that phony colonial anymore for fifty thousand the season."

Waiters, wearing black bow ties and white naval mess jackets, began changing the dinner plates.

Prince Ludovic scowled at the design on the soup dish. "It's the Habsburg coat of arms—what's Holcombe trying to tell us?"

"Rank is rank," Countess Marina said. "It simplifies the seating at dinner."

"I don't entirely agree," Gordon Dobbs said. "It seems to me it's a question of celebrity who sits where. I can remember when George Plimpton and Andy Warhol were hot seats to be placed next to. Now it's that Letterman man and Madonna."

Betsy Vlaminck shook her head. "You can't go by celebrity—that's a pure boom-and-bust market."

"I couldn't be more in agreement," Prince Ludovic said. "Look at the people on this ship. How many of them will have any social desirability at all in three years? No more than half."

"I doubt half have any desirability tonight," Countess Marina said. "Holcombe's given Tina two birthdays, and this is the B party. The A party was last month, when he flew twenty of us to his schloss in the Austrian Alps."

"I don't go to B parties," Ash Canfield said.

"Oh yes you do, darling," Betsy Vlaminck said. "Count the number of publicists here tonight. Tell me it's not a tax writeoff."

"Holcombe's shrewd, that's all," Ash said.

At that very moment a waiter was going around the table, ladling court bouillon of lobster from a silver tureen.

Lady Ash said "No, thank you" to a waiter offering more wine, and Sir Dunk placed his own glass at Ash's hand. Cardozo noticed the switch, and Dunk noticed him noticing. Dunk's eyes became pools of hostility.

"What do you think of Jeannette Cowles?" Prince Ludovic said. "I mean, leaving her husband to marry a *homosexual?*"

Betsy Vlaminck arched an eyebrow. "You mean leaving her husband to marry a man who has AIDS."

"He couldn't have AIDS," Countess Marina said. "People have been spreading that rumor for years and Oswaldo Straus puts out a marvelous collection every spring and fall."

"Kid you not, Oswaldo Straus has AIDS." Gordon Dobbs raised his right hand in a Boy Scout oath. "Once a month Sloan-Kettering drains him and changes every drop of fluid in his body. They're barely keeping the disease at bay. He's had to have plastic surgery three times on his Kaposi."

"He must have contracted it from that lover," Betsy Vlaminck said, "that boy who was smeared all over Times Square in those big hunky naked ads."

"No one could date the lover without getting on Ozzie's evil side," Prince Ludovic said.

"No one could date that lover," Gordon Dobbs said, "without getting AIDS."

"Then Jeannette Cowles is going to be the first woman in the Social Register to come down with it," Prince Ludovic said.

"Not quite the first," Gordon Dobbs said. "Some ved-dee prom-i-nent ladies have already succumbed to the plague." He named the ex-wife of the man who had founded the first radio network in America.

"But that was from a transfusion she had five years before," Prince Ludovic said.

"Remarkable isn't it," Gordon Dobbs said, "how there's always an alibi when it's anyone who's anyone. Believe me, there's a lot more going on than the Center for Disease Control is letting on."

The waiters served capon suprême in ginger and raspberry vinegar sauce, with side dishes of wild rice and French beans amandine.

Before helping herself, Ash reached for her glass, slopping it and noticing but not caring. She banged an elbow against Cardozo's ribs and in that split second he saw that she had become someone else: the face and voice were still Ash Canfield, but something had come unbridled at the center, something defiant and loud.

"Waiter," she said, "would you please hold the fucking platter straight?"

Betsy Vlaminck mentioned the duke of Windsor.

"The smallest dick in the British Empire," Ash said, spilling beans on the deck.

Betsy Vlaminck stopped, eyes veering toward Ash. "How do you know that?" she said.

"The duchess told me."

"How did *she* know?" Countess Marina said.

Ash laughed. "Because she went down on the whole empire."

"Really," Countess Marina said, not quite convincing in her disapproval.

"The duke and duchess were no better than a couple of call girls," Ash was saying. She was trying to cut into her capon, but it kept skidding away from her knife. "All those stories about their sending bills for coming to dinner or staying for weekends are absolutely true."

A not-very-convincing frown drove Countess Marina's lips together. "That is a lie, and it was started by Helena Guest because the duke and duchess stopped going to her place in Old Westbury after she divorced Winston."

Cardozo shot Babe a glance. The mood at the table was getting to him.

"Never mind that," Gordon Dobbs said. "Why was the duchess so dotty? Was she having strokes?"

"The problem was face-lifts," Ash said. "After she reached age seventy-three, no responsible plastic surgeon would touch her. At eighty-five, just after the duke's death, she imported that society surgeon from Brazil to do the job. Her *eighth* lift. At the last moment she told him to do the eye pouches. He had to keep her anesthetized three hours, and that's too long at that age. He warned her, but you know Wallis."

"What happened?" Countess Marina said.

"A quarter of her brain cells died and she came out partially aphasic and totally incontinent. Word was put out that she had Alzheimer's, which of course wasn't the case at all. What she had was necrosis of the parietal lobes. And it spread, like timber rot. She regressed. She began thinking of herself as a child again. Do you know what she wanted for Christmas? It's so pathetic. She wanted toy trains. Can you imagine? *Toy trains.* Of course her retinue was absolutely terrified."

"Terrified of what?" Countess Marina asked.

"You don't know?" Ash said, looking round the table.

Dunk poured more champagne into his wife's empty glass. "Ash, don't," he said.

"Come on," Ash said, "everyone knows anyway."

"*I* don't know," Countess Marina said.

"Well, you're the only one who doesn't."

"*I* don't know either," Gordon Dobbs said.

"Nor do I," Betsy Vlaminck said.

Ash fortified herself with a long swallow of champagne.

"Ash," Babe said, "do you need that?"

Ash's eyes turned. "Get your own, sweetie." She addressed the table. "The duchess of Windsor began life as a man."

"A *man*?" Countess Marina set down her fork.

"A cross-dresser," Ash said. "Who but a man of exquisite sensibility would have had Wallis's taste in clothes? Or in interior design?"

"But that's ridiculous," Countess Marina said. "Wallis married three times."

"What does sex have to do with marriage?" Ash said, and there was laughter. But Cardozo didn't laugh. He was paying less attention to what Ash was saying than the way she was saying it, the way her husband was watching her.

"Why in the world," Ash said, "do you think Churchill and the archibishop of Canterbury were so dead set against Wallis's marrying the king? Not because of what she had in her past—but in her crotch."

"How did they know?" Gordon Dobbs said.

"They'd been to bed with her—him. Winnie was a little—you know."

"Did the duchess ever have a sex change?" Gordon Dobbs asked.

Ash nodded. "During the Second World War. She and David went to occupied Denmark. They were collaborators, you know; no problem getting in or out of the Reich. She was a trailblazer—crossed over years before Christine Jorgensen."

The waiters brought lemon soufflé with chocolate sauce. When Cardozo passed Ash the crystallized rock sugar for her coffee she ground her cigarette out in it.

"Doctors can't give a man ovaries," Countess Marina said, "and Wallis had children when she was Mrs. Simpson."

"Samson was the *real* name," Ash said, "and the sons were adopted from a Jewish relief agency in Palestine."

A sudden hush fell on the ship as Holcombe Kaiser walked to the bandstand and adjusted the level of the microphone. "Testing, testing, can you all hear me? I want to announce an absolutely marvelous artistic and historical find. After eleven years' searching, Sotheby's has located the original tin soldiers belonging to François Charles Joseph Bonaparte, better known as l'Aiglon, the son of Napoleon Bonaparte and Marie Louise."

A swell of murmurs and applause swept the deck.

"These are the very toy soldiers that the infant Bonaparte played with at age five when he was confined to the court of Vienna. After restoration by master craftsmen from the Swiss firm of Birsch and Loewen, these soldiers will be exhibited at the Holcombe Kaiser Museum of Toy Soldiers in Hartford, Connecticut. Any of you who wish to become cofounding sponsors of the Hartford Kaiser Museum may do so by filling out the pledge cards attached to your menus; furthermore, anyone contributing one thousand dollars or more may request society's premier troubadour, our own Scottie Devens, to sing any song he or she desires."

Holcombe Kaiser stepped back from the mike, bowing sideways toward Scottie Devens, already seated at the Steinway.

"Maestro," Kaiser cried, "commence!"

Doria Forbes-Steinman strode through the tables. She slapped a pledge card on the music stand of the Steinway.

Scottie Devens nodded, then angled toward the mike: "An old sentimental favorite that set grandma's toes tapping—I'm sure you all remember."

He riffed an upward arpeggio and in a smooth, slightly neutered baritone began singing "Baby Face."

Heads reangled themselves in a wave toward the table where Babe and Cardozo were sitting.

Cardozo felt Babe stiffen beside him.

"She did that on purpose." Babe's eyes looked dark and furious against the sudden whiteness of her skin. " 'Baby Face' was Scottie's and my song, and everyone here knows it. Vince, I'd like to go."

From what Cardozo had seen tonight of what the gossip columns called society, it was no different from the street; and the one thing you didn't do with a thousand eyes pinned on you was walk away from a challenge.

He reached for the nearest menu and ripped the pledge card from the bottom.

"What are you doing?" Babe said.

"Praying the bank comes through with my home equity loan."

"Vince—don't."

She reached for him but he was already up from his chair, making his way through the hooting and laughing guests to the piano.

He handed Scottie Devens the card. " 'You Took Advantage of Me' —know it?"

Scottie riffed to a new key. "Naturally." Scottie spoke into the mike. "For Lieutenant Vincente—or is that Vincent, Lieutenant?"

"Vincent—like it's spelled."

"For Lieutenant Vincent Cardozo of New York's Finest, an old Rodgers and Hart favorite."

Scottie's amplified voice floated over the deck.

Cardozo returned to the table and sat. "Kiss me," he told Babe. "Right now while every buzzard on the ship is watching."

Babe kissed him. "You know something?" she said. "You're god-damned wonderful."

Cardozo's attention went to the reactions of the guests around them. At the exact instant that he noticed the woman at the next table, she noticed him noticing her.

She had wide-set eyes that were green and sparkling and a little dangerous. At the back of her neck a green velvet ribbon that matched her eyes caught her long, straight, dark hair. She was keeping herself at the edge of the conversation, lifting a pale white hand to her pink mouth. An enormous ruby-and-diamond ring glittered sharply.

There was general laughter and applause when the song ended, and then Countess Marina filled out a card and dispatched Prince Ludovic to request "I'll Follow My Secret Heart."

"Who's that woman at the next table?" Cardozo asked Babe.

"You mean wearing the black silk, cut on the bias?"

"What do I know from bias and black silk? The woman that's staring at me."

Ash overheard. "That's Countess Victoria de Savoie-Sancerre and that Adonis next to her is Count Leopold."

The count was much older than his wife, with a tanned face and hawk eyes. He was swigging bourbon neat instead of wine.

"She's a dyke," Ash said, "and he's a fag."

"She's not looking at me like she's gay."

"She doesn't think anyone knows," Ash said. "They married because he couldn't inherit the estate without an heir. They've had a son by artificial insemination. She's always thumping around in big butch leather boots."

For a moment Cardozo was puzzled, knowing he had seen the countess somewhere else, somewhere very different from this yacht.

After dinner and liqueurs there was dancing on the aft deck. Babe and Cardozo stayed at the table and watched couples crowding the dance floor. Many were boozed or stoned or coked, and they turned to movement as though it was a continuation of the high. The deck swirled.

Babe directed Cardozo's attention with a nod.

Sir Dunk and Lady Ash had cleared themselves a patch of floor-space, and a circle of guests was standing around clapping and cheering them on. The Canfields were either play-acting or smashed—loud, funny, with big gross motor movements—stomping around doing an odd Highland fling with complete abandon.

A woman's voice with a slightly French accent said, "Excuse us, darlings."

Cardozo turned. Countess Victoria and her armadillo count had stopped by to chat.

Cardozo smiled hello as Babe made introductions.

While the countess went at the gathering with her battering ram of a tongue, the count looked moodily into space, his balding head crossed with hairs and wrinkles.

Finally the countess turned her gaze to Cardozo, giving him an easy, offhand look. "Since Babe isn't dancing, would you care to?"

"I'll sit with Babe," the count volunteered.

Babe shot Cardozo a helpless, what-can-I-do look. "Go ahead, Vince. Please."

Cardozo found himself dancing tightly against Countess Victoria.

"Tonight's so exquisitely vulgar," she said. "No one knows how to enjoy themselves so well as the nouveaux riches, don't you find?"

"You like it that much, hey?" Cardozo said.

She said, "Yes, I like everything, food, drinking, dancing, meeting new people, Bach, Mahler, Stevie Wonder, sex, speed, coke, tequila —preferably all at once."

"The rich at play," he sighed.

She gave him a scowl. "I wish everybody would give up that silly belief that we're so very rich. It's not true. We lead a quite average, everyday sort of existence."

"Sure you do."

She leaned her head back, assessing him. "I like your contempt. You're a very sexy man."

"I'm sexy, there's no doubt about that."

"And conceited—just my type. Am I yours?"

"Possibly. Where have we met?"

"We haven't yet." She melted a little against his shoulder, then frowned. "I've never heard of erections in the *armpit*. What have you got there, a gun?"

"Mmm-hmm."

"Mmm-*hmm*." She snuggled closer, close enough to run her tongue over his chin. "I want to see you again."

"What would the count say to that?" he said.

"The count is a man of very few words."

From across the deck came a whiplike crack of shattering glass. Cardozo turned his head.

The music stopped and there was a second crash.

The crowd froze. The night suddenly vibrated and a slash of movement cut through the surrounding immobility.

Cardozo glimpsed a figure plunging rigidly forward and then Ash Canfield came barreling out of the crowd.

Under her frothing cap of bronze and gold curls she looked like a crazed pixie. Her breath came in short, steep gasps. She stretched her arms out slowly, arcing them up from her body, and then her hips slipped into a wild syncopation and her hands clawed the air crazily, fighting fog, slapping mist.

"Cocksuckers!" she screamed, her voice swollen with pain and hate.

Delighted shock whipped through the crowd.

"You're all walkers and pillheads!" Lady Ash collapsed onto the deck and tried to get up but fell back, her limbs suddenly boneless.

Cardozo pushed through the crowd. By the time he reached Ash, the ship's doctor was crouching beside her.

The doctor was wearing rimless spectacles, and the gaze behind them was coldly professional. He raised one of Lady Ash's eyelids, then the other.

"What happened to her?" Cardozo said.

"Seizure." The doctor slipped together a syringe. He filled it from a blue cartridge. The fluid was colorless.

The guests, hungry as a flock of TV news minicams, watched avidly. There were nudges, whispers.

The doctor straightened Lady Ash's arm, administering the injection into the vein. He signaled two waiters. They lifted her onto a stretcher and fastened her arms and wrists with canvas straps.

Cardozo stood looking down at Ash. There was nothing moving in her now. She had the stillness of a dead machine. So much for his hopes of having Ash Canfield identify the figures in the photos.

Sir Dunk came out of the crowd and hovered, hands adjusting his black satin bow tie.

"Does that happen a lot?" Cardozo asked.

"It's been getting worse," Sir Dunk said. "I can't bear to see her when she gets like this."

Cardozo felt disgust. "Then don't feed her booze."

Ten minutes later a helicopter lifted Sir Dunk and Lady Ash Canfield from Holcombe Kaiser's yacht up into the fog.

Countess Victoria flipped a look Cardozo's way. She crossed to him, her step confident, her glance warm. "I'm not in the book," she said. "Have you got something to write on?"

Cardozo shook a business card loose from his wallet. It turned out to be Melissa Hatfield's.

Countess Victoria took out a small lipstick brush and wrote her phone number across the back of the card. "Call me. I give divine head."

40

EVERY DAY BEFORE WORK, BABE PRACTICED TWO HOURS. SHE lined up chairs at three-foot distances and struggled from one to the next without support. When she could manage three feet, she respaced the chairs four feet from one another, and then five and then six, evaluating her every step in the mirror. Eventually she dared to risk a turn to the left, a turn to the right, and finally she pushed the chairs to the wall and at long, long last—after fall-downs and stumbles and uncounted hesitations and swayings—she walked with no help or hesitation whatsoever from one end of the room all the way to the other.

Babethings was showing its new line of cruisewear the first week in September at the Park Avenue Armory; Babe had made it her goal to appear at the event without her cane.

She chose her ensemble for the event carefully—a black crepe suit that she had designed herself and a single piece of jewelry, a large emerald brooch that her grandmother had left her. The brooch had brought her good luck years ago, all the times she had showed her line at the Pierre, and tonight she kissed it before pinning it on.

Billi arrived for her at quarter to eight. She met him in the ground floor hallway. Luckily—because she might just need a little help with the steps at the armory—Billi did not intend to spend any of the show backstage. Instead he would sit in front, getting the pulse of the audience.

"Don't you look ravishing, Babe." Billi, whose eye rarely missed a detail, didn't notice the absence of the cane. That fact gave Babe confidence—it meant she was moving naturally, not showing her nervousness.

Billi kissed her on the cheek and held the front door. The black Mercedes limousine stood idling at the curb, eight feet away.

A pulse of uneasiness beat in Babe's throat as she took her first unsupported step on concrete.

The driver touched a gloved hand to the brim of his cap and swung the passenger door open. "Good evening, Mrs. Devens."

She turned to smile at him. In that instant of inattention one leg shot out from under her. She slammed painfully against the door. Momentum propelled her forward, and a split second later she had landed on the floor of the limousine.

The driver quickly helped her up. She stood blinking, angry and humiliated and not quite believing what had happened.

"My God, Babe, are you all right?" Billi possessed an aristocracy of face that usually hid whatever was going on in his mind, but at this moment, concerned and solicitous, he was watching her with undisguised pity.

Babe shook her head. "I'm fine."

Billi bent to help her brush off her skirt. "No rips, no tears on you or the suit?"

"I'm fine."

"No wonder," he exclaimed. "You forgot your cane!"

"How foolish of me." Babe's vision was filming and she did her best to hold tears at bay.

Billi snapped his fingers. "Carlos, be good enough to get Mrs. Devens's cane? It's in the house."

On the approach to the armory, the car had to maneuver around clots of stopped limousines. Gawking crowds pushed against police sawhorses. Police patrolled on foot and on horseback, struggling to keep order.

Searchlights mounted on wheeled platforms strafed low-hanging clouds, and as Billi took Babe's hand to help her to the curb, dozens of flashbulbs popped. "God save us from New York's brigade of professional event watchers," Billi shouted.

With his help and the help of her cane, Babe climbed the red-carpeted steps.

Inside, extraordinary-looking women milled about with their escorts. They had obviously dressed to make a statement, but the clothes Babe saw struck her as loud and careless, probably overpriced as well, and they made her feel like a limping refugee from a time capsule.

People swarmed to Billi in flurries of adulation. "You remember Babe Devens," he kept saying, "my partner."

Yes, they remembered Babe. *Hi, Babe.* But they loved Billi. *Billi, phone me and let's set up that lunch. . . . Billi, when are we going to have dinner? . . . Billi, you owe me a Michael Feinstein after that hideous Lohengrin!*

Kiss kiss.

Darling's and *chéri*'s and *caro*'s peppered the cooing and shoving. Babe kept smiling and nodding, fighting to keep her balance and fighting to keep the fight from showing. To reach their seats Billi had to pull her through wall after wall of fashion hangers-on.

By the time they found their places in the center bleachers, Babe's breath was harsh and hurting in her chest.

She had reserved the seats next to them for Ash, but Dunk arrived with Countess Vicki instead.

"Ash is still in detox," Dunk shouted. "She can't even have visitors yet."

"So you'll just have to put up with me." Countess Vicki planted a kiss on Babe's cheek. "You look glorious, Babe, as always, and so sweet and sentimental in that frock." She leaned across to scream at Billi, *"Also liebe Billi, der Tag ist jezt, nicht wahr?"*

Billi smiled. *"Ja, ja."*

When the building lights dipped, a wild wind of applause gusted through the armory. There was a moment of darkness and stiff silence and then, with a thirty-speaker blare of recorded music, banks of stagelights came up, flooding the runway.

The first mannequin came strutting out, hands on hips.

"Billi!" Countess Vicki screamed. "Su-*blime!*"

Babe frowned. The mannequin was wearing an outfit of skintight blue satin pants with passimetrie swirling around the buttocks. She had pump heels, a low-cut lavender silk blouse with four oversized loops of oversized fake pearls and a big scoop-brim blue fedora squared over her eyes. She was wearing craters of black eye shadow and too much lipstick, and her hips moved with a hard, angular syncopation to the fender-beat music.

A creamy-voiced British actor delivered the amplified voice-over.

Applause mounted as the mannequin strutted to the end of the runway.

Before she had even turned, the second mannequin bounded out onto the runway. On her pencil-thin red-stockinged legs, swathed in yards of fuchsia boa from her neck down to her ripped-off gray sweatcloth exercise tights, she looked like a pair of burning stilts holding up a cloud of acid rain.

Once the fifth mannequin strode onto the runway, Babe found that the dresses and ensembles overlapped in a discordant blur. Though tradition had it that you viewed only one mannequin at a time, Billi put as many as twelve on the runway at once. For Babe the effect was bewilderingly like a Broadway show—too much movement, too many lights, too much music.

She squirmed as Billi's eighty-five mannequins filed on and off the runway, their outfits progressively more hostile and aggressive, and it all began leaving her with a taste of mega-hyped insincerity.

The big outfit of the line—the one that got the greatest applause and that seemed to be the clearest statement of the house's esthetic —was a chartreuse blazer of crumpled silk linen. The jacket had been loaded with beading and more passimetrie than a Turkish dress uniform, and it was falling off the mannequin's shoulders, too big even to be called oversized. The dress underneath, shocking pink, was much too tight and almost pornographically short, and the heels on the black pumps were four inches—far too high.

By some miracle of luck or coordination, the mannequin was managing to keep her balance. Incredibly, she was chewing gum, and her face was set in a theatrical sneer.

"Well, Babe," Billi cried over the mounting applause, "what do you think of our little girl?"

It took Babe a moment's shock to recognize that the mannequin was her own daughter. "Well, Billi, you certainly have turned things inside out."

"What the hell else is tradition for?" he laughed.

The one tradition he had stuck with was to close the show with a wedding gown.

The lights dimmed suspensefully and came up again on a runway that was, for the first time since the evening had begun, empty. The speakers blared an eerily electronic Bridal Chorus.

Billi's tallest, skinniest mannequin slithered into the light, glistening as though she were oiled.

Babe sat rigid, not moving. What she saw went through her brain like a knife.

A sheath of black leather—cut tight down to the pelvis, flaring into a skirt below the knees—covered the mannequin from neck to ankles. Around her throat she wore a diamond-encrusted ankh, fastened upside down to a platinum-link chain. Billi's designers had studded the gown with steel zippers and outcroppings of black crow's feathers. For the veil they had used miles of black illusion, for the boots, black-dyed baby lamb.

Babe's blood was beating a drum in her head. The image of a steel-mouthed mask flashed before her.

"The bride wore boots!" Countess Vicki yelped. "Billi, I want that gown—the count and I are going to confirm our vows this spring, and *that* is going to be the look!"

The next few moments passed like caterpillars crawling over Babe's skin.

Applause exploded and a spotlight swept the bleachers, searching for Billi and finally, when he rose, escorting him down to the runway through a congratulating roar of high-fashion color and gemstone.

Bowing, Billi exuded pride and satisfaction. Letting his eyes drop half closed, he spread his arms wide, embracing the crowd.

The dinner afterward was at Lutèce, and Babe did her best.

The buzz at the tables was that Billi's line was glitzy, sexy, funny, compelling, expertly paced, slick, ironic, full of Hollywood decadence and offbeat charm, sure to be a winner.

Everyone said Babe must be so pleased for her company, and she made a pleased face.

Champagne was served with the meal. The guests toasted Billi and Babe, and somewhere down the line of toasts someone made a speech about Cordelia's wacky charm.

Cordelia remained imperturbably there, a perfectly coiffed presence with a cigarette dangling from her lips.

Babe had two espressos, hoping one of them would persuade her she still had the capacity to think. As dessert soufflés were being served, she excused herself.

Billi's dark eyes questioned her.

She promised him she could get home safely. "It's just a little headache from all the fun and excitement."

As Babe lifted the phone in her bedroom, her mind was finally made up. She felt energized, as though all her synapses were at last firing.

It took twelve seconds for the call to click through.

"*Allo?*"

"Mathilde, it's Babe. I'm sorry to call you at this hour, but—"

"*Bonjour, chérie! Ça va?*"

"Mathilde, I'm going to start my own atelier again, and I want you to come back and oversee the first season."

"But I explained, it's not possible."

"How much did you say that farmhouse is going to cost you? I'll pay you three times the amount. Your bank will have the money tomorrow."

There was a hesitation in Mathilde's voice, a missed beat.

Babe doubled the offer.

Babe and Cardozo followed a nurse down an ornate marble hall, their footsteps echoing like drum taps. Since the showing it had taken Babe another week of practice to walk without her cane, and there was still a slight limp in her left leg.

The nurse led them past a landing with a door opening onto what must once have been a ballroom. Patients in pajamas and robes formed hushed groups, shuffling in paper slippers beneath a blazing crystal chandelier.

"How is she doing?" Babe asked.

"She's still hanging on to a lot of denial," the nurse said. "At meetings patients are supposed to use their first name—you know, 'Hi, I'm Joe, I'm an alcoholic.' She says, 'Good evening, I'm Lady Canfield, delighted to be here with you.' Like she's dropped in from the Rockefeller Foundation."

The nurse took them as far as Ash's door.

Ash was sitting in a chair wearing a simple black silk dress and long strands of pearls. Her right arm was in motion, braceleted and white, moving through lamplight that glinted off the plastic fork in her hand.

She was working her way through a raw vegetable salad topped with nuts and seeds, with a glass of Perrier on the side. She ate with an elegant weariness, looking frail and very tired. The white of her skin contrasted starkly with the blue veins in her temples, and she was wearing her hair pulled straight back, with the earphones of a Walkman fitted over it.

As Babe bent to kiss Ash she noticed with strangely pained surprise how old and tired her friend looked.

Ash reacted slowly, recognizing Babe, smiling, pulling off the earphones. She got to her feet, and it saddened Babe to see how she had to make the effort in stages.

"I didn't hear you come in," Ash said. "I was listening to Bobby Short singing some beautiful old Vernon Duke songs."

Babe and Ash held each other.

"My first nonfamily visitor in over a month," Ash said. "Oh sweetie, I've missed you."

"Ash," Babe said, "you remember Vince Cardozo."

Ash glanced sidelong at Cardozo, studied him, then cast him a disarming smile. "Do I?"

"You and Vince met at the party on Holcombe's yacht."

Ash looked at Babe. There was something speculative in her gaze. "Should I remember a party on a yacht?"

"Well, you were there," Babe said, "and it was memorable."

Ash's eyes took on a wary expression. "I'm sorry. I suppose I misbehaved." She coughed a deep, dry cough. "What do you think of my temporary headquarters? It's *très* glam, *n'est-ce pas?*"

There was a tiroir of pale ash with ebony handles. The four-poster bed had a cream-colored cover. A Raggedy Ann doll that was at least as old as Ash lolled against the enormous fluffy pillows in lace cases.

"This is a place for drunks, you know," Ash said. "But my problem's not drink. I only drink because of other problems."

"How are you feeling?" Babe asked.

"I'm fine—cured. Back to normal and bored. I'll probably check myself out tomorrow."

"Can you do that?"

"I'd better be able to do it. It's my money that got me in, my money can damned well get me out."

Beneath the bravado, Babe heard the voice of a frightened child.

"Where's Dunk?" Ash said.

"I saw Dunk at the showing," Babe said. "He was fine. Don't worry yourself. Get your rest, and you'll pick up the threads of your life in no time."

"What in the world are you saying? I never dropped the threads of my life."

There was a strained silence. Ash's eyes traveling from Babe to Cardozo. Babe could feel they were entering a dangerous emotional zone.

"Well?" Ash said.

"Well what?" Babe said.

"The purpose of this visit."

"Must it have a purpose? We came to see you."

"No, no, no, no." Ash pointed at Cardozo. *"He* didn't come to see me. He doesn't even know me."

"Lady Canfield," Cardozo said, "last month we showed you these pictures."

He handed them to her. Her gaze was flat, empty of reaction.

"We asked you if you recognized any of them." He handed her the last photo: the girl with the confident stride, with the strong nose and jaw, the blond hair and brown eyes, the girl with the package who had gone into Beaux Arts Tower at 11:07 A.M., Tuesday, May 27, and never came out again. "You said you recognized this one."

For a moment Ash appeared to be lost in a mist between worlds. She shook her head. "Never saw her blond before. I can see I'm going to need to refresh my memory."

She went to the tiroir where she had arranged her Countess Lura Esterhasz skin care bottles. She brought three tumblers and a bottle of moisturizer to the bedside table. She tipped Babe a crafty glance.

"Remember when we used to do this at Farmington?"

She uncapped the moisturizer and tilted it over one of the tumblers. A clear amber liquid poured out.

She poured two fingers in each tumbler. "They don't give you ice here. But this is Jack Daniel's, it tastes terrific neat." She raised her glass. *"Santé,* everyone."

She stopped, conscious of Babe's cool disbelieving stare.

"Ash," Babe cried, "for God's sake don't drink that!"

"I most certainly shall." Ash emptied the glass in a single swallow.

She sat on the edge of the bed, staring vaguely in front of her. After a moment she reached to the table for a second tumbler.

Babe made a move to stop her.

Cardozo put out a hand. "Let her do it. It's what she wants."

Ash nodded. "Babe, your friend's a wise man."

Ash downed the second glass.

"On the house." Cardozo pushed the third tumbler toward her. She stared at him, then at it, then at Babe.

The lids sank over her eyes. Her face began crumpling. She put a hand to her mouth and burped softly, and then she was vomiting through her fingers, vomiting over her pearls, down her dress.

Ash studied her vomit-stained hand as though it were an object that had materialized from another universe. She blinked back tears. A spasm racked her and she made a gagging sound.

This isn't my friend, Babe thought. *Ash Canfield is not puking on the detox floor.*

Ash was sliding off the bed to her knees, bending forward, dragging herself slowly through the fouled pile of the carpet.

Babe stared at her childhood friend, crawling across the carpet like a squashed slug.

"Get out," Ash whimpered. "Please just get the fuck out."

41

IN THE TAXI CARDOZO COULD FEEL THE PAIN IN BABE AND HE knew she was trying to hold back tears.

"I'm sorry," he said. "It's a damned shame."

Babe nodded, teeth pressed down on her lower lip. He put his arm around her and drew her against his shoulder.

They rode on in silence.

After a while he looked at the photo again, thinking of what Ash had said: *Never saw her blond before.*

And suddenly the mystery woman wasn't a mystery anymore.

The butler led Cardozo into the big, pricey pad and threw open the huge cypress doors of the livingroom.

"Your Ladyship, Mr. Vince Cardozo."

Countess Vicki sat curled on the enormous velvet sofa, one leg beneath her and the other swinging shoeless. The shoes lying on the Persian carpet matched her brown silk dress.

She was talking on the telephone and trying to clasp an emerald bracelet. Sapphires and diamonds blazed at her throat and wrists and ears. Her slender, oval face turned in Cardozo's direction, full-lipped and hinting, and she shot him a smiling, brown-eyed glance of welcome.

Like the countess's dress, the enormous livingroom with its three marbled pillars and two crystal chandeliers seemed to have been designed to set off the owner's dark coloring. Bookcases were filled with gold-tooled leather bindings and glittering figurines and intricately ornamented porcelain plates. Tables wore bright shawls and were dotted with china bowls and silver-framed pictures of current celebrities, most of them autographed.

Cardozo took a leisurely stroll to the fireplace. Engraved invitations were stuck in the mirror over the mantel. They were also, more surprisingly, stuck in the frame of a Renoir.

"Too divine," Vicki said. "Call you later—love you much." She set the phone receiver back in the cradle and rose from the sofa.

"How angelic of you to remember my phone number." She came across the room and took Cardozo's hand. "I honestly thought you'd forgotten me."

Cardozo smiled. "Never."

The countess bent down and pulled the phone cord out of the wall jack. "We don't need that anymore. Would you like something to drink? I have some leftover cappuccino—or would you rather get drunk?"

"I could live without cappuccino."

The countess, a dark silhouette against the glow of the pantry doorway, spent three minutes trying to press extra ice cubes into the blender. "I hope you like slush margaritas," she called. "And if you don't, please pretend."

The blender screeched and she came out of the pantry carrying two champagne glasses filled with what looked like chopped icicles. "Maid's day off—forgive."

He sipped. "Tastes great."

She sipped. "It's usually hard for me to meet new people. But with you it's different, I felt that right away. I can be myself with you—and you can be yourself with me—and neither of us is going to judge the other. I think that's the way a man and a woman should be, don't you?"

"It's not a bad idea."

"Why don't we find a more private locale?"

Dark hair billowing, skirt swaying, she led him down a seemingly endless corridor, the walls tiled with Utrillos and Jasper Johnses.

Drink in hand, she stood by the door, her bright mouth smiling now, her large eyes inviting him into the still, cool, dim interior of the bedroom.

He accepted, moving past her.

The walls had been done in a dizzying variety of *faux* marble and *faux* wood and trompe-l'oeil. There were cut begonias in a Chinese porcelain vase on the dresser and a telephone console with eight buttons on the bedside table. On a chest of drawers were three wigs on stands—a red, a gray, and a blond.

Clothes had been laid out on the bed: a mauve evening gown, silk stockings, a sequined purse, a short fur jacket.

"Are you going out?" he asked.

"I was planning to." She swung out one of the mirror wall panels and took a cushioned hanger from the closet. "But why go to a dull party when I can stay home and have an exciting one?"

"I guess you're pretty good at state-of-the-art partying."

"I guess that's a compliment." She finished her drink and slipped a CD into the player. Tinkly music filled the room. "I love the naive magic of Mozart—don't you?"

She switched off the lamp, leaving the room half lit by streetlights slanting through the Roman shades. She drew the thick damask curtains, and a moment later she lit a scented candle and placed it beside the phone.

"Make yourself comfortable," she said.

He sat down on the bed.

She sat beside him, solemnly reading his face. She put her arm around him and drew him against her breasts.

He felt the involuntary response of his body, the deep-down beat of his heart speeding up.

"It's a beautiful thing, don't you think, our being so intimate—complete strangers?" She unbuttoned his shirt. Her tongue touched him softly. "Why do you have the gun? What kind of crime are you in?"

"I'm a cop."

She smiled, accepting the answer without believing it. "And I'm the Ayatollah."

"Don't joke—he's a holy man."

"Are you a Moslem cop?"

"The force recruits minorities."

She bent down and laid her head lightly on his lap. She had a troubled moment with his zipper.

He was only halfway hard.

She pulled up and kissed him on the mouth, giving him a tiny grin, and then she went to the mirrored closet and got a little Tiffany salt cellar of cocaine. She took a tiny spoonful of coke up her nostril and then offered him one.

"Pass," he said.

She stared with hungry dark eyes at him and then she dove.

He could feel an acute attack of integrity coming on. "Look, this is a little sleazoid for me." He freed himself and stood.

She pushed her hair out of her face. Her eyes were bright with sudden noncomprehension. "Then why did you come here?"

"I told you. I'm a cop."

He showed her his shield. The silence hung there, blazing.

"I resent this invasion. I've never broken the law."

"Cocaine's not breaking the law?"

She was sitting with sudden, furious erectness. "Half a gram. Personal use."

"Aiding and abetting isn't breaking the law?"

"Aiding whom? Abetting what?"

He reached into his jacket and brought out the photograph of Countess Victoria de Savoie-Sancerre in her blond wig striding into Beaux Arts Tower with the little package. "You bought a leather mask from the Pleasure Trove in Greenwich Village the Tuesday after Memorial Day. Who did you take it to?"

A twisted look came into her mouth and a network of fine lines suddenly crisscrossed her face. "You've got fucking nerve spying on me!"

"You and your friends have been running between raindrops a long, long while. But this time you're all going to get soaking wet."

"Fucker!" she screamed. "Motherfucking copfucking sucker!"

She dove for the door and wrenched it open.

Count Leopold de Savoie-Sancerre, his flushed face looking very much surprised, was crouching at keyhole level on the other side.

Cardozo and Sam Richards were discussing a fifty-nine-year-old Hispanic by the name of Avery Rodriguez who had taken two .38 slugs in the head that morning in the men's room at Bloomingdale's. They were reviewing Avery's rapsheet, a thesaurus of petty felonies, when Sergeant Goldberg shouted from the squad room that Cardozo had a call on three.

Cardozo pushed the blinking button and lifted the receiver. "Cardozo."

A woman's voice said, "Would you hold for District Attorney Spalding, please."

A moment later Al Spalding's voice came on the line. "Vince, the Downs case is closed. Why are you hassling people?"

Cardozo signaled Richards to hold on a moment. "Who says I'm hassling them?"

"Countess Victoria de Savoie-Sancerre."

"I didn't realize you were a friend of hers."

"Let's say I'm an acquaintance of an acquaintance. This isn't an official call, Vince, but if you don't lay off, the next call's going to be official and it won't come from me."

"I don't have any idea what Countess Vicki de S. and S. is talking about."

"Vince, don't play dumb with me, please. I'd appreciate it if we could clear up this matter with this phone call."

"Just tell me who said Downs case? Who used those two words, *Downs case?*"

"She said you did."

Cardozo knew he hadn't mentioned the Downs case to Countess Vicki. She'd made the connection herself. Big slip. "Okay, Al. It's cleared up." He hung up the phone. "Be right with you, Sam."

Cardozo opened his desk drawer and found Melissa Hatfield's business card. On one side there was printed black lettering; on the other, the countess's unlisted phone—seven smudged red digits punctuated by a dash.

Something not very pleasant had happened to Lou Stein's face. Cardozo's glance slid incredulously along the bruise running from the right eye down to the mouth, the barely healed multiple abrasions on the cheekbone. "Kissing a meat grinder?" he asked.

"Disagreement with a stranger on Fifty-eighth Street," Lou muttered through swollen lips. "He thought he had a right to my wallet, I disagreed."

"Who won?"

Lou Stein, who came to work each day to do his little bit in the age-old combat between dark and light, sat there for a second just looking balding, stocky, discouraged. "I kept the wallet. Did I win? Is losing a tooth winning? I had fifty bucks in the wallet. I had five hundred invested in that root canal."

"So you'll get a false tooth. You're insured."

Lou's left hand waved Cardozo to a chair. The air conditioning inside Forensic wasn't working. It was one of those hot New York fall days when the atmosphere has stagnant weight.

"Did you file a complaint?" Cardozo asked.

Lou fixed him with an incredulous gaze. "You kidding? I got enough aggravation. So tell me what sorrow you're bringing to brighten my day?"

Cardozo plopped the sandwich-sized evidence bag down in the middle of the papers on Lou's desk. "Is there enough lipstick on that cigarette butt to do a chemical analysis?"

Lou Stein picked up the evidence bag tagged with the number of the Jodie Downs homicide. He frowned at the inch and a half of crushed cigarette inside the plastic. "Maybe."

Cardozo held up the evidence bag that he had tagged VINCE C. SPECIAL. "Tell me if the lipstick on that cigarette and the lipstick on this business card are the same."

Lou Stein phoned Cardozo four days later. "Both lipstick samples contain glycerine, beeswax, yeast protein, red dye six, orange dye two, purple dye two, rose oil, and trace amounts of hydrocortisone acetate—which in simple English is cortisone."

"Cortisone—is that usual in a lipstick?"

"No. And it ought to be illegal. In the old days, you'd have needed a prescription. But now cortisone's sold over the counter in mild concentrations—point four, five percent. It's an anti-inflammatory agent. Masks minor irritations such as you'd get from applying this mishmash to a chapped lip."

"You're telling me it's not your usual mass-produced commercial cosmetic."

"No way. The cortisone requires FDA registration. This so-called blend, or formula, is concocted exclusively by a coven of warlocks calling themselves Countess Lura Esterhasz Products, and it's available only at the Esterhasz Eternelle Boutique on Fifth Avenue, do you need me to spell that."

"I can manage. Thanks, Lou."

"Oh, Vince, you'll get a kick out of this. The sample on the cigarette butt has one trace ingredient I couldn't find on the calling card. Guess. You'll never guess. I'll tell you. Honey."

"Honey?"

"Yep. I have a hunch that's the evening flavor."

Cardozo strode down Fifth Avenue, dodging chestnut vendors and messengers on skates with Walkmans and junior execs in jogging shoes.

It was the kind of day he loved. The air was extraordinarily clear. The show windows of Bergdorf Goodman and Tiffany and Harry Winston glinted in the sunlight and the sky was the deeply saturated blue of autumn. The lengthening shadows of late afternoon reverberated like echoes and fitful gusts of wind blew along Fifty-seventh Street.

In front of the Esterhasz Eternelle Boutique women were climbing out of limousines. It was a gentle perpetual twilight inside the boutique, the air cool and blue, sweet with soft light and music and elusive perfumes and the aroma of money.

The salon had been decorated in muted tones of blue and beige and rust, with clean, shining surfaces. Each square glass counter had two or three salesgirls waiting on one or two customers. The salesgirls were as well dressed as the clientele, and twenty to thirty years younger.

But the customers had the slightly unreal beauty that only wealth could bestow. They seemed golden, like a memory of the past, their jewels sparkling with points of light. They moved like ripples in water. The murmur of upper class, ever so slightly back-in-the-throat voices, perfected during Newport summers and private-school winters, sounded like a record slowed down to a seductively wrong speed.

Tea and sherry and Madeira and British water biscuits were being served at small tables in an alcove. Cardozo felt he'd walked by mistake into the ladies' room. He approached the lipstick counter and coughed discreetly.

The salesgirl's hair was long, straight, and pale—the color of champagne. "May I help you, sir?"

"I need some information. Are your products ready-made?"

She approached him, a cool, self-possessed young woman. "Absolutely not, sir. All our products are custom-made, and each is unique for the customer. You see, skins are like fingerprints. No two are exactly the same."

"What about lips?"

She looked at him with a slightly amused expression. "No two pairs of lips are the same. Are you interested for yourself or for someone else?" .

He felt his cheeks flush under the steadiness of her gaze. "For someone else."

"It's more usual for the lady to inquire herself."

"I have her formula." Cardozo produced the piece of paper. "All I need to know is her name."

An expression of doubt clouded the salesgirl's face. "I'm sorry. We can't give out that information."

He showed her his shield. He felt he had brought a machine gun to trap a butterfly. "I'd appreciate it if you could make an exception."

A frown darkened her forehead. "Just one moment, please." She took the formula and went through a doorway and returned three minutes later. "You'll have to talk with Countess Esterhasz—could you come this way, please?"

Cardozo followed the salesgirl into an office. There were two small Hockneys on the wall, and a tray of liqueurs on a red lacquer table.

"Would you care for a drink?" the girl offered.

"No, thank you."

"Countess Esterhasz will be with you directly."

Seven minutes later Countess Esterhasz entered through another door. Tall, sturdily built, she appeared to be a little past forty but was probably well past sixty and a testament to her own beauty products.

She smiled in greeting. She had clear pale skin and black hair falling straight to her shoulders. She was wearing a lavender silk dress and a strand of pearls, and the hand with the three-strand matching pearl bracelet was holding the piece of paper that Cardozo had given the salesgirl.

"How may I help the police?" she said in a pleasantly accented voice.

"Do you recognize that formula?" Cardozo asked.

She shot him a half-lidded glance. "Our clients rely on our discretion. Sometimes, following certain types of surgical reconstruction, the skin develops sensitivities. A hypoallergenic cosmetic may be called for. A woman—and sometimes a man—prefers to deal with such problems privately—in confidence." She sat in a gilded beechwood armchair. Her eyes were a keen, intelligent green. "What do you do for your skin?" she asked.

"Nothing."

She studied him, prolonging the slightly uncomfortable silence. "You should use a collagen moisturizer with calf placenta. It would help those lines around your eyes."

"I don't mind the lines."

She smiled, and charm lay on her like a veil. "You will in ten years."

"If you'll tell me who you made that lipstick for, I won't need to take any more of your time."

"How convenient to be a man. You keep your looks without devoting your life to it. As for the lipstick, we never reveal clients' records." Her mouth came together with firmness.

"Are you a doctor?"

"I hold a doctorate of biological science from Budapest University."

She pointed to an impressively framed document on the wall. It was a fine example of Hungarian language calligraphy and it had been hung just beneath a very old autographed photo of a plump, young Marlene Dietrich and a very new one of Ronald Reagan, Jr., whose eyelashes seemed to be grinning.

"Since you're not an M.D.," Cardozo said, "your records aren't privileged."

He could feel the mounting wave of her annoyance.

"My associate, Dr. Franzblau, is a dispensing chemist."

"There's no such thing as chemist-client confidentiality in New York City," Cardozo said.

She mused on that and nodded. "Why do you need this information?"

"I'm investigating a homicide."

Her face stiffened. "You realize you've given me two different formulas."

"I realize one has honey in it. I suppose that's for kissing."

She was not amused. "What we call type-C labial tissue requires glucose—which you may choose to call honey. What we call type H-three does not require glucose."

"I take it the formula without glucose is lipstick for Countess Victoria de Savoie-Sancerre."

Countess Esterhasz smiled. "You have a very good accent, Lieutenant. And that is correct. It is her exclusive formula, devised by our chemists and dermatologists to meet her unique needs."

"Then the other is hers too?"

"Absolutely not."

Cardozo's eyebrows went up and Countess Lura Esterhasz had his attention.

"The formula containing glucose would react most harmfully with Countess Victoria's sensitive alkaline tissue. That lipstick was perfected for another client—Lady Ash Canfield."

"Do you recognize this man?" Cardozo held out the photograph of Jodie Downs.

Ash Canfield's blue eyes gazed out from under a fluff of graying hair. Her eyelids were heavy and low, the eyes sunken in, dark and lifeless, like ice cubes made of stagnant pond water. The whites of her eyes were startlingly luminous. She had developed night sweats after detox and had spent three weeks in intensive care, battling 106-degree fevers. Her doctor hadn't allowed Cardozo to visit till today, when her fever was down to 101.

"Who is that?" She had a blank, baffled look.

Next, Cardozo showed her the photo of Claude Loring. "Do you know this man?"

Ash had been cranked up to a sitting position. The pillows she was propped on kept slipping awry. She was wearing a beaded ivory silk satin nightgown over white satin pajamas.

"He . . . should . . . dress . . . better."

An IV had been inserted into a vein in her forearm and from it a tube looped up to a steel pole, where a plastic bag of glucose hung. The clear fluid seeped drop by drop into her bloodstream. Through another tube oxygen ran from a wall outlet into her nose.

Cardozo held out the photo of the black leather mask. "Have you ever seen this mask?"

She smiled. "Halloween."

"You saw this mask on Halloween?"

"Mary," she said. "Mary Queen. Queen of Scots."

A medicine tray on the table beside the bed held a collection of pills that looked like the purse of a hophead on a spree. There were little paper cups of Valium and phenobarbital, enough to make even an elephant feel vague.

Cardozo leaned closer and spoke very clearly. "Did anyone ever borrow your lipstick? Or steal it? Did you ever lose it?"

Ash's breathing became more rapid. She stared at him, and now she was smiling.

"She's no good today," Babe said from the chair in the corner of the room. Her face was worn and exhausted and pale.

Cardozo didn't want to look at that. It hurt him too much to look at the pain she was feeling for her friend.

There was a knock on the open door, and without waiting for an answer, a well-dressed woman came into the room. Long-faced and tanned, with crisply waving auburn hair, she moved tall and slim and light, with a horseback rider's grace.

She crossed to the bed and kissed the top of Ash's head, laying her cheek for an instant on the damp, downy hair. "How are you feeling, Sis?"

Ash smiled.

"Dina," Babe said, "this is a friend of Ash's and mine—Vince Cardozo. Vince, Dina Alstetter—Ash's sister."

Mrs. Alstetter smiled politely at Cardozo. She had keen, take-in-everything blue-gray eyes. There was something urbane and intelligent in the set of the mouth.

"How do you do." She had the sort of New York voice that insinuated all sorts of money and ease, and she gave Cardozo the feeling that she wanted something—maybe nothing more than to be alone with her sister, but still she wanted it very badly.

She began pulling goodies out of a Channel 13 totebag, holding them up for Ash to see.

Ash's gaze moved slowly, following each object: a beautifully wrapped package of Opium perfume. Hugely oversized magazines and newspapers—the newest *Interview*, the newest *W*. A half dozen ripe pears, sitting in a basket of excelsior. Walkman cassettes, which Mrs. Alstetter named as she brought them out and set them on the table. "Bobby Short, Bobby Short, and a Furtwängler reissue—Schubert. Just the stuff you need to get well again."

She lifted the cover from Ash's untouched dinner.

"What kind of specials are they tempting us with today? Looks like roast pork with sweet red cabbage and . . ."

She dipped a pinkie into the other vegetable and tapped her tongue to the tip.

"Squash puree. Any of that appeal to you?"

"She wasn't hungry," Babe said.

"We'll see." Mrs. Alstetter took the knife and fork and began expertly dissecting the meat into baby-bite pieces. She held a piece of pork to Ash's lips.

Ash shook her head.

"She won't touch a thing," Babe said.

"Okay, starve yourself to death." Mrs. Alstetter stuck out her tongue at her sister. "Feel like talking?"

Ash shook her head again.

Mrs. Alstetter took the copy of *W*, deposited herself in a chair, and lit a cigarette.

"You shouldn't," Babe said. "Ash is on oxygen."

"I won't wave it in her face."

The fourth cigarette was one third ash when the doctor came into the room, trailed by an assistant and a nurse. "Now, now, Mrs. Alstetter, no smoking while your sister's on oxygen."

"Sorry." She stubbed out her cigarette.

The doctor greeted the others with the sort of friendliness that wasted no time, then leaned over his patient. He lifted Ash's wrist and timed her pulse against the digital second readout of his gold chunk of a Rolex watch.

He patted Ash's arm encouragingly and whispered something to the nurse, who made a notation on the patient's chart.

"Could I trouble you people to leave the room for a moment?" he said.

In the hallway Cardozo watched Dina Alstetter light another cigarette.

"Ash isn't looking well," Babe said.

Dina Alstetter's lips pulled together into a thin, frustrated line. "She's getting the best treatment—Dr. Tiffany's tops, he's state of the art."

"What's the matter with your sister?" Cardozo said.

"Would you believe that after all the blood tests and X rays and biopsies and bronchoscopies, all the EKGs and CAT scans, they still don't know for sure? There's a possibility of Tourette's syndrome."

Cardozo had a cousin with Tourette's who broke into facial tics and uncontrollable cursing at odd moments; but the man weighed a hefty two hundred twenty pounds. "Isn't the weight loss a little out of line with Tourette's?"

Dina Alstetter nodded. "Some kind of brain disorder is bringing on the seizures, but if anyone knows anything more than that, they're sure as hell not telling me. I'm not next of kin, you see." Bitterness curled her voice. "Dunk is next of kin. He gets the news, not me. It's so damned unfair. Dunk and Ash are practically divorced and he's still next of kin."

"What are the doctors telling Dunk?" Babe said.

"Who knows? The bastard's in France, can you believe it?"

The doctor and his team came out of Ash's room.

"How's she doing?" Dina Alstetter asked with a bright tone and an anxious, uncertain smile.

Judging by the doctor's expression, and discounting for the medical profession's ability to maintain a poker face, Cardozo estimated that Lady Ash's prospects were somewhere between negligible and none.

"She's tired," Dr. Tiffany said. "You'd better let her rest."

Dina Alstetter absorbed the lack of information quietly. "May we say good-bye?"

"Of course. Just don't take too long."

With hugs and assurances Babe kissed Ash good-bye. "See you tomorrow, sweetie. Be good."

Dina Alstetter stood staring at her sister, and then, slowly, her eyes began to tear over. "You two go along," she said. "Don't wait for me. I want to sit with Ash."

Halfway to the elevator, Babe said, "She's acting as though Ash were already dead."

"How long has Ash been this way?" Cardozo asked.

"I honestly can't say. It's all been so damnably *gradual*. Ash has always been crazy—you've seen her, you know how she can be—infantile rages, no discipline, no realism at all. When she was a child, everyone said 'It's a stage; she'll grow out of it.' Then they said 'It's adolescence, she'll grow out of it.' Later they said 'It's her drinking,' and no one said she'd grow out of *that*. Then her conversation got more and more bizarre. She'd change mood or subject right in the middle of a sentence. Go from laughter to tears, from the King of Siam to the cost of living in eight syllables. Everyone said 'See what happens when you do too much coke?' In the last few months it got far worse. There've been times she didn't recognize people, or couldn't find the word for something that was right in front of her, or called things by a completely wrong word—like *giraffe* for *coffee*. There wasn't even Freudian sense to it."

"Have the doctors ruled out stroke?"

"They haven't ruled it out, but they say there's got to be something more. Stroke wouldn't explain the weight loss."

It was sunny outside the hospital, with puffs of white clouds looking like splats of Reddi Wip in the blue sky. The winds of autumn were here, nipping like little dogs, and the trees were beginning to give up their leaves.

Babe turned up the collar of her coat. Crossing to the parking lot, Cardozo took her arm. They stopped at the gray Rolls.

"You love her very much," he said.

"She's my childhood. She's my youth. She's all the years I missed."

"Do you want to talk about it?"

"I hate to say what I'm thinking. I hate myself for thinking it."

"Think it. Say it."

She stared at him, her eyes wide, her head slightly lowered. "The way she was today—it's something new, and it's bad . . . and it's not going to go away."

He put a finger under her chin. "Hey, what ever happened to hope?"

Her mouth opened a little wider, and she nodded just a little.

He reached for her quickly and she clung to him, pressing her face into his chest.

42

IN ROOM 1227 OF THE VANDERBILT PAVILION, DINA ALSTETTER
sat on a small armchair two feet from the bed, watching the IV drip
into the anorexic bundle of bones that her sister had become.

She stubbed out her seventh cigarette.

She loaded a fresh cassette into her recorder and pulled the chair
nearer to the bed. There was no sound in the sickroom but the faint
whirring of the tape.

She held the recorder two inches from Ash's mouth.

"Ash, can you hear me? This is important. Please try to focus. I
have to ask you something."

There was a stab in Gordon Dobbs's heart when he saw Ash looking so *tiny* in that bed, smiling her heartbreaking, lopsided little grin.

She must have lost forty pounds, he calculated. Her hair was a
gray-blond wisp bound with tortoiseshell clips. Shock welled up in
him, and he put more wish than conviction into his greeting.

"Ash—great to see ya, hon."

There was a deep haze in the blue skies of what had been her eyes
and he wasn't sure she recognized him.

He slid into a chair near the bed.

Ash was still smiling at him with that eager, childlike quality of
hers, as though he were the magician at a birthday party who was
going to pop a furry white miracle out of a top hat for her. He
adjusted the press in his trouser legs and reached across to pat her
hand.

He decided to begin with fluff. There was nothing like fluff for
teasing smiles out of an invalid.

He talked to her about debs, show biz, newcomers, duchesses and gossip columnists, the two news anchors on different networks who were having a hot lesbian affair that was the talk of Mortimer's.

He was trying very hard to be an easy person to be with, but she looked at him as though his clothes were slipping off.

"What happened to Mama's dog?" she said.

He blinked, his face aching from the ready-to-guffaw expression he was powerless to keep it from taking on. "How many guesses do I get?"

She stared at him.

The impulse to flee was beating in his veins.

"What's going on?" she said.

Whatever she meant by that, he decided to take it as a cue for a description of the week's top parties—the usual smorgasbords of pedigrees, brains, fame, and nouveau Nueva.

She seemed to be following, but he couldn't be sure.

"Look, I figured I could stop at Integral Yoga and get two pounds of tofu," Dobbsie said, "or I could dig up some really fun yummies. So guess where we're going. We're going to Archibald's! Faith Banks has reserved us the front table! Shall we start with an aperitif?"

He clapped his hands, and Felicien, the maître d' from Archibald's, entered, carrying a silver tray with a bottle of Evian and two small glasses. Sal, his young assistant, brought the ice and lime and laid two formal lunch settings—one on Ash's hospital table and the other on a portable buffet table for Dobbsie. With a flourish, Felicien poured two glasses of mineral water.

Dobbsie raised his glass. "Health."

"I'll drink to that," Ash said.

The appetizer was petite pastry shells heaped with gray beluga caviar, each topped with a quail egg. He watched Ash, wanting to be able to tell Tina Vanderbilt how well she was handling a fork. She didn't touch her food and she didn't chuckle once at his stories.

"There's a new game," he said, "making up names for people—but it has to be an article of clothing. Are you ready? The Von Auersbergs are the Newport blazers. Isn't that too much? Well, you remember those parties they gave at Clarendon Court last summer. The Pendletons are the Saratoga breechers, that's cheating a little, but Merce de la Renta thought it up and it really fits. The Fords are the Grosse Pointe loafers. Get it? Okay—who are Bill and Pat Buckley?"

No reaction.

"I'll give you a hint. Stamford."

She sat in a deep lethargy, saying nothing.

Dobbsie wolfed his dessert, fresh raspberries with crème Chantilly flavored with just a zeste of Benedictine—a secret he'd coaxed out of the chef at Grand Vefour in Paris. He managed to keep a semblance of patter going, but it was like playing both sides of the tennis net at once.

"I mean, you see Henry Kissinger's Frau curtsying to this princess who is dressed so grotesquely, and you have to ask yourself, who is fooling whom? Well, they're not fooling us old foxes, are they, hon."

There didn't seem much purpose in continuing what had become a monologue, especially when the audience had drifted away to some other universe.

He wiped his mouth and carefully folded Mrs. Banks's beautiful Pierre Deux napkin.

Ash was staring, of all things, at a lipstick tube. It shocked Dobbsie to see what an effort thinking had become for her. Her brow was drawn painfully, her eyes were blinking.

"Dobbsie," she said, "you know everything. Who was it who was asking me about this lipstick?"

"I don't know, hon." He leaned close, but didn't kiss her. "Bye-bye —kiss kiss. Don't worry about the dishes, Felicien's man will be in to pick them up. Love you much, hon, come back to us soon."

Stepping into the hallway, Dobbsie felt he'd come out of a sweatbox. He loosened his silk cravat. His shirt must have shrunk a full size in there.

Felicien's man—everyone knew his name was Sal, but they called him Felicien's man—was waiting in the hallway, reading the princess of Yugoslavia's memoirs.

"You can clear the plates," Dobbsie said.

He found Dina Alstetter in the hallway, smoking a cigarette.

"And look at you, Deenie, in your green plaid Scaasi suit all jazzed up with that platinum Bulgari squiggle pin."

"We have to talk." She seized his arm.

The visitors' waiting room was a ferociously cheery place cluttered with striped blue and yellow chairs and matching inflatable animals. There was a pot in the coffeemaker. Dina closed the door, leaning her weight on it.

"I talked a lot of froufrou," Dobbsie said. "That story about Alice Mason—I could have used that in a column, but I gave it to Ash instead and people are going to just adore her for it."

"I wanted you to see for yourself how sick she is," Dina said.

"They're saying her blood gas is very low—she'll have to be put on a respirator."

"Jesus—is she terminal?"

"There's no way she can recover."

Dobbsie poured himself a Styrofoam cup of coffee that he absolutely did not need and dumped in two teaspoons of sugar that he absolutely should not have had.

"That bastard Dunk hasn't visited, hasn't phoned, hasn't written. He's dumped her."

Cream, Dobbsie decided. *What the hell, go for it.* "I must say, even for Dunk, that's remarkable."

"He can't be allowed to get away with it. Promise you won't let him."

The one subject Dobbsie had ever known Dina Alstetter to wax a tad tiresome over was her brother-in-law—all because Dunk had taken her to bed a few times and then married her sister. Why couldn't Dina forgive Dunk his preferences and let the story die, instead of constantly drawing the whole world's attention to what was really a rather pedestrian jilt-and-switch? A woman who had published in *The New Yorker* had no business obsessing over a man who had gone to Harrow on scholarship.

"Deenie dearie, what the hell control do I have over Dunk?"

"You can put it in your column—after she's dead."

The little nightlamp cast a pale circle of light around the sick woman.

Her breathing made a sound as though her ribs had cracked, each inhalation digging a splinter of bone deeper into her lungs.

Dina Alstetter sat motionless, slightly slumped in a chair with her hands folded in her lap.

Babe knelt next to Ash, whispering "I'm here," stroking her arm, staring at that thin, beautiful, very old, and strangely, unexpectedly wise face. It was the face of Ash at thirty-six, but it was also Ash at ninety-six, Ash who had leapt in two weeks to that brink of farewell.

The gray New York dawn slid through the canted blinds, striping the hospital bed where Ash Canfield lay in coma. She had developed embolisms in both lungs. Beneath the blue satin De la Renta robe her body was covered with monitoring electrodes.

Her temperature registered 105.5 Her pulse made a faint, irregular blip on an amber screen. The respirator beside the bed forced air through a tube into her throat and down into lungs that had long since given up all effort.

Ash was moving her lips, trying to force sound out.

Dina leapt up. "Ash!"

"Nurse!" Babe cried.

A nurse and an intern hurried into the room. The intern removed the respirator and the nurse held a glass of water to Ash's lips.

Ash forced a swallow and tried to speak. Her voice was scarcely a whisper. "When this is all over, we'll all live together, won't we?"

Babe's tongue was helpless and her throat was dry.

"Yes, darling," Dina said, "we'll all get a lovely house together."

"I want my viewing . . . in the best suite at Frank E. Campbell's. . . . Get my hair done . . . a little rinse over the gray. Dress me in that . . . pale blue gown . . . Babe made me. And give me . . . a really grand send-off . . . at Saint Bart's."

"Yes, darling," Dina said.

"I'd like to be alone now. Dunk will be . . . on the phone, and I want . . . to be ready . . . Would you turn out the lights?"

Dina turned out the light.

When Babe looked back from the doorway, all that was left of her friend was the unmoving shadow of a shadow.

43

BABE AND CARDOZO SIGNED THE VISITORS' REGISTER. THE ROOM was softly lit. The immediate family formed a receiving line: Dunk, doing his best to muster a sorrowful charm; Dina, with a look of mourning dignity; Ash's parents—DeWitt Cadwalader, a tall, gray man dressed in power; Thelma Cadwalader, a slender bejeweled woman with eyes warm and large and a benevolent smile; and Dina's son, Lawson, a grave little six-year-old.

The count and countess de Savoie arrived directly behind Babe and Cardozo. They scattered condolences to the family, and then the countess saw Cardozo.

"Well hello, Dick Tracy."

"Hi, your highnesses."

The countess kissed Babe. "Quite a turnout. And live piano music —*quelle élégance*. But 'Hey, Look Me Over'? Whose joke is that?"

"It's not a joke. It was Ash's favorite song."

"Crazy, crazy gal. You just gotta love her."

There was a mood in the place that was strange to Cardozo. This wasn't an Irish cop's wake where old women wept and men wearing their one good suit grabbed one another by the shoulder. Here the clothes were expensive and elegant and the room had the buzz of gossip. There was a glitter of polished oak and crystal, of jeweled women who had trundled to the viewing in the warm dark of limousines. Servants circulated with trays of wine. It had more the air of a party than a viewing.

The viewing line advanced slowly, past slipcovered sofas and wingback chairs, handsome antique tables laden with flowers.

Gordon Dobbs sauntered over and kissed Babe's cheek.

"Hi, sweetie. Hi, Vince. Isn't this a blast? One of Ash's greatest parties—she knew it would be. I got the whole death scene. She was fabulously brave, fabulously serene. And wait till you see her—she *looks* absolutely great. The family had Raoul Valency Concorded over from Paris to do her. What a character. What a life. Catch you later."

When they reached the casket, Babe kissed her fingertips and touched them to Ash's folded hands.

Staring at Ash in her blue gown and bangle bracelets, Cardozo felt he was face to face with human fragility and insignificance and the one final earthly certainty, solitude.

Babe was shaking as though a wave had hit her.

He put an arm around her. "There's a chair over here." He steered her through the crowd around to a wingback chair.

"I just need to rest a moment," Babe said.

"Sure—you rest."

Something made Cardozo look up. Dina Alstetter was standing by the fireplace, staring at him. She motioned him over.

"Thanks for coming," she said with an offhand tone.

"I'm sorry about your sister. She was a good person."

"Thanks." Her eyes held his. "There are some things I need to talk to you about."

"Feel free to phone me."

"I mean now."

"I'm listening."

"Not here." She took a glass of wine and Cardozo followed her into the hallway.

They entered another viewing room. In the corner a woman was laid out in a silk-lined mahogany casket. She had pear-shaped ruby earclips and brown hair waved to her shoulders and she was wearing an evening gown. A hand-lettered plaque announced that her name was Lavinia Mellon Fields. The visitors' register on the bookstand was blank. A sort of stillness submerged everything.

"Should we be here?" Cardozo said. "It doesn't seem respectful."

Dina Alstetter replied to that notion by sitting in a chair, very much in the manner of a cat staking out its turf, and lighting a fresh cigarette. "Vinnie Fields was the banal widow of a banal San Francisco billionaire and I very much doubt she'll have any callers."

"What do you want to tell me?"

She breathed in, breathed out, and said, "I have evidence." She opened her purse and drew out a mini-cassette recorder.

Cardozo had to wonder, *What kind of woman would bring a tape recorder to her dead sister's viewing?* and the only answer that came to him was, *This kind of woman.*

Dina Alstetter pressed a button. There were two voices on the tape.

One was Dina Alstetter's. "You know he stole your clothes."

The other voice was a shadow of Ash Canfield's. "Did he?"

"I'm asking you. Did he? Say yes or no. You have to say it, Ash. This isn't a videorecorder."

"Yes."

"Dunk stole your clothes. Duncan Canfield stole your clothes and jewels and sold them."

"Yes."

"He was flagrantly unfaithful to you. You knew he was unfaithful to you. He made no secret of it. He humiliated you and made you miserable."

"Yes."

"He introduced you to drugs and provided them."

"Yes."

"You wanted to divorce him and you still do."

"Yes."

"It's he who wants the reconciliation, not you."

"Yes."

"And you haven't slept with him since the separation."

"Yes."

"You haven't, Ash. Say you haven't if you haven't. Or have you?"

"No."

"Do you regard him as your husband?"

A long silence.

"No."

"You've intended to divorce him since the separation and you've never wavered in that intention."

A long silence.

"No."

"Is it your intention that Duncan Canfield remain in your will?"

"No."

"Is it your intention to modify your will and to bequeath Duncan Canfield no more than one dollar? Is that your intention, Ash?"

"Yes."

Cardozo listened and frowned, and when the tape had whirred to a stop he looked at Dina Alstetter. "You recorded that in the hospital?"

She lit another cigarette from a burning stub. "Yes."

"Why?"

"To prove she was going to disinherit him."

"Was she?"

"For God's sake, is the tape in Chinese?"

"On that tape you're stuffing words into a dying woman's mouth."

"We had discussions long before Ash took ill. She knew all about Dunk and his gay party set."

"What gay party set?"

"The count and that loathesome Lew Monserat."

"What did she know about them?"

"That they were carrying on, doing drugs, throwing orgies. That's why she filed for a separation. She was in full possession of her faculties when she filed. Dunk has no right to her money."

"I don't get it. You certainly don't look like you need the money."

"I don't have to need money to want justice."

"No, but you sure seem to need his scalp. What the hell did he do—jilt you?"

"I know you only mean to be rude—but if I didn't need a favor from you, I'd slap you for that."

Cardozo frowned. "You're in love with that airhead?"

She drew in a breath and let out a sigh. "Since you insist on having the background, let's just say Dunk and I used to be friends and one day we stopped."

"Be a pal, use someone else to stir up trouble for him. This doesn't involve me."

"But it most certainly does. He killed her and my feelings about Duncan Canfield don't even enter the picture because that is a rock-bottom fact."

"A disease killed her."

"He gave her the disease."

"Now how the hell did he do that?"

"The autopsy will show how."

"There's not going to be an autopsy. Your sister's embalmed. Mrs. Alstetter, you have all my sympathy, and I'll throw in some advice. You haven't got a case, and you sure as hell haven't got any evidence. There's not a doubt in my mind that the son of a bitch wanted his wife dead. But there's no such crime as malice. At least, it's not my department, and if there is, you're as guilty of it as he is."

She snapped her purse shut. "All right—if I have to prove it to you by getting her medical records, I will."

"Examination of head reveals left eye missing. Left eye socket is site of bullet entry wound." Dan Hippolito was dictating into a microphone suspended over the examining table. "Exit wound is in left posterior parietal area."

Dan glanced over and saw Cardozo. With his hand gloved in skin-hugging bloodied plastic, he moved the microphone aside, then lifted his curved Plexiglas face shield.

"Hiyah, Vince, I'd shake hands but you caught me in the middle of things."

Cardozo looked down at the body of the one-eyed young male Hispanic. "Am I interrupting?"

"The patient will keep. What's up?"

"Got time for a cup of coffee?"

"Sure."

They went to Dan's office, a small stark white subterranean chamber. Dan popped his hands out of the gloves. He took off his rubber apron and surgical smock and hung them on the coat stand.

There were two chairs and a desk and a table with a hot plate and a coffee pot. Dan had arranged a small forest of plants against one wall. Another wall was lined with shelves of medical books.

Cardozo took a seat. "Dan, would you look at a medical report for me?"

"Hey, there's sloppy work in this department, but I don't want to snitch on a colleague, okay?"

"Not to worry, this isn't an autopsy."

Dan came back from the hot plate with two Styrofoam cups of coffee.

Cardozo handed him the folder.

Dan turned pages. "What are you looking for?"

"A general impression. Is it kosher?"

"You know, my practice for the last twenty years has been dead people."

"This woman *is* dead."

Dan Hippolito sipped coffee and kept turning pages. "That begins to be evident. Catastrophic weight loss—fulminating fever—uremia . . ." He looked up, open curiosity sparking his dark eyes. "Friend of yours?"

"Friend of a friend."

"Okay, let's start at the beginning." His eyes scanned. "Valium, Dilantin, phenobarbital . . . Was this female an alcoholic?"

"Yes."

"So we're medicating for alcohol-induced epilepsy." He read on. "Stereomycin is an antifungoid, Dilantin is an antiseizure, Dramamine is an antinausea . . . Okay, a rabbi I am not, but this is about as kosher as a pig's foot. What were they doing, experimenting? You wouldn't prescribe this combination to a chimpanzee."

"Why not?"

"The drugs counteract one another." Dan flipped through more pages. "Procaine to desensitize the trachea."

"Why are they doing that?"

"It's generally done prior to a bronchoscopy."

"What's that?"

"Go down the throat and cut a little tissue from the lungs to biopsy for cancer. Except they're doing a dye test on the brain artery." Dan swiveled in his chair. "These records would make sense if she had lung cancers entering the bloodstream and metastasizing to the brain. That I could buy, but—" He stopped at the next page. *"Methadone?* Are these pages for one patient? Because methadone has one use and one use only, purely political, to shift addicts from free-market heroin to government-owned heroin. Was she a junkie?"

"She did a lot of drugs."

Dan shook his head. "I don't see a consistent diagnosis. Gamma globulin you give for hepatitis, but what's the blood analysis? There's no cell count, no sedimentation rate, nothing. These records are incomplete."

He whipped through pages and came to something that made him stop.

"Now this is downright interesting. Tegretol. That's specific for temporal lobe infection. Which means it's not a tumor attacking the brain, it's an organism." Dan frowned. "What kind of brain infection did she have?"

"I'm asking you."

"I'd have to section the brain and put it under a microscope. They must have done that at the hospital. Go back and ask if they ran a brain section p.m."

"This lady was a socialite, they don't autopsy socialites."

"This socialite they should've. Either the infection moved incredibly fast or the initial diagnosis was way off. They're all over the map, treating morphine withdrawal, hepatitis, heart fibrillation, epilepsy, and meantime something very hungry is having a picnic on her brain."

He closed the folder and pursed his lips thoughtfully, the pencil in his hand tapping the desk edge.

"Assuming these doctors aren't jerks, something that began as a blood disorder crossed to the brain. And the blood-brain barrier is not easy to penetrate. You have to be the size of maybe two electrons to get through. But without the blood sheets, there's no point even guessing."

"Any chance of unnatural causes?"

"These are infections, not bullets."

"Could someone who knew medicine have infected her?"

"Not even Josef Mengele. This kind of disaster is like a five-plane midair collision. You can't plan it, you can't control it. You trying to make a case?"

"Just wondering."

"If she was sharing needles, there could have been contributing negligence. But that's luck of the draw, not murder."

"I don't think she was sharing. Too classy for that."

"Get me her blood charts. There's definitely grounds for curiosity."

"Sorry to keep you waiting, Lieutenant."

Dr. William Tiffany rose from his desk and stretched out his arm, offering a handshake. He was the same stout, Nautilus-pumped man Cardozo remembered from Ash's sick room, dressed in a well-cut dark suit and striped tie.

It was a roomy corner office, with a black leather couch and two comfortable matching chairs. Cardozo chose the chair nearer the window.

Dr. Tiffany closed a folder and took the other chair.

Between the doctor and the detective was a table of woven bamboo, painted a ripe peach and heaped with magazines—*Town and Country, Yachting, Vanity Fair*, the French edition of *Réalités*.

Dr. Tiffany smiled, exuding the confidence of a man who dealt every day with the lives and deaths of people with very deep pockets. "You said on the phone you were a friend of Lady Ash Canfield."

"Yes, I was."

"That makes two of us. Terrible loss. And you're a friend of Dina Alstetter as well?"

"She asked me to speak with you."

"Yes? Concerning—?"

"Lady Canfield's medical records. My coroner says they're not complete. There are no blood analyses."

Dr. Tiffany's eyes were intelligent, shrewd. "Lady Canfield's husband has the right to keep them confidential."

"Mrs. Alstetter says Lady Canfield was going to divorce her husband. As next of kin, she'd like to know what killed her sister."

"Congestive heart failure."

"My coroner says something got across the blood-brain barrier. He says you're protecting yourself. Mrs. Alstetter wants to know your side of things before she takes legal steps."

The doctor looked toward Cardozo with that built-in coolness of his profession. "Nothing could have saved Lady Canfield. Lieutenant, have you heard the term *HIV*?"

"It causes AIDS. Is that what Lady Canfield had?"

Dr. Tiffany leaned back in his chair.

"AIDS manifested in Zaire twelve years ago," he said. "Cuban troops brought AIDS to this hemisphere and to Central America. American mercenaries and military advisers brought AIDS from Central America to New York, where it entered the gay community and the heterosexual swinging community. Because gays are a small population, living in three or four ghettos across the country, the number of repeat exposures was enormous, and the disease followed a spectacular, fulminating course. What people are just beginning to grasp is that AIDS may have spread just as rapidly among heterosexuals. Because it's had the entire American population to fan out through, repeat heterosexual exposures have been far lower than among gays. On the other hand, total exposures have been enormously higher, given that heterosexuals outnumber gays ten to one. We do know that one repeatedly exposed heterosexual group, non-IV-using female prostitutes, is showing double the rate of infection that male homosexuals in New York City did four years ago. If you extrapolate from that statistic, we have a holocaust down the road."

Dr. Tiffany shook his head and paused and sat there just looking at Cardozo.

Cardozo sat there looking back.

"Are you Catholic or Fundamentalist or born again?" Dr. Tiffany asked.

"Does it matter?"

"I don't want to offend you."

"You couldn't even begin."

"With the virus as widespread as it is, and the Catholic hierarchy and the Falwellians dead set against educating the public, the caseload is doubling every six months. Over a tenth of the population has been exposed, and possibly a third of those exposed will die within seven years. How does that grab you, Lieutenant?"

"Doctor," Cardozo said, "you don't need to shout. Put me on the mailing list. I'll contribute. Could you just tell me if you tested Ash Canfield's blood?"

Dr. Tiffany rose and walked to his files. "Would you mind coming over here, Lieutenant?"

Dr. Tiffany pulled a gold keychain from his pocket and unlocked one of the file drawers. The drawer slid out smoothly on noiseless rollers.

"There's a lot of agony going on out there, Lieutenant. Not just the kind you police deal with. These are the records of tens of thousands of blood tests, X rays, CAT scans, examinations by dozens of our doctors. They go back five years."

Cardozo stared at the alphabetized folders, aware that something alien and menacing was passing under his eyes.

"The men and women in these files have suffered physical degradation you could not begin to imagine. Over half of them are dead. And the others don't have long."

Cardozo ran his eye from the back of the drawer forward to the C's and then along the names. CLEMENS, CANNING, CANFIELD.

"In these drawers you'll find the ex-wife of the head of the largest communications conglomerate in the country. A nun. Top fashion designers. Children. Infants. Grandfathers. Firemen. Pro football players. Some of your own coworkers. Some of mine. Famous actors. Actors who were never famous and never will be. Soldiers—men who survived Vietnam. Help yourself."

Cardozo drew out the folder marked CANFIELD, ASH, and stared at the photograph of Ash Canfield at nearly full body-weight, at the sheets of computer-generated graphs and printout.

"I don't understand these graphs," he said.

"Lady Ash Canfield had no T-cells and her blood tested positive for HIV antibodies."

Cardozo dropped the file back into place. An awareness was pressing at the margin of his consciousness. Something to do with the drawer, a deep drawer, the letters running back through the early H's. He saw that the last name was Hatfield.

"What about this one?" he drew the folder out. The photo showed a wholesome-looking man in his mid-thirties. HATFIELD, BRIAN. "Dead or alive?"

"Brian was one of mine," Dr. Tiffany said. "He died last summer."

Cardozo drew out the neighboring folder. HALLEY, JOHN. His stomach tightened as though a fist had slammed him. The face in the photograph was Jodie Downs's.

"Tell me about this patient," Cardozo said. "John Halley."

"John was one of my outpatients. He had ARC—AIDS-related complex. He dropped out of the program a little over five months ago."

"Is ARC infectious?"

"We don't know. Some people seem to be able to transmit the virus without coming down with AIDS themselves. I'd have to answer that one with a guarded yes."

"What's the incubation period?"

"There's a lot of misinformation in the press on that. We don't know what triggers the virus once it's in the blood. There could be cofactors we're completely unaware of. So far as we know, the disease can manifest anytime between exposure and death. So I'd put what you call the incubation period at anywhere from an hour to forty years."

"Then if someone was playing around with John Halley's blood, there's a chance that person might pick up the disease?"

"Blood is the major vector. But that depends what you mean by 'playing around.' "

"Light cutting."

"Cutting through the skin?" Dr. Tiffany sounded perplexed.

"Yeah. Ritual stuff. S.m." Cardozo remembered a case from eight years back. Two fifty-year-old angel-dust freaks who'd thought they were vampires. "There may even be some—uh—drinking."

"Drinking Halley's *blood*?"

"Possibly."

"Anyone behaving that way in this city today runs an excellent chance of already having the disease." An excellent chance, Dr. Tiffany's tone of voice seemed to say, and a richly deserved one.

* * *

That evening at home Cardozo opened the Manhattan telephone directory. He turned to the *H*'s, counting Hatfields. There were eleven.

He sat a moment, feeling a thickening layer of certainty. It couldn't be chance, he told himself. Chance never took such perfect aim.

44

CARDOZO SEARCHED THROUGH HIS ROLODEX TILL HE FOUND *Beaux Arts Properties, Ltd.* He propped the card against the phone as a reminder to call Melissa Hatfield when her office opened—ten A.M.

He settled down to read yesterday's fives on a corporate takeover lawyer whose body had been found a week ago in the park at Sutton Place. Monteleone's spelling, as usual, was atrocious.

At 8:37 Cardozo's phone rang.

"We have to have a talk, Vince." It was Mel O'Brien, the chief of detectives. Usually phone talks with O'Brien began with his hatchet man, Detective Inigo, and then thirty to ninety seconds on hold before you got through to Himself. It was a rare thing for the CD to place his own call, and it was a dangerous thing when his voice was as easy and congenial as it was now. "Nine o'clock, my office, okay?"

Which gave Cardozo exactly twenty-two minutes to bust his ass getting through morning rush-hour traffic down to One Police Plaza.

Mel O'Brien stood at the window, gazing out at the fall sky and the glow it cast on the high rises beginning to encircle Chinatown. "What are you up to, Vince? Spending all your time in the field? Out-Sherlocking your own men?"

"No, sir. Unless it's a task force, I don't go into the field."

"How many hours have you logged in the precinct this last month?"

"It's in the log."

"I wouldn't mind knowing what cases you're on."

"You do know, Chief."

The CD turned and looked at Cardozo. "You were tying up the

computer a few weeks back—running a lot of lists through—what was that all about?"

Cardozo had a sense that his head was about to be held under a bucket of bureaucratic horsepiss. "It related to an ongoing homicide."

"What homicide?"

"Sunny Mirandella, a stewardess. She was murdered in her apartment up on Madison."

Which wasn't exactly a lie, but it was pretty thin ice.

"You had Babe Devens into the precinct for a slide show." O'Brien's gaze moved over Cardozo with the coolness of a stethoscope. He was making it very obvious that he'd been checking back over Cardozo's movements, that he had the power to do it and that he had a damned good reason to do it.

"I was showing Mrs. Devens slides from the Downs case."

"You thought Mrs. Devens was involved?"

"I hoped she could give me some help."

The CD sat down in his big upholstered swivel chair, shaking his head from side to side. "Jesus Christ, Vince, Devens and Downs are closed. You closed them. We've got five new homicides a day in this city and we're not even making arrests in three a week."

"Chief—you don't have to worry about me."

"Because that wasn't the only time you were seen with Mrs. Devens." O'Brien was studying Cardozo, watching to see what his reaction would give away. "You two were at a viewing at the Campbell Funeral Home."

At that point the whole picture changed.

Cardozo had known he was taking risks: even though he hadn't let his ongoing caseload slide, if he reopened closed cases without a good cause and a fast result, and the wrong people found out, the price could be his shield and his pension. He could find his ass busted back to patrolman. But now he saw that if he *did* show cause and produce results, the price could be all that and a little bit more too.

"Ash Canfield was a friend," he said. "She died, she had a viewing. I went."

The complaint had to have come from Countess Vicki. Again. Which showed Cardozo how the chain of communication ran—from the countess to someone who was probably Ted Morgenstern, to the D.A. to the CD.

"And Babe Devens?" O'Brien asked.

"Mrs. Devens is a friend too. If there's something wrong with our going to a funeral home I wish you'd tell me."

"Did you go on job time?"

"It was a viewing, for Christ's sake. It wasn't like I was going to a party."

"It wasn't like you were going to a homicide, either."

O'Brien gave him a long, dark look. It galled Cardozo to be reminded that this man had an absolute right to tell him what to do; it galled him to accept that sometimes in this job nothing was wanted or tolerated but obedience.

"What was the case you were discussing with Dan Hippolito last Tuesday?" O'Brien asked. "Was that job-related too?"

The CD was a master in the use of words. That little syllable *too* said it all.

"I was in the neighborhood—I stopped by. Dan and I go back a long way."

"You got a lot of friends."

"I'm lucky."

"What about that kid murdered outside the Metropolitan Museum this morning?"

The call had come in on 911 at 8:10. Cardozo had assigned the case. "O'Rourke is on it," he said.

"Why don't you get on it too."

Cardozo drove back to the precinct, sorting it out. Calling the CD on him meant someone was scared, using up big favors, taking big risks—and that meant that very soon someone would be wanting Vince Cardozo silenced.

In his cubicle, Cardozo phoned Judge Tom Levin. He got the judge's secretary.

"Amy, can you tell the judge I've got to see him tonight. Nine o'clock, his place, unless he leaves word otherwise."

"I'll tell him, Vince."

Cardozo jiggled the cradle, got a dial tone, and punched out the number on the Rolodex card that he had left leaning against the phone.

"Beaux-Arts-Balthazar." It was Melissa Hatfield's voice, with the husky, offhand tone that he remembered.

"Melissa, it's Vince Cardozo. How you been?"

"Oh, life's been stumbling along as best it can."

"What I'm calling about, could I come up and see you after work? Your place? Six, six-thirty?"

Cardozo would have been on time for Melissa, but at 12:30 Larry O'Rourke burst into his office.

"Vince—we got an ID."

O'Rourke had Irish red-blond hair and intense green eyes. He was short and slender, but his body was all muscle and tendon and he worked out at a gym to keep it that way. He'd just made detective and if he seemed a little excited it was because the dead girl found outside the Metropolitan Museum that morning was his first homicide.

"Her name's Janet Samuels. The stepdaughter of Harold Benziger." O'Rourke was standing there as though the name should mean something.

"Sorry," Cardozo said. "Bell's aren't ringing."

"Real estate. He spearheaded the I Love New York campaign. Gives the mayor a lot of financial support. I mean a *lot.*"

Cardozo had often thought that the money spent putting celebrities on TV singing that jingle could have renovated a few thousand units of decayed housing. "Oh yeah, *that* Benziger."

Two hours later the CD telephoned Cardozo again. "I want you personally to tell the Benzigers that their daughter's been murdered."

"It's O'Rourke's case, Chief."

"I'm not sending a rookie in there. That would be complete disrespect of the Benzigers' stature in this community."

"O'Rourke isn't a rookie."

"Christ's sake, he just got his gold. Harold Benziger is a force in this town. He gets a lieutenant to bring him the bad news. His secretary says she can't reach him, but he'll be at his home at seven tonight."

It was eight thirty by the time Cardozo pushed Melissa Hatfield's doorbell.

"You've changed the color scheme," he said.

"I'm trying to."

Melissa Hatfield invited him in and offered him a drink.

"Melissa, would you mind sitting down?"

"Sure." She didn't sit. "What is it?"

"Who was Brian Hatfield?"

After what seemed a long time, though it might have been only ten seconds, she said, "Brian was my brother."

"Tell me about him."

"He died."

Cardozo looked in her eyes. "Dr. William Tiffany was treating him in the Vanderbilt Pavilion, am I right?"

Melissa's teeth came down over her lower lip.

"You thought you recognized Jodie Downs's photograph. You said he reminded you of someone you'd seen in an elevator. Someone you'd seen regularly but couldn't place. Later you backed away from that. Said you'd made a mistake. I think you *did* place his face. I think Jodie Downs was an outpatient in the same program as your brother. I think you saw Jodie in that elevator regularly when you went to visit Brian."

She reacted as if she were living in slow motion. She moved to one of the windows, stood with her hands resting on the air-conditioning unit.

"I was ashamed," she said.

"Ashamed that your brother had AIDS?"

Melissa dropped her head. "There are people who get ashamed. They can't help it. And then they have to be ashamed of being ashamed. Hasn't that ever happened to you?"

For a long moment the room was hushed.

"Jodie Downs was ashamed," she said softly. "You know what he told me his name was? John Halley. That's how he happened to be in Brian's group. *F* to *L.* Imagine being ashamed that you're dying, having to pretend you're someone else, that the person with your name would never have a disease like that."

"Was Brian ashamed?"

"Brian wasn't ashamed, not of AIDS, not of anything. He was Gay Lib militant and triumphant. Right to the end. I tried to be like him. Every evening I'd go and sit by the bed and pretend it was all right, that dying was just part of life and if he wanted to accept it that was just great. We read Kübler-Ross together, and when his eyesight went I read it to him and he held my hand. Oh, Brian was a real champ at acceptance. But *I* couldn't accept it. I still can't."

She looked up at him. "I could use a drink. What about you?"

A sense of her isolation engulfed him.

He shook his head. "I'm sorry. I have a date with a judge and I'm late."

*   *   *

"What do you expect me to do about it?" Webbing out from Jerry Brandon's red-rimmed eyes were the fine lines of overwork.

"Tell them," Cardozo said.

"AIDS is already endemic in the prison system."

"Tell them anyway."

Brandon moved the long extendable arm of the lamp out of the way and sat at his desk. He lifted the phone and dialed. In a minute he was talking chummily to a prison doctor and all of him was in motion—his bony head, his big shoulders, his square jaw.

"You've got an inmate up there by the name of Claude Loring, L-O-R-I-N-G as in George. He ought to be tested for AIDS."

It must have been a long reply, because Brandon listened for over three minutes. "You're sure? When?" His eyes flicked up at Cardozo's and he picked up a ballpoint and began scribbling quickly. "Thanks."

Brandon hung up the phone and stared at Cardozo. "Vince, this is going to surprise you."

"I'm never surprised."

"Claude Loring's not in prison."

Cardozo sat forward. "What the hell happened to him?"

"It seems to be a very long story. I couldn't get all of it. The governor commuted Loring's sentence a week ago."

Cardozo's stomach was getting tight. "On what grounds?"

"Compassionate medical."

"For AIDS?"

Brandon shook his head. "Loring's mother is sick. He's her sole support."

Cardozo couldn't believe what he was hearing. When he moved his head the room seemed to tip. "How could the governor fall for that bullshit?"

"Rumor is a lot of heavyweights interceded for Loring. He must be one popular guy."

"Who interceded?"

"It's just rumor. The archdiocese of New York—some real estate moguls by the names of Nat Chamberlain and Harold Benziger— Cyrus Hastings, president of Citichem Bank. Know any of them?"

"No—and neither does Loring."

"Why the hell did you make the deal with Morgenstern?" Cardozo said. "Now we've got a killer loose, skipping around spreading AIDS."

District Attorney Alfred Spaulding rose, crossed the office, and closed the door. He returned to his desk and gazed imperturbably at Cardozo. "To clear the Downs case we had to deal with Morgenstern; he happened to be defending the accused."

"Who the hell wasn't he defending?" The words came hurtling out of Cardozo's throat. "I questioned the dealer who sold the mask, Morgenstern's associate rushed in, you can't do this to our client. I questioned the doorman who was running coke in the building, Morgenstern's associate rushed in, you can't do this to our client. I arrested the killer, Morgenstern came rushing in, you can't do this to my client. Morgenstern was wired in to this from the very start, before we even knew who the dead man was. He would have defended the hooker on the ninth floor if we'd accused her of farting. Ted Morgenstern was ready to defend anyone connected in any way with this killing. Why? Who paid him? You're going to tell me this was *pro bono,* this coverup, this fix?"

"What the hell are you calling a fix?"

"The director of Citichem bank and the Catholic archdiocese of New York and the two guys who own every building in Manhattan that Donald Trump doesn't—they all petition the governor to commute Loring's sentence. You think that comes free? You think those people even *know* who Claude Loring is? Ted Morgenstern was calling in favors. He's represented the archdiocese against the city, he's represented Citichem against the city, he's represented Benziger and Chamberlain before the zoning commission. Those are major call-ins. For a punk. Doesn't that even make you curious?"

"Vince, we've talked about this."

"Let's talk some more."

"The case is closed. A guy was killed, we caught his killer. My curiosity stops there. In case you haven't heard, this city isn't exactly operating in the black. If we can clear a case without coming to trial that's a saving. Yes I did a deal, and I saved time and money. It was in line with city policy and I'm not ashamed of it."

"There's more to it than that, Al. Three weeks after Judge Davenport imposed the sentence he signed a piece of paper suspending it. No publicity, nothing in the papers."

Either Spalding already knew or he was doing a good job of not showing surprise. "Judges have the discretion to suspend sentences."

"Jesus, wake up. We're deep in the valley of the shadow of dollars. Withersoever Counselor Morgenstern walks, money goes. You know it and you're *still* dealing with him, and I'm not just talking plea bargain."

"Are you accusing me of something?"

Cardozo was staring at Alfred Spaulding, thinking about power—about the people who owned it and the things they chose to do with it. "What the hell do I need to accuse you of—you fucking admitted it when you phoned and told me to stop hassling Morgenstern's friends. His friends are killers, Al. You gotta know it. You're not a dumb man. Not dumb that way."

Spaulding's eyes narrowed into thin wary slits. A shadow played across his face. "Who did they kill?"

"They killed Jodie Downs."

"Claude Loring killed Jodie Downs."

"A bunch of Morgenstern's freak friends did it and that's why Morgenstern's calling you to call me off, and that's why you're calling the CD to call me off. You *know* it, Al. And you're *still* letting it go down, and that puts you in the same shit as the rest of them."

Spaulding was shouting. "There was *one* killer in the Downs case!"

"There was a *bunch!*" Cardozo shouted back. "I have a witness!"

Something in the D.A.'s face opened just a crack, letting out a thin wisp of fear. "Vince, drop it. *There weren't witnesses.*"

"There *were* witnesses, there were *accomplices.* Why do you think Loring walked? That was the deal they paid Morgenstern to cut. Loring confessed, Loring walked, *they* stayed out of sight."

Spaulding expelled his breath, sharply. "Who's your witness?"

"You think I'm going to tell you? You think I can even trust you? I can trust you to do one thing, and that's to go straight to Morgenstern. So why don't you go straight to Morgenstern, and you tell him that last night I moved my files out of my office and put them in the hands of someone who knows how to use them if anything happens to me."

"What the hell do you think could happen to you, Vince?"

"You know damned well what could happen—I could get sent to Park Slope, I could get my pension lifted, I could get dead."

"Look, Vince, I honestly think you're getting a little paranoid—"

"And *you* lay off the CD. Because I'm going to close this case. And if the CD or anyone else starts asking you about me, you tell them I'm working on special assignment for you."

"Hold on, Vince. That's just not believable."

"*Make* it believable! Al, it's your ass I'll be saving. Your office fucking miscarried with Babe Devens and Jodie Downs. But it doesn't need to come out that you *knew*. You cover for me and I'll cover for you—that's the deal, okay?"

Spalding sat for a long time, staring at Cardozo, staring at his desktop, staring again at Cardozo.

"Okay."

"You can't go in there," the secretary said primly. "He's in conference."

Cardozo pushed through the door.

Morgenstern looked up from his desk, his eyes barely visible through the lowered slits of his eyelids. "Got a problem, Cardozo?"

"I want Claude Loring."

"Ever heard of double jeopardy? You can't touch Loring."

"He can be indicted for obstruction, and so can you."

"Bull."

"You hand Claude Loring over to me for questioning or I will personally tail you and bust you for possession of coke or sucking the cocks of minors, whichever you do first."

Morgenstern's eyes pinpointed in cold fury. The office suddenly had the suffocating stillness of a plastic bag.

A petite woman was sitting on a corner of a chintz sofa. She had iron gray hair and she wore a stylish dark silk dress and she had the unflappable look of someone who was always being photographed and reported on.

She was watching Cardozo with an interested, completely calm expression, waiting expectantly for more.

Morgenstern sprang up from his chair.

Cardozo leaned across the desk and grabbed the knot of his blue-and-gold regimental. "You think that pardon's going to hold?"

Morgenstern wrenched loose. He seized an ivory letter opener.

Cardozo allowed a smile to open on his face. "You think the Republicans are going to let our Democratic governor get away with that?"

"You're not going to harass my client!" Morgenstern was backed against an étagère loaded with Kiwanis citations and autographed celebrity photos. His cobra-lidded eyes were blinking rapidly and an artery was pulsing in his temple. "We happen to live under a system called the law, Mr. Nazi, and you just get the hell out of this office and don't come back without a warrant!"

"And let me tell *you* something, Clarence Darrow. You may be a whiz when it comes to engineering compassionate commutations for cold-blooded killers, but *this* commutation just boomeranged, because yesterday in Central Park some freak ripped the panties off of Harold Benziger's stepdaughter and murdered her."

"There's no fucking connection!"

"What do you bet the *Daily News* can find a connection—like poetic justice? And shit will the press love the archdiocese tie-in. I'd like to see how fast His Eminence gives you the gate."

"I don't rat on my clients, and if any lies about any commutation appear in any newspaper, I'll have you off the force! I will personally have your ass!"

"You'll personally have my ass in your face, snake gills." Cardozo turned to the little lady on the sofa. "Nice to see you again, Ms. Vlaminck."

"Have we met?" she said pleasantly.

"We were at the same table at Holcombe Kaiser's party for Tina Vanderbilt."

"Oh, yes," she said. "Oh, yes, indeed. Nice to see you."

"We fought like we've never fought before. I told him, don't do crack, it makes you crazy. He threatened me with the bread knife."

Faye di Stasio sat there a long time, her breasts rising and falling with the rhythm of her memories.

"I had to get him out. I couldn't let him stay, crazy like that."

Tears flooded her eyes. There was a defensive tone in her voice, but she didn't look defensive. She looked crushed, as if all defenses had failed her long ago.

"I changed the locks. I can't even begin to tell you the stuff he did." She began to tell him.

Cardozo listened patiently. She had something he needed and he was willing to flatter her with attention, even kindness if necessary, to get it.

"The cat—he killed the cat." She looked at him blankly. "Who'd do a thing like that? Killing a cat?"

They sat there in silence. She lowered her eyes. She seemed shrunken. She was breathing hard, cigarette idling in one hand.

"Faye—where's Claude now?"

"Gone."

"Where?"

"I'm too tired, too confused to even want to think where."

"He got a compassionate commutation to take care of his mother. Think he could be with her?"

She floated him a look. "His mother's been dead three years."

Cardozo breathed deeply, feeling frustration like a weight across his back. "Will you let me know if he shows up?"

"He won't show up." Her lower lip was trembling. "Not if he wants to stay living."

Cardozo touched her cheek. "Don't kill him. Phone me and let me do it for you, okay?"

Eight hours later, thinking Claude Loring might have returned to play in his old pigpen, Cardozo personally dredged the Inferno. Mission unsuccessful. It was four in the morning when he decided to call yesterday a day. He pulled himself groggily up the stairs and out into the street.

After the Inferno, New York smelled clean. Mist was closing in, washing the colors out of the buildings opposite.

Cardozo walked slowly south, stepping over fetid pockets of gutter water. The echo of his footsteps followed him. He passed a few moving figures on the sidewalk, a few zonked-out forms in doorways.

At the corner of Little West Twelfth and Gansevoort streets a truck blared its horn, blasting Cardozo out of his thoughts.

He stepped back and watched the driver negotiate the turn. There was a grinning steer painted on the side of the truck, and below it the message SAM'S BEEF—NOBODY BEATS OUR MEAT.

Cardozo crossed the street. His feet were aware of edges and uneven surfaces, and he looked down and saw that the pavement had changed from asphalt to cobblestones.

His eyes came up and he was struck by something, a sign attached to the warehouse on the corner ahead of him.

He paused to read the weathered black lettering.

SHELLS	SOBRELOMO
RIBS	LOMO
HIPS	PALOMILLA
KNUCKLES	BOLA
EYES	BOLICHE
TOPS	CAÑADA
SHINS	JARRETE
FILLETS	FILETE

To the right of the sign a doorway was tilting ten degrees off the vertical, leaning toward the Hudson River.

Cardozo stepped back and took a long, careful look. The building was six-storied, wood-framed, in poor repair. There were places where the shingle siding had begun to drop off.

Every bone in his body vibrated with the conviction that he knew this building.

"Where are these meat trucks, Babe?"
"In the street."
"What street?"
"Outside the building."

Cardozo was sitting in his livingroom, sipping a Bud, his hand dipping into a bag of Nacho-flavored Doritos.

On the table Babe Vanderwalk Devens's voice spooled out of the cassette player, dreaming, disembodied.

"The building is on the corner. The cobbled street meets the asphalt. The building is falling apart. The sign is in English and Spanish. Body parts of cows. The doorway is on the left. That's where I go in."

45

MATHILDE LHEUREUX HAPPENED TO BE NEAREST WHEN THE
phone rang. "Babe," she said, one hand over the mouthpiece, "for
you—a Mr. Cardozo."

Babe took the receiver and lifted the cord over the head of one of
the seamstresses. "Vince? It doesn't sound like you."

"It's me. What are you doing?"

"Eighty-two things at once."

Babe felt Mathilde Lheureux's old humorous frowning gaze fix on
her. Mathilde's gray hair had turned totally white and she wore it
pinned back from her forehead, but she still had the shrewd, naughty
eyes of a playful monkey. Babe found something infinitely reassuring
in that familiar smile and in that dear old face, only slightly aged
from the face she remembered.

"Can you fit in an eighty-third?" Cardozo said.

Babe sighed. "Vince, it's crazy here."

Which was putting it mildly. She had been able to rent a little
space for her own atelier in the penthouse of the Babethings building. Lawyers were working on the papers—for the moment she had
a verbal agreement with Billi—and she and Mathilde had started on
her summer and fall lines. Naturally, they hadn't been able to put
together their old group—but they'd found one of their old seamstresses, and one of the beaders, and two of the tailors.

"I guess I didn't put that right," Cardozo said. "I need your help.
Can you meet me?"

Damn, Babe thought. "When?"

"Soon as possible."

*   *   *

They crossed Gansevoort Street through the bright sunlight—
Babe in her pale blue Chanel, and Cardozo with his .38 in the armpit
of his seersucker jacket, holding a tape recorder.

The wind had swept away the fog, and the sky had the blinding
colorless brightness of a scoured frying pan.

Babe's eyes scanned the derelict buildings. A perplexed expression
hovered on her face.

Cardozo pushed the button on the cassette player. Babe's voice
came sleepwalking out. *"The building is on the corner. The cobbled
street meets the asphalt."*

He took note of her reactions. Her hand tightening into a fist. Her
mouth pulling shut. Her eyes narrowing, as though fending off images.

Next to the warehouse was a construction site: three stories of
girders, and from the look of it many more to come. The steel was
already rusted, as if it had been recycled from another structure.

One of the two signs was crudely painted on plywood:

DEMOLITION BY ZAMPIZI BROS.
347 FLOWER STREET, BROOKLYN N.Y.

The other was professionally lettered in flowing script:

THIS SITE WILL BE THE LOCATION OF THE LUXOR
A THIRTY-TWO-STORY LUXURY CO-OP
BROUGHT TO YOU BY BALTHAZAR PROPERTIES
READY FOR SPRING OCCUPANCY
OFFERING BY PROSPECTUS ONLY

Workers moved slowly about on foot and machine. The zonked
winos of the neighborhood had gathered on the opposite sidewalk, in
front of the Espanita meat-packing plant, to watch and cheer.

The air smelled of rancid oil and decomposing animal parts with a
faint understench of diluted sewage.

He paced himself to her, slow and easy.

In front of the warehouse, dappled in the sunlight, a pile of broken
plaster waited in a dumpster. A man wearing a filthy I Love New
York T-shirt and barber-pole-striped skivvies was picking bare-
handed through the rubble.

Cardozo pushed the cassette button again.

"The sign is in English and Spanish. Body parts of cows."
Babe stopped to stare at the sign.
"Familiar?"
She shook her head. She shuddered. "How can they eat eyes?"
"The doorway is on the left. That's where I go in."
Beside the shadowy doorway a trickle of water seeped from a split in the brick wall, zigzagging across the sidewalk.
The entrance area was dim and windowless, smelling of darkness and mildew. There was a bank of eight tarnished buzzers, four of them labeled. Cardozo copied down the names.
"Up the stairs in the dark. One flight."
He led the way, climbing slowly up the peeling stairs. Babe guided herself up behind him, hand sliding lightly along the banister.
The stairway had cracked plaster walls, a ceiling fuzzy with spiderwebs. Heat beat stiflingly against the boarded windows. The narrow steps hadn't been swept in years, but then the people likely to use a stairway in a building like this were apt to have other things on their minds than hygiene.
At the first landing Cardozo glanced down the crumbling hallway. Electric wires dangled from the ceiling. A junkie was sprawled in a doorway, snoring.
"Another flight."
They went up a second flight of decaying stairs.
"I can hear voices."
"Whose voices?"
"Mickey Mouse. Richard Nixon."
Three steps led from the next landing to the corridor.
The hallway was two doors deep, with windows on one side. Hexagonal wire ribbing reinforced the panes.
"I open the door."
"Which door, Babe?"
She stared at the first door. Her head came around. "That one."
Cardozo crouched at the second door.
Babe hung back.
He inserted his MasterCard in the crack between the door and the jamb.
The door panels were the color of tapioca pudding that had been left out of the refrigerator for thirty years. Paint was peeling off the woodwork.
His hands moved carefully, silently, jiggling the latch open. The door swung smoothly inward.

She came down the corridor hesitantly.

She waited at the doorsill, staring. The room had been freshly painted a bright, flat white. It was stripped of all furnishing.

She went in first and he closed the door behind them. He slid the bolt.

She stood at the window and looked at the view across the low roofs of the surrounding warehouses to the higher roofs of Greenwich Village's rowhouses. In the distance loomed the peaked high rises going up along the river and the glass towers of the financial district.

Cardozo began at the top. His eyes roamed the ceiling, noted it was freshly plastered, then slid over walls, freshly plastered and painted. The floor was oak boarding, polyurethaned to a mirror gloss. He noted long, parallel rows of new scratches, as though the wood had been freshly clawed by a dragon.

It was the sort of place that made nighttime sounds during the day: waterpipes talking to themselves, floorboards squeaking, things pinging in the walls.

His eye was troubled by dead spots on the floor where the light didn't reflect. He crouched and made out a spattering of rust-colored deposits, barely visible.

"They don't hear me. John Wayne is passing champagne. The man is naked." "What man, Babe?" "The young man. I don't know him. He has blond hair. He's lying in the corner."

"Which corner, Babe?"

Babe walked slowly into the other room. Also empty. Also white. There were two paper cups by the radiator, lying on their side.

Cardozo picked one up and saw the dry ring of coffee in the bottom. A bit further along a bottle top glinted. He stooped. Heineken beer.

"Winnie the Pooh and the Mad Hatter pick him up and tie him to the H."

Now she snapped around and stared at the north wall. Something about it absorbed her. She was holding herself slightly forward of the perpendicular, trembling, on the brink of something.

His eye scanned, picking out details where there had only been featureless white. Ripples in the plaster. Lumps in the paint. A small elephant-shaped stain, a little below shoulder level, the color of rust. Next to it two holes, each a quarter inch in diameter. Someone had bored through the plaster into the wood beam beneath.

Below the two holes, at knee level, another pair of holes, identical to the first. Four feet to the right, two more pairs of holes, similarly spaced.

There was another rust-colored stain at ankle level, this one shaped like a tiny map of South America.

"Vince," she said, her voice tight and shaking. "I'm going to be sick. I have to get out of here."

Cardozo dialed Melissa Hatfield's work number.

"I see you people are putting up a condo in the meat-packing district. Charming neighborhood."

"Tell me," she said.

"Would you have time to run another real estate trace for me? Two lots down from your new condo there's a warehouse. Five eighteen Gansevoort."

"I know the building. It's your basic abandoned firetrap."

"You sure it's abandoned? There are names on half the mailboxes."

"Those are welfare drops. Standard scam with the Department of Human Resources, getting aid for nonexistent dependent children. No one lives there. We wanted to buy, so we checked. The owner's holding out, listing bogus rent-control tenants. You can't evict anyone under rent control. The land rights are going to skyrocket and the owner thinks he can make a killing. He's got a surprise coming. The city's reassessing all the property on that block. The taxes will quintuple and he'll have to sell. Nat Chamberlain's going to be the only bidder the city allows. So you see, it pays to contribute to the mayor's reelection campaign."

"The owner's got more than welfare phantoms in there. Somebody's been using the front apartment on the third floor. And I think they had a lease, because they made improvements. I need to know who."

"I suppose the owner could have leased to an actor or artist—something temporary. Anything's possible. I'll check."

"You ever see anything going on in that apartment?"

Cardozo pointed. The warehouse appeared dead, remote, the clouds behind it a menacing smudge.

The old man's eyes narrowed blearily beneath a shock of white hair. A varicose, hawklike nose dominated his face. He shrugged, not bothering to lift himself from the doorstep where he had made himself a pallet of newspapers and old rags. A smell of animal blood rose from the pavement.

Cardozo opened his wallet and pulled out a ten-dollar bill and dangled it.

The old man reached up a trembling hand and took the money. The rip in his undershirt widened and another fold of white torso blobbed out. "Used to see things. Hasn't been anything going on up there since they moved out."

"When did they move out?"

A soot-caked fingernail scratched white cheek-stubble. "First week in June."

"Remember the name of the moving company?"

"Shit, I don't remember my own name."

"What kind of furniture?"

"Couches, tables, lamps, cameras, black leather shit."

"What kind of black leather shit?"

"Black leather shit like they got in all those asshole clubs around here."

"What kind of cameras?"

"Video. You could hock 'em for maybe eighty bucks."

"Did you see the people who used the place?"

Silence.

Cardozo opened his wallet again.

A prostitute wobbled past on high heels, slowing to stare at the ten-dollar bill. The skirt was ass-hugging tangerine stretch nylon and the blond wig could have been swiped from a department store dummy.

A ship's horn bleated on the river.

The old man took the money; the prostitute immediately picked up speed, calves rippling with muscle.

"They had parties. Fridays, Saturdays. Limousines parked up and down all along here." The old man's hand indicated the deserted street.

"Every weekend?"

"Just now and then."

"What kind of people?"

"What kind of people ride limousines? Rich assholes. Scared they're gonna get mugged or bitten by a rat."

"How were they dressed?"

"Tuxes, dresses, costumes."

"What kind of costumes?"

"Leather."

"Any idea what they were doing up there?"

"I dunno." The old man broke out laughing. His breath was an explosive mix of beer and tooth decay. "They never invited me."

"Come on, earn that twenty. You must've heard something, seen something."

"Couldn't see nothin'. They closed the curtains. Heard music. Singin'. Once in a while screamin'."

"Screaming?"

"Sounded like screamin'. Music was so loud couldn't be sure."

"What kind of screaming? Like someone was singing, or drunk, or hurting or what?"

"Screamin' like someone was screamin'."

Cardozo stared at the warehouse. The one streetlight still working made the block look all the more abandoned.

"Did you ever see a body carried out?" he asked.

"All they did was carry each other out of that place. Some of them arrived so stoned they had to carry each other in."

"You never saw a *dead* body?"

"How you gonna tell the difference? They were dead on their feet. Haven't seen 'em in a month. Since those movers."

Cardozo patted the old man on the shoulder and crossed toward the warehouse. He had almost reached the other sidewalk when a blue Pontiac swerved around him, pulling to a stop in the middle of the block.

A black-and-white cat mewed from the gutter.

The blond wig turned. The prostitute stepped with exaggerated elegance off the sidewalk, clacked across the cobblestones, and bent down to confer with the driver.

After a moment the driver threw open the passenger door and the prostitute hopped in.

Tony Bandolero, from Forensic, was waiting in the shadow by the warehouse door. He was frowning, running a hand through his curly brown hair. "Why are all transvestite hookers black?"

"Are they?"

"That one is."

Cardozo watched the Pontiac pull across Washington Street. "Why are the customers all white, why do they all have New Jersey license plates?"

"Do they?"

"That one does."

Cardozo pushed open the door and flicked on the flashlight. They went inside and up the stairs.

"What do those hookers charge?" Tony Bandolero asked.

"I hear fifty bucks."

"Fifty bucks for a blow job? No wonder the country's going to hell."

A rat froze for an instant in the light, then scurried.

Tony Bandolero held the flashlight and Cardozo opened the door with his MasterCard.

In the dimness of the apartment the shadow of the window ribbing made a slanting pattern on the floor. Cardozo crossed through the puddles of light. He gazed out through the panes. The moon was glowing on the roofs of the city.

"These scratches look like someone was moving something heavy." Tony was squatting close to the floor. The flashlight lay on its side, lighting up a triangle of polyurethaned planking. "Refrigerator, maybe."

"I want to know what those stains are," Cardozo said.

"Let's find out." Tony opened his toolkit and selected a scalpel. Working the blade around the stained wood, he loosened a fragment, lifted it, and deposited it in a plastic evidence bag.

He played the flashlight along the floor, found other stains, took scrapings.

In the doorless doorway between the rooms he crouched to gaze at the doorjamb. The flashlight beam was showing him a rust-colored stain at knee level, a tangle of whorls and spirals.

"Hold the light for me, would you?"

Cardozo squatted beside him and took the flashlight.

Tony chiseled a cut around the stain, loosened the wood beneath it, lifted the stain with tweezers, and placed it between two sheets of glassine.

Cardozo played the light along the jamb. There was a similar stain on the neighboring surface, at the same level.

"What I think we got," Tony said, "is fingerprints. Funny place for prints, down there."

"Unless the body was slung over someone's shoulder."

Tony nodded. "Coming through the doorway he tried to grab."

"He would have been alive, then," Cardozo said. "Conscious."

"Have to be. Grabbing like that isn't reflex. Wherever he was being carried, he wasn't in any rush to get there."

"The scrapings are human blood," Lou Stein said. "Type O."

"Jodie Downs's type," Cardozo said.

"Bear in mind it's a very common type. Eighty percent of the human race—"

"I know, I know."

"The marks on the doorjamb are a thumb and partial index."

Cardozo's hand tightened on the receiver. "Whose?"

"They match Jodie Downs's prints."

"So he was there in that apartment. He was cut and carried out alive."

"Looks it."

"Thanks, Lou." Cardozo hung up the receiver. He didn't know how many minutes he sat absolutely still in his chair, running people and events in his mind, freezing images, going back, comparing, fast-forwarding, trying an image here, trying it there, finding the place where it fitted.

The pattern expanded before his eyes, opening to include all those pieces that had never fitted in before, all the brightly colored expensive people who had been hovering over the mud and blood from the beginning but who had never quite belonged to the same ugly, brutal universe.

The images linked and locked:

The apartment in the meat-packing warehouse–sex club area where glittering people had come in limousines. Babe Devens's memory of cartoon characters torturing Jodie Downs. Loring carrying Downs out of the apartment into Faye di Stasio's van, leaving bloodstains; parking the van in the garage at Beaux Arts Tower; taking Downs up the service elevator to apartment six. Snuffing him there.

"You were right." There were dark circles under Melissa Hatfield's clear gray eyes, as though she'd been putting in too much overtime. "The apartment on Gansevoort Street was rented. A man called Lewis Monserat had a three-year lease on it."

"The art dealer?" Cardozo said.

They were sitting in the rear booth at Danny's Bar and Grill on East Sixty-seventh, nursing two coffees. It was cool and dry here. The weather on the other side of the plate glass window was drizzle shot through with sunset.

Melissa nodded. "He had three two-year leases before the last lease. He broke it May thirty-first. It had a year and a half to run. Actually, he vacated four days earlier, May twenty-seventh."

The first business day, Cardozo reflected, after the body had been found in Beaux Arts Tower. "The apartment couldn't have been his residence."

"No. But the lease was residential. So it was some sort of pied-à-terre."

"Unusual neighborhood."

"He must like having a pied-à-terre. He put a binder on a loft in a co-op five days later." She was watching Cardozo with an odd intensity. She had a habit of smiling with her mouth and retracting the smile with her eyes. "Four thirty-two Franklin Street. Apartment four-A. Down in TriBeCa."

He nodded, thinking. "Makes sense. Same sort of neighborhood—warehouses and small businesses."

"It was for three minutes. Then the artists fleeing SoHo rents moved in, and then real estate moved in, and now it's *the* section of town for young established types—college professors, financial consultants, lawyers. People who think it's square to live uptown."

"How much did Monserat pay for the new place?"

"Too much and a half. The bank put up seventy-five percent, and he still can't afford it. He needed a cosigner."

"How come he couldn't swing it on his own? I thought his gallery was one of the biggest in town."

"So what? Who's going to pay two hundred thousand for an eight-by-eight of a pickle? You can hit on the New York State Foundation for the Arts once, twice, then your market's dried up. Monserat's gallery is a penny-ante laundering operation for dope money."

"Then he's rich."

"He likes to think he is."

"Who cosigned for Monserat?"

Melissa looked at Cardozo. She was going through some kind of pain. "I'm in sort of a conflict-of-interest situation here, Vince. This isn't easy for me. When you showed me that dead boy's photograph it didn't come to me at first where I knew him from, and then I remembered and I thought about picking up the phone and telling you everything. Then I thought about not telling you anything. And I guess I came down in the middle and now I'm moving off center and I'm a little scared."

"Jodie Downs and your brother had something to do with Lewis Monserat's cosigner?"

"In a way. Lew Monserat's cosigner was Balthazar Properties. One of our corporations."

"How come?"

"Because Ted Morgenstern has shares in Balthazar."

Cardozo's brows arched down at the name Morgenstern. "Why did Morgenstern want to help Monserat?"

"He wasn't necessarily helping. Morgenstern uses fronts for his property. You'd have to dig to the bottom of a manure pile of shell companies to find out who really owns that loft. The one thing I'm sure of is it doesn't belong to Lew Monserat."

"Who do you think owns it? Educated guess."

"Ted Morgenstern has handled a lot of society divorces and he's covered up more than a few society murders; and when it comes to dirty mergers and forced acquisitions and real estate takeovers, he's king of the hill. He renders a lot of special services, and any one of his rich clients might want a discreet little one-bedroom under a false name. And any one of his poor clients would be willing to provide the cover."

"Any chance Morgenstern owns it himself?"

Melissa nodded. "From what I know of him personally, he could have an interest in it."

"What kind of interest?"

"My hunch is it's a pleasure pad, trick pad, whatever you want to call it. But in the upper reaches of depravity, as opposed to the upper reaches of politics, it's hard to know who holds the real power. It could be that Morgenstern's the master and the place is his, or it could be that Morgenstern has a master and the place is that person's."

"You're talking master-slave s.m. stuff?"

"It's a possibility, is all I'm saying. On the other hand it could be Morgenstern just has a habit of hiding property because he's lived that way for thirty years. Nothing he owns is in his name. The yacht, the town house, the cars, the paintings—they're owned by his firm, not him."

"Why's he so anxious to avoid ownership?"

Melissa waited for the waitress to refill their cups, and then she glanced around the room. The booths next to theirs were empty.

"Three reasons," she said. "One, Morgenstern deals real estate for the archdiocese, and they don't need scandal. Two, he's been under tax indictment for the last twenty-two years and the feds could seize everything he owns. Every cardinal since Spellman has tried to get the indictment lifted, but IRS isn't Vatican City."

"That's two reasons. What's the third?"

"Vince, can I trust you? This could mean my job. It could mean my kneecaps or my face or my life. They can't know it came from me."

"You can trust me."

Melissa regarded him with her deep-set eyes. "Morgenstern is dying. He'll be damned if he's going to pay a penny in estate taxes to any government."

"What's he dying of?"

"He's in the same program at Vanderbilt that my brother was."

"He's got AIDS?"

"Early stages. They give him three years."

"He's gay?" Cardozo said. "He's an IV drug user? What?"

"All of the above. Morgenstern uses my boss as a drop for liquid amphetamine. I never heard of anyone drinking liquid amphetamine, though I suppose you could. Balthazar buys Morgenstern callboys through a charge card service. Nat keeps the records because it's a tax deduction. As a favor to Morgenstern, Nat also provides callboys to religious figures in the community. As a result some high-rankers have AIDS. Less said about that the better."

"How many shares does Morgenstern have in Balthazar?"

"Thirty-five percent. It's held by Astoria Properties N.A. That's a Dutch Antilles company. As far as the meat-packing district scheme goes, as far as any of his scams go, he's technically clean. But Morgenstern's real power is that he's dying. He doesn't have to care about anyone. He's a terrorist wearing a vest that's wired to explode. The only thing he cares about is, he doesn't want it publicly known he's gay. No, there's a second thing he cares about. He doesn't want to go to hell."

"Do Jews believe in hell?"

"He's Catholic. Spellman baptized him. Morgenstern hates Jews."

"Did Spellman give him a plenary indulgence?"

"How did you know?"

"I didn't."

"Spellman dealt everything—real estate, POW's, indulgences."

"How do you know all this stuff about Spellman and Morgenstern?"

"Everyone knows Spellman had a weakness for pretty little Jewish boys. Which Morgenstern was before he turned into the portrait of Dorian Gray."

"I mean the inside stuff. How did you get it?"

"I had an inside track." There was a pause, just a beat of silence, as if she were deciding how far she could trust him. "My brother and Morgenstern were lovers. It's a long story."

"I've got time."

"Some gays cruise subway johns and get caught, and some gay lawyers cruise police lockups. Morgenstern got Brian off a soliciting charge. He liked Brian's looks, he liked Brian's style: Brian was the kind of person he could take to Gracie Mansion and the Archdiocesan Palace and the Harmonie Club without everyone snickering."

She lit another cigarette, looked at it with hatred, and decapitated it against the edge of the ashtray.

"Brian was always looking for the big break. He said New York is a who-do-you-know town, Morgenstern knew everyone, if he slept with Morgenstern he'd know everyone. He'd even have contacts in the federal government, because Morgenstern had a town house in Washington, D.C.; it was a partying pad for him and his government connections, walking distance from the Capitol. It was stocked with booze and boys, and Morgenstern stayed there whenever he had to put in a congressional fix or bribe a government agency. Brian was impressed. Dolce vita with a power twist. The downside was, he wasn't happy with Morgenstern. Sexually or emotionally or any way. Morgenstern's very controlling, very closeted. He comes from that period of powerhouse antigay gays—cardinals and J. Edgar Hoover and Joseph McCarthy. The right-wing establishment gave those guys permission to be gay provided from nine to five they were gay-bashers, black-bashers, communist-bashers—you name it, they'd bash it. Brian was very open with me. There were no taboo subjects between us. He told me all about the sex Hoover and the cardinal and Morgenstern liked. It was very punitive, very naive and sick. They had to be drunk. They liked getting hit, taking verbal abuse. Hoover had a racial wrinkle—he liked blacks. Morgenstern adds a whole anti-Semitic wrinkle, he likes his lover to dress up in SS clothes —he thinks Nazis are sexy. There's something wrong with Morgenstern's skin. Even before the AIDS he had a sort of advanced psoriasis —the lesions bleed unless they're kept oiled. Brian used to oil his back for him. Sexy, hey? So every time Brian made it with Morgenstern he had this compulsion to go trick on the outside with—how did he put it?—a mammal."

"So what was in the relationship for Brian?"

"He hoped he'd get a little power. What he got instead was AIDS."

Cardozo sat there watching Melissa Hatfield stare at him. He couldn't buy that she had learned so much from her brother, or that

Brian's AIDS and his liaison with Morgenstern were the secret he'd sensed her holding back. "Melissa," he said, "what don't you want me to know?"

She looked surprised. "What are you talking about?"

"There's something else. From day one I've felt it."

"It doesn't have anything to do with this."

"Then why don't you tell me?"

"Vince, I like you." It seemed to embarrass her to make the admission. "I even thought . . . maybe . . ." She looked down at the paper place mat printed with drink recipes and began running her fingernail back and forth through a banana daiquiri. "I wanted you to like me."

"I do like you."

"Would you like me if you knew I was sleeping with my boss? Nat Chamberlain, who's put up half the overpriced firetrap co-ops in Manhattan and took more graft than any politician in this city?"

The picture finally came into focus. "Why would I blame you for him?"

"Last spring there was a fire in one of Nat's flagship co-ops. A policeman died from burns he got rescuing a woman."

"You didn't build the building—you didn't set the fire."

"But somebody set it. And the insurance paid Nat another forty-four million." Melissa was silent a moment. "I feel dirty."

"Welcome to the real world."

"That's all—welcome to the real world?"

"If there's any other answer, I don't know it." Cardozo sighed and signaled for the check.

46

Cardozo phoned the Lewis Monserat Gallery.

The woman with the prim voice said gallery hours were Tuesday through Saturday, 11 A.M. till 6 P.M. —except Thursday, when hours were 12 till 8 P.M. She added, "We're closed Saturdays during the summer."

"Nothing like a long weekend," Cardozo said.

Cardozo examined the facade of 432 Franklin Street.

It was a typical conversion, a six-story industrial building with a column of windows marked Shaftway where the freight elevator ran. No amount of sand-blasting would ever turn the brick walls into brownstone, any more than fresh black paint would ever turn the fire escape into wrought iron art nouveau.

A sign swinging from the lowest cross-walk of the escape announced LUXURY CO-OPS AVAILABLE.

He pushed through the unlocked gray iron security door. A hand-lettered sign taped to the mailboxes inside requested, FOR YOUR OWN SECURITY PLEASE LOCK FRONT DOOR AFTER 11 P.M. THERE HAVE BEEN INCIDENTS.

Cardozo studied the building directory. Fewer than half the apartments were occupied, and there was no name in either fourth-floor slot.

The owners had installed an inner door of plate glass, the latch controlled by an intercom buzzer system. He pushed the buzzers for both sixth-floor units. An instant later two loud rasps clicked the latch open.

A glance at the first floor told him that the A apartments were at the front of the building, the B's at the rear.

He took the stairway to the fourth floor, two quiet steps at a leap.

The lock on 4A was a Medeco—not pickproof, but certainly MasterCard-proof.

"Who's there?" a woman's voice called irritably from upstairs.

Cardozo returned to his car, parked twenty yards down the opposite curb of Franklin Street, and took up his vigil, staring up at the dark windows on the fourth floor of 432.

He observed relatively little movement on Franklin. The street looked as if it had originally been an alley between two rows of warehouses. Judging by the garbage cans, most of the buildings had converted to residences. There were no stores, no restaurants, no reason to wander down the poorly lit pavement unless you happened to live there or needed a quiet wall to piss against or wanted a little semiprivacy to screw in.

Hudson, the cross street, was obviously the place for action. There was something aimless but urgent about the human movement, as if this was the now spot, the place to get sucked into the whirl of high-media exposure. The dress code was expensive sleaze, punk as modified by the fashion dictators. From his vantage point Cardozo couldn't see a person over thirty on the sidewalk.

Porsches and BMW's, Mercedeses and stretch limos crawled along, battling pedestrians for right of way. The cars changed colors like chameleons as they passed glitzy show windows and flashing neon logos.

Besides boutiques, card shops, and health food eateries, there was a disco called Space on the corner, guarded by an unsmiling seven-foot albino dressed in blue mylar. Next to it a restaurant sign flashed LA CÔTE BLEUE; through the window Cardozo could see the big circular glass bar mobbed with customers waiting to be seated.

The intersection smelled of sex and fashion and money—the things that made New York New York.

A little after eleven, a cruising police car hooked a turn down Franklin. The blue-and-white pulled alongside Cardozo.

"Hey, you." A woman leaned out the passenger window, red hair peeking out from under a police officer's blue cap. "No parking."

Cardozo flashed his shield and the woman got flustered.

"Sorry."

" 'S okay."

Fifteen minutes later a man leaned down and rapped on Cardozo's window. He had thick black hair and a beard, an earring, piercing dark eyes.

"Hey, man. I got grass, crack, PCB, coke, ludes, THC, uppers, downers, opium, hash, morphine. Try before you buy."

"Not tonight, thanks."

The man gave Cardozo a look as though he had to be crazy or a cop to be parked on that street not trying to score drugs.

A little before midnight thunder belched and Cardozo's rear view told him that the sky was turning a darker shade of night. The Empire State Building, lit art-deco blue and white for the night, was beginning to get lost in swirling clouds.

Rain spattered down, and pedestrians dodged into doorways. The line waiting to get into Space had to stand there and get soaked.

Cardozo's eye ran along the fourth story of 432 Franklin.

The windows were dark.

They stayed dark for that night and the next.

It came with no warning. Cardozo had been watching, waiting three nights for it.

Hudson Street bustled with the Friday night crowd. The heat of the day had yielded to the heat of the night, dense upward-rippling waves tinged pink and yellow by neon and headlights. The revolving door of La Côte Bleue was emptying four customers in a spin. The line waiting to get into Space stretched halfway down Franklin Street.

The alley beside 432 was so dark that Cardozo almost didn't spot the faint stir of movement.

Between the huge black garbage cans behind Space and the small silver ones behind La Côte Bleue three figures detached themselves from the shadows.

The three stood in the mouth of the alley, lighting a pipe of crack, passing it. When the pipe was consumed they moved unsteadily toward the door of 432.

The woman was pretty in a fading sort of way, wearing floppy safari trousers and a Hell's Angels denim vest. She had the look of someone too much had happened to, someone who had no more reactions to offer.

The Hispanic was skinny and dark-faced, with a V of paleness at his open shirt front.

Lewis Monserat wore an Eisenhower army jacket, cap, and designer glasses. He didn't look well. He was thin, the cords of his neck drawn taut, and he carried himself as if he had a headache, as if the very act of inserting the key in the lock required the coordinating of muscles he had barely the strength to control.

The door slammed behind them and three minutes later the lights on the fourth floor went on.

A car horn tooted, disturbingly close to Cardozo's ear.

He stirred to consciousness in the driver's seat of the Honda, hands folded across his chest. His sleep had not been deep, but he felt as if he had died in it.

The early morning light was flat and strange and it gave objects an eerie, unreal shimmer. The black Porsche sedan waiting at the door of 432 could have materialized from a dream. There didn't seem to be anyone, not even a driver, behind the tinted windows.

The horn tooted again.

The door to 432 opened. The woman and the Hispanic were dressed as they had been the night before, but Monserat had changed into an old T-shirt and a worn pair of jeans. He wore loafers, no socks. *Miami Vice* style.

He held the car door for the others. He looked around him before getting in. His dark eyes, high cheekbones, and jutting chin combined into a strikingly emaciated face.

Cardozo allowed the Porsche to make the turn onto Hudson before he turned the key in his ignition.

The Saturday morning traffic was light. He kept a two-block distance across town and down Broadway.

The sun was stroking the tops of glass buildings.

The Porsche turned left on Wall Street and continued to the East River heliport. Cardozo pulled to a hydrant a half-block away and watched.

A helicopter was waiting on the tarmac. On its door was emblazoned the logo HAMPTON HELICAB.

The Porsche drew to the metal fence.

Monserat and his companions got out and walked to the copter. A mechanic closed the door after them. The rotors blurred into invisibility. The copter lifted, throwing off motes of light.

Cardozo found a phonebooth on the corner of William Street.

"Hampton Helicab, good morning."

"This is Lieutenant Vincent Cardozo, NYPD. You have a Lewis Monserat and party flying with you this morning."

Cardozo spelled the name, and it took the agent a moment to confirm.

"Does Mr. Monserat have a return flight with you?"

"Yes he does, sir. Monday at seven forty P.M."

Cardozo broke the connection and dialed a second number.

"Waldo, it's Vince Cardozo. How about a cup of coffee, my treat?"

Twenty minutes later Cardozo and Waldo Flores were sitting in Kate's Cafeteria on West Seventeenth Street, on opposite sides of a Formica-topped table.

Waldo's large brown eyes stared above the edge of the coffee mug. "Man, you keep asking me to break the law. I'm straight now. Not pushin' drugs, not runnin' girls, no B and E. Why the hell don't you let me alone?"

Cardozo tore the edge off another packet of Sweet 'n Low and let it snow down into his coffee. "We've been having complaints about robberies at some East Side doctors' offices. Papers missing. Drugs missing, too." The drugs were a guess, but he trusted his intuition of the Waldos of this world.

Waldo's eyes came up in a hurry. "All right, I helped myself to some Valium, it's a crime?"

"Yeah, Waldo. It's a crime. What are you going to tell the judge? I asked you to go in?"

First puzzlement, then terror replaced the lost reluctant look. "Man, you never let go, do you."

"It's a Medeco. You can open it in your sleep. There's no one home till Monday night, only one other apartment on the floor, we jimmy the front door with a charge card."

Waldo bent toward the lock, his face furiously concentrated, everything focused on the signals reaching his fingers through the little steel rod.

A door banged four flights down. Steps were audible, then the sound of the elevator wheezing to life.

"Motherfuck," Waldo grumbled. "C'mon, c'mon, c'mon." He inserted a second rod, then a third.

The elevator passed and stopped one floor above.

Waldo froze.

Steps echoed. A door slammed.

Waldo straightened up, the tension dropping off his shoulders. He twisted the handle and gave the door to 4A a triumphant push.

Cardozo entered the apartment. Waldo followed.

They walked along a hallway, the only sound the crackling of Styrofoam packing pellets snapping like peanut brittle beneath their feet.

Cardozo opened doors.

Waldo stood watching him.

Lewis Monserat's home away from home had everything: a Jacuzzi in the bathroom, a blood-stained towel thrown behind the toilet, an answering machine blinking in the bedroom, a VCR and an eighty-inch projection TV in the livingroom.

Cardozo had started across the colorful rya rug that stretched before the TV screen when he saw a silver tray holding plastic-sealed syringes on the secretaire that stood beneath a gold-framed mirror. Other evidence of fun and frolic was lying about: an empty two-litre bottle of Gilbey's gin, pipes, mirrors, silver straws, single-edged safety razors.

It looked as though last night had been a quiet evening at home with booze and coke and crack, video and the Smithsonian collection of dildos and handcuffs.

"The maid's gonna have a lot of cleanin' up to do," Waldo observed.

Cardozo moved the TV screen. Four black two-by-fours had been screwed into the wall, forming an H with two cross beams. He could see scrapes on the wood, and rust stains.

Waldo prowled the room, picking up mirrors and sniffing white dust from them, scooping up red-capped plastic vials that had fallen behind sofa cushions.

Cardozo figured out how to work the VCR and ejected the video tape. The cassette label was hand-lettered: GAMES. He pocketed it.

"A lot of grass in the freezer," Waldo called from the kitchen.

"Don't take so much it's obvious," Cardozo said. "We may want to come back."

"Shit, I ain't comin' back here."

Waldo went quickly through the bedroom into the bathroom, sniffing bottles in the medicine cabinet.

Cardozo found that the bedroom closet had a Fichet lock.

"Waldo, come here."

Waldo sauntered out of the bathroom, heaping fistfuls of Quaaludes and Valiums into his pockets.

"Open this."

Waldo studied the lock, frowned, opened his toolkit, selected an eight-inch rod.

"Stand back, amigo."

Waldo probed, listened, inserted a second rod.

Cardozo glanced at the magazines on the bedside table. *Hustler. Honcho. A Child's Garden of Sex.* Last May's *Reader's Digest,* with a marker inserted at "The Seven Telltale Signs of Loneliness: Are you Suffering From the Disease That Cripples More Than Three Million Americans Annually?"

Suddenly a board creaked in the hallway. The apartment door opened, slamming against the wall.

Waldo spun around, eyes huge.

"Yoo-hoo! Yoo-hoo?" A man's voice. "Yoo-hoo, God damn it."

"Il n'y a personne." A woman.

Count Leopold de Savoie-Sancerre, bloated in flowered surfer's jams and a yellow silk shirt, passed the bedroom doorway, followed by Countess Vicki in a fiery pink skirt.

Cardozo motioned Waldo to pack up his gear.

Count Leopold's voice came from the livingroom. *"Mais c'est un bordel!"*

"T'affolles pas," Countess Vicki said. *"Il y a eu une fête, c'est tout."*

Cardozo eased the front door open. He and Waldo slipped into the corridor.

First came the sound: a woman's voice singing "I Could Have Danced All Night," high and piping and almost laughably pure. *My Fair Lady,* the original cast recording, badly scratched. Julie Andrews.

An image began to appear on the television screen, lights and darks, the curve of a woman's shoulder, gloved fingers stroking the lower part of her face.

The camera pulled back jerkily.

The woman wore a glittering evening gown. She was strangely, disturbingly ugly.

The room behind her had stark white walls. There were two Queen Anne chairs. She sat.

Vague silhouettes passed through the background. A man in evening clothes stepped into focus. He bowed gallantly.

He took the woman's hand and she rose. They began moving together. The movements never quite became a dance, but still there was a sort of pattern to it, as though the actors had rehearsed certain postures and facial attitudes.

Cardozo's eyebrows were creased in the effort of understanding.

The picture changed to a different woman, standing naked against the same blank walls.

Cardozo tried to guess her age and figured she was shading sixteen.

A man in evening clothes entered the frame. He kissed the girl's eyes, her cheeks, her ears, then lightly brushed his lips against hers. They spoke, but the words were garbled—only a tone came through, joking and teasing and laughing.

Three other men in evening clothes entered the frame.

The girl began deep-throating one of the men.

Something in the image put Cardozo on guard. The three men not involved in the sex act were aware of something, seeing something the girl could not.

Suddenly the men pushed the girl to the floor. Her reaction was unstaged: surprise and pain.

Two of the men held her down. Without warning, something slopped down on the girl. It took Cardozo a moment to recognize what he was seeing: animal intestines from a slaughterhouse.

There was mindless terror in the girl's kicking and thrashing.

Cardozo knew what she was thinking—she believed these lunatics were going to kill her. That was what they wanted her to believe, that was what they wanted to get on film.

At the same time there was a bell going off in his head: the animal intestines triggered an association that wasn't quite making it to the surface.

And then it came to him.

The butcher shop viscera that Nuku Kushima had encased in lucite and made part of her art.

Connections began spinning off one another in Cardozo's mind.

Intestines in Kushima's art and intestines in Lew Monserat's home video, and Monserat was Kushima's dealer.

Claude Loring killed Jodie Downs. Doria Forbes-Steinman recognized Loring as a friend of Monserat's.

No big deal—a lot of New Yorkers were friends.

Monserat and Loring both frequented the Inferno.

Still no big deal—more than a few New Yorkers were into kink and anonymous sex.

Count Leopold and Countess Victoria de Savoie-Sancerre had a key to Monserat's new party pad. The countess had put on a blond wig and walked into Pleasure Trove, paid cash for a bondage mask, and carried it into Beaux Arts Tower.

Was that a big deal?

Putting on a disguise, giving a false name, paying cash—yes, that was a big deal. Buying the mask the first business day after the killing meant it was a replacement for the fifth Kushima mask, the mask found on the victim.

Monserat had said the fifth mask didn't exist, but this contradicted the artist's first statement. As dealer for Kushima's work Monserat could easily have owned or borrowed the fifth mask and destroyed the records.

Since Monserat didn't live in Beaux Arts Tower, that raised a question: who had Vicki given the mask to? Obviously it could have been anyone, even the doorman. All the well-heeled people in that building probably dealt with Monserat—and transporting a mask was not an offense like transporting drugs or a minor across state lines for immoral purposes.

And then there was Babe.

Babe Devens recognized Monserat's former party pad—abandoned four days after the Downs killing—as the scene of a masked party where a young man had been tortured in exactly the same way as Jodie Downs. Babe had been dreaming, but that was another story —or question. The tape in Monserat's VCR showed disjointed snippets of other sadistic parties, some masked, some not. So dreaming or not, Babe had been right on the money.

A lot of pieces, a lot of holes.

What to do?

Consult the dreamer.

47

IT WAS QUIET EXCEPT FOR THE HISSING ON THE SOUNDTRACK, AND in a way that hissing made the room even more silent. Babe's wide green-blue eyes followed the movement on the screen.

A man in evening clothes crossed the screen. Behind him four black beams attached to the wall formed the letter H, with two crosspieces, almost as tall as he was.

"That's Lew Monserat," Babe said.

Another man in evening clothes entered the frame.

Babe leaned forward. "That's Binny Harbison." She sounded astonished. "This must be an old tape."

"Who's Binny Harbison?"

"A designer. I heard he died three years ago."

Now the woman in the gown appeared. She put a cigarette to her mouth. Both Binny Harbison and Lew Monserat offered lights. The woman took a light from Binny. She crossed to one of the Queen Anne chairs and sat.

Babe's face was suddenly an oval of concentration. Her gaze played over the hard jaw, the high forehead, the widely spaced dark eyes, the aquiline nose. "There's something . . ."

The woman leaned back against the chair, watching the column of smoke from her cigarette drift up into the unstirring air.

"There's something wrong with her hair," Babe said. "It's fake. She's wearing a wig. Could you stop the film?"

Babe peered at the TV screen.

"The picture's so bad. Even the nose could be false. But still there's something . . ."

Babe got up and went to the door. "Mathilde, could you come here a moment?"

A white-haired Frenchwoman with a swatch of blue cloth in one hand and a pair of pinking shears in the other stepped into the room. Babe introduced Mathilde Lheureux, her assistant, and Cardozo said how do you do.

"Do you recognize that dress?" Babe asked.

Mathilde approached the TV screen. "You designed that dress. It is red, with hand-stitched sequins."

"Of course." Babe took Cardozo through a workroom where eight women were working sewing machines and into an office. She shut the door. "Excuse the confusion," she said, "we've hardly moved in."

She went to the deep bookcase that held art folders. Tall, moving lightly, she was showing more and more of the grace that had been locked up in her for seven years. She studied labels, found the folder she wanted. She unlaced the strings and laid it open on the drafting table. She turned sheets of paper with a little snap.

"This one," she said.

Cardozo looked down at a delicate sketch of a faceless woman in a gown that was warm, ripe red, the color of a perfect strawberry.

"I designed it for Ash Canfield," Babe said. "She wore it to my party the night I went into coma."

Babe felt silence, motionlessness in the house. Every piece of furniture seemed to say *Ash is gone.* She looked about the room, seeing the moody Corot woodscape over the fireplace, all the small doodads and objets that had been Ash's enthusiasms and now, without her, semed pitiful and meaningless, like abandoned pups.

"First stop, a drink, yes?" Dunk said.

"Isn't it a little early for that?"

"You know what the Countess Rothschild used to say—'Oh, well, what the hell.' "

He mixed martinis, strained them carefully into two glasses, and garnished them with garlic olives. He came across the livingroom and handed Babe one. They settled onto facing couches.

She studied his face, the squarely set eyes, the bobsled nose and dimpled chin, the long curling lashes, all the physical details that had been Ash's obsession. And Dina Alstetter's. And, once upon a time, hers too. It seemed peculiar: Ash gone, the obsession surviving.

"It's sweet of you to come by," he said. "You look more and more terrific every day."

There were dark lines under Dunk Canfield's eyes, accentuated by his deep tan, and they seemed to speak of weeks of sleeplessness. A yachting cap sat rakishly atilt his hair, bleached from the Corfu sun.

"How are you, Dunk?"

"It's been one of those days. It's been one of those lives." His posture sagged and his head hung forward. "I loved her. I was a rotten bastard to her, but I loved her. We weren't always the best lovers or the best friends—as you well know—but damn it, we knew how to have fun. She was my best playmate ever. And we were just getting back together. And this time it would have worked. I know it would have."

Babe was silent.

"I walk through these rooms—they feel so lonely, so empty."

"What are you doing with yourself? Aren't you getting out at all?"

"I was out with Vicki the other night—she took me to some of the discos—it's not a lot, but it's a toe in the water. I really don't feel up to dinners, meeting people, making chitchat. There's always that obligatory I'm-so-sorry and I'm so tired of it. And every damned little thing reminds me of her. I order Château-Margaux and I remember when she and I last drank it. I play a record and it's her favorite. I try to read and the words on the page start a chain of associations and I wind up thinking of her. Look what I found, going through her things."

Dunk pulled a pack of glossy photographs out of a manila envelope and handed them to Babe.

She looked at them—candids of Ash, appearing rather tipsy in some airport or other. One showed Ash dancing on a VIP lounge couch, a gaggle of nuns staring in open shock.

"Our trip to Bavaria, remember?" Dunk said. "When we all went to Caroline's schloss and at Shannon they announced 'Boarding all passengers on Aeroflot to Moscow and all passengers on Mr. Getty's jet to Bad Nemetz.' It's one of those silly moments you never forget."

"I remember." Babe remembered being embarrassed, but it was obviously one of Dunk's golden moments and she wasn't going to say anything to tarnish it.

"Speaking of mementos . . ." Babe opened her own envelope and handed Dunk her sketch of the red gown. "Do you remember the dress I designed for Ash?"

He shook his head. "I got rid of all her clothes. The day after she died I phoned the Junior League thrift shop and told them to send a truck."

* * *

Cardozo held the door for Babe.

The air inside the Junior League thrift shop smelled of floor wax, camphor, and the perfumes of forty different millionaires' wives. The women floating up and down the aisles did not seem to be shopping so much as strolling, enjoying a break in lives that were all intermission to begin with, pausing to examine a froth of petticoat or an onyx bookend. They had a bored air, but there was a seriousness in their boredom, as though they were pursuing highly competitive careers.

"How do you tell who's selling and who's buying?" Cardozo whispered.

"The saleswomen are wearing originals," Babe said.

Cardozo glanced along the racks of dresses and evening gowns, seemingly crushed together helter-skelter, all exuding an aroma of last decade's chic; shelves of figurines and glasses and vases; stacks of books coming apart at the bindings.

"Garth, look!" a woman cried. "Depression glass candlesticks!"

Babe examined the sleeve of an oxydized mink that had gone the color of an old toupee.

A young woman approached. She wore slacks and a silk blouse with a patterned scarf, her reddish-brown hair pinned behind one ear with an emerald clip. "May I help you?"

"Who takes deliveries?" Babe asked.

"Cybilla handles those. I'll see if she's free."

Everyone in the store looked free to Cardozo.

By the window, he observed two women discussing a flared rust-and-black patterned dress.

The younger woman was thin and blond, bright-eyed, agitated, a princess with a small p, doing coke or possibly prescription speed, worried about her age, her body, her left contact lens.

Her opponent was a tall, slender woman with steel-gray hair softly waved over an intelligent face.

They were disagreeing. It was clearly a collision of life-styles.

Cardozo understood what the young blond woman did not: the Junior League boutique was not Crazy Eddie's; you didn't *hondle* with the help, who in any case were not help but Park Avenue volunteers.

The woman in slacks spoke to the gray-haired lady, who came smiling across the shop.

"Great to see you, Babe. You're looking just terrific."

"So are you, Cybilla."

"We're going crazy. Three cartons of *tip-top* junk just came in from Truman Capote's old garage and we're understaffed."

"Cybilla," Babe said, "this is Vincent Cardozo. Vince, Cybilla deClairville—a good friend of my mother's and mine."

Cybilla raised her left eyebrow. She held out a perfectly and unobtrusively manicured hand. One gold band and nothing else. "You look familiar to me, Mr. Cardozo. Have we met?"

"Your home was robbed eleven years ago," he said. "They almost killed the butler. How's he doing?"

"Very well, thank you."

"The Bonnard is all stitched up?"

"As good as new, Mr. Cardozo."

Babe showed Cybilla her sketch of the red dress. "Do you have this dress?"

Cybilla studied the sketch. "I'm afraid we don't. It's a bit out of our league."

"But it came in with Ash Canfield's things."

Noncomprehension lines knotted Cybilla's brow.

"I designed it for her," Babe said. "I'd like it for sentimental reasons. I'll buy it, of course."

"We don't have any of Ash's things," Cybilla said.

"But Dunk gave you everything."

"No he didn't. Dunk hasn't said *boo* to me in three years."

Countess Vicki de Savoie-Sancerre joined the conversation, tall and leggy in an orange jumpsuit. "Hello, Babe, you're looking glorious, as always."

"I didn't know you worked here," Babe said.

"Every Thursday this month, taking over for Betsy."

Cybilla handed Countess Vicki the sketch. "Have we had a dress like this?"

Countess Vicki stared at the sketch. "Oh, Dunk Canfield brought it in and it was purchased the same day."

"Do you happen to have the receipt?" Cardozo asked.

Countess Vicki smiled and held out her wrists. "Lieutenant, handcuff me. I didn't make out a receipt. I just put the money in the register."

For an instant Duncan Canfield's face glowed from the entire screen, patterned pinpoints of vibrating light and dark.

Charley Brackner pushed a button that split the screen.

From the bottom half Canfield's image sent out sharp glints like sparks from a flint. In the upper half appeared the message:

WELCOME TO IDENTI-KIT COPYRIGHT 1985
HERE IS YOUR MENU OF CHOICES:
    [1] MALE
    [2] FEMALE

"Female," Cardozo said.
Charley Brackner's brown eyes glanced up at him. "Female?"
"Read my lips. Female."
Charley pushed another button. A new message appeared:

HERE IS YOUR MENU OF CHOICES.
    FACE SHAPE
    HAIR
    EYEBROWS
    EYES
    NOSE
    CHEEKS
    LIPS
    JAW
    CHIN

"How would he disguise himself," Cardozo said, "if he wanted to be a woman for the night. For Halloween. For a joke."
"Okay. A wig, eyeshadow, lashes . . ."
The cursor began snatching options from the top half of the screen and moving them down onto the face. Feature by feature a drifting current of superimpositions redrew reality.
"How good is our man at this stuff?" Charley said.
Cardozo studied what was coming up on the screen. "Better than you are."
"Sorry about that. Lipstick?"
"Definitely lipstick. I could even give you the shade."
"Color we don't have."
Fleetingly the smile left Canfield's face, then returned with Cupid's bow lips.
"Less like a hooker," Cardozo said.
New lips, more lady-like, fell into place. Gradually a change passed over the face. The likeness to Canfield began to die and the likeness

to someone else, to *something* else, began to spread. There was a precise moment when the balance tipped, when the human being faded away, when all gentleness in the face had gone, and suddenly the image seethed with almost theatrical violence and anger.

"Try adding more hair, earrings—you know, women's things."

The hair dropped from her ears—for she was now definitely some kind of she—to her neck to her shoulders.

Cardozo stood there, staring. There was still a faint stain of doubt, a sensation that something was missing.

"Give her a dress."

Suddenly she was wearing a severe dark dress.

"Make it lighter, flouncier."

"Vince, we only have a limited line of dresses in this program. Saks Fifth Avenue we are not."

"I can draw you the type I want." Cardozo drew it on a piece of scratch paper.

"Vince, never go into fashion."

The dress toppled into place.

Charley Brackner pressed a button and now the face occupied the entire screen, casting a hard glow, like sunlight on snow.

"That's good," Cardozo said. "Can you print that face?"

Charley pushed a button.

Seven minutes later Cardozo was sitting in his cubicle staring at Dunk Canfield transformed.

He angled the picture under his desk lamp. Specks of dust floated in the grayish flicker. Light vibrated on the face. The face was trapped in fluorescence. The eyes stared back at him, cheerless and vacant.

Unless Canfield had an identical twin of the opposite sex, there could be very little doubt: Sir Dunk was the same person as the ugly woman in the videotape wearing Ash Canfield's dress.

Cardozo heaved himself up from the desk. He went into the squad room and studied the bulletin board. "Who took down the flyer for the Gay Cops' Dance?"

Monteleone whooped. "You going, Vince? Take me along?"

"The CP ruled that that flyer stays up."

The CP had issued an edict affirming the right of any and all organizations on the force to post notice of peaceful assemblies.

"Look under the Uniformed Sons of Erin novena. Under, Vince. Underneath."

Cardozo undid the bottom thumbtacks on the novena announce-
ment and found the gay cops' flyer.

Technically, hiding the gay cops' flyer under the Uniformed Sons
of Erin's was not a violation. Nevertheless, after he had made a note
of the name and precinct of the organizer, Cardozo tacked the flyer
over the latest communique from the CD's office.

Sergeant John Henning, president of the Gay Policemen's Caucus
and organizer of the Gay Cops' Dance, shook a Marlboro loose from
the packet. He looked across the coffee shop booth at Cardozo. "Do
you mind?"

"You're going to die that way."

Sergeant Henning lit his cigarette and signaled the waitress for
another round of coffees. "You always draw morals?"

"Never. Am I going to insult you if I ask you about drag queens?"

For just a flash, Sergeant Henning's eyes narrowed. Then they
crinkled into a blandly diplomatic smile. "The only insult is asking if
it's an insult. What do you want to know?"

"I want to know if I'm getting too far from reality."

Cardozo showed Henning the photograph of Sir Duncan that Ellie
Siegel had clipped from *Town and Country.* "This is what this guy
looks like in—let's call it real life." He laid down the computer-
modified portrait beside it. "I'm almost a hundred and two percent
convinced that this is the same guy."

Sergeant Henning was a powerfully built young man, serious-look-
ing and clean shaven, with keen blue eyes and a full head of black
hair curling back from a face that was prematurely lined and drawn.
His eyes wrinkled and there was a flicker of something—not exactly
surprise, more like distaste caught off guard and not wanting to show
itself.

"Strike you as reasonable that a man who looked like that would
want to look like a woman who looked like that?"

"Reason doesn't come into it," Sergeant Henning said. "I have no
trouble with it."

"Say this guy is doing drag acts in his wife's old clothes. The wife
doesn't know. Didn't know. Thought her old clothes were going to
charity."

"A lot of TV's keep it secret for a whole marriage."

"TV?"

"Transvestite."

"The guy may not be a transvestite exactly. The real point may be something else—a sort of s.m. that involves play-acting and gender switching."

"All possible. Not frequent, but possible. Usually TV's and s.m. are two very different worlds. Psychologically and socially."

"But it could happen?"

"Sure."

"The guy may dress up and act out these scenes in front of a video camera. Possible?"

"Very frequent."

"But he doesn't keep the camera at his home. There's a special place where he gets together with like-minded friends. They do drugs and dress up and party and make these videotapes."

"It's very common for TV's or s.m.'s to have a special apartment for their celebrations. Trick pads. The way some married guys have apartments to meet their girlfriends."

"Okay. Where does he keep his clothes, the drag clothes?"

"Most guys would keep them at home. If they're married and the wife doesn't know, they'd keep them someplace where she wouldn't be apt to look—the toolchest, the workshop, maybe even a safe."

"But if he lives in a Manhattan apartment, how does he get across town without being noticed?"

"Is he rich?"

"Very."

"Hire a limo."

"Then the elevator man knows. The doorman knows."

"He changes into drag in the limo. The driver's in on it. That happens a lot. There are special limo services. He could even stash the drag with the limo company."

"But it's fancy drag, he wants it to look good. A real woman wouldn't dress in a limo, make herself up in the back seat—would this guy?"

"Either you don't know the things some women do in limos, or you don't know what state-of-the-art limos are like. They have Jacuzzis. Beds. Mirrors."

"But say these games and videotapes—say the s.m. in them is really rough. Maybe someone's even been killed."

Henning's eye flicked up and fixed on Cardozo. "We both know that happens."

"This guy doesn't want anyone to know he does drag—not anyone on the outside, certainly not a limo driver. He doesn't want anything showing that connects to that side of his life."

"Then if he's smart he changes in the place where they make the films. But there are no rules. A lot of guys aren't realistic in this one area. They don't want to be found out, but they take asshole risks. Maybe that's part of the unconscious thrill. You see Manhattan publishers, bankers, lawyers, guys with two-hundred-thousand-dollar-a-year salaries, walking past the doorman in leather. Leather, for Christ's sake. They gotta be crazy if they think they're leading a double life, but they do it."

"But drag?"

"Drag—no. They don't go past the doorman in drag. Not the older generation. Not if it's secret. If it weren't for the wife, I'd say your friend takes the drag with him in a suitcase. But married, I don't know what he tells her—he's going to Chicago on business for six hours? Unless the wife isn't around much, or they lead separate lives, like she has a lover or she's always out Thursdays at the opera."

"What about keeping the drag in the secret apartment?"

"Frankly, Lieutenant, I know more about leather than drag. But if we're talking high drag, the gear is very expensive—it runs a few thousand dollars. And the people that do these things, the drugs, the games—they're not the kind you'd trust with something you valued. So unless this secret apartment was his own place, no one else coming and going, I don't think he'd keep the drag there. Also, how does it get cleaned and repaired, who takes care of all that? There's a lot of logistics to drag, a lot more than to leather."

"You don't know any guys who have this kind of profile?"

"Making snuff films in drag?"

"You might have heard something."

"Sure, you hear things, but take it with a grain of salt."

Henning started to speak, hesitated, worked his lip.

"Okay, I've heard of somebody, he does drag, and he's in a situation where it would wreck his life, his friendships, his career, everything, if it ever came out."

Cardozo flashed that Henning was talking about a cop. Not himself, but another cop. A member of the Gay Caucus.

"It's a compulsion, a need. And he needs a place where he can act out and it can't be at home, because at home he drinks Bud with the boys, watches ballgames. A coworker could open a closet and see Scarlett O'Hara's ballgown and blow the whole thing. So what's he going to do? We know what rents are, who can afford one apartment, let alone a secret pad? So he shares with some other TV's, who are not exactly reliable people. I don't mean in general, but these particular TV's are dips. So he keeps a locker in the pad. It's a secure locker, you could put jewels in it. Dynamite couldn't get into it."

Cardozo flashed that Henning was talking about his lover. "Kind of like keeping your own bottle of liquor at an after-hours club?"

Henning nodded. "Right."

48

"I NEED TO GET INTO LEWIS MONSERAT'S FRANKLIN STREET LOFT," Cardozo said.

"But he lives on Madison," Babe said.

"His playpen is on Franklin."

A hesitation came over the phone line. "Has he done anything wrong?"

"I'll know after I search. Can you keep him busy two hours?"

"He's showing a new artist at his gallery this Wednesday evening, he'll have to be there at least three hours."

"Are you going?"

"I can."

"Is Duncan Canfield going?"

"Do you want him to go?"

"Him and Count Leopold and Countess Vicki."

"The count and countess never miss an opening of Lew's. And I can ask Dunk to take me."

"Be your most—what's the word they use in gossip columns?— captivating. Make sure they all stay."

At 8 P.M. three men in the brown uniforms of the United Parcel Service approached the doorway of number 432 Franklin Street. Two were empty-handed and the third carried a large carton marked SONY TRINITRON.

The tallest of the delivery men glanced both ways along the street. The thin crowds of early evening had begun milling up the block on Hudson Street, but except for the three UPS men, Franklin was deserted.

The shortest of the delivery men removed a plastic card from his wallet and worked it into the crack between the inner door and the metal jamb. A moment later the door swung free.

Babe's eye played across the crowd.

The Monserat Gallery was full of guests, and more were arriving by the minute. Handsome women in smart gowns, men in tuxes who were obviously going on to other events mingled with young and not-so-young people in jeans and T-shirts and flouncy gypsy skirts with peasant tops.

For those who couldn't brave the crush to the elaborate buffet tables, waiters circulated with drinks and food. Deftly placed speakers pumped discreet post-punk energized trance music into the party.

"Lew!" Babe waved.

Lew Monserat had a little slow smile for her as they drew toward one another, and he kissed her on each cheek.

He was elegantly dressed in a blue blazer, vellum-colored shirt, ecru flannels, but his face was gaunt, his eyes exhausted, and he moved with a sort of stoop.

"It's been so long," Babe said.

"We haven't talked in eight years—can you believe it?"

"Well, I know how to fix that." Babe took his arm. "Tell me about your new artist and introduce me to everyone."

Waldo Flores's assbones ached from sitting on the hard wooden chair, and he had a crimp in his neck from leaning forward to listen for a click that never came.

But this time there was a click. It was so faint he couldn't tell at first whether he had heard it or just wished it.

He slid a steel piece between the rods and pressured it slowly clockwise.

The lock made a friendly sound as the bolt slid back.

An hour of pain dropped off his shoulders and he swung the door open.

Cardozo found the light switch and flicked it. "Jesus Christ," he said.

It startled Waldo to see Richard Nixon wearing a Frederick's of Hollywood black lace panty-bra with the crotch cut out. The mask was that realistic.

Mickey and Minnie Mouse and the other cartoon character masks looked real in their own way, but it was a different way, not shocking, just ugly with the black lingerie and black leather dangling on hangers beneath them.

But Nixon and John Wayne, those were shocks.

Cardozo bent down at the bottom shelf in the closet, pulled out a videocassette, and studied it. The neatly hand-lettered label read FUN 'N' GAMES HALLOWEEN 7.

He carefully peeled off the label and stuck it onto the spine of one of his own blank cassettes. He put the labeled blank on the shelf in place of Monserat's cassette.

He wrote FUN 'N' GAMES HALLOWEEN 7 on a fresh label and attached it to Monserat's cassette. He dropped the cassette into the Sony Trinitron carton.

Tony Bandolero stepped around Cardozo and took a gown down from the clothesbar. There was the powdery crackle of a plastic bag opening.

The gown was deep red, with sequins. Because flashes would be visible through the blinds, Tony was using room light. He scanned the gown with his digital light meter and adjusted his camera aperture.

There was a click as the shutter opened and shut and then a faint whir as the film advanced.

Cardozo's felt-tip pen carefully wrote FUN 'N' GAMES HALLOWEEN 8.

Cardozo stared through the filtered darkness, registering the slow, silent passage of the camera's gaze across a white wall.

Weird figures took shape on the TV screen, ghostly inhabitants of a world of electronic phantoms and dreams, moving and swaying in the flickering light, acting out their secret rituals.

A sensation of unformed dread grew in his belly.

And then, in front of his eyes, it was real.

His gaze slashed for one disbelieving instant at the image on the screen. The blood drained sickeningly from his head.

He reached a shaking hand for the phone and dialed.

"Hippolito."

"Dan, it's Vince. I need your opinion on something. It's urgent."

Cardozo's livingroom was dim with the rapid shifting of lights and darks. Dan Hippolito, mild and grave, watched the TV screen with a look of disdain.

"Morgenstern's gay?" he said in a tone of amazement.

"A guy sucking a guy's cock, I'd call that gay," Cardozo said.

"Why the hell did he let it be filmed?"

"He didn't know. There are two types of movies in this collection: one where the camera's moving around in the party and everyone knows they're stars or hired help. Then there's another type, like this, where the camera doesn't move. Which means it's hidden, operated remote or automatic. The people wearing masks know what's happening. The object is to get the goods on the people who don't know."

"Jesus, he gives deep throat. Vince, if you don't mind, I find Ted Morgenstern kind of revolting under the best of circumstances. Chowing down on a nine-foot Watusi in a Wehrmacht uniform I think he's to puke."

Cardozo pressed the fast-forward. The actors plunged into a comic, sped-up dance.

Naked on a stepladder, the dark-haired girl free-based while a chivalrous gentleman in a Popeye mask held the flame of an acetylene torch beneath her bulbed glass pipe. A ponytailed young man wearing see-through black lace panties flung himself into doggie position on the floor, sniffing through a silver straw at a hand mirror zebra'd with lines of white powder.

A man wearing a Richard Nixon mask snapped flash pictures of an industrious young woman who was blowing a man in a Lone Ranger mask and simultaneously fondling the genitals of two other men in Mickey Mouse and Donald Duck masks. Seated on two Queen Anne chairs sipping drinks, two extraordinarily ugly drags ignored the couplings and thrashings. One of them was moustached and the other was not. They both wore elaborate gowns.

"Charlie Chaplin goes porno." Dan Hippolito lit a cigarette. "So help me, Vince, you better not have dragged me down here to watch home movie orgies. I have real trouble empathizing with driven behavior."

"You may have more than a little trouble empathizing with what comes next."

What came next was a startlingly beautiful Latin woman with the face of a Madonna, lying naked and absolutely still on a thick quilt that had been spread on the floor between the two Queen Anne chairs.

Something had happened to Dan Hippolito's expression. "Stop the frame." His voice had the even, dead strain of on-guardedness.

He moved forward, sitting in the hard glow of the frozen TV picture. He seemed to be searching the actors' faces for some explanation. But the Madonna's face was absolutely serene and her abusers' faces had only a drugged, wow-I'm-not-here look.

"Take it backward."

Cardozo ran the tape backward.

"Forward again. Real time. I'll tell you when to stop-frame. There."

For an unending moment stillness submerged everything.

Finally a sigh came out of Dan. "She's a young female Hispanic, I'd say twenty to twenty-two years old, good physical condition, five foot one inch tall, scale weight probably one hundred ten pounds."

"And?" Cardozo prodded.

Dan walked over and gently put an arm around Cardozo's shoulders. It was a spontaneous, unthinking gesture, compassionate, as though he were preparing his friend for some very bad news.

"Don't get hispanical."

"What do you mean, hispanical?"

"I mean the way you are now—hispanical. Just relax."

Dan began talking about lividity and rigor. The words came at Cardozo like a slow bucket of swamp water.

"Dan, just tell me yes or no—is she dead?"

"She's dead."

"From start to finish, she's dead?"

"Do you mean are they killing her on camera? No. She's been dead two, three days before this even began. And I don't think she was murdered."

"How do you figure that?"

"Suspicious death there would have been an autopsy. Nothing has cut this girl, except the drainage catheters in the forearms. And that's professional. Which means there was a death certificate. She's embalmed. You don't have amateur embalmers. Certainly not loons like these. The girl's from a funeral home."

"They took a body from a funeral home?"

"It's called necrophilia. It happens."

"I hate these guys."

"It's not a homicide, Vince. There's no trauma to the body. It was a quick easy death. Most likely an OD. To tell you more that that, I can't. Not the way she looks. Not what you're showing me. All I can give you is an educated guess."

"Give me your educated guess on this." Cardozo sprang the videocassette out of the VCR and inserted another. "It's going to be a little more than you want to see."

"Every day I see more than I want to."

The image this time was a thin young man stumbling across the screen in faded blue jeans and white sneakers, goofily grinning, blissed out.

The young man stripped clumsily to the buff and lay belly down on a banquet table.

Porky Pig and the Lone Ranger, nattily dressed in white tie and tails, moved into the frame. They lashed the young man's hands to the legs of the table.

The kid was grinning. Fun and games.

Porky and the Ranger passed lengths of bicycle chain around the young man's ankles, made the chains fast to the other two table legs. Now came a ceremonial padlocking of the chains.

The kid turned and smiled at the camera.

The Lone Ranger stepped off camera and returned holding a jumbo-sized jar of Vaseline and a six-inch clear plastic tube of one-inch diameter. He presented both to the camera's inspection.

The Lone Ranger stepped off camera again. He returned holding in one hand a wooden tongue depressor. He showed it to the camera.

Now he showed the other hand. His palm held a small clump of wet fur. The fur was alive, skittering, the size of a new-born rat. It had long hind legs and a long skinny tail and tiny bright black eyes and two white needles of incisors in the upper jaw of its chattering miniature mouth.

The boy looked around. His expression changed to puzzlement.

What happened next was difficult to believe.

"How much of this is there?" Dan said.

"The tape runs a few hours."

"Jesus, I don't want to see this."

Cardozo killed the film. A commercial for AT&T long-distance dialing came up on Channel 7 and he killed the TV. "These are intelligent, wealthy people," Cardozo said. "The wealthiest people on earth, and look at the things they do to other people. I can't get that out of my head. People with everything, nothing good left to want, so they have to want bad things. And their attitude. It's like they're saying, what's so special about a human life? Why should we respect it? Let's wipe it out. Want to see it again? Run the tape back. See it sped up or in slo-mo? Just push the button."

"Vince, no one got killed."

"You better believe these nuts killed someone. You don't get that close to the borderline and not step over. Just once. Just to see what it feels like."

"You still can't indict the whole class."

"Why not? The whole country worships them. They're glamorous. Powerful. Rich. In. They're the people everyone else wants to be. And look at the pattern of their existence. Going to parties, posing for photographers, hoping they'll make the gossip columns, waiting for something different to happen. Well, nothing different's going to happen, so they decide to make it happen."

"Vince, on those tapes you have two things coming together that weren't meant to. You have an instinct—sex—and a class of substances—drugs."

"It's not that simple, Monsignor."

"Okay, I'm Catholic, and it *is* that simple. Simpler. I see it five times a week on the autopsy table. Separately, drugs and sex can go either way—good or evil. But put them together, use them for kicks —and there's no limit to the evil."

"Sometimes I get the feeling that you've got so many answers that none of this shit bothers you."

"Of course it bothers me. I'm human. But I'm a doctor. I've seen how it works. There's nothing demonic about it, nothing that proves Karl Marx was right. It's an impulse—a sort of 'what if?'—you don't even imagine it clearly—under ordinary circumstances, that impulse would slide right by, like a bubble—but you take a drug, the drug freezes that moment, that impulse, and the what-if turns into a why-not and then you're doing it and the drug's telling you it's not you doing it. And believe me, even what's on those tapes isn't the worst. It's the surface of the cesspool. You don't know what else is down there."

"No, Dan. *You* don't know. I've seen the rest of these tapes."

49

"DRUGWISE," THE STAR WAS SAYING, "THESE ARE THE GLORY days."

Cardozo watched from the doorway. He admired the woman. She had been there. She had had the guts to go public and take the celebrity edge off the drug cult. At fifty-two she looked better than she had at thirty-two, and even at her most drugged out she had always been a beauty.

"Coke is cheaper, purer, and more abundant than ever before. Doctors use it. Lawyers use it. Investment counselors use it. And God knows, senators use it. How else do you explain those votes on Salvador and Nicaragua? Coke keeps you awake, but contrary to popular belief, it does not make you smart, and it sure as hell doesn't help you lose weight."

There was laughter, and the star grinned back at her audience, but her violet eyes stayed serious.

"So what are you going to do the next time your host passes a mirror of flake at a sit-down dinner? Why not do what I do. Say 'Fuck you.' That's a good clear way of sending a *no* signal, and it's a sure way of not being invited back by assholes."

More laughter.

Cardozo's eye kept going back to Cordelia Koenig, tucked into the fifth row of folding chairs. She was glancing around to see who was arriving and who was leaving and who was watching whom.

The guard noticed Cardozo. He crossed to the doorway. "Can I see your card?"

Cardozo showed his shield.

The guard frowned and backed off.

The star lifted a tumbler of ice water from the card table and took a healthy swallow. Then she was into her homestretch.

"There are people who believe that Twelfth Avenue may have problems. A Hundred Third Street may have problems, but Fifth Avenue and Fifty-seventh Street will never have problems. Well, we know the problem is everywhere. Above all, it's right here. And we know where the answer is. Same place. God bless you all and thanks for listening to me—and keep coming back."

There was applause, which the star cut short.

Hands went up.

The star began taking comments from the floor.

The guard was pointing to his watch.

The star got to her feet. "Would those who care to please join me in the Lord's Prayer."

Cordelia kept looking around, not joining in the prayer.

The meeting broke up.

Cordelia's dress flashed like blue fire as she headed for the other exit. Cardozo quickly followed her slender back, the hollow between the shoulder blades where a cashmere tennis cardigan from C. Z. Guest's new collection dangled like a mauve flag.

She hurried down a flight of stairs, heels castanetting in the stone well. The side door of Saint Andrew's Protestant Episcopal Church slammed.

When Cardozo came out onto Fifty-third Street, the night was a dark bruise behind the skyline of Manhattan. She was sitting on the fender of a chauffeured BMW, chatting and laughing with friends.

Her head moved with easy humor, and her blond bangs swayed.

Cardozo interrupted. "Miss Koenig?"

Her gaze came up at him, pale blue and drop-deadish, as if he were no more to her than an autograph hunter.

"Can we talk privately?" He showed her his shield, making it clear this was official.

The others saw it too—the dark-haired girl with her Locust Valley lockjaw voice, the young man carrying an initialed pigskin briefcase and a squash racquet.

Silence fell like the slam of a coffin lid.

"What's this about?" Cordelia's voice was suddenly high-pitched and fluty.

He motioned her to step aside with him.

She slid silkily off the fender and, hesitating, followed him down the sidewalk, past double-parked limos to his double-parked Honda.

Across the sidewalk the glass silhouette of Beaux Arts Tower gleamed as if it had been dipped in black ink.

Cardozo opened the passenger door for her.

"Please get in. I need you to identify someone."

She looked at him with terrified child's eyes. "Has something happened? Oh my God, who is it?"

Cordelia's gaze wandered, straightforwardly appraising every *tchotchke* in the apartment. It was the gaze of a curious child still seeing the world for the first time.

Watching her—her every movement studied, every glance precise, the upward tilt of her head like a pharaoh's—Cardozo saw his home through her eyes—the down-scale, budget look of the fold-out sofa from Castro, the tables from the Sloan's closeout, the lace curtains from the latino bodegas on Fourteenth Street.

She had a special unguarded glance of disbelief for the painting of the Valley of Lourdes hanging over the TV.

Matisse, he had to admit, it was not.

"You live near Space," was her only remark.

Now she moved through the room like an actress on a film set, knowing where the light was, catching it exactly with her smile. She dropped easily into the overstuffed chair, as if it belonged to her.

"The way you were talking, I thought you were taking me to the morgue to see my mother's body."

"No, I want you to identify a man."

"Bring him out," she said cheerfully. She was like a chameleon— by turns defensive, childlike, and now ever so slightly flirtatious. She was a mirror giving him back what she thought he wanted.

"He's on tape," Cardozo said. "Would you like some coffee?"

"Have you got honey?"

"No."

"Then I'll have any kind of caffeine-free diet soda."

All the refrigerator had was nondiet 7-Up. Cardozo doubted her tastebuds would know the difference.

They didn't.

She sipped and smiled as he lowered blinds, turned down lights, and pressed the start button on the VCR remote.

Images came onto the screen, hazed as though with the passage of time. The walls of a room painted stark white. The black rectangles of closed shutters. The gracious curves of a Queen Anne chair. A table. A second chair.

A slim figure moved awkwardly into the frame. At first indistinct in the uncertain light, it suddenly resolved into a young girl.

She looked bizarre and beautiful and vulnerable in an ultrasophisticated silk gown. There was something touching and wild, endearing and silly about the way she wobbled on high heels—as though she had raided mommy's closet. Except the dress fitted. Fitted those fledgling twelve-year-old breasts perfectly.

She wore makeup—lashes and lipstick, additions to the perfection of youth that seemed garish because they were unnecessary, a mockery of nature. She wore diamond earrings and triple strands of pearls, probably courtesy of her mother, who probably didn't know she'd extended the courtesy.

The girl took off one earring. Licked it lingeringly. Placed it in an ashtray.

On the table beside the ashtray, neatly set out as though for a formal dinner, were a syringe, a small silver chafing dish, an eyedropper, a bowl of clear liquid, and several glassine envelopes of powder.

She took off the other earring and repeated the ritual.

There was no sound in the room but the buzzing of the VCR.

Cardozo watched Cordelia sitting there, alert in the flickering cone of light. He could smell her tingling state of puzzlement.

It was like meeting an old friend at an unexpected time and place, out of context—not at first recognizing them—taking a moment to remember that there's a thing called time, that it changes us, that the stranger we're looking at now could be the friend of years ago.

A spasm twitched the muscles of Cordelia's face, and at that instant Cardozo saw her recognize the little girl.

It was herself, seven years ago.

From the whiteness of her face he understood that she had had no idea any of this had been videotaped.

She felt his attention, glanced over, looked quickly away from him.

A man stepped gracefully into the picture on the TV screen. He wore evening clothes and a half mask, a domino, over his eyes. He could have been the Lone Ranger in a tux.

He began fondling the girl. He kissed her cheeks, her eyes, her forehead, her throat, each ear, and then brushed his lips against hers. Once, lightly. A second time, lingeringly.

Now, working with the unhurried care of a maître d' personally preparing crepes suzette for a favorite marchioness, the Lone Ranger readied the dope. He lit the flame in the chafing dish, melted the white powders down into a liquid, drew them up into the syringe.

Without prompting, the girl held out her arm.

He tied a length of rubber tubing around her forearm. A vein rose, delicately pulsing in the shaded crook.

He pressed the tip of the needle into the vein, slowly depressed the plunger, emptied the chamber into her bloodstream.

All the while she gazed at him with blank-faced adoration.

Over the next sixty seconds the dope took hold. A beat slipped into the girl's movements as she shed her awkwardness and shyness.

Her head tipped back invitingly. The man kissed her throat, his tongue passing over the milk-white patch faintly hollowed by a shadow. At the same time he undid the zipper down the back of the gown.

The silken fabric fell to the girl's waist. She wriggled, and the dress slid past her slender hips and lay in a shimmering puddle on the floor. She stepped out of it. She was wearing no undergarments.

There was only the faintest darkening of pubic hair at her crotch.

She reached up and unhooked the pearl necklace. Letting it slide slowly through her hands, she dropped it on the table.

The tip of her tongue appeared in the corner of her mouth.

She knelt.

First she took the man's right hand. She kissed his fingers, one at a time. Then the left hand. Same m.o.

Then she opened his fly, drew out his circumcised penis, manipulated him to erection. She began blowing him. It was a slick, experienced blowjob, like the work of a hooker who'd been at it for half her lifetime. Only there was real enthusiasm to it. The kid got a kick out of dick.

The man stepped back, erection wagging. He undressed, folding his clothes and laying them neatly on the Queen Anne chair, putting his shirt studs and cufflinks into the ashtray on the table.

His attention came back to the girl.

She tilted her face toward him. He drew her head up. She went on tiptoes, closing her eyes.

He swiftly covered her neck, her shoulders, in kisses. His lips moved more slowly over her mouth, her cheeks, her closed eyes. His hands softly stroked her throat, then went to her breasts, to the perfect pubescent nipples, teasing them to erectness.

His face dove and smothered the breast, his mask a slash of black like a knife wound across her flesh.

He lowered her into the chair, spread her thighs, and began intercourse.

The camera never blinked.

Cardozo froze the image with a little snap. He waited, letting the
silence widen.

Cordelia was in some sort of twilight, looking at the screen in a
musing way. Her face had become an unmoving mask, all expression
paralyzed: the only thing that showed was the emptiness in her eyes.

"Well?" he said, staring at her, not letting her look away.

She raised her eyebrows at his tone. "Well what?"

"Who's the man?"

She shifted and her dress made a silky sound. She lit a cigarette and
exhaled a plume of smoke. She sat gazing at him, not answering, an
impudently poised nineteen-year-old. Her eyes seemed to say, *I
make three hundred thousand a year on my own and I'll inherit
thirty million and I'm a New York Vanderwalk. Who the hell are
you?*

He sensed it was a performance, far from the truth of what she was
feeling.

"Are you threatening me?" she said.

"No."

"Good." She gathered up her cigarettes and silk purse. He could
feel her fighting her fear with a show of bravado. "I'm going to go
now," she said.

"No you're not. There's something else you're going to see."

He changed videocassettes.

The images shimmered, the only source of light in the darkened
room.

Her hand hovered like a hummingbird just above the arm of the
chair, and then she sank back, holding on to the arm very hard.

The tapes were a voyage to a very strange part of a country called
Hell.

Cordelia watched in utter stillness, a belt of moisture forming
across her forehead. Without warning she jumped and grabbed the
remote control from him and jammed off the picture.

"Who is he?" Cardozo shouted.

Her breath was coming in little shakes. The channel on the screen
began changing eratically.

"Those are human beings!" Cardozo screamed. "Ripped and gone,
like pages of last year's calendar, crumpled and tossed into the incin-
erator! And you think the man you're shielding is human? You think

he's even a man? Let me tell you something, he's not human, he's not a man, he's prehistoric slime!"

He twisted the remote control from her hand and flicked the cassette back on. He felt totally out of control, and what was more dangerous, he was enjoying the feeling.

"Some species survive because they taste horrible, because they're poisonous . . . because they have no predators." Cardozo thrust his thumb at the man frozen on the TV screen, gray skin pulled taut over his cheekbones, eyes behind the mask halfway to sockets. "He's one of them! Tell me that shithead's name! It's Monserat, isn't it! Your downstairs neighbor!"

Cardozo stood there, rage building up to critical mass, and she still didn't answer, and pumps began thudding in his skull.

"He gave you the insulin to inject your mother—didn't he! He taught you how to use a syringe—didn't he! And did you know he's a sadist and a necrophile, did he invite you to any of his parties where torture was the entertainment or a dead body was the guest of honor?" He stopped the picture. "You're lucky you're fucking alive, you know that?"

She spoke in a half whisper. "You're getting me very confused."

His eyes hooked hers and the resolve seemed to drain out of her.

"I was only a kid," she whispered.

"You're not a kid now."

"I didn't have anything to do with—those other things."

"Then stop shielding him."

He stared at her until she looked down.

"Why are you doing this to me? It wasn't my fault! I never had a chance!"

"You have a chance now."

Cordelia turned away and put a fist to her mouth. He could feel her breaking, and he had a sense of encroaching light as though he were on the very edge of hearing her say the man's name.

But her flow of emotion broke off, suddenly suspended.

He felt a third presence, a shape at the end of the dark entrance corridor. He followed the direction of Cordelia's gaze.

His daughter Terri had come into the room.

He felt a fist go into his heart. He didn't know how long she had stood there, how much she had seen or heard.

It may have been nothing more than the shock of the moment that made Terri look at him like that, a kid—sweet and thin, like a forlorn remnant of a doll—watching him with large sad injured eyes. He had a dizzying sense of levitation.

"Terri," he said, wanting to explain, wanting to apologize.

Cordelia brushed violently past him. There was a slam, and she was out the door, her heels clattering crazily down the stairs, and then came the deeper, more distant thud of the street door.

"Terri," he said.

The silence was spreading out too far, too fast.

"It's all right," she said.

There was something about her that seemed unsoiled. Cardozo realized that he knew nothing about this girl, this young woman, this daughter. He had no idea where she drew her strength from.

She came into the livingroom and flicked on a light, gazing at him. "Daddy, come here, you need someone to hug you."

50

"WE'VE GOT TO TALK." CORDELIA'S VOICE CAME OUT OF HER throat clogged, muffled. The hand holding the receiver was so shaky she had to steady it with the other hand, and her bracelets were rattling.

"This is such a volte-face." The deep voice flowed creamily across the line. "For months you avoid me, and now at the very moment I'm going out to dinner you have to see me."

"I haven't been avoiding you. I've just needed time to think."

"I'm glad you've completed your thinking."

"Look, I'm spooked. A friend of my mother's showed me some pictures and told me some really sick lies."

"What were these really sick lies?"

"About me—and you—and other people."

"Who is this friend of Babe's?"

"You've met him, that policeman she's seeing."

There was an instant's silence. "What was his purpose?"

"He wants me to tell him about you and me. And you."

"I wish you could be a little clearer about these lies."

"Not over the phone."

"Wait for me," he said. "Wait right there. I'll come as soon as I can get away from Tina's."

Cordelia was tired of waiting. The livingroom seemed oppressively soundless and empty and the figure in the mirror very small and alone.

She had to go walking. Just for a minute's breath.

She put on pink-dyed jeans and a man's Hawaiian shirt and a

Racquet and Tennis Club necktie loosely knotted, and oversized beads and earrings that were all wrong. That was to be the look tonight—all wrong.

She made herself a cup of instant coffee and looked in the refrigerator for the half-and-half. That was when her eye fell on the vials of crack.

No, she thought. *I've got six days in Cokenders. I'm not going to.*

She tipped half-and-half into her coffee and as she put it back she looked at the vials again and she knew it was going to happen.

She sipped her coffee and loaded up the crack pipe and smoked.

A sweet buzzing went up to her head and all her fears faded. After another vial of crack she felt centered, high-spirited, and reckless.

She went down into the street and walked through bubbling activity. A roar hung over Hudson Street. Traffic crawled and horns blared and pedestrians jaywalked as though they were exercising a constitutional right.

She walked south on Broadway. Bad images kept coming up in her head. Those people on the videotapes, screaming, begging, bleeding . . .

The more she thought about it the shakier she felt. She saw a phonebooth on the corner and she went to it and dialed her shrink's number.

She waited through three rings, hoping she wasn't going to get the machine.

A man passed the booth. He was in his mid-twenties, tall, dark. He was wearing Banana Republic safari trousers and a Mostly Mozart sweatshirt and he carried himself with a swagger. He turned as if he were surprised to see someone inside the phonebooth.

His mouth had a tough defiant twist, but looking at her his expression turned into a half smile. The half smile turned into a slowing stride, and the slowing stride turned into a full stop.

She shot him a glance from under her eyelids. He was a great-looking guy, just great.

"Hi," he said.

"Hi," she answered.

Cordelia handed back the pipe.

The young man sucked in a deep drag.

They were sitting on an unmade bed. He took her fingers. He massaged her knuckles with his thumb, then squeezed her palm and raised her fingertips to his mouth.

"Go down on me," he whispered.

She felt a skip in her heart. "Just a second." She reached onto the floor for her purse and took out the mask. "Put it on."

"What?"

"Please, just put it on."

"Sure—next Halloween."

He tossed the mask aside and in extremely slow motion he grasped the sides of her head with both hands. He pushed her down toward his cock.

"Come on, baby."

He was holding a coke inhaler in her nostril. She had a sudden medicinal rush in her nose, as if she had inhaled mouthwash.

She broke away and pulled up to sitting. "I'm sorry. I can't do it— unless you wear the mask."

He sat watching her. "You're bullshit, man."

She gathered up her clothes.

"What's with the fuckin' mask? Something wrong with my face?"

"Look, sometimes it doesn't work—nothing personal." She was aware that her voice was too clear, too loud for ordinary speech.

He settled himself in a chair, legs apart, cock dangling, hands clasped across his stomach. "I know who you are," he said. "I recognized you. You're bullshit."

"I was honestly moved by you," she said, "and then you made me feel embarrassed about the way I chose to respond to you. That wasn't necessary."

"That mask is kindergarten games. You're scared, man. I'll bet your daddy fucked you when you were a kid and that turned you off sex, right?"

She struck him. He struck her back instantly.

"Get out." He began pushing her.

She struggled and kicked, fighting him with everything that had built up inside her. He pulled the door open and shoved her into the hall.

The door slammed.

"I personally know very few people who would spend two thousand dollars for the dubious privilege of dancing on the same floor as Jacqueline Onassis," Lucia Vanderwalk said. She was sitting at Gwennie Tiark's dinner table, and she was talking to Ambassador Post, whose wife was rumored to have just left him. "It shows a blatant disrespect for the value of money, don't you think?"

"But if it's for charity—" the ambassador said.

"Rubbish. Charity is visiting the wards, not devouring quail."

A maid came to the dinner table and whispered to Lucia.

"What a bother." Lucia glanced at her diamond pavé and gold-faced dinner watch on its black satin band. "A phone call for me."

"Have them call later," Gwennie Tiark said.

"Apparently it's an emergency. Excuse me."

Lucia pushed herself up to her feet and followed the maid past the circular marble staircase, down a mirrored, plush hallway. Gwennie Tiark's Fifth Avenue duplex apartment had once belonged to the Rockefellers, and Billy Baldwin had completely redecorated it. The rooms had good detail—parquetry and carved lintels and mullioned windows—but Lucia thought the Titian was a little showy and large for the library wall and totally the wrong color.

The maid handed her the telephone.

"Yes?" Lucia said.

"Mrs. Vanderwalk?"

"To whom am I speaking?"

"This is Dr. Flora Vogelsang."

Oh dear, Lucia thought. "Yes, Doctor?"

"I'm sorry to interrupt your dinner, but I've had a sad and very distressing call from Cordelia. Although I don't approve of capitulating to her manipulations, in this case I feel she needs help."

Cordelia stumbled through the doorway at the rear of the restaurant.

A black-tie gala was in full swing.

Cordelia kept one hand extended in front of her, as though searching for a wall. Her disheveled hair cascaded over her eyes and she was walking a very slow, very deliberate zigzag.

When Babe turned and saw her daughter, her hand—holding a champagne glass—froze.

Cordelia's hip struck a table. The little candelabra with delicate rose-printed lampshades almost toppled, and Cordelia fell face-forward.

"Excuse me," Babe apologized to Henry Kissinger.

Cordelia broke loose from the waiter who had helped her up. She dashed through the bar and stumbled down three marble steps.

Babe had to elbow her way. "Excuse me—excuse me."

Cordelia came to a dead end, a wall of plum Lalique glass. She dropped onto a sofa and sat trembling, arms locked around her knees.

Babe came into the little room. "Cordelia," she said.

Cordelia looked up. Her face twisted.

"What is it?" Babe sat beside her. She saw tears in her daughter's eyes. She hugged Cordelia to her. "Tell me."

Cordelia dropped her head into her hand. "Forgive me."

"Forgive you what, darling? There's nothing to forgive."

"There is. There is."

Lucia came into the restaurant.

A man in a butler's cutaway asked for her invitation. She waved him aside, saying it was quite all right, she wouldn't be needing one.

She took three steps toward the crowd. Festivities appeared to have accelerated to a full tilt. Peering, she saw her daughter and granddaughter.

She came into the room without a sound and settled into a seat. "So here we all are. The three sisters." She asked Cordelia, "Are you all right, my dear? I was worried."

Cordelia rose shakily from the sofa. "Yes, Grandmère, I'm fine. I'm going to go home."

"Yes, do go home. Rest. Take a taxi." Lucia opened her purse and handed her granddaughter two fifty-dollar bills.

"Thanks, Grandmère. G'night."

Cordelia kissed Lucia and threw a glance back at her mother.

Babe started after her.

"Don't go yet," Lucia said. "We have to talk."

"Mama, I—"

Lucia stared without comment at Babe's strapless pink satin Lanvin. "Sit!"

Babe froze in her tracks. Obedience consumed her. "Mama, please. I can't let Cordelia run off like that."

"Cordelia is precisely the reason I am here." Lucia regarded Babe steadily for a moment. "I've just spoken to her psychiatrist and she's very near clinical depression."

Babe sank onto the sofa. "I didn't know Cordelia had a psychiatrist."

"I'm sure there are many things about your daughter you've never bothered to know."

Babe struggled to control herself. "Never bothered to know? You never told me!"

"And why should I have played go-between? It was your job to be close to your daughter, to share her trust and confidence. Under normal circumstances the relationship is built up over time. It's called love."

"What are you saying?" Babe stared at the judgment blazing in her mother's eyes. She felt a rush of injustice. "Because I was sick, because I wasn't there, I didn't love my daughter? I refuse to be made guilty for something that was in no way my fault!"

"Who's discussing fault? Who's discussing guilt?"

"You are! You're heaping it on me! You're sitting there in your first tier box, reveling in this drama!"

"I'm hardly reveling. I'm deeply concerned when I see someone I love suffering the way that child is suffering."

Babe stared at this woman, her mother, and a wound so deeply buried in her, so silted over that it was almost mute, came gradually to the surface, taking on words. "Do you really love Cordelia? Or is loving her just another way of not loving me?"

"Not loving you! I cared for you for seven interminable years! I kept you alive when half the specialists in the country were saying, 'Pull the plug, let her die.' How many mothers would have done that?"

"A million! What no mother would have done is hold back information affecting my daughter's health and happiness!"

"How could we have told you? You'd let too much go wrong for too long. There were limits to the strain we could put you under."

"That excuse seems to cover your every deception. You kept me in the hospital when there was no need for it. You lied about how I got there. And it was always to save me from strain. Well, give me your strain and spare me your saving!"

"Someone had to defend you."

"From what?"

"The consequences of the life you led before your illness."

"There's nothing wrong with the life I've led."

"Your exalted opinion of yourself is obviously not shared by the person who tried to murder you."

Babe felt amazement wash the colors from her face. "You think I *deserved* an attempt on my life?"

"You lived in such a way as to make misfortune inevitable. You ignored your husband, and he turned against you. You ignored your daughter, and she developed severe emotional problems."

"Her problems are my doing?"

"Your lack of doing."

Tears stung Babe's eyes, tears she hadn't even known were pooling there, ready to betray her. "All right. Maybe I didn't do enough. I'm sorry."

"As if that was any help."

"Mama, I'm not the person I was then."

"How so?"

"I've changed. There *are* experiences in life that change a person."

Lucia sighed. "Beatrice, you have a habit that truly tests my patience. It's when you turn righteous and saccharine like that. You spout a blend of Sigmund Freud and Norman Vincent Peale that is quite your own. They were both fine men in their day, but this *is* almost the end of the century, even if you have managed to sleep through most of the decade. In my opinion your seven-year nap has in no way transformed you. You are the person you always were. As is Cordelia. She's had to be in arduous psychotherapy for many, many years. They call her a borderline personality. It's a technical term. She's struggling against terrific emotional odds and you have never helped. You are not helping now, and quite frankly I don't believe you ever will be able to help."

"How do you expect me to help something I'm not even told about?"

"What do you need to be *told*? If a car breaks down you don't wait to be taught the principles of internal combustion. You see the trouble and you take the car to a good garage and you get it repaired."

"Cordelia is not a car. She's my daughter."

"And she is my granddaughter. And I want you to give your father and me custody."

A wave of rage swept over Babe, tightening her throat. "I can't *believe* you said that."

"Do speak in a normal voice," Lucia said.

Determination came to Babe like an electric bolt. She rose and walked to the door.

Lucia reached out and with one braceleted arm blocked Babe's way. "We haven't finished."

"But we have finished, Mama. The answer is no, never." Babe thrust her mother's arm away.

There was a phone in the coatcheck room. Babe lifted the receiver and punched out the digits of Cordelia's number. She waited while the call clicked through.

She could hear Cordelia's phone buzzing. She counted seven rings. The machine answered.

"Cordelia," she said, "if you're there please pick up."

No one picked up. She broke the connection and dialed Vince Cardozo's direct line.

His voice answered. "Cardozo."

"Vince—it's not a police matter, but—"

"You're not talking to the police, you're talking to me. Tell me about it."

She told him and he listened.

"Babe," he said in a calm voice, "this isn't your fault. Cordelia's a statistic waiting to happen. If we're lucky she's on her way to her place. What's her address?"

Babe gave it to him.

"Go there. If she's not home, wait for me. I'll meet you in fifteen minutes. I'm leaving right now."

51

CARDOZO DISCOVERED IT WAS A MISTAKE TO HAVE DRIVEN WEST on Prince.

Traffic was barely moving; double-parkers clogged the lanes, and partying yuppies sat on fenders with plastic wineglasses from somebody's art opening. In three minutes he covered half a block, and then the congestion brought him to a standstill at the intersection. A sign was hanging from one of the corner buildings: FOOD. He'd read about the restaurant; it served nonsteroid chicken and all-organic tofu fruit pies.

Through the plate glass window he saw Cordelia Koenig, in jeans and a Hawaiian shirt, sitting alone at a table with a plate of pie.

He pulled in behind a double-parked, empty Mercedes whose horn and front lights were blasting and flashing in sync. He put his police card in the window.

Cordelia brushed her hair off her forehead and looked up as he approached.

"What's your phone number?" he said.

She told him and he went to the payphone and dialed and got a busy signal. He waited a minute and tried again. Still busy. He came back and sat at the table and looked at her.

"You didn't know he was taping you, did you," he said.

She shook her head.

"Why do you think he made those films?"

"I don't know," she said softly.

"He made them to show to other people. He's not protecting your secret, Cordelia, so why are you protecting him?"

"I don't have a secret."

"But you think you have. You really believe no one besides you and that lunatic knows what you did seven years ago."

Babe saw from the street that there was no light in Cordelia's apartment. Either Cordelia was on her way home, or already asleep.

Babe used her key to get into the apartment.

She turned on the light.

She looked in the bedroom. Empty.

She went into the kitchen and searched cabinets and made herself coffee. She saw from the cup in the sink that Cordelia had already made coffee that evening.

She sat in the livingroom, waiting for her coffee to cool.

A mirror hung on the wall opposite her. Something in its glow, some movement, caught her eye.

She saw the reflection of a man.

He was walking slowly and deliberately out of the motionless darkness. He stopped beneath a flood of overhead light, letting the light and shadow play over his close-cropped hair and staring eyes, his strong bare arms hanging from the sleeveless Levi's jacket.

There was something proud and brutal and dangerous in the way he stood there, the cords of his neck drawn taut, his eyes taking hold of her.

She recognized the face gradually: Claude Loring, the man she had wanted to draw, the man charged with murder who had shouted at her.

His pupils were huge, blue dazzles of light whirling around on themselves.

She stood slowly. "What are you doing here?"

"I'm sorry." His voice was pleasant. "It's nothing personal, but I have to kill you."

He was standing between her and the front door.

She was absolutely unmoving for a moment. She gauged his strength and his madness and realized she had at best a little courage, a little cleverness to muster against him.

She whirled before he could react and she sped through the hallway into the bedroom, flinging the door shut and twisting the key in the lock. She ran to the phone.

Her lungs were pulling in ragged breaths.

There was no dial tone. She jiggled the cradle. The line was dead. She stared at the receiver disbelievingly. She realized Loring had yanked the cord from the wall.

"Jesus," she gasped.

She ran to the bedroom window and snapped the Levolors open. The windows were dark across the airshaft. There were lights on two floors below, but rock music was screeching into the night and there was no chance anyone would hear her if she yelled for help.

A crash whirled her around. The bedroom door shot open, smashing into the wall.

Babe froze.

Loring stood panting, silhouetted in the doorframe. His right hand held a sledge hammer.

Lifted on a jolt of panic, Babe dashed into the bathroom, flinging the door shut and jamming the bolt into place. She stepped back, her eyes fixed on the door, realizing it offered at the outside no more than thirty seconds' protection.

A crash filled the brightly tiled space around her. Jars and bottles chattered on the bathtub shelf. The panels of the door buckled and parted and the gray head of the sledgehammer jutted through, swung back, forced deeper entry.

The realization shot through Babe that her one chance was to go outside.

The window lock had been painted shut and she had to jab the paint loose with a nail file from the cabinet.

Behind her, with each deafening smash, the hammer widened the breach.

She shoved the window up and crouched on the ledge. Holding to the window with one hand, she swept through the dark with the other. Another wall of the building ran at right angles to the bathroom and her fingers contacted wood. It was a cutting board propped on its edge, holding the livingroom window open.

She reached one foot for the other ledge, found it, shifted her center of gravity out over the airshaft. She grabbed the livingroom window and pulled herself through. She could feel brick scrape through her gown.

At that instant she heard the door panel give in the bathroom.

Loring had switched off the lights in the livingroom. She fell down from the window into darkness. Her foot caught on a table leg and the table went crashing to the floor.

She raced across the livingroom and pulled at the front door. She remembered putting her purse on the chair by the door. She felt for it, found it, wrestled again with the knob.

The door flew open with the third yank.

She darted into the corridor, slammed the door. She rummaged in her purse, found the key, locked the deadbolt.

That would give her another ten seconds. If he didn't have a key, maybe another sixty tops.

She ran down the corridor and pushed the elevator button. She could see from the floor indicator that the elevator was climbing up from the ground floor.

She heard Loring pulling at the front door of the apartment, and then she heard the hammer crashing.

She pulled at the door of the fire stairs next to the elevator. It was unlocked. She shot into the stairway. The only light bulb was on the landing below, and she slipped in the dark. Her high-heeled shoe twisted beneath her, sending a sickening wrench up through her calf.

Her balance was gone. She lunged forward, fell three concrete steps, managed to catch the steel railing.

She pulled herself upright. Burning pain was shooting through her ankle. She took off her shoes. Clutching purse and high heels, she scrambled down the stairs to the next landing.

She dashed into the corridor. The indicator showed that the elevator was still rising, just passing the second floor.

She stood jabbing a finger at the call button. She heard Loring break through the door upstairs, and then the thudding of his workboots across the floor.

She sped back to the fire stairs. She ran down another flight to four and into the corridor.

The indicator showed the elevator still climbing, passing three now. She pushed the call button.

The elevator came to a stop.

Making as little sound as possible, Babe drew the elevator door open. She reached for the grill and attempted to pull it aside. It refused to yield.

She hammered at the grill with the heel of her shoe.

Finally, taking its time, the grill opened.

She slipped into the elevator. There was no light and the walls were covered in heavy industrial bunting.

She tried to yank the grill shut. Again, it was automatically timed and there was no way she could speed it. She began jamming buttons —*down* and *close* and *emergency call* and *floor one.* The grill slowly closed and the elevator cable shuddered.

She could hearing Loring two floors above, hear the staticky clicks of his finger on the call button.

The elevator hesitated between the up and down calls—and then with a thin screaming sound it began lumbering downward at a maddeningly unhurried speed.

Babe heard footsteps crashing down the stairs, doors slamming.

The elevator crawled to three, and she glimpsed Loring's face as he peered through the elevator door and then dove into the stairwell. His workboots thunked down the concrete steps. The elevator dropped past three.

And suddenly he was there, swinging his hammer, shattering an opening in the elevator door. The sledgehammer crashed through the breach. The gate began buckling.

The elevator continued its downward crawl past two. The hammering suddenly stopped.

As the elevator reached the first floor, Loring darted into view. The sledgehammer struck two battering blows at the door.

Babe pressed her weight on the up button, trying desperately to reverse the elevator's direction.

She searched frenziedly through her purse for some object of defense. She had nothing.

Babe dropped her purse.

Loring yanked the door open and slammed the grill aside.

His face was inhumanly twisted.

Babe held her shoes in front of her, toes out.

He lifted the sledgehammer, and twenty pounds of raw iron arced through space.

Babe ducked.

The hammer smashed into the wall behind her, ripping down bunting, then lifted again.

With the toes of both shoes angled directly at his eyes, Babe thrust.

As Cardozo and Cordelia entered the building there was a buzzing sound of voices. A small crowd stood in the hallway. At first they seemed to be the overflow of some party, chatting, and Cardozo half expected to see that they were holding glasses of wine.

But one of the men was holding up Babe Devens.

Her hair was tangled across her face and her evening dress was ripped. She stretched out a hand to Cardozo. The hand held a shoe, held it tightly, like a weapon. There was blood on the toe.

Cardozo opened his arms and she stepped in against him and he hugged her. Then Babe put both hands on Cordelia's head and kissed her.

"What happened?" Cardozo said.

A professorial man in his late forties stepped forward. "I saw it." He was gray-haired with a world-battered, intellectual sort of look, wearing an open-necked shirt and blazer. "A madman was going at her with a sledgehammer. If we hadn't walked in when we did, he would have smashed her head open."

"It was Loring." Babe's breathing steadied. "He was waiting upstairs."

"Are you okay?" Cardozo asked.

"Okay now," she said, but there was a look in her eyes and it was light-years away from okay.

Cardozo took Cordelia and Babe up in the elevator to the sixth floor. A hole had been hammered in the apartment door and splintered wood littered the hallway. He pushed the door open.

The structural columns in the apartment glowed in the light coming through the windows. He flicked the light switch. Half the furniture in the room had been shattered.

"My God," Cordelia whispered, and put her hands to her face.

"He was waiting here to kill you, Cordelia," Cardozo said. "You, not your mother. And you know who sent him."

52

LUCINDA MACGILL, TALL AND SLIM, CARRIED HERSELF FROM THE car to the doorway with a purposeful stride. "Do you have any idea what this is all about?"

"Vince told me to find you." Monteleone leaned his thumb on the buzzer. "That's all I know." His pale, heavy-jawed face stared impatiently between the bars of the wrought-iron grill.

A moment later Cardozo opened the town house door. He looked agitated. "Glad you're both here. I appreciate it."

He took MacGill and Monteleone upstairs to a room with cherry-wood paneling. Lucinda MacGill glanced at the French impressionists on the wall.

"Your surroundings have improved, Lieutenant."

"Thanks. Have a seat."

MacGill sat down in a silk upholstered bentwood chair and surveyed Cardozo with a steady eye.

"Let me just give you some idea what's coming down," Cardozo said. "I have two very nervous ladies in the next room. Tonight an attempt was made on the life of one of them, but it was meant for the other. You know the mother, Babe Devens. She's the one who almost got taken out. I don't think you know the daughter, Cordelia Koenig. Cordelia has been through a lot. A *lot*. She's at the breaking point, and she's ready to tell us just about everything we need to make an indictment. Is your tape recorder loaded, Counselor?"

Lucinda MacGill slid her Panasonic out of her purse. "With a ninety-minute tape."

"We're going to need every inch of it. Let's go." Cardozo showed the way to the room next door.

Cordelia was sitting on the deep plush sofa, not moving, tensed, her eyes fixed on the green marble fireplace with its brass griffin and irons. Babe was sitting in the chair beside her daughter, and she shifted nervously while Cardozo made introductions.

Lucinda MacGill adjusted herself in a comfortable chair. Her eyes took in the dark oak paneling, the oyster-colored silk curtains, the Boesendorfer concert grand piano. Bowls of cut roses and gardenias lightly scented the air.

"Anytime you're ready, Cordelia," Cardozo said.

Lucinda MacGill started her tape recorder.

Cordelia seemed to lose herself for a moment, blinking and gazing around the room as though she had gone to sleep somewhere else and just woken up in a place she'd never seen before. When she finally spoke, her words had a once-removed, hearsay quality, as if everything she was describing had happened way offstage to someone else.

"We started making love when I was eleven. I didn't really know about sex and I didn't know what we were doing and I didn't know he was filming it. He gave me drugs. He said he loved me. He said we'd get married when I was sixteen."

Her uninflected tone told of a life of anguish and solitude, a life so screwed up that there had never been any point not screwing it up further.

"He said Mother would be drunk that night and so would Scottie. All I'd have to do would be to go into the bedroom and put the needle into her arm and empty the syringe. My mother and stepfather came home drunk and they passed out. I went into their bedroom and I put the needle into my mother's arm."

Babe was sitting there, erect and slender against the back of her chair, looking at her daughter with eyes that were wide and pained.

"I only gave her half the dose," Cordelia said.

"Just a minute," Lucinda MacGill said. "You did what?"

"I gave her half." Cordelia blinked hard and a confused frown made tiny lines in her face. "I don't know why. I guess I couldn't kill her all the way."

Lucinda MacGill rose. "Miss Koenig, don't say another word to me or to Lieutenant Cardozo or to Detective Monteleone or to any member of the police force or district attorney's office."

Cardozo's head snapped back into a disbelieving stare. "What the hell are you pulling?"

"Lieutenant," Lucinda MacGill said, "we need to have a word."

He followed her into the hallway.

"It's tainted." Lucinda MacGill spoke with flat finality, sliding the glass-paneled door shut behind them. "Nothing that girl says is admissible."

"You got to be crazy."

"Cordelia is confessing to the attempted murder of her mother. Her evidence is self-incriminating. She should be represented by counsel when she talks to the police." Lucinda MacGill's manner was precise, unexcited, unemotional. The perfect justice machine. "No counsel on earth would permit her to make those statements."

"She chooses to waive her goddamn rights."

Lucinda MacGill's eyes said Vince Cardozo was an idiot. "You can read her her Miranda twelve times and she can waive her rights thirteen times, she's still got to have a lawyer because otherwise this is not going to be allowed as evidence in *any* court of law."

"We're not indicting *her* for Christ's sake! We're going after the man who seduced her and gave her that syringe."

"Has she told you his name?"

"Not yet."

"Good. Don't let her tell you."

"I *want* to know his name. I want to nail him. That's why I got you here."

"You got me here and I'm spelling it out to you. Do this the right way, Vince."

"What the hell is this, a minuet?"

"You're dealing with an emotionally unstable girl—I know she's young, I assume she's unstable. Legally, she's doubly incompetent. If all you've got is her testimony, and her testimony involves one word of what I just heard, get her a lawyer right now. Otherwise the D.A. won't touch this megillah and your criminal's going to walk." She continued to fix Cardozo with a burning gaze. "I'm sorry. Whoever he is, he sounds like a real louse, but even if he doesn't live under the law, we do."

"Lucinda," Cardozo said wearily, "what you're not grasping is the human cost—the contamination this guy is leaving in his path."

"Believe me, Vince, I do get the picture."

There was no point going straight home. Cardozo knew he was too furious to sleep. He stopped off at the precinct.

He poured himself a coffee. It must have been sitting in the pot since 3 A.M. of the day before. His first sip added to his sense that his life was not only unreal but disgusting.

He went to his cubicle. There were four new directives from the PC's office. He sailed them over to the open file cabinet drawer. They plopped on top of last week's.

Now he was staring at a flyer that someone had put on his desk: MADAME ROBERTA—FORTUNES TOLD—ASTRAL READINGS

He was about to crumple it when he saw handwriting on the back: *Vince C., call Faye.* He went to the door.

"Who the hell is Faye?"

"She said you know her," Sergeant Goldberg answered.

"You took this message, Goldberg? There's no date, there's no time, there's no last name, there's no number."

"Hire a secretary," Sergeant Goldberg grumbled.

Cardozo could think of only one Faye—Loring's friend Faye di Stasio. He got the number from Information and dialed. On the seventh ring a clouded voice said hello.

"Faye? This is Lieutenant Vince Cardozo. You phoned me?"

"You asked me to keep an eye out for Claude. He's set up a coke buy—tonight, two A.M., outside the Inferno."

"Who's he selling to?"

"Me."

Claude Loring held his arms and rubbed them: the weather was growing too cool for a sleeveless Levi's jacket. Faye di Stasio followed him to the van parked across Ninth Avenue from the entrance to the Inferno.

Claude reached into the glove compartment and took out the little black paper bag. Faye dug into her pocket and pulled out a roll of twenties.

There was a pinging sound like a pebble striking a hub cap. Claude spun around.

"Freeze." A man stood there, holding out a gold shield. "Lieutenant MacFinney, narcotics."

Claude whirled and ran. Another cop stepped out from behind a parked Chevy, gun drawn. "You heard the man, Claude."

Claude stopped in his tracks. A cinderblock was forming in his stomach. The cop knew Claude's name. It was a setup—had to be.

"It's not my coke, it's hers." Claude pointed. "Faye di Stasio, she's a dealer, I was holding for her."

The cop who'd said his name was MacFinney turned around. "Faye—go and sin no more."

Faye stumbled into the darkness.

"Open the bag," MacFinney said.

Claude opened the bag.

The other cop came forward, dangling a pair of handcuffs. "Up against the wall, fella."

Claude turned himself toward the wall. There were two clicks and he felt the icy burn of metal against his wrists. The cops steered him to an unmarked car. Another cop was sitting inside in plainclothes. Recognition hit Claude like a slap.

Vince Cardozo slid over to make room. "We have to discuss a few matters with you, Claude. Possession with intent to sell and a homicide you attempted two nights ago."

"I want to see my lawyer."

"You don't need a lawyer. It's not you we're after. Tell us who sent you to kill Cordelia Koenig."

"I was at the Inferno talking to a guy with a green mohawk." Claude Loring had a chain smoker's rasp to his voice. "Then Jodie Downs came up and started butting in and being real obnoxious and I thought okay, punk, you just won the lottery, you're it. I took him up to the van to smoke some crack and after that first hit he was mine. I told him I knew where we could get some more crack, and I took him up to Monserat's party pad. I was the scout for Lew's parties —I dug up the entertainment."

"What kind of entertainment?" Cardozo said.

"People. Kids, guys, girls. Dead bodies."

Lucinda MacGill was usually a bright, self-possessed young woman, but her upturned face stared at Loring in horror. "Where'd you get the dead bodies?" she asked.

"Monserat had a deal with a funeral home."

"What funeral home?"

Claude Loring named a well-known funeral home. "They'd loan him the stiffs overnight. He paid two, three hundred dollars per body. He paid more for the dead bodies than for the living. I got a hundred for every guest I delivered. And all the drugs I wanted."

"Were people tortured at these parties?" Cardozo said.

"The dead bodies we had to be careful with, because they had to look good from the neck up, you never knew who was open casket. But the people who weren't dead, sometimes they got roughed up.

Monserat says the way you get to the soul of another person is when you produce panic in them. You have someone there at your mercy and they're panicked, think they could die any moment and it's completely up to you, how you flip a coin."

"Sounds like it excited you too," Cardozo said.

"Yeah, it excited me. Everyone was getting off on everyone else getting off. Like a circle jerk."

A blank, almost disgusted incredulity showed in Lucinda MacGill's face.

"Anyone ever get killed at these parties?" Cardozo asked.

Loring had to think for a moment. "Not that I recall."

"Where did the black bondage hood come from?"

"It was Monserat's. It was a work of art, he used to say. Anyone who wore it became a masterpiece. He said masks were the real reality. He had lots of masks—different types—Halloween masks, joke store masks. But the bondage mask was special."

"Special how?"

"That mask was reserved for the victims. If Jodie Downs hadn't been wearing that mask I could never have hurt him. I'm a gentle guy, I don't hurt people. But once Jodie had the mask on, for me he wasn't human anymore. He turned into something else. When I looked at him in that mask five percent of me said he was a man and ninety-five percent of me said he was a monster. That mask had a nightmare look. Like anyone wearing it would cut your head off if you gave them the chance. They had to be killed. It was self-defense —you or them."

Claude Loring flexed his hands nervously. Sitting in his jeans and I LOVE NEW YORK T-shirt, he looked taller than his six feet two, huge and rawboned, and those hands looked as though they could snap a human neck as easily as a celery stalk.

"Tell us who was at the party that night," Cardozo said.

Claude Loring named names. Lucinda MacGill took notes.

"Who was wearing drag?" Cardozo asked.

"Two, three of them. That Duncan creep, Sir Dunk—he was wearing one of his wife's red dresses—real glitzy number, shimmer and shimmy."

"Was he wearing lipstick?"

"The works, rouge from his eyeballs down to his jowls. Believe me, some guys should not do drag. It's beyond grotesque."

"Was Duncan Canfield smoking?"

"Yeah, he smoked."

"Cigarettes?"

"Cigarettes, pot, crack."

"Did he put out a cigarette in Jodie Downs's hand?"

"Yeah, and it was weird, Jodie hated it but liked it, Jodie held on to that cigarette, he was moaning like he was coming."

"Was Jodie killed at the party?"

"No—he was cut, but not killed."

"Describe how he got killed."

"It was my job to dump the merchandise after the parties. If it was a dead body, I'd truck it back to the funeral home. If it was a kid, I'd take them back to where they were staying, pay them off. I was supposed to take the mask off Jodie and take him back home. But he was calling me a dumb fag and a lot of things—so I decided Jodie, you're a two-time winner, and I took him to Beaux Arts Tower to have a scene alone with him. We smoked some more crack and Jodie kept saying 'Do it, do it.' "

"What did he mean, 'Do it'?"

"Kill him. You have to understand—I was on crack. And he was asking for it, begging for it. So I choked him."

Claude Loring mopped his face with a red-checked handkerchief.

"After Jodie was dead I guess I panicked."

"Because you'd killed him," Lucinda MacGill said.

"Because I'd killed him and I was out of crack and I needed to keep going. There I was with this body in this evil mask and what the shit was I going to do? Talk about drawing a complete blank—I knew I had to get a second wind, get it together, I couldn't just sit there with this body scaring the bejeezus out of me. And then I remembered my coke dealer was on duty at the front door."

"Hector," Cardozo said.

Loring nodded. "Son of a bitch didn't want to let me have any. But I pushed his buttons and he let me have a lid. I snorted it and then it was like no problems. I saw what I had to do—cut the body up and drop the pieces in different garbage chutes. There was a saw up on seventeen, they were remodeling up there. So I started to cut him up and I got one leg off and it was really hard work, and I was beat, so I thought, okay, time off. I was planning to come back in a few hours, but I passed out."

He began sobbing.

"I hate myself and I hate what I did. But it's like it wasn't me. Monserat gave me drugs and once I was high I was like a dog on a chain. Wherever Monserat wanted me to go I would go. I tried to fight, but I guess I was really weak."

Now he was playing the cocker spaniel, all soft and appealing, with great big blue eyes, begging for understanding.

The spring in the swivel chair groaned as Cardozo leaned forward. "Okay, Claude, that will be it for now."

Greg Monteleone took Loring back to the lockup.

Lucinda MacGill was shaking, a survivor who had barely made it across the border of the damned. She had to plant the soles of her shoes on the floor until she was steady, and then she stood.

"How are you?" Cardozo asked.

"Older," she said. "You think you know all about the unbelievable. And then you hear a story like that and your brain wants to shut down."

"Loring is willing to repeat all that in exchange for immunity."

"From what? He's already been convicted of killing Downs."

"He can still be tried for dealing crack. For assaulting Babe Devens with intent to kill."

Cardozo felt the cool, deliberate touch of Lucinda MacGill's attention.

"Loring's claim that Lewis Monserat sent him to kill Cordelia Koenig—that bothers me," she said. "Do you believe him?"

"Damned right I do. You don't?"

Her expression was concerned, serious. "Loring could be saving his own skin."

"He's got no reason to go after Cordelia or her mother. It's got to be Monserat."

"Why? You say Monserat wanted Babe dead and Scott Devens convicted so Cordelia would inherit and he'd marry her and get control. . . .I don't know, Vince. He's forty years older."

"And money's money. And Monserat loves money. And Cordelia loved Monserat. He gave her drugs. He gave her strokes when no one else was giving her anything. You heard her last night. She *wanted* to marry him."

MacGill's eyes were a cool, boiling green. "Legally, Loring is just as useless as Cordelia. What you've got is two attempts to murder Babe Devens and the unsupported testimony of two confessed would-be murderers. Loring claims Monserat put him up to it, and you claim Monserat put Cordelia up to it, and what Cordelia claims we're not going to know till she gets a lawyer. But she's a drug addict and barely legal age, and Loring is a drug addict and a convicted killer.

You can't even bring Monserat in for *questioning* on evidence like that. Morgenstern will crucify you."

"What if we just take portions of Cordelia's statement?" Cardozo said. "The sexual acts with Monserat while she was underage and the drugs he provided her?"

"Vince," Lucinda MacGill said, "I spent last night saving you from that. It's not going to hold up."

"What about the kiddie porn?"

"He's masked in all the films you showed me. Unless you're holding some footage back, you haven't got an ID."

"Cordelia will come around," Cardozo said. "She'll ID him."

"And all you'll have then is the same uncorroborated, totally inadmissible statement you began with." Lucinda MacGill sighed.

"She was there, for God's sake," Cardozo said, belligerent now.

Lucinda MacGill's eyes reached out patiently. "She was a child, she was drugged, it was seven years ago. She absolutely has to be corroborated."

"The videotapes are corroboration," Cardozo said.

"I wouldn't be in such a rush to use those tapes. They show drug use, which impeaches Cordelia's judgment and memory, and they show sodomy, which impeaches her character and credibility. The tapes might not even be allowed into evidence if the court rules that she can't waive self-incrimination. And if it can be proved the tapes are seven years old, they get Monserat off, because the statute of limitations on the offenses has run."

"Jesus Christ," Cardozo muttered.

"The long and the short of it is, the sex and drug charges are going to backfire. So forget them."

"So how do we get to Monserat?" Cardozo said.

"I'm fresh out of bright ideas," Lucinda MacGill said.

Out in the squad room, the television had been moved onto the Mr. Coffee table. It was the bottom of the eighth. The count was three and two. The Mets had men on second and first. The St. Louis Cardinals were ahead by one run. A shout went up from the detectives as Gary Carter struck a two-base hit.

Cardozo felt a sharp dagger of pain behind his eyes.

"Vince, stop making faces as though I'm the one who makes up these laws."

"You're the one who keeps springing them on me."

"That's my job."

"Monserat tried to kill Cordelia. He's going to try again."

"Then give her a guard. Vince, you can't bring him in on Loring's evidence. Be realistic. Loring is a felon, a convict. He'd do anything for his next hit of coke. He's tainting some very important people. You hear a lot of those names in real estate and arbitrage and junk bonds and corporate takeovers and restructurings and political fund-raising."

"You're saying because these people are tied in with money, with real estate, with politicians, because they have dinner with the Rockefellers and get photographed with Brooke Astor, they can't be touched? The city's bombing out socially and economically, but so long as there's gold to be made playing three-card monte with the ruins, it's okay to chop up anybody you want and jack off over the videotape?"

"You're saying that, not me. What's this thing you've got? Poor people commit murder too. It's not just the rich."

"Poor people don't have Ted Morgenstern. They get caught."

"Loring had Ted Morgenstern. He got off with two months."

"I don't care about Loring. He's a windup doll. I care about that fuck of an art dealer."

"Ease off, Vince."

He thumped a hand against the desk. A drawer splintered. "I don't believe what this city's become. This used to be my home. Now you need ten million for openers in this city."

"What the hell has that got to do with anything? You're off on a tangent, Vince."

They were screaming at one another now.

"You bet I'm on a tangent." Cardozo snatched up the phone and punched out a number. Over the noise of the ball game a phone rang in the squad room. "Greg—I want you and Siegel and Malloy to tail Monserat. Round the clock. I want a tap on his phone. I want to know where he goes, who he talks to, and I don't want him near Cordelia Koenig."

When he hung up, MacGill's eyes were waiting for his, narrowed and concerned. "You can't do that."

"Screw can't," he said.

53

"I NEVER THOUGHT I'D SPEND A NIGHT IN THIS HOUSE AGAIN."
Cordelia's voice came wonderingly across the room.

Babe looked up and smiled. "It's like the old days to have you back
—even if it's only till the carpenters put up your walls again."

The two of them had been sitting there for over an hour. At first
they had talked, and then, yielding to a sort of insinuating gravity,
they had let the faint fingers of drizzle against the windows lull them
into increasingly longer silences.

"Strange," Cordelia said. "This place still feels like home to me."

"I'm glad."

"It makes me remember." Today Cordelia had tied her hair back
with a wide blue band that matched her eyes. In the soft cone of
dimmed light her hair was the color of fresh cornbread. "It makes me
think how life could have been—and how lousy it turned out instead."

The sudden vehemence in the girl's voice caught Babe unprepared. "Nothing's turned out lousy," Babe said.

"I have."

"That's not true."

"How can you stand having me here?" Cordelia cried. "How can
you sleep in that bed knowing I'm only a room away? How can you
stand me at all?"

Babe crinkled her eyes in puzzlement. "You're my daughter. I love
you."

"That's not possible." With a crackling of slick paper Cordelia
threw her magazine to the floor and sprang to her feet. "You can't
love me after what I did."

"You didn't—" Babe drew back, taking a moment to choose her words, to find the tone for them. "You needed someone to show you the way. I should have been there for you and I wasn't."

"A lot of mothers aren't there for their children." Cordelia hugged her arms around herself. "But their children don't give them lethal injections."

Babe drew in a long inhalation and slowly let it out. "You did what you were told to do. You trusted someone, and he didn't deserve your trust. You were a child. You were used."

Cordelia turned, her eyes sharp and challenging. "You really believe that."

"Yes I believe it, and I hate Lew Monserat for what he did to you. I'll never forgive myself for abandoning you to people like him."

Cordelia shrugged. "Don't blame Lew. He hasn't hurt me."

Babe was astonished. "He sent that man to kill you."

Cordelia flicked her a glance. "It's not the way you think. It's not Lew's fault."

Babe felt a darkness in her stomach. "Aren't you even angry?" She rose from her chair. "Or frightened?"

"I suppose I'm frightened." Cordelia's voice was curiously flattened. "But why should I be angry at Lew? He can't help anything." She moved toward the piano. In deliberate slow motion she played with the chrysanthemums in the vase. "He's no worse than me."

Amazement gathered in the wrinkles of Babe's forehead. "You can't seriously put yourself on the same level as him."

"I know my level. A man seduced me and gave me drugs and I loved it and I loved him. Now he wants to kill me and I don't feel any differently about him. I'd let him kill me."

Babe's heart hit her a blow under her throat. "You don't mean one word of that."

"I still love him," Cordelia said quietly, "and I don't want to hurt him. That makes me as bad as him, doesn't it?"

A sense of the utter hopelessness of the child invaded every pore of Babe's body. *He can't have that much power over her,* she told herself. *How could anyone have that much power over another human being?*

"When you fell in love," Babe said, "if it was love—you were alone and helpless—and a child. You turned to someone you thought would protect you."

"And what a good child I was. He handed me a syringe and told to kill my own mother. And I did it. What a good, obedient child."

"But *you didn't do it.*" Babe's voice was pleading. "That's the difference between you and him. You couldn't kill."

Cordelia thought for a moment. "But I could do other things just as bad." Then she added, "And don't think I haven't."

"It wasn't you doing those things. It was drugs doing them."

"Drugs don't create evil—they only fertilize it." Cordelia raised the lid from the piano keyboard and rolled her knuckles across a cluster of black keys. A bright, childlike sound pinged through the livingroom. "I have evil inside me."

"That's untrue," Babe said.

Cordelia shook her head. "It's there. When I close my eyes it shows me pictures. Evil pictures. Sometimes it's like a television set jammed to one channel. There's no way I can turn it off."

"Just because you imagine something evil doesn't mean that you've done it or that you're going to."

Cordelia struck another clump of black notes on the piano. "Do you see things like that inside your head?"

"Everyone does."

Interest hung behind Cordelia's neutral expression. "Everyone?"

"Sure. Sometimes I see crazy mixtures of kindergarten and Marquis de Sade."

The reaction on Cordelia's face was held back. "Tell me about them."

There was just an image in Babe's mind, so small and shadowy that she had to work to keep hold of it. "Ever since my coma I've kept seeing a sort of cocktail party in a candlelit room. The guests are wearing evening clothes and joke store masks—Porky Pig and Minnie Mouse and Alice in Wonderland and Richard Nixon."

Cordelia's eyes snapped around.

Babe made a little laugh. "That shows you how whacked-out my mental processes are."

"I don't see what's so evil about joke store masks," Cordelia said.

"It turns evil," Babe said.

She moved to the window and Cordelia's gaze moved with her.

"There's a young man in the room," Babe said. "He's naked—unconscious. I think he's drugged. These people in the masks bind him to a sort of rack. They put a black leather hood over his face. And then Richard Nixon—"

The way Cordelia was standing there, folded in a curtain of shock, made Babe stop.

"Takes a knife from the table," Cordelia said, "and cuts a circle in his chest."

A jolt went through Babe. "How did you know that?"

Behind Cordelia's bright shining eyes something fierce and excited was growing. "And then Richard Nixon cuts a Y inside the circle?"

"That's right." Babe couldn't exhale. A kind of dreaming unreality invaded her.

"And you tell yourself it's not really happening," Cordelia said, "but then the Y starts bleeding and you know it's real, and the young man screams through the mask and the scream is real too."

A damp static crawled slowly across Babe's skin. "And then Minnie Mouse . . ."

"Minnie Mouse puts her cigarette out," Cordelia said. "She puts it out in the young man's . . ."

"Hand." Babe said.

Silence sank down onto the room.

"I don't believe it." Cordelia's eyes took hold of her mother. "I *saw* them doing those things. I was *there.* I was standing at the door to his loft. I watched. And when I couldn't stand watching any more of it I turned and ran and when I stopped running I was in your hospital room. You were the only person I could tell it to."

A wave of icy heat washed up Babe's spine. "You—told me?"

Cordelia nodded. "While you were in coma—I told you everything. I pretended you could hear me." Pressing her lip between her teeth, Cordelia walked to the fireplace and stood gazing at the unlit logs. "I pretended you wanted to hear me—lying in your bed, so peaceful, always waiting for me, never running off anywhere. You were my best friend. And I was yours." Cordelia's voice developed an almost childish, singsong lilt. "I'd ask, Mother should I do this, should I do that. There'd be a catch in your breathing, because you heard me, and I'd count your breaths till the next catch. An even number meant yes and an odd number meant no. That was our code. And before I went home, I'd bend over you and kiss you and I'd say *Mother I love you, I'm sorry I've hurt you—and if you ever get well I'll never hurt you again.*"

Cordelia stared a moment at her mother. She turned away again.

"And you'd say *I love you too, Cordelia.* At least that was what I liked to pretend."

Her words came out in gulps and she began to lose control of her breathing.

"That day—after what I saw in the loft—I begged you: *Mother—come back.*"

Her voice took on the tone of a child begging.

"I need you. I don't have anyone now."

Cordelia started to cry, little sobs that she fought back and then couldn't fight back any longer.

"And you opened your eyes. For just that one second you were looking at me."

Cordelia clutched a fist to her mouth.

"I called the nurse. I said, 'Mother heard me.' The nurse said, 'No, she can't hear anything.' She said opening your eyes didn't mean you were seeing."

"But I woke up," Babe said.

Cordelia nodded. "That night."

At last Babe found the first foothold of understanding. The thing that had haunted her was not a dream, not a psychic flash; it was Cordelia standing by the hospital bed and pouring out all the pain of her terror and loneliness and need as she would have to a tombstone. And because Babe had been alive, not dead, some faculty standing sentinel over her sleeping mind had heard her daughter's call. And, like a hysterical ninety-pound mother lifting a two-ton VW off her crushed infant, she had answered the call—rising back to wakefulness, remembering the words that had summoned her, but taking them for the voice of her own mind, not knowing till now how it was or what it really was that she remembered.

"Cordelia," she said, "if you hadn't come to me that day . . ."

Cordelia's teeth closed on a knuckle. She blinked and stared from behind a fist at her mother.

"If you hadn't stood by my bed," Babe said, "if you hadn't called me—I'd still be in coma. It was *you* that brought me back."

The sad, hopeful, questioning smile on Cordelia's face seemed to float across the room and reach out to her.

"Thank you," Babe said. "Thank you for needing me. Thank you for saving me."

Babe laid her hand against the girl's cheek.

"Cordelia—you said I was your best friend when I was asleep. And you said you were my best friend. Now that I'm awake—could you trust me to keep on being your friend? Do you think we could try?"

Cordelia stood stiff and silent and awkward. Then she swallowed and sniffled and nodded, and very slowly, her arms closed around her mother.

* * *

"I'm moving home," Cordelia announced.

Cardozo lifted a stack of reports off one of the chairs, clearing a place for her to sit. "The plasterers fixed your apartment that fast? Give me their number."

"No. I'm moving home to my mother's house."

"Oh. That's terrific."

"I think so. So does she." Cordelia was silent a moment. "That's not why I'm here."

"How many guesses do I get?"

"I'm not going to shield him anymore."

Cardozo gave her a long glance. He found a pad and picked up his ballpoint and squiggled it on a piece of paper to make sure the ink was flowing.

"Do you have a lawyer?"

"No."

"Until you have a lawyer, don't tell me anything that's going to incriminate you, and don't tell me the names of any people who've committed crimes. For the time being I'm not supposed to learn this kind of information from you. My expert tells me that's the law."

"Funny law." Cordelia sat gazing at him.

"Doesn't leave much to talk about, does it. Okay. Excuse my directness, but if there's a polite way to phrase this question I sure don't know it."

"You don't have to start being polite with me."

"Did you sleep with Scottie Devens when you were thirteen?"

"I never slept with my stepfather."

"So there's no way you could have caught gonorrhea from him?"

"Not unless it spreads telepathically."

"Did you know you had gonorrhea when you were thirteen?"

"I knew I had something. I didn't know then what it was. I know now."

"Do you know how you got it?"

"Yes. So do you."

"How many men did you have sex with before you were infected?"

"You're giving me too much credit. There was only him."

Cardozo's mind played with the new piece of information.

What it came down to was that Ted Morgenstern had done his usual snoop job on the chief witness against his client. For a few hundred bucks slipped to a pediatrician's nurse, he'd turned up paydirt: the kid was being treated for gonorrhea. He raised a tzimmes in court about her sanity, had her sent to a psychiatrist, who by law also had to be an M.D., and got the gonorrhea introduced into evidence as part of the psychiatric report. At the same time he sent Scottie out to incriminate himself by catching an independent dose.

All the Vanderwalks had to buy was that Cordelia and Scottie had been walking around infected with the same dose.

Cardozo reflected that a dose of the clap was a pretty cheap price to pay for a plea bargain. Especially a plea bargain that cut a thirty-year sentence to three months. Throw in a lifetime annuity of a quarter million, and it was a deal no defendant—not even an innocent one—could afford to refuse.

And that's what people pay lawyers for.

Cordelia was smiling, showing unusually white teeth. "Lieutenant —do you hate him?"

For a moment Cardozo wasn't there. "Hate who?"

"The man I'm not supposed to name."

"Hate takes time. I'm a busy guy."

"I hate him." Her index finger went skimming in a back-and-forth motion along the edge of the desk. "I know how we can trap him."

Cordelia gave him a look, and Cardozo waited for whatever it was that was going to spring out of that head.

"I can get his confession on videotape," she said. "He has the equipment."

"Somehow I don't think he's going to sit still while you set up the lights for the quiz."

Cordelia's finger slowed. "He likes to tape sex. We'll have sex with the sound recorder on. I'll get him to talk. We'll both be high. It'll be easy. He's a real jabbermouth when we have sex."

Cardozo leapt up and his feet went down on the floor with a thump. "Jesus Christ. No way. Don't even say it."

When Greg Monteleone got home and gave his wife Gina a kiss, she didn't give him one back.

"Tell me, Detective," she said, "what would you say to a beautiful strung-out young girl in your livingroom?"

Cordelia Koenig was sitting idly on the sofa, turning the pages of *Time* magazine much too quickly even to be speed-reading them. Monteleone felt his heart squeeze into the space meant for his Adam's apple. He prepared a smile and came into the room.

The girl was on her feet nimbly and quickly. "Hi—remember me? We met the other night?"

"Course I remember you, Miss Koenig."

"I hope you don't mind my asking the precinct where you lived." She stood there, with her tumbling taffy-blond hair and her perfectly upturned nose and her brightly lipsticked mouth, smiling a smile that he sensed was a lie. "I knew the minute you walked into Mother's livingroom that you were a man I could talk to."

Her eyelids with their long black lashes came down, pale and uncontrollably fluttering against the darker skin of her face. Monteleone knew immediately she was on speed.

"Sure, you can talk to me. Have a seat."

"There's a criminal I know. You know him too. He's hurt a lot of people."

Her large blue eyes stared at Monteleone. There was a kind of nonnegotiable determination in them, and he realized the kid wasn't just on speed, she was on major speed.

"Let's get him," she whispered huskily.

54

"SOMEBODY BROKE INTO MY APARTMENT AND ATTACKED Mother," Cordelia said. "But it was me they were after."

"Who do you think it was?" the voice on the phone asked.

"My dealer. He had to have sent one of his goons. I'm a little behind on my coke payments."

"Naughty, naughty."

"It's not my fault. The U.S. Trust won't let me sell my Connecticut Light and Power and my IBM doesn't pay dividends till next month."

"But you can't let a debt to your dealer ride. Not if he's sending his collectors."

A slight pause. "I thought maybe if you could lend me three thousand till Monday . . ."

He sighed. "You only phone me when you need rescuing."

"It's the last time I'll ever ask."

"Well . . . Maybe just this one last time . . ."

"Cash?"

"Why don't you come to my new place on Franklin Street?" He gave her the address. "Tomorrow morning, nine o'clock. We can enjoy ourselves."

It was ten after ten and Cardozo's head ached and for two hours he'd been wanting to go back to bed. He'd had no sleep at all the night before and he'd come in this morning to find Monteleone's latest fives even worse spelled than Greg's usual atrocities.

A call came in on three. "Cordelia's been gone since last night."

Babe had the voice of a mother doing a very poor job of not sounding frantic.

"She hasn't phoned?"

"Not a word."

"She say where she was going?"

"I think she was lying."

"What was the lie?"

"A flutist called Wilson, Ransom Wilson she said, a concert at Alice Tully Hall. I found a pad of paper by her phone—the writing went through to the next sheet. I think she was copying down some times."

"What are the times?"

"If I can read her writing—six to six thirty, it says, fifteen-dash-thirty-four-dash-twelve."

"Twelve?"

"Excuse me, twelfth."

"Anything else? Does it say E or F?"

"No."

"There's no subway stop? Does it say Woodside?"

"No, just fifteen thirty-four twelfth."

"Okay."

"Vince—there's a bottle in her bathroom."

"What's the label?"

"No label. Little black pills."

"Like BB gun pellets, about an eighth of an inch across, a tiny line down the middle?"

"What are they?"

"Look, if they're in the bottle they're not in her. Stay by the phone. I'll take care of it."

Cardozo hung up and shouted for Greg Monteleone.

"Called in sick," Sergeant Goldberg shouted back.

"What's Monteleone's house number—fifteen thirty-four sound right?"

"Fifteen thirty-four on unforgettable Twelfth Street, the Avenue Foch of Woodside."

"What the fuck's an Avenue Foch?" someone shouted.

Cardozo picked up the phone and dialed Monteleone's home number. He asked Gina to put her husband on.

She sounded surprised. "Monte's on assignment."

Cardozo sensed a cold current around him as he sank back in his swivel chair. "What assignment is that, Gina?"

"That kiddie porn thing you put him on. Cordelia Koenig."

Cardozo slammed a fist into the desk and his knuckles instantly regretted the gesture. "Right. *That* kiddie porn thing." He hung up and sat looking at his hand. "Son of a fuckin' bitch!" he shouted.

Eight minutes later Cardozo was running along Franklin Street.

Across from 432, he saw the Con Ed truck. He beat his fists on the rear door and when Monteleone opened it an inch he yanked it wide and stormed in. He had come to kick ass.

"Congratulations, Greg, you just fucking blew it."

"She volunteered, for Christ's sake."

"We can't use it."

"We can't use *this* tape, but there are two tapes—he's making his own up there and we're tapping into the signal. Pete here is an electronic genius, it was a piece of cake."

The technician turned to acknowledge the compliment. He had plain features, a little slope to his nose. He was a quiet man, competent-looking.

Cardozo's gaze moved slowly from one face to the other and then to the monitor with its shadowy play of shapes. "All you've got is a lousy TV hookup. You've got no control over what happens."

"You haven't seen this girl in action. Sit down, Vince. Watch. She's amazing."

Cardozo didn't sit, but he watched.

The sound was crackling and the middle third of the picture rippled. The technician fine-tuned. The image on the monitor resolved into lights and darks, the curve of a woman's shoulder, her arm touching the lower part of her face. Cordelia.

"She's too close," the technician said.

"He knows," Monteleone said. "He'll back her off. He wants this film to turn out as good as we do."

He wants to kill her, Cardozo thought. *He sent a man to kill her the other night. He hasn't changed his mind.*

"Come here," a man's voice said.

She moved back, and now the camera saw a man sitting on a sofa, wearing a half mask over his eyes and a striped dressing gown. His arms went around her. He folded his hands on her breast. He drew her down. He kissed her eyes, her cheeks, her throat, and then lightly brushed his lips against hers.

"I've missed you." She unbuttoned her blouse. She wasn't wearing a bra.

He couldn't kill her, the thought came back. *Not oncamera.*

"Why have you been staying away?" the masked man asked.

But the man's a necro. He wants jack-off films of people dying. What could be hotter than this, a home movie of yours truly killing one of the country's top models?

"A lot's been happening." Cordelia let her skirt drop, then peeled her panties off. They slid silkenly down her.

The man put his face close to Cordelia's. "It's good to see you."

"You too."

"Do you forgive me for the other night?" the man asked. "Tina's party went on forever. I tried to phone you but there was something wrong with your machine."

"That's okay, I went out."

He sniffed at her mouth, her eyes, her hairline. He sniffed at the tops of her breasts. His hand moved along her leg.

As Cardozo watched, something crawled through him.

The man's dressing gown fell open.

"I have a confession to make." Cordelia began stroking his penis. "I ran out of coke Memorial Day weekend. I went to your old place to borrow some. You had a party going on. A dude was tied up."

Memorial Day weekend, Cardozo thought. His mind had been working on it but it wasn't till now that it came together.

"You were torturing him," Cordelia said. "It freaked me. Because it turned me on. I've never been turned on like that."

Cordelia had seen them torturing Downs. And Cordelia must have told her mother while Babe was still in coma. The time sequence fit. *That* was Babe's telepathy, her dream. The puzzle dissolved into the simple image of a panicked child telling her mommy the terrible thing that had happened, pleading with mommy to make the world right again.

On the screen, the man took Cordelia's hand away from his hard cock. "Not yet," he said. "Let's make it better."

He got up and disappeared from the frame. A moment later he returned and laid out his banquet on the coffee table: four glassine envelopes, horn-handled scissors, four red-capped vials, a soup spoon, a chafing dish heater, a silver caviar cup, red rubber tubing, an eyedropper, a cigarette lighter, a bottle of mineral water, a syringe.

"Have you ever killed anyone?" Cordelia asked.

"Of course."

"Tell me about it. Get me hot."

"She's great," Monteleone said. "She's handling it."

Monteleone could have been watching a game show. He wasn't feeling what Cardozo was feeling. Cardozo had a sense of a change in the man's expression. Something shifted behind the eyeslits.

The man lit the heater, then with the eyedropper measured mineral water into the cup. "I fought in the Second World War. Many people were killed." He placed the cup over the flame and slowly tapped the crystals from the four vials into the water.

"Not that kind of killing," Cordelia said. "I mean for kicks."

"There are kicks in war. You'd be surprised." One by one the man snipped the corners off the four envelopes and tapped their powdered contents into the mix.

"He's cooking a speedball," the technician said.

"That's no speedball." Cardozo didn't believe it. He saw it happening in front of him, and he couldn't believe it. "He's melting down crack. That's a fucking speedball express. Once that hits their bloodstream they're going to be out of control."

The man filled the syringe from the cup, drawing the liquid up into the transparent chamber. He laid the syringe on the table. He held out the red tubing, smiling.

Cordelia came toward him, smiling back at him. She stretched out her arms, palms toward the ceiling.

"Eenie, meenie, minie, moe," the man said. "Where oh where shall the goodies go?"

"You choose which arm," Cordelia said. "You always bring me luck."

The man carefully knotted the tubing around her upper left arm. The swollen dark vein jutted in the crook.

Cordelia turned slightly, so that the man had to reorient himself. As he touched the tip of the needle to the pulsing vein, he was facing the TV camera.

Cardozo could feel something wordlessly taking shape. There was a tiny preparatory movement on the man's part, and then with a quick jab he sank the needle tip into the vein and began to lower the plunger.

White-hot realization shot through Cardozo. "He's giving it all to her! It'll kill her!"

Cordelia's free hand whipped up. Her fingers dug under the mask, clawing it up off the man's eyes. His pivoting gaze froze. For one blinking, unbelieving moment the unmasked face of Baron Billi von Kleist stared straight into the camera.

Of course, Cardozo realized. *Not Monserat. Von Kleist. The suitor, the guardian, the best friend.*

Cordelia stretched out her hands to grab the syringe. The needle was shooting glittering droplets into space. Twenty fingers twisted around one another, tangoing across the screen, zooming in and out of focus, grappling for possession.

The baron bent Cordelia backward over the table. The lit heater wobbled and went over. Flame jetted across the tabletop.

The baron reached with his right hand for the mineral water.

Cordelia, using both hands, twisted the syringe from his left hand. She took three steps away from him and stood at the edge of the screen.

The baron doused the flame in Evian. When he turned again to face Cordelia, he raised the scissors in his right hand.

It was a face-off, the needle with its payload versus the scissors with their cutting edges.

Panic and determination were mingled in Cordelia's expression. Now she was circling out of camera range, and the baron was turning, eyes tracking her.

"No way I'm going to let this happen." Cardozo flung open the truck door and bounded across the street.

He dove into the building entrance and leaned on the buzzer to 4A to spook them, maybe to stop them, anyway to buy time, and he leaned on all the other buzzers to get into the building. A rattling buzz answered and released the lock and he yanked the inner door open.

The indicator showed the elevator on the third floor.

He took the first flight of stairs in a blind run. His legs thrust him up past two and three in a single continuous lunge.

On four he swerved into the corridor, his shoes slapping and skidding on the tiled floor. He faced the door of 4A, tested the knob, stepped back. He drew his revolver and took dead aim at the lock and fired one shot. Wood and metal shattered. Holding the gun with both hands at eye level, he kicked the door in.

The baron was swaying in the livingroom at the end of the corridor. In the colors of real life his bathrobe was maroon and ochre. His feet were splayed apart and he was trying to steady himself by gripping the back of a chair.

His back arched and cords stood out at the base of his suntanned neck. His breath was a whinny, a struggle for air. Red foam was bubbling from his lips.

The chamber of the empty syringe was jutting out of his throat, like a grotesquely oversized tiepin that had been shoved in twelve inches too high. The needle had dug in to the hilt.

Above the pale and trembling lips the large staring eyes turned toward Cardozo. The baron's pupils had become pinpoints of disbelieving, dwindling light. The moment became a silence. The baron's eyes closed and his hands lost the chair. He fell in a sideways heap.

Cordelia had retreated to a corner, hands covering her face as if to choke back the whimpers coming from her.

Cardozo crossed to her. Her fingers closed around his.

"Did I kill him?" she whispered.

Cardozo glanced over at the corpse. "Somebody had to."

"All I wanted to do was get his confession on film."

"Was it Von Kleist who gave you the insulin and syringe to kill your mother?"

Cordelia nodded.

"He gave you dope, had sex with you from the time you were twelve?"

"Everything."

"And Monserat?" Cardozo asked.

"Lew never touched me." Cordelia staggered to the couch and dropped onto a cushion. "Lew was just one of Billi's fronts. Billi had a hundred of them." She was looking at her panties hopelessly; they were a riddle she couldn't solve. The dope was in her blood, fogging her. "People thought Billi was . . . was attractive and . . . got involved and then . . . couldn't get . . . ."

Cardozo was thinking that it had taken one scared immature drug-addicted girl to do what no policeman, no court could ever have done, to make Billi von Kleist pay in kind for the pain and murder he had strewn, to ensure that he would never twist or take another life.

"I loved him." She was staring at the corpse, leaning down to touch the lapel of the robe. "I still . . . ."

She was beginning to nod out. Silent tears were tracking down her cheeks. The tear from the right eye was already at her chin and the tear from the left was only halfway to her mouth.

Cardozo wondered why that was, why one tear was faster than the other, what force in the universe decided things like that.

Her head dropped. Cardozo caught her before she could hit the floor. He eased her back onto the sofa. "You're going to be okay," he soothed.

She had passed out. He had no idea how the hell he was going to get her out of this. A flying carpet was all he needed.

55

THE PRINT MAN FINISHED DUSTING AND THE PHOTOGRAPHER FIN-
ished taking pictures and the men from the M.E.'s office zipped
Baron Billi into a body bag. They filed out of the loft, leaving the
chalk outline of a dead man in the floor.

Cardozo phoned Ted Morgenstern. "Get down here to Lew Monserat's loft. Cordelia Koenig has killed Baron Billi von Kleist. You're
going to defend her."

Twenty minutes later Ted Morgenstern identified himself to the
sergeant guarding the crime scene. He stalked into the apartment
with the confidence of a predator.

"Where's my client?"

"In the hospital. Have a seat."

There was an edge of command to Cardozo's voice. Ted Morgenstern's face betrayed a rush of irritation, but he sat.

Cardozo pushed buttons on the VCR, and the TV set bathed the
room in ghostly voices and images.

Morgenstern did his best to stay frosted, and when the tape had
run he put on an air of smug, lighthearted adventure. "Who made
that tape? The police? It's inadmissible."

"Baron Billi von Kleist made it. Kleist's last tape."

Morgenstern's face was calculating. "Can you prove that?"

"I can prove the baron had a habit of giving sex-and-torture parties
and taking candid tapes of them. There are seven years of tapes right
here in the closet."

Something changed. Morgenstern's eyes were on Cardozo and
there was the first flicker of fear in them. A thread of excitement
moved in Cardozo's body and he was almost ashamed of it.

"Some of the tapes are going to interest you, Counselor. You star in them."

Ted Morgenstern had started to rise from the sofa but now he sank back again.

Cardozo ran a two-minute selection from the tapes—enough to give Morgenstern a taste.

Morgenstern was ashen and shaking. "Those tapes aren't relevant," he said.

Lucinda MacGill came out of the bedroom, carrying a videocassette in each hand. "The tapes *are* relevant, Counselor," she said. "Anything found on the scene of the crime is relevant and admissible. People of New York versus Cudahy, 1953. Upheld by the Supreme Court, 1958."

Ted Morgenstern looked as though he'd been slammed in the stomach with a baseball bat. "Are those the only copies?"

"There are dupes," Cardozo said.

Morgenstern was sitting there, dead. "The police have them?"

"The cops don't know the dupes exist. They don't even know the originals exist."

"Who has the dupes?"

"I do. In a bank vault."

Ted Morgenstern closed his eyes.

"I've been thinking about Cordelia's defense," Cardozo said. "You know how I think you should handle it? Offscreen. Like in the Downs case and the Devens case. You flashed Jodie Downs's medical file at his parents. They didn't want it made public and they accepted a plea bargain and Loring got off. Seven years ago, Cordelia Koenig caught the clap from Baron Billi. You had Devens catch himself a dose. You flashed the medical records at the Vanderwalks, they saw a connection between her gonorrhea and his. They weren't going to let that get into the newspapers, so they let Devens walk. Are you following me, Counselor?"

"Not exactly." The resolve had drained out of Morgenstern's voice.

"People take your suggestions. With your clout you can get the D.A. to accept a plea of justifiable manslaughter."

"Excuse me," Lucinda MacGill interrupted. "Why not head this off at the coroner's office and go for accidental death?"

Her balls took Cardozo's breath away.

"With accidental," she said, "there'll be a hearing, no charges, no trial, and the existence of the tapes won't even need to be known."

Ted Morgenstern sat there cracking his knuckles. "It'll mean calling in a few favors. But accidental is definitely the way to go."

"Okay," Cardozo said. "In exchange for accidental in the Von Kleist killing, you get Baron Billi's tapes." He felt a strange elation. He had never thought he would be holding the power to influence events, to make the world jump like a trained dog as the Ted Morgensterns and the Vanderwalks and the D.A.'s of New York routinely did. But for the first time in his life he held that power, and it was more potent than a loaded magnum and more addictive than a jeroboam of crack.

Morgenstern rose and walked to the window and stared at police and reporters swarming down in the street. "And what do you want for the duplicate tapes?"

"That's simple. Baron Billi's groupies get visas to Paraguay and they have till Saturday to use them."

"You're joking."

"Here's another laugh. Sir Dunk turns his wife's estate over to the AIDS foundation."

Cardozo phoned Jodie Downs's parents from the precinct. Lockwood Downs answered.

"Jodie's death wasn't simple murder," Cardozo said. "Claude Loring was working for other people. We just caught them."

It took Lockwood Downs a moment to speak. "I wasn't expecting this. Meridee and I had just about given up hope that anyone would ever pay."

"These people are going to pay."

"I'm sorry. I don't mean to sound ungrateful. I just don't know what to say."

"You don't have to say anything. I just wanted you to know."

"Thank you for keeping on it, Lieutenant. We both thank you."

Sixty seconds later Cardozo told Babe everything, not attempting to sweeten any of it. The telephone receiver pressed the silence of her shock into his ear.

"Where have they taken Cordelia?"

Cardozo gave Babe the address of the hospital. "Look," he said, "I know it sounds like the end of the world, but worlds are ending every day and it's not always such a bad thing. Other kids have gotten off drugs. Cordelia can do it. Just remember I'll be there beside you."

"Will you, Vince? Be beside me?"

Vince Cardozo, he asked himself, *what the hell are you doing?*

He realized he was in love with her, dreaming of some kind of happily ever after that just didn't exist. He and Babe Devens were from two different planets on opposite sides of the sun.

He thought about that and decided, just for today, to forget happily ever after.

"Yeah. I'll be right beside you," he said. "Meet you at the hospital. Fifteen minutes."

He hesitated, then decided he had time to make one last call. It was Terri's lunch break. She'd be home. He dialed and his daughter answered on the fourth ring.

"Remember that day we got called away from the beach? I'm going to make it up to you."

"Daddy, you don't have to make anything up to me."

"I want to. How about this weekend? Would you like to go swimming?"

"It's too cold."

"It's not too cold in the Virgin Islands. I have three days off. What do you say? No way the precinct can beep me in Saint Thomas."

"I love you, Daddy."

"I love you too, and that's not an answer. Do we have a date?"

She was silent only a moment. "You twisted my arm. It's a date."